THE NIGHT FIRM

KARPOV KINRADE

http://KarpovKinrade.com

Edited by Joseph Nassise, Ellie Adams,
and the Novel Fixer

~ ~ ~ ~ ~

Published by Daring Books

~ ~ ~ ~ ~

First Edition
ISBN: 978-1-939559-07-4

~ ~ ~ ~ ~

I AM the WILD

BOOK ONE

CHAPTER 1: THE WANTED AD

BEING A CANDLE IS NOT EASY; in order to give light, one must first burn.
~ *Rumi*

Underwater, the world doesn't feel like itself anymore. It becomes more like a gateway to another reality. It's an in-between place, water. Same with air. And dreams. They are all in-between places where so much possibility lives.

I often get my best flashes in the water. Some would call them premonitions, but they aren't nearly that defined. They're more impulses with a slight tingle to them. The kind I've learned to listen to.

A flash is what led me to turn right instead of left on my way home yesterday, which took me past a homeless person I gave change to, who then gave me their newspaper as a thank you, which had a strange advertisement for a job, which resulted in an interview today.

It read:

ASSISTANT NEEDED FOR UNIQUE FIRM.
Must be willing to work at night, travel, and live on-site.
Strong stomach a perk.

1

Compensation generous. Will train.

If you're reading this, you're the person we're looking for.

IT LISTED a number but no name. When I called, a woman answered the phone with a chipper, "The Night Firm, how may I direct your call?"

I told her I was calling about an ad in the newspaper for a job. She paused. Became very quiet for a moment, and then said, "Please hold," with less chipperness than before.

When she returned, her voice was nearly robotic. "Be at 333 Alley Lane at 10 p.m. tomorrow," she said, before promptly and unceremoniously hanging up on me!

I sat staring at my phone for several minutes, unsure of what had just happened or what I should do.

A quick Google search for The Night Firm revealed only skin care creams and a questionable website that showed women bent over with minimal clothing. I instantly decided I wasn't going to go. It was stupid, possibly dangerous, and surely not worth it.

But then I set my phone down and wandered my two-bedroom apartment with the secondhand, mismatched furniture that smelled like cigarettes and body odor, the carpet that hailed from another epoch, and the couple above I'm certain are professional dancers who also like to breathe loudly during sex, and I changed my mind. Rather, my flash changed my mind. I got the tingly feeling, and I knew I had to go.

So here I am, applying one more coat of mascara before heading out the door in a suit I can't afford and will be returning first thing tomorrow, in hopes of landing the most mysterious job ever.

How do you dress when you have no idea what the job is that you're applying for and don't know anything about the company? I figured it would be better to be professionally overdressed than under, thus the blue Prada suit. The woman at the store insisted I wear it, despite my objection that the feather cuffs were a bit much. She assured me it was all the rage, and I must confess I do look rather striking in it. My dark hair is pulled into a French twist, and I accented my blue eyes with a charcoal powder. Red lips provide the finishing touch.

They can't possibly judge me for my choice of presentation when they didn't give me any hints as to what they are about.

With one last glance in the mirror and a fake smile that I hope looks sincere, confident and competent, I turn off the light in the bathroom and grab my well-worn leather bag as I head to the front door.

I don't open *his* door this time as I pass it, though I do run my hand over the knob briefly, even as my mind unpacks the memories stored there. Memories of before. Memories of us. Always us. "It's us against the world, Evie," he'd always say, his blue eyes, so alike to mine, peering straight into my soul in a way no one else could. My hand lingers a moment longer, then slips off, and I tuck the memories back into their mental box and shove them away.

I'm clearly not over it. Not ready to entirely move on. Still, there's some progress. I think even Jerry—my former therapist—would agree.

Former because we ended up sleeping together and it took me longer than it should to realize how unhealthy that was. He took advantage of me during a low point in my life, and I let him, because I was in too much pain to say no to something that looked enough like love.

His true colors bled into our relationship slowly, and by then it was too late. I was already under his thumb.

I don't even cry every night anymore. Not about my brother and not about my therapist/love/ex/asshole.

But when my phone bings, the familiar panic sends a surge of unneeded adrenaline through my bloodstream and my heart quickens as I swallow back bile.

Because I know it's Jerry.

And I'm not wrong.

I'd love to be wrong. Just once.

PLEASE, babe. Give me another chance. We're perfect together. I love you. Isn't that enough?

. . .

I SQUEEZE AWAY the tears forming in my eyes as I look around for something to anchor me to the present moment. The silver door knob. The Ansel Adams print hanging in the hall. The spider crawling in the corner of the ceiling. I breathe in. Breathe out. In through the nose two counts, out through the mouth four counts. I am safe. Whole. One with all. I am safe. Whole. One with all.

As my body settles and my mind calms, I continue my breathing until the panic abates.

It's getting easier to recover from these unexpected contacts. I screenshot the exchange, put it in the file I created specifically for this, and block the number. Again.

The gesture is beginning to feel pointless. He just finds a new number. I think he's got a year's worth of burner phones for the sole purpose of harassing me daily. I've already deleted all my social media and gone dark in every way that I can. My phone number is unlisted and I change it every three months. I would move if I could, but I haven't been able to afford it since Adam died. The authorities are fairly useless. Which leaves me on my own to deal with my ex.

So here we are.

I drop the phone into my bag and let myself out of my apartment, which involves unlocking four separate deadbolts I insisted my land-lord install for me. I take a few moments to lock up, suck in my breath, and turn to face my future.

THE SUBWAY this time of night is shockingly less crowded than I would have expected, much to my relief. Rush hour is long past, but still, New York is overcrowded at any time, day or night. Yet our train is only moderately full, mostly of people who look to be heading out for a good time or coming home from one.

I find a seat as far from everyone else as I can, pull out my sketch-book and pencils, and look around for the perfect subject.

I'm about to settle on a beautiful older male couple holding hands and talking quietly with their heads close together when I see him.

My body's response to him is physical, visceral and immediate. It takes me a moment to remember how to breathe. It's as if all the oxygen has been sucked from me, and when it returns, I gasp, then cough to cover up the sound.

He hasn't noticed me—the god-like specimen across the train— and I'd like to keep it that way.

Never have I seen someone so perfect, so symmetrical, so angular in all the right ways, so handsome but also devilishly sexy at the same time. I feel a tightening in my gut as I study him, an awakening of something dormant within, something I haven't felt in a very long time. I shove that feeling aside and focus on the art as my fingers work quickly to sketch his form.

He's tall, maybe 6'4" or 6'5", broad shoulders, tapered waist, all wrapped in a suit that looks custom-tailored just for his body. His dark hair is wild, falls past his collar, and compliments his forest green eyes, and I have to look away quickly before he catches me staring. A viral energy emanates from him and he fills the train with a kind of magic that belies his expensive suit.

The woman to his left can't take her eyes off of him and is practically straining to get closer even as the man she's with wraps his arms around her possessively while he shoots dark looks at the stranger. Two college girls give up their seats to stand closer to him. Even the men respond, some with anger and fear, their bodies betraying their desire to get as far away from him as possible.

It's not just his attractiveness or the wealth he oozes with every detail of his bearing and clothing. He doesn't look as if he belongs on a New York subway. In fact, he doesn't look as if he belongs in the beautiful but grungy city of New York at all. He looks like a photo-shopped magazine cover come to life, but whether that magazine is GQ or National Geographic is hard to say.

I watch, amazed, as some people scoot away from him, even as I fight every instinct inside me to move closer, as if he has a force field around him, repelling and attracting, pushing and pulling. He's drawing me in without even knowing it. I could be invisible to him, but suddenly he's become the only thing I can focus on.

I work almost mindlessly, letting the art and inspiration flow through me. This has always been my release, my way of connecting to the creative movements of life. I minored in art after my college boyfriend convinced me an art major wouldn't be worth the paper my degree was printed on.

I chose a more practical route and kept my art a side hobby, a passion, a secret obsession at times.

I don't completely regret the choice. It turns out I'm damn good at what I do. Sometimes, I even like it. Though finding joy in anything for the last few years has been hard. Even my art has been more therapy than pleasure.

My fingers are smudged black by the time I complete the portrait. I stare at it for a moment, happy to discover I caught that undefinable energy he has, even while standing still. It's like he's always in motion. A hunger driving him. Almost imperceptible, but still there. I normally like to put stories to the people I draw on the subway, but he seems to defy my silly storytelling. He's telling his own story with every breath, every movement of his head, every glance at his over-priced watch.

I'm completely lost in my drawing when a baritone voice with a British accent shocks me back to the present.

"That's an incredible likeness."

I look up and into his forest eyes—and I feel suddenly lost in sensations of the wind and earth and tall trees and wilderness. My flashes are buzzing like a trapped bee in my gut. I'm flustered, which isn't like me. "Thanks," I manage to mutter, though I can't seem to pull my gaze from his.

"You just drew this? In the last few minutes?" he asks, pushing the reluctant conversation forward as he takes the seat beside me. I move my bag to give him more room, and now our thighs are touching, and I suck in air like I'll never have the option again.

I nod in answer to his question, my jaw locked stubbornly in place. Come on, get your shit together. Stop acting like a tongue-tied teenager.

"Yes. It's a hobby of mine while on the subway. To draw people I find interesting in some way." There. A complete sentence. We're making progress.

His lips form a smirky little smile. "And what did you find interesting about me?"

I manage to pull my gaze away from his to glance down at my drawing as I consider his question. Obviously he's smoking hot, but I actually see a lot of sexy men in New York, and yet they generally bore me as subjects for my work. It's not his incredible good looks that drew me in. "You seem juxtaposed against life," I say, as if that makes sense to anyone but me.

He raises an eyebrow. "Do tell," he says.

Great. Okay, how to explain. "You stand out. Most people fade into the fabric of life. They are colors blended into the whole, washed out by the pulse around them. You...you don't blend in. You stand out in sharp contrast, like you don't entirely belong, or maybe you're the only one who truly does belong and everyone else is just faking it. If...if that makes any sense." My mouth is dry now and I reach desperately into my bag for my water.

I pull out the bottle and suck down half the contents just as our train lurches to a halt. My hands, sweaty from stress, can't maintain purchase on the plastic, and it slips from my grasp. For a split second I'm aware that my entire sketchbook—and my lap—is going to to take a bath it won't recover from.

I'm about to decide that this fiasco will end any chance of me attending my job interview when the stranger next to me reaches out and catches the water bottle before it spills even a single drop.

The movement is so fast I don't even see it. I only see the aftereffect of him holding the bottle that a fraction of a moment ago slipped from my hands.

My eyes widen. "You have quite the reflexes," I say, taking the water back from him and slipping it into my purse after making sure the lid is secured. "Thanks."

He nods but says nothing, just continues staring at me. "You're an unusual woman."

I shrug. "I get that a lot."

7

"Where are you headed?"

"A job interview," I say.

"Something in art, I hope?" he says.

I chuckle. "No. Haven't you heard? There's no money in art."

He frowns but doesn't say anything, so I continue. "Business," I say. "I chose business, and that's what the interview is for. Though it's far from what I really want to be doing, to be honest."

I have no idea why I'm telling a total stranger this, but again, here we are.

"Don't settle," he says, "Trust me when I say you don't want to get stuck in a life you hate." His gaze settles on me, his eyes searching mine for secrets. "Hold fast to dreams, For if dreams die, Life is a broken-winged bird That cannot fly."

"Hold fast to dreams," I say, finishing the poem, "For when dreams go, Life is a barren field Frozen with snow."

He raises an eyebrow. "You know your poetry. Are you a fan of Langston Hughes?"

"I actually don't read much poetry anymore," I say. "But I took a class in college and I have a good memory."

"Better than good, I would say."

The train slows, and I realize we're at my stop. I stand, regretting the break of contact with his thigh, and he stands with me.

"Looks like we're both getting off here," he says.

I nod and grab my bag, then walk through the doors with him just a step behind me. I can feel him with every movement. My own body actually seems to be orienting itself to his movements, which annoys me, so I take an extra-large step to the left and let him catch up to me as we walk up the stairs and into the chill night air.

It's an awkward moment. I don't want to leave him, but I can't be late to my interview.

He nods. "Good luck," he says, turning away from me.

I can't help myself. I call out before he walks too far, "Wait!"

I run up to him as I tear the portrait out of my sketchbook. "For you. I usually give my subjects their portraits when I'm done."

He takes it from my hand, studying it and then studying me. "You always give your art away? Without compensation or recognition?"

I cock my head. "I don't do it for money or recognition," I say. "I do it because it drives my soul in a way nothing else does. And I give it away because it brings joy to people. It brightens their day to know someone has truly seen them, even if just for fifteen or twenty minutes during a subway commute. Everyone has a light to give to the world, and that's mine. *In lumen et lumen.*"

"What did you just say?" he asks.

"*In lumen et lumen.* It's Latin for '*In the light, of the light.*' Something my dad used to say to me and my brother, that we should always strive to live in the light and be of the light. It's always been a kind of guiding mantra for me."

I cock my head and smile. "You never told me your name," I say, holding out a hand. "I'm Eve."

"Sebastian," he says automatically, bringing his hand to mine.

When our palms touch, a shock of electricity shoots through my arm and into me, and my eyes widen. So do his, or maybe I'm imagining it.

"Well, Sebastian, it was a pleasure meeting you tonight. I just have one more question for you before we part ways."

"And what's that, Eve?"

"What's your light? Do you know?"

HE MIGHT STILL BE BACK THERE, PONDERING my question, or watching me walk away. I don't know, because I refuse to look. Back straight, chest up, I am confident and smart and I am not blowing a potential job for a cute face. Besides, no way am I ready to date after my last shitfest of a relationship. I'm happy enough single.

I stick to my resolve. I don't look back.

But I won't lie, my fingers are itching to draw him again.

And to touch him.

But I shove that inappropriate thought aside and continue on.

On the way to the office, a meow interrupts my thoughts, and I pause and kneel to give an orange tabby some love. The cat pushes against my hand, purring and demanding affection, which I'm happy to accommodate. I always have time for cats, and they always seem to have time for me.

I arrive at my destination after a five-minute walk, the tabby following me until I reach the front door. It's a tall glass and steel office building with blacked out windows and no sign other than the address. Very mysterious.

When I walk in, the mystery only deepens. The front lobby is a blend of modern and zen. Clean lines, minimalistic décor, everything in beige and white. The wall behind the receptionist's desk draws my eye—an indoor waterfall flowing over stone. A man and woman, both unnaturally beautiful, both dressed in black, sit behind the desk typing on sleek computers. They look up simultaneously when I walk over, and I'm struck by their matching hazel eyes set against their dark amber skin. Even their bone structure is similar, and before I can stop myself, I blurt out, "Are you twins?"

They each nod once, briefly, and then the woman asks, "How can I help you?"

I recognize her voice from the phone call. "I'm Eve Oliver. I have an interview right now."

I don't give more details because I don't have more details to give.

She frowns, then taps a small silver device on her ear. "She's here." She nods. "Have a seat. They will be with you shortly."

I pick a spot close to the front desk so I can do some sleuthing and see if I can find out more about this company. It occurs to me I should try asking. "Excuse me?"

The two look up in unison and my heart lurches at the familiarity of that synchronized connection one can only have with a twin.

"What does this company do exactly? What position am I applying for?" I feel stupid asking, but I'll feel even more stupid going into the meeting knowing nothing.

"They will tell you what you need to know during the interview," the woman says. I still haven't heard the guy speak.

"You can't give me any info?" I ask, perplexed. "A brochure, maybe? Website URL? Anything?"

She gives one curt shake of her head and then returns to her computer.

I sigh, give up, and pull out my sketchbook. I take a deep breath and quiet my mind, closing my eyes, letting stress and worry flow off of me like water. It doesn't take long for my attention to return to Sebastian. I envision every detail that I can recall. The different shades of green in his eyes. The aristocratic slope of his nose. His smooth brow and sharp cheekbones. I don't open my eyes as I sketch. Sometimes drawing blind helps me hold the vision.

I don't know how long it takes me to finish, but when I open my eyes, I'm staring into his. Well, not really his, but his likeness on my paper. Even in charcoal and pencil he's breathtaking, and I'm ridiculous, lusting after my own drawing. I close my sketchbook and check the time, shocked to see I've already been here over an hour.

"Excuse me," I say, drawing the attention of two sets of impatient hazel eyes. "My interview was some time ago. Do you know how much longer I'll be waiting?"

"Until they call you up," she says, unhelpfully.

"Great. Thanks."

It's after midnight, and I've played more Candy Crush on my phone than I'm willing to admit, when the woman finally leaves her desk and gestures for me to follow.

She says nothing as we walk through marbled halls featuring modern paintings and I'm led to a boardroom. "Sit. They will join you shortly."

Lovely, more waiting. I take a seat at the long, mahogany table and stare out the window overlooking the New York harbor.

When I hear the click of the door, I stand, straightening my skirt and wiping my sweaty palm against my jacket. Taking a deep breath, I put on my best professional smile as the door opens.

My smile falters when I see the man standing there. The man whose eyes have haunted me since the subway.

"Sebastian?"

My pulse quickens and I feel a sinking in my stomach. I wanted to see him again, it's true. But not here. Not like this.

Not after I just confessed that I don't really want the job I am here applying for.

A job…apparently…with his company.

CHAPTER 2: THE INTERVIEW

THOUGH MY SOUL may set in darkness, it will rise in perfect light; I have loved the stars too fondly to be fearful of the night. ~ Sarah Williams

ANOTHER MAN PUSHES past him into the room, turning to face Sebastian, then glancing at me. "You two know each other?" he asks. He has the same British accent as Sebastian.

"No," Sebastian says, pulling his eyes away from mine and taking a seat as far from me as possible.

It takes me a moment to really see the other man, but when I finally look at him, I have to do a double take.

I might be in a room with the two sexiest men that have ever lived. And I'm not even exaggerating.

Man #2 is just as tall as Sebastian, though his build is leaner. His hair is a lighter brown and shorter, cut stylishly, and his eyes are ocean blue rather than the forest green of Sebastian's, but the two men share the same sharp cheekbones and nose.

He smiles at me, and I'm dazzled by his charm and his dimpled chin as he introduces himself. "I'm Derek Night," he says as he takes my hand to shake it. The moment we touch, I'm lost in his eyes, adrift in an endless ocean, nearly drowning in him. I can almost smell the salty spray.

I realize I'm holding my breath and I suck in air as my head spins.

He pauses a moment, staring into my eyes as if he also feels this connection. Cocking his head, he releases my hand. "Curious," he says under his breath, before taking a seat near me. "This is my brother, Sebastian, but you seem to already know his name?"

I nod, returning to my seat. "We briefly met in the subway a few hours ago." Brothers. That makes sense. Damn, they come from good genes, though.

Derek raises an eyebrow at his brother. "You took the subway?"

Sebastian shrugs and still doesn't look at me. He seems pissed, and I'm assuming it's because he thinks he's wasting his time interviewing someone who doesn't even want the job.

But I do *need* the job. And I can probably do the job, once I figure out what the job is.

Derek sighs as if he's used to his brother's mercurial moods. He returns his focus to me. "Once our other brothers arrive, we can begin. I apologize for the long wait. We had an emergency with a client that took longer than expected."

My heart hammers hard in my chest at the thought that there are more of them. Isn't two enough? "What kind of business is this that it handles client concerns in the middle of the night?" I ask.

But before my question can be answered, the door opens and two more men walk in. The air around me crackles with unseen electricity and I wonder if I'm the only one who can feel it. The four of them together overwhelm my senses and I brace myself against the table, my flash buzzing under my skin and in my head, making me dizzy.

Derek stands, smiling at the new arrivals. "Everything go okay?"

The tall blond with eyes such a pale blue they're almost white nods. "It's handled." He looks my way. "You must be Miss Oliver?"

I nod.

"I'm Elijah Night." He doesn't offer to shake my hand, and I'm equal measures disappointed and relieved. He's taller than the others, lean, and his light blond hair is longer and pulled back into a tie at the base of his neck. He's pale with a face that looks to be carved from marble. He pours himself into the chair with ease and grace, like a wild animal settling in.

In fact, all four brothers have an animalistic energy to them. Wild and untamed, despite the expensive suits and polished exterior.

The last brother steps forward and extends his hand, a small frown on his face. "I'm Liam Night," he says. "Welcome to The Night Firm."

He studies me with golden eyes that look like twin suns as we shake hands. He's shorter than his brothers, but only by an inch or so, which still makes him quite tall, and he has wild, dark auburn hair that is stylishly disheveled. When we touch, it's like touching fire but without the pain. A deep burning in my soul, a warmth that spreads through me. I'm melting under the heat of it, under the heat of him.

I pull my hand away as graciously as I can. "Nice to meet you."

He holds my eyes a moment longer, then takes a seat.

Four sets of eyes are on me, and I sit back down, trying not to fidget. The collective stare of the Night brothers is disconcerting. Each of them is entirely unique. Entirely original. And yet, I can feel their connection to each other. I can see the family resemblance. I can feel it in their intensity and power.

"We realize this is a bit of an unusual interview," Derek says, smiling. "Thank you for agreeing to come."

I nod. "I'm certainly intrigued. Do I now get to find out what kind of job I'm applying for?"

Once again, the most critical question I need answered is interrupted when the door opens, and a woman pushing a cart walks through. She is tiny, standing not much taller than four feet—if that—with long silver hair pulled back into a braid that rides down her spine. She wears a white robe tied around her waist with a knotted sash. Her face is lined with age and softened by kindness. Her silver eyes are clear and piercing. When she sees me, she smiles as if she's been expecting me—like we are old friends becoming reacquainted. She leaves her cart to take my hand in hers. Her skin is thin and soft, like aged crepe paper.

"It's such a pleasure to finally meet you, my dear," she says in a different accent than the brothers. More Irish than British. "I'm Matilda Night, the grandmother of these boys. If they give you any trouble, you just let me know. I brought snacks and drinks for everyone."

She gives a pointed look to her grandsons before passing out drinks. The brothers have glasses of what look like red wine. An odd choice for a job interview. She hands me a cup of tea and a plate of cookies.

"Thank you," I say, my curiosity about this job and this family ever growing.

Matilda pats my hand and shuffles out the door with the cart, closing it behind her, but not before she gives me a mischievous wink.

I pick up the tea, grateful for something to keep my hands occupied, and blow on it, then sip, surprised to discover it's chai, my favorite, with just the right amount of cream and sugar. Interesting.

"Your grandmother is sweet," I say to the silent room. The brothers exchange secret glances that clearly hold hidden layers of meaning I'm not privy to—the kind of sibling communication I used to have not so long ago—and the pang of seeing it still alive in others causes something in my gut to clench. I squeeze my eyes closed a moment, putting Adam out of my mind.

"To address your question," Derek says, "the role you're applying for here is a bit unusual."

Well, there's a shocker.

"We need someone to manage schedules, help with clients, and assist with any investigations, emergencies or events that arise."

I nod. "Okay. I mean, I'm definitely capable of doing that, but… " I pull out my resume from my bag and place it before me while he continues speaking.

"And we're not an ordinary firm. You'd be working from sundown to sunup, and our location frequently changes, so it's something of a live-in position."

"Live-in? I'd have to live here? In an office building?"

"No. You'd live in our home. With us."

"Just the four of you?"

"And our grandmother and other staff," he says.

My nerves tingle, and my flash hits me with a wave of light that makes me almost vomit. "Where is your home?" I ask, trying to mask the effects of my gift. That's what Adam always called it. A gift. "We're secret superheroes," he would whisper to me when I would cry myself to sleep every night after our father's death. "No one can hurt us."

"That's also complicated," he says.

"This is a waste of time," Sebastian says, speaking for the first time since this meeting began.

Derek looks at him. "What do you mean?"

"She doesn't even want to be here. She doesn't want this job. She told me herself. She's wasting our time. She's not qualified."

My face burns red as blood rushes to it, and that mental barrier that's supposed to keep people from blurting out what's on their mind at inappropriate times snaps in half. "Not qualified? What could you possibly know about my qualifications? Or anything about me at all? You haven't asked about my work history or seen my resume. You have no idea what I'm capable of." I stand, to the surprise of all four of them, and walk to Sebastian, shoving my resume in his face. "I'll have you know I'm more than qualified to work for you. In fact, I'm overqualified. I graduated from Harvard's MBA program with honors. I was Managing Director of the last company I worked for. I'm probably more qualified than you to run your business, whatever the hell it is. You should be working for me." As soon as the words are out, I regret them, but it's too late. Words, once spoken, cannot be reined in. They take on their own life, which is why it's so important we choose with care which ideas or words we give birth to. My father tried to teach me that, but I'm clearly still learning the lesson.

Sebastian shoves the resume aside. "And where did you get your law degree?" he asks with ice in his voice.

"What?" I ask, confused.

"If you're more qualified than me to run my business, you must have a law degree. After all, we are a law firm. Where did you get your law degree? I don't see it on your resume."

"This is a law firm?" I ask, more confused than ever. "What kind of law firm does interviews at midnight?"

Derek shoots Sebastian a stern look and takes the resume from him. "We offer our services to a niche clientele. One you will have to become familiar with, should you choose to accept this job."

"Who are your clients? Vampires?" I say with a laugh, but none of them smile. Sebastian smirks and leans back in his chair. I want to smack that grin off his beautiful, perfect face. Derek narrows his lips and glances at the others. This is too weird. "It was a joke. I obviously don't think your clients are vampires. Sheesh. Tough crowd."

Still, nothing but uncomfortable stares and awkward silences.

"She's not the one," Sebastian says again, and I'm stung by his rejection, despite my qualifications, despite the connection I thought we had on the train, and despite the fact that I'm not even sure I want this stupid job.

I ignore my flash that's pushing me to stay and glare at Sebastian. "You're right. I'm not the one. This would be a huge step down in my career. Perhaps if your creepy receptionist gave me an inkling of what this interview was for, I could have spared us all the waste of time. Good day."

I grab my bag and make my way to the door, pulling it open in one harsh movement, but then I stop and glance back at Sebastian, leveling him with my stare. "Harvard," I say.

He narrows his eyes at me, confused.

"My law degree," I clarify. "It's from Harvard as well. I didn't put it on my resume because I didn't take the bar, and I was never told what kind of firm this was." And with those closing words, I storm out and slam the door behind me.

The moment I do, tension builds inside me, buzzing on my skin, in my head, like spiders hatching within my body. I've felt this before, in the past, when I ignored my flash, but it will go away. I just need to get out of this soulless building and away from these men who make me crazy in too many ways.

But the tension doesn't fade as I walk the halls. It builds. It builds so much it scares me. I search for a bathroom and see a door ajar down the hall. My brain feels like it's swelling and tears prick my eyes at what's to come. This hasn't happened in so long. Not since...not since that day. I thought this was under control.

I knock gently on the door and it opens slowly. I expect to see any number of things—a broom closet, a standard office or waiting room, but what I find is nothing that should exist in this building.

It's as if I've been transported to a castle in an age of magic and wizards. The room is windowless and covered on one wall with floor to ceiling shelves filled with leather-bound books that look like they should be under glass at an important library. Another wall has shelves full of jars with different colored powders, roots, and other strange objects. In a corner sits a round table carved from jade and etched with ancient symbols. A fire burns in the center, though I see no source to feed the flames. And the flames are blue, rather than the standard red or orange. While I know blue flames can occur in nature—wood saturated with sea salt can produce blue flames—I don't know of any that can dance atop solid stone like that. Must be a chemistry trick, though why it would be in a law office is beyond me.

The room smells of spices and wood and earth. Against another wall is a desk covered with scrolls, with books and jars resting above it on shelves. A large chair sits in the center of the room in front of a blazing stone fireplace with a strong fire burning within. There's no chimney, no way for any of this to work.

"Hello there, dear, can I help you?"

I jump at the sound and turn to see Matilda standing in the doorway.

The pressure in my brain is building. I don't have much time to find somewhere private. Damnit.

Black spots appear in my vision. Light dances before my eyes as pain explodes in my head. I only have time to say, "Help, please!" as my eyes fill with tears and I grip my skull and sink to my knees, a sob escaping my throat.

Matilda rushes over. "Oh, my dear, it's all right, love. Come now." She rests a cool hand on my forehead. "You're burning up!"

I know. I always do when these hit.

And it's not over yet. It's just starting.

She helps me to the chair, supporting my body weight as sweat slicks my skin, and I shiver. I am both cold and hot. The pain hasn't reached its climax yet and I'm not looking forward to when it does. I won't be able to stop what happens next, and that terrifies me.

"I have to leave," I say between breaths, grinding the words out through the pain.

"Of course you can't leave. Not in this condition."

I reach for my bag, knowing I don't have enough time to get out of here, hoping I still have the strip of leather I used to carry just in case. I fumble, my sketchbook falling out, still opened to the page of Sebastian's sketch. Matilda notices it but says nothing as I find what I'm looking for and stick it into my mouth to keep from screaming.

Just in time, too.

The pain breaks my skull open, shattering my mind into a million pieces, undoing me, removing from my consciousness any memory of who I am or where I am. All I know is pain. And I bite down, moaning, muffled screams escaping through the leather.

My body convulses, and I experience a moment of a flash, and a vision so dark and terrifying fills my mind that I let the scream burst forth, spitting out the leather in the process, my body thrashing.

Something is pressed against my lips. Hot liquid pours into my mouth, a trickle at a time. It's bitter. Vile. I cough and try to spit it out, but a hand holds my head, and a soft voice soothes me. "This will help, my dear. Drink it all. It will help, I promise. You poor thing."

As more of the liquid makes its way down my throat, I feel its effects. The vision fades. The pain ebbs. The vise-like grip on my brain eases. And I slip into the darkness.

HE IS ALWAYS THERE, in my dreams. In my sleep. In my mind.

This time we are children. Nine or ten years old. I'm in bed, sweat beading on my forehead, the pain in my small body building. Adam is lying next to me, holding my hand, his face contorted in pain as well, but it's not his pain he's feeling. It's mine. "Why is this happening?" he asks our father, his voice a scared whine.

My father places a cool washcloth on my forehead and tenderly brushes away the wet hair clinging to my skin. "Every superhero has to go through hardships to come into their powers," my father says, his smile sad, untold secrets living in his dark brown eyes. Eyes my twin and I do not share. We have our mother's eyes.

"When will I go through my hardship?" Adam asks, with equal mixture of fear and excitement.

Adam wanted to be a superhero more than anything. And he felt sure we were meant to be just that.

Our father's smile slips, but he catches it in time and pastes it back onto his face. "Someday, my boy. Someday you, too, will go through your own transformation. *In lumen et lumen.* Always remember to stay in the light."

～

I TRY to cling to the vision of my brother and my father—two men now lost to me forever—to the memories that feel more real than the present sometimes, but consciousness steals him from me once again. When I come to, my head is still pounding, but it's no longer splintering into jagged edges. It's just a normal headache. My mouth is dry and bitter tasting, and I am curled up on a huge chair in front of a fire. It takes a moment for the preceding events to flow back into my mind. When they do, I shift my body and move to stand, but a wave of dizziness forces me back into the chair. Okay then. I have to take this slower.

I've never been hit with a headache that bad before. I'm dreading the recovery length of this one. I don't have time to be laid up. Moving slowly, cautiously, I lift myself upright, using the back of the chair as support. A wave of nausea passes through me, then recedes. I got this. I inch forward on the chair, my nails digging into the leather upholstery.

Voices in the hall give me pause. I strain my ears to listen, then slowly lift myself to standing and creep towards the door, retrieving my bag along the way.

"She's a mundane. She'll never fit into this world. It's not worth the risk!" That sounds like Sebastian, his voice deep and commanding. A voice that leads armies, that men and women will follow into battle and die for.

"She's exactly what we need—did you see who wrote her letter of recommendation? Do you want to tell Richard Dwarvas that his protege isn't good enough for us?" Derek pauses dramatically, and I almost laugh. Rick would have laughed.

"Even if she weren't," he continues, "we are out of time. He'll be expecting us by week's end."

"She is hot-tempered and ill-suited to this world." I think that one is Liam.

"You're one to call someone out for being hot-tempered," Derek says haughtily. "And if any of you have a better idea, now's the time to give it voice. We need her. You know we do."

"The four of you need to pipe down," Matilda's voice interjects. "The girl passed out and is in my office."

"What?" Sebastian says with a fierce growl.

"Oh, calm yourself, boy. She'll be fine. I gave her some tea to help. Poor thing. She'll feel it when she wakes up though."

I don't need to hear more. I just need to get the hell out of this office of horrors. Coming here was a giant mistake, one I intend to immediately remedy.

Slipping out of the office quietly, I head down the hall in the opposite direction of their voices. I see the shadows they cast from around the corner, but can't see them, so unless they have eyes in their shadows, they can't see me either.

I do my best to move confidently through the halls, but I haven't recovered from my episode, and I really need to be at home in bed right now.

I'm forced to pass through an open office space with cubicles, where people in suits are busily working on what look like important matters. There are law books open, phone calls being made, frantic typing on sleek, modern computers that match the space in which they dwell. I'm at least dressed the part, though my face must look ashen and my eyes sunken. Likely my makeup is smeared as well. I try to touch up my eyes with the pad of my index finger as I walk, avoiding the gazes of anyone who might glance my way.

I wonder what will happen when Matilda and the Night brothers discover I've left. Maybe nothing. I'm surely not special in the grand scheme of things, despite my impressive letter of recommendation. As I walk down another hall trying to find a stairway or elevator to take me back to the first floor, I notice a glass meeting room with what looks like clients and their attorneys. At first my glance is just that, a casual noticing, but then I turn back, slowing my step to reassure my brain I didn't just see what I think I did.

My breathing quickens as I try to stay casual and totally normal. Inside the room, one woman stands apart from the rest, and no one seems to acknowledge her presence. It takes me a moment to register what I'm seeing. She has long silver hair down to her feet, styled into hundreds of tiny braids. Her skin is a deep black, dark as midnight, with freckles on her prominent cheekbones that glow silver like stars in the night sky. Her eyes are wide and large and are entirely silver. And on her forehead is a delicate silver horn.

I know the moment she sees me. The moment we see each other. Her presence washes over me like a waterfall on a warm day, inviting and cool and so refreshing. I hear the soft whisper of my name carried on the faintest drift of air, or maybe it's in my head, I can't tell. But as my name enters me, I feel peace even through the pain.

A tear rolls down my cheek and she smiles, revealing large white teeth, and in my mind's eye I see her in a brilliant emerald glade, prancing through the thick grass, but her body is not that of a woman, but a unicorn.

I walk as if in a daze, somehow finding the elevator and making my way to the first floor. The twins both stare as I walk out and hail a cab, my mind spinning with all that I saw, but my heart is full from that brief glimpse of the woman with silver eyes.

CHAPTER 3: THE OFFER

I AM NOT YOURS, not lost in you,
Not lost, although I long to be
Lost as a candle lit at noon,
Lost as a snowflake in the sea.
~ Sara Teasdale

I MAKE a quick stop at the grocery store, tipping the cabbie generously with money I can ill afford to spend so she'll wait as I pick up the necessary supplies for my evening plan. It should be sleep, since it's almost two in the morning at this point, but this is New York, a city that's always awake. And I don't sleep much at any rate.

When the cab pulls up to my apartment, I tip once again, mentally counting down how much—or rather how little—money I have left. I slink into the building, hoping the manager isn't around. It was a nice place once upon a time, and the architecture is still breathtaking, but lack of care has worn it down. You can feel the spirit within has given up the fight. Even still, the rooms weren't cheap to come by. New York is New York, no matter what neighborhood you live in.

At my old job, the cost was no big deal. In fact, I had my sights set on something much grander before.

Now...

I'm just about to the elevator when I hear his voice. "Miss Oliver, I was hoping to run into you. Can we talk privately in my office a moment?" he asks, while placing his hand at my elbow and giving me a pointed stare.

It's not a question, it's a command, and I resent him and myself for the fact that I feel like a misbehaving child as he leads me to his office and closes the door. He sits behind his desk, and I stand, giving me a good view of the balding spot on his head, the light bulb overhead flashing against pale skin. Roger Lemon's parents own this building, which is his only qualification for managing an apartment complex. He's got a skinny mustache across a thin lip that makes him look Hitleresque but without the gravitas to lead a country.

"Miss Oliver, your payments are now several months past due. You have gotten my notices, I trust?"

"Every single one of them," I say through gritted teeth.

"Then you know this cannot be allowed to go on. We will have to take, dare I say it, drastic measures, if you do not get your account in compliance."

Compliance. I've always hated that word.

"I should have the money to you soon. I had a job interview today that looks promising."

His thin lips pinch together, forming a crease between his eyebrows. "I sympathize with what you've been through, but I think we've been patient long enough."

"I'll get you your money," I say. "I just need a bit more time."

His dark beady eyes bore into me. "You have until the end of the week, Miss Oliver. If you are not caught up on all your payments—including interest, you will be locked out of your apartment and all of your belongings will be confiscated and sold to pay your balance."

I seethe with rage, but I can't act on it. Not yet. "I'll get you your money by the end of the week," I say, then I turn to leave, but he grabs my arm, and when I whirl around to face him, he licks his lips.

He hands me an envelope with a red "PAST DUE" stamp on it. "There are other ways you could work off what you owe," he says.

It's not the first time he's pulled this shit, and it likely won't be the last. I yank my arm out of his grip, knowing his fingers will leave bruises. "I'll get you your money."

I can feel his eyes watching me as I go, and I force myself not to shiver.

Once in my apartment, I triple lock the door behind me, draw the curtains, and head to my bedroom. It only takes me ten minutes to change into my pajamas, scrub my face, and warm up a blanket in the dryer. While the blanket heats, I dig through my bag of goodies and pull out my current romantic threesome. Ben & Jerry. My rebound guys. Always here for me. Never disappointing. I grab a spoon and fill a glass generously with red wine, then head to the couch.

But the past due envelope snags my attention, and I rip it open in frustration, my eyes burning when I read it through once, then twice.

That bastard is charging an insane amount of interest. I owe twice what I thought, which was already more than I know how to get.

Not only will I lose my home, I'll lose everything in it.

Once I have my blanket, I tuck in for a few hours of watching horror movies as I try to mentally process what I saw, heard, and now suspect about my job interview, and what I'm going to do about this new deadline.

I would move out, if I could. But I don't have the money for a first, last, and deposit. Hell, I don't have the money for boxes to pack my shit. And after the last year, my credit is shot. The only way I don't become homeless in a week is to find a job that will give me an advance large enough to get caught up on my payments.

I think back to The Night Firm. We never got around to talking salary. Even if I was willing to work for them. Which I'm not.

I try to remember why I'm not, but my thoughts are muddled. It's becoming harder and harder to pull out the details of my exchange. I blame it on the wine, the sugar, and the haunting soundtrack of the movie I'm watching. My massive breakdown earlier. Speaking of, I should be feeling much worse right now. I don't understand how I recovered so quickly.

Halfway through the movie and the bottle of wine, I've nearly got myself convinced that my mind was playing tricks on me. I've been under tremendous stress for over a year now. I'm exhausted. I'm probably malnourished. That can do things to the brain. I just need to move on. Tomorrow, I decide, refilling my glass, tomorrow I'll go online, search for more jobs, find more interviews. I'll stick to 9-5 listings only!

With that decided, I give all my attention to the movie, and am mildly disappointed when I try to pour more wine and only a reluctant drop comes out. But I planned for this and bought two bottles.

A bit wobbly, I head back to the kitchen to uncork the other bottle, when I'm interrupted by a knock at my door and the ringing of the doorbell.

This shocks me almost more than anything else this evening.

No one comes to visit here, certainly not in the middle of the night. If it's Roger, that slimy bastard, I'm going to sue his ass for harassment.

In my alcohol-muddled mind, it doesn't take me long to convince myself that's exactly who's behind the door. Roger thinks if I'm desperate enough he can have me. He doesn't seem to get I would literally rather be homeless than let him touch me.

I school my face into one of a fierce warrior, then I march to the door and swing it open, ready for battle.

"You can go shove it up your ass if you think I'm going to—"

"Hello, Eve," Sebastian Night says, standing in my hallway with a pissy expression on his god-like face. "I see your outburst in the office isn't a one-off."

"I thought you were someone else," I say, my wine-addled brain sluggish. "What are you doing here?" I cross my arms over my chest, feeling suddenly self-conscious in my cat slippers and matching robe.

He hands me an envelope. "I was sent to give you this."

"What is it?" I ask, taking it from him. As I do, our fingers touch, and that sense of an earthquake rocking my insides overwhelms me again, though not unpleasantly. It's just intense. Passionate. Buried passion. He flinches at the touch, so I assume he feels something, too, but isn't thrilled with it.

"It's a job offer," he says, ignoring whatever is going on between us.

"Are you serious?" I ask, completely shocked. "After that interview, why would I work for you, and why would you want me to?"

He shrugs, avoiding my eyes. "It wasn't my decision." He turns to walk away, then pauses, glancing at me over my shoulder. "But if I were you, I'd burn that paper and pretend you never heard of The Night Firm. Stick to the light like your father said."

I watch until he disappears around the corner, then close my door, locking up once again. Back on the couch, I stare at the thick cream envelope stamped with a wax seal. How pretentious, but kinda cool, too. I break open the seal and unfold the letter. It's handwritten in calligraphy, so formal it feels like a summons from a king, not a job offer from a law firm.

THE NIGHT FIRM would like to offer Miss Eve Oliver the job of Manager of Operations, to begin immediately, or as soon as Miss Oliver can avail herself of the position. It is a full time, live-in position, with generous compensation and benefits. We await your decision.

IT ENDS with each of the four brothers' names and signatures and stamped with an "N" matching the wax seal.

There's a second page, this one indicating a generous signing bonus, salary, benefits and spending budget for wardrobe, food, and more.

The numbers make me gasp.

I sit there in a daze, staring at the letter to make sure it's real and not something I'm imagining.

This is enough to get caught up on my payments and then some. Though I realize that since it's a live-in position, I wouldn't actually need this place anymore.

Tears burn my eyes. This job could save me from bankruptcy and homelessness.

Two years ago, if you'd told me this is what my life would look like right now, I never would have believed you.

I was happy, at the top of my career, in love with someone I thought was a great man, living in a luxury apartment in the heart of New York's poshest neighborhood. I had it all.

Then I lost it all the day my brother called with the news.

I didn't know it at the time. Not yet.

But certain events in life have the ability to strip you of everything so slowly you don't realize it's happening until it's too late.

Now I'm single, deeply in debt, unemployed, and as unhappy as I've ever been in my life.

I glance down at the thick parchment, shaking my head. This could solve all my problems.

I can't believe I'm considering it. That place was insane. Even if I was only imagining parts of it.

After all, the strange things I saw did happen after my explosive headache. I've never had one that bad, but even in the past I've had moments of seeing things that weren't there. This might have felt more real, but that's likely due to the severity of the episode.

So, what's really the problem with taking the job? I reach for my wine glass but realize I never finished opening the new bottle. Damn.

The worst thing is that a few of the brothers clearly don't want me there. Especially Sebastian.

So what? I climbed to the top at my last job despite men like that, not because of them. I could do it again. Would do it again.

I consider waiting until morning, but I realize this is now my new work day, if I really am going to do this. *Am* I really going to do this?

Apparently I am.

I dial before I change my mind. The female twin answers. "This is Eve. May I please speak with Derek?"

I decide to use his first name since Mr. Night would bring all the boys running, and I only want to talk to the one who actually fought for me to be there.

"Hello, Eve," his warm voice says a moment later.

"I'll take the job," I say hurriedly, before my liquid courage fades.

"I'm delighted to hear that. Can we expect you to start tomorrow evening?"

"You said this requires a live-in situation, yes?"

"Yes."

"I might need a few days to get my belongings packed and my things in order. But I have...a favor to ask."

"What might that be?"

I bite my lip, hating that I have to ask this. "Is it possible to get my signing bonus now?"

"Of course, that can be arranged." He pauses, and I hear some clicking in the background. "The money has been transferred into your account. You should see it there now. Is there anything else I can do for you?"

I'm dumbfounded. I set my phone to speaker and click open my banking app to check. Sure enough, the deposit was made. "But, I didn't give you my account information."

He chuckles. "You will find we have significant resources at our disposal. You don't think we offered this job to you without doing a thorough investigation into your life, do you?"

"That's...that's invasive!" I feel vulnerable and violated, but not enough to take back my acceptance of the job. I can't totally blame them. I always encouraged background checks on new employees. Of course, they would look into me, especially if I'll be handling sensitive client information or dealing with large amounts of money. And if I'm living with them, then that's a whole other deal. They'd certainly want to know the person they were bringing into their home.

I should be so diligent, but I can't seem to find anything about this company or this family online, which is just strange, and I don't know what that means. How do you run a business, a successful one by the looks of it, without having some online presence these days?

"I apologize for the personal intrusion, but given the sensitive nature of our work, I fear we had no choice but to be thorough. As for your relocation, I can send a moving team to your apartment tomorrow to help you pack and move whatever you want. I can provide a storage unit, or if you'd rather, I can arrange for whatever you'd like to be sold and the money sent to your account."

"Um. Thanks. Yeah, I guess that would be helpful."

"Very good. Can I expect to see you Thursday evening, then?"

"Yes, that should be enough time."

"Wonderful. We look forward to having you as part of our family. I'll send a driver for you and your belongings at 7 p.m. Anything you'd like sent to our home, please let the movers know tomorrow and it will be here waiting for you."

"Can I ask you one more thing?" I rush the words before I lose my nerve. This may be a bad idea, but what the hell. I'm full of those tonight.

"Anything," he says.

I explain to him what I need and I can hear the smile in his voice. "It would be my pleasure to assist in this."

He ends the call, and I sit staring at my phone. Have I completely lost my mind? I kind of feel like I have.

I yawn, and the adrenaline rush of seeing Sebastian and making that call crashes over me, leaving me weak and tired and ready for bed.

I abandon the second bottle of wine and retire to my bedroom, falling onto my mattress like the drunk, exhausted woman I am.

That night my dreams take me to a grove of trees near a stream. The moon is full and reflects off the water. A woman shrouded in a robe stands in front of a blazing fire, her long, dark, hair — untamed and curly — whips in the wind as she raises her arms.

"I am the woman in the wild!" she screams into the shrieking wind. As she speaks, the wind thrashes, the water becomes brackish, the fire blazes, and the trees seem to bend into her.

"I am the blood sister of the moon! I am the call of the night and her secrets. The radiance left from a star. I am all that you need and more than you know. I am the hidden that shall now be found. Tell my story. Set me free. I am the magic that you seek. I am the wild!"

As her robes fall off, she stands naked, her face covered by her hair, the flames dancing off her pale skin, moving around her. She controls the flames, sending them forward. Sending them into me in a flash of heat and searing pain.

My heart slams against my ribs as I wake with a start, gasping for breath, clutching my chest.

I lie in my bed, staring at the ceiling, replaying my dream. It felt so real. So visceral. Like I was standing in the clearing with her. I could feel the heat of the flames, the splash of the water from the stream. I could smell the wood burning and the mulch from the forest. I could feel her power flowing in and around me.

My breathing slows and I check the time. It's not even seven in the morning yet, but I know I won't be getting any more sleep.

I slide out of bed and am about to head to the shower, but I decide to take a run instead, despite my hangover, either from the bottle of wine or the headache, likely both. Still, it's been too long since I worked out. I need this.

On my way to the door, I pause outside my brother's room and take a deep breath. Some days are easier than others. All days are hard. I push it away most of the time, but when I'm home, I allow myself a moment for our memories. Just a moment.

Then I leave the building and begin running.

With music blasting in my ear, and the pounding of the pavement under my feet, I don't pay too much attention to where I'm going, so I'm a little surprised when I end up at The Night Firm.

But I'm not nearly as surprised as when I poke my head in and see it's empty. Not just no one at the front desk, but totally empty. No sign. No furniture. No cool zen decorations. No fountain overflowing.

I pull out my phone and call the office number. The creepy twin whose name I should probably learn answers. "The Night Firm."

"Derek, please, it's Eve."

She puts me on hold without a word. As usual. If I were them I'd put someone more personable up front as the first contact, but that's just me.

"Derek Night here," he says in a distracted voice.

"Hi, it's Eve," I say. "I'm um…I'm confused."

"About what, Eve?"

"I'm at the office, only The Night Firm no longer exists here. Is this some kind of scam?" I ask.

"How could this be a scam?" he asks. "I've sent you money. Isn't a scam usually the other way around?"

He's got a point there.

31

"So you relocated in the few hours I slept?" I ask. "How's that even possible?"

"With the right motivation, anything is possible."

I don't know what to say in response to that.

"And we did make it clear that this job was live-in and involved travel. We go where our clients need us."

"That's a highly unusual way for a law firm to do business," I say, which is honestly the biggest understatement in the history of under-statements.

"We are a highly unusual firm, Miss Oliver, as I'm sure you've noticed. But I am glad you called. The movers will be at your house in two hours. They should have everything done by noon."

That seems unlikely, but I don't say as much. After all, anything is possible according to this guy.

We end the call, and I run back to my apartment and shower before the movers arrive.

If they really are on their way, I need to hurry.

I pause in front of my brother's room, my hand resting on the cool, metal doorknob. I haven't entered his room since the day he died. I know that sounds foolish, but it's like Schrödinger's cat. There's a box with a cat in it, and the cat has an equal chance of being alive or dead. But once you open the box, it's over, the truth staring at you. As long as I keep the door closed, I can pretend my brother yet lives. At least in my own mind. Once I open the door and face the emptiness, it'll be over.

Still.

It's time.

I twist the knob and close my eyes, then push the door open.

His scent—cinnamon and honey—hits me first, and it shocks me so much I crumple to my knees with a whimper. It's as if he was just here. How is that possible?

I open my eyes and see that the room is empty, as expected. It looks exactly as it did when he was alive, minus the hospital bed we rented for him. Now, in lieu of a bed, there are deep grooves in the carpets where the wheels had pressed in. But everything else is untouched. The bottles of medication on the side table. The open book lying face down, holding his page as if he might come back to it at any moment. His favorite socks folded just so next to his shoes.

A breeze catches the curtains of his window, blowing through the room gently, carrying more of his scent to me. I could have sworn the window had been locked. It always was.

Adam and I fought about it constantly. He needed fresh air, but he refused to let me leave the windows open. "I don't want to stink up the rest of the world with the scent of my death," he'd said.

And so his scent grew stronger in our home, turning from the beloved and comforting and familiar to a mutated version of itself, similar enough to inspire a fresh wave of grief, but more rancid and laced with rot. A reminder of what was to come.

I suck in my breath and cross the room in ten steps, stopping in front of the window. When I touch it, I feel the pull of a flash, but it fades before I can follow the thread. The window slams shut quite suddenly, and without my aid, or the aid of anyone as far as I can see.

It must have been the wind.

I turn towards the bedroom, to face what remains of my brother. There are some things I cannot let someone else pack, or even touch. Not until I am done.

And so I begin one item at a time, savoring the memory each of his belongings brings up in me, even as it slices a fresh wound in my already eviscerated heart.

A sweet torture.

In the end, I only keep one thing.

His ring.

He always wore it. To the very end.

I gave it to him the day we both graduated college.

I slip it onto my middle finger and then leave his bedroom for the last time.

I DON'T KNOW how it happened, but Derek wasn't wrong. The movers have everything cleared out by noon. I am left in an empty apartment, save for my personal items. I've decided not to store anything, and to take only what I truly need and a few keepsakes.

A fresh start, as it were.

Letting them into my brother's room was the hardest part, but I know it's time to move on. He would want me to if nothing else.

When the movers leave, I take out my checkbook and march down to Roger's office. He grins when he sees me. "I see you've come to your senses and are ready to discuss my terms," he says, his smile a lascivious sneer.

He licks his lips and I shudder. I clench my fist around my checkbook, then smile. "Why, that's so sweet, but you see I've come to pay off what I owe."

His face pales. "Well, that's great news, but surely you don't need to spend all that money when there are other ways to satisfy the debt."

I slap the check onto his desk. "Here is my payment in full, plus interest."

He looks at it and the sides of his lips curl up. "It seems you're several thousand dollars short."

"About that," I say, shoving a letter into his hands featuring The Night Firm letterhead. "It seems it wasn't contractually legal for you to hike the interest after we'd signed an agreement. I've paid what was originally agreed upon. Nothing more. It's also not legal to extort sexual favors as payment for a debt, you miserable sleaze-ball. If you have any questions, you can contact my lawyer."

I let myself gloat as I walk out of his office, leaving him gaping.

I owe Derek a big thanks for that one.

TOMORROW MY NEW LIFE BEGINS. Today, I'm going to pamper myself and use my new expense card to make sure I have the right wardrobe for this job.

I want to enjoy the shopping, the makeover—god I've needed a new haircut for ages—the pampering. But my mind keeps turning back to Sebastian and his brothers. They mesmerize me even as they confound me. And I still don't really know what this bloody job is. My life feels entirely too surreal.

Back in my hotel for the night, I push myself to stay awake until morning. It's time to get used to my new sleep schedule.

I spend the night sketching Sebastian in different poses. Tired of my obsession, I move on to other subjects. First, I sketch Matilda leaning over that strange table with the fire. Then I sketch the scene that dances in my mind like a dream, of eyes glowing silver in a face of midnight, that delicate horn in the center of her forehead.

I manage three hours of sleep before waking in the afternoon. I realize I'm ready to go. This is too much waiting. I pass the time exercising in the hotel gym, taking a bath, eating, watching movies. Finally, it's time. I check out with all my belongings and wait in front of the hotel for the driver Derek promised. It's been awhile since I've owned a car, and I've never had a driver. This is quite a change of status for me.

A limo pulls up at precisely seven p.m. and a perky young woman bounces out and smiles widely at me. "I'm Lily. I'll be your driver from now on."

Lily has pink punk rock hair, multiple facial piercings, and wears a driver uniform that's bright neon colors mixed with tie dye. It's quite the combination and it stands out starkly against her ebony skin. I'm instantly drawn to her sparkly personality.

"I get a driver all the time?" I ask.

She laughs. "Of course, silly. You're part of the family now."

I don't know what she means by that, but she opens the door for me to get in, and then proceeds to pack my luggage into the trunk.

Once we're both settled, she asks if I want the middle window up or down. "It's sound proof. You'll have complete privacy."

"No, I like talking to you," I say, as I study the limo. I've been in one before, but this is especially nice. "Where are we going?"

"I don't know," she says sheepishly.

"You don't know where we're going? Then how will we get there?"

"The GPS is programmed with the current address," she says.

"Current address? They have several homes?"

"No, well, yes, but that's not what I meant. The home changes locations as needed for security or work."

A shock of horror fills me. "Am I going to be living in a mobile home?" I ask.

She laughs. "No way. Wait till you see it. It's not that kind of mobile. It's...really hard to explain. You'll have to wait to get there and see for yourself. It's going to blow your mind." She snaps her mouth shut. "But I'm not supposed to say too much. They want to tell you everything themselves."

"Everything like what?" I ask, hoping I can get more out of her.

"I'm sorry, I can't!" She squeezes her lips together and shakes her head.

I sigh, letting her off the hook. I don't want her to get in trouble.

"Can you at least tell me if they're a good family to work for?"

She smiles broadly. "Oh, yes. Granny Night rescued me when I was little. I was practically raised with the Nights. The brothers are like my uncles. They can seem a bit gruff at first, but they each have a soft spot worth searching for. Don't give up on them."

It's good to hear someone speak well of them. It makes me feel less nervous about relocating my life into theirs with so little warning.

I resign myself to my own thoughts and wonder idly who Roger's next victim will be. A thought occurs to me, and I call Derek.

"Hello, Miss Oliver, I trust your driver is taking good care of you and that the movers were helpful?"

"Oh, yes, to both. And call me Eve. I... have another favor—and it's... unusual."

"Oh, I'm intrigued," Derek says.

"My former landlord is a sleaze to women. I'd hate to imagine another woman getting that apartment and being harassed by him. Is there anything you can do to...I don't know, make sure that doesn't happen?" I don't even know what I'm asking, and I feel like a moron. "Maybe somehow ensure it gets rented to a big, buff dude or something?"

Derek chuckles. "I like your style, Miss...Eve. You'll fit right in, I think. I can definitely handle that. Anything else?"

"Um, I don't think so. You've already been more than generous."

When we hang up, I check my bank account again to make sure my eyes weren't deceiving me before, but the money is all there. I know the check I wrote will clear soon, but that still leaves a comfortable savings and a decent buffer fund should this job go south fast. That gives me a little room to breathe. I worked so hard to build a stable financial structure, never imagining that one year of medical expenses could wipe it all out so quickly.

Cancer kills in more ways than one.

It destroys everything about a person's life.

I shake my head, unwilling to dwell on that now. I'm turning things around. Making progress with my life. I think.

I hope.

I close my eyes and let myself try to doze until I feel the limo slowing.

"Are we there already?" I ask, surprised the drive went by so fast.

"Not exactly," Lily says. "We have one more passenger to pick up." She says this sheepishly, and I realize why when the door opens and Sebastian slides into the back, newspaper in hand.

The look of irritation doesn't appear on his face until he sees me.

Naturally.

Seriously though, what did I do to piss this guy off?

CHAPTER 4: THE DRIVE

WE GROW ACCUSTOMED to the Dark—
When Light is put away—
- Emily Dickinson

I SIGH as he picks a seat as far from me as he possibly can. Fortunately, there's plenty of room back here, and we don't have to sit too close to each other.

Not that my body isn't craving being just a little bit closer to this insanely attractive man. But my brain knows better, and I'm sticking with my brain for now.

He gives me a curt nod. "I hope you do not mind, since we are both going to the same location."

"It's fine," I say. "I mean, obviously. This is your car and driver. I just appreciate the ride. And the job," I add, almost as an afterthought.

He grunts and opens his newspaper to begin reading.

"You don't find it tedious to read the news that way?" I ask, as Lily starts the limo and gets us back on the road.

"No. I do not."

"You can find all that and more online," I say, holding up my smart phone.

He sighs in exasperation and lowers the paper to glare at me. "I prefer analog to digital. Call me old-fashioned."

Lily giggles and doesn't seem the least bit intimidated when Sebastian casts his standard glare at her. She just laughs harder. "Oh, Uncle Seb, stop being such a brat."

I'm surprised to hear her teasing him like that, but not as surprised as I am when his face lights up in a smile and he laughs in return. It's the first time I've heard him laugh, and it's deep and husky, and makes his face even more handsome. Damn him.

The moment passes, however, and when he returns his focus to me, his energy shifts.

And not for the better.

"Look," I say, ready to settle this between us once and for all. "I know you think I'm not serious about this job because of what I told you on the subway, but I am. I don't even think I'd want to do art for my career. If I had to worry about drawing for others, for money, I might not get the joy from it I do now. I meant what I said during the interview: I'm smart, educated and resourceful. Granted, I'm still not entirely clear what my job is, or how your law firm even operates effectively if it's only open at night, but I can promise you I will learn everything I need to, and quickly. I work hard, study hard, and always excel at what I do. Always. So, if you'll just give me a chance, you'll find that I'm an excellent employee."

I say this all in one breath, and when I'm done I slump back into my seat, emotionally spent.

He stares for a moment and then says, "Do not presume to know my thoughts, Miss Oliver." And with that he finds the next page of his newspaper and turns away from me once more.

I've clearly been dismissed.

Determined to make some use out of what is proving to be a long car ride with an unpleasant companion, I pull out my sketchbook and close my eyes. I take a deep breath and mentally count backwards from ten. As I do, I follow a staircase in my mind down, down, down until I'm standing before a large red door. Opening it, I step through into a secret garden where I instantly connect to my muse. She glows within a swaying willow tree, her form moving through the bark and branches, her hair falling around her in waves of green. Her voice echoes in the wind and the rustling of leaves.

She sings me a song. I catch it and smile. Then open my eyes and draw.

I don't think too hard about what I'm drawing. I just let my muse's voice speak through the charcoal and pencil.

Everything around me is silent as I work, and I don't realize until the drawing is complete that Sebastian is staring at me.

Or rather, at my drawing.

I study it myself, now that my focus is returning to normal and my head is clearing. Four men—clearly the Night brothers—stand back to back, forming a circle around a woman, surrounded by a dark and menacing wood, with trees that look alive and hungry in the worst possible way. The brothers hold drawn swords, steel glinting in the moonlight.

I am the woman they are guarding.

We're all standing in the center of a pentagram burned into the grass beneath our feet.

Sebastian is still staring, and I quickly close my sketchbook and slip it into my bag, embarrassed that my boss saw what I drew. Embarrassed that my subconscious pulled that image out of my mind for this exercise.

And more than a little unnerved at what that image might mean.

"How did you learn to do that?" Sebastian asks.

"Do what? Draw?"

"Well, yes, that, too. But how did you learn to induce a trance state so easily?"

"Um. I taught myself. Both things. As a kid I loved drawing, and the obsession never went away. I drew on anything I could with anything I could. By the time I was ten, I was selling my drawings to the neighbors. My brother was my business partner and marketer," I say with a smile. "He could sell shoes to a shoemaker. He'd go door to door, and by the time he would come back all my art would be sold. I didn't learn until much later that he was the one buying most of it, because he didn't want me to give up on my dreams." I suck in a breath to keep myself from rambling even more. He doesn't need to hear about my childhood. And I don't need to dive into stories about my brother right now.

Instead, I turn to his original question. "As for the trance, it's just a silly self-hypnosis trick. It helps put me in a more creative mindset. It's nothing, really. Anyone can do it. Just Google a YouTube video."

He scoffs at that. "Trust me, it is not 'nothing' as you say. And I do not watch the YouTube."

I snort-laugh at that in a very unladylike way. "What are you, ninety years old? *The* YouTube? Oh dear. You have so much to learn."

"No offense, but I highly doubt there's anything you could possibly teach me," he says and then he snaps up his newspaper and proceeds to ignore me again.

"How could I possibly find that offensive?" I ask, with a sharp dose of sarcasm before I turn away from him, folding my arms firmly across my chest to reinforce my point.

I press my lips together, biting my tongue to avoid saying something hot-headed and stupid to my new boss who already doesn't like me. The boss I now have to live with.

What have I gotten myself into? I wonder, not for the first time and very likely not for the last.

The minutes tick by slowly, and the exhaustion of the last couple of days seeps into my bones. Just as I'm about to doze off, my flash buzzes in my head. My eyes blink open as my body slams forward. My seat belt tightens around my waist and chest, digging into my skin even through my clothes, pushing out all the breath in me.

And then my world is spinning. Spinning wildly, toppling end over end, crunching and slamming and crashing into itself.

Pain shoots through me, but I can't tell where on my body it specifically hurts. My nerves dance, lit up like current pouring through live wires. I feel everything until it becomes a kind of nothing.

When I can think clearly again, I find I'm hanging from my seatbelt, upside down in what's left of the car, my head spinning and my breathing coming in short gasps.

There's a voice, but I can't find the face it belongs to.

He's saying my name.

"Eve. Eve, focus on me. Eve. Stay with me."

I blink. Something thick drips into my eyes, stinging. The face in question comes into focus, and though my mind is sluggish, and words and names come reluctantly, as if being dragged through tar, the visceral response of my body is instant. Warmth floods me, and I feel myself sinking into him, like into quicksand.

"Sebastian," I say with a raspy throat. "What happened?"

"We hit a deer. The limo flipped. I need to get you out of here. I'm going to unbuckle you, but I need you to hold onto me. Can you do that?"

I lick my parched lips and nod. His words sound like they're coming from underwater, but I think I understand.

He reaches for me, one hand wrapping behind my back, the other hand over my waist. "Are you ready?" he asks.

I nod, then mumble, "Yes."

My heart quickens—in fear? anticipation?—as he unlatches the seatbelt. Gravity takes over and I fall unceremoniously into his arms. The removal of pressure causes blood to rush into my extremities, leading to pain.

A whole lot of pain.

I look down and see a metal rod sticking out of my right leg. "Holy shit!" I scream as my leg spasms.

I reach to pull the rod out, but Sebastian stops me.

"It's safer to leave it for now."

I'm fighting to breathe, my ribs aching with the effort to move oxygen through my body.

I bury my face in his chest, closing my eyes against whatever is happening outside his embrace. Fear pulses through me, tainting my body with the sour smell of it.

Everything slows, and there's an unearthly quiet outside for a moment before a loud *whump* comes from somewhere behind us and heat begins penetrating the back seat, filling it with smoke.

For a moment I contemplate my own death, that this might be my last moment on earth. I find I'm not as scared as I always expected I would be. I will be with my parents and my brother. With my family.

But I don't die. Not now, anyways.

Sebastian holds me close to him, crouching in the ruined limo.

"I need you to trust me," he says, his mouth pressed against my ear.

I nod.

"Good. I'm going to set you down so I can pry the door open. Stay close to me."

I nod, ignoring the panic rising in my chest and the pain spreading through me.

My lungs fill with smoke and I choke as he puts me on the floor – actually, the ceiling since we're upside down - beside him, my head pounding, my vision dancing with specks of light.

I glance toward the front of the limo, where Lily was, but she's not there. Did she get thrown out of the car when we crashed?

Sebastian grunts, pulling my attention back to him, as he uses his muscular legs to kick the door. I'm about to tell him that's not going to work, but my mouth clamps shut when the door flies off the hinges and into the street.

I stare in confused wonder and awe, the pain from my injuries subsiding at the distraction of seeing Sebastian perform superhuman feats of strength. I've read stories about this. About the adrenaline surge that can happen during a life or death crisis. How it can give ordinary people extraordinary strength for a few moments to accomplish the impossible. And Sebastian certainly isn't ordinary. He's anything but.

Before I can process much more, he's lifting me into his arms. I grab my bag and clutch it to my chest as he extracts us from the wreckage of the burning limo. And then he runs. I expect to be jolted around like a sack of potatoes, but the motion is smooth, seemingly effortless, which is mind-boggling.

"Wait! Lily! We can't leave her. We have to go back!"

"Lily got away," he says, showing no sign of weariness. "She knows what to do. We have to get out of here." His pace does not slow, and I'm beginning to worry he's going to try to run all the way to our final destination.

Whereas his adrenaline may be everlasting, mine, alas, is not. It crashes, leaving me writhing in pain.

I scream as I feel the deep wound of the metal bar plunged into my leg.

Sebastian glances down at me, his brow furrowed. "You are not dying. I know it hurts, but you will live. Help is coming."

As if on cue, I hear the sound of an approaching vehicle and glance around to see a black sedan pull up beside us. Sebastian nods to it and somehow opens the back door, laying me gently in the backseat. I expect him to take the front seat, but he surprises me by scooting in next to me, careful not to bump my injured leg.

I'm shocked to see that Lily's the driver. She somehow got away completely unscathed and found us a new car. There's definitely more to her than meets the eye.

Lily hands Sebastian a small black bag, flinching when she gets a good look at me.

"Is it that bad?" I ask. I feel beat up, bloody and miserable, so yes, it probably is.

"You'll be okay," she says with an encouraging smile.

Sebastian pulls a jar of green goo and a strip of leather out of the bag. "This will hurt. A lot. But then it will be better." He hands me the leather and then gently pulls my injured leg onto his lap. "Bite on this."

Still somewhat dazed, I do what I'm told, taking the leather and placing it between my teeth, thinking, is this really necessary?

It only takes a moment to realize...it's necessary.

My teeth dig new grooves into the leather as Sebastian pulls the rod out of my leg and proceeds to smear the putrid-smelling green goo over it.

The sensation vacillates from fire to ice as the ointment is absorbed into my flesh and blood. I feel infected. Feverish. The pain is so fierce I lose sense of anything else.

He brushes my hair to the side and rubs more of the ointment into my head wound. The smell is nauseating, and my headache, already a level ten, ramps up until I have to close my eyes to keep from vomiting and passing out.

I fade in and out of consciousness for some unknowable amount of time, until finally the pain eases and then disappears entirely.

With its departure, I come back to myself and open my eyes. I let out a deep sigh of relief and tentatively test sitting up on my own. Nothing terrible happens. Yay.

I extricate my leg from the delicious lap of Sebastian Night and am stunned to see that the gaping wound that was there just a few moments ago has now knitted itself back together.

"How?" I ask, any other words failing me.

"You'll find out soon enough," he says, though he doesn't sound happy about it.

"That's all you have to say? I'll find out soon enough?" I respond, incredulous.

"Why did you take this job, Eve?" he asks, deflecting.

"You answer my question first," I counter.

And then I wait. Silently. Eyes on him as he weighs what he wants more.

"There's a lot I'm not telling you, though not by my choice. There is risk with this job. We make enemies. And our latest client is something of a high-profile celebrity in certain circles, and that comes with additional risk."

"Who's the client?"

"You'll find out soon enough. Your turn, Eve. A deal's a deal."

I nod. "That it is. Very well. I took the job because everything about who I am changed the night my brother died."

"From cancer. I was sorry to hear that. My condolences."

I clear my throat and continue. "He didn't die of cancer. Not officially," I say, the words alive in my throat, like bees demanding to be let out. Words I have never spoken to another living person. But words I tell myself every single day.

"My brother, Adam, had cancer, yes. But it had been in remission. We were happy. Celebrating. Planning for the future. Or so I thought. I got the call at 4:34 a.m. on Friday the Thirteenth. No joke. On Friday the thirteenth, of all days, I got the call that my brother had died by suicide. He'd gotten the results from his latest scan. The cancer was back. He left me a note explaining it all. How he knew this had

45

already wiped me out financially. How I'd put my career on hold to stay home and take care of him. How my health was going to shit and I needed to take better care of myself." At this point, I can't stop the tears. They flow, and the emotion sticks in my throat as I speak. "As if losing my twin, my best friend, my other half, as if losing him would ever make my life easier in any way at all."

What I don't say is that I already knew he was dead when the call came in. I had the worst flash of my life that morning. And I knew.

Sebastian doesn't look away from my grief when our eyes meet, and I can see in his eyes that he's known his share, too.

I wipe my tears and calm my breathing, centering myself before I continue. "After that, going back to the life I had before, well, it just seemed pointless. And painful. My brother is everywhere in my old life. There was no aspect of our lives that didn't intersect in some way. I needed something different."

Sebastian lets out a sudden, humorless laugh. "You definitely got different."

Our car slows and Lily turns to look at us. "We're here."

I've been so caught up in my story, and in Sebastian, that I failed to notice the scenery around us changing.

We are in the middle of the country, surrounded by the ocean on one side and forest on the other, and there is a house—nay an estate—lit by thousands of candles, with a manicured topiary garden lining the path to the front of an actual castle made of white stone and complete with four towers and several turrets. In the center, above the draw-bridge, is a jaw-dropping rose window made of stained glass that shimmers even in the darkness. The castle is surrounded by a moat with koi splashing within.

"This looks like something you'd find in Europe on a tourist to-do list," I say through breathy excitement, momentarily forgetting about my freshly healed leg and Sebastian's evasiveness. "Is this where I'll be living?"

"It is," Lily says when Sebastian doesn't answer. "Welcome to your new home, Eve. Welcome to the family."

CHAPTER 5: THE NIGHT ESTATE

THERE ARE darknesses in life and there are lights, and you are one of the lights, the light of all lights.
  ~ Bram Stoker

MY SPINE TINGLES the closer we come to the castle. Lily pulls the sedan up to the front and Sebastian lets himself out before the car has hardly had a chance to stop. As an afterthought he glances back at me. "Lily will take care of you." Then he leaves, rushing across the small bridge over the moat as if his pants are on fire.

I let myself out as well, and Lily rests her hands on her hips and frowns. "Hey, that's my job!"

"Sorry. I'm not used to people opening doors for me."

"You'd better get used to it in your position."

"What? As glorified secretary?" I ask with a not-so-subtle snark in my voice.

Her eyes widen. "You think you're a glorified secretary? Wow, they really haven't told you anything, have they? I'm surprised you took the job with what you know."

"You and me both," I say. "But I needed the money."

She nods. "I get it. Oh, your stuff arrived earlier today. It's all been taken to your suite."

"I have a suite?" I ask.

She giggles. "You have no idea what you have!"

The door opens as we approach and Matilda comes out to greet us, arms held open for an embrace. Tears burn my eyes when she wraps her surprisingly strong arms around me. I have to lean over to hug her, but it's worth it. Her hug makes me feel like I'm being hugged by the universe. Unconditional love flows through me and I instantly love this old woman I already knew I liked.

She wipes a tear from my cheek and pats my hand. "Don't worry, dear. You're home now. With family. I'm so glad you decided to trust yourself and come, despite everything."

Her words are layered with double meaning and I get a strong sense she knows more about my life than I realized, even factoring in the extensive background check. "I hope you and I can be friends," I say, surprising myself.

"We already are, and have always been," she says kindly. "I heard what happened on the way here. That's certainly not an ideal first day on the job, is it?"

I half laugh through brimming tears and shake my head.

Lily is glancing worriedly from me to Matilda, bouncing on her tip-toes. The girl can never seem to stay still for long. I put her in her mid-20s, though she looks younger.

"Lily, dear, you handled the situation perfectly. We're all very proud of you and grateful."

Lily beams, and her eyes practically glow with the joy the compliment inspires.

"Would you mind showing Eve to her room? I've got to meet with the boys," Matilda says to Lily, then she looks to me. "I suspect you'll want a few minutes to get settled and orient yourself. The boys are in a meeting but will speak with you when it ends. They wanted to be here to greet you themselves, but on top of discussing what happened on the way here, we're meeting with a big client tomorrow and they have a lot of work to do. So will you, once you familiarize yourself with your job."

"About that," I say. "When will I learn more about what my job entails?"

"Tonight. I promise many of your questions will be answered tonight. I hope you like your suite. I designed it myself just for you."

I thank her and follow Lily through an entryway that's larger than some apartments in New York. Two grand staircases wind up to a second floor, meeting in the middle. There's a door to the right, a door to the left, and a hall beneath the stairs that leads to another part of the castle. Lily leads me upstairs and down several hallways. I try to memorize the path, but quickly lose track. I feel like I should be leaving bread crumbs to find my way back.

We stop at a door that looks the same as several others we've passed. "This is your suite. Just ring the bell if you need help. It's a big place and easy to get lost in when you're new."

"Do you live here, too?" I ask.

She nods. "You're going to love it."

She walks away, leaving me with my bags, but turns back to face me before I enter the room. "We're all really glad you're here, Eve. You're just who they need."

She leaves for real this time and I wipe my palms on my pants and turn the knob, letting myself in.

I expect to walk into a bedroom, but I actually step into a sitting room with a loveseat and chair positioned in front of a fireplace with a coffee table between them. There's a patio with a cream-colored silk curtain dancing in the wind coming in from the open glass door. Along one wall, a desk with my some of my books stacked on it waits and the rest are lined up on the shelves next to it. My personal items have been dispersed through the room just as I would have placed them, including a sketch I drew of my brother framed on the fireplace mantel, right next to my brother's urn.

Seeing it brings more tears to my eyes. I place my bags down and walk over to it, running a finger down the side of the urn, my heart contracting with the grief that threatens to overwhelm me daily. It still doesn't seem real, and yet it's altogether too real at the same time. Grief is like that, I've learned. It lives on the impossible edge between real and unreal. Between waking and dreaming. And that makes it all the more crushing. Not understanding what happened to the brother I knew. How his body, the fullness of his life, could be reduced to a handful of ashes.

I turn away from his remains and focus on exploring the rest of the room. The hand-painted tile flooring is partially covered by thick rugs to take the chill off, and the blazing fire in the hearth warms the space. A large bookshelf covers one wall and is filled with books, some of them mine, some new. Well, old, actually, but new to me. Mine stand out as the only ones without leather covers.

In another corner is a two-person table with a bowl of fruit and a jug of juice or wine atop it. There's another jug with water, and a bar with stronger drinks to the side. I step through a door and into my bedroom, which boasts another lit fire with two comfortable leather chairs in front of it, and a huge four-poster canopy bed carved from a beautiful light wood and decorated with cherry blossoms. A thick purple velvet comforter covers it and I push my hand into the bed and sigh at how luxurious it feels. Way better than the bed I just sold. There's a large wardrobe that reveals all my clothes unpacked when I open it, plus other clothes, very fancy dresses and suits, that I've never seen before but are all in my size with matching shoes. The new clothes are gothic and Renaissance in style, which is unusual, but beautiful and clearly expensively, made with the finest craftsmanship and fabrics.

I've been well off in the past, comfortable enough to live in a nice neighborhood in New York, buy nice clothes, and go to restaurants when I wanted. Granted I had to sell anything of value to help pay Adam's medical expenses and relocate to a much cheaper apartment, but I still remember that life. But as I look around, I realize this is a whole other level of wealth that most people can only dream about.

The bathroom is spacious, with a huge tub in the center of the room. One wall is made of stone and hides the shower behind it. There's no door, just stone walls and floor with a window overlooking the grounds, though I'm high enough up that I don't think anyone can see me from here. It's not immediately clear how to operate the shower or tub, and I make a mental note to ask someone how to work all of this.

I return to my bedroom and realize there's one box under the bed that hasn't been unpacked. I pull it out and find a note on it, written in formal script. "I thought you might want to unpack this one yourself, so I had the movers leave it." It's signed Sebastian. I open the box and discover that it contains my brother's belongings. I pull out his old college hoodie. A sob chokes my throat as I put it on, hugging it around me. His scent has surely faded after all this time, but I can still smell him. Maybe it's in my mind, but I cling to it, nonetheless.

"Oh, Adam. You were too young. This shouldn't have happened."

There's another balcony door in my bedroom, and I step out and realize the balconies are connected into one large one, with a small table and two chairs outside, and several beautiful plants adding an earthiness to the space. It's dark, but the sky is full of moonlight and the stars are bright. I take a deep breath of the crisp late fall air and close my eyes, listening to the sounds of the night creatures. I always loved the night, the darkness, the eye of the moon on me. It never occurred to me I would end up in a job that required me to live in the night, but I'm finding myself excited by the prospect. The moon holds the secrets the sun cannot see. But I want to see them.

I want to know all the secrets the moon holds.

I want to see the wild woman again. I want to feel the power she held.

And, I realize, I also want to get to know my new home.

Slipping my phone into my pocket and grabbing my sketchbook, I leave my room and hope I'll be able to find my way back. I keep track of where I'm going by drawing a map as I go. Most of the rooms I try are just guest suites or bedrooms, and I worry I will come across someone's lived in quarters but I always knock first, and so far they've all been empty.

The place is huge, and I use more and more pages of my sketchbook to map it, making notes when I find bedrooms, bathrooms, random meeting rooms, storage rooms. I'm sticking to upstairs at the moment, but I know there will be so much more to explore downstairs. The dark, windowless halls are lit by torches on the walls, though they are not flames but rather some kind of strange bulb. At least, I assume it's a bulb. There's no actual evidence of one. Just a ball of pale blue light that is cool rather than warm.

There's a flurry of activity happening near one suite. It sounds like several people are working, but when I glance in, I see only Matilda. "Is someone else coming?" I ask, since she is clearly preparing this suite for someone who doesn't already live here.

"He arrives tomorrow. We must prepare." She is distracted and looks around as if trying to find help.

"Who's he?"

"No time to explain. We'll talk later, dear." She rushes off, so I keep exploring, turning corners, studying portraits and paintings that line the walls, until I find myself in a hall that has no doors or windows, though it's very long. At the very end is one red door, intricately carved. I reach to turn the knob, forgetting my own rule about knocking, when a voice barks at me.

"Do not open that door! This wing isn't meant for you." I turn to face Liam, and his eyes are alight with simmering rage. Dude has issues.

"I'm sorry. I was just trying to get my bearings here. What's in the room?" I ask.

"None of your business."

"Is it like your sex dungeon or something? The red room of pain?" I laugh, but he doesn't. Again. Tough crowd.

"That would be a different red door," another voice chimes in. Derek arrives, with Sebastian and Elijah following. "It seems our meeting has started without us."

"She has no business being here," Liam says harshly. "This is a mistake. She could ruin everything. She's a mundane."

"I've heard that twice. Mundane. What does that mean?"

Derek sighs. "We have to tell her sometime. It's not like we can keep this a secret for long. Not with him coming tomorrow."

Sebastian crosses his arms over his chest but says nothing.

Elijah nods. "The decision is made, now we must make the best of it."

Liam looks furious, but says nothing as Derek pulls a key out of his pocket and opens the door. "There's something you should know about us, and this company, Eve." He steps into the room, and I can't help but stare.

"Do you also run a funeral parlor?" I ask, because there are four beautiful coffins side by side in the darkened and windowless room. "Or this really is your sex room and y'all are super kinky? I mean, I'm not judging, to each their own, but I don't really think I need to know about this part of your life. We can have some secrets, don't you think?"

Sebastian laughs, but it's more of a disappointed sound as he shakes his head. "You don't get it, Eve. This isn't a funeral parlor. We weren't drinking wine at your job interview, and there's a reason we only work at night."

"Are you... ?" I swallow, thinking through the ramifications of it all. Realization finally sets in, but it's a hard pill to swallow. "Okay, I get it. You're really deep into the lifestyle. I mean clearly, solidly committed. Structuring your law firm around it is pretty intense, but it's cool. I've met some people with vampire and bite kinks. None who took it quite this far, but enough that I know it's pretty serious for some. Is this why you need me? Because you want to stick to your role? No going out in daylight and all that? I'm down with going along, to an extent. I don't want to, like, participate though. If you catch my drift." I show my teeth. "No bitey bitey on me and we're all good."

Sebastian throws his hands in the air and turns away, sighing. Elijah presses his lips together, and Derek frowns.

But not Liam. He clenches his fist, and what happens next is too fast for me to do anything to prevent.

Before I realize what's happening, my body slams into the wall, knocking the breath out of my lungs, and Liam is pressed against me, his rock-hard form crushing my breasts, his hands gripping my wrists tightly, pushing them over my head. A guttural growl, inhumane in its sound, emanates from him, and I see his teeth are elongated far beyond what's normal or natural. Then his mouth is at my neck.

I feel pain, fire burning in me, through me, as his teeth sink into my flesh, then a kind of strange bliss washes over me, even as fear leeches into me, trying to find purchase in all the confusion.

There's no time for panic to take me. My heart slows as my blood is drained, my head spins, and my body feels disconnected from my mind, unable to support itself. Liam is holding me up at this point. If he pulls away, I will crumple to the ground, a pale, bloodless ghost.

My thoughts flicker to random moments in my life. My last fight with Jerry. My last hug from my father. My last long talk with my brother. So many lasts. We seldom know what moment will be the last of something. We celebrate the firsts, but we don't think of the lasts. They are the memories that stick when all else is gone. Those final footprints in the snow, covering all others. The last words, last laughs, last tears. It's only in hindsight that we see how precious those moments were.

I close my eyes and give into this moment. Savoring it. Savoring my life, what little is left. Will I see my brother soon? My parents? That won't be so bad. Death is the ultimate last and first, all at once. It encompasses it all.

Someone shouts, and Liam is pulled away amidst argument and fights. My body crumples to the ground, but strong arms catch me and lift me. My head rests against a muscular chest. His breathing is heavy, his anger solid and intense.

Sebastian.

"Why?" I ask, with the airy breathlessness reserved for those whose life is leaking out of them. "Why are you always angry at me?"

I pry my eyes open to meet his, finding him staring at me, his jaw clenched, his face conflicted.

I hear more arguing, and someone shouts, "Get her out of here. Take care of her. We'll handle Liam."

Sebastian grunts and we begin to move. My body is limp, like fresh noodles, but Sebastian doesn't seem to have any trouble managing it.

He takes me to a room with a fire and lays me on a bed. It's not my room or my bed, but I'm too out of it to care.

I feel his hands on my body, on my neck. Water, something cold, then something that stings. Then his wrist is at my mouth, and he forces thick, viscous liquid down my throat. I gag and try to spit it out but he doesn't let me.

"Drink. You need this. Trust me. Drink."

My eyes flicker open and closed, the world swirling in a confusing array of light and color.

A cool cloth on my forehead.

A gentle hand brushing away my hair from my face.

A body next to mine in the bed.

"It's not you I'm always angry at," I hear as my mind drifts away and my thoughts scatter into dreams.

CHAPTER 6: THE NIGHT BROTHERS

I AM A FOREST, and a night of dark trees: but he who is not afraid of my darkness, will find banks full of roses under my cypresses.
- Friedrich Nietzsche

"SHE NEEDS TO LEARN. Do you think *he* will be as gentle if she mocks him the way she mocked us?"

The voice wakes me from my sleep, but I don't stir or open my eyes. I don't want anyone to know I'm conscious. I hope to glean more feigning sleep than I've managed to learn thus far while awake. Though pieces of the mystery are starting to fall into place, I still can't make sense of any of it. Nothing I've experienced with this family makes sense, actually.

"She wasn't mocking." That's Derek. I appreciate how he always defends me. He seems to be the only one who's really been on my side since I was interviewed and subsequently hired to this job I'm beginning to regret.

There's a deep ache in my neck, and my brain is still trying to put it all together in a way that doesn't make me sound crazy.

"It's to be expected," Derek continues, "that she would have trouble embracing the truth immediately. We have to give her time, not attack her and make her fear us. You nearly killed her!"

"That's nonsense," says the first voice. Liam.

Flashes penetrate the fog in my brain and cut through the pain in my throat.

Liam, his teeth unnaturally long.

Liam pinning me against the wall with superhuman strength.

Liam's teeth sinking into my neck.

Blood.

I feel nauseous and quickly sit up, afraid of choking should I vomit. I see a water basin on the dresser by the bedside and grab it, leaning over it to retch, though there's little in my stomach to empty. Still, my body convulses, and I feel bad for whoever has to deal with my mess.

My head spins, my throat burns and aches, like my muscles are tearing, and I close my eyes, moaning in pain as the hell continues.

Cool hands touch my face, and I open my eyes to find Sebastian standing beside the bed.

"Eve," he says, gently, but I recoil from his touch, scrambling away from him until I'm pushed up against the headboard, as far from him as I can get without leaving the bed.

"Don't touch me!" I tell him, the memories of what Liam did to me still fresh in my mind. Layered over other memories of abuse. Pain. Betrayal.

I glance toward the door, wondering if I can cross the distance to it before Sebastian can catch me, and he seems to read my mind.

"It's okay, Eve. I'm not going to hurt you."

"Right," I tell him, as anger slowly begins to replace my fear. "And you expect me to believe that after what Liam did to me?"

He frowns. "I am not Liam."

"No, but you're a vampire just like he is!" I respond hotly, realizing even as I say it that I've given a name to the elephant in the room.

There's no denying the truth of my statement and, thankfully, he doesn't try. It would just have been embarrassing for him if he had.

He sighs and mentally seems to be counting to ten. Then, "What Liam did was wrong, and I apologize for it. It shouldn't have

happened. I've brought you something to help with the...after effects."
He hands me a glass of something purple and fizzy. "Drink this. You'll
thank me."

I pause. "Why should I trust you?"

"Because I only wish to help."

Carefully, I take the drink and sniff at the contents. The sweet
smell has me nearly drooling despite myself, so I guzzle it in one shot
—and nearly puke it back up. How can something that smells so good
taste so very awful? I gag, but force the vile brew down my throat, at
the quiet promptings of Sebastian, who takes the cup from me when
I'm done and hands me a cold rag for my head.

Eyeing him cautiously, I lie back down.

He hesitates, then gestures at the space next to me on the bed.
"May I?"

I'm still ticked, but nothing's going to be gained by staying mad at
him. He's right; he's not Liam. He saved my life, in fact. Never have I
had a twenty-four hour period where my life was in such peril with
such frequency. Still, I nod and stiffen only a little bit as he climbs into
the bed next to me.

He doesn't speak for several minutes, and I close my eyes and
enjoy the silence, and, I'll admit, the feeling of his body so close to
mine.

It happens in a wave, like water washing over me, and as it does,
my body buzzes with energy. The pain recedes, the aches dissipate, and
I feel a kind of euphoria that leaves me relaxed and grateful for the
relief.

"You are feeling better." It's a statement, not a question.

I nod with my eyes still closed, a small smile on my face. "Thank
you," I whisper.

His thumb gently rubs against my temple, all the way down to the
line of my jaw, tracing it to my collarbone. His touch leaves a trail of
fire in its wake, and I sigh at the contact, though my heart and body
are confused by his on again, off again attentions. And my brain is
trying to convince me that whatever these feelings are that I'm having
for my boss, they need to shut the hell down right away. I'm done with

unhealthy power dynamic relationships. They've already messed up my head too much.

The euphoria I was feeling wears off too quickly and I'm left with my doubts and confusion. I sit up quickly and instantly regret it, my head spinning a bit as I look around. "Where are they?" I ask.

"Who?" Sebastian says.

"Your brothers. Their voices woke me. I heard them talking."

Sebastian frowns. "They're in the right wing where I left them. This is my room, in the left wing. There's no way you could have heard them talking," he says.

"Huh. It must have been a dream." I twist to face him, and our bodies are so close—and in his bed, no less—that it's driving me to distraction, but I ignore it, or try to. "What's going on? Maybe those voices were a dream, but the rest of it isn't, is it?"

"No. It's not."

"So, it wasn't the adrenaline..."

Sebastian frowned. "Sorry?"

"After the accident. The door was jammed shut by the crash. You not only kicked it open, but sent it flying off its hinges. At the time I thought it was due to a sudden, massive burst of adrenaline, but it wasn't, was it?"

A slight shake of his head. "No."

"And then you ran with me, carrying me miles, as if I weighed nothing."

He nods again.

"You have coffins in a locked room."

His gaze bores into mine.

"Liam drank my blood."

"Yes. All of this true. Which is why you should have turned down the job. Why you still should. It's not too late. Not yet. You can leave now. I can help you."

"What do you mean it's not too late yet? When will it be too late?"

Before Sebastian can answer, the door slams open and Elijah stands there, an intensity to his eyes. "He's on his way right now!"

Sebastian straightens at that. "What? He's not due to arrive until tomorrow."

Elijah shrugs. "Seems he's come early."

"Bloody hell," Sebastian says. "She doesn't even know everything yet."

Elijah looks at me, then back at Sebastian. "You'd better fill her in fast. He'll be here in twenty."

Elijah leaves, closing the door behind him, and I turn to face Sebastian. "Who's coming? What's going on?"

"We have a new client," he says. "An important client. When you meet him, it's critical you are careful. He's very...dynamic. And dangerous."

"Who's the client?"

"If I told you, you wouldn't believe me. You're having a hard enough time believing what you've seen with your own eyes."

"What I've seen is impossible," I say.

"There are more things in heaven and earth than are dreamt of in your philosophy," he says, quoting Shakespeare.

"Funny, you don't strike me as the Shakespeare reading type," I say, deflecting the seriousness of the situation.

"There's a lot about me you might be surprised by, Eve," he says, and I can't help but love how my name sounds on his lips. "We both need to get ready for his arrival, but first, let's be absolutely clear about what's going on here. You are correct; we—my brothers and I—are vampires. And The Night Firm isn't just any firm. It's a law firm for paranormal creatures. We have our own justice system and court of law. Humans could never keep us in check, so we do it ourselves."

"Paranormal creatures," I say, in a breathy whisper. "So there are more than just vampires?"

He nods. "But you knew that already. You saw others when you left your interview, did you not?"

It's my turn to nod, as I remember the woman I saw as I left the building that night.

"They were real. Just as I am real. This is a dangerous place for you, Eve. You asked before why I'm always mad at you. I'm not. I'm mad you're here, because I worry you will not be safe. Especially now."

Everything he's said and done since we met is suddenly seen in a new light, and all the attraction and pent up desire I feel surfaces. My eyes fall to his lips, and I can see by the way his body tenses, he feels the energy in the room shift as well.

Our hands are touching, skin brushing against skin on the silky sheets. My hip is pressed against him.

Panic wells in me and I pull back. "The accident wasn't an accident was it?" It's all starting to click into place.

"No, it wasn't," he says, regaining his composure quickly. "We make enemies. Our clients make enemies. Especially the client you're about to meet. You will be in constant danger if you stay."

It's clear he wants me to leave. But...where would I go? I have nothing left to return to.

I slide off the bed and adjust my clothes. "I think I'll take my chances," I say, though I have a million questions. "And I should probably get ready, if he's on his way." I need an excuse to leave, because I can't stay in the room with him any longer and not act on the desires building up in me.

Before I leave, I turn, a question on my mind. "Why do you have coffins if you also have a regular bedroom?" I ask.

"We don't regularly sleep in the coffins," he says. "They're for emergencies. If we have to travel during the day or heal from serious injury. They are filled with dirt from our homeland, from before our vampire lives."

I nod, processing that, and he doesn't speak to stop me as I turn to leave.

I wander around the mansion trying to find my room until I bump into Lily, who's wide-eyed and jittery. "I've been looking everywhere for you. We have to get you dressed. Come on!"

She practically drags me to my room, and once there, opens my closet and starts pulling out dresses. "It needs to be perfect. This is a big deal."

I can't tell if she's excited or nervous or both. I'm not sure how to feel. The Night brothers seem pretty powerful. Who could they possibly be this jumpy about seeing?

My mind is still reeling from my conversation with Sebastian, and now I'm supposed to play dress up? I sit on the bed as Lily fusses with my hair.

"Is it true?" I ask Lily. I assume she knows everything. How could she not?

"Is what true?" she asks, twisting my hair expertly into a Dutch braid any hair stylist in New York would be jealous of.

"You're all vampires."

She freezes, and then moves to stand so we are face to face. "Not all of us."

A blink.

The pink hair is gone. The dark complexion changed.

The being that stands before me is naked, skin a deep-moss-green. Hair thick like vines, adorned with white flowers and auburn branches. Eyes like emeralds.

The smell of spring's first rain overtakes me.

And as quickly as it appeared, the vision is gone.

Lily smiles across from me, rosy hair falling over her shoulder. "Now let's add some make-up."

I nod, unsure of what I just witnessed, curiosity and fear mixing within me. "What about Matilda? Is she a vampire? Or is she...like you?"

Lily retrieves a blue eyeshadow and begins applying it to my face, pursing her lips. "Granny Matilda is something else, but that's her story to tell, not mine."

"Is it rude to ask what you are? I don't mean to be impolite. This is all just so new to me."

She smiles, and I see a shadow of the wild woodland creature she truly is.

"I'm a dryad," she says simply. "A creature of the forest, the soul of a tree."

I'm not sure if I should be relieved or worried. Everything poses more questions than answers. "Am I safe here?"

She narrows her eyes. "The Nights won't let anything happen to you."

I scoff at that. "Liam just tried to kill me."

She rolls her eyes. "Liam can be a giant ass sometimes. He's hotheaded, impulsive and prone to reckless acts. But if he wanted to kill you, you'd be dead. That much is certain. No, what he did, it was a warning."

"Nothing like getting into a near deadly car accident on my way to my first day, then getting attacked and bitten by my boss." The snark is strong in my voice.

Lily sighs. "I know it doesn't make sense, and it's a crap way to start your work here, but I promise it will get better. Give them a chance."

I don't know how to respond, so I stay silent as she finishes helping me dress in a sapphire blue gown that matches my eyes and is cinched at my waist and flared at my hips, cascading down my legs in layers.

When she's done, she pulls back to admire her handiwork. "You look incredible. And you have such perfect porcelain skin. You could pass for a vampire if you smelled different," she says, wrinkling her nose.

"Uh, thanks?"

She laughs. "I'm so glad you finally know. It's been agony waiting for those dummies to tell you everything."

"I hardly think they've told me everything," I say, slipping my feet into a pair of heels that match my dress.

"It's a lot for some people to take," she says. "Sometimes it's easier to get it in pieces than all at once."

As Lily leads me out of my room, through the labyrinth of halls and towards the library, I ask a question that's been prickling my mind since discovering the truth. "Why did they hire me?"

Lily shrugs. "Your resume impressed them, I guess?"

"I don't mean me specifically. Why did they hire a human? Why not stick with vampires or...whatever else? Keep it in the family so to speak. Why expose this world to an outsider for no reason?"

She stops and turns to frown at me. "I could tell the moment we met that you belong here. If I can feel it, they can definitely feel it. And besides, you wouldn't have even heard about the job if you weren't the right person."

With that she continues to walk, but once again I'm left with more questions. "What do you mean? I would have seen it in the paper like everyone else."

She laughs. "That's funny."

When she realizes I'm not laughing she stops again. "You're serious. Oh dear. There's just so much you don't know. Granny spelled the advertisement so that only the perfect candidate for the job would find it. In fact, they're the only one who would even be able to see it. You had the job the moment you called the number. You were the only candidate."

We're moving again, and I try not to stumble over my dress as I work to keep pace with Lily's power walk. "She spelled it? Like with magic?"

"Yup. She's got all kinds of spells up her sleeves. She even showed me how to make a potion that changes my hair color, which is really fun for when I'm out clubbing."

I don't have time to unpack that statement as we have finally arrived at the library where the Night brothers and Matilda are waiting. Sebastian gives me a brief nod and a slight smile of encouragement. Liam doesn't make eye contact with me. Coward. Elijah's eyes hold mine for a long moment, and it's as if a cool breeze dances against my skin when he looks at me like that. I feel an uncomfortable stirring in my body as I consider the quietest of the four brothers. Elijah always seems more contemplative. I can practically see his mind working even as he locks eyes with me.

Derek heads to the bar, pours a drink and walks over to me. "For your nerves," he says, handing me the glass. "You look beautiful."

"Thank you," I say, for the drink and the compliment. A glance at the bottle he poured from shows this is an expensive whiskey. I savor each sip, enjoying the way it burns as I swallow.

"I had hoped to have more time to explain everything," Derek says, his smile faltering. "This has all happened faster than we expected. I wanted to apologize for my brother. He will never do that again. I give you my word."

Despite his promise, or perhaps because of it, the anger bubbling inside me spills out. I'm not just upset, I realize. I'm royally pissed.

"Damn straight he won't or I'll shove a wooden chair leg through his heart faster than he can blink!"

Derek stares at me wide-eyed, jaw slack.

Before he can say anything, I turn and glare in Liam's direction.

He's studiously ignoring me.

That won't do.

Won't do at all.

Downing the rest of my drink, I set the finely etched crystal glass on the table slowly and deliberately and then head straight to over to Liam, getting right in his face so he can't avoid my gaze anymore.

I can feel everyone in the room staring at us.

I stab my finger into his ridiculously muscled chest as I speak with all the authority and rage I can muster. "You had no right to do that, and you will never, ever touch me like that again, am I clear? If you so much as think about doing that again, I will stake your ass so fast you will wish you'd never been born...er...unborn. Or made undead. Whatever. You get my point. Do. Not. Do. That. Again." I say, pushing my fingernail harder against his chest with each word. "Also, you owe me an apology. Or I walk. I'm not working here without one."

He blinks. I don't. I wait. Eyes focused. Heart pounding. My neck is completely healed, not even a scratch, but the memory of the pain still haunts me.

"I apologize," he says, breaking the silence in the room. One of his brothers makes a sound of surprise, but I don't look away from Liam to find out who.

His eyes burn with heat and his muscular chest probably did more damage to my finger than I did to it.

"Why did you do it?" I ask in almost a whisper. For that moment, as his gaze pulls me in, it feels as if we are the only two people in the room.

"To show you the danger you're in. Be careful, Miss Oliver. We're the good guys, and even we aren't that good."

He turns away just as Matilda enters the room. The look on her face is more serious than any I've seen so far. Addressing the brothers, she says, "Your guest has arrived. Shall I show him in?"

"Please," Derek replies. He glances at me quickly, winking flirtatiously before turning his attention back to the library entrance.

The tension in the room ramps up. I have no idea what to expect, since everyone here is so damn tight lipped, but I know it's something big.

My palms are suddenly sweaty, but I can't wipe them on my dress, it'll stain. I consider surreptitiously wiping them on the nearby chair, but I can feel Sebastian's gaze upon me and I do my best to resist. A moment later he passes me his handkerchief.

"Take a deep breath," he says. "We have our reasons to be worried, but you needn't fear for anything," he whispers as I gratefully wipe my hands dry.

And then all eyes are on the doorway as Matilda returns, our guest in tow. "May I present the eminent Count Dracula," she says solemnly.

CHAPTER 7: THE GUEST

IT WAS IN MY FLAWS,
I found a much deeper truth—
and it is from them,
I bloom: a black rose.
~ Segovia Amil

THE BROTHERS GIVE CURT BOWS, while I stand in shock as a tall, lithe man walks into the library.

The man—Dracula—wears a tuxedo reminiscent of older times. A long cape, coal-black on the outside, crimson on the inside, drags behind his leather boots. His pitch-black hair is slicked back, though one strand falls lose over his eyes, which are almost as dark as his hair. His skin is the palest cream, and though unlined by years, he feels ancient, powerful, and his presence fills the room.

It's almost suffocating, being in the same space with him. I take a step back instinctively, which is a mistake, as his eyes jump to me, devouring me in one glance.

I feel naked.

Uncomfortable.

And way too exposed in a room full of vampires.

Derek steps forward first, taking the lead. "Vlad, welcome to our home."

He nods. "If only this visit were under better circumstances," he says, his accent Slavic and his voice deep.

"We will sort out all that," Derek says with confidence, though I can sense a flicker of unease in him, despite his valiant attempts to hide it.

"And who is she?" Dracula asks.

Derek gestures for me to step forward. "This is our new associate, Miss Eve Oliver. Eve comes highly recommended by Richard Dwarvas and has both an MBA in business and a law degree from Harvard University."

I'm not entirely sure why he's trying so hard to sell my credentials to this guy—to Dracula—but I do appreciate the reminder to everyone else in this room that I am damn well qualified to be here. Aside from me being super frail and human. And I suppose, mundane.

Still. I can hold my own.

I put my hand forward to shake his, but he brings it up to his lips and brushes it with a soft kiss. "A pleasure to make your acquaintance. It seems my sons have certainly done well for themselves."

"Sons?" I say, my eyes flickering to Sebastian, who grits his teeth and clenches his fists.

"We aren't your sons," Liam says, stepping forward, his anger on full display.

Dracula shrugs. "Your birth father gave life to you. I gave you immortality and power beyond measure. Which one sounds like more of a father?"

Click. Pieces falling into place. Dracula turned the Night brothers. I'm having a serious holy shit moment. I feel a bit as if I'm in a farce, playing the part of the only person who doesn't know the joke's on them.

But that bite on my neck. That was real.

I glance at Liam, who looks toward me, as if he knows I'm thinking about him, then he returns his attention to Dracula. "We are paying our debt to you now. We will keep you from being buried alive for all eternity, and you will leave us the hell alone. Forever."

The tension is so thick in the room I can barely breathe. Everyone is frozen, waiting for what will happen next.

"If you deliver justice," Dracula says, "then our blood debt will be cleared. You will be free of the sire bond."

The brothers exchange glances and everyone nods. Well, nearly everyone.

"I need to hear him say it, first," Liam says. "I need to him to look me in the eyes and tell me he didn't do it." Liam walks over to Dracula and stands inches from him, their eyes deadlocked. "Tell me you didn't kill Mary. Convince me of your innocence."

Dracula's face changes, morphing from calm and collected to monstrous in his rage. And I realize I'm seeing Vlad the Impaler right now. He lifts Liam by the cuffs of his shirt and pushes him forward, slamming him against the wall in much the same way Liam did to me earlier. I can't help but feel a little bit gloaty about that.

But when I see the crack in the stone from the impact of Liam's body, I cringe. Ouch, that's gotta hurt.

Dracula growls at Liam, his teeth elongated, full on vampire mode. "I did not kill my wife. I would never harm her. She was my heart and my soul. I am nothing without her."

With those words, the anger and rage drain from Dracula, and he drops Liam to the ground and sways back on his heels before righting himself. He seems to come back to the awareness that he is not alone, and his face, previously so full of raw emotion, clamps down instantly, the mask so effective it's tempting to think I just imagined anything but the haughty, cold, measured way he assesses everyone and everything.

Dracula looks at all four of the Night brothers. "Prove my innocence, and you will get what you want. Fail, and I will not be the only one suffering an eternity of torture. You have my word on that."

Dracula turns to me and bows. "Miss Oliver, a pleasure." He shifts to Matilda. "Madam Night, good evening." And then with a click of his heels, he turns and marches out.

Apparently, he knows his way around the castle.

As soon as he's out of earshot, the room seems to exhale the breath it has been holding for far too long.

"This was a mistake," Liam says. "We will either be freeing the monster who murdered Mary, or we will be at war with Dracula himself. Neither option is optimal."

"We have no choice," Derek says with a shrug. "He pulls our strings until he breaks our sire bond. Until then, we are beholden."

"Is that how it works?" I ask, breaking everyone's focus. Four sets of eyes move to meet mine, as if just realizing I am still here. "If you turn someone, you can control them?"

"Not entirely," Derek says. "But close. It's a compulsion that's hard to resist. And if you resist too long, it can cause serious pain. But it takes energy from both parties, so it's not used as often as you might imagine."

"But he's using it now? For this?"

Derek nods. "He's been formally charged with murdering his wife and unborn child and draining them both of blood."

I gasp. "Why would he do that? Why would anyone do that?"

The silence that greets my question tells me all I need to know.

"If he's been charged, that means there will be a trial. Are you defending him?"

"Yes," Elijah says.

"What if he's guilty? Will you really work to prove his innocence to save yourself?"

Liam glares at me. "We have no choice. It's not the pain that's the problem. Eventually the compulsion will work. No one is strong enough to resist, especially not when it's Dracula himself. And besides, it's not our job to determine guilt or innocence. After all, who are we to judge?"

"Then let's get to work," I say. "I need to bone up on my knowledge of your legal system. Where do I start?"

They all stare at me, and a flicker of a smile appears on Matilda's face. "Elijah, dear, why don't you take Eve to your study and give her an overview, then direct her to the right books so she can get started."

Elijah nods. "Would you like to change first?"

I look down at my formal gown and nod. "Yes. I would, actually. Thank you."

It doesn't take more than ten minutes for me to change and find my way to Elijah's office. It's a cozy room with wall-to-wall books and a few comfortable chairs in the center near the fireplace. There's a desk to one side piled with more books, and ladders to reach the highest shelves.

I take the seat offered, and Elijah brings over a pile of books and places them next to me. "Our kind are tried similarly to the American justice system, by a jury of our peers, with a proper defense and prosecution, and a judge to oversee it. The biggest differences are the laws—what's illegal and what's not—and the punishments. Out of necessity, given the power many of us have, the punishments are harsh and often permanent."

I nod. "That makes sense, I suppose."

He raises an eyebrow. "The punishments can seem medieval and even inhumane to someone not used to our ways," he elaborates.

"Yeah, I get it. Like Dracula will be put to ground while still alive, presumably in a way he can't escape, for all of eternity."

He nods. "Amongst other things, yes, that is one example. Though other punishments are much more gruesome, and often the guilty do not live through the experience. Paranormals tend to liken themselves to the gods of old and are just as capricious with our punishments."

I shudder at the images that come to mind, but then I shake it off. This is my life now. Better acclimate fast. "Gotcha. What else?"

He leans forward, studying me. "You surprise me, Miss Oliver."

"Just Eve is fine, thanks."

"Eve, then. You're not what I expected."

"What did you expect?"

"Not you," he says, a smile playing at his lips.

My heart skips a beat at the look he's giving me right now.

"You have a sharp mind," he says. "That much is clear. And courage, for standing up to Liam like that. That hothead is going to get himself killed someday if he's not careful."

"He needs balancing," I say. "Too much fire. He needs water to cool his engines. Earth to ground him."

"What did you just say?"

"The elements? You know, how we all have these qualities in us, and if they get out of balance it can create an excess of certain personality traits. Honestly, you guys should check out Google more often. You might learn a few useful things about the 21st century."

"Yes, of course. Well, you do have a keen eye, Miss Oliver, er, Eve. But I'm afraid I must retire. Sunrise is upon us, and contrary to popular media, we do not function during the daylight hours. Not in this world."

"Oh, right." I stand as he does. "Um, is it okay if I stay and read? I have a lot to learn and not a lot of time in which to learn it."

Elijah nods. "As you wish. Until this evening, then." He touches my arm gently, letting his fingers slide over my skin, before walking away.

My skin tingles where he made contact, and it takes my body a beat to settle down from the effects of his attention.

These Night brothers might be the death of me, in more ways than one.

I attempt to read, to study the pile of texts left for me, but my mind keeps returning to the enigmatic Elijah, his clear blue eyes holding keen intelligence and secret knowledge. Giving up, I pull out my sketchbook, which I take with me everywhere, and begin to draw from memory the eyes that I can't put out of my mind. I draw him as I saw him when I entered his study, sitting at his desk, a book before him, his expression one of lost reflection as he looks up at the noise of me entering his space.

When I'm done, I study it and smile. It's as if he's sitting before me, mid-interruption, just before he's about to speak. I tuck the sketchbook back into my bag and refocus my attentions.

For the rest of the morning, I read. And let me just set the record straight, in case there was any confusion about this, reading law books is about as exciting as watching paint dry. Paranormal law books are no exception, though a few of their laws raised my eyebrows.

For example, there's a law that werewolves aren't allowed to leave their clothing on private property not belonging to them, or on public lands, during full moon shifts, unless they request a special permit, which has to be signed by a judge. The penalty for breaking this law is one full moon cycle locked up in silver chains.

I make good work on the books. One of the ways I was able to graduate with both my MBA and law degree so fast was my ability to speed read and retain the vast majority of the material I take in when I do. When I told the Night brothers that I was smart, I wasn't being vain or exaggerating. I'm a member of Mensa, after all.

At around three in the afternoon, I'm in the middle of a thick book on court procedures when I get a flash that I'm needed in the topiary garden. I have no idea by whom or for what, but there's no resisting the sensation. I decide to take a stroll outside to enjoy some sunshine and Vitamin D before my planned slumber.

There's a gentle breeze that carries the scent of wildflowers, and the sun is so warm and bright that I feel sorry for vampires who can no longer feel the kiss of daylight on their skin. What a sad existence that must be, to be forced into darkness, never again experiencing nature's light.

I make my way through the garden, passing bushes molded into fantastical beasts straight from fairy tales, following my instincts and marveling at the artistry that went into creating the landscape around the castle as I go, until I hear something coming from one of the bushes. A meowing, tiny and faint, but there.

I squat down to peer into the bush, and stuck there between two branches is a tiny black kitten with big yellow eyes staring at me plaintively. It meows again and looks to be at the end of its rope. Careful not to hurt the fur ball, I maneuver it out of the bramble and scoop it into a pouch I make of my sweatshirt. I give the kitten a quick exam to see if there are any obvious injuries.

"You look in one piece," I say. "And it seems you're a boy."

He holds eye contact with me and purrs each time I pet him. He looks at me with such love and devotion my heart melts, and I'm determined I will keep him. Hopefully I don't have to go battle with the brothers over this, but I will if I must.

I head back to the castle and I find Lily, bringing her into my plan. After a high-pitched squeal of delight, she goes off in search of food and supplies to care for him.

I bring him back to my room and take a warm cloth to his fur, brushing away bits of sticks and dirt. He purrs the whole time.

When I'm done, I hold his face up to mine, nuzzling him with my nose. "You're going to need a name," I say. "What shall we call you?"

Lily comes in, carrying a bowl of food and one with water, and I ask her the name of the bush he got stuck in.

"It's called a Moonweed," she says. "Though it's not really a weed. And it can only be grown with magic."

I look into the kitten's eyes again, studying him. "I'm not going to name you Weed. But I like the name Moon. What do you think?"

He purrs and licks my nose. I laugh. "I think we have a winner. Lily, meet Moon."

She claps and then sits next to me and gives him some love. "I don't think we've ever had a pet in the castle before. Especially not a cat. This is going to be so fun!"

"Do you think the brothers will give me a hard time about it?" I ask.

Lily shrugs. "Who cares? What are they going to do to stop you? Take him to Granny first. Once she's on board, they're powerless. Everyone thinks they run things around here, but it's really Granny. Always has been."

I yawn, the day, or rather night, catching up with me. Lily nods sympathetically. "It's a hard schedule to get used to," she says. "My kind are drawn to the sun, but fortunately we also don't need much sleep. But humans do. Get some rest. Tonight is going to be a busy day."

I laugh at that and nod, my body suddenly feeling as if weights have been added to my arms and legs.

Lily pulls the curtains in my room, sending it into complete darkness, and stokes the fire to ward off the constant chill in the castle. I always dreamed of living in a castle when I was a little girl, but I never realized how drafty they could be.

Before Lily leaves the room, I call after her. "How do I use the plumbing in the bathroom?"

I'm looking forward to a long bath once I'm not so exhausted.

She smiles. "It's not plumbing, it's magic." She makes a series of symbols in the air. "Use those and you'll be fine."

I practice a few times and she nods. "You've got it. Goodnight, Eve."

She closes the door softly and I crawl into bed with Moon, who curls up on my shoulder in the crook of my neck and purrs contentedly.

It only takes moment for me to fall asleep after my head hits the pillow.

My dreams turn dark. I'm in the woods, alone at night. Naked. Bleeding. Scared. Moon is trapped in barbed vines and I can't get to him. He's crying, meowing to get out, but every time he moves he gets cut.

My hands and arms are covered in bloody gashes, but I've made no progress in getting him free.

Then a tall man walks up to me, black cape flowing behind him. It's Dracula, his pale face shining in the moonlight.

He walks with a black ebony cane tipped with jade at the handle, his dark eyes taking everything in.

When he reaches me, he smiles, but his eyes remain hard, cold, calculating. Taking another step, he places himself between me and Moon, then leans in, sniffing me. "You smell different," he says. "How have they not noticed?"

Then he pulls my body towards him, his pupils dilating as he brings my bloody hands up to his mouth. His tongue flicks out, licking one of the wounds, and he smiles. "Ah, now I understand."

He laughs, dropping my arm, and reaches into the vines to pull out Moon. He does not get cut, but rather seems to repel the barbed plants away. I reach for Moon, grateful he's okay, when Dracula clutches the kitten around the neck. He stares at me for a moment. "Never trust us," he says, then he snaps Moon's neck.

I wake with a scream, and Moon startles from my shoulder, meowing and stretching as I jerk up in bed. I see him grooming himself and relief floods me. It was just a dream. But my flash is screaming at me, buzzing under my skin in a way I can't ignore.

Dracula is dangerous.

That much I know.

The question is how dangerous? Dangerous enough to kill and drain his wife and unborn child?

Dangerous enough to be a threat to the Nights and to me and Moon?

That's the question I need answered.

And soon.

CHAPTER 8: THE LEGEND

IF YOU WANT THE MOON, do not hide from the night. If you want a rose, do not run from the thorns. If you want love, do not hide from yourself. ~ *Rumi*

THAT NIGHT I wake from a restless sleep full of strange dreams as my subconscious tries to process all that I've learned.

Moon is off exploring our suite, and the fire in my bedroom is dying down, leaving the room with a deep chill. I decide it's time to test the magical plumbing and take a bath.

I handle my morning business then stand before the large bathtub and draw the symbols into the air that Lily showed me. Immediately, hot steaming water begins to fill the tub. I test it with my hand and sigh at the warmth, then quickly strip and step in. It's a heady experience, playing with magic.

The heat fills me, penetrating a layer of chill I thought would never leave. I add scented oils to the bath and scrub my body with a soft sponge, then lay back with my eyes closed, enjoying the peace. My relaxation is brought to an end when I hear Moon hissing at something in the other room. I step out of the water that stayed hot the entire bath—much to my surprise—and wrap a thick robe around myself before making my way to my kitten to see what's upsetting him.

There's nothing obvious out of the ordinary, but the bed is made and the fire is stoked, bringing heat back into the space. This wouldn't seem that odd in and of itself, except that last night I locked the door to my suit from the inside, and it's still locked.

No one could have gotten in to do these things, and Moon is still hissing at something that I can't see.

I pick up the angry kitten and soothe him as I dress, then the two of us make our way to the dining room for breakfast.

Matilda, Lily, and the four Night brothers are already seated around the large table. The brothers each have a goblet of crimson liquid. Blood, presumably. I shiver at the thought and wonder where it came from. And though they don't eat real food, the center of the table is filled with platters of bacon, fruit, yogurt, granola, eggs, pancakes and biscuits, a pitcher of orange juice and a pot of freshly brewed tea.

"Are we the only people who live here?" I ask, marveling at the plethora of choices before me.

"Dracula's a temporary guest as well, but generally yes, why?" Lily asks.

"Were any of you in my room earlier?" I ask.

Everyone says no and continues with their conversations.

While Moon sleeps in the pocket of my cardigan, I get a cup of tea and dish up some fruit, yogurt and granola before taking a seat between Matilda and Elijah, my mind still on the mystery of my made bed and stoked fire.

Elijah smiles at me. "I saw you put the books I gave you back. Give up? They can be very dry."

I shake my head, swallowing a bite before answering. "No. I mean, yes, they're dry for sure. Dear god they're dry. But no, I finished them all and am ready for more."

His eyes widen. "What do you mean you finished them?"

"I mean finished them. You know, read them."

"All of them?"

"Of course, all of them. Hopefully I put them back in the right places." I shrug. "Anyway, I need more." I'm saying all this in between bites because I realized with all the excitement last night, I never got dinner and I am starving.

"How's that possible?" he asks.

At this point, everyone else at the table is paying attention as well, so I explain about my speed-reading and my near photographic memory. "Didn't you wonder how I got so many degrees at such a young age?" I ask.

And I realize no one at the table even considered the fact that I actually am the age I look. I have not lived multiple lifetimes. Just the one.

"So in twenty-five years—and you started as an infant, yes?" Elijah asks, in all seriousness.

I laugh so hard I spit tea out and turn bright red as I clean it up. "Yes. Of course. You don't get around humans very often, do you?"

"It has been awhile," he says with a soft smile. "So, in that time, you had to grow to adulthood and you still got your degrees?" he asks, again, clarifying.

"Yes," I say, smiling at the strangeness of this conversation.

He gives me an appreciative appraisal. "You really are quite a find, Miss Eve Oliver. Quite a find. But I have a hard time believing you retained any of that knowledge. That would be—extraordinary."

"Try me," I say. This was my favorite game in college and grad school. My roommate and I would go to college bars and start talking about our classes. Inevitably some know-it-all mansplaining dude would come up and try to instruct us on what so-and-so meant when they wrote this or did that. We would then challenge him to a duel of knowledge. We'd find a book, (or he'd provide one, which usually made him even more confident), I would read through it, then our friends would quiz us on the content. I would quote complete passages. He would muddle through. I would win $100. He would walk away calling me a bitch.

Good times.

Elijah takes me up on my offer and begins to quiz me on the history and laws of the paranormal community.

Lily leaves the table first. Impressed, but bored. Then Matilda, who kisses my head and whispers something in another language in my ear.

Liam and Derek are quick to follow. Sebastian stays the longest, surprisingly. He's studying me as I recite and give my opinion on entire passages in their complex law and history books. But even he eventually gets bored and leaves.

At last, Elijah pauses, cocking his head. "Extraordinary. It's been many, many years since I met anyone with a mind like yours."

That perks my attention. "Really, who was the last one?" I ask.

"Al," he says. "Al had a brilliant mind. I begged him to let me turn him before he died, but he refused, insisting that all life must cycle from dust to dust. Such a waste though."

"Al?" I ask.

"Albert, actually. He hated when I called him Al. Albert Einstein."

My mouth drops. "You knew Albert Einstein?"

He smiles. "Yes."

I don't know what's giving me the full body buzz right now. The fact that I'm sitting in a house with beings who have lived with some of the most amazing talents and minds our world has ever seen, or the fact that he just favorably compared me to Albert Einstein.

I feel giddy either way, and it's nice.

Just then, my phone rings, and I answer on instinct, though the number isn't one I recognize.

"This is Eve," I say, holding a finger up to Elijah, who nods.

"You finally answered."

Jerry.

Though I've only been in my new life a few days, already my old life feels light years away. Like an old dream I struggle to remember but find the details fuzzy at best.

"You need to stop calling me," I say. "Whose number is this?"

"It doesn't matter. You keep blocking me, so I had to find a way to get through. I went to your apartment, but they said you moved. That's an extreme reaction, one propelled by grief. One you will regret in time. I spoke to the manager of the building. He and I agreed it would be best if you came back. He will return your money and you can keep your apartment. We can get you better, Eve. Have you had any more episodes?"

I frown, anger bubbling in me. "How dare you! How dare you show up at my place! How dare you speak to anyone on my behalf or imply I'm not stable enough to make my own decisions. I didn't report you to spare you your career, but there's still time to change that, Jerry. The statute of limitations hasn't expired. I do have a law degree, if you'll recall. I know my rights and I know what would happen to you if everyone found out what you've been doing with your patients." I let my threat hang in the air, lingering there like a bad scent. I want him to feel uncomfortable in the silence. I want him to imagine what his life would be like if I followed through on my threat.

"Eve, you don't want to do that," he says, his anger brimming to the surface. I know what would happen if I were there.

Explosive anger. He would attack, verbally and physically. Afterwards he'd apologize, justify, tell stories about his abusive childhood, anything to avoid facing what he'd done and who he is. He could never handle looking at his true reflection and seeing the monster he was underneath the handsome exterior.

"I'm hanging up now and blocking this number. Do not contact me again. I will call the police if you do." I end the call and block the number, but not before taking screenshots. My hands are shaking and my breathing is labored.

I nearly jump out of my skin when Elijah puts a hand on mine.

"It's all right," he says in a calm, soothing voice, like a gentle breeze on a warm night. "You're safe."

My panic attack settles into something more manageable as I use the tools I learned—ironically from Jerry himself. I find something to look at. The wood pattern of the dining room table, with its variation and imperfections that make it all the more perfect. Something to listen to. The clicking of the grandfather clock in the next room. Something to feel. I grip Elijah's hand more tightly, noticing how soft his skin is, and how long and elegant his fingers are. Something to smell. I inhale and am rewarded with the scent of fresh coffee brewing in the kitchen. And something to think about—my happy place. My sanctuary.

With Elijah's hand still in mine, I dive into my mind, controlling my breathing as the winding staircase comes into focus. I follow it down, down, down, so far down, until the red door appears. I open it and smile, relaxing into the beautiful environment I now find myself in. Nature. Running water. Birds chirping. The sun shining. Flowers swaying in the gentle breeze. And her. My Muse.

She reaches for me with a long-branched arm, leaves for fingers, and brushes them against my face gently. The wind rustles in her branches and I hear a message for me in them, but I cannot make out the specific words. It's just a feeling. I settle into that feeling, and then open my eyes.

Elijah is waiting patiently, his hand still holding mine, his eyes seeking out my own. "You are very skilled at that," he says.

"I went through a bad spell," I say. "This helped. Still does."

"And that man who called?" He frowns, worry lines forming on his smooth face.

"My ex. And former therapist."

"Does he need to be dealt with?" Elijah asks.

"Who needs to be dealt with?" Sebastian asks, returning to the dining room, his eyes seeking mine the moment he enters.

"Eve's ex is bothering her," Elijah says with clear malice.

Sebastian's face hardens and his eyes lock onto mine. "In what way is he bothering you?" His words are slow and controlled, but there's a power behind them and I almost want to laugh at the pickle Jerry would find himself in if I unleashed the Night brothers on him.

"He just called. It's not a big deal."

Elijah flashes me a look and frowns. "It sent you into a state of panic. Did he hurt you?"

Of the four brothers, Elijah is in many ways the easiest to talk to. He has a calmness and gentleness to him that is missing in the others, but it doesn't take away from the raw force of his charisma or power. He's just as mesmerizing, and just as dangerous, I'm sure. I certainly see that danger in his eyes now, and even though it's not directed at me, it still makes me shudder.

Sebastian puts a hand on my shoulder, and his stability and solidness center me. I lean into him, relishing the touch, closing my eyes as I think back to memories I'd rather not revisit.

"I met him while my brother was sick. I was having panic attacks and they were interfering with my work and life enough to worry Adam. He convinced me to go see a therapist, thinking it would help. At first it did. Jerry was good at his job. We talked about medication, but I was able to manage it with some self-hypnosis tricks I learned online and tools he taught me to center myself back into my body and into the present moment. I should have stopped seeing him then, once my panic was under control," I say.

Elijah's hand tightens around mine and Sebastian squeezes my shoulder in support.

"But things were so hard. I was constantly cutting my hours to the point that I had to take a leave of absence as Adam got worse. My bank account was drained, but the bills weren't slowing. I thought having someone to talk to would be helpful. He took advantage of that. I see that now. He preyed on my vulnerability and need for someone—anyone—to step in and help bear some of the load I was carrying. It started innocently enough. A run-in at the coffee shop which lead to lunch at the cafe next door, which led to another plan for dinner the following week. Slowly it built, until I was convinced everything I was feeling was real and that I'd found my prince charming. Then it turned dark."

I suck in a breath, take a sip of orange juice, and continue. "He would lash out at the smallest things, then apologize and make it up to me with lavish gifts he couldn't afford. Then the money stress would create another cycle of abuse. He'd choke me, belittle me, twist my fingers until they almost broke. He never full on hit me though. So I didn't think it was abuse. At least, at first."

There's a low growl emanating from Sebastian, and Derek and Liam return, but I continue.

"But Adam walked in once when…when we were fighting, and he lost his shit over what was happening. Nearly beat Jerry to death. He ended up in the hospital with stitches—Jerry, not my brother—and I cut him out of my life from that point on. When Adam died, I almost caved and called him back. I was so lonely and Adam had been my only real friend. But I resisted, knowing Adam would have been so pissed if I'd done that. But now Jerry won't leave me alone. Though the solution is easy enough at this point."

I surprise them all by standing and tossing my phone to the floor, then stomping it with my feet. I expect a dramatic spraying of glass and metal as the phone explodes, but I'm disappointed. Nothing happens. Not even a crack.

"Seriously?" I ask, picking it up and examining it. "I dropped my last phone on my bed and it sustained more damage than this."

Liam holds out his hand. "May I?" he asks.

I pass it to him, and to my utter shock and astonishment, his hand lights on fire, flames peeling out from his palm and engulfing the phone in dancing golden flames. The phone melts, and he drops it onto the table and takes a napkin to wipe his fingers.

I'm staring bug-eyed at Liam, but no one else seems phased. "This is something you can do? Shoot fire out of your hand?"

Liam glances up at me, but it's not him who answers. In fact, it's not any of the Night brothers. It's Dracula himself, but today he's dressed in jeans and a band t-shirt and I do a double take because it's so incongruous with his appearance yesterday that I can scarcely picture him as the same man.

Dracula steals the room with just his entrance. His voice commands attention. "Have they not told you? They always were too modest with their gifts."

He walks closer to me, delicately sniffing the air as he does. I nervously wonder if I remembered deodorant. And then I wonder why I care what this prick thinks. And then I go back to being nervous. This is exhausting.

But I won't be baited. Not by him. I don't give him the satisfaction of asking what he means. He laid the trap, but I won't walk into it. I long ago learned the value of silence.

I keep my mouth shut and I wait.

After several moments during which I have to frequently give a gentle shake of a head to warn one of the brothers away from breaking the silence first, Dracula raises an eyebrow and continues. "You're quite

a treasure," he says with a gleam in his eye that makes me uncomfortable.

"An often underestimated one," I say, deliberately catching the gaze
of each of the brothers.

"Quite so," Dracula says. "Very well, then. The Night brothers are
not just ordinary vampires. No. There is nothing about this clan that is
ordinary."

Liam growls low in his throat, his muscles contracting and his
stance shifting to attack mode. Elijah lays a hand on his brother's
shoulder and leans to whisper something in his ear. This seems to take
Liam's rage down a notch or two, which eases some of the tension for
everyone. But it's clear that the brothers do not want Dracula to tell
me whatever he's going to tell me.

It's equally clear Dracula doesn't give a shit and is going to tell me
anyway.

So I wait.

"The Night brothers," he continues, his long, elegant finger raised
to rest contemplatively against his chin, "were once Sacred Druids of
the Holy Order, a secret sect devoted to the higher calling of the gods
of nature. But they were banished from the Order and cursed with the
Unforgivable Curse. They were each branded with the darkest, most
evil aspects of the elements they held in such reverence—earth, air, fire
and water—dooming them to a life of pain and hurting all those they
had sworn soul vows to help. The inner conflict of their new demons
drove them mad!"

Sebastian flinches at his words, his hands clenched to his sides.

"They made a suicide pact and did what they could to end their
lives. I found them just before the last vestiges of life had left their
bodies. I saved them. Turned them. Made them practically immortal,
though they could still be killed under the right circumstances. I didn't
want them falling to their basest instincts and attempting self-destruc-
tion again, so I compelled them to never attempt anything that could
lead to suicide or imminent and foreseeable death. I compelled them
to live."

Derek glances away, his shoulders slumped. Liam refuses to make eye contact with anyone. Elijah is studying a book in his lap, though I suspect he isn't actually reading it.

Only Sebastian looks me in the eyes, with a small nod of the head. He wants me to know the truth. He doesn't want to hide from me anymore.

The implications of what he's said settle into me in layers. The first is that they are under constant compulsion, which to my understanding is a drain on everyone. I can't imagine having a compulsion running 24/7 for like, ever. That's gotta create some serious baggage.

Second, that the brothers are magical ancient Druids. So they have magic. Maybe not all they possessed before, but something.

And Dracula collected them like dolls and ordered them to stay alive even when their lives had turned into their worst nightmares day in and day out.

What pain must they be in? And how long have they endured this?

In a flash, their personalities come into focus, and I can see the wounds hidden beneath the anger in Liam, the stubbornness in Sebastian, the stoic intellectualism in Elijah, and the flirtatious charisma of Derek.

They each carry their sorrows in their own way.

And I wonder if part of my job is to help lighten those sorrows.

If only I understood how.

CHAPTER 9: THE IMPALER

LOOK at how a single candle can both defy and define the darkness. ~ Anne Frank

THE ATMOSPHERE IS uncomfortable in the dining room as Dracula finishes outing the brothers and their secret past.

I'm wrapping my mind around the Druid part. If they each represent an element, then Liam is obviously fire. I study the other three, wondering what they are. My eyes land on Sebastian and I flash to the drawing I did of him when we first met, with a mountain range behind him. He must be earth, with his stubbornness and inflexibility. And Elijah is the thinker, the intellectual, full of ideas…that would make him air. Which leaves water for Derek. I wonder how those all manifest negatively. With fire and earth it's easy enough to see, but water and air? I'll have to pay more attention to the four of them. As if my thoughts aren't entirely consumed by them already.

Derek clears his throat and walks to the entrance of the dining room. "Shall we all retire to the library where we can discuss the case and get started? The trial will be starting soon. We need to be ready."

We all quietly shuffle out the door and follow Derek to the library.

That's when Moon wakes up and begins meowing in my pocket. Everyone turns to stare at me.

"Are you aware that your sweater is meowing?" Elijah asks.

"Yes, uh, about that." I pull out the kitten, who hisses at the brothers fiercely. "I rescued him yesterday from the Moonweed bush. I'm keeping him."

I stare at each of them, daring them to challenge me.

None do.

"Very well," Derek says. "But he has to stay in your room while we're working. Cats don't like vampires."

I exhale, relieved it was that easy, and use a bell in the library to summon Lily, who is more than happy to take the kitten and keep an eye on him for the evening.

Matilda comes in pushing a tray of goblets filled with blood and a pitcher of tea with cream and sugar for me, then winks at me as she leaves.

We each take a seat—I choose a chair that gives me a good view of everyone without being in the way—and I grab a legal pad and pen, ready to take notes.

Derek pulls out a file and places it on the coffee table between him and Dracula. "This is the police report," he says. "At 2:23 a.m. on November 4, your wife, Mary, was found dead in your home. She was drained of blood. The child—a boy—was beheaded and also drained of blood. Mary was still alive when all this happened. She died last."

The gruesomeness of it startles me, and I study the faces of the men in the room, looking for emotional cues.

Dracula's jaw is clenched. Liam is full of thinly veiled rage. Derek and Elijah are all business. Sebastian is…well, Sebastian. Brooding.

"You are being charged with two counts of murder, two counts of unlawful draining of blood, and two counts of violating the Non-Violent Vampire Act," Derek says.

I'm already rattled by my mental image of this crime, but then he pulls out a crystal and says something in Latin. Before my eyes, an image, like a holograph, appears and begins to move. It's a bedroom covered in blood, with the corpse of a woman and the beheaded infant she recently gave birth to lying in the center of it all.

I find the nearest trash bin and empty my stomach.

As if on cue, Matilda arrives with a cold washcloth and a new trash bin. I raise an eyebrow at her, and the men in the room are all locked in some kind of power play staring contest and don't even seem to notice I'm over here losing my breakfast.

"I'm going to ask you one more time, Vlad. Did you kill her?" Derek says.

"I did not kill my wife and child," he replies through gritted teeth, his eyes fixed on the projected image. "But I will make the person who did this pay. They will feel the wrath of Vlad the Impaler as no one has ever felt it, and they will know pain before I let them die. *If* I let them die."

There's a cruel gleam in his eyes that sends shivers up my spine. It's not hard to imagine him being responsible for the deaths of tens of thousands of people, as history says he was in Romania in 1462. Whether he was defending his home region or is a truly sadistic monster, history can't agree, but looking at him now, I can imagine both. He may have been fighting for a greater cause, but he also reveled in the bloodshed, savored ripping the heads off his enemies and drinking their blood as it poured out of their skulls. He enjoyed it, and still does.

"Then tell us what happened," Elijah says, flicking off the crystal. "How did someone manage to kill your family in your own home and leave without you knowing or seeing them?"

Dracula's spine stiffens. "The night that it happened, I had left to find someone to feed on—within the rules and bylaws established, of course—and when I returned, I found them dead. My butler didn't see or hear anything, and no leads have turned up since. I am the only suspect as far as I can tell."

"We will need a list of your enemies," Derek says, making a note on his legal pad.

Dracula laughs. "That's going to be a longer list than we have time to investigate," he says.

Derek sighs. "If you don't cooperate in your own defense, we can't help you. I need a list of anyone who might have such a grudge against you, or Mary, that they would do this. A list of anyone who worked for you at that time. Household staff. Anyone who had access to Mary or your home."

The count sighs and digs into the briefcase at his side. He hands Derek a file.

"That should have everything you need."

Derek flips it open and scans the contents, then nods and closes the file. "We will begin our investigation first by talking to the coroners and visiting the crime scene. We need the name and contact information of the person or persons you fed off of that night as well as anyone who can provide an alibi or character testimony on your behalf."

Dracula shakes his head. "I have no alibi, not anyone useful at any rate. I was hunting for blood. I didn't ask for their name and number. I fed, wiped their memory and left. They will be no help."

Sebastian shifts in his seat. "We still need to know where you were. An accounting of every minute. Other people could have seen you that night and they may be able to vouch for your whereabouts."

"Can you bring human witnesses into your courts?" I ask, speaking for the first time.

All eyes shift to me. Elijah answers. "Not specifically, no. But we can use a Memory Catcher—like the one you just saw—to capture their memory of the night in question, and that's admissible as eyewitness testimony."

I'm torn between being impressed and dismayed. "So you steal memories from people without their knowledge or consent?"

"Not exactly," Elijah says. "It's more like we are picking up the impression of the memory that's left. If it's strong enough, it will give us a clear indication of what happened." He gestures to the crystal they just activated a moment ago. "That memory was lifted from one of the Enforcers who first responded to the murder."

"Then can't you do that with Dracula? Catch his memories to prove what happened?"

"Paranormals can tamper with memory imprints, so they are not admissible in court unless they are expert testimony used to establish the facts of the case, such as an Enforcer or coroner's memory," Derek says. "Otherwise only human memories can be used. We will do a

Memory Catch of the crime scene, but it's unlikely to yield anything useful since we don't have any non-paranormal memory prints to pull."

"This is your whole plan?" Dracula asks. "Throw some magic around and hope for the best?"

Derek scowls at his sire. "We will do everything we can to win this case. We want to be freed of you as much as you want to be freed of this mess. Maybe more. But we have to work with what we have, which, at the moment, isn't much."

"Very well," Dracula says, standing. "I will find you a character witness. In the meantime, you will find the evidence that proves me innocent and identifies the murderer." This is a statement, not a question, and with a sharp turn he walks out of the library.

Derek stands. "Elijah, you and I will work on the paperwork we have to file for court." He looks to Liam next. "Put your ear to the ground, brother. See if any of our sources know anything about the murder or the nature of their relationship."

Liam nods. "I'll report back later," he says, leaving the room.

Derek looks to me and Sebastian. "I need you two to talk with the coroners and examine the crime scene for anything the Enforcers might have missed."

Sebastian glances my way, but his face is impartial, and I can't get a read on his emotions. I, for one, am nervous and excited to be assigned fieldwork. I assumed I'd be stuck in an office all day doing paralegal grunt work.

Elijah leaves and Derek approaches me with a frown on his face.

"Are you comfortable doing this?" he asks. "I know you're getting thrown in head first. It can be overwhelming."

"It can be," I admit. "But I'm ready. I want to go."

I'm about to turn away, when I pause. "Is there any chance we can make a detour on the way back? I need a new cell phone since Liam melted mine. And I'll need a new number, so Jerry can't call me again."

"About that," Derek says. "We will be moving, and where we're going, you won't need a cell phone."

"We're moving? Now? I don't understand."

Derek glances at Sebastian. "You'll see what I mean shortly. Is there anything else I can do for you? I am, as always, at your disposal."

"No, I'm good." Answers. All I want is more answers. But I feel as if I've found a magic lamp with a genie who is granting me all my wishes, and though this new life comes with a heavy dose of danger and mystery, it's kinda worth it. Something about all of this crazy fits. I feel like this is where I belong.

Derek reaches for my hand, and the touch sends a shiver up my spine. "Never hesitate to let me know if you need anything at all." His gaze holds mine for too long, and I look away first, blood rising to my cheeks.

"Thank you," I say sincerely, forcing myself to look him in the eyes. "For everything you've done for me. I appreciate it. I...I've been worried that you'll regret hiring me. Because I'm...mundane."

He frowns. "It is...unusual, especially since we work within the legal system of our community. But it's not unheard of. There's a precedent if I need to justify your presence. I know Lily told you about the spell on the ad. You shouldn't have been able to see it at all as a human, but you did. That's significant. You're meant to be here, Eve Oliver. That much is clear."

He says this with such conviction and authority that I know he believes in what he's saying and will fight for me. I can hear it in his voice. See it in the hard set of his jaw. He really believes I belong here.

I smile and squeeze his hand. "If you're sure."

He nods. "I'm absolutely sure, Eve."

Sebastian approaches us, hands in his pockets. "Ready?" he says, though he looks none too happy to be doing this, whether because I'm going or because of where we're going I can't say. Either way, being with mister grump is going to be less than awesome if he's going to be in a bad mood all day.

I link my arm through his and smile my most charming smile at him as he leads us out the library. "Come now, you can't spend your whole existence growling and grimacing at everyone. You really need to lighten up and enjoy life more."

He snorts at that. "Lighten up? That's your advice for me while we're investigating the highest profile murder case in the paranormal community?"

I nod. "That's exactly my advice. There will always be something that gives us an excuse to be miserable. Our job is to find the reasons to be happy. To make joy and gratitude more of a habit than misery and excessive amounts of stress and worry."

He looks down at me, his face unreadable. "You're very wise for such a young human," he says.

I make an exaggerated scrunched face. "I'm not that young. Sheesh. You old guys think everyone is young."

"Old guys?" he asks, his stern facing cracking into a small smile despite himself.

"You are male, yes?" I give him an appraising look with a bit of a flirtatious edge.

He rolls his eyes. "Yes, I am male."

"And you are old, yes?"

He glares at me a moment, but then nods. "I suppose by some standards you could consider me aged."

"Some standards? By whose standards would you not be considered ancient?" I ask.

"Dragons," he says without hesitancy. "To them everyone is young."

I nearly choke on my tongue at that. "There are dragons?" I ask.

He nods. "There are dragons, yes, and so many other creatures. Was that not in the books Elijah gave you?"

I shake my head. "Nope. They were just dry, boring, law books."

"I have a book for you. If you'd like to read it." He says this almost shyly, and I'm intrigued.

"Definitely. I most definitely want to read it. Thank you."

He nods and leads me down a corridor I haven't seen before. An archway lined with moss and branches and vines climbing up the walls. Lily joins us, though I don't see her arrive or what direction she comes from.

"Aren't we going to the limo?" I ask.

He shakes his head. "It's time to move the castle."

"Move the...castle?" I remember Lily mentioning something about their home changing location. "Is this what Derek meant when he said we're moving?" I ask.

He grunts, as if that tells me all I need to know.

I roll my eyes. "Lily? Care to elaborate?"

"Sure, bosswoman," she says eagerly. "My uncles have clients all over the globe. We go where needed. And right now, we're needed in the Otherworld."

"The Otherworld?"

"It's where I was born. Where most paranormals are born these days." She pauses, losing her chirpy composure for a moment. "My tree was still young in the dryad grove when a land-bound mermaid with a penchant for arson started a fire that burned for a fortnight. My home was destroyed in the blaze, killing my family and nearly killing me. But Granny Matilda saved a seed from my tree, a seed of my soul. She saved *me*. And when she planted the seed in the castle, it flourished, and so did I." She finishes with her natural spunk and pulls open a heavy wooden door.

My next question catches in my throat at the sight before us. A massive tree grows at the center of the room; bark white as snow, roots digging into the glass floor, spreading out endlessly into the darkness below. Leaves of all colors, emerald and crimson, burnt-orange and deep purple, reach toward the ceiling, except there is no roof, but a whirlpool of stars and clouds swirling above.

I am frozen. Transfixed by the impossible imagery.

Sebastian squeezes my hands and steps forward onto the glass floor, which stays firm beneath his heavy body. "It will be all right," he says.

I nod with a smile and join him in the room. From here, I cannot see where the world ends, and I feel suspended, floating in the night sky, the tree glowing like the moon.

"It takes a great deal of energy to move an object the size of the Night Castle and surrounding property," says Sebastian, leading me to the base of the trunk. "Lily's tree provides the fuel."

I look at her compassionately. "Is that difficult?"

She shakes her head. "Dryad magic is meant to be used. Traveling is like a rollercoaster ride for me. But I suppose I would get tired if my tree teleported a bunch of times in a short while."

"So how does it work?" I ask. "Do we need to do anything special or…"

"Lily's the only one who needs to be here. But if you lay your hand on the bark, you can feel the power," Sebastian says, placing his palm flat against the tree. I do the same, and when I touch the wood, a sense of easy comfort fills me, like drinking warm tea by the fire on a cold night.

"You both ready?" asks Lily, her hands scrunched up, her face bursting with anticipation.

Sebastian nods.

"Ready," I say.

The dryad places her hand on the tree, and the stars above begin to swirl around us, covering my vision with blinding light.

I close my eyes.

And a flash comes over me.

Three figures stand on a cliff. Their faces hidden in darkness. I can barely make out their forms in the night, until lightning strikes, and they look like shadows, hungry and cruel. Rain falls heavy and thick, and a stormy sea swirls below them.

I can't breathe.

I can barely think.

I am here. Standing on the shore at the base of the cliff.

One of the figures leaps down, cape billowing in the angry wind. They land before me, and for a spilt moment lightning strikes, and I see their face, their beautiful face. Blood red lips. Eyes like the ocean. Hair dark as night. It is a woman, I realize, and she reaches forward and grabs me by the throat. Her nails rip into my flesh. "You should have died with your mother."

I scream.

And strong arms reach around me, holding me close.

A soothing voice whispers to me.

"Shh…you're safe. You're safe, Eve. No one is going to hurt you."

He grips me firmly; my head is against his chest. My tears stain his shirt.

I try to adjust my breathing to match his. Slowing it, steadying it.

A warmth flows through me and my head fills with images of the mountains and tall trees reaching for the sky. I feel my body settle into the earth, like my soul is being grounded, tethered gently to something strong and sturdy, something immovable.

Eventually my shaking stops, my breathing normalizes, and the panic subsides, leaving in its wake a massive headache.

I open my eyes and see that I am lying in Sebastian's arms at the base of the dryad tree. The swirl of stars is gone. Lily stands uncomfortably to the side.

Now that I'm feeling a bit better, embarrassment floods me and I pull away from Sebastian and wipe my eyes. "I'm...sorry about that. I get panic attacks from time to time, though they seem to be coming in more frequency recently. I think the lights triggered something—"

"You have nothing to apologize for. This isn't your world. And it's dangerous. You're smart to be scared."

I frown, looking at both of them. "That's just it. I'm not scared. Of any of this. I know I should be. And I keep waiting for it to hit, but so far, nothing. If anything, this feels like home. Like I've finally come home after being gone for far too long."

I look at the endless darkness below me, at the roots reaching into nothing. "Adam and I never felt like we belonged anywhere. Our father did his best to make us feel special, since we weren't very normal. But after he died, it was hard. Foster homes and other people's agendas and expectations of us. And then Adam died and it was like the last tether I had was cut. I was floating away until I found this job. This life."

"Your father sounds like he was a special man," Sebastian says softly. "Foster care must have been hard."

"He was," I say. "And most of the foster parents weren't bad people. But they didn't understand us or our relationship. They didn't understand why we never fit in."

I look over at him again, our eyes locking. "Is it weird that this is the place I finally feel like I belong?" I ask.

He shrugs. "Who's to say what's weird or not? Life is full of impossible dreams, often wrapped in the ordinary."

"You're very wise for such an old vampire," I say, teasing him with his own words.

A quiet laugh escapes his mouth. Reluctantly, I think. "Touché," he says.

I chuckle and stand, smoothing out my clothes with my hands. "So did we do it? Did the castle travel?"

Lily beams. "See for yourself." With a spring to her step, she leads us out the door we came, and to the front entrance of the castle. When we step outside, I gasp.

Green lights dance across a dark sky. Shimmering and coiling like a snake. "The northern lights," I whisper.

"Perhaps," says Sebastian. "Here we call it the Dragon's Breath."

I study the shapes in the sky, like green fire amongst the stars. "Are we near the northern hemisphere, or the southern? It doesn't seem too cold."

Sebastian shrugs. "No one knows, save the dragons. They created the Otherworld as a safe haven for all paranormals of the earth. Elijah suspects we are near the Antarctic."

"And you?"

He shakes his head. "Personally, I believe we are in a different world altogether. The sky here never changes. It is always like this, both darkness and light. A place where both creatures of the night and creatures of the sun can live in balance."

He guides me forward. Where once stood a driveway, now the land is covered in cobbled streets, and instead of a black limo, a dark carriage awaits us. And not just any carriage, but one fit for a man of Sebastian's wealth, with sleek lines and a polished mahogany frame that's pulled by a team of four horses. Something about the majestic beasts doesn't look right, however, and when I step closer I understand what it is.

The horses have six legs each and manes of glistening silver and gold hair!

Past the moat, golden lights drift in the sky like fireflies. They are lanterns, I realize, illuminating buildings torn from a different century. Manors that belong in medieval France. Villas reminiscent of Spain. Gothic cathedrals with sharp angles and stained glass.

The sky turns moist and rain begins to fall, soaking us, but I don't care. I'm too entranced by what I'm seeing.

Lily opens the carriage door, and Sebastian helps me in.

"Ready to experience the Otherworld?" he asks with a wink.

I nod, my mind exploding with the possibilities of what my life has become.

CHAPTER 10: THE MORGUE

DEATH, be not proud, though some have called thee
Mighty and dreadful, for thou art so;
~ John Donne

LILY GIVES a sharp cry from the driver's seat outside and the carriage shifts into motion with barely a jolt.

Sebastian is quiet as we travel over cobbled roads, and I don't disturb his silence with the million questions buzzing through my mind. Instead, I stare out the carriage window, marveling as we leave the Night brothers' estate behind and enter the town proper. The northern lights, or Dragon's Breath as they call it, casts rays of color against the rain-slicked streets. The buildings around us resemble something straight out of a Bavarian village, with peaked roofs and colorful shutters. They're pushed up close to the edge of the cobble-stone streets, leaving narrow walkways on either side for pedestrians.

And, despite the late hour, there are people making use of them, too. We pass several couples headed in the opposite direction we are, as if coming back from an evening event. They're dressed in a style that reminds me of the fashions of Victorian England; formal vests, coats and hats for the men, narrow-waisted skirts and bonnets for the women. Many of them look as human as I do, but when I examine them more closely I can see evidence of their supernatural heritage, from the twitch of a tail that peeks out from beneath one man's topcoat to the gleam of vertical pupils in the yellow eyes of a woman who looks up at me as we speed past.

It is almost too much to take in.

I sit back and run a hand through my damp hair, shivering a bit as I attempt to wrap my mind around the new world I'm now inexplicably a part of.

"Everyone lives together peacefully?" I ask, finally breaking my silence.

"As peacefully as humans do," Sebastian replies.

"Right. So that's a no, then."

"We have our justice system, as you know," he says, finally turning to look at me. "And there are communities of paranormals here, with their own rules and laws. Overall it works. But we do have our conflicts and occasional wars, sometimes between different races, sometimes amongst our own ranks. If it's an internal conflict, the dragons usually leave the community to handle their own as long as it doesn't spill into the rest of the Otherworld. If it's between factions, the dragons will get involved and arbitrate before things get too out of hand."

"Dragons. Those are judges, right? And they're like, real dragons? Big flying dragons?"

"Yes. Big flying dragons. There are six. One born of each of the elements that shape this world."

I shift in the carriage as we go over a bump and my hip hits a sharp edge of wood. That's going to leave a bruise. "I thought there were only four elements? Earth, air, fire and water?"

"In our world there are two more. Light and darkness. Vampires are born of darkness."

"Makes sense," I say. "So, the dragons rule all?"

"They created this world. They came together to create a place that would protect paranormals and humans alike."

"Like from the witch trials? That kind of thing?"

He smirks. "You caught no real witches during your massacre," he said. "All of those killed were human. Witches are too powerful to get caught up in such a human mess."

"Right. Well, I'm anti-witch hunt, just for the record."

He nods. "The witches will be glad to know it."

The carriage slows and then comes to a stop in front of a cemetery. The rain has faded to a slight misting of the air, and fog hugs the earth around the ancient-looking tombstones, setting a sinister tone.

Lily opens my carriage door and offers her hand to steady me as I climb out. I'm about to tell her I can manage without aid, but then I slip and nearly land on my ass in the mud. She rescues me with a strong arm around my waist, surprising me anew with her dexterity and strength.

"Thanks," I say with a smile.

"It takes some getting used to," she says, and I don't know if she means carriage riding or magical otherworlds, or both. I'm going with both.

"Why are we at a graveyard?" I ask. "I thought we were going to the coroner's office?"

"We are," Sebastian says without further comment as he begins walking.

I follow, but Lily stays behind with the carriage, giving a little wave and wink as we walk away. "Don't be scared," she says. "They're harmless."

"Well that's not ominous at all," I say under my breath. I catch up to Sebastian and grab his arm. "What am I not supposed to be scared about?" I ask. "Who's harmless?"

"You'll see soon enough."

Ugh. If I get that answer from one more Night brother, I'm gonna punch one of them.

"Can none of you actually answer questions in a straightforward manner? Is it part of your curse, to be so annoyingly vague?"

He grunts at that. "We shouldn't have to explain this world to you. You should already be part of it. I don't know how you saw the ad or got this job, but it's a giant mistake."

That stings, but I try not to let it show. "Well, as it happens, I did

101

see the ad and I did get the job. So now I need you guys to actually answer my questions and tell me shit or it's going to be hella hard to do my damn job."

We are walking across the muddy cemetery towards a mausoleum. It's a massive structure, far larger than I would have expected. The towering gothic building casts a long shadow over the dead with its clustered columns, sharply pointed spires and flying buttresses. The stained-glass windows give added color to the Dragon's Breath in a magical display as we approach the entrance.

Sebastian pauses between the two intricately carved stone gargoyles guarding the door.

I wait, unsure of what we're doing. "Are we going in or...?"

"We will. In a moment. Once we have permission." Sebastian clears his throat and says something in a language I don't recognize.

It kinda sounds like "*oobolacky jambonick kay.*" But really, I'm totally guessing about that.

At his strange words, a sound like grinding stone startles a pair of birds perched on one of the leafless trees near us. And then the gargoyles blink!

I blink as well, thinking maybe I imagined it. But no, the stone gargoyles are definitely moving. One yawns, its mouth opening and stretching, revealing dozens of large stone teeth.

My flash is blinking in my mind, but it doesn't feel like a danger warning as much as something auspicious I'm being alerted to.

"What does the Son of Night seek in the place of the dead?" one of the gargoyles asks, its voice like gravel.

"Greetings, Akuro. We seek the wisdom of the Infrits in our investigation of a wrongful death," Sebastian replies.

The second gargoyle then leaps down from its pedestal, wings spread, tail wrapping around itself as it lands before me. It's at least twelve feet tall with a fierce face full of sharp teeth. It's nearly identical to the other gargoyle, with only subtle differences that most would miss on a casual glance. It bends its head down to sniff me.

I inhale sharply, and the scents of stone and earth and air mixed with cedar hit me.

"I know she is human, but she is under my protection," Sebastian says. "She works for The Night Firm."

At his words, both gargoyles begin to shake and make a sound that resembles rocks being thrown at a boulder. It takes me a moment to realize that they're laughing!

Sebastian frowns, clearly perplexed by their reaction.

"The Sons of Night have much to learn," the gargoyle in front of me says. This one's voice is lighter, more feminine.

Each of the gargoyles' eyes are the size of my head, and I have a hard time knowing which one to look into as it lowers itself further to make eye contact with me.

"Tell me what you know," she commands.

Somehow, I know it's a she.

I'm about to say I don't know what she's talking about, that I don't know anything, when her mouth gently rests on my forehead and a vision overtakes me. I am no longer in the cemetery, but on the highest imaginable mountain. At the peak, the two gargoyles are together, and the one that spoke to me shoots into the air, flying higher, higher, higher. She screams as something within her pushes out, and a baby gargoyle slips into the wind, falling into the other gargoyle's arms.

I see the baby gargoyle, feel into it, and then the vision disappears as quickly as it came. I fall, my legs too weak to sustain myself, and feel strong arms catch me before the earth does.

"What did you do to her?" Sebastian demands, drawing closer and reaching for me.

I place a tempering hand on his arm. "I'm fine."

With his help I stand, leaning against him for balance, as I look into the eyes—or at least into one of the eyes—of the female gargoyle before me. Sebastian gasps as I place a hand on the gargoyle's face gently. "Your child will be born atop a mountain, and she will be healthy and safe and beautiful."

The gargoyle nods, huffing into my face. "Thank you, Wise One, for that blessing."

With that, the gargoyles return to their posts and resume their stone-like slumber as the door before us swings open.

"What was that all about?" I ask, my heart jack-rabbiting in my chest.

"I do not know," he says, casting a suspicious glance at the gargoyles before leading us into the darkened hall of the mausoleum. "Akuro and Okura have been guardians of the dead for as long as I can remember. But they've never behaved that way before." He looks at me with wonder and confusion. "How did you know she was pregnant? Gargoyles rarely breed. It hasn't happened in thousands of years, that I know of."

I shrug. "When she asked me, I saw a vision and I knew. I've always had hunches about things, and sometimes I have ideas that I write about, but never anything so clear, or about someone other than myself. I always assumed I was just making them up." My mind flashes to the vision of the brothers defending me against the evil forest. I assumed that was just a fantasy, but what if it wasn't?

"Who are you, Eve Oliver?" he asks, his arm still around my waist in case I collapse again.

I shrug again, feeling stupid. "I don't know how to answer that. I'm just me."

"Indeed," he says, skeptically.

"Indeed," I repeat, with an edge to my voice. "Do you think I'm lying to you?"

"No. But I do think there's more to you than is immediately evident."

"Isn't that true of everyone?" I ask. "None of us are what we first appear. We all have layers, depth, secret pains and hidden desires that subtly shape who we are. Why would you ever presume to know someone with so little effort?"

I step away from him and suck in a breath of air. "I can walk now. Shall we?" I say, before he has a chance to respond. I'm still shaken with what just happened and I don't really want to talk about it with skeptical Sebastian, at least not until I have a chance to think on things.

He's still eyeing me strangely as we walk through the darkened halls. It smells of death and dust and old flowers and cold marble, and every step we take echoes in the large, sparse space.

Even our breathing sounds too loud as I walk beside him. He seems to know where he's going, so I stick close as I look around, trying to take it all in. The walls, ceiling, and floor are all made of white marble. There are no pictures, no furniture, nothing but arched doorways with heavy doors appearing every so often. "Where do the doors lead?" I ask.

"Various places. Examining rooms. Storage. Broom closet."

I do a double take to see if Sebastian is actually making a joke, but I can't tell. His face is stoic. And they probably do need broom closets here. So he might have just been being very literal. But do I perhaps notice a corner of his mouth twitching ever so slightly?

The man is maddening.

We stop before a large arched double door and Sebastian reaches for it very cautiously. "Stay behind me," he says softly, as he opens the door.

I do as I'm told because I am not stupid and my survival instincts are alive and well.

The door swings open, and I feel the flames before I see them. Warm and dancing on the edges of the marble, casting golden light everywhere.

Sebastian clears his throat and the fire dies down, though the room is still uncommonly warm as we enter, and sweat beads on my skin, sliding down my spine uncomfortably.

My eyes widen. In some ways it looks like a standard morgue, with bodies lying on tables, but that's where the resemblance ends. The rest of the place looks like something out of a mad scientist's laboratory, with seemingly miles of glass tubing connecting beakers of bubbling liquid and a strange apparatus whose purpose I can't immediately discern. Specimen jars line the shelves of multiple cabinets and here and there I think I can see something moving inside them.

But they're not the most remarkable nor eye-catching part of the room, not by a long shot.

No, that honor is reserved for the two men on fire standing in front of us.

They are both leaning over a table, the body of something that looks like a cross between a stag and man before them, its chest cut open as the two flaming men probe and poke and pull things out of the cavity they've created.

I squint and realize they aren't on fire; they are literally made from fire. It's a part of them. It *is* them. One of the men glances over at us, his eyes like small fireballs burning brightly in his face of flames. "Oh, how rude of us!" he says with a chuckle and a wave of his hand.

Immediately, the flames encasing both of them die out, and, as I blink, they turn into normal-ish looking men.

Normal-ish because their exposed skin is still a burnt orange-red in color and their eyes still glow like fire. They both have red hair, but one man is bigger, more muscular than the other, who is shorter and leaner. They're dressed in identical white lab coats.

The shorter one walks over to us and holds out a hand to shake mine. When I hesitate, he glances at his hand and only then realizes that it's covered in blood and guts. "Sorry about that, truly. It's been *a week.*"

He saunters over to the sink and washes his hands. "Elal, tell them about the week it has *been!*" His words are over-enunciated and exaggerated and he shakes his hips for emphasis.

The big one, Elal, covers the body on his table with a sheet and removes his coat, revealing the white shirt and pants he's wearing beneath. Miraculously, and unlike his lab coat, his clothing is free of bloodstains. "It has been a week, as Ifi said. The werewolves have a problem on their hands. One of their own has been leaving unauthorized half-eaten corpses both in the mundane world and Otherworld. The dragons are in a fit for us to wrap this up. The vampires, are, of course, loving this. No offense," he says, glancing at Sebastian.

Sebastian nods. "None taken. Everyone knows there's no love lost between our kinds."

"Indeed," Elal says, with a nod.

Ifi joins the three of us, sans lab coat, and there's not a speck of blood on him either. He wraps one arm around Elal's waist, while holding out a hand to shake mine. "Let's try this again, shall we? I am Ifi, Ifrit of the High Kingdom of Furor, Lord of the Flaming Backlands, son of the Great Flame herself."

I raise an eyebrow and accept his hand, which is hot to the touch. "I'm Eve Oliver, Managing Director at The Night Firm."

Elal and I then shake hands. "I'm Elal," he says, simply.

"No other titles?" I tease.

Elal laughs. "Ifi made those up. He likes how it sounds to strangers."

Ifi pouts and bumps Elal with his hips. "It's not as fun when you tell them. And besides, I am the son of the Great Flame herself."

Elal rolls his eyes. "As is every Ifirit born of the Flame. That's hardly noteworthy." But then Elal glances down at who I assume is his romantic partner, and his face softens. "But you are the flame of my heart, and always will be. You are the only one who can claim that title in all the worlds."

Ifi's frown turns into a beatific smile and the two share a moment, and a kiss, until Sebastian, the party pooper, clears his throat.

"Sorry to break up the foreplay, boys, but you've done the autopsy on Mary Dracule, Vlad Dracule's wife, yes?"

The two Ifrits glance at each other, frowning. Ifi answers first. "Yes. We did. Her and her child."

I flinch at the memory of the crime scene projection. So gruesome and senseless.

"We need to know everything you found," Sebastian says.

They nod, and Elal points at the door of a refrigeration unit on the other side of the room, which pops open at his command and disgorges an exam table, complete with a cloth-covered form, that rolls swiftly to his side without a sound. Together the two morticians reach down and pull back the sheet, revealing the body of Mary and her newborn baby. I'm stunned to see that the pair have been put back together in the wake of the autopsy with precise care. It's impossible to even see where they were cut into.

"The child was killed first, while she watched, most likely," Elal says, soberly.

"The child's head was ripped off and his blood drained," Ifi says, continuing. "Mary was then drained of her blood and left for dead."

My eyebrow shoots up at that. "So the killer might have left before she died?"

Sebastian looks at me and gives an imperceptible nod. Oh, did I finally do something to maybe impress him?

"Or the killer watched her die slowly," Elal says. "But the creature who killed her didn't drain her entirely. They left enough so she could bleed out on her own, holding the pieces of her dead child in her arms as she did."

Vomit burns the back of my throat and I swallow it down. This is heinous. "You said 'creature'. So it's not necessarily a vampire?" I ask.

"A vampire would be the most likely culprit, but there are some unusual inconsistencies," Elal says.

"Like what?" Sebastian asks.

"Her blood not being entirely drained, for one. It would take a lot of self-control for a vampire to leave her alive like that," Ifi says. "And the bite wounds were slashed, so it's hard to tell exactly what killed her."

"And what of paternity?" Sebastian asks. "Have you been able to confirm whether the child is Vlad's?"

Elal shakes his head. "That test will take longer, I'm afraid. We will turn those results over to both you and the prosecution as soon as we have them."

Sebastian doesn't look happy about that, but what can he do?

"Were you able to extract her dying wish?" Sebastian asks, as if this is a totally normal and common request.

"Dying wish?" I ask, when it seems clear no one is going to offer an explanation.

"We are Ifrit," Elal says.

"And?" I ask.

Ifi grins and sashays over to me. "Oh darling, you're so new it's almost painful, in a delightful kind of way. We are Ifrits. Genies of the fire. Elal and I have the special gift of discovering the dying wish of the recently deceased."

"What do you do with their wishes?" I ask, imagining the massive problems that could occur if every person's dying wish was granted.

Ifi shrugs. "Usually nothing. Most beings are entirely uncreative and boring. Sometimes we pass it on to the authorities and let them handle things. And sometimes," he says, with a gleam in his eyes, "sometimes, if it's interesting enough, we grant them."

"All legally, of course," Sebastian says gruffly.

"Of course, Mr. Night," Ifi says, moving closer to Sebastian seductively. "Always legal."

Ifi tweaks Sebastian's nose like a schoolboy then laughs and returns to Elal's side.

"All right, enough monkey housing," Elal says. "Show them the wish."

Ifi sighs dramatically. "Fine, fine. Step back a moment. Wouldn't want to hurt anyone. Humans and vampires are so delicate when it comes to fire."

Sebastian stiffens by my side and pulls me back as Ifi bursts into flames.

The fire burns around us, and I sweat profusely, the air hot and heavy in my lungs.

Ifi begins chanting in a language I've never heard. His voice seems powered with magic. It becomes layered with other voices, the vibration of them shaking the room. I clutch Sebastian's arm to avoid falling over, and he braces me as everything rattles. I worry the building will cave in on top of us. I glance at the vampire by my side with frantic eyes, but he looks calm, collected, like this is par for the course.

I take a breath and calm myself. A loud screeching fills the air. Flames dance against the marble walls and ceilings. And then the body of Mary Dracule begins to shake as flames flow into her, animating her from within.

She sits up and turns to us, color filling her cheeks, light and soul filling her eyes. She locks her gaze with mine, a plea on her face as she clutches her dead baby to her chest.

"Save them. Save my babies. Please! Save them!"

And with that, she drops back down to the table with a loud thunk. The fire leaves her body, flowing back into Ifi, who staggers to the side and is in turn caught by Elal. Ifi returns to his more human form and the temperature in the room drops about thirty degrees, though I'm still sweating profusely. I'm dizzy, too, though whether that's from the heat, the fire, or the dead woman coming back to life, I can't rightly say.

With everything going on, it takes a moment for Mary's last words to register.

"Are dying wishes considered reliable?" I ask.

Elal nods. "Generally. We can tell if someone's spirit is too broken to make sense. Why do you ask?"

"Because Mary only has one child. So why was her wish that her babies—plural—be saved?"

CHAPTER 11: THE CRIME SCENE

HE WHO DARES NOT GRASP the thorn should never crave the rose. ~ Anne Bronte

THE COLD AIR of the rainy evening hits me as we exit the mausoleum. The gargoyles, Okura and Akuro, do not come to life to greet us again, but I feel Okura's eyes on me as we walk away, and I swear she winks at me.

"What do you think it means?" I ask, referring to the final wish of Mary Dracule.

Sebastian shrugs. "Perhaps she had a child in the past no one knew about? We'll have to look into it. Maybe something at the crime scene will give us a clue."

Lily greets us with a cheery smile when we return to the carriage. "Aren't they amazing?" she says, gushingly.

"The gargoyles or the Ifrits?" I ask.

She considers. "Well, both, but mostly I meant the Ifrits. The gargoyles don't talk much."

"I've never met an Ifrit before," I say, which is true of all of them actually. First dryad, vampire, Ifrit and gargoyle. And whatever Matilda is.

"They're fun. You should come clubbing with us sometime. They know the best spots for partying."

Sebastian huffs at that, and this time I'm on the side of the boring vampire. "That's probably not my scene," I say diplomatically.

We climb into the carriage and Lily guides us over cobbled paths towards Dracula's place.

The tightly packed town becomes more spread out the longer we drive, turning into farmland and then larger estates.

The carriage comes to a stop, and I look out the window and see a Spanish-style villa sprawled out over acres of beautiful land with a view to kill for. "This is incredible," I say. "Clearly Dracula lives on the right side of the tracks."

"Tracks?" Sebastian asks.

"It's an expression. He's rich."

"Vampires get very good at acquiring wealth," he says.

"I assume that applies to you as well?" I say, thinking about their freaking castle and cars and all the things.

"Yes," he says simply.

"Then why do you still work as lawyers? You could just retire on your wealth, couldn't you?"

"We could. But even vampires need purpose. Being immortal is a long time to live, and for that life to have meaning, we need work that fulfills us and makes a difference."

"That makes sense," I say. "But why law? Specifically, why defense?"

"The paranormal legal system can be finicky. Dragons are generally decent judges, since they are considered wise and long-lived even by our community standards. But their perspective can get skewed as a result and they can be overly harsh in their judgements. It's our job to make sure our clients get a fair trial. That they aren't unnecessarily punished beyond what is reasonable for the crime they committed, or, if innocent, that they are not punished at all."

"And Dracula? Do you really believe he's innocent?" I ask.

He shrugs. "I don't know. I don't think he would kill Mary, but then again, I can't be sure I'm being impartial when it comes to him. As I'm sure you've gathered, our history with him is complicated."

"Yeah, that is pretty clear."

Lily opens my door and I slide out, with Sebastian following. I notice a ruined cathedral opposite Dracula's manor. A mighty structure of gray stone, its twin towers almost reaching the Dragon's Breath. Half of its roof is caved in, and chipped gargoyles perch on what remains, their gazes old and tired.

Sebastian follows my eyes. "The place has been in disrepair for so long, most call it the Broken Cathedral now," he says.

"What was it called before?"

He shrugs. "I don't partake much in religion."

Somehow that doesn't surprise me. "And what sort of religions exist in the Otherworld?"

"The same as in the mundane world. The cathedrals are open to all faiths carried over into this place."

I nod, and we make our way to the villa. It's even more stunning up close. There's a beautiful garden in the courtyard we pass, and Lily squeals at the flowers blooming under the shifting lights of the Dragon's Breath. "This place is amazing," she says, clearly delighted.

"Remember, we're here to investigate a murder, not to have afternoon tea," Sebastian says.

I frown at him. He really needs to learn to lighten up sometimes.

Lilly doesn't take any offense. "I know, Uncle Seb. I just think it's pretty here. That's all."

Yellow eyes peer at us from behind a bush, and I kneel and make a clicking sound, luring a beautiful Egyptian Mau out of hiding. The cat hisses at Sebastian but nuzzles against me, purring. I give the sweet thing some love and then stand when someone comes out to greet us.

The butler Dracula mentioned. "You must be from the Night Firm?" he asks.

We nod.

"The Count said to expect you. Please, follow me."

The cat scurries away as the butler leads us through an open living room, and upstairs into a master suite larger than some apartments

I've lived in. It would be a gorgeous room if not for the bloodstains soaking the bed and staining the white silk sheets.

"This is where the mistress and her child were killed," the man says quietly.

"What's your name?" I ask.

He looks up in surprise. "Leonard," he replies.

"Thank you, Leonard. Would it be possible to get some tea and blood? Lily can help you."

He looks at me with an expression of relief. "Of course. Yes. I can do that. Will you two be okay here?"

I nod, smiling, and he leaves Sebastian and me alone in the bloody bedroom with a look of relief. Lily follows him out.

"We are going to need to Memory Catch him," Sebastian says once they are gone.

"He's human?"

"No, so it can't be used in court, but it can give us useful information regardless. Even if his memory's been tampered with, that in itself can be a clue."

"Can you tell if he's messed with it?"

"We can, yes. Usually. Someone has to be really skilled at memory manipulation to deceive us. We've been doing this a very long time."

I nod and study the room, imagining Mary's final moments of life, bleeding out on the bed, her dead baby in her arms. Who did this?

"Are there no surveillance cameras?" I ask.

"No, we don't use technology of that type here. That's why I said you wouldn't be needing a new phone. The Otherworld is... slow to change. Technology is frowned upon. There are no cell towers or electricity. Everything is powered by magic."

"Huh. Wow. Do you prefer it here?" I ask.

He shrugs. "There are advantages and disadvantages. Certain technology is useful and is considered contraband here. You can get into legal trouble for owning so much as an electric toothbrush. But here, I am not subject to the whims of the sun, and I do not have to hide who and what I am."

"Good thing you have a magic castle that can go anywhere, then."

He smirks. "Yes, good thing."

I scan around the room, refocusing on our task. "So, what are we looking for?"

"Anything that might give us a hint into Mary's life. Did she have other lovers? Other children? Enemies? Any letters? Journals?"

I nod. "Do I need to wear gloves or avoid touching anything?"

"No. The area's already been examined by the Enforcers."

I head to her closet as Sebastian checks the dresser and bedside tables.

Everything in this room and in the closet appears to belong to her. "Did Dracula sleep somewhere else?"

"Yes. They had separate rooms. We can look there next."

I shiver at the thought of going through the personal items of *the* Dracula. That's just so wild my head can't fully comprehend it. And yet, it's astonishing how quickly we can adapt to new life circumstances, no matter how outlandish they might be. We are remarkable at survival, for a species with so little physical protection.

Mary has a lot of fancy dresses that show little to no wear, indicating that they were rarely used. Same with the shoes and hats I find. It's not until I get down to the bottom drawer of her dresser that I find the clothes she preferred. More casual clothing. Cotton pants and blouses. Comfortable clothes that aren't stylish, or appropriate for the Otherworld from what I've seen.

"Did Mary like living here? Being with a vampire?" I ask, coming back into the bedroom holding jeans and a Grateful Dead band shirt.

"I don't know. She and I weren't close. But she wouldn't have been allowed to wear those in public." He glances away, and I leave it at that for now.

We continue searching her room for a few more hours. We find nothing and are about to give up when a flash gives me pause. I walk to the fireplace and run my hand over the stones, feeling for something but not sure what. So far nothing. Frustrated, I push a sitting chair over and stand on it, balancing myself against the wall as I feel the along the stones I couldn't reach on my own.

"What in the blazes are you doing, woman?" Sebastian says, grabbing my hips and nearly causing me to topple from the chair.

"I'm checking something."

I ignore the warmth of his hands on my hips, his fingers digging into my flesh, as I strain to reach the top stones. Finally, my persistence pays off. One of the stones is loose. I struggle to pull it out and then reach into the dark hole and smile as my hand touches a box. I take it and replace the stone.

Sebastian helps me down, and still has his hands on my waist as I hold up the box to show him. "She was hiding this. Let's find out why."

It doesn't take us long to realize Mary was hiding a secret.

I hold up a letter and read:

My dearest love,

It pains me to stay away for so long, to not hold you or caress you or see your face every day.

When can we be together again?

Yours,

L

We read through a few more, and they are similar. None are dated. None are signed with anything other than an L.

"Who's L?" I ask, putting the letters back into the box.

"I don't know," Sebastian says, frowning. "Given we don't know when these were written, they might not mean much."

"Is there a way to determine how old they are? Science or magic or..." I shrug, still so new to this world that I don't know the right questions to ask yet. In the absence of knowing what is possible, I choose to believe nothing is impossible. It keeps more options open that way.

"Elijah might have a contact that can help. We can check after we're done here."

Having exhausted all options in Mary's room, we move to Dracula's. Despite there being less blood, I'm suddenly anxious about entering his space.

His room is lighter than I expect, with gray and white the dominant color scheme amidst splashes of turquoise. "I expected his go-to color would be red," I say.

Sebastian chuckles. "That is the vibe he gives off."

There are a few surprises in Dracula's room.

First, we find a stack of romance novels by the bed. I raise an eyebrow. "Unusual reading preference for the most famous vampire in the world," I say.

Sebastian shrugs. "He always did have a taste for the romantic. It would explain his success with women."

We also find a journal written in his hand. I glance through it, then hold it up. "This could prove insightful," I say.

Sebastian nods in response.

Other than those two things, however, we find little else of note.

Sebastian glances around one last time and seems to come to the same conclusion I have. "Time for the butler."

I have to admit I've been morbidly looking forward to this part of the investigation. How does a Memory Catcher work? What does it do? I've seen the final result, but I'm looking forward to learning the rest.

We find Leonard in the kitchen with Lily, where the two of them are chatting over tea.

He jumps up when we enter, his face paling. "Pardon me. I was just about to bring you refreshments," he says, wringing his hands, clearly stretching the truth as there are no refreshments prepared.

I step forward. "I'm feeling a bit sick to my stomach after being in that room. I couldn't eat a thing. But thank you for your kindness."

He smiles in relief, and the stress in the room palpably lowers as he sighs.

"It has been hard living here since her death," he admits. "She was a fair and kind mistress. What happened to her is an abomination."

Sebastian pulls a chain out his pocket. A clear crystal set in a base of gold hangs from it and I can see intricate designs etched into its various faces. "I assume you won't mind sharing your memories in hopes it will help us find who did this?" Sebastian says to Leonard.

The butler nods. "Of course not. You may have everything in me. Though I don't know that it will prove useful. I wish I knew something helpful, but I'm useless. Absolutely useless." He wrings his hands again, his face crinkling in despair.

I reach a hand out and place it on his. "You never know what little clue might lead to something. It might not even be a memory you realize is important. Don't give up hope. The light shall reveal the truth. *In lumen et lumen.*"

My words seem to soothe him and his agitation stills as he stands straighter. "I'm ready," he says, with as much bravery as he can seemingly muster.

Sebastian places the crystal in front of Leonard and steps back, then utters the word *revelare.*

The crystal begins to glow, casting rainbow shards against the polished tile floor and countertops, and then an image appears before us, like the one I saw earlier. It's the perspective of the butler as he goes about his day, cleaning, acquiring blood, cooking and caring for Mary. It's startling to see her alive, to see her laughing and smiling and hear her voice through his mind and memories. It makes the memory of her corpse that much more tragic.

Seeing Mary through the butler's eyes makes one thing very clear.

He adored her. Worshipped her. You can feel it in every look he gives her. It's nearly stifling. He would do anything for her. That much is clear. What I want to know is would he do anything *to* her? If his affections were rejected? His name does start with an L.

Sebastian says "*ante*" and the scenes speed up, like fast-forward. We watch through it all, and I work to catch as many details as I can, but I see nothing out of the ordinary. Leonard was right; he didn't see anything helpful, at least not that I can tell.

"Thank you, Leonard," I say when Sebastian removes the crystal and pockets it. "This was extremely useful."

His eyes brighten at that. "It was?"

"Of course. Mary would be proud."

He smiles.

"Just one more thing," I say. "Would you mind giving us a writing sample? We're asking everyone to supply them just in case we have need of them later."

"No, of course not. What do you want me to write?" he asks, retrieving a note page and pen from a nearby utility drawer.

"Oh, I don't know. How about 'I love being on vacation but hate being away from home so long'?" I suggest, thinking about the note from earlier and trying to get some of the words to match without making it too obvious.

Leonard doesn't question the line at all, just dashes it off with a quick flourish and hands the paper over without a word.

We leave him with a tear in his eye and a heavy heart. Is it just grief that weighs on him? Or does he also carry guilt? Is he the man behind the letters?

Once outside, Sebastian pauses to look at me. "His memories weren't helpful."

"I know," I say.

"Then why did you tell him they were?"

"One, because he needed to hear it. And two, because you can't determine the worth of something so quickly. There are many ways to ascertain something—or someone's—worth." I glare at him pointedly. "In this case, his willingness to give up his memories helped us, even if the memories themselves didn't."

"How so?" Sebastian asks.

"Because he was clearly obsessed with Mary. He could have written those letters. That's why I asked him for the writing sample, just to be sure. He could have killed her in a jealous rage. But unless his memories have been tampered with, he was willing to let us pry into his mind. He probably didn't do it. That's useful information and further narrows our suspect pool, doesn't it?"

He nods. "That's impressive thinking, Eve. And you're right. If his memories haven't been tampered with, then he's most likely eliminated himself as a suspect. Though it doesn't mean he didn't write the letters."

"True. What kind of information can we get about them?" I ask.

"That's Elijah's department. He's got a contact, but they'll only work with him."

Something interrupts my attention, darting past the periphery of my vision, and I spot the cat I saw earlier, slinking behind a bush. I put a hand on Sebastian's chest to pause him, not taking my eyes off the feline, an idea percolating.

"Those Memory Catcher things. Do they work on animals?"

"They can work on any living thing," Sebastian says. "Except plants. We tried that once. A plant witnessed a murder and we thought we could catch a memory. It...didn't go well."

That sounds like a story for another time, so I press on. "The cat we saw earlier is still here. Which likely means it hangs around the villa a lot. What if we catch its memory and see what it knows?"

Sebastian cocks his head. "That's bloody brilliant. If you keep it still long enough. Cats don't typically like vampires very much."

"Why's that?" I ask, remembering his brother said the same thing when I found Moon.

"Maybe they remember how we fed on them when humans were scarce. Especially during times of plague and famine."

"Ew. Gross." I shift and squat to my knees. "Stay away then. Give me a minute. And give me the memory catcher."

"You don't know how to use it."

"Do I need magic?" I ask.

"No," he says.

I hold out my hand, palm up. "Then I know how to use it."

He sighs and places the crystal in my hand. I wait for him to move away and then creep forward, making clicking sounds with my tongue. "Hey, kitty. Come say hi."

The cat peeks out of the bushes and then saunters forward. I hold out my hand and let it come to me. It rubs against my hand, then my arm.

Soon the cat is in my lap purring happily as I scratch its chin and make cooing sounds.

Slowly I set the Memory Catcher in front of it and repeat the word Sebastian used earlier. Once again the crystal glows, then images begin to appear. The perspective of a cat is harder to sift through. They aren't interested in the things we would be, and so I get a lot of small dark spaces and some rats. I whisper "*ante*" and the images speed up, but still show nothing interesting. As the cat's vision pans to another set of feet, I'm about to call it a night when Sebastian steps forward.

"*Prohibere!*" he says, freezing the memory.

"What is it?" I ask.

He points to the image, which show a pair of feet in expensive shoes. "We've seen Mary's, Leonard's and Dracula's feet so far. These feet don't belong to any of them."

Upon closer inspection I see that he's right, though I hadn't noticed it before. "Then whose feet are they?" I ask.

"I recognize the shoes," Sebastian says, turning his head toward me. "They belong to Liam."

CHAPTER 12: THE CONFRONTATION

HE THAT SHUTS LOVE OUT, in turn shall be shut out from love, and on her threshold lie, howling in the darkness. ~ Alfred Lord Tennyson

I ASSUME we're heading back to the castle, but Sebastian has Lily stop at a pub on the corner with a wooden sign hanging outside that reads "The Naked Dwarf." He opens the door for me and I step into a smoke-filled den full of raucous laughter.

The pub itself is decorated in dark wood-paneled walls and black onyx flooring with dim red lighting giving it an eerie vibe. Sebastian finds us a seat in the back corner near the large fire pit that does a decent job of keeping the place warm despite the slightly damp and mildew-smelling seats. It is as private as we can be in such a place.

"I assumed you might be hungry," he says, as he slides into the booth.

I sit across from him, enjoying the warmth and the smell of freshly baked bread coming from the kitchen. My stomach rumbles and he smiles at the confirmation.

A man comes by to take our order and I have to school my face to not drop my jaw. He's human from the waist up, but from the waist down he's all horse. As I live and breathe, it's a centaur.

"What can I get the two of you?" He eyes Sebastian a moment and says, "Blood?"

Sebastian nods, then they both look to me.

We never got menus, though, and I have no idea what they serve. "Um, what do you suggest?" I ask.

"The stew is good. Vegetable or meat. With fresh bread."

I'm about to order the meat, but Sebastian shakes his head. "Get the vegetable," he says.

"Okay, I'll take the vegetable stew and bread, and some water, please."

"Not water. We'll both have a glass of Elf Juice," Sebastian says, causing the centaur to raise an eyebrow and smile.

"Coming right up."

When he leaves, I face Sebastian. "Why not the meat?" I ask.

"They often use meat sources that humans would find unfavorable," he says.

"Oh. Um. Okay. Such as?"

"All manner of animal. As long as it doesn't talk or shift, it's fair game," he says. "Cats, dogs, horses, pigs, goats, cows, chicken. They're all the same here."

My stomach turns and that delicious smell now inspires a wave of vomit to climb up into my throat. "In theory, I get it. Pigs are smarter than dogs. So why do we eat one and not the other? But in practice, it's too ingrained. I can't."

He nods. "You humans become quite attached to your domesticated animals. But inconsistently so."

"It's true. Looks like I'm becoming vegetarian while we're here."

The centaur returns with bread and two blue fizzy drinks.

"What's Elf Juice?" I ask, studying my glass goblet.

"An incredible and rare concoction made by the Woodland Elves from a hard-to-grow berry found in the highest mountains. This is the only tavern in town that's allowed to serve it," he says.

I take a small sip first, then sigh in pleasure and drink more deeply.

It is a perfect blend of sweet and tart and it makes my vision swim just enough to enjoy. "This is the best thing I've ever tasted," I say, with a more relaxed smile than I've had all day.

Sebastian returns the smile, sipping his own drink, which is the same blue, but as he drinks it begins to turn purple as it mixes with a red at the center. "Does yours have blood in it?" I ask, enjoying the swirl of color in his glass despite myself.

"It does," he says.

I nod. "It makes a cool color."

He raises an eyebrow and continues drinking as I look around, studying the other diners.

There's a couple who look like they're on a first date. Rough choice of place, dude. She doesn't look happy. She catches my eye and we share a knowing look and rueful smile. I'm only slightly surprised when I look more closely and notice her eyes aren't human, but rather more like those of a fish. Then I notice the sheen to her skin isn't a trick of light, but a reflection off of the iridescent scales on her skin.

"Is that... " I ask Sebastian, my words trailing off.

"A mermaid? Yes. Though she won't be able to remain on land too long."

"What is the guy she's with?" I ask.

"Werewolf," he says with distaste. "Odd match. I doubt it'll last."

I snort at that. "I agree, but not because of their species difference. He's not impressing her at all."

"Not surprising. He is a werewolf, after all. They're a rather brutish bunch."

The centaur arrives with my food, and I poke my spoon at the thick stew. "You sure this is safe?" I ask.

"I'm sure."

"And these are normal vegetables? Nothing strange or sentient?" I feel like a real lawyer, finding the loopholes in everything.

"Yes, normal vegetables. You have my word." He's got an amused glint in his eyes and I squint at him in distrust, but then decide to take him at his word. I take a small bite, teasing it with my teeth and tongue. "It's quite chewy," I say, when I can finally swallow. "Like a tire."

Sebastian laughs. "So not a fan, then."

I push the bowl away. "Not so much."

I study the man across from me as we drink our Elf Juice and I nibble on bread. His green eyes are intense, his body full of energy.

"Why would Liam be visiting Dracula?" I ask, refocusing our attention back onto the case.

"He wouldn't," Sebastian says, gritting his teeth and clenching his fist.

"You don't think... you don't think Liam is the letter writer, do you?" I ask.

"I do not know. For the sake of this case, my brother, and everyone involved, I certainly hope to gods not."

It's a tense drive back once we've finished our drinks, and Sebastian stalks into the castle. I brace myself for the confrontation I know is about to happen.

We find Liam in his personal quarters, head bent over his desk as he writes in a journal. He slams it shut when we enter, then curses as he knocks over a vial of ink onto a stack of papers. "What do you want?" he growls, avoiding eye contact with me.

Sebastian doesn't say anything, but instead pulls out the crystal and projects the memory of the cat. "Those are your shoes," he says, pointing to Liam's feet. Sure enough, the shoes match.

"So?" he asks.

"So, this memory occurred inside Mary Dracule's bedroom. What the hell were you thinking, Liam? Were you having an affair with our sire's wife?"

Liam stiffens, then stands. I step back, not wanting to get between two vampire brothers, but not wanting to miss anything important either. A flash tingles in my mind and flows down my body like electricity. Something is happening.

"What I do is my business, not yours," Liam hisses, his face inches away from his brother's.

Sebastian laughs mockingly. "Really? Because this sure as hell looks like it's all our business now!"

"What's all our business?" Derek asks, walking in with Elijah by his side.

"Private meeting. Go away," says Liam.

"Is that any way to greet your brother?" Derek asks with a charming smile, not the least bit put off by Liam's attitude. "I came to find out if you tracked down anything about who might have it in for our beloved sire, but it seems I've walked into something much juicier. Pray tell."

Liam jerks his head at Elijah. "And what are you doing here?" he asks, ignoring Derek's question.

Elijah holds up a journal. "Research. I needed to borrow a book and happened to arrive at the same time as Derek."

"How convenient," he says, then glares at me as if it's my fault. "What did you do?"

"Me? Nothing. What *could* I do?" I ask.

He scoffs. "As if you don't know."

Now everyone in the room is confused. "What are you talking about?"

"Did you think you could hide the truth from us?" Liam asks.

He shifts positions and stalks to me. The other brothers step closer, presumably to protect me if hothead here loses his shit again.

Sebastian glances at me, then grabs Liam's arm. "Stop trying to change the subject. It's just as well everyone is here so I don't have to repeat it." He turns to address Derek and Elijah. "Liam, here, has been paying visits to Mary behind Vlad's back. We also found love letters she had hidden, signed by the letter L. I'm trying to determine if he was having an affair with her."

"I wasn't," Liam says.

"But you were visiting her?" Derek asks, crossing his arms over his chest.

There's a long pause, and it's clear Liam is debating how much of the truth to tell us.

"Let me remind you," Sebastian says, "we have evidence you were at their house."

"What kind of evidence?" Derek asks.

"A memory," Sebastian says.

Liam scoffs. "Those are easily tampered with and you know it."

"It was the memory of a cat," I say, speaking for the first time. "Unless cats in this world are something quite newsworthy, I doubt it's been tampered with."

"Show me," Derek says, frowning and glancing suspiciously at Liam.

Sebastian plays the memory, pausing at Liam's shoes.

Derek and Elijah lean in, studying the frozen projection.

"Your penchant for custom clothing might be your undoing after all," Elijah says dryly to his fuming brother.

Liam finally nods curtly. "Yes, I was there. Okay? I was there. But not for the reasons you think."

"Why, then?" Derek asks. "What could possibly justify you going against our sire like that?"

Liam steps back and paces in front of his fireplace. "It's not what it looks like. Mary reached out to me. She needed help and didn't know who else to ask."

"What did she need help with?" I ask.

Liam glares at me again. "Her baby. She was worried about her pregnancy and needed a healer. So she called me."

"You're a healer?" I ask, the astonishment clear in my voice.

"I was," he says. "Before the curse. She thought that since I'm a vampire who was a healer, I could help her. She was very sick and worried she wouldn't make it through the pregnancy alive."

A pause descends on the room as the brothers take each other's measures.

"Why risk it?" Elijah asks. "Why risk everything for Vlad's wife?"

"I took an oath, before the sacred groves of our ancestors." His voice is plaintive, broken. "I vowed to provide healing to those in need. How could I refuse her?"

"Who else knows?" Derek asks, and I can see his mind working, trying to sort out how best to contain this in the midst of the trial.

"No one," Liam says. "We were beyond careful."

"Why meet at her house?" I ask. "Why not somewhere else, where you were less likely to get caught?"

"This isn't your business," Liam hisses at me.

Derek opens his mouth, but I beat him to the punch. "Actually, it is. I work here. I'm working on the defense team. That makes it my business whether you like it or not."

Derek's mouth snaps closed, and Sebastian smiles despite himself. Elijah raises an eyebrow and gives a brief nod of his head in encouragement.

Liam, seeing no one else will be coming to his defense, relents. "Vlad had her house-bound. He claimed it was for the safety of her and their unborn child, but he was just jealous and paranoid."

"Seems he was justified in his paranoia, assuming he's as innocent as he claims," Sebastian says.

Liam just grunts at that.

"What about the letters?" I ask.

Liam frowns. "What letters?"

Sebastian pulls the missives out of his leather satchel and hands them to his brother, who studies them. "I have no idea what these are," Liam says with what appears to be genuine confusion.

"You didn't write them?" I ask.

"No, I didn't write them. Why would you think I had?"

I roll my eyes. "Really? Because you were there. In secret. They are signed with an L. And you're acting awfully defensive."

He shoves the papers back into Sebastian's hands. "I didn't write them. I've never seen them before."

I cock my head and study him. I don't know if he's telling the whole truth, but I don't think he's lying about the letters. "Do you have any idea who might have written them?" I ask.

He shakes his head. "I can't even imagine who might have. She was pretty isolated."

Great. A dead end.

"We need to contain this," Elijah says. "If the prosecution gets ahold of this information, it's going to make our defense a hell of a lot more complicated."

Sebastian nods. "Agreed. I'll put the Memory Catcher in our safe. It's immaterial at any rate. But we still need to have these letters analyzed. We need to figure out who wrote them and when."

Elijah steps forward. "Then you'll be needing my assistance."

Sebastian hands them to his brother. Elijah glances at them, then looks at me. "It is too late in the evening for a visit to my contact. But Eve, would you like to join me tomorrow night? It could be educational for you."

"Yes, I would love that, if I'm not needed elsewhere?" I look around, not entirely sure who I'm supposed to get permission or direction from.

Derek speaks first. "That's an excellent idea. You should spend time with each of us, in order to get a complete picture of what we do and what the Otherworld is like. For now, let us all make our way to dinner and then prepare for a good day's rest."

"Where's Dracula?" I ask, as I follow the brothers to the dining room.

"Did he not meet you at his house?" Derek asks.

"No," Sebastian says. "It was just the butler."

"And the cat," I say, with a smile.

Sebastian holds my gaze a moment, then smiles. "And the cat. Eve has quite a way with the felines it seems."

"Speaking of cats," Lily says, coming down the hall towards us, "this little guy has been missing you."

I squeal and hold out my hands for Moon, who nuzzles against me, purring the moment I have him in hand.

"You're not going to bring him to dinner, are you?" Elijah asks, with a frown.

"He needs to eat, too, don't you, little guy?" I say, nuzzling his nose. "Besides, he misses me."

Dinner is a quiet affair. Only Lily, Matilda, and I eat food. The brothers, of course, feast on blood, and Moon enjoys his cat food on a small plate by my feet. No one is much in the mood for talking, though Liam keeps casting suspicious glances at me, for reasons I do not understood. I'm relieved when dinner ends and I retire quickly to my room, exhausted and with much weighing on my mind.

Moon curls up on my lap as I sit in front of the fire with my eyes closed. The heat warms my face and hands, which are perpetually cold from the drafts in the castle. In the distance, I hear the music of a violin playing a haunting melody. My skin buzzes with my flash as the music slides into me, calling me.

Even my kitten takes notice, jumping off my lap and stalking to the door in curiosity.

I stand, wrapping myself in the knit blanket from my chair, and follow the notes through the halls. I feel a presence behind me and turn, expecting to see Lily or Matilda, but no one is there.

I keep walking, and again, I feel like I'm being watched, or followed. I turn again and catch the hint of a white dress turning the corner. I follow it, calling out, but when I look, no one is there.

Perplexed, I resume my hunt for the beautiful music and find myself before a heavy door that is slightly ajar. I knock softly, though I am loathe to interrupt the masterful playing.

The door creaks open just enough for me to see inside.

I am stunned to see the man behind the magical music is none other than the hot-headed Liam Night, bane of my existence and perpetual pain in my neck...literally.

Emotions of irritation and admiration war in me as his music sucks me in. His body sways in time to the melody, his eyes are closed, his concentration solely on his instrument. He is naked and his muscular upper body glints in the silver light of the Dragon's Breath shining through the large window that he is silhouetted against. He works his violin like a true master, coaxing each note out like a lover bringing his partner to climax.

I want to turn away and leave, to put as much distance between me and this arrogant bastard as possible, but his music has paralyzed me. I feel rooted in place, transfixed by the complex emotions this unfamiliar piece evokes.

When the song ends, the silence comes slowly as the last notes fades into nothing. I'm brought back to myself and flush a scarlet red as I turn to leave, but I am not fast enough.

He opens his eyes and sees me before I can make my escape.

"Stop. Why are you here?" he growls, holding his violin in his left hand, the bow in his right, as he stalks over to me. He seems unconcerned with his nudity, but I don't know where to let my eyes land.

I know where they *want* to land.

"I heard someone playing and wanted to be closer to the music," I say, hating how dwarfed I feel by him.

He doesn't seem to know what to do with that answer, so he turns away.

That just gives me another enticing view I shouldn't be noticing.

"What piece was that?" I ask, not sure why I want to continue this conversation as I force my eyes to stay on his upper back and no lower.

"Something I wrote," he says reluctantly, and my heart thumps loudly in my chest at this unexpected tenderness that arises in him when he plays.

"It's beautiful," I tell him honestly. "I'm sorry to bother you. I'll leave you be."

"Wait," he says, turning. He frowns, staring at me. "Do you really not know?"

"Not know what?" I ask.

"What you are?"

I gulp, unhappy with the direction this conversation is taking. "I'm human. A mundane, as you call it. Haven't I been reminded of that often enough?"

"But you aren't really, are you? At least not fully. You could read our ad."

"Yes. That's been established."

He puts his violin on its stand and hangs the bow, then turns and walks towards me. My kitten meows and hides behind my legs as Liam comes so close I can feel his breath on my face. His body emanates heat and his eyes burn with barely contained passions, though for pleasure or pain it's hard to tell. I've only experienced pain from him thus far.

"You could not have read our ad as a mundane. I do not know why you smell like one," he says, leaning in to inhale my neck, his mouth a hair's width from the vein pulsing in my neck. "But I have tasted you, Eve Oliver. You are no human. There is power in you. Deep and dark and wild. You are dangerous," he says, his voice a low growl. "Who sent you?"

"Who sent me?" I ask, repeating his question. "No one. You did. I don't know. Fate, if you will."

131

He steps back, his eyes narrowing on me suspiciously. "You confound me. And I do not like to be confounded."

"I don't like to be bitten against my will. I guess life is just rough sometimes, isn't it?" The sass is back in my voice, naturally. Because that's never made a problem worse.

"You are guileless. Which makes you innocent of your own heritage. Or extremely well-trained in the art of subterfuge." His golden eyes bore into mine as if trying to read my soul.

"Um, I'm gonna go with guileless, I think. That seems the safest bet." I bite my lip as something comes to me. "How do you know I'm not mundane? Because you drank me? How did that tell you anything? What do you think I am, if you don't believe me?"

"You are nothing I have tasted before, so I cannot give you a name. But I know power when I taste it. I have been feeling it within me since that moment. And it is showing no signs of fading. If other vampires knew what effect you could have on them, you would be served up as the appetizer and main course at an all-you-can-eat vampire buffet. There wouldn't be enough left of you to identify."

His words send shivers up my spine, and I steel myself against the implied threat, but he's not finished yet.

"You need to figure out who you are before someone else figures it out first. The Otherworld isn't a safe place for someone who tastes like you. Watch your back."

"Yeah, well, thanks for the warning, I guess. I'll keep an eye out for hordes of vampires wanting to drain me. I'm sure that heads up will be all I need to rise victorious over beings that much stronger, faster and more powerful than me." The sarcasm drips from my voice, and though I am grateful for the warning and knowledge, I'm annoyed at how useless it is. If vampires want me, at the end of the day—or night, rather—there's not much I can do to stop them.

At least...nothing I know of. But what if there are more things I don't know? Because that's absolutely true. There's a shit ton I don't know and that lack of knowledge could get me killed.

I know who I have to talk to.

Liam has already turned his back on me as he picks up his violin and prepares to play again—still naked as the day he was born. Vampires clearly have no modesty. Or this one doesn't, at any rate.

I avert my eyes and slink out of the room, closing the door firmly behind me before his music pulls me back.

I search deep within myself for a pulse or flash of some kind to help me figure out where I can find Grandmother Matilda. But it turns out, I don't need a flash. Moon is already on the trail, and so I follow the tiny thing until we reach the old woman's suite. I knock once and the door opens of its own will.

Matilda is leaning over the fire, stirring something in an iron pot. "Come in, and close the door, my dear. The hallways are always so drafty. I keep telling the boys to upgrade the ventilation system, but they are always too busy."

She speaks as she stirs, and Moon and I walk over to her. "I'm sorry to bother so late, but—"

"You have questions," she says, standing and turning, wiping her hands on a black apron around her waist. "So many questions, buzzing around in your mind like a swarm of wasps."

She gets two soup bowls with handles and fills them both, handing one to me. I sniff it and smile. "Apple cider?"

She nods and sits in one of the chairs before the fire, gesturing for me to do the same.

Her suite is one very large room, where her desk, bookshelves, work shelves, bed, wardrobe, small dining table and chairs all share space.

"Take a seat, dear. It's time we talked."

I do as I'm instructed and sip on the cider, enjoying the sweet, earthy taste of it.

"When Liam bit me, he said he could tell that I'm not entirely human, but he doesn't know what I am. Do you?"

Matilda stares into the fire, as if it holds the answers to all the questions. The fire makes me think of Liam, of the warmth of his body, the way his muscles moved as he played his violin in an almost feverish trance.

When she speaks again, it is with a different voice. Matilda but not

Matilda. A prophetic voice. A voice that gives me chills. A voice I know will haunt my dreams.

Her eyes are alight with the flames of the fires as she says, "Beneath the silence of the golden bell, the wolf will hunt the lamb and the stones will feed on the blood that freely flows."

CHAPTER 13: THE EX

LIKE A BLACK ROSE, her darkness was beautifully fatal.
  ~ e. corona

MATILDA and I sit in silence, drinking our cider, for a long while. I think over her words but cannot put voice to the many questions running through me. I'm too tired. Too weary of the way everyone speaks in puzzles. I'm not even sure they realize they're doing it. To them, this is how one communicates. To me, it's utterly maddening.

When I return to my room, I intend to go straight to sleep, but the image of Liam playing the violin has me enthralled. Blood rises to my cheeks as I remember him as he looked, standing against the lights of the Dragon's Breath, his full body on display.

I can't get him out of my head, so I pull out my sketchbook and begin to draw.

I use shading and smudging to capture the contoured muscles of his chest and the movement of his body as he allows the music to consume him. I draw with intricate detail, with thought to motion and sound. His power, his rage, his fire and passion, all captured in the intensity of his expression and the way he holds his instrument, as if speaking through his music, pouring parts of himself into it.

I study it once it's complete, sucking in my breath. I can practically hear his music as I look at the drawing.

Once the image is out of my system, I crash into bed and sleep restlessly, haunted by dreams and visions and voices of doom. I rise several hours later with bags under my eyes and knots in my hair from tossing and turning.

There is a hot bath drawn for me when I rise, filled with the same scented oils I used before. Once again, I'm perplexed. I locked my door. No one could have gotten in.

This castle is starting to creep me out.

I'm not hungry, so instead of going to the kitchen after bathing, I head to the library and retrieve the letters we found in Mary's room. We never asked Dracula about them and going on a gut instinct and a bit of my flash, I decide it's best I talk to him alone.

His relationship with the brothers is too complicated. None of them are seeing each other clearly.

I remember the suite Matilda was preparing for Dracula's arrival, and I head there, my hands sweating from nerves.

I find the legendary vampire sitting before a grand piano, his long, tapered fingers gliding over the keys, playing a sad, melancholy song in a minor key. It's haunting, and I pause, not wanting to disturb him. When he finishes, his shoulders slump forward and he seems lost in his own grief. I knock gently, and he turns sharply, all signs of sadness gone. In its place is a cold curiosity as he studies me.

"Miss Oliver, do come in. I had hoped we would have a moment alone together at some point."

I pause, momentarily regretting my impulsiveness in coming here alone. But then I force myself to step forward. After Jerry, I vowed I'd never let another man intimidate me again.

That includes Dracula.

Smiling, I take a seat in a comfortable chair by the fire. He sits across from me and pours himself a goblet of blood. "I would offer you something to drink, but... "

"I'm good," I say, wrinkling my nose. "I just had a question for you, if you don't mind."

"By all means," he says, leaning back elegantly as he sips at his drink.

He has a regal stillness about him that sets my nerves on edge. I pull out the letters and place them before him. "Have you ever seen these?" I ask.

He takes them and studies them, frowning as he does. "No. Why? Where did you get them?"

I gulp, nervous about his response. "From Mary's room."

He sets the papers down and stares into the fire, saying nothing, offering nothing.

"Do you think Mary was cheating on you?" I ask outright.

His response surprises me. "I am not an easy man to love. I know this. Especially for one such as Mary."

"What do you mean, one such as her? A human?"

He steers his gaze towards me. "Yes. Being human is part of it. Humans have a different moral compass than those of us who are immortal. Life has a different flavor when it only lasts a few short years. To us, time is immaterial. But more than that, Mary was a sensitive soul. She could not always handle the peril inherent in the Otherworld."

"Did you never think to turn her?" I ask.

"Of course. She was the love of my life. But we wanted a child together," he says. "If she were vampire, we would not be able to have one. I was going to turn her after our son was born. We would have spent eternity together."

His voice cracks at the end of that, and he turns away, schooling his face into something unreadable.

"I'm so sorry for your loss," I say, standing. "I'll leave you in peace. Thank you for answering my questions."

He doesn't speak again as I leave the room and head downstairs in search of Elijah. We're meant to see his contact tonight about the letters. Hopefully they can shed more light on the mystery or at least turn us towards another potential suspect. Reasonable doubt. Even in the Otherworld, that's all we need.

Derek joins me as I look over the other paperwork we have on the case.

"Anything come to you?" he asks.

I tell him about my conversation with Dracula and he frowns. "That was risky, but brave. And useful, I suppose. He doesn't talk very openly to us."

Matilda comes in, interrupting us. "You have a visitor. The prosecution is here with a settlement offer. In the sitting room."

My heart thumps against my chest as I follow Derek down the hall.

I haven't heard anything about the prosecution yet, and I have no idea what to expect. Another type of creature I've yet to meet?

I'm imagining all manner of beings. Gnomes. Giants. Sprites and fairies.

I'm not expecting a beautiful tall blond woman. Her hair is perfectly kept; not a single strand out of place. So, too, is the rest of her; from her makeup to her nails to her perfectly schooled expression of irritation for the job she's come to do. Unlike most women I've seen in the Otherworld, she's wearing a style more suited to the men. Trousers and a cloak. She nods to Derek and then glances at me with a frown.

"Moira, this is Eve Oliver, our Managing Director. Eve, this is Moira Van Helsing, lead prosecutor on Vlad's case," Derek says, by way of introduction.

"Van Helsing?" I say. "As in *the* Van Helsings?"

"Yes," Moira says, with such force it feels like a slap. "Now, if we can get onto business? Derek, I come with an offer. A generous one, I might add," she says with clear distaste.

"I take it this wasn't your idea," Derek replies with a chuckle.

She glares at him. "You know it wasn't. But I'm forced to make the offer. If Dracula pleads guilty and surrenders his holdings to the council, his punishment will be reduced to ten thousand years underground rather than all of eternity."

Derek laughs sarcastically. "*Only* ten thousand years. How truly generous. You know my client will never agree to it."

"I hope he doesn't," she says, "because we've got him by the balls and I'd personally like to see him pay."

"I'll relay the offer at any rate," Derek says, ignoring her last comment. "Is there anything else?"

"No, that was all. You have until tomorrow to accept."

"Duly noted," he says. "May I escort you out?"

"I can find my own way," she says, stalking out of the sitting room and heading straight for the front door.

Once she's gone, I turn to face Derek as we head back to the library. "Maybe we should advise him to take it," I say reluctantly.

He raises an eyebrow. "You don't think we can win?"

"With what we currently have? I'm not confident."

He smiles. "Maybe this will boost your confidence, then. We've received word from Vlad's ex-wife. She's agreed to meet with us. Vlad is sure she'll be an excellent character witness."

"When?"

"Right now," he says.

Dracula enters the library and pauses when he hears what we're discussing. "Lilith and I had a special bond," Dracula says, and it takes a moment for the name to register.

"Lilith?" I ask. "*The* Lilith?"

Dracula nods. "I was human when we met and fell in love. She, of course, was the first of our kind, created by the Night herself, when a moonbeam hit a rare black rose at just the right moment, and that rose turned into a beautiful woman, pale as moonlight, lips red as blood, hair black as the night herself, teeth sharp as thorns. The first vampire. And the first woman, before Eve. Adam's true love."

He has us spellbound with his words, with his voice, so hypnotic and melodious. "But Adam betrayed her, and she left him in the garden alone while she roamed the earth in search of others like herself. When she found none, and as humans began to populate the world, she realized she would have to turn them herself, to create her own family. And so she did. First Able, when he was left for dead by his jealous brother. They were lovers for many centuries. Then many after. Until me. But alas, we wanted different things in life. I wanted children, and so we divorced, and I met Mary and gave her what was left of my cold, undead heart."

So Lilith is the mother of all vampires. And I'm about to meet her.

~

ONCE THE DECISION is made to visit Lilith, we don't waste any time. Derek and I climb into the carriage and Lily gets us underway without a moment to lose.

I stare out the window as we leave the lowlands behind and climb high into the mountains to the east. The road is narrow, with a staggeringly steep cliff falling away to one side as we make our way into the dark peaks ahead of us, and I'm suddenly thankful that our trusted steeds have an extra pair of legs each to keep their footing secure as Lily drives them onward.

After what feels like forever—at least to my height-addled nerves—we pass through a narrow canyon and emerge into a wind-swept valley high in the mountains. A Mediterranean-style villa sprawls across the lawn ahead of us, lights beckoning from its windows like a thousand sparkling fires. Dozens of servants work the grounds, tending to roses and lavender, trimming shrubbery into the shapes of dragons and horses. The tail end of a dark coat catches my eye, then disappears instantly behind a pillar of white stone. I wouldn't be surprised if we're being watched. Our movements accounted for. After all, a manor like this must have security.

Lily stops the carriage in front of a grand red door, and soon Derek and I are seated in a spacious gathering room inside the main building as Lilith's servants bring us drinks. Everything is gold-crusted or rimmed or framed, and I feel a bit like I've been transported inside an Oscar statue.

Lilith herself is nothing short of divine. Her long black hair is worn in tight curls beaded with gold stretching down her back. Gold powder on her lids brings out the gold in her tiger-like eyes, and gold lipstick shines against her pale skin. Her gown is a matching gold, flowing down her slim frame like a waterfall of sunlight. To look upon her is to look upon something sacred.

"He was a terrible husband," Lilith says frankly of Dracula, to the disappointment of Derek and myself. "He had an unparalleled thirst, which is my fault, really. I knew the kind of man he was in war; the blood of his enemies flowed in his veins. I just overestimated my ability to control him. He was violent, prone to flashes of temper that required me to use compulsion on him. He could never harm me, of course, but by the gods he tried." Lilith takes a delicate sip of blood from a gold-rimmed wine goblet before continuing. "I'm convinced he killed his wife and child."

Derek sighs and looks at me. I shrug. We both know what this means. Not only is she not going to be a good witness for us, she'll be a great witness for them.

Then she grins. "Is that what you fear I'll say, when the prosecution calls me to the stand?"

Derek blinks and I narrow my eyes. She's playing with us.

"I could say that," she says, leaning back gracefully and crossing one leg over the other. "There is truth in my words. We all carry within us shades of dark and light. What fun would this drab world be without it?" She glances at my fingers. "You know, my dear, do you not? An artist, more than anyone, appreciates the shades of gray."

I glance at my fingers, but I can't see any visible charcoal smudges on them. "How—"

"You have the eyes and the hands of an artist," she says, leaning forward. She reaches for a parchment and hands it to Derek. "The Van Helsings are out for blood. They want me to say what I just told you. With as much emotion and wringing of the hands as I can muster."

I wondered when I'd see the corruption creeping in. You can't have a legal system without corruption. It's partly why I chose business over law. Both are corrupt, but at least business doesn't try to pretend it's upholding something sacred.

"What did you tell them?" I ask.

"I haven't decided," she says. "There are so many sides to the man you call Dracula. Who am I to say what's the truth?"

"What's the other side?" I ask.

She winks. "All in good time. First, tell me, what are you?" Her gaze is locked onto mine and I hold it, playing this game of wills with the oldest vampire in the world.

Lilith smiles at me like a cat playing with a mouse and she walks over, sliding up against me on the couch, draping her arm around my shoulders. "You are a curious creature, are you not?" She slides a finger down my cheek so gently I almost don't feel it, then licks her finger, closing her eyes.

"Curious. You are a tasty little mystery, aren't you, my dear? What I wouldn't give for just one true taste, to know for certain—"

Derek stands and pulls me against him, leaving Lilith on the couch alone. "That's enough. You know the rules, Lilith."

She licks her finger one more time and stands, sighing. "I wasn't going to hurt her, Derek. Not without consent. You Night brothers are all far too serious."

"However," she continues, turning to us with another mischievous smile. "I will make a deal with you. Give me a taste of your blood willingly, my dear, and I will tell the court the story of a loyal and kind man who was the love of my life. But for his desire to have children I could not give him, we would have spent eternity together. But I loved him too much to tear him from his fate of fatherhood and so I set him free. He will make a strong and yet tender father, just as he did a husband. I will have the jury and judge alike eating out of my hands. What say you?"

"Which story is the truth?" I ask. They are both entirely too compelling.

She laughs. "The truth? Why, all of them. And none of them. We are each a truth unto ourselves."

I realize I'm willing to say yes, despite the warning Liam gave me, despite my own revulsion to the idea, despite the fact that I don't know what game she's playing. I'm willing to do it, if it helps our case. Because her testimony could make or break us. And if it breaks us, the Night brothers will be forever tormented.

Derek must see how close I am to offering myself up, because he stands between us once again and shakes his head. "No deal. You know I can't allow that."

I tug at his sleeve. "But we need—"

"No deal." His eyes are hard.

I nod.

Lilith pouts and reclines back to the couch. "Pity. See you in court then."

∽

WE SIT in the carriage in silence. I'm breathing heavily. Everything feels surreal.

"Why didn't you let me do it?" I ask.

"It's too risky. You could have died. You could have become her obsession, in which case we couldn't protect you. She'd turn you and you'd have no say. Also, it's not ethical. It would be considered buying a testimony. We could be disbarred."

"Those are a lot of good reasons," I say breathlessly. And I'm an idiot, I add silently. I clearly have no self-preservation instincts. What the hell is wrong with me?

When we get back to the castle, I excuse myself to my suite to collect my thoughts. And to sketch.

I first draw Lilith, the way her neck curves in just such a way, and the way her large cat-like eyes take everything in. She misses nothing in the going-ons around her, and I suspect she's always several steps ahead. She and Dracula must have been quite the potent power couple.

And then I draw Derek the way he looked when he was refusing Lilith to protect me. My hands fly across the page as I capture his stance, the strength in his frame as he stands between us, a living barrier to whatever mischief Lilith had planned for me should I have agreed to her offer. I don't think I could have imagined any of the Nights as white knights, but something in the way he holds himself brings that image to mind, and I know there is more to all of them than I have yet imagined. I know he gave the argument of being disbarred as a reason for turning down Lilith's offer, but their legal standing isn't going to matter much if they lose and become tormented until insanity by their sire. He was protecting me, at the cost of everything, possibly.

The trial is starting soon and our case isn't yet strong enough to guarantee a win. We need more.

When I finish Derek's drawing, I admire the determination in his eyes, the slope of his nose, the way his jaw tightens when he's serious.

Pulling out of my self-induced trance I realize it's time to find Elijah and head to his contact to study the letters.

I'm putting a lot of unearned hope that this will be the clue that breaks the case.

And hopefully in our favor.

CHAPTER 14: THE GRAPHOLOGIST

SHE'S mad but she's magic. There's no lie in her fire. ~ Charles Bukowski

I FIND Elijah in his study, surrounded by books, which is not surprising.

His pale blond head is bent over a large leather-bound tome, and he mumbles under his breath as he reads something in Latin.

"Not summoning any demons, I hope?" I ask jokingly, and then I realize we are in a world that likely has demons and all manner of other creatures, and suddenly my little joke isn't so funny.

"Not at the moment," he says in all seriousness. "That requires more candles. And a virgin sacrifice."

It takes me a beat to realize he's joking. He winks at me, and I exhale and then laugh awkwardly. "Ah, the classic virgin sacrifice joke. Good one!" I clumsily punch him in the arm, then step back and screw my mouth shut and plaster my arms to my side, because I am being entirely too weird.

"It was a joke, yes?" I ask after a moment.

"Yes," he says with a softer smile. "We don't use virgins anymore.

Too hard to find." I frown at that, and he tugs at one of my braids. "Don't take it all so seriously or you'll make yourself crazy."

"Right. So, where are we off to today?" I ask as he grabs a cloak and drapes it over his shoulders.

"I have a contact. She's a graphologist—of sorts—and will be able to tell us about the letters. When they were written. How old they are. Possibly who wrote them."

"That reminds me," I say, pulling a piece of paper from my satchel. "Here is a writing sample from the butler. As far as we can tell, Dracula, Liam, and the butler, Leonard, were the only three men who came in contact with Mary in the months leading up to her death. But the author of the letters may not have seen her in person, so that might not be very helpful."

"Any new information is helpful," he says, taking the paper from me. "It all gives us information with which to narrow down our defense."

"And what is the defense going to be for Dracula?" I ask as we walk through the castle and out the front door, into a cold evening still damp from rain.

I shiver and pull my cloak more tightly around my shoulders when I realize we won't be taking a carriage but will be walking instead.

"Lily is taking Derek and Sebastian to the courthouse tonight, so we will be on foot. I hope that's okay?"

I nod. "I could use the exercise. Is it always so cold here though?" As I ask, flakes of snow form in the sky, landing on my skin and dissolving into tiny puddles. I can feel the cold in the back of my throat and I inhale a deep breath.

"Winter is nearly upon us," Elijah says, as we walk briskly down the cobbled path to town, tall trees lining each side and reaching towards each other above us form a living tunnel through which we walk. "It's only going to get colder. Soon we will have the Midwinter Festival. You'll enjoy that. There's all manner of food, live music, dancing and huge bonfires as we welcome winter. It's traditionally a gift-giving time in our world as well."

"Sounds like Christmas," I say. "Without the dogma."

We make it into town, and despite the snow, booths are set up and there are many townsfolk shopping and going about their evening. "Is the town this busy during daylight hours as well?" I ask.

"There's no real distinction between night and day here, so we all keep whatever schedule suits us. Since most creatures don't have the same sleep needs as humans, the town is bustling at all times."

I pay attention to the people as we walk. There are all manner of beings; some with horns, some with skin like dyed leather, some with body parts that aren't human.

Elijah takes us through an alley and as we pass, someone throws out their bodily waste through the window, creating a trail of odor that has me gagging.

Elijah sighs, and with a flick of his hand, the wind picks up, carrying the scent in the opposite direction and clearing the air for us. "We have more efficient sanitation systems in place now—and that took a lifetime to get the council to vote in—but some creatures are entirely too stubborn for their own good and refuse to leave the medieval era behind where it belongs. Thus we are forced to endure their filth as they cling to the old ways."

"How unpleasant," I say, glancing back at the brown puddle left behind.

"Indeed."

I look at Elijah, wondering about him. "Can I ask you a question?"

He nods. "Of course."

"You're air, yes? That's the element that's part of your curse?"

His lips tighten together. "Yes."

"Well, I can see how Liam's fire makes him hot-headed. And Sebastian is stubborn as an old goat."

Elijah snorts at that.

"But what downside is there to air?"

He frowns, considering. "I have always been more in my head than my brothers. More lost in ideas. In thoughts. In books. But it was always balanced by my love of people. By my desire to bring new ideas to the world. After the curse, and then once I was turned, I found it hard to…" He stops walking and turns to face me. "I found it hard to connect. To care. Ideas have become their own end goal. Books are a world unto themselves. I struggle to find the passion I once had to

147

help others. It has made me cold. Vacant, if you ask my brothers. Aloof."

"You seem very self-aware. That's a good step," I say, surprised by his honesty.

He nods his head. "We have had many years to become such. Even Liam, were you to gain his trust, would admit to his own shortcomings. We all know, but we struggle to do anything about it. We are stuck in this inertia, unable to move forward. It's maddening, particularly when our Druidic Order focused on spiritual and personal growth in order to be of service to all. Our curse has put us at direct odds with our oath. Our purpose. It has left us rudderless at sea. At the whims of our egos, rather than guided by our higher nature."

"Are there other Druids still around?" I ask.

His face darkens. "We are the last of our kind. Our Order was killed."

He turns sharply and continues walking, clearly uninterested in continuing the conversation.

When we reach a black door hidden in shadows in the crook of a winding alley, he stops. "We are here."

The door is plain, with an eyehole in the shape of an actual eye in the center.

Elijah knocks sharply three times, and to my astonishment, the eye opens, revealing an obsidian eyeball that flits between the two of us, taking our measure.

"Tell Kana that Elijah Night is in need of her assistance."

The eye blinks once, then closes.

"Magic?" I ask.

Elijah's lips curl up in a small smile. "Yes."

The door opens a moment later revealing a beautiful woman in a red kimono with a glowing ball around her neck as a pendant. Her glossy black hair is pulled up in an elaborate bun and her voice is soft and trickling, like tiny bells. "Elijah, so good to see you again. Please, come in. Both of you."

We enter through a hall decorated with simple ink drawings of lotus flowers and move into a spacious room. To the right is a desk with piles of scrolls covering it. In the center of the room are tatami mats for sitting, with a sunken hearth in the floor between the mats and a fire below that is meant to heat tea during a Japanese tea ceremony. I participated in one during a trip to San Francisco years ago for work and recognize some of the elements.

Kana guides us to sit on the mats as she lowers herself onto one across from us. She places some aromatic wood on the fire and then begins to mix a green powder, creating the base for our tea.

We sit in silence as she works with measured movements. Her body flows with such grace and elegance that I'm mesmerized by her. I've never seen anyone move like she does, and I wonder at it, realizing she is likely not human, given where we are. She sets the cups before us, but Elijah places his hand over my cup before I can drink.

"Pardon the interruption, Kana," Elijah says, "but will this be safe for my associate, who is thought to be mundane?"

He removes his hand, and I frown at the tea as I realize something is moving within the delicate porcelain cup. A tiny sea creature of sorts, long and slim like a worm but with green scales and tiny black eyes. I shiver as it splashes in the green liquid.

Kana sips her tea, swallowing deeply, then looks to me and with a wink says, "She may drink."

That seems to be enough for Elijah, and he takes a long drink from his cup. His eyes encourage me to do the same. I have so many questions, but it's clear this is expected before we can do business, so I say a silent prayer to any gods that may be listening, and I drink.

Whatever little creature was in my cup is now slithering down my throat, and I nearly gag and vomit it back up when Elijah's hand comes to rest gently on mine. The touch sends a cool breeze through me, calming my throat reflexes and allowing the tea—and mini sea creature—to stay put. For now, at least.

My face flushes and my skin begins to tingle, but this isn't a flash. It's something else entirely.

As I blink, the room changes. As if a new lens has been added to my sight. I see things that weren't there before. Furry creatures scurrying around books. Paintings that move and shift and change designs. A room that looks more like a den or cave, and pillows that are now furs. When my gaze lands on Kana, she is no longer a beautiful woman in a kimono. Or she is, but she is also a fox, lovely and white, with several tails splayed behind her and large eyes that stare deeply into mine.

"Kana is a Kitsune," Elijah says, "a magical fox who often takes the shape of a beautiful woman. She only shows her true form to a rare few."

I nod my head to Kana. "Thank you for the honor," I say, my skin buzzing again, this time with a flash.

"And you as well," Kana says, with a nod towards me. "It is not everyday we have one such as yourself visit here."

I glance at Elijah, wondering what she means. But he's already digging through his satchel to pull out the letters. "We were hoping you could help with these," he says, handing her the stack of letters. "We need to know everything you can decipher about them."

She closes her eyes and holds them in her hands/paws, then sighs and opens them. "I fear you will not like the answers. But I will provide them nonetheless. Do you have my payment?"

Elijah nods and reaches into his bag again, this time handing her a vial of blood.

My eyes widen. "Whose blood is that?" I ask.

"Mine," Elijah says. "It is the cost of doing business with Kana."

She slips the blood into a mysterious gap in her kimono, the image of her fox form still superimposed over her female form. I remind myself to ask about this later. What does she do with the blood? In the normal course of affairs, this would be odd enough? But in this realm? With magic and mystery the norm? Here, I'd be extra worried.

Kana takes the papers over to her desk, which with the second sight looks like a stone boulder with runes carved into it. She works quietly, studying the papers, turning them over, examining them from all sides and comparing them to each other. She frowns, then takes a pouch and pinches a bit of black granules that she blows onto the papers. A spark of light ignites in the air above them, then fizzles out into a dark cloud of dust.

The entire process takes quite a long time. Maybe hours. Elijah and I sit silently for so long my feet go numb. I try to discreetly wake them back up with subtle shifts of weight, frowning as pins and needles overtake the numbness.

Elijah smirks at me like he knows what's going on and finds it amusing.

When she finally brings us the letters back, she looks tired. "They were written over the last year. They do not match any of the handwriting samples you brought me. The author is old. Powerful. Ancient. And dangerous."

She hands Elijah the letters. "I cannot give you a name but I know that this isn't a person to trifle with or to take lightly."

"What other man could she have been in contact with?" I ask, looking at Elijah.

He shrugs. "She was fairly isolated. I can't imagine many people had access to her."

"I should clarify," Kana says. "The writer of the letters wasn't male."

We turn and look at her, surprise on both of our faces. "So the writer was female?" I ask.

"Yes. A powerful female."

"Is there anything else you can tell us?" I ask.

"Like what?" she asks with a wry grin.

I shrug. "I don't know. Like, who might have read them?"

She cocks her head. "Curious question. The emotional imprints are few. The writer of the letter, clearly. Several from your firm. And...a woman. A pregnant human woman."

"Can you tell if Dracula read them?" I ask. "Earlier. Not recently."

"He hasn't, no," she says. "Will there be anything else?"

Elijah and I stand and bow. "Thank you," he says.

As we leave, she slips something into my hand. I look down and see a crystal pendant with a fox carved into. "For protection. You are going to need it, one thought to be mundane. Watch yourself," she says, then closes the door behind us.

When we step outside, the cold slaps me in the face. The office, or den, was so warm that I'd forgotten about the impending winter awaiting us. My nose burns with the cold as we walk quickly through the streets. It's snowing more harshly outside, and neither of us speak right away as we bundle against the cold. I slip the pendant around my neck, studying the craftsmanship.

We walk in silence for a few moments before I turn to Elijah. "If the writer was female, maybe Mary wasn't the intended recipient. Or she had a female lover."

"Those were my thoughts as well," he says. "But I do have a suspicion. The letters are signed with an L. Written by a powerful, ancient woman. Who do we know who is involved with this case and fits those criteria?"

And then it all clicks. "Lilith."

ELIJAH ISN'T EXPECTING it when I suggest that I go see Lilith alone.

To be honest, I'm a bit surprised by it myself. I'd nearly succumbed to her entreaty once before, and here I am volunteering to put myself back into harm's way without one of the Nights to protect me this time?

My companion must be thinking the same thing.

"Not a chance," he tells me, without even a glance.

But I'm not content to leave it at that. I reach out, grab his arm, and pull him to a stop.

"It is our best option and you know it. She'll have her guard up if you or one of your brothers show up on her doorstep full of questions and we won't get anything out of her. But if I go alone, she'll be too intrigued to worry about what I'm actually doing there. She's underestimated me—everyone does—and that will give us out best chance to get the information we need from her."

"Eve..." Elijah begins, but I cut him off.

"You know I'm right. There's no sense in arguing about it."

He looks off into the distance, an expression of exasperation on his face, and I know in that moment that I've got him.

Which is how I ended up sitting in Lilith's living room a few hours later, waiting for her to join me, my hands sweating from budding anxiety. My nerves are a bit rattled, and I'm starting to regret volunteering myself like this, but it's too late to turn back now.

I stand as she glides into the room, resplendent in her gown—
which is now a blood red floor-length design that hugs her body like
she's been dipped into it, with matching lips, and long hair shimmering down her back like an inky waterfall. She raises an eyebrow
when she sees that I'm alone.

"No Night brother to guard you against my dangerous appetites?"
she asks with a mischievous spark in her eyes.

"Should I be scared?" I ask in reply, in what I hope is a confident-
totally-not-scared-at-all attitude.

"Not of me," she says, sliding gracefully into the chair across
from me.

She sips at a wine glass full of blood as red as her dress and then
smiles at me. "What can I do for you, Eve?"

She says my name slowly and with meaning, and given who she is,
I wonder about her life. Her adventures. Her history.

"I had a few more questions I was hoping you could help me
with," I say, pulling out the letters.

I had a whole speech planned, but under her intense gaze, my
mind is a bit tongue-tied, as it were.

When she sees the letters, her eyes widen a fraction and she sets
her glass down. "May I?" she asks, holding out her hand.

I give her the stack of parchments and study her as she flips
through them.

"Where did you find these?" she asks.

"Mary Dracule's bedroom," I say.

She raises an eyebrow. "I underestimated her."

"So you don't deny that you wrote these?" I ask.

"No. I don't. But they were meant for Vlad. How did Mary get
them?" she asks, but the question is clearly rhetorical.

"Dracula never saw them," I say, wondering if I'm telling her too
much.

"How can you be sure?" she asks.

"He denied knowing what they were," I say, "and we had a third
party test them."

"That explains so much," she says, looking almost relieved.

"Like what?"

"Like why he never contacted me, even to tell me to bugger off. It's not like him to ignore me so entirely."

"Why did you send these?" I ask, cocking my head to the side slightly as I study this enigmatic mystery before me.

"I missed him. I still miss him. Vlad is my match in every way. He is the love of my many lives. He is my personal sun, the light and warmth I thought I would never experience the joy of…that's what he has always been for me." Her expression is that of one lost in memory, blind to what is in front of her, trapped in the past.

"If that's true…why did you break up then?" I ask, curious about her side of the story.

"I knew he wanted a child of his own blood more than anything. Maybe even more than me. But he would not betray me in that way. He could not. Not with our sire bond. So…"

A single tear slides down her perfect cheek and she makes no move to dry it as she continues. "I ended things between us and freed him to find a human with which to procreate. Something, despite all my years on this earth, I will never be able to do. A vampire's womb is full of death. It is too barren to carry a child to term."

She leans forward and slips a hand under the cushion of her chair and pulls out a box of cigarettes and a lighter. Noticing the surprise on my face, she shrugs. "Don't tell the brothers. They'd frown at my flagrant use of contraband. Not that I give a single shit about their fragile boy feelings, but I'm not in the market for trouble at the moment."

She pauses to light a cigarette and takes a deep puff, closing her eyes, a look of sublime joy passing across her face before she exhales and then refocuses her gaze upon me. "I'm sure you've wondered about this world, and why any of us would spend time amongst mundanes, given the limitations of the sun, the risk of being discovered?"

I nod. "Yes, that's true. I have wondered." I'm not surprised she surmised this about me. Given her lifespan and clear intelligence, I imagine she is quite the master manipulator, which means she has a keen insight into others. And the tragic irony isn't lost on me. Eve was the mother of humanity, but also blamed for the fall of humanity. The creator and the destroyer. The savior and the villain. Lilith was the mother of all vampires, but never a mother herself. For some, that could be a great and painful burden to bear for so many lifetimes.

"There are perks to your world," she says, taking another hit from her cigarette. "These, for instance." She smiles. "Technology, sanitation, style, and comfort of living. The mundane world has it all. Yes, it comes at a price, so those of us with means have homes in both worlds, to move back and forth through them as we like. The best of it all. Sometimes the Otherworld can be frustrating with its artificial limitations of advancement and growth. Its backward ways." She blows smoke and it coalesces into the shape of a dragon storming the sky with billowing fires. "It will soon be time to set the worlds on fire, Eve. I wonder if you'll be ready."

I swallow, shifting uncomfortably on the couch. "Ready for what?"

"For the role you will be asked to play. And for the role you are destined to play. Women with great power make sought-after targets. Men do not like to yield power to anyone, let alone a woman. And women who have chosen to align themselves with the enemy in order to gain favor above their sisters do not like the system they have erroneously chosen to be toppled, so you will have many enemies, even amongst those you think are trustworthy." She snuffs out the cigarette in a crystal ashtray I hadn't noticed before.

"I don't think I am who you think I am," I say. I know I'm different, but I'm definitely not the explosive powerhouse she's painting me to be.

"You have no idea who you are," she says plainly. "But then, I don't know either. I assume that will be your next question and I'm sorry to say I don't have an answer for you. Though that in itself is its own kind of information. I know much of many beings. But I do not know you."

My heart is beating hard against my chest and I feel heat pulse through my veins. "What does that mean? If you of all people don't know what I am, how can I ever find out?"

A new desperation fills me. This has been eating at me like a cancer, not understanding the core of my own being. Having a sense of something living in me but not understanding what that means and having no one outside of Adam to share that with. And now he's gone and there is no one.

A flash.

Just a blink.

Did I really see it or just imagine it?

Isn't that always the question?

The woman with the silver freckles. The silver horn glowing in the soft swirls of the Dragon's Breath colors.

A cooling of the heat.

A calmness.

Lilith smiles. "So she has visited you. Good. You are not as alone as I had feared. There might be hope for you yet."

CHAPTER 15: THE COURTHOUSE

IT IS during our darkest moments that we must focus to see the light. ~ Aristotle

WHEN I RETURN, all four brothers are waiting for me.

"Well, did you get anything useful?" Elijah asks, without preamble.

"She confirmed the letters were hers, written to Dracula," I say, giving a recap of the conversation.

Derek paces the library, thinking. "It's risky, but we could cast a shadow of a doubt on her. She has means and motive," he says, with a frown. "But she's a powerful enemy to make."

"She didn't do it," I say. "She was at a ball that night. She gave me a list of individuals who can confirm her presence. It should be easy enough to check."

"Then we've still got nothing," Liam says with a clench of his jaw. "We still don't know who killed Mary or why."

Derek shrugs. "While it would be useful to identify the actual killer, it's not necessary for our purposes. We just need to prove Vlad didn't do it. And we don't have much time left, so let's get to work."

~

We spend the next few days diving into law books, preparing for Dracula's legal defense. We've sussed out all the evidence we can, and at this point, his guilt or innocence will largely be circumstantial. The final verdict will rely on compelling testimony and closing arguments.

Derek is lead counsel, which is how I find myself alone with him late one night in his office as he practices in front of me.

"Feel free to speak your mind," he says, after going through his opening statements.

"I don't know your legal system well enough to give helpful feedback," I say, biting my lip.

He cocks his head. "That's rubbish. I can tell you have thoughts. Speak them. You won't offend me." He offers up a charming smile as proof that his feathers won't be ruffled.

Of all the brothers, he's the easiest to be around, I've found. Maybe it's the water element in him, but Derek is less rigid than Sebastian, less volatile than Liam, and less mentally distracted than Elijah. With Derek, I feel I am the center of the universe when he looks at me, like I'm drowning in him, but not unpleasantly. His dimpled chin and ocean blue eyes pull me in, and his charisma is organic, consuming the room and me with it. It's no wonder he's lead counsel. He could charm anyone. He reminds me a lot of my brother, which sends a twinge of pain through my heart.

Adam would have loved it here. He always believed there was more to the world than what we could see. This would have vindicated him and those beliefs.

Being sent from foster home to foster home was tough on both of us after our dad died, but it was especially tough on him. He didn't keep his ideas about monsters and superheroes to himself, and not all the foster parents appreciated his creative interpretation of the world. He was beaten a lot for his stories. And though I did my best to protect and defend him, it usually just led to both of us getting the belt across our backsides. One time he was hit so hard it split his skin clean open. I had screamed louder than him when I saw what our foster father had done in his drunken rage. Adam couldn't sit for weeks. We were sent to a new home, but it wasn't much better.

I shake my head, ridding it of past memories, and focus on the man before me. "You're trying to make a case for Dracula's innocence, right?"

Derek nods. "Obviously."

"But you're trying to soften him. To paint him as a regular Joe blow who couldn't possibly commit such a heinous crime."

"Well, yes," Derek says, scratching the dimple on his chin.

"I assume Dracula's reputation proceeds him, even here?"

Derek chuckles. "You could say that."

"Then it won't work. The jury, the judge, they're already going to have ideas about Dracula. They may have even decided he's guilty. I don't know how impartial the system is here, but in my world it's pretty corrupt."

Derek narrows his eyes but doesn't challenge me. "What would you suggest?"

"Play up his reputation. Lay it all on the table. The prosecution goes first, yes? They're going to paint him as a monster. So let them. Encourage it. Bring out the monster in him."

He begins pacing again. "How will that help win the case?"

"Because you'll be showing the jury and the judge you know the truth of your client. You'll be creating a bond of trust. Then, you show Dracula's intelligence. His cunning. His ability to plan and implement acts of cruelty." The ideas are coming to me quickly as I consider his best defense.

"Okay... " Derek says slowly.

I stand from the chair I've been curled up in and pace the room as Derek pauses to watch and listen. "And once you've done all that, you show how this crime, this crime scene, is sloppy. It's messy. It's lazy. It's not the crime of a genius monster like Dracula. It's a bad frame job that's too poorly done to be him at all. Prove that Dracula is too evil, too monstrous, too good at his killing to have done this crime. Then, you can use the Ifrit's testimony to cast doubt on whether a vampire committed the crime and argue that he wanted a child more than anything and would never have killed his."

Derek's eyes widen, and in two long strides he is by my side pulling me into an embrace and kissing my forehead. "That's genius, Eve Oliver. Pure genius!"

Our bodies are pressed together, and the light moment of celebratory breakthrough turns into something else, something that stirs desires in me as once again I am lost in this man's eyes.

I pull away, and his gaze follows me as I take my tea and sit again, trying to ignore the color rushing to my cheeks. "Do you think it'll work?"

Derek is already at his desk rewriting his argument. "I think it's the best chance we have, either way."

I nod, scanning over the notes I've taken at my side. "So much has come to light, and yet we don't really know what happened to Mary. Who killed her? Why? Perhaps we've been running in circles. Perhaps Dracula is guilty all along."

Derek pauses, looking up, his fingers stained black from the ink of his feather pen. "Does it matter? Don't the guilty deserve someone advocating for them?" he asks, in response.

"I guess it depends on what they did," I say.

"What crimes are too heinous to justify a fair trial?" he asks, curious.

"Rape, certain kinds of murder, child abuse and molestation," I say, checking off the big deal breakers for me.

"And what of extenuating circumstances?" he asks.

"That's why I said, certain kinds of murder. There are times it can be justified. But how can you ever justify rape or hurting a child?"

He nods. "We are selective." He shrugs. "Usually. But we do believe everyone deserves to have someone in their corner. We can't always ascertain guilt or innocence. Part of our job is to uncover the truth. The rest is to make sure our client isn't unfairly sentenced, even if they are guilty. The guilty were all innocent at one point, and many of them became monsters because of what was once done to them."

A voice in the hall interrupts us. "Time to go!" Liam.

I stand, as does Derek. "One more question," I say, laying a hand on his arm before he opens the door. "Would you have taken on Dracula's case if he hadn't compelled you?"

"Yes," Derek says.

"Why?"

"Because the prosecution isn't objective when it comes to him. They have a long vendetta against him. I don't believe he'll get a fair trial in this world, and I believe he deserves one, regardless of who he is."

The door bursts open and Liam is there looking smoking hot in a scarlet cloak and golden vest. "Time to go. Can't be late. We've been assigned Judge Dath'Racul."

"Shit," Derek says under his breath.

"What's wrong with this judge?" I ask.

"He's the fire dragon. If you think Liam is hot-headed, wait until you meet Dath'Racul."

Liam scowls at Derek at that, but I just smirk. "He's not wrong," I tell the auburn-haired fire Druid.

"Let's just go. We're already on bad footing with him from that Leprechaun case."

"Leprechaun? I'll have to get more details about that later."

The four brothers and I, carrying leather satchels with legal briefs and papers, squeeze into the carriage and Lily drives us to the court-house. "Where's Dracula?" I ask.

"He's meeting us there," Sebastian says.

This is my first time in this part of the town, but I know the court-house the moment I see it. It's the tallest building I have ever seen, dome-shaped, made of gray stone, stained glass windows throughout. You could fit several baseball stadiums and a couple of high-rise build-ings into the structure and still have room to spare.

"It's huge!" I say, gasping.

"That's what she said," Derek quips, and I nearly choke on my tongue.

"That's some serious teenage boy humor for an immortal and wise vampire," I say.

He shrugs. "We have to stay relevant and current with the times." He winks at me, and I flush.

Elijah speaks without looking up from the book he's reading. "It has to be this large to accommodate not only the judges, but also all manner of creature who may need to come to court. About 100 years ago the giants petitioned for the doors to be made larger, because though the dragons can fly in from the top, the giants had a hard time getting in through the regular entrance. It was a whole drama that eventually resulted in the building being remodeled. Now everyone is more or less happy, though some of the flower fairies complain it's too big and they get tired trying to find their way. You can't please everyone it seems."

The carriage is silent as we pull up to the front. The doors are made of stone. Everything is stone. No wood. I assume because of creatures who breathe fire or burst into flames.

Elijah finally looks up and smiles. "It's time."

We pile out and make our way in. I idly wonder who opens and closes these doors each day, but then I see that one of the guards is a an actual giant and my question is answered. He towers over us, easily the size of a tall tree, and I can barely make out the features of his face. "Are you carrying any weapons, magicks or forbidden items?" the giant booms at us.

"No. We are here for the defense," Derek says.

"You may enter."

The space within is just as huge as it seems from without, and has benches of varying sizes, presumably to accommodate all manner of creature.

I try to take it all in as the brothers rush us to our courtroom. We travel through long hallways with impossibly high ceilings until we reach our destination. It's set up more like a throne room than a court-house, though there are nods to the latter with the defendant's box and jury box.

I already know from my reading that the jury selection is different here. The judge chooses the jury based on a pool of interspecies candidates who have been given legal training and have been vetted for impartiality. The lawyers are stuck with who they get, unless there are no jurors from the defendant's race.

The courtroom is packed already with bystanders who want to see Dracula. It's more of a celebrity spotting than a court of law. The judge's seat is a huge stone platform big enough for a dragon. There is no ceiling, and yet the snow that is starting to fall more heavily outside doesn't enter the chamber. There's some kind of magical field that keeps out the weather but allows a view of the sky and the swirling colors of the Dragon's Breath. We take our place at stone tables and super uncomfortable stone benches. Derek explained to me that court cases here are different than in the mundane world. Here, there are breaks, but court isn't dismissed until the case is complete. Which means we could be here for days. And the accommodations are less than comfortable.

And I'm a human who actually needs a reasonable amount of sleep.

I glance at the prosecution and see two women and a man conferring with each other, their backs to me. One of them is familiar. She came to the house offering the plea. The Van Helsings.

I glance at the jury box and study the thirteen chosen to hear the case. Elijah explains that the three dwarvish-looking fellows with the craggy faces and long beards are druegar, from the diamond mines in the far north. The naga has the upper body of a woman–and a beautiful one at that–but the lower body of a monstrous python, and next to her, in a special tank to accommodate their aquatic nature, are a pair of selkies that the average person would have a hard time differentiating from a couple of seals. I ignore the others and ask the question that's been on my mind since entering the room. "How many vampires do we have?" I ask.

Derek glances over. "Three. That could be to our favor, or not. Dracula has a mixed reputation amongst our kind."

Speak of the devil, Dracula enters the courtroom and everyone falls silent as he makes his way to us, his black cape flowing behind him like a macabre wedding train.

"Cutting it rather close, aren't you?" Liam hisses as Dracula takes a seat at our table.

"I am here. That is what matters."

"Where have you been? We could have used your help in preparing your defense," Sebastian says.

Dracula glares at the Night brother. "I had business to attend to. I trust you made do in my absence."

A very tiny woman comes out of what looks like a hole in one of the walls. She's so small she could fit in the palm of my hand. She must use some kind of magic to amplify her voice, because when she talks, it fills the whole room.

"Hear ye, hear ye. Judge Dath'Racul residing. Court is in session in the matter of the Otherworld vs. Vlad Dracule on two counts of murder, two counts of unlawful draining of blood, and two counts of violating the Non-Violent Vampire Act."

With that, there is a great whooshing sound and the air around us is whipped into a frenzy as a huge red dragon descends from the sky and into the chamber, wings spanning the length of the space as he lands upon the platform, his giant claws digging into the stone as he does.

I gasp and clutch at Sebastian's arm. It's one thing to imagine a dragon, it's quite another to see one up close and in person. His scales shimmer like gemstones and his large ebony eyes scan the courtroom.

"Rise," the dragon says with a deep, thunderous voice, a puff of fire spurting from his nose.

We rise, my legs still wobbly from being in the presence of an actual freaking dragon!

"Who stands for the defendant?" the dragon asks.

"The Night Firm," Derek says.

The judge nods his giant head. "And who stands for the Otherworld?"

"The Van Helsings," one of the women says. "Moira, Anna and Able."

"Very well, begin with your opening arguments."

The Van Helsing woman steps forward, and the tiny woman who is now seated at the side of the dragon waves her hand and an iridescent cloud appears above us. When the prosecutor speaks, her voice is also amplified.

"Your Greatness, we intend to show that Vlad Dracule, also known as Dracula, has a history of violent and bloody crimes against others. That he was abusive to his wife, and when he found out she was having an affair, he killed her and her child in a most brutal fashion."

Derek stiffens and the brothers look at each other.

Dracula's eyes narrow. His nails scrape at the stone bench, leaving grooves in their wake.

I lean in toward the Count, speaking softly. "They'll need proof of an affair. Otherwise, it's just speculation."

He nods, his hands clenched.

Moira calls her first witness. "We call Lilith to the stand," she says.

The courtroom door opens and Lilith walks in like a celebrity on the red carpet. Her dress is white silk and has a long train that trails behind her. She looks like a bride, innocent and virginal. Dracula stiffens, his eyes glued to her.

Liam hisses. "I thought she wasn't going to testify for them?"

Lilith catches my gaze and winks, and I put a steadying hand on Liam's arm. "I don't think she is," I whisper.

Lilith takes the stand and the tiny woman next to the dragon brings a giant book for Lilith to swear on.

"Who is that woman, and what is that book?" I whisper to Sebastian.

"She is a gnome and is the right hand of Judge Dath'Racul. And the book is an ancient book of magic that is said to hold the secrets of the dead. Everyone swears on it when testifying."

"What is your relationship to the defendant?" Moira asks Lilith.

"I am his sire, and he was my husband for several hundred years," she says, with a bell-like voice that carries through the courtroom.

"And how would you describe your relationship to Dracula when you were married?" Moira asks.

Our entire table holds our collective breath as we wait to see what her answer will be.

"We were as close as two people could be. It was the happiest time of my existence." There's a sad melancholy to her voice and I know this is her truth.

Moira frowns. "Would you describe Mr. Dracule as violent?"

"Objection, Your Honor," Derek says, standing. "Leading the witness."

"Ms. Van Helsing, you know better," the judge says.

"I'll rephrase," she says, turning back to Lilith. "How many people has Vlad killed?"

"I couldn't say. You'd have to ask him."

Moira looks frustrated. "How many did he kill while you were married?"

Lilith's lips twitch. "Again, I couldn't say. I wasn't his keeper. We were equals. Partners."

"How would you describe his temperament?" Moira asks.

"Intriguing, brilliant, thoughtful," she says.

Moira sighs and looks to the judge. "Your Honor, permission to treat Lilith as a hostile witness."

"Granted," the dragon says.

Moira looks back to Lilith, her eyes hard. "Isn't it true that you've claimed Vlad was abusive and volatile?"

"He was never abusive," Lilith says. "And I found him more calculating than volatile. Vlad never let his temper get the best of him."

The rest of her testimony is more of the same. She paints her ex in the best possible light, explaining that they only separated so Dracula could fulfill his desire to have a child.

When Derek stands to cross-examine Lilith, he asks only one question. "Based on what you know of Vlad, do you think he's capable of killing his wife and child?"

"Not in the least," Lilith says. "He wanted a child more than anything. He would never have harmed Mary or their baby."

The testimony went better for us than expected and the prosecution doesn't look happy.

Moira looks through her notes, then speaks. "We call Jerome Van Helsing to the stand."

Derek stands. "Objection, your honor, this witness is not on the list provided to us."

"Your honor, new evidence only recently came to light. Jerome is being called as an expert witness to testify to the defendant's frame of mind surrounding this new information."

"I will allow it," the dragon says.

The courtroom doors open and I turn, studying the man called Jerome Van Helsing.

My blood runs cold.

My hands tremble.

My breathing becomes rapid. My vision blurs with the burning of tears.

I'm sitting between Sebastian and Derek, and both of them notice my body tense and shake.

"What is it?" Sebastian asks, his lips glancing against my ear.

"It's him," I say. "It's Jerry. My ex."

CHAPTER 16: THE PAIN

Submit to you—
  is that what you advise?
  The way the ripples do
  whenever ill winds arise?

~ *Ono no Komachi, loose translation by Michael R. Burch*

"How?" asks Derek, eyes wide.

I shake my head, a rising panic flooding my senses. "I don't know. But that's Jerry."

I would know him anywhere. The dark eyes and black hair that's perfectly coifed. The long, brown coat he always wears. The cruel glint in his eyes.

Sebastian curses under his breath. "I heard he had a practice in the mundane world, but I never imagined the two of you had met. It can't be coincidence."

"What do you mean?" I ask. "He sought me out as a client?"

"Or perhaps Matilda's ad sought you out because of him. I'm not sure." His eyes look dark. His brow furrowed in worry.

Before we can say more, Jerome—Jerry—Van Helsing passes us by, smiling and winking at me. All four brothers stand and call for an objection at the same time.

"Your honor," Derek says, as the other brothers sit, "this is highly unusual. This man has never met with my client professionally and has a history of violence against women. He's unsuitable to be their expert witness."

At the words "violence against women," I shrink into myself, my mind clouding with the unreality of it all. What's he doing here? How is this happening?

Sebastian reaches for my hand under the table and squeezes it. The touch, the strength in it, soothes some of the frantic fear out of me, but I'm still left perplexed by the situation I now find myself in.

Moira Van Helsing stands, glancing at me before she speaks to the judge. "Your honor, my brother is an expert in the field of psychology, has given professional testimony in this court before, and is more than capable of studying Count Dracule's file and giving his expert opinion on the accused."

"Objection overruled," the dragon bellows. "You may continue."

Derek frowns and sits, his hands clenched into fists at his side.

Moira smiles and nods to the judge. "Thank you, Your Greatness."

She faces Jerry with a flourish. "Dr. Van Helsing, please recount your qualifications for the record."

My head fills with the sound of whooshing water and I feel like I'm going to vomit as Jerry stares at me while elaborating on his skill and training, including being pack therapist for the Van Helsing werewolf clan.

My ex is a werewolf?

He then goes on to testify about Dracula, that he's hot headed, dangerous, abusive, feels himself above the law. All the expected attacks that we prepared for.

But we didn't prepare for what happens next.

First, the courtroom door opens and Elal, the coroner, comes in and hands a slip of paper to Derek and to Moira. He looks apologetically at us, then slinks away.

Moira's eyes widen when she reads it, and her smile is damning.

Derek looks it over and swears.

Moira admits into evidence a Memory Catcher. The crystal looks familiar.

Derek objects but is overruled again, and Moira hands the stone to Jerry, who proceeds to show the image.

"This is the memory of a cat," Jerry says. "One who lives on Count Dracule's property." Jerry speeds through until he gets to the part where Liam's shoes are clearly visible. "And these are the shoes of Mr. Liam Night, for the defense. He was there, with Mary, while Dracula was away."

The court goes wild. But the gnome woman screams for everyone to settle down, and Moira, before she loses momentum, submits the paper Elal brought in as evidence.

"And can you tell the court what this document says?" Moira asks Jerry.

Jerry smirks. "It says the child wasn't Dracula's. Which means Mary was having an affair."

Dracula stands and flips over a stone table in sheer, uncontrollable rage. He dashes to Liam and pins him to the floor, stepping on him with his boot. "How dare you betray me this way after everything I've done for you!"

Liam thrashes under the weight of his sire. The dragon bellows fire into the air with a loud screech, and the tiny woman with the big voice walks over and grabs Dracula by the cuff of his pants. It's all she can reach. But I watch, wide-eyed, as she yanks, and Dracula is pulled into the air and smashed against the marble flooring with a loud thud.

"There will be silence in the court," the little woman screeches to a stunned audience.

Dracula stands, dusting himself off, and nods to her, showing a deference I've never seen in him. He stands quietly, holding his rage tightly around him like a cloak against the winter winds.

Liam climbs to his feet, backing away from Dracula, a sneer on his face. "I wasn't having an affair with Mary."

"Silence!" the woman screams. "Court is adjourned for fifteen minutes. Counselors, the judge will see you in his chambers. Only one from each side."

Moira follows the gnome towards the dragon, and Derek steps forward, telling us all to behave until he's back. His jaw is locked in anger.

Elijah has retreated to his book, Liam looks ready to murder everyone, and so it is left to me to reprimand Dracula himself. I stand and face him, eye to eye. "You need to chill your shit immediately. If this case wasn't already damned by their testimony, your outburst was surely the nail in the coffin. Unless you want to spend the rest of eternity underground, calm the hell down now."

His teeth elongate, and he eyes my neck like it will be his dinner, but I don't back away. "Calm. The. Hell. Down."

Finally, Dracula nods. "You are right. This display has not helped us. I will save my anger for later." And with a flourish of his cape, Dracula strides out of the courtroom without another word.

We follow him into the main hall and find a few benches tucked away in a corner, hoping for smidgen of privacy. Liam, Elijah, Sebastian, Lily and I sit on one bench. Dracula is alone on the other.

"Let Liam explain," I say to the Count, then glance at the red-haired vampire. For once, he almost looks grateful.

"I was her healer," Liam says calmly. "She was worried about the baby and didn't want to trouble you, so she asked for my help. We were not having an affair, and I had no idea the baby wasn't yours."

The rage on Dracula's face evaporates into grief so deeply profound and heartrending I have to look away. The sobs shake his body as all the pain of this loss consumes him.

It's too much. No one moves to offer him comfort, so I do.

I take a seat by his side and put an arm around his broad shoulders. With a soft, soothing voice, I give him what solace I can. "The grief will destroy you if you let it," I say. "I know how hard this is, and I'm truly sorry for the loss you bear."

I ignore the brothers. I even ignore my own wariness about this man—this vampire. Instead, I connect with the part of him that is in all of us. The heart and soul, the pain and sorrow. In this we are the same.

In this, Dracula and I share the same unsealing wound.

When he looks up and into my eyes, there is new understanding there. We are now kindred, bound by pain, through pain. Bound in the darkness of grief.

Bound.

"Thank you," he says softly.

I nod and step back, giving him space, and take a seat between Sebastian and Liam to discuss strategy. "That crystal looked awfully familiar," I say.

Sebastian nods. "Indeed." He motions to Lily. "Return to the castle. Check the safe."

She nods and sprints away, disappearing down the hallway.

I lower my voice. "You don't think the prosecution stole it, do you?"

Sebastian grits his teeth. "We shall see. But in my experience, the Van Helsings will do almost anything to punish Dracula. He caused much pain to their family, back in the days when we were not governed by laws."

I look to the Count, but he says nothing, his eyes fixed on a fireplace crackling amongst the gray stone.

"If the baby wasn't Dracula's, then who was Mary involved with?" I ask aloud, though no one answers.

Dracula just clenches his fist.

Liam looks ready to set the building on fire.

Elijah and Sebastian have no more answers than I do.

Derek steps around the corner, looking drained of all life—even for the undead. "It's not good," he says, speaking to all of us. "If another outburst occurs, we will each be fined. Heavily. And..." he pauses, looking uneasy.

"And?" asks Sebastian. "Spit it out, brother."

Derek takes a deep breath. "And for the remainder of the trial, due to his entanglement in the case, Liam isn't allowed in the courtroom."

"What?" roars the fire Druid. "I've done nothing wrong."

"Be that as it may," says Derek coolly, "the judge believes things will proceed more...smoothly...if you are not present."

Liam leaps to his feet, pacing next to the fireplace and sparking the flames with his fingers. "Fine. Go and protect this monster," he says, gesturing to Dracula. "I took this case for Mary. And we don't even know who actually killed her yet. So go. Go play lawyer. And while you do, I'll be here focusing on what really matters. Finding the truth!"

He clenches his jaw, and the fire roars at his back, casting him in crimson light. Steam mixes with his breath.

"Perhaps," Elijah says plainly, "if you had been honest with us from the start, we could have avoided this problem."

"It wasn't that simple," hisses Liam.

"Listen," I say, looking at everyone calmly. "We could argue all day, but that's exactly what the prosecution wants. Dracula's outburst set us back profoundly, as did the paternity test. We need a new plan. We need…" I swallow, this next part hard for me to say. "We need to discredit their expert witness. I have to take the stand, to testify to what Jerry did to me."

My words have the intended effect, and all their fury at each other seems forgotten.

"No!" Sebastian says roughly. "We aren't putting you through that."

"We can find another way," Derek says.

Elijah shrugs. "If she's willing, I say we let her."

"You would say that," Liam spits. "All head and no heart."

I can see the wound his words create in Elijah, though I suspect no one else can. It's covered up so quickly.

"Then what do you suggest?" Elijah asks Liam, who has no response other than to glare and turn away.

"It's the only way," I say. "If you want to win. And…I can do this. I need to do this. And not just for the case."

One by one they seem to understand what I'm not saying. That this is my way of fighting what he did to me. This is my way of standing up for myself.

Each of them nods at me in turn.

Then Lily returns, breathless, her suit stained with sweat around the collar, pink hair disheveled. "The crystal wasn't there," she says between heavy gasps. "It's gone."

"Shit," curses Sebastian. "How did they get past our security?"

"Perhaps they didn't," says Dracula, his voice defeated. "Perhaps the Van Helsings aren't the only ones who wish to see me imprisoned."

Liam's eyes narrow at Elijah. "You," says the fire Druid. "You gave them the crystal." He sounds more shocked than angry.

"Why would I do such a thing?" Elijah asks, his voice cold and calculating. "What would be the reason?"

"Because you are no longer committed to our oath," Liam says. "You would rather see us lose, see us forever bound to Dracula, than find us released from our compulsion."

Elijah looks at me worriedly, then back at Liam. "It's true that I have reservations about a plan we made so very long ago, under wildly different circumstances." He clenches his hands and frowns. "But I would never betray our firm. You must know that. It wasn't me."

Liam scoffs. "I've read your journals. Your misgivings."

"Those were private—"

"You betray our oath."

"Never."

This isn't the first time I've heard them talk of oaths, and it makes my stomach cramp at what I suspect is their intention. But I need to know for sure. "What oath?" I ask through trembling lips.

Elijah looks to me, compassion in his eyes. "When we were cursed—"

"Shut the hell up, Elijah," Sebastian says, with a warning.

"She deserves to know. Isn't this why she was hired? To help with the last piece?" Elijah casts a challenging gaze at each of his brothers, and an understanding passes between them. The passion in their eyes drifts away, replaced by a quiet resignation.

He looks back at me, his voice thin and morose. "When we were cursed, the power consumed us. Made us crazy. We lost ourselves in the excess of our gifts, in the excess of each element. It turned us cruel. Monstrous."

Elijah looks away, gazing at the fire, his words far away. "There are many sins laid at our feet from those days. We set fire to homes, villages, cities. I cannot even count the innocents we killed.

"We couldn't contain our power. Earthquakes erupted wherever we went, uprooting trees that had lived thousands of years. Ravaging towns and collapsing mountains.

"We were the apocalypse incarnate. Flooding followed us, drowning anyone and anything in our path. Destroying livestock and farms. Killing wildlife and humans without discrimination."

Elijah nods in remembrance, his words full of sorrow. "And we brought the winds. They howled and shook the earth, blowing away homes and destroying whatever might be left. We tried to separate, as our collective power was too great, but we just spread our destruction farther. We tried living alone, as far from anyone as we could, but it was no use. We were too strong. Too out of control."

"And so we made an oath," Derek says, cutting in. "A suicide pact. If we could not control the powers we had been cursed with, we would end our lives and spare those around us. But we are not easy to kill. Only a great power can kill one such as us. We had to create a perfect storm, using all the elements, to end our lives."

"And it almost worked," Sebastian says bitterly.

"But Dracula found you," I whisper.

They nod.

"I gave you control," says the Count. "I gave you life."

Liam frowns. "You sucked our power away, leaving us shells of our former selves." He holds his palm out and a single flame ignites on it, glowing. "This is all that's left of who I was."

I shake my head, confused. "But then...if vampirism solved your problem, why do you still want to end your lives?"

Sebastian looks over to me, his eyes heavy with too many lifetimes of grief.

They say nothing. But I think I understand.

Some sins are too much for anyone to bear. Some crimes too heinous to forget.

I understand.

But I don't agree.

"So you plan to die when this trial is over?" I ask, my voice cracking. "And I'm supposed to help you somehow?"

"You're supposed to help us win this case," Derek says, not making eye contact with me. "That is why Matilda's magic chose you. Perhaps

175

because of your relationship with Jerome, or perhaps because of some yet unknown reason, you are critical to the outcome of these proceedings. You will help us win. Then Dracula will free us from the sire bond, and we will handle the rest."

"The rest? As in killing yourselves?"

They stay quiet, avoiding my gaze.

"I won't do it," I say, standing up, my entire body shaking with fear and anger and sadness. "I won't help you. If you lose this case, Dracula won't release you, and you won't be able to cause any harm to yourselves."

Derek shakes his head, finally meeting my eyes with his own. "If we lose, Dracula will be tortured for all time. The sire bond will remain, and we will feel his pain as our own. We will go mad from an eternity of torment. No. Whatever your wishes, it will be done by midwinter."

I look to the Count, my eyes pleading.

"They are not wrong," says Dracula.

"Please," I beg. "Please. Even if we lose, don't make them suffer."

"Why not?" he says, staring at his own hands, his long sharp nails. "Have I not suffered? Have I not lost all I hold dear?" He closes his eyes, a single tear falling down his cheek. "Even so, it does not matter. If the sire bond remains, they will feel what I feel. And if I free them, then they will carry out their oath. As you can see, Miss Oliver, the Night Brothers have chosen their fate."

There's only one way then. We have to win the case. But before we do, I must convince the Night brothers to abandon their plan.

"It's time we return to the courtroom," I say simply, checking the giant copper clock at the end of the hall. I take the lead, my stride quick as the others lag behind. Someone walks up beside me, and I'm surprised to see Matilda, dressed in a green gown, beads in her hair, keeping pace with me. "I thought you were staying at the castle?" I ask.

She nods. "I was."

"Then what changed?"

"I was needed here," she says, a kindly smile on her face. Then her features turn grim. "You understand now, what my boys intend to do."

"We have to stop them. You have to stop them. They'll listen to you," I say, firm determination in my voice.

"I have talked to them, and in most things, they do listen. But not in this. Their pain has been too great. Their losses too deep. They cannot fathom a life of eternal darkness. They've yet to see how light can still live within them, even if they cannot live within the light."

"*In lumen et lumen*," I whisper.

Matilda nods. "You are their light. You are the only person who can change their hearts in this matter. That's why the spell called to you above all others."

"Wait a second." I raise an eyebrow. "Derek said the ad chose me to help win the case."

The old woman waves her hand dismissively. "Oh, that is what they all think, yes. That is what I told them. But they are wrong, Eve Oliver. I made a spell to find the one who can save the Night brothers. The one who can remind them of who they truly are." She winks mischievously and steps back, chatting with Lily.

Somehow, the woman's words always manage to cheer me up, and I walk a bit straighter then. As I near the door to the courtroom, a man cuts me off, his brown trench coat old and rugged. Jerry. He wears a wolfish grin.

"How nice to see you again, Eve," he says smoothly, as if we were old friends. "How have you been?"

His easy manner makes me boil with rage, but I keep my anger below the surface. "Better and better since I stopped going to therapy," I say, crossing my arms,

"Glad I could help."

I nod, my voice sincere. "You were a prime example of what not to do."

A hint of a frown touches his lips. Quickly gone. He gestures behind me. "I see the Night brothers have roped you into their little game. No doubt to tell lies about me. Come now, Eve, I thought you had more integrity than that. Tell me, what did they promise you?"

I shrug. "I don't have to tell you anything." And with that, I walk past him and into the courtroom.

CHAPTER 17: THE WILD

You may shoot me with your words,
You may cut me with your eyes,
You may kill me with your hatefulness,
But still, like air, I'll rise.
~ Maya Angelou

WE ALL RETURN to our seats, with the exception of Liam, who remains out in the hall. The other Night brothers crowd around me protectively.

"Are you all right?" Derek asks gently. His eyes shift to Jerry for a moment, then back at me. "I heard what he said."

"I'm fine," I say, though my gut is buzzing like angry bees. "And I don't care about what he said."

"He will never harm you again," Derek says.

"He will die if he tries," adds Sebastian.

I can't help but smile at their determination to keep me safe. "I'll be okay. Don't go losing your law license over me."

"Our actions would be of a noble nature," says Elijah. "Besides, it's not as if we don't know any lawyers to bail us out."

We all chuckle lightly.

"I can sneak into Jerry's house if you'd like," whispers Lily. "Summon moths to eat through his clothing. Cause his garden to wither. Make his food go rotten."

"Wouldn't that be nice," I say.

She grins.

"Wait," I add. "You know I was joking, right?"

"Right." She winks.

Before I can say anything else, the judge returns, and the prosecution resumes their case.

They spend what feels like a thousand years parading witness after witness to talk about all the bad things Dracula has ever done.

It's...a lot.

And makes me sick to my stomach.

But just because he did all those things, doesn't mean he killed Mary and the baby.

The baby that wasn't his.

Considering his outburst, I doubt he even knew the true paternity at the time of the murder.

When the prosecution finally closes their case, my palms are sweating and I'm close to having a panic attack.

I'll be the first witness Derek calls.

I will have to tell everyone in this courtroom the details of my abuse at Jerry's hands.

And pray it will be enough to discredit him.

When Derek makes his opening statement, he is mesmerizing. He owns the courtroom with his confidence and charisma, and I am pulled into his powerful presence.

To take my mind off what's to come, I pull out my sketchbook and begin to draw him in his element. Talking to the jury, making his case, explaining how this crime is too sloppy for the likes of Vlad Dracule.

I draw his eyes, full of intelligence and cunning, and the strong slope of his nose and jawline. The dimpled chin that deepens when he smiles. With shading I create the solidness of his body, the way he fills a space.

He says something funny and the jury laughs. They are putty in his hands. So am I.

And then it comes time for me to testify.

I take the stand with wobbly legs.

Jerry stays in the courtroom, watching. Studying me.

It's unnerving, and Derek lays a hand on mine as I pass him. "Just keep your eyes on me," he says.

I nod, swallowing through a dry mouth.

I'm sworn in by the small gnome woman and then Derek begins his questioning. "How do you know Jerome Van Helsing?" he asks.

"He was my therapist in the mundane world," I say.

And then I explain how Jerry seduced me during the most painful part of my life. How he used our relationship in therapy to become my lover. And how he abused me.

"The first time it happened he was drunk," I say. "He came over to my apartment and demanded to be let in. He accused me of cheating on him and began choking me until I nearly passed out."

I can still feel his hands on my throat. The panic as I couldn't breathe. The belief that I might die.

"The abuse escalated from there," I say. "In another instance he broke my finger when I got angry at him for driving erratically."

It had healed, eventually.

I recount more instances of abuse, my eyes locked on Derek's.

But the real panic doesn't hit until Moira stands to cross-examine me.

"If the abuse was so bad, why didn't you report it?" she asks.

"I was scared," I say. "I also wanted to believe him when he said it wouldn't happen again. I didn't want him to get in trouble."

My excuses sound weak. Lame. But it's so messy when you're in the middle of it. So complicated. It's not as easy to walk away as people think.

"So he was awful and abusive, but you didn't want him to get into trouble? That's odd, don't you think?"

"Objection," Derek says, standing.

"Sustained," the dragon says. "Keep the questions relevant."

"Apologies, your honor," Moira says, refocusing on me. "Why didn't you leave?"

"I did," I say through clenched teeth.

"Why didn't you leave earlier?" she clarifies.

"My brother was dying of cancer. I had no one else to turn to. I was scared, alone, and heartbroken."

"It sounds to me like it wasn't that bad at all," she says, through Derek's objection. Moira smiles. "Withdrawn."

"Jerry didn't just abuse me," I say. "He continued to stalk me after I broke up with him."

Moira cocks her head. "Do you have proof of this?"

"Yes," I say. "I saved screenshots on my phone."

"Can you produce this phone? I'm sure the judge will allow contraband for the purposes of evidence."

Shit. "No, the phone broke," I say.

"How convenient. One final question, Miss Oliver. Isn't it true you're making this up to help your new bosses with their case? That my brother actually broke up with you, and this is your attempt to get revenge for a broken heart?"

"No, that is not true at all," I say, my rage simmering. "Jerry abused his position as my therapist and abused me before I finally broke up with him just before my brother died. Then he continued to stalk me."

I'm shaking. Tears are streaming down my face. I can't breathe as I'm excused from the witness stand and rejoin the Nights at their table.

Sebastian takes my hand the moment I sit, squeezing it reassuringly. His face is hard, his jaw locked as he glares at Jerry and the other Van Helsings.

Derek now presents our case.

We debated about having Dracula testify, but decided against the idea. It could too easily turn against us. Or the Count could have another outburst. Instead, Derek calls Liam to testify that he wasn't having an affair with Mary but was actually the doctor helping with her delivery. He calls Elal, the coroner, to testify that it might not have been a vampire who killed her. He calls Leonard to testify that the

Dracules had a good marriage, that Dracula was excited about his baby and in love with Mary.

And then he pulls the arguments together. He talks about how this crime was too messy to have been orchestrated by the great Vlad Dracule. How the Van Helsings hold a grudge against the count going back centuries.

He is both persuasive and powerful in his presentation, but the jury doesn't look swayed. In fact, they seem to sneer at Dracula more and more. When the time comes to make a verdict, I suspect they will be driven by emotion rather than logic.

Derek wraps up his speech, and we receive a short five-minute break before closing arguments begin. Each side is allocated thirty minutes. Finally, the end is in sight. Though I dread it more and more. If we lose, and I don't see how we won't, Dracula and the Night brothers will suffer for all eternity.

The prosecution goes first. Moira summarizes the facts of the case, reaffirms Dracula's cruel reputation, and replays the memory from the cat. She fast forwards to the relevant part of Liam's shoes, and as she does, something catches my eye. Something I hadn't notice before. As the feline scrambles up an ancient stone gargoyle, I see a speck in the distance, a crop of twigs in the abandoned cathedral opposite of Dracula's manor. The image lasts less than a second, and the picture is a muddy blur, but I'm sure of what I saw. Someone else was nearby that day. Someone may have seen what happened.

"I need to check on something," I say quickly, getting to my feet.

"Is something wrong?" Sebastian asks.

"No. It's about the case. It might be nothing. Or it might help us."

"I'll come with you." He starts to stand, but I gesture for him to stop.

"Stay here." I look at all three brothers and Lily. "Work together on the closing argument. And…buy me time. Make a commotion if you need to. Liam will come with me."

They each nod in unison, though they don't look too happy as they return to their notes.

I rush out of the courtroom, in the most polite-yet-quick walk I can manage, and find Liam pacing by the fireplace. "What's happened?" he asks, red-hair disheveled, as if he's been running his hand through it over and over again. "Is the trial over?"

"Not yet." I grab his hand and pull him toward the exit. "Come on."

~

I'VE LOST track of how long it's been since the trial began. Since I was last outside. Since I had any sleep. At least a few days. And when I step out onto the stone square of the courthouse, a storm greets me. Winter has come in earnest, it seems, and brought with it all the pent-up energy of waiting for fall to end. The wind lashes at my face, causing my eyes to tear. Ice, thin and sharp, falls from the sky, beating across my skin. I wrap my arms around myself, shaking, my breath a fog before my eyes. Liam yanks off his cloak and throws it over my head like a hood, then pulls me close, shielding me with his figure. An unnatural warmth radiates from his body and the chill inside me fades away. Liam is so close, his scent overtakes me. Charcoal and wood and the feeling of coming home to a roaring fire. Other feelings begin to rise in me as well, but we don't have time for those right now.

"Quickly," I yell over the wind. "To the carriage. We need to get to the Broken Cathedral."

Liam nods, leading me to a grand stable, fit for fifty horses, opposite the courthouse. Over the last three days, Lily took breaks from the trial to feed her steeds and take them out for rides. There are stable hands in service to the court who do that as well, she told me, but she prefers to do it herself.

Once in the stable, we're offered some respite from the cold, but it doesn't last long. The smell of straw and manure fill my nose as Liam quickly finds our carriage and opens the door for me. I shake my head, pointing to the driver's seat. "We need to be able to talk."

He nods, and together we take Lily's usual place behind the horses. A part of me wishes I had asked her to come with me, so I could sit cozy in the back with Liam, but when it comes to delaying the court with a distraction, I have more faith in Lily than anyone else. She's not a lawyer. She doesn't have as much to lose due to bad behavior. And from what I've heard, she's good at mayhem.

I just hope all of this is worth it.

Liam yanks on the reins and we're off, rushing down the cobbled streets of the Otherworld, the harsh winds piercing even the warm protection the fire Druid provides.

"What's going on?" asks Liam. "What happened?"

"I...saw...something," I say, teeth chattering, making my words stilted and broken. "In the memory. There...might be another witness. Someone who saw the truth. But I'll need your help. I'll need you...to catch them."

⪼

WE ARRIVE at the Broken Cathedral, the Otherworld sky darker than I have ever seen before, the storm clouds blocking out the Dragon's Breath, and no lanterns to light our way. I nearly trip climbing off the carriage, and Liam raises his hand, his palm lighting with a soft flame, illuminating our near surroundings. "Thanks," I say. "I'm surprised you didn't do that earlier. How could you even see the roads?"

"I can see better in the dark than I once did," he replies quickly. And I remember what Sebastian once told me, that vampires are creatures of shadow.

"What are we looking for?" asks Liam, holding his blazing hand up higher.

"A gargoyle. I'll know it when I see it."

He nods, and together we run into the cathedral ruins. In the main hall, half of the roof is gone, making way for snow and ice, and I walk carefully to avoid slipping. "Are the gargoyles here alive? Like in the mausoleum?" I ask, as we keep searching.

"They were once," Liam says somberly. "But when the earthquake that brought this building to ruin came, the gargoyles gave their life so that some of the cathedral could remain standing. They are just stone now."

I shake my head. "That's terrible. Why die to protect a building?"

He sighs. "It is what gargoyles do. And they saved many lives that day. You see, the cathedral was still in use at the time."

I pause, studying a gargoyle near a broken window. It's not the one I seek, but I take a quick moment to thank it silently, before continuing on.

"It is said," Liam continues, "that when the cathedral is restored, the gargoyles may return to life."

I raise an eyebrow. "Is that possible?"

He shrugs. "Such things have happened before."

We climb higher, searching for the ancient gargoyle in the memory. My heart nearly stops when I see it, perched at the edge of one of the great towers, looking out at the world below. We are near the top of the cathedral now, surrounded by the stone pillars that hold up a solid ceiling. They are spaced far apart, making the area open to the wind and sky, to the dark clouds swirling above. We are so high up, I feel I can almost touch them, these thick rolling masses of thunder and ice.

Here the wind comes swiftly and harshly and leaves just as quickly. Snow has piled on in tall mounds near the pillars. Thick ropes fall from pulley systems built into the ceiling, coiling at our feet, and a golden church bell hangs over our heads, engraved with runes, wider than three horses, so enormous not even the storm can sway it.

I run to the gargoyle, pulling myself up on its wings, much like the cat had done in its memory.

"This is madness," says Liam. "You'll fall."

But I don't. I stay steady as I climb up over the head of the ancient statue.

And there, at the top, I see it.

A coil of branches and twigs, nestled safely against the crook of a stone wing.

A nest.

Filled with speckled eggs.

Liam climbs up behind me, wrapping his arm protectively around my waist. His hand is no longer on fire, but it's easier to see this close to the Dragon's Breath. "What are you doing?" he asks. "Have you gone—" He freezes, his eyes landing on the nest. "You don't think—"

"There's a bird nearby," I say, my breath heaving, the cold in me burned away by adrenaline. "And maybe, just maybe, it saw what happened." I look up, and there, amidst a swirl of dark cloud, I see a raven descending to protect its home. "Your babies are safe," I say softly. "We mean no harm." I turn to Liam. "Catch it. But be gentle."

He nods, and in a flash, he runs up the stone pillar, three steps straight up a horizontal wall, and leaps into the air, catching the bird and holding it like a precious gem. He lands across from me, balanced on the gargoyle's wing, a space only three inches wide. He sits down on the heels of his feet, steady as a rock, and lowers his hands in front of me. The bird, held firmly between his palms, meets my eyes, curiosity in its gaze. It stays still, quietly content, and not thrashing about as I imagined. There is an ease between us I can't quite understand.

I pull out the memory catcher Sebastian gave me and say the necessary words, praying to see something useful. There are many memories, of flying above Dracula's manor, of hunting for worms in the dirt, but I feel something inside me, a flash, guiding me to what matters most. There. The memory.

It is dark. The Dragon's Breath dim in the sky.

The bird sits perched on a tree near Dracula's front entryway. The door opens, spilling golden light into the shadows, and the Count himself steps out, wrapped in black. But before leaving, he turns back, holding up a gentle hand, and putting it to a woman's face. Mary. She stands in the doorway, dressed in a white gown, belly large, dark hair messy but beautiful all the same. She looks happy and radiant and a woman ready to bring joy and life into the world. She laughs at something Dracula says, then stands up on her toes and kisses him on the lips. With a final smile, she closes the door, and the Count walks away. The moment is intimate and peaceful, and it will never happen again.

The bird takes flight. It drifts through the quiet air, returning to its nest, studying its eggs. *No*, I think. *That can't be it. There must be something more.*

Something.

To save Dracula.

To save the Night brothers.

But there is nothing. The bird doesn't leave the nest.

I sigh, my energy dissipating, the cold creeping back into me.

"I'm sorry," I say, lowering the memory catcher, my eyes blurry as I look at Liam. "I thought I could save you. I thought—"

In the memory, the bird turns toward the manor, and I gasp with astonishment. Somehow, the image of the Dracula's home, though at least a mile away, is crystal clear.

"Photoreceptive cones," I mumble, laughing to myself, my eyes filling with tears.

"What are you going on about?" asks Liam.

"Photoreceptive cones in the retina," I repeat, louder, the strength back in my voice. "Birds have far more than humans. Some can see four or five times further. I read it once."

Liam smirks.

And the memory continues.

A figure walks toward the Manor, moving briskly. They wear a long brown coat. Their hair is a mess of dark curls.

It can't be...

And yet, Jerome Van Helsing enters the Dracule Manor on the night of the murder. Several moments later he steps out, his clothing soaked in blood.

My hands shake at the sight, and I almost drop the crystal. Instead, I lose my balance and Liam catches me, steadying me, and gently lowers the bird to the ground. It jumps into its nest, sitting calmly near its eggs.

"We need to get this back to the courthouse." I turn, looking over the snow-covered fields below, and a stone sinks in my throat. It will take a long time to climb back down the cathedral and even longer to ride back to the courthouse. There's no way we'll make it back before the trial is over. No way, unless...

"Go," I say, pushing the Memory Catcher into Liam's hand. "You're faster than me."

He pauses, still holding me with his other hand. I expect him to argue, to spew warnings about my safety. Instead, he meets my eyes, a fierce determination in his gaze, and nods once slowly.

And then, he leaps off the cathedral.

∽

THE EARTH CRACKS where Liam lands, kicking up dust and snow, and leaving veins of black in the stone. He bends his knees to absorb the impact, and stands up without hesitation, red hair wild in the storm. He doesn't take the carriage. He just runs, faster than I have seen anyone run before.

I turn away from the dizzying sight and crouch, staying low as I climb back down the statue and make my way under the great bell, looking for the stairs. Without Liam's fire to guide me, it's near pitch-black inside. I almost reach the stairs when a warm orange glow spills out from their depths. For a second, I freeze, bewildered, and then I realize someone is coming, carrying light.

My first thought is Sebastian must have come looking for us. But then I see the man step onto my floor, blazing-torch in hand. The man from my nightmares.

"You found something, didn't you," says Jerry, his face half in shadow, the other half cast in red angry light. "A memory." These are not questions. Just statements.

"I need to return to the courthouse," I say, trying to step around him.

He blocks the path, the heat from his torch too close to my face, too hot on my skin.

"I can explain," he says, brown coat billowing in the wind. "I received a letter. Signed by Mary. She asked for my help. That's why I was there that night."

I take a deep breath, trying to keep my emotions in check. Though I find it hard to look at him, I meet his eyes, looking for sincerity. For kindness. He does not have these things.

"Where is this special letter then?" I ask.

He bows his head. "Not here."

"Then go get it."

"I can't. It's gone. Went missing."

I snicker, unable to contain my sneer. "Well that's very convenient for you, isn't it?"

"It's the truth," he says, and for once, he looks broken, weak and

188

fragile and human like I have never seen him before. But that doesn't mean he's earnest.

"Then prove it to the court," I say, pushing past him.

He grabs my arm, hard enough to bruise. "They'll never believe me. Not after your testimony. You need to withdraw your statement. Say you were manipulated. Say you were confused. I don't care. Say you were wrong." He growls, and the sound from his mouth is nothing human.

"I wasn't wrong," I say. "The things you did to me were horrific. And you will never do them to anyone else again."

He snarls, grabbing me by the neck and yanking me close, so close the stench of his breath is on my face, and I see his teeth are sharper than before. Mouth dripping with saliva.

"Say you were wrong," he repeats, his voice low and guttural and beastly. "Or I will squeeze the life out of you." His grip tightens. Nails that were once short and neat now dig deep into my flesh like claws.

"You're a monster." I spit in his face. And knee him between the legs.

He yelps, letting me go for an instant, and I rush away toward the stairs. A shadow flies across the floor, and Jerry lands in my way, clothing stretched tight over bulging muscles too large to be human, long claws sprouting from thin veiny hands. He must have dropped the torch and jumped over me, all before I could take three steps.

Words flow out of me, quicker than thought. "If you kill me, the Night brothers will make sure you suffer for all eternity. You will stain your family name. You will—"

"Where's the crystal?" he roars.

"Not here. But I can get it." I'd never give it to him, but I need to make him think I will as I work out a plan to escape.

"He has it," says Jerry. "The one with red-hair. I saw the both of you leave together."

"Yes, but—"

"Then it's too late. He's at the courthouse by now." Jerry bows his head, defeated. He talks slowly. "Do you know, Eve, the greatest pleasure a werewolf can feel?"

I shake my head rapidly, my entire body vibrating with fear.

"It is the hunt," he says. "The chase of prey. Digging your teeth into a ripe, plump, juicy neck. Feeling the blood spraying into your mouth. Feeling the pulse of your query slow. Feeling the life leave them." He looks up, eyes mad and hungry. "If this is to be my last day of freedom, then I shall feel the hunt once again."

He pulls his head back and roars, muscles ripping out of his clothing, skin turning dark and matted with fur. All the charm of his face is torn away, replaced by a wet snout and purple lips, long ragged ears and too many barred teeth. He turns into the monster I know him to be.

And then I run.

A howl on the wind.

A beast on my heels.

~

I TAKE THE STAIRS. Not down, as I would have liked, for Jerry blocked that path. But up.

The torch, left at the base of the room, is dimming now and provides me little light as I climb. The staircase, which has railings but isn't surrounded by walls, zigzags toward the ceiling, and I realize I will soon reach the roof with nowhere else to run. That won't do. So I look out to my side, to the beams and pulleys holding up the church bell. Below, a shadow moves to the base of the stairs. He is taking his time, creeping in the darkness.

I carefully climb onto the railing, reaching out for a rope. My arms aren't long enough. I'll need to jump. And quietly, because I need Jerry to still think I'm on the stairs.

Gritting my teeth, I take one slow breath, and leap forward, hands fumbling clumsily in front of me. They find purchase, but slip, the coarse rope burning my skin as I tighten my grip to stop from falling. My descent slows and I hang near the ceiling, biting my lips shut though my entire body needs to scream.

The rope steadies. I allow myself one more breath. Slow. Quiet.

Then I pull myself higher and clasp one of the wooden beams holding up the church bell. My muscles straining, cold and restless, I climb up onto the beam, and lie flat as I crawl forward toward a rope at the other end. Then I can slide down and take the stairs.

One breath. Two.

I'm almost there.

The stairs behind me creak.

And I know he's standing where I stood a moment ago.

Keep moving, Jerry. Just keep going up.

He doesn't.

A sniff.

Another.

Like a hungry dog locked onto a scent.

I climb forward.

The torch is below me.

The rope within my reach.

I climb forward.

And something digs into my arm. Hot and sharp. A piece of splintered wood I hadn't seen. I suck in my breath, burying all the pain blooming under my skin, and reach forward, my hand slick with blood, and grab hold of the rope.

Silence.

The quiet before the storm.

The moment before the predator's leap.

I let myself fall, sliding down the rope, skin tearing from my palms in my haste.

The beast flies over me.

Landing where I was just a moment ago.

I made it, I think, for one ludicrous second.

And the wooden beam cracks under his weight.

The rope goes slack in my hands.

And we both fall to the ground.

I land with a crunch, my head hitting stone, my body collapsing near the burning torch. Spots blur my vision. Nausea fills my gut.

Two sets of claws land before me.

I am laying at the beast's heels.

Broken and weak. And suddenly, I am taken back to another time, another me, one who was beaten and choked. One who was left alone to weep on the floor and wonder what she did wrong. But that is me no longer.

The pain leaves me, burned away by a surge of strength. My mind is clear and light. My skin has forgotten the cold. And I stand, feet steady as rock, and I look the monster in the eye.

"You will never hurt me again," I say. "Know that. Even if you kill me now. Even if you rip me apart. I will feel nothing for you. Not anger. Not sadness. Not fear. Nothing." I take a breath. "I am not afraid."

The beast tilts his head, as if he hears something I do not. And then he charges.

One bite.

Deep into my neck.

My throat closes shut with blood.

My eyes twitch.

All I think is…

Nothing.

The beast rears its head. Letting me go. And I fly across the room. Past the pillars. Out into the sky.

I am falling, and yet I know, I will not fall.

I know it with a certainty I have always had. A certainty for things yet to come.

And a flash overtakes me.

More powerful than I have ever felt.

I don't fight it. Not as I have before.

And as the energy courses through my body, I realize, it is not just visions I have. Not just a feeling of what will happen. It is power. Raw, uncontrolled power.

It takes hold of me.

And I do not fall.

I fly.

I AM ME, and yet I am not. There are things I do, and things done through me. My voice is mine, and not my own.

. . .

"I AM the woman in the wild!" I scream into the shrieking wind. As I speak, lightning flashes, the fire of the torch blazes, and the clouds swirl around me. The pendant from the kitsune blazes at my throat. I am suspended in mid-air. My skin and clothes glow white, smooth and clear of any blemish, illuminating the dark sky. Illuminating the werewolf, who stands at the edge of the cathedral, jaw slack with wonder.

"I am the blood sister of the moon! I am the call of the night and her secrets. The radiance left from a star. I am all that you need and more than you know. I am the hidden that shall now be found. I am the magic that you seek. I am the wild!"

The wind thrashes at my words, so hard it pushes the beast backwards. He growls, barring his teeth. He bends his knees, preparing to leap.

"Do not move," I warn. "Do not try."

He howls one last time.

And jumps.

He swipes his claws forward mid-air, aiming for my neck.

He is nearly at me, when I raise my arm, and a gale of wind strikes down from above, so fierce and quick, it draws the clouds toward it like a tornado and sends the beast falling down.

He does not land smoothly.

One might say, he does not land at all.

His body hits the tip of a gargoyle wing.

And the stone pierces his flesh, bursting from his chest.

I don't recall the gargoyle wing being there. It wasn't there last I looked.

But perhaps I'm wrong. I'm not myself right now.

I am the radiance of a star, burning away. And as the energy fades, I glide back toward the tower. The power is gone before I find my footing, and I collapse, not quite on solid ground. I reach to grab the edge.

Someone grabs me first.

Strong arms pull me close.

"I'm here," he says, his warmth seeping into my body. "I'm here."

And I drift away.

And dream of nothing.

CHAPTER 18: THE FIRE

THROUGH LOVE, burning fire becomes pleasant light. ~ Rumi

MY CONSCIOUSNESS COMES and goes in waves. I'm aware only of strong arms carrying me through the streets of the Otherworld, of Liam's voice alternating between chastising me for my foolishness, cursing himself for leaving me, and offering words of comfort. All of this comes in fragments, until it's as if I'm with a different man altogether each time I awake.

Liam is a man at war with himself.

There is no winner in a war against yourself.

The storm around us grows in fury and hail the size of snowballs falls from the sky, the temperature dropping dangerously fast.

I shiver, my body convulsing without guidance from me in its attempt to warm itself.

Liam curses and a warmth spreads through me, blazing through his skin and into mine, fighting the chill that's settling into my frigid body.

When darkness overtakes me once more, I see Jerry's face, his anger and hatred, his desire to see me suffer even at his own demise.

And when I open my eyes again, I see the golden eyes of Liam studying me thoughtfully, his expression unreadable.

This time I feel more-clear headed, better in control of myself. Like I can actually keep my eyes open for longer than a few seconds, despite the pounding in my skull.

"Where are we?" I ask, trying to sit up and failing miserably.

"Move slowly," he says. "You've been through a lot."

He offers the support of his arm to prop me up, and I see we are in his bedchamber. A fire warms the space, dancing in shadows off the walls.

A familiar purr brings a smile to my face as Moon nudges against my leg and then curls up next to my lap. I pet the fur ball. "You're a sight for sore eyes," I tell my cat.

Liam snorts. "The beast wouldn't shut up. Howled outside my door for hours on end until I finally let him in. He can't stand me, but he wouldn't leave your side."

I give Moon extra love for that level of loyalty and devotion.

"What happened?" I ask, my mouth dry and thick.

Liam hands me a goblet of water and I sip it gratefully. He's sitting on the bed next to me, his arm still supporting me, our bodies pressed closely together, the heat between us tugging at my gut, sending a tingle up my spine.

Our fingers brush against each other on the bed, and his pinkie covers mine. We both studiously avoid looking at our fingers, but my every nerve is focused on how his finger feels brushing against mine.

"What happened?" he asks.

I search my memories, but it's all a bit fuzzy. "Jerry. He...he tried to kill me."

Liam's jaw clenches, and he nods. "He must have followed us from the courthouse."

"He's dead," I say. It's not a question. I remember the sound he made, a last, thin exhale as life left him. The last sound he'll ever make.

"Yes." Liam brushes hair out of my eyes and examines my face with one hand, while keeping the other on the bed touching mine. "How do you feel? Something...something happened to you. I came at the end, but for a moment I saw. You glowed like the moon." He looks almost frightened.

"I don't know," I say. "I still can't entirely remember." And then I suck in my breath as more details come back to me. "What happened in court? Did the judge see the memory of Jerry covered in blood?"

My heart beats frantically against my chest as I realize we need to get back, to tell the others what happened. But Liam moves his hand to cover mine, our fingers intertwining, the heat between us growing —and this time it has nothing to do with his Druid powers.

"The trial is over," he says. "The jury has reached a verdict and my brothers are at court now to hear it. I gave them the Memory Catcher in time." His lips curls in a smile. "Though apparently there had been a delay. Something about a dryad running naked through the court-room. She got away though, her face unseen."

I chuckle lightly, but it hurts my ribs and turns into a groan.

Liam stiffens at the sound of my pain. "I came back for you as soon as I could," he says. "I brought you home, and Matilda sent word to the court of your altercation with Jerry. She explained, in great detail, how you acted in self-defense."

I pause. "But if you only arrived at the end, how could you know what happened?"

A playful smile crosses his lips. "I may have told the enforcers I saw the entire attack. With your previous testimony, and the memory of Jerry covered in blood, it was not hard to convince them of your inno-cence. You will, however, have to answer some questions eventually. The Enforcers will need your first-hand account."

I nod. "So the court saw the memory?"

Liam nods. "They know everything."

"So they have to find Dracula innocent, right?"

"It does seem likely, though you never know until the end. It's just the way of things." He shrugs like it doesn't matter, but I know it does. It matters in so many ways.

"What will you do?" I ask. "When the sire bond is broken?" I hold my breath, waiting for his reply.

"I do not know," he says, turning away from my gaze. "There is much we need to consider."

Is he thinking of me, I wonder? But his eyes are far away. Fixated on the fire. There is someone else tugging at his heart. And I think back, to all the things Liam said these past months. *I took this case for Mary. I was her healer.*

"You were more, weren't you?" I ask hesitantly.

"What do you mean?"

"More than her healer." I place a hand on his face and pull it back to me gently. "The baby. He was yours, wasn't he? You weren't just helping Mary deliver her baby. You were helping her deliver *your* baby."

His eyes glisten with unshed emotion and he nods. "Babies," he says, in such a whisper I almost don't hear him.

"Babies?" I ask, sucking in a breath, thinking of Mary's last wish. That her babies would be protected. "There was more than one?"

He nods. "Twins. I... "

He pulls away from me and stands, pacing back and forth nervously. Cold rushes in where his warmth once existed and I find myself missing having him close.

I take another sip of water and place my goblet down, then slowly rise, moving carefully so as not to pass out. I take a step towards him, then another, until I have reached him.

"Liam. What happened?" I keep my voice soothing and calm, like I would if talking to a wild animal. He has that power in him, that wild, untamed madness that all the Night brothers have so much of.

"I was too late," he says, his voice breaking. "I knew something was wrong, but I didn't know what. When I showed up, she was already dead, covered in blood, the baby killed. It was a massacre. It took me a moment to realize..." he sucks in his breath, then lets it out in one long, slow exhale before continuing. Each word costs him a piece of his soul to say. "She was still in labor."

It's my turn to suck in my breath. I had several theories, but this wasn't one of them. I reach for his hand, taking it in mine, my icy fingers thawing at his touch, as our fingers once again intertwine. I stay still and silent, creating the space he needs to tell his story.

"She was pregnant with twins. She didn't want anyone to know. Didn't want to jinx it. She said she'd had nightmares that one of the babies died. So she refused to speak about the children to anyone but me." He pauses. "We weren't close, Mary and me. Not really. Our time together was one of passion, but little else, and each time I regretted it. Still, for some reason she trusted me. Trusted me with the truth above all others." With his free hand he runs his fingers roughly through his wild auburn hair. "I...I delivered my daughter into the gore of her mother and brother's deathbed. And then I ran. Like a coward, I took her and I ran, telling no one."

His grief breaks him, and I pull him into a fierce embrace. His arms wind around my waist as mine wrap around his neck, and he presses his body into me, his face buried in the crook of my neck, his tears drenching my shoulder as his sobs tear free from him.

The pain he's been holding in and using to feed his rage pours out of him, and I catch it all, staying strong enough for the both of us so that he can break, just for a moment.

I don't speak again until his body stills and his breathing returns to normal. Then I ask the burning question on my tongue. "Liam, where's the other baby now? Where's your daughter?"

"She's somewhere safe," he says, pulling back from me to wipe his eyes and compose himself. "Somewhere Dracula won't find her. She is being cared for well. Better than I ever could." His face hardens, and he looks at me. "If Dracula ever finds out about her, he'll kill her."

I swallow, believing him. "We will keep her safe." I say, knowing it's presumptuous to assume he wants or needs my help in this matter. But also knowing it's the right thing to say. The necessary and true thing to say. However it happened, whatever it might mean, the Night family has become my family. I will not abandon them to the darkness that lurks so closely at their heels.

"Liam," I say with all the tenderness in my heart, "you must know you were not a coward. No man should ever be put in the position you were in, and yet you delivered your daughter, you saved her and kept her safe. You did what Mary would have wanted. You were brave. You were your daughter's hero."

He flinches at my words. "I am a danger to her. She's better off without me." He moves to turn away from me, but I stop him.

"She's not," I say. "I promise you, she's not. You have so much to offer her. To teach her. To give her. Starting with your love. She needs her father. Trust me. This comes from a girl who would give anything to have her own father back, even for a day."

This softens him, but it's not enough. I know I need to show him the truth of himself. "You're so deeply enmeshed in your own self-hatred you can't see past it. But you're only seeing the shadows, not the light. There is light in you, Liam. In all four of you. And yes, there is darkness, too. But that's true of everyone. We all carry within us the entirety of existence. The light and the dark. The noble and the ignoble. Sometimes we have to walk in the shadows, but we must always strive to come back to the other side. Your daughter needs you to find your way back. Your brothers need you." I pause, hesitating, assessing my own feelings, and then I speak, knowing it is the truth. "And *I* need you."

Our faces are inches apart. My right hand is in his, my left hand now resting on his chest. Our fingers are intertwined and I'm suddenly keenly aware of the contact, of flesh on flesh, of his breath mingling with mine, of all my senses responding to his.

"What are you, Eve Oliver?" he asks, sliding a finger down my cheek.

"I don't know," I say honestly. "I just know that everyone deserves a fair trial and a strong defense. So I'm fighting for you and Sebastian and Derek and Elijah. Even if you won't fight for yourselves."

The mood in the room has shifted. The tension between us is visceral.

Every nerve in my body is on fire as he moves closer to me, his head bending down, his lips brushing against mine.

The kiss starts softly, gently, a teasing only. When I move in closer, I surprise us both.

My arms wind back around his neck and he pulls me against him, his hard chest pressed to my breasts, his nails digging into my back as his lips claim mine again, this time with all the heat and power of a Druid turned vampire.

He tastes of warmth and honey and my body responds to his with all the desire that's been pent up in me since starting this job.

I moan into his mouth as I feel his body further harden against me, in clear evidence of his excitement.

My mind clouds with passion and I know where this is leading. And still, I don't pull away. I have fought against my own desires for so long, out of fear. Fear of being hurt. Fear of losing another person I love. Fear of getting too close.

I can't live in fear any longer.

Liam gazes deeply into my eyes. "You look oceans away," he says softly, his lips so close to mine I can feel them moving, our foreheads pressed together.

"I was just thinking about the nature of love," I say, and then I kiss him again.

Our passion moves us across the room, where he presses me against the wall and moves his mouth down my neck, his teeth gliding against my pulsing vein, my pains and aches forgotten for the moment.

My breath hitches, and I can't tell if what I'm feeling is fear or excitement as pleasure wars with past memories of a violent Liam tearing into my neck.

He pauses, lips brushing against the flesh of my ear. "Is this okay?" He asks breathlessly. "Tell me to stop."

"Don't. Stop," I say.

And he wouldn't have, had Matilda not come to the door at that precise moment.

CHAPTER 19: THE OATH

WE CAN EASILY FORGIVE a child who is afraid of the dark; the real tragedy of life is when men are afraid of the light. ~ Plato

LIAM and I pull away from each other like guilty teenagers caught making out in the basement.

Matilda gives us both knowing looks and smiles. "It's good to see you two getting along with one another at last," she says in the under-statement of the year.

Liam coughs and I hide a smile, my body still buzzing with need for him. It's almost painful to not be touching him right now.

"I came to tell you the verdict." She pauses dramatically, letting us both compose ourselves. "Dracula was found innocent of all charges."

Liam and I both exhale at the same moment, smiles playing across our lips.

Matilda continues, looking directly at me. "Eve, the Van Helsings are beyond mad with anger and grief. I expect Moira will want to see you punished for Jerry's death, but the law is on our side in this matter. You have nothing to fear in this regard." She says it in that way she has about her. As if she knows things the rest of us don't.

She turns to Liam. "Your brothers had a final meeting with Dracula at the courthouse. They should return shortly."

He nods, and her lips curl in a smile. "Very well then. I shall leave the two of you to your...celebration." And with that she walks out the door, Moon meowing as she does, then winding around my legs and purring. As soon as we are alone again, Liam steps closer, pulling me back into his arms, a wide grin on his face. "I can hardly believe it," he says. "We won. We...we could never have done this without you, Eve. I hope you know that."

"I know." I lean in to kiss him once more.

Then suddenly, Liam does something I have never seen him do before. He loses his balance.

And topples towards me, and I catch him as best I can, both of us falling into the wall.

"Are you okay?" I ask. "What happened?"

He raises his head, rubbing his forehead with his hand, when the door bursts open, and the rest of the Night brothers rush in, still dressed in the fine suits and vests they wore to the courthouse, but looking rather disheveled. "Have you felt it too, brother?" asks Sebastian.

Liam nods, his eyes widening in awe. "He's released the sire bond." He smiles at me, the broadest smile I've ever seen on his face. "We're free!"

Elation wars with fear in my gut, and I hold Liam close and look to all of the brothers. "Does this mean you will..." I can barely say the words. "Does this mean you will go through with your plans? Will you—"

Sebastian rushes towards me and grabs my arms gently with his rough hands, studying me with his forest-green eyes. "Are you well? I would have stayed at your side, but Liam vowed to look after you while I was needed at court."

"I'm fine."

Before I can add more, Derek stands in front of me, his five o'clock shadow a little more beard and a little less shadow than usual over his dimpled chin. "I'm so sorry," he says. "We swore to protect you from that monster, and yet we failed."

"I kept myself safe," I say.

"Indeed," agrees Elijah, running a hand through his blond hair, joining his brothers around me. "The evidence you procured also won the trial. We are in your debt, Miss Oliver." He bows dramatically, with a flourish of his silver cape.

I chuckle despite myself, then sober quickly. "So…what about your oath?"

Liam looks to each of his brothers, an understanding passing between them. Then he turns to me with his amber eyes and runs a hand softly across my cheek. "There are more important things now," he whispers. Finally, he lets me go, standing straight and speaking to all his brothers. "We have all done heinous things. And we all carry that pain differently. But I think the time has come to stop seeking an end to our lives and to instead search for ways to atone for our sins."

They all nod somberly.

All except Elijah, who lifts up one finger thoughtfully. "So what you're all saying is…you agree with me? And I was right all along?"

A contagious laughter takes us all.

As DAY-TIME APPROACHES, we are all tired beyond imagining and yet none of us feel inclined to be alone.

An idea sparks in my mind, and it's so silly and stupid that I love it instantly. "Let's have a sleepover," I say.

We've all relocated to the library and are sitting on plush red chairs talking. The four of them look at me as if I've gone mad.

"Hear me out," I say. "We'll pull some furs over to the main hearth, light the fire, grab some of that whiskey Derek keeps hidden in his desk," I wink at him and his shocked expression, "and we'll tell stories until we fall asleep."

Liam grunts. "Fine, but there will be no braiding of hair."

I nearly choke on my own laughter, and I tug at a long strand of his auburn mane. "But you'd look very fashionable in a fishtail," I say.

Now Derek is laughing, and that giddiness spreads to us all. Elijah nearly falls off his chair, chuckling so hard he's holding his stomach.

Matilda and Lily come in just as we're settling down, bearing a plate of food for me and goblets of blood for the boys. The old woman is all smiles as she hands me a dish full of baked greens and ripe cheeses, then gives a hug to each of her grandsons.

Lily places a hand on my shoulder, beaming proudly. "I knew you could do it," she says.

"Save the trial?" I ask in between bites, feeling ravenous after such a long and grueling night.

"Save my uncles," she says, her eyes a tad watery as she looks at the Night brothers. Then she wraps me in a tight hug and I almost drop my plate, putting it down beside me.

"I couldn't have done it without you," I say. "Your delay of the court proceedings was perfect."

She shrugs, and when she pulls away, Matilda takes her place. She hugs me long and hard. "You did it, my girl. I knew you would. You brought light back into my boys."

"*In lumen et lumen*," I whisper.

I feel wet tears on my neck and then she stands to leave, wiping her face with her hand. I invite them both to the slumber party, but they graciously decline. Lily will sleep in her tree as usual and Matilda says she is too old for such ways, but I think she secretly wants me to spend more time with the boys alone. She's a crafty one, that old lady.

It doesn't take us long to set up everything, and Sebastian surprises me with two gifts. "Tomorrow is the Midwinter Festival," he says. "And...well, here."

The gifts are both wrapped in gold and purple ribbon and I open the first, finding a book of poetry within. My eyes light up. "You remembered."

He nods. "You aren't the only one with a good memory," he says with a shy smile.

The second box contains my heart's desire. Gourmet chocolates.

I throw myself into his arms. "Thank you. This is perfect."

He holds me tightly, and I rest my head on his shoulder, enjoying the solidness of him, the assurance of having him in my life. He is my rock. My mountain. I know he will have my back no matter what.

There's so much to explore with him. With each of them. I'm rather overwhelmed by it all, but there's time.

Now that they've decided to stay, to give life a second chance, there's time for it all.

DEREK IS TELLING a story about a great serpent that wraps around the entire world when sleep takes me. My dreams are not easy things. A wolf devours a lamb, spraying blood on the golden bell of the Broken Cathedral. And the wolf has a face I would rather forget.

When I wake, it is with a gasp, my body covered in sweat.

And I find four men on the alert, ready to comfort me, to hold me, to let me cry.

"It's not your fault," Sebastian assures me, pulling me back into his arms as Liam uses his power to give a fresh blaze to the fire.

The flames steal the chill from the air, and I scoot back under the furs, enjoying the feel of Sebastian and Liam close to me, with Elijah and Derek on either side of them. I could stay like this forever. Perhaps I will.

Something moves at the corner of my eye. A fire iron poking at the fireplace, igniting the wood into brighter flames. But no one else is here. The fire iron moves mid-air on its own. I freeze, clutching Liam's hand.

"What's that?" I ask, pointing at the fire iron. "More of your magic?"

Liam follows my gaze. "What, them? They're just the castle ghosts."

"Ghosts? You mean, there's ghosts in the castle?"

"Yeah, who do you think cleans and cooks and does all the work around here?" He says it so casually, I can't help but laugh.

"I had wondered about it," I say. "But this wasn't what I was expecting. Who are they?"

"These two are called Mable and Cili," says Liam.

Derek rolls his eyes. "You call all of them Mable and Cili."

"True, but only because we don't have a great way to communicate. We can share general ideas, but not specifics."

Elijah sighs, elaborating, "They are ancient beings. Ones who worked for this castle for centuries before we took residence. It would have been rude to kick them out, so instead we made a deal. They keep the castle tidy, and in exchange we maintain their unmarked graves on the grounds. As well as light candles for their souls once a year when the veil is thinnest, allowing them to join the living for a night and celebrate the pleasures of the flesh, as it were."

"Wow," I say. Sometimes simple words are best.

We lie quietly then, all of us bundled up together, gazing into the fire, none of us ready to leave. After a while, I feel Liam tensing beside me, something painful building within. His voice is fraught with nerves when he speaks. "I have something to tell you all. Something you should know about me and Mary."

The truth is hard for Liam to admit, especially to his brothers, but to their credit they remain quiet as he tells his story. "By the time we found out she was pregnant, we were no longer having an affair," he says. "But I had to stand by her to the end. And now, I must stay and stand by my daughter, whatever might come."

"So you're a father," Derek says, with a small smile. "Imagine that."

"Who is taking care of the babe now?" asks Sebastian.

"The Ifrits," says Liam. "Ifi and Elal."

Of course, I realize. *They're granting Mary's last wish.*

Eventually, the natural urges of waking take effect, and I excuse myself to use the bathroom, and we all begin our day. I'm pretty sure it would be night in the mundane world at this hour. But here, in the Otherworld, the schedule of the sun matters little and I've lost all sense of that rhythm. I'm finding a new rhythm in the Otherworld.

As I finish freshening up, Lily bounces into my room, insisting we go shopping for new dresses for the Midwinter festival. I agree, and we make plans to meet the Night brothers at the festivities. At 4:00 a.m. sharp.

Lily offers to take me in the carriage, but I insist she refrain from driving people around on the holiday. Besides, the weather is lovely today. Though snow covers the roads, the air is gentle and warm, the Dragon's Breath burning bright in the sky.

Lily guides me to a nearby market full of odd trinkets and food. Together, we find a deep blue gown with tiny rhinestones sewn in around the collar and cuffs. "This," she says eagerly. "This is perfect. You'll look like the sky at twilight."

I smile and buy the dress, using Otherworld money my job at the Night Firm provides. Gold and silver and copper coins.

Lily buys a dress for herself as well. A leaf-green gown adorned with white flowers. She guides me to the changing room where we can both dress ourselves and then we head out to the center of town.

We can hear the festivities before we see them. Live music filling the streets. Fireworks filling the sky. The smell of freshly baked treats in the air. There are carts and stalls set up along both sides of the street, a hundred different merchants with wares for sale, and I'm practically overwhelmed by all the choices that confront me. We move from stall to stall, taking in the dazzling displays before moving quickly on to the next. My cheeks hurt from so much grinning as I pull Lily ahead faster, excited to let off some steam and party like it's 1699.

We arrive earlier than planned, and the brothers are nowhere to be seen as Lily walks off to grab us drinks. I do notice some familiar faces though.

"Look who we have here," Ifi says. "If it isn't the little mundane who isn't."

Ifi and Elal walk over hand in hand, sipping on purple drinks, their skin aflame with golden fire that they let fade into nothing as they approach.

"I was worried I wouldn't know anyone," I say. "It's so good to see you."

"Elal here thought you'd be long gone by now, but I assured him you're here to stay, isn't that right?" He winks at me.

Elal huffs at that. "I said nothing of the sort. Stop your nonsense, love, and just play nice."

I chuckle at them both. "I am here to stay it seems," I say.

"Consider us your first friends in the Otherworld then," Ifi says, but he's interrupted by another voice, this one low and booming and coming from the sky.

"I believe that title belongs to me." Okura descends from the sky, her stone body massive compared to ours. And near her belly, in a solid pouch that wasn't there before, sits a baby gargoyle. Her mate lands beside her, while Ifi and Elal stare at the youngling, jaws hanging wide open.

"She's beautiful," I tell the doting parents, who are clearly smitten with their creation.

"Thank you for your blessing on her," Okura says.

I still don't know what exactly I did, but I nod and smile, glad it could help them at any rate.

Ifi turns back to look at me. "You're quite full of surprises, Miss Oliver. Working with you will no doubt be entertaining." With that, he takes Elal's hand, and the two of them wonder off to refill their drinks. The gargoyles depart as well, walking to admire the great glowing tree at the center of the square.

I look up, checking the massive iron clock that hangs on a nearby tower. It's 4:00 a.m. now. The brothers should arrive any second.

Lily returns with cups of golden liquid, and the drink tastes like warm honey with a touch of brandy. We explore the festival, watching as a group of gnomes participate in a challenge of strength, smashing a hammer into a golden disk for points. Five minutes pass. Still the brothers do not arrive.

"They're late," I say.

Lily shrugs. "Liam probably just saw a pair of shoes he couldn't resist."

I nod, and we continue, walking past an Ifrit, burning brightly, sitting above a tank of water, as human-looking girls throw balls at a red target connected to a mechanism which would make him fall.

"Are they young werewolves?" I ask.

Lily shakes her head. "Young dryads."

A light rain begins to fall, and another five minutes pass with no sign of the brothers. I start to get irritated. Then worried. "Do you know where they went?" I ask.

Lily shakes her head. "No. But Uncle Liam did mention they had something important to do. I suppose he was a bit more secretive than usual."

Something important to do.

My gut twists into a knot, but I tell myself I have nothing to fear. I'm just being silly. The Night brothers are safe and well.

Another five minutes pass. The rain falls down harder, so much so that we buy cloaks off a vendor at the festival to keep ourselves dry. A chill enters the air and I find my teeth rattling.

Several more minutes pass and the knot in my gut is now a storm of worry. I wonder at where they could be, and I remember something I had forgotten. Something Derek had said at the trial.

It will be done by midwinter.

There is a pain in my chest, and my stomach burns like acid. I have felt like this once before. When my brother left me his final note.

"What's wrong?" asks Lily.

But I have no words in reply, my mind a flurry of doubt. Have they gone through with it? I wonder. Had the smiles and laughter been easier for them than telling me the truth? Had the sleepover been a way of saying goodbye?

I notice a familiar face in the distance. Matilda, wearing her cloak tight around her against the heavy rain. Matilda, who said she was too old for such parties. Matilda, who is coming toward us all the same, her face dark and grim.

A sob begins to break from my lips.

And just as it does…

I hear them.

"What's wrong, Eve?"

"How can we help?"

"What happened?"

"I swear, if someone hurt you…"

I turn around, seeing the four Night brothers crowding around me. And my heart breaks open with tears of happiness.

"Perhaps she's just upset we're late," says Elijah.

"Sorry about that, Eve," says Derek. "We had a bit of an emergency. You see…" He gestures to his brother.

And Liam moves aside his cloak, revealing a little baby girl, hair red as flame.

"She's beautiful," I say, the tears subsiding. "May I hold her?"

"Of course," says Liam, handing me the baby.

"We picked the little thing up from Ifi and Elal an hour ago," says Derek. "And we would have been on time, if Liam hadn't—"

"If Liam hadn't seen a bit of poop and thought she was dying," says Sebastian.

The fire druid shrugs. "What? It was an unordinary amount of excrement. And such a strange color. That can't be normal."

"We had to pick up diapers," concludes Elijah. "And console poor Liam's soul."

I laugh, holding the baby close in the crook of my arm, playing with her little fingers. "Does she have a name yet?"

Liam glances down, looking slightly embarrassed. "I'm naming her Alina. It's Greek for light."

I look down at the cherubic face and smile. "It's perfect. She's perfect." I look at Liam. "Does this mean we're keeping her?"

He nods. "I think it does. She needs her father, after all."

"What about Dracula?" I ask.

"We will keep her safe," Liam says fiercely, and I know this little girl will be the most loved child in any world.

"You look incredible, by the way," says Derek.

"Thank you," I say, with a grin. With my worries subsided, I take a moment to admire the Night brothers properly.

Elijah sports a look I haven't seen on him before. A black coat with purple buttons, a top hat covering his blond hair, a silver cane in his hand. He looks every bit the sophisticated gentlemen, pulled straight from the Victorian era.

Derek has shaved since I last saw him and wears a finely tailored suit, a red scarf wrapped around his neck.

Sebastian is a little more rough around the edges. His jacket and boots are black leather. Simple. Sturdy. But he does sport an elegant pink tie at his neck.

Liam is dressed as he often is, but not any less impressive. Custom designed shoes with fine embroidery. An emerald green cloak that compliments his auburn hair perfectly.

I hand the babe back to Liam as Matilda comes to join us. We exchange greetings, while Elijah and Sebastian begin discussing the finer points of Otherworld law. I link arms with them both and laugh. "You guys, it's a party. No work today. Let's enjoy our victory and our evening, shall we?"

Derek smiles. "Right you are, Eve. Right you are. I for one plan on drinking my body weight in liquor. Who's game to join me?"

"I think that might kill me," I say. "But I will partake in a drink or two." I look at Matilda. "I'll definitely need your hangover cure tomorrow."

The old woman winks knowingly. "I've already prepared a batch for all of you. Now go have fun, my dears."

We make our way through the festival, and I notice it stopped raining almost as quickly as it started. Lucky for us. But as Sebastian tries his hand at the strength competition, the earth seems to shift under my feet, and the Ifrit above the water tank loses balance and falls in.

"A small earthquake," says Elijah. "Nothing to fear. They happen from time to time."

Everyone seems to resume their activities without a second thought, and so we do the same. Derek and Lily make a beeline for the bar to grab everyone drinks. Sebastian offers to acquire sustenance of some kind for me. "If that includes chocolate, yes, please," I say with a wink.

Liam sees someone he knows and excuses himself to say hi, handing the baby to Matilda who has been vying for her chance to give the little one love. Elijah sits down by the huge bonfire with a book in hand. I shake my head at that. I'm a book nerd myself, but even I know when to let it go for a night.

From the corner of my eye, I notice a familiar black cloak disappear behind a tree. Interesting. I didn't expect to see him, not so soon after everything that happened. Curious, I snake away from the celebration and towards the shadows, where I find Dracula waiting.

He holds a hand up before I can speak. "I wanted to say goodbye.

I'll be leaving the Otherworld for a while, to let all the gossip die down. But I wanted to thank you. You were instrumental in proving my innocence. That won't be forgotten."

I don't know what to say, so I just nod, relieved he'll be leaving. That should make protecting Alina easier.

His eyes are dark, intense, and locked on mine as he speaks. "My sons have a unique bond with you. I haven't seen them like this with anyone else in their long lives. I hope you know what you've gotten yourself into."

"I know enough," I say a little tersely.

"Oh, but, my dear, there is so much yet to learn. How great is your capacity for forgiveness, I wonder? I suppose we'll find out in time."

Another tremor rocks the world around us, sending waves of movement through the land. Most of the partiers don't notice, too lost in the revelry and booze. But a few do, and this time they look around, alarmed.

A small smile creeps onto Dracula's lips. "It has begun. Guard yourself, Miss Oliver. No one in the Otherworld is truly innocent."

I shrug. "The same can be said of anyone anywhere. I choose faith and love over doubt and fear. It's a happier way to live."

He nods, then lifts my hand to his lips, kissing it softly. "Then I bid thee farewell. May you hold onto that optimism as long as you can."

And with that he disappears into the shadows, and I wonder if we'll ever see him again. I think of Liam's baby daughter and hope we don't. She's safer that way.

I'm about to turn and head back to the party when something in the grass glints in the light of the Dragon's Breath. I bend down to pick it up and see it's a Memory Catcher.

Curious, I activate it.

I see a familiar room before me.

Cream walls.

White carpet.

I appear to be looking at things through a window.

Looking straight into Mary's chambers.

There's a scream, and the image tilts to the side, revealing Mary on the bed, dressed in a white gown, half-way through labor. Alone. Crying, calling out for help.

I know what happens next.

Jerry will come in soon. He will kill her and the baby, though a young girl will live. I am ready to stop the memory, unwilling to see the gruesome sight, when a person comes through the door.

A person who isn't Jerry.

The man wears a long black cloak I have seen before. When he walks, his steps are achingly familiar.

And when I see his face, my entire body shakes.

This is impossible.

It can't be real.

And yet the memory unfolds.

He steps closer to the bed, silent, expression cold, and Mary pulls back, frightened, confused. Racked with pain.

As she delivers her own baby, the man grabs the child and—

I look away.

I can't have that image in my mind forever.

But I hear it.

What he does with the child. What he does to Mary.

And when I look back at the memory, she is dead. They both are.

A few moments later, Jerry arrives, a letter in hand he quickly shoves into his pocket. He runs to Mary's side, screaming, trying to revive her though she is clearly dead. When he finally realizes his efforts are futile, he notices the blood all over his jacket, his hands. And then he runs.

Minutes pass. Minutes that feel like hours.

I see her belly moving after a moment, and then Liam runs into the room, a look of utter horror on his face as he witnesses the devastation.

I stop the memory, not needing to see more. I know the rest.

I fall to my knees, a sob building in my throat. My nails dig into the wet earth as I feel the pain wash in waves through me.

This has to be a trick.

The memory has to be a fake.

Otherwise, everything I have ever known will shatter.

And then I see his feet, dark, mud-caked boots.

Then his legs.

And I pull myself up, my beautiful dress covered in dirt, as I face the man I thought I knew.

The man I thought I could trust.

And I face Mary's real killer.

A scent of cinnamon and honey catches on the wind, and I am racked with sorrow as blue eyes I know better than my own look back at me. And when he holds out his hand, my heart lurches in my chest.

"Hello, sister."

My voice catches in my throat. "Adam?"

KEEP READING FOR BOOK 2...

I AM the STORM

BOOK TWO

CHAPTER 1 : THE FESTIVAL

WHEN YOU COME out of the storm, you won't be the same person who walked in. That's what this storm's all about. ~Haruki Murakami

"ADAM?" My heart races as my mind tries to process what I'm seeing. My knees dig into the ground, mud from the recent rains soaking into my blue gown. Tears wet my cheeks, and I make no effort to wipe them away.

With shaking legs, I stand to face the man before me.

To stare into the eyes I thought I'd never see again.

The same blue eyes as my own.

My brother cocks his head and smiles crookedly. It's such a familiar gesture that my heart lurches and I take a step forward. Surely, I'm imagining this. Or it's a trick? There's still so much I don't know about the Otherworld. Could someone be impersonating my twin for some cruel reason?

"I know what you're thinking," he says, his long, black coat whipping in the wind as he runs a hand through his dark hair. "But it really is me. I'm sorry, Evie. Sorry about everything."

I narrow my eyes at him, pieces of the past clicking together into a troubling picture. I've seen this coat before. At Lilith's mansion. While I was shopping one day in town. He's been following me, and I never got a good enough look at his face to realize it was him. All this time, I've been seeing my brother in every stranger's face I pass, but I failed to see what was right in front of my eyes.

He reaches for my hand, and as we touch a small jolt of power shoots up my arm. We both widen our eyes in surprise, but we don't let go of each other.

"How?" I ask, my eyes burning with tears. "You were dead. I have your ashes on my fireplace mantle. I mourned for you. I still mourn for you," I say through a heavy wave of emotion, my voice cracking.

He pulls me closer to him, into a hug, his arms wrapping around me, and I lay my head on his chest and hear his heart beat. He feels strong, healthy. The smell of him, of cinnamon and honey catching on the wind, brings me back to childhood memories I had forgotten. Skipping stones on the river. Playing hide and seek by the willow tree. I want to hold onto him forever. To bask in the familiarity of his arms. But then I remember the Memory Catcher.

Mary.

The baby.

And I pull back, shaking, all sense of security shattered. "You're not my brother," I spit, the rage at this deceit boiling up within me. "My brother would never kill anyone. Especially not a child."

He bows his head in the way that always meant he was sorry, and my heart cracks at the familiar gesture. "I had to, Evie," he says, voice soft and yet cold. "The child could not be allowed to grow up."

"What are you talking about?" I ask, tears stinging my eyes. "He was just an innocent baby—"

"No," Adam cuts me off sharply. He speaks quickly, his eyes darting around as if he sees something I do not. "The boy would have killed thousands. On his twentieth birthday, his mother, Mary, is murdered for copulating with a vampire. Murdered by her own fellow humans. Dracula seeks revenge against the killers—destroying them and their families. Anyone who was part of it. But that's not enough for Mary's son. He is the most powerful vampire ever created, and he deems all humans to be treacherous, weak beings. He begins to slaughter them by the hundreds. And those he doesn't kill, he enslaves, like sheep in a pen. His sister tries to stop him. She fails. Then…" He pauses, his voice growing pained as he meets my gaze with bloodshot eyes. "You try to stop him. You fail."

He reaches for my hand, but I pull back and catch a glimpse of the hurt in his eyes.

"How can you possibly know this?" I ask.

"After I died," he says, "I came back. I don't know how. But when I woke, I was not only healed, but… different. Our father was right, Evie. We do have powers. Mine just took longer to manifest than yours." He sounds excited, like the little boy I remember. The boy who stayed at my side as fevers took me after my flashes. "Now I see things," he continues. "Things that have yet to pass. They flow past my eyes like ghosts. Like the future and the present are layered over one another. Both for me to discover. To change for the better."

My jaw clenches. "How could you do it? You…who used to save bees from the hot tub? Who took spiders outside of the house on a napkin?"

He cries then. And despite myself, I wrap my arms around his shoulders and let his head rest in the crook of my neck.

"Evie," he whimpers, his tears running down my skin. "I see horrible things…things I would not wish upon anyone. They are like nightmares, but I can never wake. The only way to stop them…is to change things." He pulls back to look at me. "The girl, Alina, will have a better life now."

At the mention of Liam's baby, my voice softens. "You fool," I say, shaking my head. "You're my best friend. My twin. I was cut in half without you. Why the fake ashes? The hiding? Why didn't you come to me?"

"I wanted to," he says quickly. "But you had to believe I was dead. Otherwise, you never would have gone to work for the Night Firm. It's…important…what you're doing. What you will do."

"What am I going to do?" I ask.

He sighs. "If I told you, it would never happen."

His words would sound ludicrous if I didn't have visions of my own. If I didn't know things I had no right knowing. I thought my brother had been spared from that fate, but it seems his powers were just biding their time.

"Whose memory was that?" I ask, holding up the Memory Catcher. "Someone watched you through the window."

He nods. "You'll meet them in time. For now, just remember..." His eyes drift away, landing on the large iron clock on the tower across the town square, then flick back to me. "I will always protect you, no matter what."

Footsteps.

The shuffling of grass.

"There you are," says Sebastian, emerging from behind the trees, carrying two glasses in one hand and a plate piled with treats in the other. "I heard raised voices," he says. "Was someone bothering you?"

My throat clenches, unsure of how to explain this. I turn back to Adam...but he's gone. Vanished as quickly as he appeared. Even his footprints are gone.

My eyes dart to the forest behind me, but there's no sign of my brother. My gut tells me I'll see him again, though. He still has questions to answer.

I turn back to Sebastian, doing my best to look festive despite the worry I feel. "Dracula was here," I say casually. "He wanted to say goodbye and thank me for my help exonerating him." It's not a lie, but it's not the whole truth, either. "Thanks for grabbing the drinks."

Sebastian smiles, his forest green eyes crinkling around the edges. Every time I see him, he steals my breath. You'd think I'd get used to it, to his earthy sexiness, his aristocratic features, his sculpted muscles and tall, lean body. But the earth Druid turned vampire has an animal magnetism that always catches me off guard. Tonight, he's wearing a black leather jacket and black pants with a white tailored tunic that does nothing to diminish his chiseled body. And his pink tie adds a splash of charm to his badass look.

He hands me a plate piled high with food—brightly-colored

pastries, éclairs stuffed with chocolate and cream, and an oddly shaped set of donuts with not one but two holes in the center—and one of the drinks. His is red—blood most likely, probably mixed with liquor. Mine is a pretty blue color and I sniff at it. Blueberries and honey.

I take a sip, following Sebastian to a stone table where Elijah, Liam, and Derek are already sitting. Liam lifts a crimson bottle to his baby, and I raise an eyebrow at it as I take a seat across from him.

"Do I want to know why Alina's milk is red?" I ask, shuddering to think of the reason.

He turns to look at me, raising an eyebrow at my muddy and disheveled state but apparently too polite to ask what happened in front of everyone else. When I refuse to answer his unspoken inquiry, his golden eyes narrow momentarily but then goes back to feeding his daughter. "She's half vampire," he says, a flock of auburn hair falling across his forehead. "She needs milk and blood. It's a special mix the Ifrits put together."

"Yum," I say, picking at my own food but not actually eating any.

Liam frowns, then winks, and my body heats up at the memory of his kisses, his hands on me, his passion teasing my senses. Our gazes are locked onto one another's as he admires the sapphire blue gown that hugs my curves and I notice the way the emerald green of his cloak brings out his eyes.

But then the bottle slips from Alina's mouth and a trickle of milky blood stains her pink dress. Liam breaks eye contact with me to tend to her, and I mentally fan myself to cool off from the memories of his body pressed against mine.

Elijah, who sits next to Liam, sips at his blood cocktail and smiles, his silver-white hair swept back in a tie, his top hat covering most of it. He's very dashing in a fine black coat with purple buttons and silver walking stick. "We should buy her red clothing, to hide the blood stains," the air Druid says. "There is much research to be done on raising a hybrid child. We've never had an infant in the family." As if his own comment inspires him, he pulls a book out of his breast pocket and begins to read. I just chuckle and sip at my drink.

"You've hardly touched your food," Sebastian says with a nudge to my shoulder. "Not to your liking? I can get you something else."

His attentiveness is touching, and I smile warmly at him while inwardly I wince. "I'm just not very hungry," I say. Seeing my dead brother has sapped my appetite, I want to add. But I can't. Not yet. I trust the Night brothers. I do. They've become my family. But they're lawyers, sworn to uphold the law. And my brother...my brother is a murderer. Who let another man take the fall for his crimes. He may be justified in his actions, or he might be insane. He could be lying, but that seems the least likely. I can't imagine him evil. Not that. Anything but that. But either way, I can't risk the Nights turning him in while I'm figuring out what to do. I already lost my twin once. I won't lose him again.

Derek, sitting on the other side of me, wraps an arm around my shoulders and leans in to kiss my head. "Don't drink too much without food in you. Matilda has tonics ready for us all after tonight, but they take time to work, and you're not going to enjoy the taste."

The charismatic water Druid stands, adjusting his red scarf as he scans the crowds. "I'm off to mingle. Don't get too crazy," he says good-naturedly.

Elijah stands as well, tucking his book into his jacket. "I will join you, brother. Ifi and Elal look like they could use a few drinking companions."

I glance to where he's pointing and see the Ifrits engaged in some kind of elemental drinking game. Derek grins and they leave together, greeting the two men with laughter and back slaps.

Around us the festivities continue. Lily is dancing in her long green gown with other dryads, their movements flowing like leaves in the wind, their true forms flashing in and out as an elf plays a fiddle and a woman who looks part mermaid with scales lining her skin sings a haunting song in a strange language. It's entrancing.

Liam stands with Alina, catching my gaze as he cradles her in his arms. "I'll see you in a bit?" he asks. I nod and he heads to a nearby fire pit where the two gargoyles, Okura and Akuro are perched, talking softy. Well, softly for gargoyles. When Liam reaches them, Okura—the female gargoyle who recently gave birth—pulls her baby out of the pouch so the two newborns can meet. Maybe they'll grow up to be friends. What a lucky childhood Alina will have.

I don't see Matilda, and I wonder briefly if she went home.

Everywhere there is laughter and great anticipation for the night that is to come. Even Lilith is here, her long dark hair slick and shiny as she raises a glass in toast with Kana, the Kitsune who helped us untangle the mysteries surrounding Mary's letters.

Beyond the town center, towering over the stalls and booths, is the courthouse. Large enough to accommodate dragons and all manner of magical creatures, casting a long shadow across the town with its gothic architecture and gray stonework.

Sebastian and I are the only two left at the table. He is my rock, my foundation in a very strange world, and as he lays a hand on mine, I want to unburden my soul. But instead I pull away, fighting every urge in me to grab onto him and not let go, to hold him close and feel his strength embrace me and erase my fear and worry.

"Everyone looks to be having a wonderful time," I say, hating myself for making small talk with Sebastian of all people.

"That does appear to be the case," he says. "But are you? You seem lost in thought."

Before I can answer, we're interrupted by the arrival of someone intent on saying hello to Sebastian. The newcomer is short, with the upper body of a man—and a very hairy one at that, given that he isn't wearing a shirt and I can still see the thick mat covering his chest and back—and the lower body of a goat. Thankfully, his lower half is covered by a pair of bright purple pants. Sebastian reluctantly engages in conversation with him, and I'm left a bit dumbstruck at the thought that I've just met my first faun.

I say a brief hello and introduce myself, then turn my attention to the party. I search each person, looking for Adam's face in theirs. Looking for my twin. But I know he's gone. The real question is, will he come back?

I'm distracted from thoughts of my brother when someone catches my eye, a beautiful man gliding through the crowd, dressed entirely in black to match his hair. When he looks my way, I suck in my breath, but I can't turn away. His eyes are dark as night, void of any color. The blackest eyes I've ever seen. And I feel a compulsion I can't explain. I want to be closer to him. To never stop looking at him. To touch him.

He stops to stand in front of a bonfire like a shadow in the flames, mesmerizing. His eyes don't leave mine and his expression is curious. He smiles and I melt inside.

I'm about to stand and walk towards him. Power beyond myself compels me to do so, but then the clock tower clangs loudly, pulling my gaze from his for just a moment. When I look back, the man is gone, and I feel a bitter disappointment.

But his image is seared in my mind, and I kick myself for not bringing my sketchbook tonight. My fingers are itching to draw him. To capture every nuance of his look and expression on paper.

The clock tower continues to chime, and as it does, an overwhelming sense of wrongness takes hold within me. A flash grips me and I stand and follow its pull towards the woods. If I don't move, if I don't obey the compulsion, I will be too sick to function. It has happened before.

Sebastian realizes I'm leaving and grabs my hand. "Are you well?"

But when he sees my face, he frowns and walks away from his conversation with the faun "What's happening?" he asks urgently.

"Something's wrong," I whisper, but it's hard to speak. Hard to form words. I just have to...move. "We have to get out of here."

I pull him with me farther away from the crowd.

The chime ends.

The clock tower explodes.

The force rocks the world beneath my feet, and it's only Sebastian's hold on me that keeps me from collapsing.

From the corner of my eye I see a familiar form surrounded by mist, her eyes sad, her mouth forming my name.

"Eve."

I hear it on the wind. The woman with skin dark as midnight and long silver braids that flow down her back. A silver horn protrudes from her forehead and her large silver eyes watch me with curiosity.

I scream as another flash seizes me and clutch my head as my brain feels as if it's squeezed into a vise. I struggle to focus, my head pounding, bile rising in my throat. And then I smell it. Smoke. Ash. Fire. The rising dust of falling debris. And then I hear the screams.

I turn to look at the town square and I see the flames, the panic, the people struggling to flee the courtyard, a brave few trying to put out the blaze with buckets of water. Smoke billowing everywhere, choking the oxygen out of my lungs. People clearing away rubble. Part of the courthouse has collapsed. The part holding the clock. The source of the explosion. And then I remember.

I look around for Lily. The other Night brothers. I don't see them. I don't see any of them. Panic seizes me. "We need to find your brothers," I yell.

"Let's go," he says, grabbing my hand.

We run towards the direction of the explosion.

I ditch the cloak that's slowing me down, and I try to pull out whatever power is in me. Can I put out the flames? Help in some way?

Enforcers dressed in black leather organize a group to help put out the fire. It spreads beyond the courthouse, taking down other buildings and many stalls and booths. The Ifrits run in and out of the blaze, pulling people from under the fallen structures, the flames dripping off them like oil. One of the gargoyles flies large buckets of water from a nearby stream, but it's not enough.

I have to find a way to help.

Anxiety clutches me and I struggle to breathe, to calm my mind. Where are the others? My mind spins with all my deepest fears of losing those I love. If they were near the blast, they could be dead, and I can't handle losing more of my family. Tears burn my eyes and the world feels like it's closing in on me.

Sebastian pauses and glances at me. "Eve?"

But I can't answer him. I'm hyperventilating and I feel dizzy and scared. Like my heart is going to explode.

Sebastian turns to me, putting his hands gently on my face, and I feel a pulse of his earth power flow into me. It's strong, steady, stable, safe.

"Breathe with me," he says, slowing his own breath and encouraging me to do the same.

"Focus on my voice. Focus on my hands on your face."

His hands do feel good, and his voice is deep and rhythmic. Calming.

Finally, I use the tools I have learned over the years to manage my anxiety attacks. I focus on my senses. On identifying and counting things I can see, taste, touch, smell, hear.

And then I feel it.

Welling up within me.

My power.

I close my eyes.

Water. We need water. I put everything I am into that thought, that feeling of covering the earth with water.

Thunder breaks through the sky.

Wind whips around us.

And then...

The rain falls.

I open my eyes, and see Sebastian looking at me in wonder. "Did you do that?" he asks, looking up at the sky.

"I think I did."

His eyes widen in awe, and he caresses my cheek. "You're incredible."

I put my hand on his and smile. "Thank you for helping me. Now, let's go find our family."

The rain continues to pour, a storm building around us. It's not enough to put out the flames entirely, but it's helping.

I call out for Derek, for Liam, for Lily. I look around for Elijah. Where is everyone?

We reach the origin of the explosion, a shattered clock and a crater in the earth, and I suck in a sob. How could anyone survive this? "Liam had Alina with him," I say in despair.

Sebastian squeezes my hand. "He'll protect her. She's part fire Druid, remember. Flames can't hurt them."

I let out my breath. I hadn't thought of that. But..."Falling rubble can," I say.

We jog along the edges of the flames, and I spot a familiar shoe sticking out from part of the collapsed stone structure. "Sebastian!" I scream, pointing.

It's Derek. Face paler than usual. Eyes glazed over. His head and feet the only part of him visible from beneath the rubble. I rush to his side. Start lifting away rocks. One is too heavy for me. My hands are cut and bleeding, but my tears aren't from pain but rather fear. Every moment he's trapped could be a moment too late.

And then a large pillar begins to rise on its own, floating into the air and landing beside me with a hard thud.

I turn to stare at Sebastian, whose forest green eyes are wide with awe. His hands are raised, and I can feel the power emanating from them.

"That was you, wasn't it?" I ask.

He nods.

I stand back as he makes quick work of the rest of the debris, until there's nothing left trapping Derek. I clutch the vampire in my arms. His body is broken, bloodied, and unnaturally still. "No!" I yell.

The flames rage around us, but I don't care. All of my focus is on the unconscious vampire in front of me.

Smoke chokes me as I tilt his head to give him CPR, compressing his chest just as I learned in the classes Adam and I took together when he first got his diagnosis.

I do everything I can, but nothing works. I look to Sebastian, panic on my face. "He's not waking up."

"He needs blood," Sebastian says, kneeling next to me, his hands supporting his brother's head gently.

I nod, knowing what I need to do. I hold up my wrist to Sebastian. "I don't have a knife, can you... "

He knows what I'm asking and takes my wrist into his mouth, biting deeply. The pain only lasts a moment, then a strange pleasure spreads through me. When my blood touches Sebastian's tongue his eyes widen, and he sucks more out before he realizes what he's doing and pulls himself away.

"Eve," he whispers, his pupils dilated, but I can't focus on him right now. I hold my wrist over Derek's mouth, letting my blood drip down his throat.

After a few moments, Derek stirs, his mouth seeking my blood, and he begins to drink.

My head spins and I feel dizzy from blood loss when strong arms pull me away from Derek. Sebastian cradles me in his arms. "You can't give him too much," he says sternly.

I look into his eyes and flick my lids. "You really are always mad at me for something," I say half-jokingly.

Then I hear Derek shift and sit up. He takes my wrist into his hand and licks at the puncture marks there, closing them.

Another explosion rocks the ground, and as terror spreads through the crowd, a figure emerges from the flames of the courthouse.

At first, it looks like an Ifrit, so lit up by fire is he, but as he nears us, I realize who it is, and I swallow a sob and run towards him.

"Liam!"

The fire Druid looks toward me, and I notice the bundle under his cloak, protected from the flames. He pulls out the infant as the fire dies around him. Alina lets out a piercing wail, and I release my breath in relief as I reach them and throw myself into his arms, burying my face in his neck.

He smells of smoke and magick, and my tears burn off his hot skin like rain hitting scalding pavement. "I feared you were both dead," I say.

His lips find mine and he kisses me deeply, his daughter between us, her tiny hand gripping onto a lock of my hair and tugging as Liam's passion consumes us both.

We are so lost in each other that, at first, I don't hear it, but then, a distant sound intrudes on my consciousness. It's faint but grows in clarity as it draws closer and before long, I recognize it as the beating of wings.

Very large wings.

As I pull away from Liam, I can feel the wind on my face, pulsing in time with the beat of those wings, and as I look up, I see a massive blue dragon descending from above. It is slightly smaller than Dath'Racul, with a sleek, elegant body and deep blue scales reflecting the light like sparkling sapphires. Each of the six living dragons embody an element, I recall, and as this dragon begins to roar, a powerful stream of icy water pours forth from its mouth, striking the flames with a steaming hiss, quenching them more quickly than anything else thus far.

Water falls on us, soaking through our hair and clothes, and from the dying flames and gray smoke, Elijah emerges, silver hair wild in the wind, head bowed, shoulders slumped. A limp body lies in his arms, with skin charred black. And when he comes closer, I see who he's carrying.

Lily.

CHAPTER 2: THE CRIME

YOU ARE A STORM IN TRANSITION, *even as these words are being written.*
  ~Nikita Gill

MY GUT CLENCHES as I run to the wind Druid, the rain I created with my powers growing stronger as emotions flood me, surging my magick. The wind grows fierce and lightning flashes across the sky.

"Is she—?" I'm afraid to say the word as my tears mix with the rain.

"She's alive," Elijah says, "but by a thread. We have to get her home. To her tree."

It takes a moment to see the smallest movement of her chest and I exhale in relief. She's still breathing, but I can barely imagine how. Her beautiful punk hair is singed, and her skin is covered in charred burns that swell with puss. If she were human, I would have no hope, but she's not, so anything is possible. You'll be fine, I think. You have to be fine. I cling to that thought as my hand falls to Elijah's back and we walk as quickly as possible to the carriage. Sebastian helps Derek stand up and Liam follows with Alina in his arms, covered by his cloak to protect her from the smoke and rain.

Elijah, Liam, and I squeeze in the back, and while I hold the baby, the fire Druid begins to examine Lily's wounds. Sebastian and Derek sit up front, and Sebastian takes the reins to guide us home.

The horses whinny at the clash of thunder in the sky, and I realize my storm is taking on a life of its own. The question is whether it's doing more harm than good at this point.

I take a breath and try to calm my emotions as the baby in my arms fusses and begins to cry. I hold her closer and rock her, whispering soothing platitudes while I watch Liam.

"How bad is it?" I ask, still marveling that Liam is the healer of the four. I would have pegged the water Druid as a man of medicine, not the fiery hot-headed vampire before me.

He glances up, his expression grim "She needs balms to soothe the burns. Tinctures to facilitate recovery. Even those...may not be enough."

I kiss Alina's head, fighting the tears as I watch one of my closest friends fight for her life.

Sebastian is pushing the horses as fast as he can, but we suddenly grind to a stop after some time of bumping along the dirt road, and Liam and Elijah frown.

"I'll check to see what's going on," I say, taking the baby with me while they stay with Lily.

Outside, other carriages and travelers have halted as well. It seems the bridge ahead is closed. Derek is still sitting up front, looking a little peaked from being buried under stones. Sebastian is standing in front of an Enforcer, arms crossed over his chest, looking pissed and impatient.

"What's going on?" I ask, walking up to them.

Sebastian gestures to the Enforcer, who's dressed all in black and has a sword hanging from his hip. "He says everyone leaving town has to be searched."

I look to the Enforcer. "Why? Is this because of the explosion?" I ask.

The Enforcer's brown eyes widen, and I wonder what his supernatural race is. He passes as pretty human. At least until I realize he has tiny horns on his forehead that were covered by the hood of his cloak.

"I don't know anything about an explosion," he says. "A dragon egg—
the dragon egg—has been stolen. By order of the Council of Dragons,
no one may leave town without a thorough search."

I place a hand on Sebastian's arm. "We need to allow it so we can
get going. Lily's not doing well."

His frown deepens but he nods.

The Enforcer pats Sebastian down, who clenches his jaw and his
fists to keep from lashing out at the man doing his job.

When the Enforcer turns to me, I sigh and pass the baby to Sebastian, who cradles her gently as the man pats me down. When he gets to
the pockets in my cloak, he pulls out the Memory Catcher Adam left
me and my breath hitches.

"What's this?" he asks.

I take it from his hand. "It's for work. We're lawyers," I say,
though technically I'm not quite a lawyer in this world.

Sebastian raises an eyebrow at me, his gaze falling to the crystal in
my hand. He'll know it's not one of theirs. He'll wonder why I have it.
And I don't have a good answer.

The Enforcer nods. "Right. You defend all the criminals. Like
Dracula."

I can tell by his voice that he doesn't approve, and Sebastian's
spine stiffens even more. "Everyone deserves a fair trial," he says
through his teeth.

The Enforcer doesn't respond. Instead he asks to see the baby.

"Seriously?" I say. "We have a friend in the carriage dying from
burns. This baby has just been through hell. We need to get them
home. Do you think we're smuggling a dragon egg in her diaper?" I'm
about to lose my shit, and the anger triggers heat to grow in my hands.
I look down at them and realizing they're hissing in the rain, small
tendrils of fire spitting from my fingers.

Sebastian notices and grabs one of them, pulling me closer to him
as he holds the baby with the other hand. He leans into me to whisper
in my ear, "Stay calm. Take a deep breath."

I do as he says, grateful the Enforcer didn't see me. He's instead
peeking into the baby blanket to pat Alina down, who doesn't enjoy
the disruption and begins to wail.

231

"What the hell are you doing to my daughter?" Liam yells, stepping out of the carriage, flames dancing around his hands.

Unlike me, he does nothing to hide his fire or stem his anger.

The Enforcer steps back, putting a hand on the hilt of his sword. "Step back, vampire. Or you'll be arrested. I need to search your carriage."

I realize that this will escalate quickly if Liam doesn't chill. I leave Alina with Sebastian and slip my arm around Liam. "We need to let him, or he won't allow us to leave and Lily could die," I say softly as I try to cool his fire with my own powers.

It seems to work, and he simmers down as the Enforcer searches our carriage and pats down the rest of us. When he's done, he sighs, looking more tired than before. "You may go to your home, but just so you know…there will be no leaving the Otherworld for anyone until the egg is found, by order of the Council of Dragons." He pauses, looking at Lily through the carriage window. "I'll provide an escort to help you move along quickly. I hope your friend recovers."

ONCE WE RETURN to the castle, Sebastian takes the baby to her crib while Liam carries Lily to her tree. Elijah and I follow at his heels. Worry for my friend consumes me. We wind through the expansive castle, the grandeur of it lost on me as my focus remains on the shallow breaths Lily is taking. They seem to be coming further and further apart.

When we finally get to the area where her tree lives, I gasp. The gorgeous blossoms of emerald and crimson, burnt-orange and deep purple, have shriveled, petals dropping to the floor, branches hanging like dead weight from the trunk, a black charred coating covering everything. "What happened to it?" I ask, shocked at the sight.

"Lily and her tree are connected," Liam says. "If she dies, it dies, and vice versa."

He moves forward and the center of the massive trunk opens like a womb. He gently places her into it then steps back.

I sit on my knees and clutch Lily's hand as the trunk begins to close around her. Vines grow over her skin and her eyes flicker open for just a moment. She grips my hand with more strength than I expected. "I saw him," she whispers. "I saw him…"

"Who did you see?" I ask.

But she's already unconscious, the vines spreading over her face. I expect a miracle. To see her charred coating fall away, replaced by fresh skin, but the tree and Lily remain the same. Near death, lifeless, charred. Isn't she supposed to be healing?

Behind me, I hear yelling. Liam's voice. Sharp and mean. "Who else would have done this? Take note of who was injured or almost injured. Our family. My daughter. The Van Helsings want revenge, and this is how they're doing it," he shouts.

"There's no proof," says Elijah, much more calmly but just as loud.

"Then I'll find some," hisses the fire Druid. "Even if I have to wring it from their stupid throats."

I turn away from Lily, my gaze following their voices to the doorway. Liam heads for the exit, but Elijah blocks his path. "You cannot go after them, brother. It will only make things worse." He places a hand on Liam's shoulder.

"Let go of me."

Elijah doesn't. "Use your head for once. If you attack the Van Helsings, you'll end up in jail. How will that help Alina?"

"At least she'll be safe with them gone." Liam raises his hand, flames dancing on his fingers. "But I'm not surprised you'd rather do nothing. You can read books about heroes all you want. But you'll never be one."

Elijah's eyes widen. "I'm not trying to be a—"

"Get out of my way!"

Liam shoves his brother aside, and then flies backwards as if hit by a car, slamming into the nearby wall. He stays there, struggling, as if pinned to the stone.

"I won't let you go," says Elijah, his black jacket drifting in a wind I cannot feel.

"Stop," I yell. "Both of you—"

But before I can finish, flames explode from Liam's hand and fly towards his brother. A whip of wind knocks it out of the air. Elijah raises his arm and—

"You will cease this insolence at once," roars Matilda. The small old lady emerges from the doorway, her pinched face filled with fury. She then grabs Liam and Elijah each by the ear, dragging them both down to her height.

"Ouch," squeal both the brothers at once. But they don't fight back. Instead, their faces turn red as they avoid Matilda's disapproving gaze as much as possible.

The wind dies down.

The fire goes out.

Matilda sighs. "I leave you alone for one moment and look what happens. You turn into naughty schoolchildren." She turns to Liam. "Lily needs your healing. Are you going to let her die?"

Liam drops his head. He, at least, has the decency to look ashamed. "No."

"If I let you go, will you behave?" Matilda asks.

"Yes," Liam says gruffly.

"And you?" she asks Elijah.

"I will," he says, still looking away. "You know I will."

She sniffs and lowers her hands, releasing both brothers. "You both need to cool off and clear your heads. And don't you dare use your powers against each other in this house again!"

"Yes, Matilda," they say in unison, rubbing at their ears.

"Now that you're done being idiots," I interject. "Something's wrong. Lily doesn't look any better," I say. "The tree isn't healing."

Liam frowns. "I need milkweed," he says, looking to Matilda.

"We are out," she says. "And nothing will be open with all the chaos. But I know someone who will have some. I'll send a message to have them bring it here as soon as they're able."

I gaze at Liam. "Will Lily be okay?" I ask.

"I won't know until I get her the potion." He sighs. "In the meanwhile, I'll do what I can." He walks back over to the tree and kneels by Lily, placing his hands over her and muttering words I don't understand.

"I'll stay with you," I say, but he shakes his head.

"Go clean up, get some food. You're going to need your strength."

I look down at my mud and ash and water-soaked dress and realize he's right. I'm a mess. "Okay, but keep me posted?"

He nods. "Matilda. Can you fetch me the salves from my room? Second drawer?"

She nods, walking past Elijah. "You should all clean up," she says to him. "It's going to be a long night."

ONCE I STRIP my ruined gowned off my bruised and tired body, I do the hand motion to turn on the magical waterfall-like shower and step into the stone enclosure. The hot water soothes my tired muscles and washes away the grime that's caked to my skin and in every crevice of my body.

Closing my eyes, I take a moment to sift through everything that's happened in the last forty-eight hours.

Winning Dracula's case.

Jerry's death.

The emergence of my powers.

That kiss with Liam.

The Night brothers choosing life over suicide when their sire bond was broken.

Liam's child coming to live with us.

My brother returning from the dead.

The explosion.

The injuries.

Lily almost dying.

How can so much happen in such a short time? In any given moment, life can change forever, and you'll never know when that change is about to hit.

How do we get through life with so much uncertainty? So much that's out of our control?

The worst of all these moments flash in my mind and anxiety creeps into me slowly, overtaking my senses. My heart rate increases, and my body begins to shake. I lean against the stone wall and wrap my arms over my chest, then sink to the floor, letting the fear and pain consume me. Sobs wrack my body and everything in me turns dark until I can't see or feel or hear anything.

There's nothing around me but emptiness. Black emptiness. I scream but nothing comes out. Panic seizes me. I try to summon the tools to calm myself, but I can't. It's too much. It's all too much!

But then strong hands grip my shoulders. A soft voice whispers in my ear. My eyes pop open and I look around.

Derek kneels before me, his body glistening with moisture, his short dark hair spiky and wet, his ocean blue eyes pulling me in. The only thing he wears is a linen towel wrapped around his waist. His expression is cautious, but his gaze is warm, and his eyes quickly trail my body then land once again on my face.

"Are you hurt?" he asks.

"I...I don't know—"

He moves towards me, closing the distance between us until our bodies are touching. I suck in a breath as I realize just how little stands between our naked flesh. He seems to have the same realization as evidence of his arousal disturbs his towel.

"I heard you scream," he says.

"I screamed? I don't remember screaming. I was taking a shower and just... thinking about everything that's happened. I guess...I don't know. It all went black."

He raises a hand to cup my face, peering into my eyes. "This is a lot to take in. More than we expected when we hired you. If you regret your choice to work here, to live here, I would understand." He looks sorrowful...almost ashamed.

Is he giving me an out? A way to leave all this behind?

The Night Firm.

The brothers.

I have no life to return to, but I could start a new life, I suppose. Manage a company in New York like I used to, or maybe travel some-where else. Maybe focus on my art. Everything would be fine. Normal.

But that's a lie.

Even if I wanted to leave the Otherworld behind, it would never leave me. Not if I kept having flashes and abilities beyond my control.

Not if I knew my brother was out there somewhere, having visions of his own.

I look Derek in the eyes. My body is practically vibrating, being so near him, and I can't help but close the last breath of space between us, my chest now grazing his ever so slightly. "I don't regret my choices," I say. "But I'm not exactly sure what you thought I was when you hired me." I think of what I did to Jerry. Of what my brother did…my eyes go to the floor, shame and fear warring within me.

"My dad always said to stay in the light," I say. "*In lumen et lumen.* In the light, of the light. What if…" I pause, unsure how to articulate what I've been feeling. "What if he knew that there was something bad in me? Something dark? What if I'm a danger to the firm? To you?" I ask, for the first time expressing the fear that's been building in me since Jerry's death.

Derek blinks, but instead of answering he leans in and claims my lips with his.

The kiss is so unexpected it takes my body a moment to figure out what to do. How to respond. But then I return his passion with my own, knowing it's been building for some time. Through all our long nights preparing for Dracula's defense, through our talks about life and hopes and dreams, through the days of fear that he and his brothers wouldn't be here after the trial.

He pulls me closer to him, shifting his hand to the back of my head, deepening our embrace as I wrap my arms around his waist and splay my hands across the corded muscles of his naked back. My right palm grazes a wound that hasn't fully healed yet, and though he doesn't flinch, I pull back to look at him, though I regret it the moment our lips are no longer touching. I can still taste him in my mouth. Smokey and minty.

"I've wanted to do that for a long time," he says in a husky voice laced with unspent desire. "Ever since you first walked into that interview."

"Then why didn't you?" I ask softly.

He laughs, and it's a rich, deep sound that reminds me of waves crashing on a shore and the warmth of the sun on my face. The smell of coconut. The taste of salt.

"I…" His words turn into a painful groan.

"You're still hurt," I say, tracing the wound on his back. A pink slash from his shoulder to his hip.

He nods. "It will heal. I would be much worse without your blood flowing through me. Eve…" he whispers my name with reverence and awe, and it melts my insides. "You saved my life."

My lips slightly part, my body mesmerized by his voice as I feel his wound throbbing beneath my fingers. "You need more blood."

His eyes widen. "We have reserves stashed away. I will be fine."

But I can feel his need as if it's my own and I tilt my head, exposing my neck to him in an unspoken invitation. My breath stills as I wait for him to decide.

And when his lips caress the vein pulsing under my flesh, I sigh in pleasure and close my eyes.

It only hurts a moment, as his teeth sink into me, but then I am flooded with ecstasy so intense my legs go weak. Derek clutches me closer to him, holding me upright as he drinks deeply. His arousal rock hard and pressing against my belly through his towel.

It takes everything in me not to shed the barrier between us and claim him. I run my fingers along his back, feeling his wound fade away, and—

A knock on the door breaks the spell between us, and Derek pulls back.

"Hurry up in there," yells Sebastian. "We need you in the study. Moira Van Helsing is here."

~

DEREK LEAVES THE BATHROOM FIRST. Even after I'm dried and dressed in a cream tunic and dark linen pants, my body still feels swollen with need. But then I recall my recent make-out session with Liam, and I'm not sure how I feel. I want Derek. I want Liam. I want both. So what do I do?

It's not like poly relationships are unheard of, even in my world, but I've never been in a relationship with more than one guy at a time and I don't quite know the rules. And well…I don't really have time to figure them out. Not if Moira's here. Not if Liam is hell-bent on making the Van Helsings pay. This could go south fast.

I pull my wet hair into a bun then head to the library. When I arrive, Elijah offers me a brandy, chocolate covered strawberries, and a plate full of food. I take the silver tray gratefully and sit on the love seat in front of the large hearth, letting the flames pull the chill from my body. Castles are glamorized in modern media, but no one ever tells you how cold they get. The hanging tapestries and rugs aren't just for decor, but for some semblance of insulation.

I notice my plate is piled high with foods rich in iron—beef, beans, dried apricot, and a baked potato—and I glance at Elijah who gives me a slightly rueful smile as he takes a seat next to me.

"If you're going to continue sharing your blood, you need to keep your iron levels up," he says in explanation, slipping his arm around me in protective manner.

At the moment, we're the only ones here, and I take comfort in his presence. Elijah is a quiet man. Thoughtful and careful with his words. A quality I appreciate about him, particularly since it's something I lack in myself.

"Thank you," I say, trying the potato. I don't think I'm hungry, but the moment I start eating I discover I'm ravenous, and I clean my plate in record time. Elijah squeezes my shoulder and nods his head approvingly.

When Derek and Sebastian arrive, Matilda escorts Moira into the study. She's wearing an impeccably tailored dark suit and a crisp blue shirt. Her long blond hair is pulled up in a bun and, as usual, not a hair seems out of place. Despite her outward appearance, one look into her eyes shows how unsettled she is.

Liam is nowhere to be seen. He must still be helping Lily. Good. His presence would only complicate things right now.

Moira looks around nervously, clutching a piece of parchment in her hand.

Sebastian faces her, his face hard. "Did you come to confess?" he asks harshly.

She blanches at his tone. "Confess? Whatever for?"

"For trying to kill us in that explosion!" he says, and I realize though he and Liam butt heads all the time, they're more alike than they want to admit. It actually warms my heart to see Sebastian taking his brother's side, even if it is escalating the situation.

"We didn't try to kill you," says Moira. "We didn't set the fire. Why would we?"

"Let's see…" Elijah says. "Your family hates us, even more so since the death of your despicable brother." His hand tightens around my shoulder with his words, and I shift towards him.

Moira pales. "That's actually why I'm here. Because…" she fidgets with the paper in her hands. "I'm here because we found the letter Jerry received. The one asking him to go to Dracula's house. I…I wanted to show it to you. To prove he wasn't the murderer."

It's my turn to lose all the blood in my face. I already know Jerry wasn't guilty of the murders, but the Night brothers do not. They don't know about Adam. And it sickens me to my stomach.

Derek approaches Moira and takes the letter, scanning it quickly. "How do we know it's not fake?"

"You can keep it," she says quickly. "Have it analyzed. Whatever you want to do. It doesn't change anything, I know. But I just…" she stumbles on her words, then turns to me. "I just wanted someone to know that though Jerry could be an asshole, he wasn't a killer. I don't know who murdered Mary and her child, but it wasn't my brother."

Derek scoffs. "This only proves he wasn't lying about the letter. It doesn't mean he didn't kill them."

There are tears in her eyes, and despite everything, I feel for her. I stand and take the letter from Derek, reading it over. When I'm done, I hand it back to Moira. "I believe you," I say quietly.

Everyone looks surprised.

Especially the Van Helsing. "You…you do?" she asks

"Yes. If Derek wants to have the letter examined that's fine, but I don't need to. I believe you." Because I know the truth. And because I know how important it is to believe that your own brother, your own flesh and blood, isn't all evil. And though I can't stand Moira, and she put me through hell on the stand during Dracula's trial, I can't let her believe a lie.

She's trying very hard not to cry as she clears her throat. "Thank you, Eve. I...I wasn't expecting that."

I don't know what to say, so I just nod.

She glances down at her shoes, then back up at me again. "I...I know Jerry hurt you. I know he..." she swallows before continuing. "I know he abused you. You weren't the first and probably wouldn't have been the last. We've been covering up his behavior for too long. I'm... I'm so sorry. You didn't deserve that."

Now I'm the one fighting tears. I thought I'd processed my shit with Jerry. With the abuse. With his death. But this kind of healing happens in layers, and there are a shit ton of layers to work through. Just when I think I've got it covered, another wave of emotion hits me. I wonder if I'll ever be rid of that asshole or if he'll always haunt my soul in some way.

"I appreciate that," I say, keeping my voice calm. She's trying, and I don't want to ignore that, but I also can't just let her think a quick 'sorry' is enough. She's part of the problem and she needs to own that. We all have to own our part in the trauma we create for others.

"Listen...Moira, the way you treated me on the stand? The questions you asked me? The victim blaming? Those things weren't okay. You became complicit in his abuse." My words are harsh, but my tone is soft.

She bows her head. "I could say I was just doing my job. It would be the truth."

"Sure," I say, agreeing. "You could say that. But is that the person you really want to be?"

She shakes her head, and when she makes eye contact with me again, the tears she's been holding back flow freely. "You don't understand what it's like to love someone, to be so close to someone who is capable of such acts. It tore my heart in two. Jerry and I were best friends growing up. How could I turn on him? I thought I could help him. Save him from his darkest impulses. He wasn't all bad." She chokes out her last words, and I do something that surprises both of us. I pull her into a hug.

"I do understand," I whisper to her. "I do."

She cries into my shoulder, and the Night brothers watch silently as I console a woman I would have considered my enemy twenty minutes ago.

Maybe she's still my enemy. We will certainly face each other in court again. Or maybe everyone we meet has a story that would break our hearts, if only we took a moment to hear it. And maybe when we hear those stories, and see those people with new eyes, we will realize none of us are all that different from one another. We all make the best choices we can with what we have. Some of us just have less than others. Some of us have more to lose.

Some of us can't handle the heartbreak again.

Eventually her tears dry, and I walk her out. Something has shifted between us. How long it lasts or what it will look like another day, I have no idea. But for now, Moira and I see each other in a new light, and I grip her hand before she leaves and squeeze it. I don't have words to offer her, but I think we both share the moment just fine in silence.

When I return, Elijah stands and pulls me into his arms.

He isn't the brother I expected to offer comfort, but I accept it. And as we hold each other close, I lose track of time and forget my worries. Even if just for a moment.

～

SOME TIME LATER, Liam joins us. No one mentions the visit from Moira. He's too concerned as it is.

"Has the milkweed come?" he asks.

"Not yet," I say. "We're waiting. How's Lily doing?"

"Not well. But no worse." He walks over to a crib in the corner of the library where Alina is sleeping peacefully, and stares down at her, his eyes softening. "Do you think she dreams? Do you think she knows what happened to her mother and brother?"

Guilt floods me at his words. Because I know the truth that he doesn't. And the secret is a cancer eating away at my soul. "I think she feels safe here. She feels safe and happy with you," I say honestly.

He smiles at me, then begins pacing the room as we all wait for the medicine to arrive. I pull out my sketchbook and distract myself with a new drawing. Without thinking, I find myself sketching the mysterious man I saw at the festival. His dark eyes and confident posture. The way he held my gaze with his. The way I felt him calling to me, connecting to me.

I'm so lost in my drawing that when someone knocks on the door, I nearly break my pencil in surprise.

I stick it back into my bag and stand. "Lily's medicine?" I ask. It must be. It's been so long.

Liam dashes to the front door and I follow, hoping desperately that this potion will cure my friend. I can't bear to think of her so injured, burned, after losing her family in a fire. I can only imagine the trauma she's experiencing right now.

Liam swings open the door. "It's about time!" He barks, then stops short when he sees who's there.

Three Enforcers, fully armed, faces hard.

One holds up a parchment. "Liam Night?" he asks.

"Yes," Liam says harshly. "What's going on—"

The Enforcer grabs him, wrapping his wrists in steel carved with magical glyphs. "You're under arrest for arson, public destruction of property, and conspiracy to steal a dragon egg."

CHAPTER 3: THE FIGHT

How do you go back to being strangers with someone who has seen your soul? ~Nikita Gill

THE WARRANT HAS BEEN SIGNED by Dath'Racul so there is little we can do but watch in silence as they drag Liam away. Inside the house, Alina begins to wail as if she knows what is happening with her father. And who's to say she doesn't?

We reconvene in the library, everyone on edge. Matilda rocks the baby, who is inconsolable.

"I'll make sure he gets out on bail as soon as possible," Derek says, sitting at the desk and pulling out a sheath of parchment and a pen.

"They must think he caused the explosion at the festival," Elijah says, scratching his chin. "It did, after all, draw away Ava'Kara, who was needed to put out the flames. The egg was stolen while she was away. That can't be a coincidence."

"That's ridiculous," I say, angry. "Liam would never do that. He and Alina were caught in the blast. He'd never risk her life that way."

"She's part fire Druid," Elijah says. "He would know she'd be fine." I glare at him and he shrugs. "But I don't disagree. I could see

Liam setting a fire by accident, if his powers or temper got away from him. But he would never do something so premeditated. It's not who he is. He was clearly framed."

"Who would do that?" I ask. "And why?"

"Someone who wanted that egg," Sebastian says. "And who wanted Liam to take the fall for it. I'll go to the crime scene and see if there are any clues pointing to the real criminal. Or at the very least, anything that could help exonerate Liam."

"I'll go with you," I say. "An extra set of eyes could be helpful."

Sebastian nods in agreement.

"I'll come, too," Derek says, jumping up from behind the desk.

But Matilda *tsks* us all, setting the sleepy baby back into the crib. "Planning on going now, are you? The streets are swarming with Enforcers who will be none too happy to see you lot. They won't let you near the water dragon's nest."

Derek sighs, looking deflated. "You're right. We won't get anywhere tonight. I'll put in a formal request in the morning."

Matilda nods, her long white braids bobbing on her shoulders. "Good. Then all of you can get some rest. You have a busy day tomorrow and Liam will need you sharp. I'll wait for the milkweed to arrive, make the potion for Lily, and keep watch over Alina."

Sebastian looks ready to argue, but Matilda stares him down. All four feet of her.

"Don't think that just because you're a big tough guy I can't still take you, my boy. You need blood and sleep, or you'll be no good to Liam or anyone else. This won't be solved in a night."

Sebastian looks sheepishly away, and I almost laugh at how fast this tiny old woman put him in his place.

With minimal grumbling, we all file out of the library and head to our rooms. Elijah, Sebastian, and Derek each nod to me as they pass, and I feel some comfort in knowing we are all in this together. But then I think of Liam, of what his night will look like, and my heart breaks. He doesn't deserve to be in jail. We have to get him out.

When I get back to my room, I notice my window is open. The wind pushes the rain through the curtains and onto the rug, sending a chill through the air despite the blazing fireplace. I wonder if one of the castle ghosts opened it. They live—if live is the right word to describe a ghost?— and work in the castle, but I have never seen them.

My bedroom door closes behind me.

And I feel him there before I turn.

Adam, standing in the corner, next to the urn that I thought held his remains, soaked in rain, and looking as healthy and strong as he did at the festival.

Moon, my feisty black cat, creeps out from under the bed and hisses at the figure by the door, fur spiking on his arched back.

I suck in a breath, my mind whirling. "Is that really you?" I ask. "Or am I dreaming?"

He steps forward. "I'm here," he says, gruff with emotion. "I missed you, Evie."

My voice cracks when I speak again. "I missed you too, Adam. So much."

There is silence between us, and I sink onto my bed, the weariness of the day catching up with me. Moon curls up near my feet, and Adam comes to sit by my side, his hand on mine.

"Did you know the explosion would happen?" I ask.

"Yes," he says.

"Then why not warn me? Or the others? So many were hurt. Some could have died." We still don't know the extent of the damage, but I wouldn't be surprised if there were casualties.

"I made sure you were safe," he says.

"How?" I ask, confused. I didn't see him when the fires started.

"If I hadn't found you, if we hadn't spoken in the forest, Sebastian would have come for you sooner. You would have sat nearer the court-house, in one of the available seats. You would have been caught in the blast."

I sigh. This is all so confusing. So hard to understand. So hard to believe. All I have is my brother's word that his visions are true. Even if he is seeing them, even if he believes them, that doesn't make them real. Has Adam gone mad? Did dying destroy his mind?

"Why not stop the explosion?" I ask, my voice tired. "My friend was almost killed. Liam's been arrested. If you have this power, this gift, why not stop it from happening?"

Adam sighs and squeezes my hand. "I know this is hard for you to understand. And I'm so sorry about Lily and Liam. But things are proceeding as they should. As they must. I couldn't stop the explosion without risking too much."

"What the hell is that supposed to mean?" I ask, angry. "Is this all part of your master plan? Did you cause the fire?" The possibility crashes into me like lightning and I feel sick to my stomach. I think of Moira and her grief at facing the truth of her brother. Her desperate need to exonerate him from whatever crimes she could, even knowing the other awful things he had done. We all wear rose-colored glasses when it comes to our loved ones. We all see what we want to be there, which makes it that much harder to see what actually is there.

Adam puts his arm around me, and I rest my head on his shoulder. "No, Evie. This I did not do." He kisses the top of my head. "But it had to happen. For the sake of the Otherworld. You will understand... in time."

I pull away, facing him, my heart torn in two. "How can I trust you?" I ask. "You murdered a woman and child and—"

"And I told you about it," he says, cutting me off. "I didn't have to show you the Memory Catcher. But I wanted you to know the truth. That's why you can trust me." His blue eyes carry so much grief, so much sadness. "I've never lied to you. And I never will. You can always trust me."

I look away, my emotions all over the place. But he's right, in a twisted way. He's never lied to me in the past. That was our sacred promise to each other. Never to lie. The promise we never broke. Ever. He didn't have to show me the memory, but he did.

So, if he's not lying...then this is all real...or he believes his own insanity. "Why are you here?" I ask. "Why now?"

"I needed to see you again. To talk to you. To be with you. I've missed you. You're my other half. We are never complete apart. You know this."

Tears leak out of my eyes and I nod. I do know this. We have always been a team.

"But there's more, isn't there?" I ask, sensing it in his voice.

He nods. "There's more. When you find the dragon egg, you'll receive an offer."

"What kind of offer?" I ask,

"To leave the Night Firm," he says. "For... another opportunity. It's important that you accept."

My stomach drops. "Why?"

"That's all I can tell you," he says.

I know from his tone I won't get any more information, so I don't try. I sit with him, safe in the circle of his arm, and I think of all the things we've missed about each other these past months.

"I killed Jerry," I say suddenly, confessing my darkest crime.

"I know," he says softly, tightening his hold on me.

"It's not an easy thing, taking a life."

"It had to be done."

And in a strange way I realize we are connected, even in this. Even in murder, in death, in ending a life.

I marvel at the macabre serendipity of it all. Growing up, Adam and I were always connected. We shared events in a very twin way. One summer, as children, we were placed in different foster homes. It was the first time we'd ever been apart and the longest three months of my life. It was agony. During that summer, my only consolation was music, and I became obsessed with a country song by Billie Ray Cyrus, "Achy Breaky Heart." I listened to that song on repeat the entire summer. Adam and I weren't allowed to call or see each other, and when we finally got a new home together in the fall, we couldn't wait to update each other on our lives. When I told him about the song that got me through his absence, he grinned and showed me the cassette tape he'd been listening to. It was the same song.

This was only one example of so many times our twin powers—as we called them—connected us in shared experiences. When I broke my ankle while on a girl's only field trip, he broke his playing basketball after school with friends. At the same time. Our foster parents were not happy.

And now, we've shared in the act of taking a life. An act that has left a scar of darkness on both of us.

The exhaustion of the last few days settles on me, and I rest my head on my brother's shoulder, my eyelids too heavy to keep open. Adam notices, and guides me gently to my pillow, laying my head down and tucking me in, just like when we were kids. Moon hisses at him and readjusts his position to stay close to me.

"Sleep now, sister," Adam whispers. He kisses my forehead as dreams pull me into their realm.

I'm standing in a dark forest, wind whipping around me. Lightning blazes in the sky and rain pours in torrents through the thick foliage. Thunder rattles the earth, and everything is cloaked in shadow, but I do not feel afraid, only curious.

Then I see him. The darkly beautiful man from the festival, his ebony eyes catching my gaze. Black leather pants hang from his hips and his chest is bare. Celtic tattoos weave across his back and torso, skin glowing in the moonlight. He smiles and I feel the pull of him, the need to be closer to him, to touch him. I can see the magic connecting us, like a smoky wire with a core of light. I walk closer, but he disappears behind a tree. I follow him, but it's like trying to catch the wind in your hands.

I reach a grove of silver flowers and then he is behind me. He grabs my hand and spins me around. His touch electrifies me. His lips move to speak my name, and then I hear another voice, a familiar voice, angry and yelling.

"What is going on?"

I'm pulled out of my dream forcefully and a feeling of whiplash rocks me as my eyes open. I sit up, confused, disoriented, trying to figure out what happened.

Adam is next to me one moment, gone the next, like smoke in the wind. The window slams shut behind him and in the doorway, I see Derek, wild-eyed and angry. He glares at me. "What is the meaning of this?" he asks.

"I can explain," I say, sitting up, my heart beating like a hummingbird against my ribs. What did he hear? What did he see? What does he think he knows?

"Your brother is alive?" he asks. Of course, he would know what Adam looks like. The Night Firm investigated me before hiring me. He knows more about my life than I do, probably.

"Yes," I say, my mouth dry.

"How long have you known?" he asks, storming into the room, peering out the window.

"I just found out. At the festival." I don't want to ask any questions for fear of giving away something he doesn't already know, so I wait.

"He murdered a woman and child..." Derek says. "Mary? And the baby? He's the real killer?"

I pause, considering my options, but I can't outright lie to him, especially when he already knows the truth. I nod, hesitantly.

"My brothers must be told," he says, turning to leave.

I shoot up from the bed, disturbing a sleeping cat in the process, and grab his hand, my actions and voice full of desperate pleading. "No. Not yet. If Liam finds out, he'll kill Adam."

Derek pauses, his face softening just a bit. "I will make sure your brother has a fair trial. I will represent him myself. But justice must be served."

"You can't," I say, my voice cracking. "He...he had a reason for what he did."

"And what reason could possibly justify the murder of a woman in labor and her unborn child?" he asks, his voice heavy with disdain.

And so I tell him all that Adam told me. About the future vision, the child who would have done such evil things. I study him as I speak, but his expression reveals nothing.

"No one can see the future," he says sternly.

"Matilda can," I argue. "She gave me a vision once."

"A vague prophesy," he says. "A glimpse of a possible outcome. Nothing this specific. No one, not even my grandmother, knows what will happen for certain. Not enough to kill others over it."

A sob wells up in my throat. "I can't lose him," I say. "Not again. I can't lose my brother again."

Tears stream down my cheeks and I can't hold it in anymore. The thought of losing Adam after just getting him back is too much to bear. Derek sees the despair on my face and his expression changes. His eyes grow distant. "Sometimes we must sacrifice those we love the most for what is right," he says. He seems to want to say more, but he remains silent.

"Please," I beg. "Don't tell them yet. My brother isn't evil. He can't be evil."

Derek sighs. "They have a right to know. Especially Liam. But... " he walks towards the door. "I will leave this choice to you. If you wish to lie to our family, so be it. I will carry your lie. But just know, it will kill me inside every moment that I do."

He walks out, slamming the door behind him. And I sink to my knees, gutted and heartbroken.

CHAPTER 4: THE PAST

THEY WITNESSED HER DESTRUCTION, Then they were left to wonder why,
She saw nothing but darkness, Though the stars shone in her eyes.
   ~Supernova by Erin Hanson

DREAMS FLIT in and out of my mind. Sometimes I know I'm asleep and sometimes it feels all too real. I see Adam, his hands covered in blood, crying. Jerry, his dead eyes staring at me, his hand raising to point an accusing finger. And then I see the man from the festival, his energy pulsing and feeling the most alive and real of anything I've ever dreamed. He seems to be reaching for me. Calling for me with a silent voice. But I can never get to him before I wake.

Sunlight streams into my bedroom as my eyes, swollen from tears after my fight with Derek, peel open. I feel like I've got the world's worst hangover, even though I wasn't drinking.

As my blurry vision gains focus, I see someone standing beside my bed holding a tray of food. They're dressed in vibrant green and wearing a red scarf. Liam.

His intense golden eyes study me. "I didn't mean to wake you," he says, a shy smile forming as he puts the platter down on the bedside dresser. "I just wanted you to have some food available when you woke."

I leap out of bed and cut off his flow of words by throwing myself into his arms shouting, "You're back!"

Relief floods me and I can't let go of him. He smells of wood and fire and feels so solid and strong, I could stay in his arms all day.

"I got out on bail," he says, his lips brushing my earlobe.

I finally pull away, though I clutch his hands in mine to keep him close. "Have you seen Lily? Is she okay?"

"She is," he says. "Matilda administered the potion, so Lily will recover. It will just take time. Dryads heal slowly. Trees are not fast at anything."

I nod. "I'm glad she'll be okay. This whole thing has been so awful."

He runs a hand through his red hair, and I notice a pink scar running up his left arm. It looks fresh, puckered, and raw. It wasn't there last night. "What happened?" I ask.

"Just a scratch." He releases my hand to tug his sleeve over the wound. "The Enforcers didn't appreciate my lack of useful information about the crimes in question. They did their level best to loosen my tongue. To no avail, obviously."

He tries to make light of it, but I can see the rage simmering behind his eyes, and I feel it boiling up in me as well. "They tortured you?" I ask through clenched teeth.

"I've had worse," he says quietly. Then he drops his head and looks away from me. "I've done worse."

I remember his curse. How his fire raged out of control before he became a vampire. But I get the sense there's more to his words. Other dark deeds in his ancient past.

I'm not naive or stupid. The Night Brothers have made mistakes, done horrible things. I chose to accept that when I chose to stay at this firm and in this family. I'm not here to judge what they've done in the past, but I sure as hell am going to judge what was done to him now. "This has to be illegal," I say, my own temper flaring, the fire in me burning through my skin.

Liam looks down at my hand in surprise as flames dance along my fingers and against his. Fortunately, he's immune to the dangers of my fire. Does this mean I'll be immune to his as well, I wonder?

"It is illegal," Liam says, still watching my hand. When the flames die down, he looks up, surprise on his face. "We should test your powers when there's time. They're growing."

"Yes, we should, but right now we need to deal with this mess. If it's illegal to torture, then they need to be brought before a judge."

Liam scoffs. "There hasn't been a new dragon egg since the creation of the Otherworld," he says. "More than a thousand years. Enforcers will do whatever it takes to get it back. And if they break a few rules along the way, who's going to hold them accountable? The dragons?"

I shake my head, disgusted with how some get away with anything while others are held accountable for more than their share. And it all has to do with race, money, and power. Some things are the same everywhere.

I glance at his arm again, at the wound there, and tilt my neck. "If you need blood," I say, the invitation clear.

He runs a finger over my neck, and I can see the desire in his eyes, but he shakes his head and kisses me gently instead. "I've already fed. I just wanted to see you. And to bring you food," he says, gesturing at the platter, which is filled with eggs, cheese and dates, and a goblet of juice.

"I'm starving actually," I say as my stomach rumbles. It's easy to forget to eat when you live with vampires, though they are certainly doing their best to remind me at every turn.

I take the tray to the table in front of the fire and he joins me in the other seat while I eat. "Don't worry," I say. "We have a plan. We'll find out whoever is framing you and—"

"I tortured someone," he says, interrupting me, his gaze lost in the fire, his mind somewhere in the past. The flames dance over his pale skin as he speaks quietly of his past. "Long ago...thirty lashes for the crime they had committed. I...I didn't want to, but it was required of me by my Order."

I reach for his hand, having finished all my food. "What was the crime?" I ask.

"They had forsaken their oath," he says, then glances at me, his eyes glistening with the pain of the memory. "They had given in to the dark Magicks. Used it to kill rather than heal. Thirty lashes," he says, returning his gaze to the fire. "And it was only the start of their punishment."

He pulls his hand from mine and rolls up his sleeve, looking at the red lines that run past his elbow. There is more than one scar and I can only imagine what the rest of him looks like beneath his clothes. "I should have refused," he says, staring at the reminders of his recent torture. "Even if it meant leaving the Druidic Order. I should have refused." He looks away, from the fire, from me, from the memory, maybe. "But I didn't. I followed my orders, even though I was a healer. Even though I was sworn to do no harm."

We are both quiet for some time, and then he turns back to face me, his eyes haunted. "I thought you should know. With...with what's happening between us, whatever it is, I thought you should know the truth of me."

"Oh, Liam," I say, touching his face gently, searching his eyes. I see the compassion in him. The healer beneath the hothead. "I do know the truth of you," I say. "And your past deeds are a part of you, but they are not the whole of you. They are not the complete truth. Believing they define you is the true lie."

For a moment, as I study his beautiful face, his soulful eyes, I wonder if maybe I could tell him about Adam. Maybe he wouldn't react in haste. Maybe...

A polite knock at the door startles me out of my thoughts. We both turn to see Elijah clearing his throat. "Apologies for interrupting. It's time to investigate the crime scene," he says to me. "That is, if you still wish to go."

I nod. "I'll be right down."

Elijah looks at his brother and smiles warmly. "It's good to have you home," he says, before closing the door behind him.

As we get downstairs, we hear arguing coming from the library. It seems every five minutes at least two of the Night brothers are going at it.

Sebastian's voice carries the loudest. "What do you mean you're not going?" he demands.

"I mean, I have a case to prepare," Derek says coldly. "Even if we find the egg, it won't be enough to exonerate Liam. They'll think he's just giving it back to avoid more punishment. We'll need to prove his innocence to the jury. Show he had no motive. Redirect blame onto other parties—"

"And we will," Sebastian says, irritably. "But in the meantime, I need you by my side. Ava'Kara likes you. You two share elemental magic. Who else am I supposed to bring to the lair of the water dragon? The fire Druid?"

We walk in and Derek glances at me, then looks away sharply. "You'll have Eve."

"Get your head out of your ass," Sebastian says. "We're going." He looks at me, frowning. "Ready?"

"Yes," I say.

We walk towards the door, Liam joining us, when Elijah grabs him by the shoulders. "Hold on there, brother. Sebastian's right. You can't go near the water dragon right now. If she sees you, it will just make things more difficult. Especially for you."

Liam's temper flares instantly. "So, what am I supposed to do?" he demands. "Sit on my thumbs while you read?"

Elijah shrugs. "If you insist. But no, I was thinking we should come up with other leads. Discuss past enemies of yours. Make a list of who else we could investigate to create reasonable doubt."

"That's a good idea," I say, brushing my hand along Liam's arm.

"Whoever murdered Mary is behind this," Liam growls, and my heart sinks at his words and at his anger.

"But that was Jerry," Sebastian says.

"You saw the note," Liam says. "It might not have been him. He wasn't lying about the note and he might not have been lying about the murders. Which means the real killer could still be out there. And now they might be after Mary's remaining baby. After my baby."

I put a hand on him to calm him. "I don't think it's the same person," I say. And it's true. I don't think Adam is behind this.

Derek looks at me, then at Liam, and his face twists in disgust. He leaves the room and heads to the carriage without another word while Liam seethes with rage. It's clear that while he may have felt sorry for hurting someone in the past, he will not feel bad for punishing whoever killed Mary and her baby. I can see in his eyes there's no room for compassion. Liam will be the death of my brother, and my heart breaks all over again. One day soon, I will lose one of the men I love. I just don't know which.

CHAPTER 5: THE DRAGON

No one but Night, with tears on her dark face, watches beside me in this windy place. ~ Edna St. Vincent Millay

We travel by carriage to the water dragon's lair. While Derek drives, Sebastian and I sit in the back as we bump along a winding road. As the castle fades from sight, and we drive past homes that have seen better days, the earth Druid raises an eyebrow and leans closer to me. "What's going on between you and Derek?" he asks.

"You noticed that, huh?" I study my hands and fidget with invisible lint on my pants.

"It would have been hard not to," he says softly.

Shit. I don't want to lie to anyone else. "I...I can't tell you. It's... "

"Between you and him," Sebastian says. "I understand. I just hope he didn't hurt you."

I realize he means romantically, like a lover's quarrel, and I shake my head. "No, it's nothing like that. He didn't hurt me. If anything, I'm hurting him." I pause, leaning into Sebastian's shoulder as his arm wraps around me. I savor the comfort of him—the warmth of his body, the subtle scent he gives off—as I say what I can without betraying Adam.

"I don't want to lie to you," I begin. "But I can't tell you the whole truth either. Not yet." I sigh, twisting the edge of my shirt in my hands. "There's a choice I have to make. Only...I don't know how to make it. I don't know what the right course of action is. People always talk about things like it's so easy to know what to do, that the hard part is doing it." I look up at his forest green eyes. "I think it's the opposite. It's easy doing the right thing. The hard part is knowing what the right thing is. That's what's paralyzing."

He nods in understanding and squeezes my shoulders. "Sometimes there is no right choice, only the choice you will regret the least." He pauses, looking out the window of the carriage. "Take your time," he says, returning his emerald gaze to me. "I'll be here to talk whenever you're ready."

A flood of emotion crashes through me and I lift my hand to his face, cupping his strong square jawline. "Thank you, Sebastian," I say. "I know you'll always be by my side. I know you'll protect me."

He frowns, placing his hand over mine. "I haven't always protected those I love."

The word love strikes me, and in a moment of abandon I erase the little distance that remains between us and press my lips to his.

He is the first Night brother I met. The first I felt this strange and unyielding attraction to. The first I craved, and yet we have danced around each other, never quite meeting in the same place. Until now.

Sebastian moans against my lips, his body tensing, and then he pulls me into his lap and I sigh at the closeness, at the pleasure that cascades through me as our kiss deepens and his tongue explores mine, his teeth tugging at my lips, his fingers pressing into my back, digging into my flesh, his body pulsing with the need I also feel.

When the carriage stops, I sit back, surprised by the intensity of our connection. His eyes are dilated, and his body is needy with desire. I ease off his lap, shaking from the euphoria of finally feeling him so close, and yet craving more. Craving it all.

He kisses me once more and glides his hand through my long hair. "You are more than I ever could have hoped for," he says.

Then Sebastian exits the carriage and I follow him, tugging at my clothes to right them.

We've arrived at a pool of sapphire water hidden in a cove. Several waterfalls pour into it from steep cliffs above, and as I step out of the carriage, my feet squish into bright emerald moss that lines the shore. Near one of the waterfalls, a mermaid rests languidly on a partially submerged boulder, her pink and purple fins glistening in the light of the Dragon's Breath.

Derek hails her from the shore. "Greetings, Mira. We are here to examine the nesting site of the egg. We have the necessary documents, of course." Derek pulls out a parchment to show her.

"You are expected," Mira says over the waters without looking at the paper. "You may enter. Do you need accommodations for entry? Or would you prefer to do it yourself? We have heard your abilities have returned, Water Druid."

"Word spreads fast around here," I mutter, and Sebastian just grunts in dry amusement.

"I will make my own path," Derek says and then raises his arms. As he does, the water before us parts, creating a dry swath of land to the center waterfall.

Sebastian and I follow Derek. I marvel at the walls of water that have formed on both sides of us. Fish and other larger creatures I can't see clearly still swim within them. I take a cautious step closer to Derek, not wanting to be left behind to face whatever is submerged beneath these waters.

When we reach the waterfall, Sebastian takes my hand. "Don't worry. You won't drown."

"I wasn't worried until you said that," I say with a snort.

Derek enters the waterfall first and it parts for him. Sebastian and I step through next, then drop into a dark stone hole slick with water and slime.

We slide down the hole like the world's most terrifying water slide, and Sebastian catches me in his arms when we land in a bubble of air made by Derek. Around us looms an underground city full of wonders that my mind can scarcely comprehend. An underground castle made of sparking stone and coral stands tall, a plethora of plant life in bright colors dotting the landscape around it. Merpeople form an impromptu line to either side of us as we float to the entrance of the castle. Some are swimming, some are riding what look like giant sea horses. Derek uses his magic to guide us within the walls of the fortress, where we no longer need the air bubble. I hear a slight pop as it dissipates around us and the thick humid scent of moss fills my nostrils. We land gently on our feet and walk to a grand door guarded by an Enforcer dressed in the customary black.

"We're here to examine the nest." Derek once again holds up the signed parchment. "We've already requested permission."

The Enforcer—who appears mostly human despite his fury tail and ears—takes the paper and examines it, turns it over a few times as if some magical words might appear—which, given where we are, might be legit—then nods. He's a beast of few words as he escorts us through the door and down a long hall lined with more Enforcers heavily armed and on alert. We get to large stone doors that require massive strength or magic to open. The Enforcer pulls out a clear crystal and sticks it into the center, and the doors part, stone grinding against stone, shaking the floor beneath us.

"It would take someone highly skilled and connected to infiltrate a place like this," Sebastian says.

I look at the Enforcer, who stands by the door as guard with the other two already there. "How many people have stones that can open this room?" I ask.

He looks down at me with an unreadable expression. "Only the Elite and the Dragon Queen herself. Five in total."

"We should look into who had access," I whisper to Sebastian, "and see if any of those crystals went missing."

He nods as we walk into the nest, and I stop and sweep my gaze over the incredible display of wealth before us. We are in a cave full of blue crystals that shimmer with their own internal light, casting fractal reflections off the gems and gold piled high everywhere. I shake my head, wondering why this level of wealth would be hoarded rather than used to enrich the lives of those in the Otherworld.

Not everyone here lives in mansions and castles. While on our drives through the countryside, I've seen those who live in squalor and poverty. Those who have lost all they have to fires or feuds with other supernatural clans. The wealth on display before me could help so many.

But that's not why I'm here, I remind myself, refocusing my attention on any clues we might discover. I walk to the nearest wall and hold out my hand to see if I can sense anything with my powers. Since I have no real idea what I can do, I'm mostly winging it, but I do feel the thrum of the magic that lives in this whole place. Across parts of the stone wall are black marks that look like deep scars in the rock.

At the end of the cave, much to my surprise, a pair of burning Ifrit are leaning over something on the ground. Flames rise from their reddened skin as from wood in a fire pit, casting everything around them in an orange glow. Looking at them, you'd think they'd smell of burning flesh—which isn't a great scent. But it's more a smoky smell, like the remnants of a campfire.

"Ifi? Elal?" I walk over to them and they turn, smiling, and dim their fires until they look almost human. Ifi, the smaller one, is dressed in a white lab coat and Elal, the taller and more musical of the two, is wearing a dark cloak and slacks underneath. They both have burnt orange-red skin and red hair that looks impossible to tame. Their eyes glow like mini suns and it's almost hard to maintain eye contact with them for long with how intense their gazes are. "What are you two doing here?"

Ifi glances at his feet and I see the body on the ground.

"Ah," I say, solemnly. "I didn't realize there were casualties."

Ifi walks over and hugs me. Fortunately, he's not covered in body goo this time. "Girlfriend, there are always casualties in life. And this is a mess of one. I know I say this a lot, but I really mean it. It has been a day. Has it not, Elal?"

Elal joins his lover and nods. "Ifi isn't exaggerating this time. It has, indeed, been a day."

Then Ifi frowns, gripping my arms. "We heard about Liam and are so sorry. How's that sweet little girl doing?" he asks.

Ifi and Elal took care of Alina after Mary's death, so of course it makes sense they would have a bond with her. "She's well. She wasn't hurt in the explosion. Seems she got her dad's penchant for fire-immunity," I say. "But I'm sure she misses you. You should come for a visit soon."

Ifi claps his hands in delight. "Yes, please and thank you." He looks to Elal. "I think we need a baby, lover. I miss Alina, don't you?"

Elal puts an arm over Ifi's shoulder. "I do miss her. And maybe it is time to expand our family."

I'm dying to ask what the process is for two gay Ifrits to have a child in the Otherworld, but one: that seems rude and inappropriate, and two: I just now notice the details of the body at their feet and I have so. Many. Questions.

The Enforcer is more creature than person. Very whip-like with hair made of tiny serpents, now dead, and a body that ends not in feet but in a long snake form wrapped in a black Enforcer uniform. Their eyes are also blindfolded. "Why are their eyes covered?" I ask.

"My dear, that is a basilisk," Ifi says. "One look into her eyes would paralyze you."

"So, she wore this while alive?"

"Yes," Elal says. "Else she would make a very ineffective guard, paralyzing everyone she saw."

Sebastian joins us, laying a hand on my back. "I've battled a rogue basilisk in the past. They are not ones to trifle with."

"How could she see anything if she was always blindfolded?"

"Their other senses are extremely honed," Elal says. "She was especially gifted. Top of her class at the academy. Her name was Ethne Brinn. She was 6'7", single, parents deceased."

Sebastian crouches to examine the body more closely. "Cause of death?"

"Stabbed in the bloody chest," Ifi says dramatically. "And the skin around the puncture wound is black, indicating it's decaying faster than the rest of the body."

"Like those black marks on the wall," I say, noting the similarities.

Sebastian nods. "This was dark magic. Not something you see often anymore." He glances at the marks on the wall and frowns. "Where are the other victims?"

"There are no other victims," Elal says. "Just her."

"Only one person was left to guard the egg?" Sebastian says in disbelief. "That seems highly reckless."

Elal nods. "There are usually a few more guards from the Elite, but the attack happened during a shift change, apparently."

Derek pauses his examination of the nest to listen to our conversation, though he doesn't join us. He's still pissed, clearly. I don't blame him.

"This was well-planned," I say, thinking things through.

Sebastian nods. "At first I thought whoever did this took advantage of the explosion at the courthouse. A bit coincidental but possible. But this happening during a shift change makes that unlikely. The timing is too perfect. The crimes must be related."

"These are dark times," says Ifi, shivering. "Earthquakes. Fires. Storms. Missing corpses."

"Wait, what? Corpses have gone missing?" I ask.

Elal nods. "Someone has been breaking into the morgue and stealing the bodies. Particularly, rare races."

"Aren't the morgue and cemetery guarded?" I ask, remembering that the two gargoyles, Okura and Akuro, were powerful deterrents to mischief when I first visited there.

"Normally, yes," Elal says, crossing his muscled arms over his chest. "But they've been on maternity leave since their baby was born. Newborn gargoyles have become rare in recent years, so they're keeping to themselves more than usual."

"Indeed," Ifi says. "I was surprised to see them at the Midwinter Festival. But, oh, that baby. So cute." The Ifrit looks up at his lover with large glowing eyes, and I smile. One way or another, those two are getting a baby sooner than later if Ifi has any say about it.

Sebastian frowns. "Rare bodies being stolen? You don't think it could be…"

Ifi nods. "It very well could be. But there's no way to tell."

"The body is ready," Elal says, interrupting the conversation. "We should extract her dying wish."

"Right, yes. Of course," Ifi says. He kneels at the head of the basilisk and lays his hands on her, then closes his eyes.

Sebastian and I back up, but Elal stays by his side.

Fire erupts from him and spreads flames all around them as Ifi chants in an ancient language. When the flames die down, the body is aglow with some kind of preternatural power.

The basilisk rises from the ground, turning her head to face us. Her voice is more snake than human, a hiss on the wind that loosely forms the words. "Do not ssssearch for the egg. Do not sssssearch."

With that, her body collapses back to the floor and we all let out a collective breath.

"Well," says Ifi. "That's not what I expected. It's more like a message than a dying wish."

"Can last wishes be tampered with?" I ask. "Like how certain paranormals can mess with Memory Catchers."

Elal shrugs. "It has never been done to my knowledge. But that does not mean a very powerful being couldn't have found a way to do it."

"There's another explanation," Derek says, finally joining us and speaking for the first time since we entered the cave. "She was in on it. She helped steal the egg."

"But...she was killed," I say.

"Her partner could have betrayed her in order to cover their tracks and eliminate witnesses. It's happened before," he says. "Not everyone is as they seem." He looks at us. "Think about it. Why were her eyes still covered? If someone was attacking, she would have uncovered them. They are her greatest weapons, after all. And how would anyone have gotten in here without a crystal to open the cave? It hasn't been damaged or tampered with in any other way that I can see. Her being a party to the crime is the only explanation I can see that makes sense."

His logic is sound. "But, why? Why would she do this?"

Derek shrugs. "Why does anyone commit a crime?" he asks. "All criminals have their justifications that they think exonerate them from their own evil."

I wonder if he is still talking about the basilisk or my brother. I try to brush the thoughts aside. "If she was in on it, why frame Liam? And what was she intending to do with the egg?"

Before Derek can respond, the Enforcer who escorted us here returns, speaking promptly. "The Great Ava'Kara wishes to speak with you," he says.

Sebastian, Derek and I turn to follow him, but the Enforcer pauses. "Only the Water Druid and the woman," he says.

Sebastian shrugs. "You go ahead. I'll keep looking around here, and I'll dig into the basilisk's past a bit. Maybe there will be a lead."

Derek and I follow the guard, and when we are out of earshot of the others, I whisper to him. "How long will you keep ignoring me?" I ask.

He smiles, and it would almost look sincere if not for his eyes. "Is this what you want? Me to pretend? While my brother is facing an eternity in prison or worse? These may be his last days of freedom and I'm lying to him for you." He spits out the words like acid, and I recoil from the anger.

"I...I'm sorry," I say sincerely. "I shouldn't have asked you to lie. You..." I force myself to say the words I know I must. The words that will damn my own brother while giving his brother answers. "You can tell him the truth if you wish. I won't have you hurting yourself for me."

Derek freezes, visibly blanching at my words as if he's seen a ghost.

"What's wrong?" I ask.

"Just...I've heard those words before. Long ago." His voice softens into memory. "So very long ago."

"Proceed inside," the guard says, interrupting us once again and pointing us through a door just ahead.

We walk into a great hall with a throne in the center made of seashells and gemstones. Behind the throne is a waterfall that opens up to a large body of water somehow magicked not to enter the throne room itself. Through the water I see blue scales, the giant body of a dragon swimming underwater, like a great sea serpent of legends.

The dragon approaches the waterfall and as she moves through it, her body begins to glow a blinding blue. She shrinks the closer she gets to the throne until she steps out of the water not as a dragon, but as a beautiful woman where the dragon had just been.

She is naked and her body shimmers a striking blue. Her hair is white and flows around her, long and wild. She stretches her dragon wings to fullness, revealing their width and beauty, then they settle at her back, becoming a cloak around her. Tiny white horns dot her forehead, and her blue eyes are large—larger than any human—and still very dragon-like.

"Good to see you again, Son of Water," she says in a silky voice. She takes a seat on her throne, crossing her long legs. "I received your petition to speak with me. You have come to argue the innocence of your brother." It's not a question, but Derek nods.

"Approach," she says.

We walk forward until we are about five feet from her throne.

"Speak," she commands.

"Liam was not part of this attack," Derek says bluntly. "But we need your help to prove it."

She cocks her head. "The Son of Fire was seen exiting the explosion unharmed. He's known for his temper. And the event was clearly a distraction for someone to steal my egg. Why should I believe he wasn't part of this conspiracy? Many would pay well for the egg of a dragon."

"We have no need of money," Derek says.

She leans forward. "Money is not the most valuable currency, as I am sure you are aware."

"Kara, you know our family. You know this is not what we trade in nor is it how we work."

Her eyes narrow. "I know many things," she says. "But foremost I know my egg is missing and there are many who would like to see the Eternal Dragons fall. I can no longer be sure who are enemies and who are friends. Someone has betrayed us, and someone will pay."

She closes her eyes for a long moment, then opens them again, the reptilian movement of them a bit unnerving on her nearly human looking face.

"While I have no doubt about that, it just isn't possible that Liam was behind this," I say, and they both turn to look at me.

"Ah, the human who is not human has found her voice," the dragon says. "Tell me, Eve Oliver, why isn't this possible?"

"This took planning. Time. Liam—and all of us—have been wrapped up in a case that only recently resolved, resulting in the reemergence of his powers. In fact, they came back that very night. And they wouldn't have come back had we not won the case. Whoever planned this wouldn't have relied on something as untenable as Liam getting his powers back. Things could have easily gone the other way and the plan would have been ruined as a result."

The dragon stares at me a long time, and I wait, knowing that sometimes it's better to shut up and let the other person make up their own mind. If I keep talking, I might inadvertently say something that pushes them in the other direction.

"Tell me, Eve," she says softly, "Do you know what you truly are?"

I sigh. "I don't. Everyone keeps asking me and I don't know."

"Approach," the dragon says once again, and this time she means that I should come up to her throne.

I glance at Derek, but he nods, so I move close enough to her that she can reach out and slide a finger along my forehead, closing her eyes as her body begins to glow blue again. A wisp of power washes through me, disappearing as soon as she pulls her hand away.

"Interesting," she says. "You are most interesting. I can see why so many are fascinated with you."

"Can you...can you tell what I am?" I ask, desperate to know myself better.

But she doesn't answer my question. Instead, she asks another. "Why do you work for the Night brothers?"

This isn't a question that I expect, and it throws me off. I flounder for an answer and then give up, trying instead to bring the conversation back to Liam. "Please can you help us find the truth?"

"Silence, girl. I am asking the questions. And you have yet to answer mine."

So much for avoiding the issue. "I started working for them because I needed a job and a new life after my twin brother killed himself. I stayed with them because they have become my family. Maybe dysfunctional at times, and full of conflict, but family, nonetheless. I would never abandon them, which is why it's so important to me to find out the truth and exonerate Liam. He is a father now. He is my friend, and something more. He is needed in our family."

She leans back, studying us, twirling a gold ring on her middle finger. After a moment, she pulls the ring off and gestures for me to come forward. "Take this," she says. "It is my mark. And it will help you in your investigation. Use it to travel through the Otherworld unhindered." She holds out her ring to me and I accept it, studying the sapphire stone and signet within.

She looks to Derek. "I am surprised you are so convinced of your brother's innocence, Son of Water. You know better than most, not all Druids follow their own code."

Derek frowns and the dragon flicks her wrist dismissively. "You may leave but know this. We are the Eternal Dragons of the Otherworld. This will not be like any other trial. Someone will pay, and if my egg isn't returned to me by the end of this, that someone will be Liam."

~

WE ARE ESCORTED out of the throne room and back to the nesting cave where Sebastian is still investigating. While we walk, I reach for Derek. "What did she mean? About Druids not following their own code?" I ask.

Derek frowns and caresses my hand with more tenderness than he's shown since finding out about Adam. "It means I too have secrets...secrets I must hold close," he says with a sigh. "And given that, I will keep your secret for now. Perhaps we are more similar than I wanted to accept."

His words don't sit well with me, but it's clear he doesn't want to talk more about it, and his words at least ease my fears of losing my brother, for the time being.

When we get back to the cave, Sebastian is finishing up a conversation with another Enforcer. "How did it go?" he asks when the Enforcer leaves.

I hold up the dragon ring. "We have some privilege, but she's not convinced of Liam's innocence. And she seems weirdly interested in me," I say.

Sebastian frowns. "As word of your powers and unknown origin spreads, more and more will become intrigued. That worries me."

Derek puts an arm around my shoulder. "We'll keep her safe, if it comes to that."

Sebastian nods, his eyes flicking to my mine with unspoken questions about the change in Derek.

"I'll keep myself safe, thank you very much," I say, smiling. "Just as I did before. Now...did you find out anything about the basilisk?" I ask.

"She was well-respected," Sebastian says. "No known enemies. A rule-follower to the letter. Not much of a personal life that anyone can attest to. There's not much to go on."

"That's disappointing," I say, and I notice the body is gone along with the Ifrits.

"There is one more thing," Sebastian says. "None of the crystals that open this cave are missing. That further reinforces our theory that she was in on it."

"We've found all we're going to find here," Derek says. "It's time to head back and regroup, see if Elijah and Liam made any progress."

Once in the carriage, Sebastian by my side and Derek driving, the earth Druid leans into me. "You two worked things out?"

I shrug. "For now. It's...complicated."

And then I turn to him with a question I've had for some time. "Is this...is this okay?"

"Is what okay?" he asks.

"Well, I've...I've got this thing..." I say, flailing my hands as if that adds meaning to what I'm trying to convey, "with all of you. I mean. I haven't like, gone all the way with anyone, but..." I blush and don't know how to continue, but Sebastian spares me with a hand on mine.

"Eve, this isn't the human world. We don't do things the same way. There aren't the same taboos. This isn't the first time we have all been in love with the same woman, though it might very well be the last."

I swallow through a dry throat, my eyes widening. "In love?"

He nods. "It's maybe too soon, I realize, to talk about that, but you must know that you have done something to all of us. You have brought light back into our world. Hope. A reason to live. What is love if not that?" He brushes wisps of hair from my forehead, his gaze penetrating mine. "There is no jealousy, only a desire to be with you, to make you happy, to protect you. And there is no pressure, not from any of us. Trust your feelings. We aren't going anywhere."

My heart expands with his words, and the fear I hadn't fully articulated turns to joy. I don't have to choose one of them! I can actually have them all. Because in truth, I can't imagine my world without any of them, and though it's taking me time to get there, I know the Night brothers are my future.

I just hope his words are true, that none of them are going anywhere. I hope we can, in fact, prove Liam's innocence before the worst can happen.

My mind wanders back to our investigation in the cave and I recall a conversation that never finished. "Who do you think is stealing the corpses?" I ask. "You mentioned someone to the Ifrits."

"He calls himself the Collector. He procures rare artifacts and sells most of them to the highest bidder in secret auctions. It's well known his means of acquiring said artifacts are rarely legal."

"Let me guess. He's rich and powerful and so he's untouchable."

"Don't forget well-connected," Sebastian says bitterly.

"It's the same in the mundane world," I say. "The powerful do as they please and they rarely even get a slap on the wrist." I shake my head, disgusted with the imbalance that exists everywhere, even in other worlds. "Do you think he stole the egg? That would be quite the item to add to his collection."

"It's possible," Sebastian says. "But this feels too risky, even for him. Still, it's worth investigating. If he didn't steal it, he might know something about who did. He has eyes and ears everywhere. In the highest levels of government and law, and in the lowest alleys."

When we arrive at the castle, we find Liam and Elijah are in the library talking.

"We have a lead," I say, grabbing an apple from a fruit platter someone has taken to leaving out for me. "The Collector."

I bite into the crunchy sweetness as Elijah raises an eyebrow curiously. "We have one as well, but it's not good," he says.

"Who?" asks Sebastian, taking a seat by my side.

"The Beggar Queen," he says, closing a book on his lap. "She disagrees with the policies put in place in the last few centuries by the

Council of Dragons and could have taken the egg for leverage in those discussions."

"Or out of spite," Liam says, folding his arms over his chest and staring into the fire.

Elijah stands and paces the room. "The problem is—"

"She won't meet with us," Sebastian says, finishing his brother's sentence as he looks to me. "We've tried before."

"It won't be easy to reach the Collector either," Elijah says. "He doesn't exactly deal with lawyers. Well, not honest ones, anyways."

We all take seats and continue discussing possible avenues to reach our two biggest leads. I don't have a lot to add to the conversation, given my newness in this world, so I listen and pull out my sketchbook to draw. I flip open to the drawing I've been working on of the mysterious man who keeps finding his way into my dreams. I add some details to his eyes and blend the shadows around him. There is something…familiar…about his features, I realize. As if I should know who he is.

As I work to make the sketch more detailed, Liam glances at the drawing, and his expression hardens. "What is this?" he asks.

I'm surprised by his intensity. "It's just someone I saw," I say. "You're not jealous, are you? It's just—"

"Where?" he asks. "Where did you see him?" His voice is urgent and angry. This is more than jealousy. Something is wrong.

"At the Midwinter Festival," I answer. "Before the explosion. Why? Who is this?" I ask, holding up the drawing so they can all see better.

The other three brothers lean in, their eyes going wide at the picture.

"It can't be him," Derek says, his eyes haunted. "It's impossible."

"Look at the drawing," Liam says, taking the sketchbook from me to study more closely. "She saw him. He's back."

Sebastian pales, his jaw hardening, but he says nothing.

"Who?" I ask. "Tell me." Lily's words come back to me then. She said she saw him. Is this who she meant?

Liam's rage turns to ice, his glare glacier as he studies me. "Our brother."

CHAPTER 6: THE BROTHER

WHEN YOU LIGHT A CANDLE, you also cast a shadow. ~*Ursula K. Le Guin*

"BROTHER?" I ask, confused.

Sebastian lowers his head, still silent. Derek shifts in his seat. Liam begins pacing again, and Elijah just looks like he wishes he were reading—or doing literally anything else—rather than having this conversation.

Finally, Derek clears his throat. "There are five of us. Five Night brothers, not four. Who you've drawn," he says, pointing to my sketch, "...that's the fifth and youngest of us. The likeness is unmistakable."

My jaw drops open in shock and I snap it closed. "Why...how did I not know this? Why didn't you tell me?"

"Because he betrayed our Order," Sebastian says with clenched teeth. "Long ago, before we became vampires, before we became cursed, our brother betrayed the Druidic order. In turn, he was punished. Whipped. Imprisoned."

I look over at Liam, who seems stung by the words, by the vehemence in them, as he stares at the recent scars on his own arms and hands. It was him, I realize. He was the one who whipped his own brother. Who punished him.

"And we..." continues Sebastian. "We were forbidden to ever speak of him again. He was to be erased from history."

I swallow the lump in my throat. The tension in the room is palpable, and I have so many questions. "How did he betray your Order?"

Sebastian takes a long swig of his drink, then looks at me. "He delved into dark magick and then used his new powers to slay a priest and his disciples. Dozens died by his hand."

I can feel the blood drain from my face. "Why? Why would he do such a thing?"

Liam rubs at the scars on his arm. "The priest was burning women," he says, staring into the fire, the flames growing under his gaze. "He and his followers. If a woman opposed them, angered them in any way, they would declare her a witch and burn her at the stake."

"What the hell? That's...horrifying," I say. "They had to be stopped—"

"Yes, they had to be stopped," Sebastian says firmly, "but not that way. Not through cold-blooded murder. That was not—is not—our way. We could have persuaded the priest to change his ways. Our brother could have—"

"Cole," Derek says, interrupting Sebastian as he stands and faces the group. "His name was Cole. And he did what needed to be done. What we all should have done."

Cole. Cole Night. The man who haunts my dreams has a name. Is this why I feel such a pull to him, because of his connection to this family?

Sebastian frowns. "I recall you having a different opinion at the time, when we found out the truth of his actions." Sebastian's voice is like ice. "Cole," he says with derision, "was punished fairly."

"Cole," Liam says softly, caressing the name like something very fragile. "I haven't spoken that name in so very long."

His tender words deflate the argument in the room. Even Sebastian softens, seeing the look on Liam's face, hearing the pain in his voice.

"It may have been Cole that Eve saw," says Elijah. "Or it may have been a look-a-like. A doppelgänger."

"Escaping should have been impossible," Sebastian says.

"And yet, isn't our very existence proof that the impossible is anything but?" Elijah asks, holding out his hands.

"It's not a coincidence that Eve saw him—or someone looking like him—the night of the explosion," Derek says, furrowing his brow in worry. "He could be seeking revenge."

"We mustn't jump to conclusions," Elijah says, "but we can't dismiss the possibility that he escaped." He pauses. "We must be sure. We must go back."

Liam scowls. "I swore I would never return to that forsaken place."

"Then you can stay," Elijah says. "But I will go."

"Go where?" I ask.

"To the birthplace of our Order," Elijah says softly. "To the place our brother was imprisoned."

"You want to travel to England?" asks Liam. "Not exactly an easy trip without a dryad. How do you propose we—"

"I can help," comes a familiar voice. Lily. She's standing in the doorway, leaning on a cane, a blanket draped over her slim shoulders. She looks weak, weary, but her skin is healed of the burns, only some puckered skin remains in the places she was injured the worst.

"Lily!" I stand and walk over to her, hugging her gently.

She chuckles. "I won't break. I'm stronger than I look."

I pull away and study her as the brothers crowd around us. "We've been so worried."

Liam—ever the healer—feels her head and her pulse and studies her carefully.

Lily rolls her eyes. "I'm well, Uncle. I swear," she says, giving Liam's hand a squeeze. "Matilda told me about your arrest, and I overheard what you said about Cole. I can move the castle to England."

"No," says Liam. "You are in no condition to travel."

"But if she can—" Elijah says, ever the pragmatist.

"No," Liam says again, this time more firmly. "I am her healer, and I say she needs at least another week of rest. I will not compromise her health for our convenience."

275

Even Elijah can't argue with this. No one wants Lily hurt more than she already has been.

The dryad moves into the study to sit on a chair in front of the fire, warming her hands briskly. "Very well," she says. "But I might know someone who can help. Another dryad. Kaya." Lily glances away shyly, her cheeks flushing. "Tell her I sent you, and she should be able to take you where you need to go."

That settles it. It is too late to visit Kaya tonight, but we all agree to touch base with her in the morning and see if she will help us. For now, Elijah gets the details from Lily about where to find the dryad, and Liam makes sure Lily gets back to her tree to rest. Which is what we all need at this point.

Rest. Not a tree to sleep in.

≈

THE NEXT MORNING, I rise early, grab my cloak and bag, and get ready for our trip. I've always wanted to go to England. I just never imagined I would travel there via dryad magic. But it sure beats international flights.

All four brothers come, as I expected, and so the five of us set out in the carriage. Elijah and Derek sit up front, leaving me in the back with Liam and Sebastian. It's a mostly silent drive as we travel through the town and into a densely populated residential area that lasts for miles before we reach a clearing that leads us to a bumpy dirt road and a lot of forest and hills.

I lean back and close my eyes, replaying all of the new information I've learned over the course of the last few days. My mind keeps returning to Cole. To his face. His eyes. His haunting energy.

When the carriage begins to slow after several hours of butt-bruising travel, I peer out the window and gasp. The Dragon's Breath that fills the sky with color seems to have created a wall of furious green fire that emits such heat we can hardly get closer without burning alive. Already sweat is beading on my forehead and dripping into my eyes. The weirdest thing is that at the base of this green wall of fire, everything just…ends. The trees, the grass, the road. It all disappears. As far as the eye can see.

"It's the edge of The Otherworld," Liam says.

"The edge?" I ask, stunned. "Like…there's nothing beyond that wall?"

He nods.

"Does it encase everything, this wall? Like in a circle or something?"

"There is a perimeter to the world," the fire Druid says. "But most of it is unreachable, at the far edge of steep mountains or great bodies of water. This is the most accessible location."

"Huh. So, it's not a globe, like Earth?" I ask. I've seen maps, of course, in the many books I've read, but I never really considered the shape or magnitude of the world. I never considered that it would have an edge. An end.

"This world is much smaller than yours," Liam says. "And no, it's not a globe."

The idea of this makes my mind spin.

The carriage stops, and we all get out and stretch. My body is bruised, tired, and achy, and I wonder at how people in my world traveled like this throughout history. It's back breaking.

We emerge into a magnificent grove of wood. In a large circle, a fair distance from the fiery edge of the world, smaller saplings sway in the hot wind, and in the middle is a tree much larger than Lily's, its snowy white leaves a sharp contrast to the green hue cast by the Dragon's Breath wall.

There's shouting coming from the center of the grove and as we move towards the conflict we see a dryad, skin green and hair red as blood, yelling at two Enforcers dressed in black cloaks, while a cloven-hooved woman holding a baby cowers behind her.

"These are my clients, and they are getting in," the dryad screams, shielding the woman with her own body. The largest center tree seems to respond to her anger, branches rippling with the dryad's words.

"Kaya," the Enforcer closest to her says, holding out a hand. "The new rules dictate creatures must have a valid permit to enter the Otherworld…"

His voice is familiar, as are the tiny horns on his head. He's the same Enforcer who stopped us to search our carriage the night of the fire.

"This is complete crap," Kaya says. "A dragon egg goes missing and suddenly everyone's a potential criminal. Unless they have enough money to buy their innocence, of course."

The Enforcer looks over to the woman with the baby. "I'm sorry, miss, but you'll have to leave the Otherworld and come back with a permit—"

The woman cries, clutching her child to her chest. "Please, sir. I must stay. We're being hunted. We won't survive if you send us back."

The Enforcer steps forward holding a black wooden rod in one hand. He reaches around the dryad to grab the woman with the other hand. "I'm sure you'll find a way."

"And how is she to get a permit, which can only be issued by your department, if she's not here?" Kaya asks.

The second Enforcer pulls Kaya away from the woman, pinning her to her own tree with his wooden rod, and as he does, it zaps with an electric magnet that shocks Kaya, causing her to scream. "That will be enough argument from the likes of you," he says through gritted teeth, his fist balled, and his body poised for a fight.

The woman in question collapses to her knees, pulling out of the first Enforcer's grasp.

She cries, cradling her screaming infant. "No. Please. I beg you. If I can't stay, take my child..." Her pleas are desperate, grasping at the last remnants of hope for her child, if not herself. She holds the baby out like an offering to a cruel god, and the Enforcer pauses, his face troubled as he glances at his partner who doesn't appear nearly as bothered by conscience. He looks back at the woman but avoids eye contact. "I'm sorry, but I have my own young ones, and if I don't follow the rules, then..."

Enough is enough. I can't watch any more of this.

"Let go of them," I say in my most commanding voice. I walk forward holding up the dragon ring I received earlier. "On order of Ava'Kara, let this woman and her child through."

The Enforcer freezes, his eyes darting between me and the ring I now wield like a weapon.

My heart is pounding in my chest, and I'm soaking my tunic with sweat, the heat of the Dragon's Breath rolling off my skin. Behind me I can feel the Night brothers staring, their eyes drilling holes in my back.

While his partner looks annoyed at my intervention, the head Enforcer looks confused as to the right course of action. "But my orders..." he says.

I think he wants a way out of this. I don't believe he wants this woman and her child to die, but he's also a man who follows the law blindly, who values his own safety and health above that of others. He is like so many in my world who refuse to challenge what is clearly wrong, who refuse to look at the whole truth. Willfully blind and just as dangerous, just as cruel and evil as those who actively seek to harm. Maybe even worse, because their evil is subtle, insidious, unintentional. It's caused more by self-interest and an unwillingness to challenge a corrupt system than by any truly evil aspiration. It is the most prevalent kind of evil, and it enrages me to see it played out with such crass openness. He justifies it to himself because he thinks he's protecting his own family. His own children. But what of this woman? What of her child? What of their lives?

"Your orders are overruled," I say. "The dragons created this quarantine, did they not?"

He nods nervously.

"Then they are in a position to modify it as the need arises. I carry the authority of Ava'Kara. This woman and her child are clearly no threat, and they just as clearly are not hiding any egg. Let them through."

"Yes," he says, glancing once more at my ring. "Let them go."

His partner hesitates, and I see the small sadistic part of him that likes this power. Likes making others feel weaker. Less than. He likes being the big man with the big stick. He doesn't like that I'm taking it away from him.

"Let them go!" the Enforcer repeats again, and his partner pulls away from Kaya and spits on the ground by the tree. Kaya rights herself slowly, her eyes locked on the man who electrocuted her. She looks pissed, and I don't blame her. I'm pissed on her behalf, and I wasn't the one manhandled.

"Welcome to the Otherworld," the head Enforcer says, tipping his hat to the woman and her child. "I apologize for the—uh—for the misunderstanding."

Misunderstanding. Right. If we hadn't been here, they would have shoved her back into a world where she was being hunted. A world that would have killed them both, likely after doing unspeakable things to her.

He turns to leave, his partner following him. As he walks past me, he mumbles a 'thank you.'

I reach for his arm and pause him. "You might want to find work more suited to you," I whisper, giving him a meaningful look. He nods and continues walking.

The woman stands and comes to me, her eyes streaming with tears. "Thank you. You saved us."

I place a hand on her shoulder. "I hope you find safety here."

She sniffs and nods, and other dryads I didn't see before now come out of their trees to care for her and the child.

"Come, love," one says, taking her arm gently. "Let's get you cleaned up and find somewhere for you to stay."

Liam steps up to me, placing a hand on my back, a small smile on his face. "You sure know how to make an entrance."

"I guess you're not the only one with a temper," I say.

Kaya walks over to me and bows her head. "Thank you. It's not often someone bearing one of the dragon's seals actually helps me. Usually they're just trying to shut down my business."

"And what is your business?" I ask, curious.

"Helping folks get to the Otherworld, even if they can't pay their way." She cocks her head. "Especially if they can't pay their way."

"That sounds like a good cause," I say, holding out a hand to shake hers. "I'm Eve Oliver. My friend, Lily, said you may be able to help us."

At Lily's name, Kaya's face lights up. "Lily. How's she doing? Still getting into trouble?"

I pause. Clearly, she hasn't heard. "Lily was...she was injured in the explosion that happened in town. But she's recovering well."

Kaya's face pales. She looks over to the brothers. "You must be her uncles?"

"We are," Derek says as the rest of them join us.

"She told me about you all," she says.

"Only believe the good things," Derek says with a grin.

Kaya laughs. "It's all good things. She cares about you a lot."

"It's mutual," Sebastian says. "She's family."

Kaya nods. "Well, Eve Oliver and Lily's Uncles...tell me what you need, and I'll see what I can do. For Lily."

Elijah explains where we need to go.

"A two-way trip, huh?" Kaya strokes her chin, thinking. "Better make it fast. I have somewhere to be."

We follow her to the center tree, the largest of the grove, and we all lay our hands upon it. The bark feels rough against my palms, but I have only a moment to notice it before everything begins to spin and my vision is filled with a blinding light.

We appear under a different sky, dark and filled with thousands of stars. It's a strange sight after being away from the mundane world for so long. I miss the colors of the Dragon's Breath, but it is good to see the stars and a brilliant full moon again. The air is moist and fresh and smells of recently fallen rain against earth and grass. There's familiarity here, this world that I'm from, but it no longer feels like home, I realize. The Otherworld has become my home. The Night brothers, my family.

"Be quick," says Kaya, leaning against the trunk of her tree and lighting a pipe that she takes a deep inhale from. "Time's a ticking."

I turn to follow the Night brothers, since they seem to know where we are and where we're going. We're surrounded by trees on all sides, deep, shady forests that have come alive with the sounds of the night, of creatures scurrying under brush and birds flitting through the branches.

We walk down a narrow dirt path that leads to old stones peeking from beneath the dirt and moss. The ruins of an ancient building.

"What happened here?" I ask, looking at half-broken columns and empty fountains.

"Time," says Elijah. "It did to this place as it does to all things."

"Not all things," I say. "Not you."

"We, too, are ruins of what we once were." He flexes his hand, and a cool gust of wind picks up. "And yet, for some reason, our powers are returning."

Sebastian nods. "I felt it, too. When I lifted the rocks off Derek."

Elijah glances down at his hands again. "Perhaps Dracula's compulsion was affecting us in more ways than we realized."

Maybe Dracula was limiting their powers, but why? What did he have to gain?

Derek moves to walk by my side, pulling me from my thoughts. "Here is where new apprentices would sleep," he says, pointing to a ruin to the left. More broken columns and shattered walls. "And here used to be the baths. A part of me wishes I could go back in time. Sink my feet into the warm water." He closes his eyes and inhales deeply, and for a moment, he seems somewhere else, a smile on his face.

I notice three statues ahead. Large robed figures, their faces devoid of features, one face broken off. The detail is exquisite. Though they are carved of stone, the fabric on their bodies looks as if it could blow away in the breeze. What artistry and craftsmanship.

When Sebastian sees the statues, he bows his head as if in reverence.

"Who are they?" I ask.

"The three Fates," says Derek. "The Maiden, Mother, and Crone. They were the leaders of our Order."

Elijah nods. "It was said that the Crone could see into the past. The Mother things of the present. And the Maiden things of the future."

I freeze, thinking of Adam and his claims of future sight. "I thought you said no one could see the future," I whisper to Derek.

"No one but the Maiden," he says. "And even then, I have my doubts."

"Where are they now? The Fates?" I ask, my heart thundering in my chest as I try to make sense of what Adam said in relation to this new information. Could there be a connection?

"Gone," says Derek. "Most likely dead. You see, when our brother was imprisoned, it was the beginning of the end. His actions, though deemed a crime, inspired the Maiden to pursue a different course. She became obsessed with stopping the horrible things she would foretell at all costs. Even if it meant doing horrible things in turn."

My thoughts again turn to Adam. To Mary and the baby, dead at his feet. I exchange a worried glance with Derek.

"I am as concerned as you," he says quietly, "regarding recent developments. But I don't know anything more. Only that, once her sisters, the other Fates, learned of what the Maiden was doing, they fought. And no one has seen them since. Without the Fates, the Order collapsed."

"Were you close to them?" I ask.

"To the Fates?" He chuckles. "Not at all. We never even saw their faces. The Fates were...more goddesses than leaders. Something to be grasped at, worshipped even, but never fully understood."

A light rain begins to fall, and it quickly picks up. I look to Derek, but he shrugs. The brewing storm isn't his doing. Nor mine. My cloak is getting soaked and Liam puts an arm around me, his fire powers warming me. "Hurry," he says, guiding me forward, the others following.

He guides us under an archway still intact, towards stairs that lead underground. Before descending, I pause to take a last look at the statues. Three silhouettes in the distance. Rain splashing on their cloaks. Lightning flashing behind them. It reminds me of a dream I once had.

Of a voice in that dream. *"You should have died with your mother."*

Shivering, I descend into darkness.

WE ENTER a tunnel that smells of mildew and old dirt and something dead. I crinkle my nose and try to acclimate my night vision, but there isn't enough light to do much good. I feel around and find old torches lining the walls, long ago made useless by time, the elements, and lack of use. But with a flick of his hand, Liam lights them all.

"You'll have to teach me how to do that," I say.

Liam nods with a smile.

As each fire comes to life, the hall lights up, revealing crumbling old stone and the remains of dead rats.

I grab one of the torches since I don't have the see-in-the-dark superpowers they do, and we travel deeper and deeper. I do my best to avoid stepping on anything dead...or alive, as we walk.

"What will you do if...if your brother is still here?" I ask, my voice echoing off the walls.

Liam glances at me, his brow furrowed. Sebastian avoids my gaze and Elijah and Derek keep walking.

"Will you free him?" I ask, pressing the issue. "If he's still imprisoned?"

"Never," says Sebastian, without looking at me. "He would be a danger to us. To you."

"We would have to vote," says Elijah, glancing at his brother with a frown.

"Over a thousand years of imprisonment," says Liam. "I think Cole has paid enough."

I look to Derek, who answers after a moment. "Perhaps Cole deserves to be free," he says. And then more softly, "Perhaps we should be the ones to pay."

I study his solemn face, his wounded eyes, and I reach for his hand and squeeze it. Despite our recent arguments, he squeezes back. It was only a few days ago that these men were ready to take their own lives in payment for their sins. Their demons still haunt them...even if they've chosen to fight on.

"We're here," says Liam, and I follow him through an opening and into an antechamber. It's a massive stone room with painted carvings in the walls, most of which have faded with time.

But there's one I can still make out.

A woman's face framed by flowing silver hair that match her eyes.

I catch Elijah staring at it, then he quickly glances away.

In the center of the room a black, steel sarcophagus hangs from the ceiling, wrapped in silver chains.

I shiver at the sight of it, and the brothers all stop, staring at it as well.

I can't even imagine what it would do to a person to be locked in that for over a thousand years. I would go mad. Anyone would.

Even the shadows seem to swirl around it as if they, too, fear getting close to the monstrous prison. There's a dark energy in this room. A dangerous poison that creeps over my skin and bleeds into me.

"The bindings have been tampered with," Elijah says, taking a step closer. "It's closed but..." He reaches out, touching the black steel. The chains around the sarcophagus drop and he pulls it open.

It's empty.

My heart leaps into my throat when someone behind us begins clapping. I spin around, and there I see him.

The man from my dreams.

Pale skin in the torchlight. Dark tattoos covering his arms. A black cloak wrapped around him.

And eyes like the night.

Eyes that can steal your soul.

Cole.

CHAPTER 7: THE BEGGAR QUEEN

A STAR'S light shines the brightest, When it's starting to collapse. ~Supernova by Erin Hanson

SEBASTIAN STEPS FORWARD FIRST, his fists clenched, muscles tense. I can feel the ground beneath us tremble with his anger. "Are you here to take your revenge?" he asks.

Cole smirks, looking unconcerned. "No, *mon frère*. I'm here to help."

His French accent surprises me. I was expecting him to sound more British like his brothers.

"Really?" Sebastian doesn't sound convinced. The tension in the room is so thick I'm gagging on it. "Then why not reveal yourself sooner? Why all these cat and mouse games? We know you were at the festival."

Cole shrugs, leaning against the wall casually. Is he really this calm, I wonder? Or just good at faking it?

"I thought this would be the more appropriate location for our reunion," he says. "A walk down memory lane, as it were."

Something in another part of the ruins crashes to the ground as Sebastian struggles to control his powers. "This is just a game to you, isn't it? You enjoy toying with people, you always have. Tell me, how did you escape?"

Cole glances at the sarcophagus, and for the first time I see an emotion other than arrogance ripple across his face. Fear. But it's gone in an instant. "A thousand years is a long time. Perhaps the binding wore off..."

"Liar—"

Derek places a hand on Sebastian's arm, giving him a warning glance. "Control yourself, brother," he says softly. "Or you'll bring the whole place down on our heads."

Sebastian takes a deep breath and steps back, deliberately unclenching his fists.

Derek studies Cole, his expression a mixture of wariness and hope. "Why help us?" he asks in a much less combative tone than Sebastian.

Cole steps forward, holding the palms of his hands open in petition. "Because I didn't do it, even though you seem to think I did. This heist was masterful...but not my own. And I would never take credit for someone else's work. You should know that about me, *mon frère*."

"That's a very generous attitude, all things considered," Derek says. "What do you want from us, in return for this help?"

"I want what I have always wanted. Peace between us, brothers. My family back." His voice cracks, and either he is a skilled performer, or he's being sincere.

"After what you did?" Sebastian spits, his words creating another shift of stone and rock around us.

Cole scoffs. "After what I did? I stopped a murdering stain on the fabric of humanity. What about what you did to me?" Cole asks, coming face to face with Sebastian. "You betrayed your own brother. Your flesh and blood? And for what?"

Even Sebastian is put in his place by Cole's words, and he looks away, unable to face him.

Liam stares at the scars on his arms, and Elijah and Derek look thoughtful. Lost in past memories.

In the silence, a flash hits me, making my head spin and my stomach clench. As I take a step closer to Cole, the effects ease, and I realize something with certainty. Something the Night brothers aren't going to like. "We need him," I say, through clenched teeth. The closer I get to Cole, the better I feel, until I am standing inches from him, our gazes locked. "We need him to solve this and save Liam."

Cole studies me, his lips curling into a smile. "Smart woman. *Et belle.* My brothers showed unexpected wisdom in bringing you into the family."

Though we're not making physical contact, I feel his touch nonetheless, as if his hands are caressing my face. I blink and take a step back, my senses rattled by this intense intimacy I'm experiencing against all logic.

"He could be useful," Elijah says. "Whether he is indeed guilty, or as innocent as he claims, he could help in gaining access to our other suspects."

Cole doesn't break eye contact with me as he responds. "What are your leads?"

"None of your business," Sebastian says, glaring at Elijah. "We shouldn't be sharing anything with him. We don't know what he's up to and we can't trust him."

Elijah shrugs. "What can we lose by seeing what he has to offer? We haven't got many options and even less time in which to solve this."

"Elijah's right," Derek says. "We must explore all possibilities, and if Cole can help, so be it."

Liam steps forward, his eyes haunted. "If Eve says we need him, I trust her."

Sebastian throws up his hands in defeat and crosses his arms over his chest, sulking as Elijah answers Cole. "The Collector could be behind this, and if he isn't, there's a good chance he knows something."

Cole nods. "And?"

"And the Beggar Queen," Derek says. "She's been at odds with the dragons for as long as anyone can remember. She had the motive and the means to pull this off."

Cole finally breaks eye contact with me to look at his brothers, and in that instant, I feel his touch—his presence—vanish from my body. I release a breath I didn't realize I was holding and shiver. Liam puts a protective arm around my shoulders, his heat and strength a comfort.

Cole paces, his finger on his chin. "The Collector will be tricky. He is hard to get close to, even for me, and keeps his secrets well hidden. But you know I can get you in to see the Beggar Queen, as you call her, though she would never refer to herself as such."

"What is she the queen of?" I ask.

"The lost and forgotten," Cole says softly.

"Indeed," Elijah says, though he doesn't sound particularly happy about it. He turns to the rest of us. "I think we may need him."

"I don't," Sebastian says, stepping forward once again. "He betrayed us once before and he will again."

I pull away from Liam to stand before Sebastian, placing a hand on his chest. "It's Liam's future on the line. He should decide."

Everyone looks to the fire Druid, who sighs and turns to Cole.

I already know what Liam will say. Not just because he wants to get out of this mess, but because he wants to atone for his own sins.

"We have no way of knowing your true motives," he tells Cole. "Even still, I say we give you a chance."

Cole smiles a wolfish grin.

"The Order would never have accepted this," Sebastian roars, causing the sarcophagus to crash to the ground, startling everyone.

Derek frowns. "Look around, brother. We are all that's left. The Order is gone."

And with that, the decision is made. We make haste back to the Otherworld with Cole in tow. Kaya seems impatient to get on with her other errands, though she catches my eye as we head to the carriage and nods briefly at me, mouthing a simple 'thank you.' The woman and child we helped earlier are both being cared for by the dryads, the child nursing peacefully as the mother rests against one of the trees, and I hope that they find a good life here. That their terror and pain will be things of the past as they try to rebuild.

We are all shaped and haunted by our pasts. I haven't yet lived thirty years, and already I feel the weight of my life tugging at my heart, clouding my mind, shaping my choices for good or ill. I can't imagine having hundreds of years piling on me, like dirt on a coffin, burying me in the darkness of my past decisions, stealing away my breath with each handful of years dropped on me.

What must each of the Night brothers be feeling as we climb into the carriage and set off to meet the Beggar Queen? What memories must be resurfacing as they all face their own darkness?

Cole sits in the front with Elijah, guiding the carriage to our destination, since he's the only one who knows where we're going. Sebastian, Liam, and Derek sit in the back with me, though all are quiet and lost in thought.

I don't want to disturb them, but I reach for Sebastian's hand, as he sits beside me, and he takes it, though he doesn't look my way. But with the touch, his shoulders seem to relax just a fraction, and I hope that he can find some peace in all this mess.

They have their brother back, and it's a mixed bag for them. I get it. All too well. I kind of have my twin back, but I still don't know how to feel about all he's done...all he's become. Is evil done in the name of justice justifiable? Do we have the right to take a life preemptively to protect future innocents? Do we have the right to take a life in righteous justice when it goes against the laws of the land? At what point do we need to stop blindly following other people's rules for what's expected of us and take a stand for what we believe is right?

Both Cole and Adam clearly believe their actions—their murders—were justified. Righteous, even. And yet I am left with questions my soul cannot answer. Questions all my reading and all my knowledge and all my intelligence cannot find a definitive solution for.

Maybe there is no answer. Maybe the whole point is to question, and to keep questioning as we strive to find our way in this messy world.

After spending too much time studying the brothers and thinking about Cole, I turn my attention to the window and watch as the landscape changes. Where before we crossed through either wide expanses of open land or crowded but comfortably situated populated areas, now we move into the type of area I haven't seen in this world before, though I'm familiar enough with it from my own. Ruined buildings scatter the landscape, climbing with ivy and covered in moss as nature takes back its own. The roads are dirt and full of holes and rocks, making the journey dangerous and painful. As we come closer to the town, the poverty and unsuitable living conditions become more glaring. Malnourished children of various races run around naked, covered in dirt and slime. Entire families live in shelters constructed with bits of stick propping up palm branches as makeshift roofs. Insects buzz everywhere, more well fed than any of the people living here. What little clothing exists consists of torn rags hanging off emaciated bodies.

Though there's plenty of wilderness, there's little in the way of farmland or food sources. It's clear no Enforcer has been here in ages, if ever. Nothing has been done to create suitable living arrangements for the people here. The world has forgotten them.

We reach the end of the road and have to disembark and make our way on foot from there. The smell hits me first. Rot and bodily waste mix with the smell of cooking grains and unwashed children. I stifle the urge to gag and take shallow breaths. Cole steps up next to me, leading the way down a small alley.

"This is what coloring within the lines gets you, *mon cher*," he says. His eyes are full of pain as he looks around at those suffering. "Playing by the rules, following those in command…it only serves those in power. These are the people who pay the price."

We reach the end of the alley where two basilisks guard one of the only standing structures in this village. They're both dressed in dirty white robes, their large serpentine bodies framing a double door made of ashen wood. They are more snake than human, and like the guard who died at the nest, they wear blindfolds over their eyes. Their reptilian tongues flick out of their mouths, tasting the air.

"It hassss been sssssome time, Cole," one says, his words coming out as a hiss.

"It's good to see you, Raz. How are the kids?"

Raz nods his head. "Ssssstrong, like their mother. And you? What do you sssssseek?"

"We request an audience with Lyx, if she is able to see us," Cole says with respect in his voice.

The second basilisk hisses and turns her face to the other Night brothers. "I know you," she says. "Traitorsssss to our causssse. You are not welcome here." Then she turns to me, testing the air with her tongue. "You, I do not know."

"Bron," Cole says to the female, "this is Eve Oliver. She's with me."

"Eve Oliver," Bron says, testing my name aloud.

The basilisks pause, and the two of them touch their heads together, whispering through hisses.

Raz raises his head to speak. "Cole and the woman may enter. The resssst musssst remain."

Sebastian steps forward and I cringe, knowing this is not going to go well.

"I'm not leaving her alone with Cole. He's dangerous," Sebastian says.

"It's my life on the line," Liam says. "I should be the one to go."

"Guys, I'll be okay. No good will come from making a scene. This is our one chance to talk to her. Trust me, okay? I can take care of myself," I say, giving both of them a reassuring hand squeeze.

Then Cole, not helping matters in the least, throws an arm over my shoulder. "And I'll be sure to look out for her, too. She'll be well cared for in my very capable hands."

The earth tremors slightly as Sebastian clenches his jaw and fists, ready to strike out at his brother.

I slip away from Cole and glare at him, then shoot a look at Sebastian. "Wait for us at the carriage," I say.

He nods, then turns sharply away. Derek and Elijah give me half-hearted smiles but say nothing.

Liam grabs my arm. "Be careful. With all of them."

I nod, then follow Cole, leaving the others behind.

We enter through the double doors into a large room. Intricate rugs are intermittently spread over the dirt-packed floors and pewter lamps with colored glass hang on the walls. The air is perfumed with burning herbs and scented oils, and at the end of the room several people are lounging on purple and red pillows. In the center of the group is the Beggar Queen—Lyx. Though she, too, sits on a pillow, a goblet of wine at her side, she stands out amongst them all. Her gown is pure white. Her hair is long and silver—the same color as her eyes. She glows like a star against the night sky. Like a diamond.

"I recognize her," I whisper to Cole. "Her likeness was carved into the ruins in England."

He nods as we approach.

The queen stands and opens her arms to greet us. Cole walks into them, giving the woman an affectionate hug. She pats his face, studying him, then tilts her head and kisses his forehead. "Watch yourself, my son. You are teetering close to the abyss."

"That's the only way to truly find balance," Cole says with a charming grin.

She laughs, and he steps aside, so I can approach.

"I have heard rumors of you," the queen says, bringing me in for an unexpected embrace.

When she releases me, I step back and clear my throat. "Good ones, I hope?"

She smirks. "Strange ones. Regarding your abilities." She raises an eyebrow, as if in question. But I have no answers for her.

"Were you a Druid?" I ask, changing the subject.

She nods. "Long ago. But I renounced that Order...much like Cole, here."

I glance at Cole, then back at her. I know why he left the Order, but... "Why did you leave?"

She sits and invites us to join her, then pours us each a cup of wine. Once we are settled, she answers, "The Order claimed to help the people, but more and more, I saw that help go mostly to the wealthy and privileged. I left to help those who needed it the most."

I take a sip of the wine, realizing how thirsty I am after all the dusty travel. "I take it you and the other Night brothers didn't part on good terms?"

"No," she says. "We did not."

Of course. This is why she won't see them. "I don't know what happened between you all...but Liam is being accused of a crime he didn't commit, and I intend to prove his innocence."

The queen takes a sip of wine. "Are you a lawyer, as well?"

"I work for the firm," I say. "And I was hoping you could help me. I'm looking for information about the stolen dragon egg."

She cocks her head, studying me. "And what makes you think I know anything?"

Well, shit. I can't come right out and say she's a suspect, but I have the sense that anything less than the truth won't sit well with her, either. "To be honest, we're short on leads and even shorter on time. You're someone with influence and authority. Someone who inspires those who don't fit into the system. Whoever took the egg likely wanted to throw a wrench into the power structure of this world. That seems like something you might know about."

"Very well put," she says with a smile. "You have clearly learned the art of speaking to the heart of a truth."

"So, will you help?" I ask again. "Liam doesn't deserve to be punished for this."

"Who is to weigh the scales on what someone does or does not deserve?" she asks. "How heavy is Liam's soul? How would it compare to the weight of this punishment, I wonder?"

"Do you believe you can know that?" I ask frankly. "Do you have the measure of every person in your presence? Let alone the measure of one you haven't seen in such a long time? You formed your opinion of Liam and the other brothers a thousand years ago. And maybe at the time it was valid. But do you not believe people can change? That they can redeem themselves? When was the last time you reconsidered your own misjudgments?"

Cole is staring at me. I can feel his dark gaze like a physical touch. But I don't turn to look at him. Instead, I stare into the silver eyes of the woman before me, unwaveringly.

Finally, she sighs, and leans back, breaking contact. "I don't know who has the egg," she says. But there are words left unspoken, as if she is not telling me all she knows.

"Please," I say. "If you know anything more, share it. They're locking down the Otherworld. Until the egg is found, people who seek refuge will be denied. As bad as is it for refugees here, imagine what they face in the mundane world. They are feared, hunted, killed. They need your help. If not for Liam or me, then for them."

"Oh child, you have no idea, do you? You really don't know."

I straighten my back, staring at the queen. "Don't know what?"

"The dragons," she says softly. "The dragons always want more power. Especially Dath'Racul. He seeks to increase taxes. Reduce support to the poor. For a while, his efforts were considered too extreme. But no longer. Not with the egg missing. Now the people embrace his ways. As does the Council."

"You think...Dath'Racul stole the egg himself?" I ask. "To tighten government control?"

She shrugs. "Possibly. Or maybe one of the other dragons. Water. Earth. Fire. Air. Darkness. They used to want to help the world. But at some point, they decided to help themselves first."

She lowers her voice. "I asked my brothers and sisters to change their ways, I begged them. But they would not. So, I am here...with those they have forgotten...and they are in their palaces of crystal and gold."

Her brothers and sisters? I look at the queen of beggars again, seeing her as if for the first time as a vision overtakes me and reveals to me the queen's true self.

In the darkness of my mind a brilliant silver-white dragon stands before me, radiant like a star, vast as a mountain. She glows with light that emanates from within, casting out the shadows with her very presence.

"The dragon of light... " I say in awe.

She nods, smiling gently. "I was. Yes. But even I was not bright enough to burn the darkness out of the Order, or out of the Council of Dragons. I am sorry I cannot help you further, but I wish you the best in your quest, daughter." She leans in to kiss my cheek, and I feel a spark between us. Her eyes widen in wonder and surprise, and she studies me carefully as we are escorted out the room and back into the alley.

"She was our mentor," Cole tells me as we walk back to the carriage where the others have gone to wait. "For a while, anyway. She taught Druids about the light. My brothers had a propensity for the other elements. Fire. Water. Earth. Air. But I..." He holds up a hand and a ball of white light appears, lighting up the dark alley.

"You were a light Druid," I say, realization dawning on me.

"Once," he says, his voice soft. Reflective. "Very long ago." He drops his hand, and the light fades, drawing us into darkness once more.

CHAPTER 8: THE FLAME

SHE, In the dark, Found light Brighter than many ever see.
  -Helen Keller by Langston Hughes

AFTER SOME DELIBERATION, it's decided Cole will come back to the castle with us.

I fill them all in on what Lyx said, and now we need to decide what to do next.

"Investigating the dragons will be tricky, at best," Derek says as we bump along the road.

I rub my backside, confident there will be bruises. "Any chance we can get some, I don't know, cushions back here? I'm going to be black and blue after today."

"If you need a massage, I have excellent hands," Cole says, holding said hands up with a wink.

He's not wrong. They are fine looking hands. Strong with long fingers. A musician's hands.

Elijah and Derek both frown.

"We can make it more comfortable," Elijah says. "I've actually been considering some upgrades to the carriage. Just haven't had time."

"Thanks," I say. "If you need help, let me know. I'm pretty handy."

Elijah raises an eyebrow. "I wouldn't have guessed."

"I'm not just a pretty face and a smart brain," I say. "I have other skills."

Cole throws an arm around my shoulders. "That doesn't surprise me at all. In fact, I look forward to learning all about your other skills."

His attention is flattering and disconcerting and I'm just glad the two hotheads up front aren't here to witness it. Though with their vampire hearing, Liam and Sebastian probably aren't missing much.

Derek clears his throat. "Back to the dragons?"

"Yes, this will need to be handled very carefully," Elijah says. "They are too powerful to come at directly. We need to be discreet in our questions, and we can't let anyone suspect that we are going after them."

"Or what?" I ask. "Shouldn't the people have the right to question their leadership?"

Cole smirks. "Not here. This isn't a democracy. This is an autocracy. It may seem the Dragon Council is balanced, but really Dath'Racul runs things and keeps the other dragons under his thumb. Lyx'Ara dissented by trying to put their focus back on the people rather than their own personal power and look how that turned out for her. The Dragon of Darkness mostly holes up in his dungeon and doesn't much care for the rest of the world. And the others are too cowed by Dath to stop him in his pursuits. Especially now."

"So, they can do anything to anyone and there's no one to hold them accountable?" I ask.

"Pretty much," Cole says.

"That's not entirely true," says Elijah, pointedly. "We do have some checks and balances. We have a legal system set up with rules. There is a way to work within the system to change things."

Cole scoffs. "Right. How's that going for you? Or did you give up helping people when you became vampires?"

"We are defense attorneys," Derek reminds him. "It's our job to help people who are in trouble."

Cole leans back, crossing his arms over his chest. "That's an interesting choice of career for men who were more than willing to throw their own brother under the bus. Where was my defense when I needed one the most?"

No one has an answer for him, and so we travel in silence the rest of the way home.

The tension is thick when we arrive and head inside the castle. Matilda is waiting by the door, her eyes red and swollen like she's been crying.

When she sees Cole, she cries out, holding her arms open. "My boy. You've come home at last."

I don't entirely know what I was expecting, but when Cole embraces her and his eyes well up with tears, I'm shocked. I had no idea they were so close. There's so much to their history I don't know. So much I will likely never know.

"*Grand-mère*," he says with raw emotion. "I'm sorry I didn't come sooner."

He pulls away and she pats him on his cheek like a child. "You look good. I know you've been through more than most, but you've always been strong. Brave. I knew you'd come out of it okay."

Cole looks away frowning. "Well, I came out of it at least."

Matilda leads him in by the hand. "I hope your tastes haven't changed too much. I've prepared all your favorite foods."

We follow them into the dining room, and my stomach rumbles loud enough to draw looks from everyone.

Cole pulls out a seat next to his. "Join me? Have my brothers not been keeping you fed? Their appetites have changed, but you cannot live on blood."

Sebastian bristles at that. "She has plenty of food to eat anytime she wants."

Cole rolls his eyes and we both sit. The others all do as well, and Matilda brings out food for those of us who eat and blood for those who don't.

Lily makes a surprise visit, joining us. She smiles shyly at Cole and holds out a hand. "We haven't met. I'm Lily. The Nights adopted me into their family, years ago."

Cole stands and kisses her hand gallantly. "*Enchantè*. It is a pleasure to make your acquaintance. I've always found dryads very magical."

She nods then takes a seat across from us.

"May I ask, how is it you have a French accent, while your brothers don't?"

There's an uncomfortable silence as they glance at each other, and it's Matilda who answers for them.

"Cole spent most of his childhood training in France," she says. "He was particularly gifted with his magick at an early age and was sent to apprentice there."

"I fell in love with the country," Cole says. "If not with my master."

Matilda frowns. "I'm sorry, my boy. If we had known… "

Cole shrugs. "It is in the past, is it not? This is the time for new beginnings."

As we begin eating, a cry interrupts us from the other room. Liam jumps up, setting his goblet of blood down. "Excuse me."

Cole looks over, confused. "There's a baby here?"

"I'm surprised you didn't already know," Sebastian says bitterly. "You seem to know everything else despite having been gone for a thousand years."

Cole sips at his wine and smiles. "I've done due diligence, but some rumors clearly haven't reached me yet." He looks to me. "Is the child yours?"

I blush and shake my head. "Liam's. She is half human, though."

Liam returns with the baby bundled in his arms. His expression softens as he looks at his daughter. "She just needed a change and a bottle," he says, feeding her as he takes his seat.

Cole can't take his eyes off of them. "I'm an…uncle?"

The four other brothers look at him, but only Liam nods. "It would appear so."

We eat in silence, and when Matilda brings us apple pie fresh from the oven, Cole moves to sit next to Liam. "May I...would it be okay if I held her?"

The two lock eyes, and I can see the war in Liam. The desire to protect his child. His suspicion of Cole. But also...his own guilt. His desire to reconcile with his brother. Finally, he nods and hands the child over. "Make sure to support her head, and here, curve your arm so she can lay in it."

Liam adjusts Cole's arm and arranges Alina in his arms. Cole sits next to Liam, studying his niece, cooing to her and letting her play with his finger.

"She's strong," he says, smiling. "A mighty grip."

She gurgles and then quite suddenly a tiny burst of flames shoot from her hands, singeing the edges of Cole's hair. He handles it in stride, laughing as he uses his free hand to pat at his head. We are all staring, wide-eyed.

Cole looks around. "I take it this is new?"

Liam nods. "She's never shown powers before."

Matilda shakes her head. "We're going to need to fireproof her room. Goodness knows what she'll be up to now."

Liam's grinning like a fool. "She's a fire element. I wasn't sure if she'd have active powers, being half human."

"She takes after her father," I say with a smile, and Liam smiles back, his happiness so pure it swells my heart.

"Speaking of powers," I say. "I've become something of the Otherworld freak. Everyone we meet wants to know what I am. What I can do. I don't know what to say, and I feel like my powers are just out of control. I need help learning how to use them. How to control them. How to even figure out what they are. Will you all help me?"

Matilda nods, finishing the last bite of her pie. "I was going to suggest this myself. It seems, my dear, that you have power from many of the elements. Maybe all of them. This is incredibly rare. It makes you a magical anomaly of sorts. I think it best you train with each of my grandsons to learn to control the different elements and under-stand your limits."

My body buzzes with a new excitement. I will finally learn what I can do. Maybe this will even help me understand what I am. Who I am. And just maybe it will also help me understand my brother better.

Deep down, in a place I don't like to look at much, I also fear what I will become if I unleash my powers.

Will I become like my twin? Willing to do anything—no matter how atrocious—if I believe it will serve the greater good? But how can anyone be assured of that? How can anyone truly, in their soul, justify evil deeds for the sake of what might be?

"I can train with you a bit tonight," Liam says, pulling my attention back to the conversation.

Derek nods. "That's a good idea. I need Elijah to help with some research. We have to start preparing for the trial."

"I can take care of the baby while you two are training," Sebastian says. "I haven't had much time with my niece."

Matilda rises. "Well now, that's been settled. Cole, your room is readied for you. Come with me, and then you and I can have a nice cup of tea and catch up."

Cole hands the baby over to Sebastian and follows Matilda out, sparing one last glance at me, his expression slightly haunted.

Derek and Elijah leave for the study, and Liam takes my hand as we head to the forge. "It's best to practice fire magic in a place suited for heat and fire. We wouldn't want to burn anything down."

I can't imagine my powers being strong enough to do that kind of damage, but it's a smart precaution.

The forge is a large building adjacent to the castle and smells of hot metal and burning wood. No one is here, but there is work being done. The fire is stoked, metal is being melted, cooled, and hammered into different shapes. I stand, gaping. "Ghosts?" I ask.

Liam nods. "They use the forge to make things useful to the castle. Every once in awhile, we'll find a new sword or knife, meticulously made in the finest craftsmanship. We believe one of the ghosts must have been a master metal worker in their time."

"That's… incredible." I swipe my forehead with the sleeve of my shirt, mopping the sweat off my brow, and I wonder if improving my fire element will help me handle heat better.

Liam seems completely fine. Not a drop of sweat on him.

"How do you do that?" I ask.

"Do what? We haven't even started yet."

"Not sweat," I say. "I feel like I'm in a sauna."

He laughs, and, god, I love the sound of it. He should laugh more often.

"I don't know. I guess it's an inherent part of my powers."

"I hope it's contagious," I say, swiping again at my forehead as sweat burns my eyes.

"Let's see what you can do," he says, standing in front of me. "Remember, I'm fireproof, so don't worry about losing control. I've got you."

That does make me feel better. "How do I start?"

"Imagine a flame in the center of your body, deep within. Tap into that flame, letting it flare within you until you can feel it in your hands," he says.

I close my eyes and attempt to do what he says, but instead of fire, a strong wind blows around us.

I sigh and open my eyes. "Wrong element."

He chuckles. "But close. Fire and air are aligned. Air helps stoke fire's flames. Fire can't breathe without air. Keep trying."

This time he stands behind me and wraps his arms around me, holding my hands in his. I close my eyes and lean into him as his body heats up. I feel his flames, simmering in his palms, glancing against my flesh, but it doesn't burn me. It warms me.

His lips are against my ear, his voice soft as he guides me. "Do you feel the fire in me?" he asks.

I nod.

"It's in you as well. You just have to find it. Unlike us, you have more than one element at work, so it might be confusing. But it's there. Let my flame light your way."

His heat burns through my own resistance and I slide deeper into myself. There, in the center of my soul, I see the elemental powers that animate my magic. My breathing hitches as I realize it's not just a few of the elements I can access.

It's all of them.

All six.

I embrace the fire and feel the balancing tonic of earth and air. The light in me is strong and powerful. But it is the darkness, lurking beneath, floating like a black cloud, that scares me. I shy away from it, unwilling to touch it lest it corrupt me and turn me into something I do not want to be. I focus back on the fire, urging the tiny flame to grow.

After a moment, I feel Liam's arms tighten around me. "Open your eyes," he whispers.

I do, slowly, and at first all I see is his fire dancing on his palms. Then I look more closely and realize my hand also holds the flame.

"I'm doing it," I say, excitement surging within me.

"You are," he says, smiling against my cheek. "Now see if you can control it. Try to throw the flame at the wall."

"What if I break something?" I ask.

"Trust me, this place has seen it all. It's indestructible. At least, by fire."

I nod and focus my mind on the ball of fire in my hand. With a flick of my wrist, I toss it, and to my surprise, I'm successful! The flaming ball flies across the room, slams into the stone wall, and fizzles out at impact.

Liam steps back and grins, his flames gone now. "You're a fast study," he says. "That took an incredible amount of control."

"That was amazing," I say, studying my hands like they might reveal all the answers. "I've never felt like that before. When I used my powers before, it was by accident. I didn't know what I was doing. I still don't know how I did what I did. But now, I could feel the control, the power. It's raw and rusty, but still...I did it."

He nods. "You'll get more proficient at it with time. Now you need to practice."

And so we do. For the next hour, Liam has me throwing balls of fire, setting things on fire, dancing flames off my fingertips, and finally, he instructs me to light a candle. This proves to be the hardest of all. I melt a few candles down to the wick in my attempts to light them.

"I can't do this," I say. "I feel like I could burn a small village down, but I can't seem to light one stupid candle."

"You're tired, and smaller things require more control. You can't just unleash it all at once, you have to learn to manage your power. You'll get there. Let's pause for tonight. You look like you could use a bath and a rest."

A bath sounds amazing, and Liam walks me up to my room, gently kisses me goodnight, and leaves me to tend to myself.

As predicted, I am bruising. Badly. I bathe, letting the hot water wash away some of my pain. Moon perches on the tub next to me, meowing to be pet as I relax, and I give him some love. Then I get out and put a bathrobe on. But I'm not ready to sleep, though I should.

Instead, I make my way to Liam's room, where I hear him playing the violin. The music seeps into my soul and brings up a flood of emotion. I wait by the door, letting the last melancholic notes fade before I knock.

He's only wearing pants when he opens it, and his eyes widen in surprise at seeing me.

Suddenly I feel self-conscious. "I was hoping—as a healer—you might have something for my bruises?"

He nods, letting me in. "Show me," he says.

I suck in my breath, and then I undo my robe and let it drop to my feet, so that I'm standing before him naked. His eyes widen, and he stares at me for a long moment. "You're...you're so beautiful, Eve." His breath hitches on my name and I feel a new kind of fire alight within me.

I turn to show him my back and it's his turn to suck in a breath. "I will make sure Elijah does something to fix the carriage before you have to ride in it again," he says, frowning. "If you lie on the bed, I'll apply a cream to the bruises that should help you heal faster."

It's cool out, with a gentle breeze coming in through the open window, but all I feel is the heat igniting within me as I lie face down on his bed and breathe in his scent. I hear him moving around the room, and then feel as he sits on the bed, his body pressing against mine.

"Is it okay if I touch you?" he asks.

Right now, I want him to do a lot more than just touch me, but everything feels as if it's teetering on the edge of something important, and so I whisper, "yes," and wait.

He's been all about consent since I chewed him out for biting me against my will.

Now I crave the feel of his teeth sliding into my flesh.

But I settle for his warm hands as he slowly rubs something minty smelling into my back. Instantly, the aches and pains begin to fade. He's skilled with his hands, massaging my muscles with expert technique, easing out the stiffness and knots that I carry with me almost always. He runs his fingers between my ribs, from my spine to the sides of my breasts. As he works his way lower, every nerve in my body comes alive. His palms caress the dip in my back and then his hands cup my ass, rubbing and massaging until the pain is completely gone, and all I feel is a desperate arousal at his closeness, his touch, the vulnerability of being naked here with him.

It's quiet as he continues down my legs, fingers grazing between my thighs, coming so close to where I really want them to be, but then pulling back. He completes the massage at my feet, then lightly runs his hands over my body once more, letting out a spark of his magic and sending flashes of warmth over me.

"How do you feel?" he asks, his throat thick with his own desire.

I turn over and lay naked, facing him. "Amazing. I hope you're going to do my front as well?"

His pupils dilate and the bulge in his pants grows. This time he begins at my feet and slowly works his way up my legs. His gaze is locked on mine as he moves over me, straddling my legs so he can be in a better position. When he reaches my hips, he pauses. "How deep of a massage do you want?" he asks, his voice nearly breathless.

"As deep as you can give," I say.

He moans softly at my words, and his hands slide between my legs. He repositions himself so that I'm spread before him, and he teases at the flesh there, grazing but not penetrating.

Dipping his head closer to me, he takes a nipple into his mouth, and the sudden wave of pleasure that hits me makes my hips arch.

He moves his lips up to my neck, raking my skin with his now-elongated teeth.

I wrap my arms around him, pulling him closer to me. "I want you," I say.

He raises his head to look at me. "I have wanted you since I tasted you," he says.

He pulls away long enough to take his pants off, and I study his beautiful—and fully aroused—body. It's a masterpiece of perfection. One that could have been sculpted from marble. I run my hand over his chest and abs as he positions himself above me. Then his hand dips between my legs, and he kisses me deeply while using his fingers to pleasure me.

As the tension mounts, just before release, he removes his hand and pushes his hips into me as he sinks his teeth into my neck.

I cry out, my body pressing against his, my fingers digging into his back, as I am gripped by the best orgasm of my life. The heat between us is so intense it's nearly smoldering.

After a few minutes, he pulls me up, onto his lap, and we face each other as we continue making love. His hands explore my body, and I am consumed by him in every way.

Another orgasm grips me, and as I give into it, so, too, does he. We ride that wave together until we are both spent.

It's only then that I realize I smell something burning, and we both look at the bed and realize it's ablaze.

Instantly, I channel the water element within me, in the same way I controlled the fire, and I summon enough to drown the flames, though I also succeed in soaking most of the bed.

"This is the first time I've set my bed on fire," he says, holding me in his arms, my head on his chest.

"Or I set it on fire," I say.

"I have a feeling it was both of us." He kisses my forehead, sighing deeply. "I've never met anyone like you, Eve. No one has ever made me feel this way before."

"Not even Mary?" I ask. I instantly regret bringing up her name, and all the joy I felt a moment before crashes into regret as I consider the awful secret I'm keeping from him. My stomach twists as I fight with myself over what I should do about Adam and Liam.

"Not even Mary," he says. "I've had other lovers. I've lived a long life. But I've never had this." He tilts my head up so I'm looking into his eyes. "I've never had you."

CHAPTER 9: THE BALL

How much can come And much can go, And yet abide the world!
~Emily Dickinson

"She has a right to make her own decisions!" Cole's voice carries through the halls and I pause outside the library door, my flash tingling through my body.

They're talking about me.

"It's not worth the risk," Liam shouts back, and I can picture the two of them—Liam and Cole—staring each other down. Liam with his fiery temper and ginger good looks, Cole with his almost eerie calmness and dark, mysterious sexiness. Cole will keep his voice level, his emotions in check, which will just further infuriate Liam.

"The egg could be there," Cole says, his voice firm but level. "And she's the only one who got an invite. Of course, she should go. If she's willing. Either way, it should be her choice, not yours."

"Liam's right," Sebastian says, undoubtedly folding his arms over his muscular chest. "She'd be surrounded by the powerful but shady elite of our society. It's dangerous."

Cole snickers. "I think she's proven she can take care of herself. You underestimate her. You all do."

I sigh and push the door open. "What's too dangerous for me?" I ask the five Night brothers, who all pause their argument to stare at me.

"Well? Anyone want to explain?"

Cole smiles, turning the full weight of his natural seductiveness towards me and causing my knees to turn to jelly. He grabs something from Liam's hand and walks over, his gaze locked on mine. "You have been invited to a ball, *mon cher*," he says with a flourish, holding out a golden ticket.

I take it from him and study it.

At first, the ticket is blank save for the shiny gold finish. Then words begin to appear.

MISS EVE OLIVER is cordially invited to the Annual Winter Masquerade Ball hosted by Lord Nicholas Vanderbilt who looks forward to making your acquaintance.

ON THE BACK is a date and time but no location. "What's the significance of this ball?" I ask.

"Nothing," Liam says.

"Everything," Cole says at the same time. "It's the who's who of the Otherworld, and anybody who's anybody will be there. Lord Nicholas Vanderbilt is the Collector, and he will be having a secret auction that night where only a select view will be invited." Cole smiles at me. "If you attend, you could charm your way into that auction and see if he's got the egg."

"Why am I the only one who got an invitation?" I ask.

Derek shrugs. "You're a novelty, despite working for us. Meeting you is too enticing for him to pass up."

"Obviously I have to go, if there's a chance we could solve the case and save Liam," I say, glancing at the fire Druid, who doesn't make eye contact with me. Men are so mercurial, it's maddening.

"That's out of the question," Sebastian says. "We wouldn't be there to protect you, and anything could happen. The Collector is not one to mess with."

"I can escort her," Cole says. "If you're so worried about her safety."

Liam scoffs. "She's no safer with you. And besides, you didn't get a ticket."

Cole shrugs. "Very well, I'll keep my distance, but she should still go."

Before they can continue this argument, I clear my throat. "You all must be confused. I'm not asking for permission. I'm going to the ball. Alone. It's our biggest lead yet. And Cole is right. I can take care of myself."

I don't feel as confident as I sound about that last part, given my lack of control over my powers and my fears surrounding them, but this is the right decision, and they can suck it if they think they get to control what I do.

I smile charmingly. "I'd better go shopping for an outfit, then."

THE NIGHT OF THE BALL, Lily helps me dress. And given the complexity of the gown I'm wearing, I need all the help I can get.

It takes us—no lie—about four hours to get me ready. FOUR HOURS!?!?!? I'm so exhausted when we're done that I don't even want to go anymore, but Lily just laughs at me and spins me to face the mirror.

I gasp.

I look…magical.

The dress is Dryad inspired, made of shimmering emerald green fabric that curves around my body seductively, with slashes cut out to reveal my stomach and cleavage. Vines—that are magicked to look real and move on their own—wind up my legs and arms and twine around my gown dotted with white blossoms. My mask is made of diamonds and emeralds that are applied to my face directly, like makeup, so that I look as if I'm becoming a gemstone. The same stones dot my hair, which is twisted into elaborate braids intertwined with thin vines blossoming with more white flowers. My lips are blood red, my eyes are painted with sparkling silver, and the rest of my exposed skin is dusted with powdered diamond magicked to sparkle all night.

Lily drives me to our destination in the carriage, which has been recently cleaned, polished, and upgraded with deep cushions and a much better shock absorbing system. I have to remember to thank Elijah—and Liam, who very likely lit a fire under the air Druid's ass.

The horses are brushed down and wearing their most elaborate gear. We are quite the splendor, arriving as we do.

With a silly curtsy, Lily leaves me at the entrance and escapes into the nearby trees to await my return. I stand before the grand double doors and take a nervous breath. I got this.

Straightening my back, I clench my ticket in my hand and ring the bell.

The doors immediately open, and an older man in a black tux, likely the butler, asks to see my ticket. I hand it to him, and he waves a hand inviting me in.

Inside the manor is a lavish display of wealth and luxury. Thousands of candles line the walls and tables, casting dancing light against the cream walls. Candelabras fall from the ceiling in intricate designs inspired by nature, creating haunting shadows on the ceiling. The ballroom has already attracted a crowd as an orchestra plays the most unusual instruments I've ever seen. A woman in the center, who seems the star, flicks the chords of what looks like a double-sided harp with the help of four extra arms.

The walls are lined with tables full of food and drink for all manner of supernatural creature. Vampires fill their goblets from the blood fountain. Mermaids in human form—their skin covered in the faintest trace of translucent scales—partake of the live seafood display. There's a table full of raw meat and small cages with live animals for the hunting carnivores. Wolves, maybe? I shiver and keep moving, making my way through the crowds, unsure of what I'm looking for.

I study the faces around me looking for a familiar one beneath the masks when I feel someone's breath against my neck, his body close to mine.

311

A hand lands on my ass as another wraps around my waist to graze my breast and I turn, shocked, to confront a man I don't recognize who wears a lewd expression.

"Get your hands off me!" I shout, pushing him back.

He's of medium build and height, with mousy brown hair and small, dark eyes. Honestly, he could be considered decent looking in another context, but right now I just want to cut off his hands.

He just smirks, tips his top hat at me, and walks away.

I'm so furious at the violation, I'm shaking as my brain tries to catch up with my body. What do I do? Do I tell someone? This isn't the New York subway. I wasn't expecting such behavior, and it's triggering every vulnerable, angry, defiant feeling I've ever had when men take liberties as if my body is their personal toy.

The awful man walks across the room, his eyes clearly set on a young, green-haired mermaid enjoying live shrimp at one of the tables.

"*Merde.* You're the third woman I've seen him pull that shit on," a familiar voice whispers in my ear. His closeness makes me jump, and I spin on him, all my ire and rage welling up in me.

"What are you doing here?" I hiss, looking around to see if anyone noticed him.

And then I forget my words when I take a good look at the sexy dark Druid. He's dressed in all black, as per usual, with a long fur cape trimmed at the collar in black bird feathers. His mask is also made of feathers, and his hair is coifed in such a way that it changes his appearance entirely. I would swear on my life he was part bird if I didn't know better, and I squint at him, trying to see the magick I know is aiding his impressive illusion.

"Can you see it, then?" Cole asks, raising a hand to my face and tracing my cheek gently. "Can you see the power that connects us?"

His dark eyes pull me in as always, and I shudder and step back, reluctantly fighting this attraction I feel. "I don't see anything," I say, but that's not entirely true, though 'see' might be the wrong word. I feel it, this tie, this thread that keeps pulling us closer together. But it scares me.

He tilts his head and smiles. "You will in time, *mon coeur*," he says softly. "What is here cannot be denied."

"You didn't answer my question. What are you doing here?"

"Disobeying my brothers, of course. And providing you with unnecessary backup. I couldn't resist the chance to see you in this gown, now could I?"

A clatter behind us pulls our attention to the table the mermaid was standing at. She drops her shrimp and flees the room with tears in her eyes, while the man grins broadly and no one steps in to do or say anything.

"He'll keep at it," Cole says. "No one will stop him."

I narrow my eyes. "Challenge accepted."

Cole grins and crosses his arms over his chest as I feel my power rise up in me. The wrath I feel, coupled with the fear and helplessness being grabbed brought up in me, makes it harder to access my power.

I close my eyes and take a deep breath, centering myself, then try again. This time, I am calm. I am cold. I am justice.

I call to the elements, and air floats up, but it brings with it the darkness, and when I dip into it, I get both elements in equal measure.

Each element I try to access also brings with it the darkness, and I know there's no way around it, I have to let that power out, at least a little.

I open my eyes and watch as the man grabs a glass of something red to drink. I focus and flick my finger. The man's eyes widen as he stumbles, spilling the drink all over his suit. With another flick, I send him into a caged aquarium of piranhas. Or at least, sharp-tooth fish that look like piranhas. He breaks the tank as he falls, and fish latch on to him, drawing blood instantly as he screams for help.

Silence falls on the room as the rest of the guests just stand and stare. No one goes to his aid until the butler hurries in and helps escort the man out of the ballroom while other staff come in to contain the remaining fish and clean up the mess. Conversation resumes, the guests acting as if nothing has happened, and Cole gives me a sly wink and a subtle clap of admiration for my revenge. I must admit I feel pretty good about it, too.

As the musicians resume playing, Cole holds a hand out and offers me a charming grin. "Would the lady do me the honor of a dance?"

I'm tempted to say no, but I can't bring myself to do it. I want it too badly. So, I take his hand and let him guide me to the center of the dance floor.

The music changes tempo as if on cue, and Cole leads me in a passionate routine of complex steps that I've never done before. I'm convinced I'll fall flat on my face, but as he spins me and dips me and synchronizes his steps with mine, I find myself matching him step for step, as if we had practiced this hundreds of times. Our bodies move in time to each other, like planets orbiting one another. His body's pulse drives me, guides me, and it is as if no one exists but us. I can't feel anyone else in the room as he holds my lower back, pulling me against him, his lips brushing against my cheek.

Black tendrils of smoke seem to rise from him, and I feel his magick, his power, wrapping around me, touching and guiding me.

When the song ends, he pulls me into an embrace and dips me deeply.

That's when I realize the dance floor cleared for us, and then the crowd breaks into applause at our performance. I flush scarlet as Cole leads me away, his arm wrapped around my waist.

"How did you do that?" I ask, as we pause at a food table that tempts me with succulent roasted chicken, pasta salad, fruit platters, and pastries.

"We all have our talents," Cole says, in an answer that really isn't an answer at all.

We both fill a plate and get drinks, then move to the balcony to catch some fresh air. Unlike his brothers, the dark Druid is no vampire. He tastes like I taste. Feels like I feel.

"I'm glad you're here," I say, taking a bite of a chocolate covered strawberry.

We eat in silence for a few minutes, watching the Dragon's Breath float in the sky. Finally, I reluctantly pull away from him. "I have to go back in. I won't learn anything out here with you," I remind him.

He takes a step forward, his head dipping closer to mine, our lips inches apart. "Oh, you would learn plenty, *mon coeur*. I can promise you that."

"No doubt," I whisper, my voice thick. "But nothing about the egg." I'm desperately trying to hold onto my purpose for attending this event. Liam. I have to save Liam. But damn, Cole makes it hard to think sometimes.

"Then by all means, go collect clues. I'll be here when you're ready."

His words are layered with too many meanings for me to effectively unpack right now, so I turn and step back into the ballroom, and I walk right into someone I wasn't expecting to see, though it makes perfect sense that she would be here.

Lilith smiles at me, her teeth so white, her pale skin luminescent, her silky black hair falling down her back like a waterfall. She's wearing a pure white gown with a long trail, and a white feathered mask that flares up on the ends like cat eyes. Her lips are as red as mine and she looks enchanted. Beautiful. Dangerous.

"Can it be possible that you are here alone? Unaccompanied by the Night brothers?" she teases, handing me a glass of a foamy white drink with red sparkles in it.

I sip the drink and enjoy the frothy sweetness, but I know to be careful with supernatural alcohol. The magick packs a punch, so I drink slowly and cautiously. "They don't have me on a leash," I say, a little snippy.

"You must give those boys quite a run for their money," she says, grinning. "How marvelous." She links arms with me, and we move through the room. "What brings you here, then? You didn't strike me as the type to attend balls. Particularly alone."

I debate about how much to tell her. Our relationship—if one can call it that—is complicated. "Liam is being accused of conspiring to steal the dragon egg by starting the explosion at the Midwinter Festival. I'm here hoping to find anyone who might know something about what really happened," I say.

She raises an eyebrow. "I take it you do not believe he's responsible?"

"No, I don't," I say firmly.

She stares at me a moment, then nods. "I agree with you. This isn't Liam's style. But it is quite damning at the moment. I do hope you find what you're looking for. Wherever that might lead."

"Do you know anything?" I ask her point blank, not that I expect an honest answer. It's been my experience that the older and more powerful a supernatural being is, the more they enjoy speaking in goddamn riddles.

"I know you won't give up until you find the truth," she says. "And I know that tenacity puts you in the line of fire, no pun intended." She pulls away as someone across the room calls to her. "Be cautious," she says. "No one is who you think they are in this world. And nothing is as it seems."

Like I said. Riddles. She walks away with a final wink at me, and I realize I'm wasting precious time that I need in order to figure out how to get an invite into the secret auction later tonight.

I head to the bar in hopes of getting another drink and maybe some helpful information from the bartender, but as I approach, a hand lands on my back. "Allow me," the tall man at my side says.

He's decked out in the richest velvet and finery, from his ring-studded fingers to his tailored clothing, wealth oozing from him like pus from an infection. He looks to be in his 50s or 60s, with flecks of silver along his temples, and he has aristocratic features that give him —at first glance—a debonair style. But it's his eyes that tell me who he is before he does.

His eyes are dead. Soulless. All the charm in the world can't take the place of a soul.

He orders two drinks, both blood red, and hands me one. I eye it suspiciously and wait for him to drink first. When he does, I take a sip, relieved it's not blood or something equally awful.

It's bitter and strong, with a sweet aftertaste.

"Miss Eve Oliver," he says, with a drawl to his voice that belies his ruthlessness. "I am delighted you accepted my invitation. Allow me to introduce myself, I am—"

"Lord Nicholas Vanderbilt," I say, smiling my most charming smile. "It's a pleasure to meet you. Thank you for the invitation. This ball is extraordinary." At least I can be honest about that last part. It truly is exceptional.

I was never a very good actor. I tried out for a play in high school once. I got understudy but never had to actually perform, which was probably a good thing. But now I wish I'd studied it a little more seriously, because tonight will take all the acting skills I don't have to pull off feigning interest in this man who makes my skin crawl. As he cups my elbow and guides me through the crowd, a wave of nausea crashes through me and I set my drink down on a nearby table.

"Was it not to your liking?" he asks, eyeing the nearly full glass that's left.

"It was lovely," I say, smiling. "I'm just pacing myself."

He nods, a glint in his eyes. "A woman of temperance. I appreciate that. It's lacking in most who prefer wild extremes."

"And you?" I ask. "Are you a temperate man or one of extremes?"

I study him, and for all intents he looks human. I wonder at his supernatural race. He must have one, to be here.

"I am a man of cultivated tastes and specific desires," he says enigmatically.

The door to the ballroom opens, distracting us both as we glance over at the newcomer. A tall man with fire red hair that flows down his back walks in. He wears a red cloak that looks to be made of a strange material, and his eyes...his eyes...

The Collector smiles and escorts me to the man, who, as we get closer, I realize isn't a man at all.

"Miss Oliver, you have met Dath'Racul before, yes? I believe in his true form."

The fire dragon looks at me, eyes narrowing, and I smile nervously and hold out a hand, unsure what the proper protocol. "Yes. You were the judge at Dracula's trial," I say.

He studies my hand but does not shake it, and I awkwardly let it drop to my side.

"Indeed. You had quite the last-minute turnabout," he says, his voice as deep as it was in dragon form.

As a man, he is beautiful. His golden dragon eyes study everything around us with keen intelligence, and what I thought was a cape is actually his wings, draped around him. His skin is a deep burnt red and his body is massive for a man. Though I imagine he feels small in this form, compared to being a dragon.

"I am surprised to see you here," Dath'Racul says to me, then glances curiously at the Collector.

"It was a pleasant surprise for us all," Nicholas says. "What a rare jewel to grace our presence."

I stifle a shudder at his strange praise, knowing from rumor how he likes to collect 'rare jewels.'

"I would think Miss Oliver would have better things to do, with the trial against her employer so imminent," the dragon says with cold arrogance. "Certainly, Mr. Night is hoping for more commitment to the preparation,"

Oh boy, this guy is really trying to get my goat.

But I won't let him.

"Rest assured, The Night Firm is doing everything in its power to prove that Liam is innocent. We have many other leads that are much more damning than Liam being in the same location as everyone else in town at the time of the explosion. That seems a pretty weak foundation to prove guilt, don't you think?" I ask the judge.

He frowns. "Not many can conjure that kind of fire."

"I don't know about this world, but in my world, us talking specifics about the case like this would be justification for change of venue. Or at least a new judge," I say with another disarming smile. Honestly, after tonight, I may never smile again. My teeth hurt from exposing them to so much slime.

Dath'Racul nods. "Of course. You are correct. But you must not have heard; I am not the judge on this case."

Finally, good news, but his cruel smile doesn't encourage me.

"I will be prosecuting the case against Mr. Night," Dath'Racul says.

Shit. Shit, shit and double effing shit. How can this even be allowed? I have to keep my cool. "I think you mean you'll be prosecuting the case against the person ultimately found responsible? Surely you are committed to justice? To exploring all leads? There have been rumors of conflict with the people of the Otherworld and the dragon leadership. It's a promising lead that might exonerate Liam by pointing the finger at the true guilty party."

I study his face as he responds to my veiled threat.

"I am sure you will find the answer is not nearly so simple. It is natural that a society would want to challenge its leaders. They do not have all the information and thus question decisions they do not understand," he says.

"Perhaps it's time they had all the information then," I say.

His face hardens, but before he can say more, Nicholas chuckles. "It's good to see you, Dath'Racul. Get a drink and enjoy the party. I'd like to show Eve off to a few more people before the night escapes us."

Dath'Racul nods curtly and walks away, grabbing a flaming fire drink from a tray carried by a beautiful woman with cat ears and a tail. She is wearing almost nothing save a see-through white body suit studded with diamonds. The same as all the young, female servers. Her eyes are large and cat-like, and her pale white hair falls down her back in waves. She locks eyes with me, and though she smiles, I see the pain in them and wonder about her story. About why she's here.

Nicholas escorts me around, introducing me to the rich and powerfully corrupt of the Otherworld. I try to be charming and smile and engage in harmless conversation. The effort is exhausting, and I find myself looking around to catch a glimpse of Cole, but he seems to have disappeared. I wish he were closer. I may not need backup, but I could use the moral support in this den of vipers.

The band begins to play a new song and Nicholas holds out his hand and bows gallantly. "May I have this dance, Miss Oliver?"

"Of course," I say, through the most insincere smile I've ever worn. How can he not see how uncomfortable I am? Or does he only see what he wants to? Maybe he's the kind of man who can't conceive of anyone finding him repulsive, so it never enters his mind that someone might not enjoy his company. I've known a few of those types in my life and most of them weren't even paranormal.

It's a slow dance, of course, and his hand slides too low down my back, making me very uncomfortable. But I'm here for answers, so I don't pull away.

As he spins me and guides me over the dance floor, his gaze locks on mine. "You are a very beautiful woman," he says.

"Thank you."

My hands are sweating, but there' nothing I can do about the one he's holding. My other hand is on his waist.

"Word has it you are human. At least, that was the story when you first got here."

There's no question so I keep silent, waiting for him to continue.

"It is clear to me you are not human at all. But then, what are you? Pray do tell. I have been dying to find out for some time."

"I don't actually know," I say truthfully. "I always thought I was human as well."

He laughs. "Playing hard to get, I see. Very well, I enjoy games more than most. What would you like in exchange for this knowledge about you?"

His question surprises me. "What do you mean?" I ask.

He plunges me into a dip, our legs pressing against each other as he does, then pulls me back up to face him, our bodies entirely too close. I finally see Cole in the background, watching us. He winks when he sees me staring.

"I mean," says Nicholas, spinning me so I no longer see the Night brother, "that I am willing to play this game and offer you all manner of treasure in exchange for your secret."

"I really can't tell you," I say.

He studies me quietly for a moment. "With anyone else, I would offer wealth. Jewels. The power of my influence. But with you..." he ponders as we continue moving in synch. "With you, I feel you value more significant trades. Perhaps you would part with your secret for information about the dragon egg you are seeking."

I glance up in surprise. "Do you know where the egg is?" I ask.

"I could find information about its location, if we have an agreement."

I frown. "You're really not listening," I say. "I don't know what I am. I swear. But if you have information about the egg, maybe we could discuss another trade?"

"You're an intriguing woman, Miss Oliver. You effectively punished a man who was causing problems for the women at my party, for which I thank you. And I apologize that you were made to suffer such indignities."

"I don't know what you mean," I say, but he knows I'm lying, I can tell.

"Indeed." He pushes his hips closer to mine and I can feel his attraction to me, and it makes me sick. "I also saw you talking with Lilith, Mother of all Vampires. You keep interesting company."

"I could say the same of you," I say, looking around.

"Touché," he says with a chuckle. "What will it take for you to trust me?"

I shrug. "I don't trust easily. Don't take offense. It's the foster kid in me."

A smile curls at his lip as the orchestra completes its song. "Thank you for the dance. I have another—more private—event to introduce in the basement. Would you care to join me? You will find a great deal that might interest you."

This is it. This is what the whole night has been about. But I can't let myself look too excited. Play it cool, Eve. You got this.

"Sounds intriguing, but I don't typically follow strange men into basements. Another foster kid thing. You understand."

I make to walk away from him, but he grabs my hand to stop me. "You will be in no danger, and there will be other select guests in attendance. I give you my word you will be safe."

I turn back to him and smile. "Very well. I'd be honored to be your guest."

CHAPTER 10: THE BIDDING

I AM darkness A moonless night Grasping for stars Any trace of light The thunder resounding The lightning will transform   I am the whirlwind I am the storm ~Jennifer Borak

As NICHOLAS ESCORTS me out of the ballroom, I see Cole watching us, his gaze burning a hole in my back until we disappear from his sight. And even still, I can feel him close to me, his presence lingering.

We walk down a long corridor that ends at a door, behind which is a circular stairway that winds its way down quite a distance. We take the stairs quickly, and my shoes clack on the stone as we walk in silence, with just magically lit torches on the gray walls to light our way.

When we reach the bottom, he opens another door, and a bouncer dressed in black greets us with a nod. He's shaped like a boulder, round and solid, and looks ready to rumble with anyone who breaks the rules.

When we reach the end of the hall, the Collector pulls away from me. "This is where I must leave you for now, to attend to my duties. Please, enjoy yourself and explore. The activities will begin shortly."

Once alone, I look around the large room with hand-painted tile flooring and white walls with murals depicting enchanting magical scenes of mermaids and dryads and dragons. An incredible chandelier hangs from the ceiling and white velvet chairs are lined up in rows.

A woman with wild curly blue hair and scales covering her skin hands me a crystal. "This projects your bid number for the auction. Hold out your hand, please."

I do as she says, and she pricks my thumb with a different crystal. "Miss Eve Oliver with The Night Firm. You are officially registered. Best of luck."

I rub my sore thumb and take a moment to look around. As I wander down a long hall, I notice doors spaced a few feet apart, and I hear the sounds of sex from within several of them.

One door opens and a man comes out buttoning his pants. Behind him I see the server I noticed upstairs, the cat girl, laying on the bed naked, her eyes empty, her smile a mask to cover her pain.

Are these women here of their own accord? Something feels off.

Another man pushes past me into the room, and the woman stands and closes the door, her eyes flicking to mine before she does.

I want to speak to her, to ask her about this life she's living, but there is no opportunity, so I walk back to the main room where other women are carrying trays around serving hors d'oeuvres and drinks. I take a glass of champagne and sip at it, then find a seat. Weariness settles over me and I wish I could just go home. But I'm finally getting closer to actual answers. I can't give up now.

Someone sits next to me and I see it's Lilith, holding her own crystal.

"So, you have made your way into the secret den," she says, softly. "Be careful not to get in over your head. You may not be human, but you've led a very short human life that has not prepared you for this world."

Our conversation is cut short when Nicholas takes the stage and addresses the crowd. The chairs are now full and everyone looks eager to see what will be up for auction tonight.

"We have five very special treats for you this evening," he says, charm oozing out of him. "So, without further ado, let us begin."

There is a chorus of clapping as Nicholas snaps his fingers and in a puff of smoke an ebony box appears on the stage, centered on a table. It's about the size of a bread box and covered in intricate carvings. It's also wrapped in iron chains and has a lock that glows blue and pulses with some kind of runes.

"You've heard of Pandora's Box," Nicholas says, smiling. "A myth, of course, but not without basis in truth. This is the origin of that myth. The original holder of darkness. Open this at your own peril, for only you will be affected. It will give you the power of the dark, but at a steep price. Can I get an opening bid?"

I stare at the box curiously as those around me bid aggressively. What would happen to me if I opened it? Would it corrupt me? Or am I already corrupted? What would it do to Adam, I wonder?

When the winning bid has been announced, the item disappears into smoke to be replaced by something new.

A gold necklace lying against black velvet. It is beautifully wrought in the shape of two serpents with open mouths that form a clasp in the front. The gold itself is studded with emeralds and diamonds that twinkle under the lights of the chandelier. It's a breathtaking piece.

"Behold the Necklace of Harmonia," the Collector says. "Anyone who wears this necklace will be granted eternal youth and beauty. But at a cost. Legend says this necklace brings great misfortune to all who wear it. Is it worth the trade? Let the bidding begin."

"Fools," Lilith says, as the bidding ensues. "They will beg to be released from the curse of that bauble before long. I have seen it happen too many times. There are better ways to attain eternal youth and beauty. Though none without a price, 'tis true."

A beautiful, slim man with raven hair and reptilian eyes wins the necklace and preens like a peacock at his prize. I wonder what tragedy will befall him should he chose to wear the cursed jewelry.

Once again, it disappears into smoke and a marble stand appears with a large tome atop it. The book is bound in leather and stamped with the symbol of a crescent moon lying on its side with a circle above it.

Next to me, Lilith straightens her back and leans forward,

clutching her crystal. It appears something has caught the vampire's interest.

"Many of you have come for this treasure this evening," Nicholas says. "I expect some animated bidding for the Book of Thoth, a text said to have been written by Thoth himself, the Egyptian god of writing and knowledge. Whether he actually existed or not, this manuscript contains powerful spells and knowledge found nowhere else in either world. Though many such books were said to have existed, this is the last of its kind. Shall we start the bidding?"

Lilith raises her crystal and a holographic number displays before her as she calls out the first bid. After that, the competition is fierce and the price climbs higher than anything that came before it.

In the end, no one wanted it more than the mother of vampires herself, and though she spends a small fortune, she clearly feels it's worth it.

"This is what I came for," she says, softly. "The greatest power in either of our worlds is knowledge. Remember that."

My curiosity is piqued, and for a moment I consider asking Lilith to see the book, but then the fourth 'item' up for auction appears and my blood runs cold.

I shift uncomfortably in my seat and don't know where to look or how to behave. This isn't what I was expecting, and I feel sick to my stomach. How can I remain silent? But what can I possibly do?

Lilith notices my distress and puts a hand on my knee. "Do not play your cards just yet, my dear. This isn't the fight you came here for."

She's not wrong, but holy hell how am I supposed to keep quiet?

This auction item isn't a cursed necklace or powerful book or box.

It's a young woman.

With cat ears.

The one who served drinks upstairs and served herself down here.

Now she is being sold to the highest bidder.

The Collector traffics in people.

Live people.

Not just trinkets and dead body parts.

No one prepared me for this.

"Feast your eyes on the splendor of this beauty," Nicholas says, displaying the girl like a piece of art. She is once again in her see-through body suit, her face neutral, her white tail twitching nervously behind her.

"Many of you have tasted of her rare pleasures. Now, she can be yours forever. Let the bidding begin."

The girl looks at me, and I can't pull my gaze from her as mostly men—but also some women—bid to own her. I can only imagine the things they will do to her.

I break eye contact with her to glance at Lilith, who is impassive in the face of this atrocity. "Please do something," I say, feeling helpless even as my powers roil beneath the surface of my skin. I could unleash them here, but then I would ruin everything. What if the egg is the last up for auction? But how can I ignore what's happening?

Lilith looks at me with unreadable eyes, then gives a brief nod and holds up her crystal, entering into the bidding.

I scoot to the edge of my chair, desperate for her to win and free the girl.

Another man in the audience outbids Lilith at every turn.

She's starting to look pissed.

"Please keep going," I say. "You can't let him have her."

"Oh, I won't," she seethes between her teeth.

When the price becomes more than my mind can compute, Lilith stands up and bids an even higher amount, then takes off a ring she's wearing, holding it up for Nicholas. "I also offer the Ring of Dispel as payment. A one-of-a-kind wonder that, when worn, dispels any enchantments. It's said to have been given to Sir Lancelot by the Lady of the Lake. I can attest to its power."

The man who had been bidding against her huffs. "That's not right. She can't do that," he complains, his lusty eyes consuming the poor girl on stage.

Nicholas can't take his gaze off the ring, and I can see how badly he wants it. "Agreed," he says to Lilith, who hands over the ring with a shrewd glance at me.

The other man storms out of the room, and the cat girl looks to me and Lilith in curiosity and fear. Likely, she is wondering what will become of her.

The girl looks at me, eyes wide, before Nicholas snaps and she disappears. "Done." He slips the coveted ring onto his finger and smiles.

"You will free her, yes?" I ask Lilith.

Lilith looks at me. "I will do something with her."

I frown. "What does that mean?"

"It means, the girl probably doesn't have anywhere to go once she's freed. But I'll sort it out." She rolls her eyes at me. "You have a soft heart, Eve. Don't let it get you killed."

"And for our last—and truly most incredible—item for auction, behold the wonder that is the Viden," the Collector says and waves his hand with a flourish. From out of the mist appears a grayish-green creature at least ten feet in length pinned to a stone slab. It has a face like a deep-sea fish and the body of a snake, dozens of tentacles sprouting from its sides.

"This magnificent being can read into the hearts and minds of any being to answer their most burning questions. But the truth isn't always what it appears to be," the Collector cautions. "Captured from the deep seas near the edge of the world, the Viden is said to be the last of its kind. Who would like to volunteer to demonstrate its powers?"

Several hands go up, but I just stare as the creature's black, beady eyes lock onto mine, and I feel the pull of the darkness within it, as if it is calling my name.

Eve.

Eve.

Eve.

Lilith nudges me, snapping me out of the trance I was in without realizing. "What's going on?" I ask.

Everyone in the room is looking at me, and the Collector is holding out his hand to me. "Miss Oliver, would you join me on stage?"

I want to say no, but if this creature can answer my questions, maybe it's worth it.

I reluctantly stand and make my way forward, then take the seat in the chair provided, directly in front of the creature.

"The Viden will answer any three questions you have. Are you ready?" Nicholas asks.

I nod and prepare myself for whatever is about to happen.

But nothing can prepare me for the creature being released from the stone slab and crawling over my head, covering my face with its body, wrapping around me until I can't breathe.

Invisible cuffs hold me to the chair, and I try to scream but nothing comes out.

Fear takes hold of me and I pull out my power, but nothing happens.

The creature's voice fills my mind.

Eveeeeeeeeee, you have questions for me. What are they, Eveeeeeeee?

I can't speak, but as I think my first question, the creature seems to understand. And though I can't breathe, somehow I do not run out of air.

Where is the missing dragon egg? I think.

The creature hums in my head as if searching for the answer.

It is nearer than you know but farther than you are. Seek it in the place you will be, when your world is about to crumble.

Of course. Of course, the answers would just be more riddles.

Next question Eveeee. I cannot release you until you ask all three.

What am I?

It seems amused.

Delightful and doubtful and despairing of truth. You are all of them and more and none of them in lore. You cannot be hidden or brought out. You are the answer and the question.

For the love of all that's holy, I'm so tired of this. Okay, I get one last question. Maybe a yes or no will give me a clearer response, though I'm not optimistic.

Is my brother evil?

The creature sniffs. *Evil is as evil does. Does motive or madness matter? Do ends and beginnings tell the same story? Nothing is at it appears. Least of all, fate's twins.*

And with the last question, the creature removes itself from my head, leaving me sticky with its tentacle goo, which has completely destroyed my mask and costume.

Nicholas notices my disheveled state and waves his hand over me. In a rush of magic, the goo disappears, and my costume is restored. He reaches for my hand to help me to my feet, and though I don't want to touch him, I'm too unsteady to rise on my own.

"Well, my dear, did you get the answers you were hoping for?"

His grin is maddening. He knew what kind of response I would get from the Viden, but I don't want to play his game. "Oh yes. It was most illuminating. Particularly in relation to what I am," I whisper.

He flinches, stepping back.

Dizziness overtakes me as I attempt to walk back to my chair, and Lilith steadies me and guides me out of the auction room and through a door leading outside. Once there, Cole greets us.

"What happened to her?" he asks, lifting me into his arms when I sway and nearly fall.

"Nicholas punished her in his own way," Lilith says.

Cole growls under his breath, and the feel of his chest rumbling is soothing to me. My head flops against his torso and the world fades in and out.

When darkness takes me, it is Cole's darkness that I feel. Cole's that I fall into blissfully, forgetting all the horrors of the night.

I regain my consciousness—and my memory of the evening— several hours later and wake to find myself in front of a fireplace in the library, a knitted blanket covering me. Matilda is crocheting in the chair across from me and smiles when I wake. "Welcome back," she says. "You've had quite the adventure."

I sit up, clutching my head as I do to keep it from rolling off my shoulders or exploding.

"There's a potion for you to drink," she says. "It will help."

I see a mug on the table before me and pick it up, sniffing. "Ugh. What is this?" I ask, crinkling my nose.

"Something that will remove the demon you brought home within you," she says nonchalantly, as if commenting about a headache.

"Demon?"

She nods. "Oh yes. He's hitched a ride and needs to head back to where he belongs now. Drink up."

I take the vile liquid in like I'm doing the longest, worst-tasting shot in the history of shots. And then my body convulses, and I see a bucket next to the couch that I grab to vomit into.

The vomiting seems to last days, but it doesn't faze Matilda.

When there's nothing left in me, I look into the bucket and see that's it's all black sludge.

She sets her crocheting down and comes to me, feeling my head and examining the bucket. Then she says some words and does a symbol above the sludge, and it all disappears.

"There. All gone. How do you feel?"

Like shit. But also…"A bit better. My mind isn't as muddled."

"Sounds like you had an interesting evening," she says.

"That's one word for it," I say. "I… think I need to go to bed. And brush my teeth. My mouth tastes like demon."

Matilda nods, as if this is all par for the course. "Sleep well, dear. You'll feel much better in the morning."

My body aches and I feel exactly as one might expect to feel after having a demon exorcised from their body. I do as promised and scrub my mouth clean until I can only remember the taste of vomiting up demon.

Then I try to undress. Holy shit. It takes me forever to figure out how to undo all the pieces of my gown, and once I'm naked I soak in a hot bathtub for a long time, letting the warmth melt away all my aches.

But a bath can't help the pain in my heart.

There were other girls there that night who were likely owned by Nicholas. Other girls he will abuse and sell and trade. I can't leave them there, but what can I do? How can I fix this?

I close my eyes, trying to sort through it all, when someone very close to me clears their throat.

330

I startle and look up to see Cole standing at the edge of my bath with a half-smile on his face.

"If I wasn't here on very important business I would be so tempted to ask if I could join you."

His words light up something inside of me, and I wonder what it would feel like to have him in the bath with me, to feel his skin against mine, our bodies becoming one.

I shake my head to dispel those thoughts. "What are you doing here?" I ask.

"I have a surprise for you," he says. "But you have to come with me."

"Right now?" I ask.

He nods. "It'll be worth it, I promise."

There's something in his eyes that convinces me it's worth going, so I stand up and his eyes take in my body as he hands me a towel. I dry and dress as quickly as I can, despite needing sleep very badly. "Where are we going?" I ask.

"Not far."

He takes my hand and pulls me into his arms. "Do you trust me?" he asks.

I look into his too-dark eyes and nod, because for some reason, despite everything, I do.

"Then close your eyes and hold on tight."

I do as I'm told, and with our bodies pressed together, I feel his power move through me, and then...it's as if for a moment we are in another realm made of air and smoke and shadow. And then I feel solid again and I'm standing in a room made of stone. A thin sheen of dust covers the walls, telling me that no one has been here for some time. A door to my right leads...somewhere. From the window I can see the top of the castle and the surrounding grounds. "Are we in the eastern tower?" I ask.

Cole nods.

And when I turn, I see what his surprise is.

Nicholas Vanderbilt is slumped in the corner, tied up, blindfolded and gagged.

"What is this?" I ask.

"A gift," Cole says. "He tortured you with that creature, sent you home demon possessed, and sells girls as sex slaves. He deserves to be punished. I thought you might like to do the honors."

I step forward, looking at the man who does indeed deserve a thousand cuts with the sharpest blade. My anger flares within me and fire appears in my palms. I hold my hands up, studying the flames. I could release them on his flesh. Burn him alive. Make him pay for all he's done.

"Can he hear us?" I ask.

"No," Cole says. "Would you like him to?"

I shake my head. I don't know what I want right now.

Cole comes up behind me, his mouth at my ear. "It will feel so good to unleash your magic on him. And he deserves it, doesn't he?"

"Your brothers wouldn't like this," I say, holding my fiery hands in front of me, visualizing the Collector burning alive.

"My brothers don't understand many things. They are limited by their own self-imposed rules. You should not be bound by those."

The temptation overwhelms me. I could so easily do it. Who would know?

"What happened to the girls he held prisoner?" I ask.

"They are free to live their own lives."

I turn to face him. "You rescued them?"

He nods, brushing a lock of hair from my face gently. "Of course."

He leans down and kisses me softly, the act sending shivers up my spine. His kiss deepens and I melt into him, into the darkness he cocoons me in like a warm blanket on a winter night.

When I pull away, he sighs, closing his eyes and flicking his tongue over his lips. "You taste as I imagined you would."

When his eyes open, they are luminous. "Eve. Do you have any idea what you and I could do together? Who we could be with one another?"

I don't answer, but I can feel it, and I want it. So bad.

But...

Shit.

I drop my hands.

"I can't. I can't be that person." I turn to Nicholas. "And he

332

doesn't deserve a quick death. He deserves to pay for his crimes. We must tell your brothers and let them turn Nicholas over to the Enforcers. The girls you freed will testify against him. He will finally get the justice he deserves."

"As you wish," Cole says sadly. "But it will not end the way you hope."

CHAPTER 11: THE DARKNESS

THE DANCE between darkness and light will always remain— the stars and the moon will always need the darkness to be seen, the darkness will just not be worth having without the moon and the stars. ~ C. JoyBell C.

IN MY ROOM later that night, I find myself in a restless state despite my exhaustion. After hours of pacing, I sit on the patio and watch the Dragon's Breath dancing in the sky as I consider whether I made the right choice.

Will the Collector get justice? Will justice be enough? Will he have a chance to harm others in the meantime? Should I have killed him when I had the chance?

Derek wasn't happy that Cole had brought him here, but the Enforcers came and arrested the Collector based on my statement of his illegal activity. Cole didn't say another word about it, but I could see on his face that he felt this plan was doomed to failure.

He might not be wrong, but just because I might fail doesn't mean I didn't make the morally right choice.

So why do I feel so hollow?

"Why so glum, sis?"

I whip around, the voice behind me startling me out of my thoughts. "Adam?"

I stand, my heart fluttering at the sight of him. I still can't believe he's back. He's alive.

He reaches over and hugs me, and I smile into his shoulder, despite everything, then I guide him to the chairs in front of the fire. "How did you get in here?" I ask.

"Magic," he says, with a flourish of his hands and a chuckle. He leans in and takes my hands. "You're so much more powerful than you realize, Evie. You have no idea." He studies my palms as if they might give him the answers to my powers, but he says nothing about what he sees. Then he pulls back and leans against the chair, crossing his left leg over his right. He used to cross his right over his left, I realize. It's a stupid observation to make, but it strikes me there is a lot about my brother I no longer know. And a lot about me he doesn't know. This is the longest we've ever spent apart from each other, and our experiences since his—well, death—have shaped us each differently.

"I have something for you," he says, pulling a small package from his cloak and handing it to me.

It's wrapped in a blue silk cloth and tied with a silver ribbon. "What's this for?" I ask.

"It's my Christmas gift to you," he says. "Or, Midwinter gift, I guess. You seem to have acclimated to this new world quite well."

His words aren't accusatory at all, just an observation, and yet I feel the sting of them just the same. What does it say about me that I was able to slough off my old life without a glance backwards?

Still, I unwrap his gift and find a small velvet box. Within is a stunning silver ring with a shiny black stone in the center in the shape of a rectangle, and red stones on either side.

"It's black onyx," he says. "It will protect you."

I slide the ring onto my finger and I actually feel a shift in the air around me, like a barrier forming. "This is so strange," I say, my mind drifting. "I had a dream about this ring. I'd forgotten it but it's all come back to me now. I found a ring just like this in a marsh surrounded by ancient trees." I look up at my brother. "It's uncanny that you would get this for me."

"We're twins," he says with a shrug. "We've always had an uncanny connection, don't you think?"

"Yes, of course, you're right." I shake off the feeling of unease with the memory of all the times our lives interconnected in strange ways. We often had the same dreams or nightmares…sometimes we'd even appear in each other's. The next day we'd remember what we did in the other person's dreams. I haven't thought about that in so long, and the memory causes an ache in my heart.

Tears fill my eyes and I reach over and grab his hand. "I've missed you." I sniff, then swipe at my eyes with my free hand. "Your remains are still on my mantelpiece."

He laughs and glances up at them, just above the fireplace. "I noticed. But you don't have to miss me anymore. I'm right here."

Then he stands, a small, sad smile on his lips. "And I will be back," he promises. "But for now, I have to go."

I rise and hug him again. "Why?"

"You know why. If I'm found here, the truth will come out about who really killed Mary and her baby and I'll be arrested. I can't risk it when there's so much to do."

"We have to talk soon," I say. "I'm having a hard time wrapping my mind around the moral conundrum you've created."

He kisses my forehead. "We will. For now, keep that ring on and be careful. I love you, Evie."

"I love you, too," I say, but before my sentence is out, he's gone. He hopped over the balcony and seemed to vanish into nothing.

A moment later there's a knock on my door and my heart beats so hard in my chest it feels like it's going to crack a rib.

If it's Liam… if he heard anything, that will put me in a sticky situation. He needs to be focused on himself. On the case that could end his freedom for good if he's convicted. Finding out the truth about Mary and my brother's role in her death could be a fatal distraction for him. I tell myself I'm keeping this from him for his own good, but, of course, I also have selfish motives. I don't want to hurt him. I don't want to lose him. What if, once he finds out, he sees my brother every time he looks at me?

But when I pull open the door, it's not Liam standing there.

It's Cole.

"*Bonsoir*, Eve," he says with a gallant bow. "I hope I'm not disturbing you." He glances behind me and frowns. "I thought I heard you talking to someone."

I try to look as innocent as possible. "No. I mean, I sometimes talk aloud to myself." I shrug as if this is totally normal.

He grins. "Did you know one of the gifts of working with the darkness is the ability to tell if someone is lying?"

Well, shit. "No, I didn't. But I thought you were a light Druid?"

I hold the door open, letting him in, and we both sit in front of the fire, where Adam and I had just been sitting.

"I was. But I found that light without darkness is an imbalance of nature. I wasn't utilizing my power to its fullest potential, limiting myself to just the one element. Once I opened myself to darkness, I grew more than you can imagine."

I frown. "So now you're a lie detector?"

He nods.

"That would be handy," I say, thinking of the ways I could make good use of that skill. With clients. With witnesses. With my personal life.

And then I wonder, is this his way of telling me he heard me and my brother talking? Should I ask? Ignore it? I'm not good at this subterfuge shit.

"I am not my brothers," he says. "Yes, I heard you and your brother talking. I heard what he did. And I do not judge. I believe we have to do the wrong things for the right reasons sometimes."

"Like killing an evil priest and his followers?" I ask softly.

He gazes at the fire and nods slowly. "Yes, like that. But that wasn't the first time I killed," he says.

I wait to see if he wants to share more.

"When I lived in France, my master, he was indeed a great teacher. I learned a lot from him." Cole pauses, and I feel his energy shift. "He was also a rapist. And I was his preferred target."

Oh god. No.

Cole looks at me, his dark eyes so intense. "I killed him with my magic one night when I couldn't take it anymore. That's when I found the darkness. That night."

He pauses, searching my face.

His story tears me apart, and I can only imagine the vast pain he's suffered, first as a child, then as a man when his brothers imprisoned him. What horror he has been dealt. What tragedy.

"I had to go to great lengths to acquire my power," he says, studying me. "But you have only to tap into what is already within you." He leans forward. "I can teach you."

My heart skips a beat and my palms become slick with sweat. I can feel the darkness below the other elements, lurking like a hungry beast waiting for its moment to strike. I pull back, looking away. "I can't. It's too risky."

"You have been so afraid of your darkness that you're stifling your light," Cole says, his dark gaze probing into me until I can't help but look back at him.

I wonder...is this why my brother is so much stronger than me? He's tapping into his darkness in ways I have been unwilling to? But at what cost?

"Isn't it reasonable to be scared of what I'm capable of?" I ask. "To fear hurting others? To be wary of this dark cancer that's in danger of consuming me?"

He brushes a lock of hair off my face, his fingers creating a trail of fire over my skin. "Only if you believe in the lie of duality. In the falsehood of either/or. I don't," he says frankly. "There's a verse in a religious text that says, 'The light shines in the darkness and the darkness has not overcome it.' And that is true. But what they don't say is that the light hasn't overcome the darkness either." He holds up his hand, palm facing me, and takes mine, placing it against his. His skin is warm and reassuring. "We are the light and the darkness. The two seeming dualities that need each other to be in balance. It is light, after all, that creates life's shadows. And it is the embrace of darkness that makes the light shine brightest."

Tears burn my eyes as I look at our hands pressed against each other. I can feel his power pulsing under his skin. I can see it in his black eyes, in the shadows that move within them. It is a dark magic, a magic practiced under the cover of night, but it is not evil. He is not evil. And maybe, neither am I. Despite what I've done, and what I might still do.

"Eve," he says softly. "You are the light to my darkness and I am the darkness to your light. We have pieces of each other within ourselves, and that is what makes us stronger together. If you can surrender to that, there's nothing you can't do."

He twines his fingers through mine and pulls us both to standing position, then bridges the gap between us. He dips his head and leans in, his lips brushing against my ear. "I need you," he says. "More than I've ever needed anything."

"You have me," I say. Because I'm done fighting this. I'm done fighting myself and my own nature. I'm done fighting him.

I am complete with him.

My light and darkness in balance.

No longer at war with each other.

"I'm not like my brothers," he says again, as he pulls his hand out of mine to wrap them around my waist. "I don't crave your blood, but I do crave your soul. You're light." He gently kisses my neck, sending shivers up my spine. "And your darkness. I want it all. I can handle it all."

I suck in my breath as a fire is lit in my belly. Need and desire crash into me, and I am consumed with them. With him.

When his lips make their way to mine, it is with slow deliberation, the passion contained in feather-light kisses that leave me breathless and desperate for more. He drops his hands to my hips and presses himself against me.

An ache grows in me and our kisses deepen.

My nails dig into his back, pressing through his shirt as I cling to him. When he pulls away, I groan, my body missing his.

"Do you trust me?" he asks.

I nod and allow him to lead me to the bed.

He undresses me slowly, meticulously, his dark eyes locked on me, his hands caressing every inch of me with such tenderness and devotion I nearly melt.

I feel no embarrassment as I stand before him naked. "You have too many clothes on," I remind him.

He strips quickly and my breath catches at the beauty of his body, perfect in every way, despite the scars he lives with. Or maybe because of them. After all, it's often our imperfections that give us our real beauty, and he is a beautiful man, with his long fingers, hard lines and sharply defined muscles.

With shocking ease, he lifts me into his arms and lays me on the bed, then produces strips of black silk cloth.

I don't resist as he ties one cloth around my eyes, rendering me blind, and then gently ties each of my wrists to the bedposts.

"Surrender to the darkness," he whispers against my flesh, his lips and hands teasing me in all the most sensitive places.

I nod, unable to speak, as I lose myself in the sensations he's coaxing from me.

When he spreads my legs and teases my sex with his tongue I nearly lose myself, but he pulls back, unwilling to let me finish so quickly.

He takes his time with my body, and as I writhe under his merciless teasing, something happens I have never experienced before. The lines between us dissipate. The boundaries of flesh give way to a complete melding of his spirit and mine. I feel him everywhere, on every inch of my body, within me, caressing me and kissing me in ways that can't be possible with just one human body.

When I can no longer hold back, he undoes the ties restraining me and blinding me, and I see a black mist mixed with gold that has become a part of both of us. We are no longer two entities, but one, and when I climax, he is in me, riding the wave with me, our bodies wrapped into each other, the light and the dark becoming one.

CHAPTER 12: THE SECRET

I WILL LOVE the light for it shows me the way, yet I will endure the darkness for it shows me the stars. ~Og Mandino

MATILDA IS SITTING in front of her fire knitting when she calls for me to enter and have a seat. There's already a steaming cup of tea waiting for me.

How does she always know?

I curl up in the overstuffed leather chair and sip at my drink as we sit in silence for a few moments.

"I can hear your mind spinning, my dear. What have you come to ask?" She smiles at me kindly, then returns her attention to the sweater she's working on.

"I used to think that right and wrong were very clear cut," I say. "But recently...with my growing powers and other things that have happened, I'm starting to wonder about that."

Matilda pauses, laying her hands on her lap, and looks deeply into the fire. "This is about Cole," she says.

"He's in my bed as we speak," I confess. After we made love, he fell asleep, but my mind was too restless. It was hard to leave his warm body for the chilly hallways of the castle, but I needed to clear my head. To talk to someone who might understand.

She glances at me, a small smile on her lips. "He is not as evil as some of his brothers might like to believe," she says. "I've known those boys their whole lives, and I can tell you that they have all done the wrong thing for right reason, and the right thing for the wrong reason, more times than I can count. In other words, they are all more human than they fancy themselves to be. You cannot live as long as they have and not pick up a few demons along the way. It's what we do about our demons that defines us. And that definition isn't static. It changes with each choice we make, with each path we choose. We are, none of us, beyond redemption or beyond change. But the longer we follow the dark path, the harder it becomes to choose the light."

"So, Cole has done evil things?" I ask.

She shrugs. "I suppose it depends on how you define evil. Many religions would argue that disobedience against their god or their god's laws is evil. But then great suffering has been wrought by those very same religions. One could conceivably argue that they perpetrated more evil than they cured. A more hedonistic view of good and evil equates those states with pleasure and pain. Pleasure is good. Pain is evil. Therefore, one must spend their life in pursuit of what brings pleasure. This, of course, can create problems. If what causes me pleasure by its very nature requires someone else to suffer, am I doing good or evil?"

She pauses, and I shift in my chair, trying to wrap my mind around it all. "Should motives matter?" I ask. "If the motive is pure, does that justify evil deeds? If a few must be sacrificed for many more to live, is that evil or good?"

"I cannot say." Matilda leans forward, stoking the fire. "The balance of our acts and our intentions must be weighed by something far wiser than myself. I just know I have lived a very long life, and it will be longer still, and what I have seen of all creatures, human and otherwise, is that there will never be a consensus on what is truly right or wrong, good or evil. For that would require all species of beings to agree on what the primary objective of life is. Is it to be happy? To live well? To leave the world better than you found it? And what does that look like? Better for whom? Who decides what happiness means? What does 'better' even mean? And so, we must all muddle along, my dear. We must all make the best choices we can with the information we have about ourselves and the world, and self-correct along the way. Perhaps, the whole point of it all isn't to be good or even happy, but to continue learning. Perhaps, we are here to evolve, nothing more or less."

"There is darkness in me," I say. "I can see it now. I can feel it. And it makes me want to do things I used to believe were wrong. It makes me want to punish people who cause others harm. My brain says I should follow the appropriate paths for justice. Work within the system. But I know the system—all systems everywhere—are inherently corrupt. I know true justice—whatever that even is—will never really be accomplished. But if we all start enacting our own brand of justice based on our personal moral compasses, chaos will ensue. However, if we keep working within a corrupt system without challenging it, complacency will ensue and those who are disadvantaged by the system will always be so. I don't know the right answer."

She reaches over and takes my hand in hers. "And you may never know. There may not be 'the right answer' as you say, only what is the best choice in any given moment, which may not be the best choice in the next moment." She searches my face and smiles. "Find your balance. Do not let any one element within you become too dominate against the others, and you will find your way."

I look at my cup and realize it's empty. I yawn and stand. "Thank you."

She nods, staring into the fire. "He is in pain," she says after a moment.

"Who?" I ask.

"Cole. He is in pain. He will hurt others in his pain, but there is love in him, too." She looks up at me and smiles. "You can trust his love."

With a lightness of heart after talking to Matilda, I rejoin Cole in bed, curling my body into his, trusting his love. And knowing that life inherently holds pain, so we must hold onto to the joy when we have it.

~

OVER THE NEXT WEEK, we discuss the various ways to mount a proper defense for Liam. The ball was a bust and did not yield an egg or any leads. The Beggar Queen raised more questions than answers. And time is running out, as Derek keeps reminding us.

"I dug deeper into the basilisk guard who was found dead," Elijah says one morning over breakfast. "As I suspected, she had some skeletons in the closet. More specifically, skeletons in the dungeon. She has a brother serving hard time there."

"How would she have been allowed to work for Ava'Kara in such a sensitive position with a convicted criminal for a brother?" I ask, taking a bite of my egg on toast. "I would think the water dragon would do a thorough background check for anyone she let in her inner circle."

"She would have," Elijah says. "I had to use...controversial methods to discover this. And it wasn't easy."

I raise an eyebrow at that but don't press further. "We should pay this brother a visit, then," I say, glancing at Sebastian.

He nods. "Grab your cloak. We can go now."

On the way to the prison, Sebastian pulls out a leather-bound book and opens it. "Elijah made notes. Ethne Brinn's brother is named Lester Cornch. It looks like Ethne changed her last name to distance herself from her family. Their parents are deceased, as was previously indicated, but their deaths are a mystery. So is Lester's reason for conviction." He closes the notebook. "It's not much to go on, but maybe he can give us some ideas about who Ethne might have been working with and why."

I nod and lean back, closing my eyes. "We have to catch a break soon," I say softly, worried at what might happen to Liam, to this family, if we don't.

Sebastian takes my hand and squeezes it. "We will."

He's silent a moment, and when he speaks again, he sounds... unsure of himself, which is unusual for the earth Druid. "I noticed you have been spending a lot of time with Cole," he says.

I open my eyes and look at him. "Yes."

344

"This isn't about jealousy. I swear. We aren't like humans in that way. This is...just be careful, Eve. Cole is dangerous."

"Everyone in this world is dangerous," I remind him. "Including me."

"That's not what I mean. He's manipulative. Conniving. And I'm still not convinced his motives for being here are pure."

"I'll be careful," I promise him.

"That's all I ask. I..." he pauses. "I know I haven't been the most aggressive in pursuing you. Liam is all fire and passion and Cole... well, he's Cole. I've wanted to give you your space. Time to heal. Time to process all you've been through. But please know, Eve, that what I feel for you has been growing since the day we met on the subway. Since the moment I saw that portrait you drew of me."

His words make my heart beat faster and when he reaches over to caress my face, my stomach fills with butterflies. He leans over and kisses me tenderly, then pulls away. "I'm not going to push myself on you, but that doesn't mean I don't want you. I want you more than I've ever wanted anything. But only when you're ready."

Dear god. I'm ready now, I want to tell him, but the carriage stops, and I realize we have arrived at the prison, so I just nod and smile and promise myself we will finish this conversation later.

We leave Lily—who is almost entirely healed—with the carriage and I follow Sebastian down a narrow cobblestone path. It's barely wide enough for one person to walk, and thorny bramble has taken over much of that room, leaving us both cut up and bleeding by the time we arrive at the massive building. Sebastian heals almost instantly, there are perks to being a vampire, it seems, but my cuts will take longer, of course.

The prison is a tall gothic cathedral made of black stone and sharp, spiky architecture. Atop it sits a massive black dragon, obsidian scales glimmering under the lights of the Dragon's Breath.

I can't tell if the dragon sees us or even cares that we're here. It seems to be content on its perch. "The Dragon of Darkness, I presume?" I ask Sebastian as we stop at the door. Beside the entrance are two skeletons, and it would have felt a bit Halloweenish except these are alive, and they scare the shit out of me when they step forward and demand to know what we want.

"We are here to see a prisoner in the course of an investigation," Sebastian says.

I flash my ring from Ava'Kara and Sebastian tells them who we want to see.

"Yes, that's the Dragon of Darkness," Sebastian says, as we follow one of the skeletons inside the building. "His name is Ra'Terr and he cares little for anything save guarding this prison. It's his magic that keeps so many creatures of different sizes, strengths, and abilities in check."

We step into a hallway lit only by torches set on the walls. It smells of brimstone and body odor and other—worse—things. I try to breathe through my mouth, but then I can taste it, and that's even worse.

Sebastian smiles sympathetically at me.

"How can you stand it?" I ask.

"I can suspend my breathing when needed," he says, and I've never been more jealous of anyone.

The skeleton leads us down long stairways that feel as if they might crumble under my feet and through long halls lined with moaning and screaming prisoners of all species. There are no bars and when a man who looks like he's in mid transformation into a wolf lunges at us, I scream and unleash a fireball at him, only to realize that there's an invisible barrier that keeps him within his cage. He hits it—hard—and is zapped back to the other wall with a cry of pain. My fire hits the wall and fizzes to nothing.

We pass a mermaid a few cells farther down, her torso resting on a mat while her tail dangles in a small bucket of water. She looks close to death and I shudder to imagine what this must be like for her. But I also wonder what she did to deserve such a punishment. She glances at me with big coral eyes and a sadness so profound I want to weep just looking at her.

Finally, we stop before a cell at the very end, and it's so dark within I can't tell who—or what—is inside. The skeleton taps on the invisible barrier. "You've got visitors."

He then leaves us alone, traveling with clacking bones back to his watch.

"I hope you were paying attention to how to get out of here," I say nervously. "It was a maze, and I didn't leave any breadcrumbs."

"I know my way around," Sebastian assures me.

A moment later, a slithering sound alerts us to the basilisk's presence. He comes close to the edge of the barrier, his forked tongue tasting the air around him. "What do you want, vampire?" he hisses.

Like Ethne, he is blindfolded. But unlike her, his seems permanently sewn into his face. Ouch.

"We came to ask you some questions about your sister," I say.

"I have no sssssissster," he says.

"We know you do," Sebastian says. "And she's been killed. We're trying to find out what happened."

At the news that she's dead, the basilisk falls back, his tail faltering beneath him.

"Ethne is dead?"

"Yes," I say. "I'm sorry for your loss. Please help us figure out who did this and why."

He laughs, but it is a cold, hard, sad sound. "What would I know of anything, rotting in here for all eternity?"

"Ethne was a guard for Ava'Kara, and was killed while on duty," I say.

"Then you have the wrong persssssson," Lester says. "My ssss-sissssster—if I had one—would never work for the dragonsssss. Ssssshe'd die first."

Interesting. "And yet, she did. Work for them. And die," I say. "Don't you want to find out how? And why?"

When he says nothing, Sebastian continues. "It looks like she was involved in a plot to steal the water dragon's egg and was killed by her partner. Any idea who she might have been working with?"

Lester laughs again, and it sounds like the laugh of a madman. "That'sssss more like my Ethne. She has avenged our family at lasssst."

"What does that mean?" I ask. "Avenged your family for what?"

Lester lunges against the invisible wall, and when it zaps him, he doesn't even flinch. He presses his forehead against the force field, his face wild, the zaps crashing into him like lightning. "They did thissss to us, didn't they? They took it all. Everyone. Everything. Left ussss with nothing but liessss. All the liessss they bury here. This isn't a prisssson; it's a cemetery for enemiesss of the dragonsss. A grave for the barely living. She died in the fight against the lies. I live in the fight against the lies. The liessss eat ussss all."

"What do you mean?" I ask, leaning in. "What did the dragons do to your family?"

His tongue flicks out and he smiles widely. Too widely. "We knew their ssssecret, didn't we? The ssssecret they want hidden forever. The ssssecret of the world. The ssssecret to ssssaving it all. Their ssssselfish, lying, evil ssssecret that fills this place with rot and shit and the carcasses of truth once sssspoken."

"What secret?" I ask.

"The ssssecret. The ssssecret. The ssssssecret." His voice escalates as he keeps repeating it, over and over.

"What secret!" I shout, trying to be heard over his insanity.

He slams his body so hard against the invisible shield that I can practically feel the zaps of electricity shooting through the wall and into him. My skin tingles with the magic around me, tapping into my own pools of power.

He flicks his tongue, licking at the invisible wall. Then he sniffs and smiles.

"You're the ssssecret. You're the ssssssecret. You're the ssssssecret." With a sudden movement, he slams his head into the shield so hard his skin splits open and he falls to the ground, writhing on the floor as the magic electrocutes him.

Sebastian pulls me away. "We have to go!"

I'm too shaken to argue with him, and it's clear we won't get any more answers from Lester, if we got anything at all.

Sebastian guides us through the maze of stairs and halls until we reach the front door.

Rather than head home, we take a detour and stop at a pub.

"You need food and we both need a drink," Sebastian says.

The Naked Gnome is indeed run by a gnome who likes to flaunt his nether regions at his place of business. Not the choice I would have made, but I shrug and go along with it.

"Ignore him," Sebastian says of the gnome who's presently dancing on the bar, doing his best free willy interpretation. "The food here is excellent."

I raise an eyebrow at that. "How would you know? You don't eat."

"I've been told," he says with a crooked grin.

"I hope his bits aren't part of the food prep process?"

Sebastian laughs. "No, he sticks to the bar. He likes the audience."

I look around at the empty pub. "Audience?"

Sebastian shrugs and when a very old and very small woman comes to take our order, I ask him to pick something he thinks I will like.

My mind is stuck on Lester's ranting. "What did he mean about a secret?" I ask.

"The dragons undoubtedly have many secrets," Sebastian says. "But what secret that could save the world? I have no idea."

"And what do I have to do with it?" I wonder. "Or was that just his insanity?"

"I would bet insanity, but we shouldn't rule anything out."

Drinks are brought to us, and I am served a plate of potatoes, meat, and a garden salad. "What kind of meat?" I ask suspiciously.

"Just eat the potatoes and salad," he says by way of answer. "We don't have cows in this world."

Yup, still a vegetarian, at least while we're in the Otherworld.

Under my plate is a recent copy of town news, and I scan the headlines until I see one that ruins my appetite and makes my blood run cold.

"What is it?" Sebastian asks.

I push the paper over to him. "Look."

Anger is clouding my judgment and when my fists turn to balls of fire, Sebastian pays quickly and escorts me out.

"How could this happen?" I ask.

"It's not a perfect system," Sebastian says.

I spin on him. "Not perfect? Not perfect? We're not even in the ballpark of perfect. We're so far from perfect right now that even adequate is out of reach. Competence is a laughable dream. This is a disgrace. This is evil!"

Lily pulls the carriage up and raises an eyebrow when she sees me. "What happened?"

Sebastian answers for me since I'm still too rage-monster to speak in coherent sentences. "The Collector was released from prison. He won't face charges."

Lily flinches as if physically punched, then shakes her head sadly.

Before we take off, I make a decision. "Lily, take us by Lilith's house on the way home. I need to call in a favor."

CHAPTER 13: THE PARTY

THERE IS nothing more important than love. And no law higher. -Lady Midnight by Cassandra Clare

MY VISIT with Lilith yields the results I expect, but I'm still struggling with my decision. Am I stepping over the line? Sliding down a slippery slope? I believe what I've done is the right choice. The just choice.

It's just not the legal choice.

Now I wait to hear back from her.

I also have a shit ton of work to do.

For two weeks, time passes at breakneck speed. We leave no stone unturned in trying to suss out the ravings of a madman, and we make no progress in figuring out what the dragons might be lying about. We already knew Ethne had no love lost for the dragons, if she was willing to betray Ava'Kara and steal her egg, so the news that their family bore a grudge against the dragons doesn't help our case any. Not unless we can figure out why, and not unless that why is connected to her motive and can also connect us to her partner/killer.

All in all, it's a waste. Our strongest argument is lack of evidence on the part of the prosecutor, but given that's Dath'Racul himself, I doubt very much that will be enough to get Liam a Not Guilty verdict.

"How can they let him prosecute?" I ask, for probably the millionth time since I found out. "He's got way too much power to make a fair prosecutor."

"It's not fair," Liam says, fire sparking at the tips of his fingers. "But nothing about this system is fair."

The other three brothers agree. Cole is the only one missing. He never attends meetings about Liam's court case, arguing he's not a lawyer and has done all he can to help. He's likely at the local pub enjoying a strong drink. I could use a strong drink myself at this point.

Matilda comes in carrying a tray of goblets and food. "You lot have been at this long enough. Have you not noticed the date?"

Elijah's eyes widen. "It's New Year's Eve tomorrow. And the court case is the next day."

Liam frowns. "There's nothing more we can do. Justice will prevail or it won't. This might be my last holiday with those I love the most," he says, his gaze locking on mine. "And I want to celebrate it. Put the law books away. And let's prepare the castle for a proper New Year's celebration."

Derek stops his pacing, hands locked behind his back, and glances at Liam. "We can't give up."

"It's not giving up," Liam says. "It's recognizing we are as prepared as we possibly can be. At the end of the day, they have no evidence against me. That's going to have to be enough. It's not our job to prove who the real criminal is. It's their job to prove it's me. And they can't." He shrugs, and as hot tempered as the fire Druid can be, he seems to be learning when to let things go.

Now is one of those times. I can see it in him. He needs to have a family celebration. Some joy. Some time with his daughter.

"I agree with Liam," I say. "This time of year is about family. Let's make happy memories while we can."

Matilda smiles gently at me, and the others finally stop arguing and stop working and we break to begin preparations for the party.

Lily sends out beautifully calligraphed invitations to our closest friends, while I work with the castle ghosts to discuss the decorations. Well, discuss might be stretching that word's definition a bit. More like, I talk to an empty room and hope someone is listening.

I have no idea if this is a gift-giving event, but I have a surprise for the family, and as I spend a few hours alone in my room, I put the finishing touches on it, admiring the polished results. A door opens and I spin around and come face to face with Cole, who stands transfixed by the painting I've been working on for weeks.

It's a watercolor painting of all of us, the five Night brothers, Matilda, Lily, me, Alina, and of course, Moon, who is presently curling around my ankles begging to be pet.

"You painted this?" Cole asks, stepping forward to study it.

"Yes."

"It should be in a museum."

I feel heat rise to my cheeks. "Thank you. I'm quite proud of it."

He smiles, redirecting his gaze to me. "You should be."

Cole cups my face and leans in to kiss me, his breath mixing with mine, his lips like velvet, and I melt into him as I feel his shadow magic wrap around me, caressing me everywhere at once.

He pulls away just enough to speak, his dark eyes so penetrating. "Leave with me," he says in a breath, and I freeze and step back.

"What?"

"Leave with me. Just you and me. We can start a new life anywhere in any world we want." He looks so earnest. So desperate for me to say yes.

"This is my home," I say. "My family. Your family."

He scoffs. "I don't belong here. I'm an outcast to my brothers. And an outsider in this world. But with you, I can be anything. Do anything. You and I are so much stronger together than apart. Can't you feel it?"

The thing is, I can. I can feel how my magic responds to Cole when he is close to me. How the power within me swells and rises, as if being summoned and magnified. It's a heady feeling, and I want to cling to it. To him. But...to leave? Just like that?

And then I remember my brother's words.

That I will be given the chance to leave, and I must take it. I must leave the Night brothers.

Is this what he meant? Is this the moment that will define my life?

I haven't seen or heard from my brother since he gave me the ring. I fidget with it as I consider my choices. If my brother truly is seeing the future, then I should leave with Cole. I should start a life with him. And it would be an amazing life, I do believe that. But it would mean saying goodbye to Liam, to Liam's daughter who has become like my own, to Sebastian, and Derek, and Elijah, all of whom I have growing feelings towards. To Matilda and Lily. The Ifrits. All of my friends here.

I haven't had time to give it much thought, but I've just realized how much I have here. How many roots I've put down. How many people I would miss, beyond just the men I'm falling in love with.

This is the moment I must decide if I truly believe my brother's visions.

If I leave with Cole, then it means I believe what my brother did by killing Mary and the baby truly will have saved many lives.

If I stay…does that mean I am saying I don't believe my brother? Which means he wasn't justified in killing them, and that makes him…evil? Or insane, but then very dangerous.

How can I decide this, right here, right now? How can I possibly have enough knowledge and wisdom to weigh those possibilities?

"Eve?" Cole's voice is hoarse.

And it breaks me.

Tears stream down my face. "Stay. Just stay. Let us all be a family. Your niece needs you. And whether they know it or not, your brothers need you."

I step forward and wrap my arms around his waist. "I need you."

"You don't know what you're asking," he says. "You don't know who I really am."

"Then stay and show me," I say. "Or stay and change. Every moment we get a chance to redeem ourselves. To reimagine who we choose to be. Use this moment now. Whatever is in your heart, whatever pain, whatever anger, whatever demons, let it go. And stay."

He kisses me and smiles. "You're truly a remarkable woman, Eve. I didn't expect you in my life."

And then he leaves, and I realize he never did promise he'll stay. I can only hope my words take root within him. This family needs to heal. And none of them can do that if Cole leaves.

~

THE NEXT DAY there is a flurry of activity as we all ready for the party. Elijah comes to my room with a long silver box. I open it and find a gorgeous red velvet dress perfectly sized for me. "Wow! Thank you."

"It compliments your complexion," he says, and then kisses my cheek and leaves quickly, as if slightly embarrassed.

Lily comes to my aid, helping me dress and style my hair. I study myself in the mirror and twirl around, smiling. It's a melancholic smile, with the looming threat of trial the next day, but I'm determined to enjoy the time we have tonight, with dear friends and family.

I wonder if Adam will show up again, or if I've seen my brother for the last time. I have no way of contacting him. No way of getting a message to him. No way of knowing if he's dead or alive. Can he even die? I have no way of knowing that, either.

Lily curls my hair and folds it into an updo, with soft ringlets let down around my face, and red holly tucked into the braid.

I stain my lips red and line my eyes with kohl, and then Lily and I walk down, arm and arm. She's dressed in green, and together we look quite festive.

I'm relieved to see Cole by the front door with his brothers as they receive guests.

Ifi and Elal arrive first, and the two Ifrits greet us quickly then make a beeline straight to the baby. Matilda hands her over and the two of them nearly set the house on fire with their excitement. I'm about to warn them to be careful with Alina, when she throws a fireball and one of them catches it and tosses it back to her.

Liam laughs and Matilda clucks her tongue. "We really need to come up with a spell to ward off fire damage, with all you fire elements running around." She looks meaningfully at Liam and me, and the

Ifrits both raise their eyebrows. Ifi thrusts his hip out and shakes his finger at me. "Girl, you are holding out. You got fire power now?"

I laugh and hold up my palm, producing a single, perfect flame in it. Then I aim at the candles lining the mantle over the fireplace and light all five of them at once. Not a single one melts on contact.

Liam claps, a huge smile on his face. "You've been practicing."

I nod. "Yes."

A knock on the door draws everyone's attention and Kana the Kitsune enters in her beautiful woman form. Her long, glossy black hair flows unbridled down the back of her floor-length, silver evening gown. As soon as she sees me, she checks that I'm wearing the amulet she gave me, and nods when she sees the crystal pendant with the fox carved into its face hanging at my collarbone.

Elijah offers his elbow and escorts her into the ballroom where we've set up tables of food and drink. It turns out the ghosts of the castle included some musicians, so we enjoy a haunted concert, as a cello, piano, bass, viola, and violin all begin to play as if on their own.

Akuro and Okura arrive next with their bundle of joy, and the Ifrits squeal in delight at another baby. The two couples head into the ballroom with the babies to let them play together.

Lily hasn't joined in the festivities and I notice she keeps glancing at the door. I find out why a few minutes later when Kaya arrives, wearing a gold dress that compliments Lily's. They both smile beatifically when they see each other, and they move into the corner to talk, holding hands the whole time.

I'm grinning from ear to ear like an idiot when Liam walks over to me and slips his arm around my waist. "You look happy, love," he says, kissing my cheek.

"I like seeing Lily happy," I say, nodding to her and Kaya.

Liam raises an eyebrow. "She does indeed look happy." He smiles. "Good for her."

He turns back to me, his face becoming more serious. "Can I talk to you? Alone?"

"Sure," I say, following him out of the ballroom and into the library. "What's up?"

He closes the door behind us and pulls out a parchment, handing it to me. "I want you to have this, in case...well, just in case."

My stomach drops as I realize what he's doing, and I squeeze the parchment in my fist, resisting the urge to give it back to him. Tears sting my eyes. "We are going to win. You're going to be fine."

"Maybe," he says. "But, maybe not. There's a strong chance I don't come out of this well. If that happens, I need to ask you the biggest favor I've ever asked anyone."

I try to swallow, but my mouth and throat have suddenly dried out. "What?"

"Take care of Alina. Adopt her. Be her mother. If I know she has you, I can face whatever is coming."

Now the tears flow, and I pull Liam into a hug, clinging to him as if the fierceness of my love is enough to save him. "You know I'll always take care of that little girl," I say. "Always."

Liam pulls back to study me. "Even if I'm found innocent, I'd... I'd still like you to adopt her. To officially become her mother, if you're willing. You're the only mother she has."

I can't speak. My heart is flooding with emotion, my body viscerally moved by his trust in me, by this shared bond that is so heavy and yet so light all at the same time. "Are you sure that's what you want?" I ask.

He nods. "More than anything. I want you and I want her. The two of you are my family."

He kisses me deeply and it feels as if it might be the last time we ever kiss like this again, though I know that's not possible. We have time before the trial. Time to steal more kisses and hold each other and talk about the future with his daughter. Our daughter.

It's a perfect moment.

Until it isn't.

A warning flash hits me first, sending a wave of dizziness through me.

Then a loud crash coming from the hall startles us both into action. When Liam and I run out, we see the front door has been beaten down and Enforcers swarm into the castle led by Dath'Racul.

He tips his head at me, "Miss Oliver." His eyes narrow when he sees Liam.

"We have a warrant to search this property." He hands Liam a scroll, and Liam studies it, singeing the edges with his fire.

I read over his shoulder and my blood runs cold.

They had a tip. The egg is somewhere in the castle, and once they find it, any defense we might have had falls apart.

CHAPTER 14: THE LIE

HOW DOES something that set fire to your heart suddenly chill your bones?
~ Nikita Gill

ENFORCERS IMMEDIATELY BEGIN to spread out, roughly handling priceless antiques as they search in the most unlikely places.

"The egg, which is the size of a medium built dog, is not hiding in a vase the size of my first," I say, grabbing the ancient hand-painted relic from an Enforcer's hand. "Are you here to destroy everything, or to actually attempt to find a dragon egg?" I ask.

Matilda, Lily, the other brothers, the Ifrits, the Kitsune, the Gargoyles and the Dryad all come to the hall after hearing the commotion. The baby is crying and the Enforcers look at each other, uncomfortable with the presence of a child, clearly.

Derek steps forward, frowning. "What's the meaning of this, Racul? You know we don't have the egg."

The fire dragon shrugs. "Then you shouldn't have any problem with us taking a look around."

My flash is still pinging in my brain, but I don't need my flash to know something smells off about this whole thing. I grab Derek's hand and pull him into another room while the others continue asking questions and generally work to keep the Enforcers from making much progress in their search.

"This is a set up," I tell Derek in a whisper. Who knows what kinds of creatures the Enforcers are, or how well they can hear.

"I assume so as well."

"Which means, the egg is here. Someone is framing Liam. We have to find the egg and get rid of it before they do, or there's nothing we'll be able to say to exonerate Liam."

Derek nods.

"You know the castle better than me. It will be somewhere that looks like it's been hidden, but not so hidden that these idiots won't find it," I say.

"The Enforcers may be idiots, but don't underestimate Dath'Racul. He's shrewd and brilliant."

I narrow my eyes. "So am I."

Derek smiles at that. "That you are."

We head to my room where I get my sketchbook and turn to the pages I drew when I first arrived here, of all the halls and rooms and secret passages I could find in the castle. Derek whistles under his breath. "I'm not sure your assessment is correct," he says.

"About what?"

"I don't think I know this castle better than you. That's the most thorough map I've ever seen."

"Let's hit up all the bedrooms as fast as we can, then head to the more remote areas."

We work quickly searching through each room—my god there are so many—and tracking our progress on my drawing. We search Liam's room more thoroughly since that would be an extra nail in the coffin if it's found in there. But...nothing.

We then head down to the lower levels, to where Lily's tree lives, to places that used to be prisons and give me the chills to be in. Moon follows at our heels, as if he understands what we're doing and wants to help.

We can hear the Enforcers hitting the places as we leave them.

When our search yields nothing, I sigh, then have a light bulb moment and grab Derek's hand. "I think I know where it is."

We've been to all the main levels, and we've been below. The only place we haven't checked is up. The stairway that winds up the tallest tower is dark and narrow, and the higher we go, the less covering we have from the storm that's brewing. Wind and rain pelt us as we reach the top platform. At first it appears we've reached another dead end, but then, in the corner, I see a trunk that wasn't here before. I show Derek, who walks over and tries to open it. "It's locked."

Derek is water, and that's not going to help us right now. "Stand back," I say, praying I have enough control for this. Because if the egg is in there, and I mess up, well, I can't think too much about that without having a panic attack.

I definitely do not want to kill a baby dragon. That's for sure not on my list of things to ever do.

I pull up the fire in me and direct it into the metal lock, heating it up until it's so hot it cracks, falling off. Derek reaches for it, but I hold him back. "You'll burn yourself."

Instead, I grab it and pull it open, knowing I am now immune to fire. My powers are growing.

And just as I suspected. Within the chest is the pulsing silver blue egg of the water dragon. I can feel the life growing within, and I lay a hand on it and close my eyes, letting the feeling of bliss from this little being wash over me.

A zapping sound startles me and Derek yelps and falls to the ground. I spin around, stunned to see Derek unconscious. I run to him and hold his head in my lap, trying to revive him. I'm about to slit my wrists to feed him when a voice stops me.

"Eve, leave him. He is not badly injured. He will wake and be fine."

I look up at Adam and frown. "What are you doing here? Why did you attack Derek?"

Laying Derek gently on the ground, I stand, facing my twin. "What's going on, Adam? Did you steal the dragon egg?"

"I had to," he says, with the same conviction he used to defend his murder of Mary and her child. "This is all happening the way it needs to. The Enforcers must find the egg. Liam must take the fall. If he doesn't..."

"What? What happens if Liam isn't blamed for a crime he didn't commit?" I ask, my patience for all this nonsense wearing thin.

"You die," he says. "You, the baby, all the other brothers, Matilda, Lily and her tree...you all die. You burn to death."

I shake my head. "That's impossible. I have the fire element in me. So does Alina. She and I can't burn to death."

He shrugs. "I've seen it, Evie. It happens. Or it would have, if I hadn't intervened. Whatever leads up to it, somehow this particular fire destroys you all. And when Liam discovers what he's done, he takes his own life. This way is better, for him and for all of you. You must let it happen."

"You want me to believe that we should play god with people's lives based on visions of a future that may or may not happen?" I ask. "I can't do that. It isn't right."

"You have always been so caught up with doing the right thing, you've never stopped to ask yourself where this idea of right and wrong even came from. Or if it even makes sense." He runs a hand through his hair and sighs. "Isn't it a greater good to save many, even if it means sacrificing a few?"

I shake my head, stepping back. "This doesn't feel right."

"Come with me, Evie. Let's leave. Together. Just you and me. Us against the world, like it always used to be." He holds out his hand, his eyes pleading. "I can't do this without you. We are stronger together. We always have been."

My heart stops. When it beats again, it fills my head with the sound. Everything slows. My breathing hitches. And then...everything falls into place and I swallow a bitter truth that cracks me open and leaves me shredded.

Adam has been pushing me to leave the Night Firm.

He showed me the Memory Catcher, which he knew would create conflict with Liam and the other brothers.

The demon the Collector subjected me to said, "Nothing is at it appears. Least of all fate's twins."

And the other night at the ball, Cole used shadow magic to change his features.

I want to deny the truth I feel in my own soul, but I can't.

"You're not Adam, are you....Cole?"

Adam sighs and a black mist floats over him. When it clears, Cole stands in his place. "I'm impressed you figured it out. Most people only see what they want to see."

"I never wanted to see my brother turn into a murderer," I say, spitting out the words. "How could you lie to me like that, then sleep with me?"

"I never wanted to hurt you," he says. "You are collateral damage in a much larger war."

"That's all I am? Collateral damage? All in an effort to punish your brothers? To punish Liam?" I feel crushed inside, but I can't give into my despair just yet. There's still the egg, and the Enforcers. "Don't you understand that Liam's been punishing himself for years? He's the one who wanted to make amends. He's a father now. He has a little girl who needs him."

Cole's face twists into an ugly smile. "They will be here at any moment," he says. "They'll arrest Liam. Hell, they'll probably arrest all of my brothers. You should leave with me now, Eve, so you don't get caught up in this mess. I still mean what I said. I need you. We are stronger together."

"The memory you showed me...did you kill Mary and the baby looking like my brother?" My only comfort in this moment is that my brother is still the man I carry in my memories. The man who couldn't hurt a fly, who was too gentle and kind for his own good. Cole nearly took that away from me.

"No," he says. "I didn't kill them. That memory was fake, created by shadow magic." He steps forward. "You could do so much with your power, Eve. I can show you. You have no idea what you're capable of with all the elements in you."

I still feel drawn to him, despite everything that he's done, and it kills me to pull away, to deny my feelings, to go against this pull that has entranced me since I first saw him at the festival.

"How did you know how to be Adam so perfectly?"

"Your dreams," Cole says. "He lives in your dreams and I can dream walk."

"What about the guard? The basilisk?" I ask. "You killed her. She was your partner and you killed her."

He shakes his head. "No. Ethne was supposed to live. She injured herself to look innocent and was meant to keep her cover. My guess is one of the dragons killed her for failing to protect the egg."

"How do I know you're telling me the truth?" I ask.

"Look at your ring," he says.

Confused, I look at my finger. The onyx is glowing, and it occurs to me Adam didn't give me this. Cole did.

Shit.

I'm going to have to go back and re-remember every damn conversation I had with the man I thought was my brother and replace that face with Cole's.

"That ring has a part of me—a part of my magic—in it. And a part of you," he says. "You can use it to tell if someone lies to you."

"How?" I ask.

He cocks his head. "Eve, I hate you."

His words are a punch to the gut, but when I look down at the ring, it's pulsing.

"Eve," he says, softly. "I love you."

The ring goes back to glowing.

"That's how," he says.

And my heart is ripped into pieces once again.

"Cole?" Derek's voice is hollow and weak, and I turn to see him sitting up. "It was you this whole time?" A tear slides down Derek's face. "We deserve this. But I deserve it the most. I may not have been the one to land the whip on you, but...I'm the one who turned you in after I found out what you did. If it weren't for me, none of this would be happening. If you must punish anyone, take me. Leave the rest of them out of it. Please. I'm so sorry, brother."

Cole scowls. "You will need to pay for that," he says. "But that doesn't exonerate the rest of them. You all played your part in my torture and imprisonment. And you will all suffer the consequences of your actions. You believe in justice? This is justice."

A black swirl appears around Cole, and I can tell he's about use his shadow powers to escape. I can't let him.

I plunge into my powers and break the wall I'd been keeping around my darkness, dipping into the inky magic that lives in my deepest depths, and I pull it up, letting it wrap around me, then I use a strand of it to tug at Cole.

Just as he's about to vanish, leaving his brothers stranded with the incriminating egg, I latch onto him and his smoke dissipates. He looks at me, wide eyed. "How did you do that?"

"I finally realized you're right. I'm more powerful when I tap into my darkness. But it has to be on my terms, even if I don't totally know what those terms are."

With my powers fully open, I feel my veins fill with all the elements, and I tremble from the influx of magic surging within me. My body rises from the ground, hovering, my arms spread, my skin glowing as the storm around us rages.

And suddenly my mind is flooded with a history of memories that don't belong to me, but I see it all, in an instant, the past and present and future are one, and my thoughts expand beyond what I thought possible.

When I open my mouth to speak, it is not my words that come forth, and it is not my voice that is heard.

"If you are going to punish anyone, Son of Light, punish me," the being within me says through my mouth. "It is not your brothers who are to blame, but myself. I was the one who decided on your punishment. I was the one who condemned you for what I thought I saw." I flick my wrist and summon a whip made of golden light, it's edge razor sharp. "If you must inflict pain on your tormenter, then whip me. Punish me." I hold out the whip, unafraid of what is to come. I accept whatever choice is made. "Or, you can break the cycle of pain and punishment and revenge. You can change the karmic path of everyone in this house and you can forgive, as I should have forgiven you. As I now do. You are forgiven, Son of Light, and restored with full honor and apologies to the Order of the Druids, should you wish to return. I cannot take away what is done, but I can offer this." With another flick of my wrist, a glowing golden light travels from my fingertips to Cole, and runs over his body. His eyes widen and he lifts his shirt, marveling as the scars from his torture disappear, replaced by healthy skin.

The magic still buzzes through me, and I see what happened to him all those years ago. The blood and tears and pain. The humiliation. The betrayal. And as much as I feel hurt and betrayed by a man I love, I also see the pain that led him down this path. And I know that whatever voice is speaking through me, I also need to follow heed and forgive, as hard as it is.

Cole leans forward, and I close my eyes, resigned as he reaches for the whip.

I will accept the lashes. The punishment.

I will accept whatever karmic end I must.

But when nothing happens, I open my eyes. The whip is still in my hand. But the egg—and Cole—are both gone.

CHAPTER 15: THE GOODBYE

GIRLS like her were born in a storm. They have lightning in their souls, thunder in their hearts, and chaos in their bones. ~Nikita Gill

WITH MY POWER DRAINED, I fall to my knees, bruising them on the stone floor. Derek's strong arms pull me towards him and keep me from hitting the ground face first. I feel as if my power, my energy, has been sucked dry. In a panic, I dive into myself, to my core, and to my relief I still see a small trickle of each element within me.

"My magic," I whisper, my eyes fluttering closed as darkness pulls at my consciousness. "It's almost gone."

Derek kisses my forehead. "You're okay. Just rest."

I WAKE in the way one does when they don't know how much time has passed or what day it is and there was something very important to do.

"The trial!" I yell, startling Liam, who is dozing in the chair next to my bed.

He rubs his eyes, then smiles when he sees I've returned to the land of the living. "You gave us a scare," he says, coming to sit on the bed next to me.

He hands me a glass of water and I down the entire thing in one gulp. He refills from a pitcher on my side table, and I drink that as well. Three cups later and I feel like a water balloon about ready to burst, but the cobwebs are finally clearing out of my head.

He hands me one more cup, and I'm about to decline, but I sniff it and realize it's not water. "Matilda?" I ask.

He smiles and nods. "You won't like it, but it will help you get your strength, and magic, back sooner."

It's worth it, I suppose. I gag it down and try not to vomit, then look around for some indication of what time it is.

"We need to get to the trial." I say, putting the cup down and trying to crawl out of bed, but Liam stills me with a hand on my knee.

"There was no trial," he says grinning.

"What? Why?"

"Charges against me have been dropped. Lack of evidence, I guess." He shrugs. "I'm free."

It takes a moment for his words to sink in, and when they do, my heart nearly bursts from the joy of it. I reach for him, sliding one hand behind his head, letting my fingers dig into his hair as I pull his face towards mine. Our lips brush against each other gently at first, then he groans and scoots our hips closer, deepening our kiss as he does.

Just as our passions rise, Liam pauses, resting his lips against my neck as he holds me close. "You're still recovering. The healer in me can't let this go further until you have all your strength back."

I sigh and kiss his neck to let him know what I think of his restraint. He groans again. "You're killing me, Eve."

Within his arms, while enjoying the scent of him and feel of him, I dive into myself again and am relieved to discover the elements within me are growing once more. I didn't lose my magic, it was just tapped out. Good to know that can happen.

And then my thoughts return to the trial, and I sit back. "I don't understand. Even without evidence, it seemed the dragons were determined to use you as the fall guy for this. What changed?"

"I don't know. But I'm grateful."

I smile. "So am I. Now Alina won't have to grow up without her father."

He nods. "What we talked about before…"

"It's okay if you want to change your mind about me adopting her," I say, though in my heart I had come to want it very badly. But still, I can't hold him to something he decided when he thought he was going away for life, or worse.

"I'm not changing my mind, Eve," he says, shaking his head as if I'm being absurd. "I'm checking to see if you've changed yours. I would understand, though I hope you haven't."

"I haven't," I say. "I want to be her mother. More than anything."

He smiles with true abandon, and it warms my heart, but then a sinking sensation steals over me. "But first, I need to tell you something, and it may affect your decision about this."

"I doubt it," he says. "But go ahead."

And so, I tell him everything. About Adam—or who I thought was Adam. About lying to him and about what came out of me when my powers activated during my confrontation with Cole.

"The weird thing was, when my powers hit, I was me but not me. Like someone else was speaking through me. I don't know how to explain it, but I said things that didn't make sense." I pause, frowning. "Anyways, I thought you should know all that before deciding on something so important. I know you're probably furious with me, and I don't blame you."

I wait for him to explode, to rage, to…I don't know, lose his temper, but instead he blinks.

That's it.

Just a blink.

"I've been wondering when you would tell me about Adam," he says, shocking the living hell out of me. "I've known for a while. I overheard the two of you at the Midwinter Festival. Though I must say, I'm so sorry my brother deceived you like that. That was cruel, even for him."

My heart lurches, both in relief that Liam isn't as angry as I thought he would be, and in renewed grief at remembering my brother really is still dead, and always was. Thinking I had him back, even knowing what he had become, gave me comfort. I didn't feel so alone in the world, knowing he was still in it.

He was the last person left alive who knew me as a child, who shared those memories of us growing up. Now, they live in me alone.

"Why didn't you say something if you already knew?" I ask.

"Why didn't you tell me?" he replies.

"Well, you are known for having quite the temper," I say. "And I didn't know what to do about Adam. He's my twin. I had to sort out what the right course of action was, and I didn't want you killing him."

A knock at the door interrupts us, and Matilda comes in. "I thought you might be awake," she says, smiling. "You have a visitor, my dear. Lilith is here for you."

"Thank you. I need a few minutes to freshen up. Can you tell her I'll be down shortly?"

Matilda nods and leaves, and Liam stands. "Do you want assistance dressing?" he asks.

I laugh. "I thought we weren't supposed to fool around? Doctor's orders or something?"

"There will be no fooling around. Strictly platonic."

He holds up his hands innocently, then slips one arm around me to help me from the bed. My legs are wobbly, and I walk about as well as a newborn colt. "How long will I feel this way?" I ask.

"It will take time for your strength and powers to return," he says as he guides me to the bathroom. "But I don't know specifically. You're a bit of an anomaly in the magical world, as I'm sure you've realized."

With Liam's totally platonic (sadly) help, I manage to bathe, brush my hair and teeth, and change into something appropriate. While dressing I notice the ring Cole gave me is missing from my finger. "Did you see my ring?" I ask. "Silver with black onyx."

"I know the one you're talking about, but no. I haven't seen it," Liam says.

Huh. It must have fallen off when my powers went all supernova.

I feel a sinking loss at that, at this one little piece I had of Cole. Despite my feelings for him being complicated, I can't change the bond we have. I can't pretend it doesn't exist, even within my hurt and anger.

Because when I think back to what he's gone through—from early childhood abuse into the adulthood that removed him from his life and family, I can see how he ended up where he did. Who's to say any of us would have acted any differently in the same circumstances.

Liam helps me downstairs and Matilda has food and wine waiting in the sitting room for me, and blood for Lilith, of course. I'm surprised to see she's brought someone with her. The cat girl from the Collector's party.

Lilith stands when I enter, then rushes to help me get seated. "What happened to you?" she asks. "You're as pale as...well, me."

"It's a long story," I say, taking a plate of food.

I glance at the girl and smile. "You look well...er, I realize I don't know your name. I'm Eve."

She nods. "I'm Sasha. Thank you. For...everything. Lilith told me what you did for me."

I direct a questioning look to Lilith, who shrugs. "She didn't have anywhere to go, so I took her in. I figured I could use a protégé. I have many businesses in this world and the mundane and no heirs. This seemed a perfect fit for us both."

I grin and offer the girl a plate of fresh bread and berries, which she accepts.

"That makes me incredibly happy," I say. "And the other matter?"

"Yes, the favor you asked of me," Lilith says with a devious smile. "It's been handled. The Collector has found himself indisposed for the foreseeable future."

"And there's no chance of him escaping or being found?" I ask. I may have crossed a line, asking Lilith to find a place the Collector could serve the prison sentence he deserves. But isn't this justice? Letting him go free to enslave and hurt others wouldn't have served anyone.

I've realized about myself two things since all that's happened with

Cole and with who I thought was Adam. One: I've got a lot more darkness in me than I wanted to admit. And two: it's okay. I can use that darkness. I don't have to stay within the lines to feel morally comfortable with my decisions, but I can't act out of vengeance and I can't kill unless I'm actively defending myself or someone else. My choices have to be just, even if they aren't always lawful.

It's an ambitious line that not all would agree with, but it's what feels right to me, at least for now.

"He will never be found or escape, of that you have my word," Lilith says. "Would you like me to take you to him so you can see for yourself?"

"No, though I appreciate the offer. I actually have something else I need to deal with right now. And I trust you."

Lilith stands. "Very well then, I must be off. But stay in touch, Eve. I truly enjoy our friendship, and despite having lived longer than almost anyone, I can't actually call many people 'friend.'"

Her words touch me. Deeply. I stand and hug her. "I value this as well," I say. "And I'll pay a visit soon. Once the dust settles with all this stolen egg business."

Lilith's eyes widen and she reaches into her bag. "That reminds me. I was asked to deliver this to you."

She hands me a scroll, sealed with a dragon mark. I break the wax and read. "It's from Ava'Kara. She wants to meet with me later today. Alone." I look up at Lilith. "Do you know what this is about?"

"I haven't got a clue," she says, "but I wouldn't be late if I were you."

Once they leave, I head to my room and stand before the mantle, staring at my brother's urn. Funny that I never got rid of it once I thought he was alive. Maybe a part of me always knew it wasn't really Adam visiting me. But like Cole said, we see what we want to. I wanted to believe Adam was alive. I wanted to believe I hadn't lost my brother forever.

I take the urn and walk outside. Moon follows close behind. Sebastian notices me leaving but sees what I'm holding and doesn't interfere.

My strength is returning to me faster than I expected. The potion must have helped. I feel strong enough to make the walk I need to. Beyond our property, just past a grove of trees, is the shoreline for the only ocean on this world. I saw it on a map and have been wanting to visit but haven't had time.

Today I'm making time.

Today I'm going to finally say goodbye to my brother.

With Moon the only witness, I stand on the shore, overlooking the horizon, where the deep purples of the Dragon's Breath dance over the waters that ebb and flow. I take off my shoes and let my toes sink into the wet sand, the salty water covering them with each tide.

As tears flow down my cheek, I taste the salt of them on my lips, I realize we are all made of the ocean. Salt and water and tides and depth and mystery and wonder. And so, I return my brother to the watery arms of the sea, to be held by her.

I open the urn and tilt it, but the air is stagnate and doesn't catch the ashes.

Closing my eyes, I dip into my power and pull just enough from the air to encourage a breeze that takes my brother's remains and sweeps them into the water.

"Goodbye, Adam," I whisper, letting the wind carry my words with his body. "Every day I think of you. Every day I wish things had gone differently for us. You should be here with me, exploring this new world, enjoying this new family. They would love you. You'd have brothers. So many brothers." I chuckle. As children, I used to dress up like a boy and pretend to be Adam's brother sometimes, so the other boys wouldn't refuse to play with us.

"I wish I could go back in time, to the day before you died, and tell you all that is in my heart. Tell you that I would have endured a thousand bankruptcies and shitty apartments to have you back. I wish I could tell you how much I love you. How much I miss you. How a piece of me died with you."

I choke on my words as the urn empties, and I watch as his ashes drift on the current.

"I wish I could tell you there were other options. Other choices. You didn't have to take your life."

I wipe my eyes and think back on all the beautiful memories we shared as children. Even the hardest times feel sweet in reflection, because I had him. "I hope more than anything that you have found peace. That whatever awaits us in the afterlife has brought you healing and joy. Someday we will be together again. Until then and always, I will carry you in my heart."

CHAPTER 16: THE SACRIFICE

YOUR LOVE WAS BORN in the wild, growing from the soft earth surrounded by trees that were surrounded by stars. That is why the forest has such a hold on you. That is why sometimes if feels like the moon knows your name.

~ YOUR LOVE by Nikita Gill

"I'LL BE WITH HER," Lily argues, setting her glass of berry juice down firmly.

Sebastian crosses his arms over his chest for the millionth time, and huffs.

I'm sick and tired of this argument. "This isn't a discussion," I say. "The note said to come alone. I'm not even sure Lily should be there."

Now it's Lily's turn to huff. "Of course, I should be there. Who else will drive you? Do you know how to effectively guide a horse-drawn carriage?" she asks pointedly.

My mouth flops open like a dead fish, and I snap it closed again and ignore her question. Because no, I have no idea how to effectively guide a horse-drawn carriage, and it's one more thing I mentally add to my growing list of shit I need to learn how to do in this world in my free time. Ha! As if I have free time.

"Besides," Lily continues, "I can just leave if it's a problem. Either way, Eve will be fine. She always is."

Lily beams at me and my heart swells at the confidence she has. But I have to admit to a certain amount of nerves. I'm about to meet a dragon face to face. Alone. For reasons unknown. That's not an everyday kinda thing, and I think I'm okay in feeling a bit flustered about it all.

What's the difference between excitement and anxiety? It's hard to say, isn't it? To the body, they are the same. It's only to the mind that they are different. One anticipates a positive outcome in a particular life event, the other anticipates a negative outcome. They are two sides of the same coin.

And so, I do my best to manage my nerves as Lily drives me to the water dragon's palace.

I have so many questions, and I wonder if I'll get any of them answered. We still don't know why they dropped the case against Liam, or what Cole did or said. I'm still waiting for the other shoe to drop. Will this be it? Will today be the day?

Ava'Kara walks down from her throne when we enter, and she doesn't even wait for the standard bows and curtseys. She takes me by the arm and guides me behind her throne into the water that I first saw her emerge from in her dragon form.

Using her powers, she creates a vortex that surrounds us, pulling us to the surface. Ava'Kara is about to use her water manipulation to allow me to breathe, but I beat her to it, channeling my own power to create an air pocket around me.

She raises an eyebrow. "I see you've come into your power. Good. That will make this all go much more smoothly."

"Make what go more smoothly?" I ask, feeling like a parrot.

She studies me with her large blue reptilian eyes. "I need a favor from you. A quite extraordinary one."

"What kind of favor?" I ask, suddenly more nervous than ever, my flash pinging like a winning slot machine in Vegas.

"The kind only you can provide."

We reach a platform made of the largest seashells I've ever seen, and Ava'Kara transforms into her dragon form, her sapphire scales like jewels flashing against the colorful sky.

"Get on," she says.

"You...you want me to ride on your back?" I ask, incredulous.

"It's the fastest way, and we haven't much time. Now!"

Not wanting to argue, but also very much wanting to argue, I ignore my own survival instincts and climb awkwardly onto her back.

She takes off into the sky, and I feel as if I'm being pulled through a wind tunnel.

"Use your air magic," she says loud enough for me to hear her.

I could kick myself for not thinking of that.

I channel my power and manipulate the air around me until it's comfortable. Smiling, I clutch her back and study the scenery below.

It doesn't take long for me to realize we are heading to the edge of the world, where the wall of Dragon's Breath prevents anyone from traveling farther.

Ava'Kara lands us near Kaya the dryad's tree, and I slide off, my legs trembling.

In the center of the grove is the dragon egg, shimmering and pulsing, and there's a crack running down its side. We are alone here, though I can feel the presences of the dryads within their trees.

"It was returned to me," Ava'Kara says, staying in her dragon form. "We know not by whom, but it does not matter. My heir is home, and she is being born as we speak."

Holy shit. Am I about to witness the birth of a dragon?

Yes. Yes, I am.

Because at that moment, the first little dragon claw cuts through the mucous and shell and pokes out, and Ava'Kara makes a strange clucking sound and moves toward her child.

I don't know how long we stand there, but slowly the baby dragon emerges, scales a lighter shade of blue from her mother's, eyes so large they look almost animated, and that newborn innocence that all babies have.

Once she's shed her shell, she takes a few clumsy steps towards her mother, then falls, hiccups, and then quite suddenly turns into a more human-looking baby. She giggles, then turns back into a dragon.

Ava'Kara glances at me. "She'll learn to control that soon enough."

I just nod.

Because holy shit.

The water dragon brings her baby to her, and they snuggle as if they have always been together.

"I need you to perform a ceremony," Ava'Kara says after some time.

"What kind?" I ask. I've read about a lot of different kinds of ceremonies, so I'm hoping it's one I'm familiar with.

"A World Expansion Ceremony," she says softly, setting her child down and shifting into her human form to approach me. "It will require all of the elements, which is why you are the only one who can do it."

"I've never heard of it," I say.

"Because it is the Council of Dragons' most closely guarded secret. Many have paid a steep price for even possessing a fraction of the knowledge I'm about to impart on you tonight," she says.

I think of Lester, rotting in prison because his family knew secrets and lies. And I'm reminded what he said about me, as well. Maybe his ramblings weren't so crazy after all.

"Why is it such a secret?" I ask, my throat dry. I know I'm about to hear something I very much do not want to hear. I feel the fear before I even know why.

"Because it involves the death of a dragon to perform," she says, and I gasp, stepping back.

"You want me to kill a...dragon?" I can't. I cannot.

"I want you to sacrifice me," she says stepping forward.

"You want to kill yourself? Why?" I should start a support group. Nearly every paranormal I've met has serious mental health issues. And for the first time I wonder if there is any kind of mental health services in this world, but I realize this is really not the time and my mind is dissociating from what is happening because I am utterly freaked out.

Eve, note to self, think about all this other shit later. A dragon just asked you to kill her.

"Why?" I ask. It's all I can think to say.

"For too long, we have flown over this world, dictating its rules, running the lives of those in our care, hoarding our own wealth and power. And now our world is crumbling. We are overpopulated and not large enough to manage the growing magical community. Someone has to step forward, and I now have an heir to carry on my element. Only I can do this."

"I don't understand," I say.

"With your powers and my sacrifice, this world will expand, and self-renew, growing as it needs in order to accommodate all of us, present and future. It's this, or so many of us die or live in slums. I can't be the one to condemn my people to that fate." She reaches for my hands and holds them, and I feel her emotions. She is desperate for me to say yes and is very much at peace with her decision. It is the only way to save the people. To save this world.

"Will you help me, Eve?"

My throat is too choked up to speak, so I just nod, glancing over at the baby dragon. She'll never know her mother.

Ava'Kara sees me looking at the baby and sighs. "It is hard to leave her, but she will be raised by someone I trust more than anyone."

The water dragon's face lights up as she glances over my shoulder and I turn around and see Lyx, the Light Dragon walking towards us, arms open. "Sister."

The two dragon queens hug.

"Take care of her for me," Ava'Kara says to Lyx.

Lyx kisses Kara's cheek. "Like she is my own."

Further back, all of the Light Dragon's people stand *en masse*, waiting quietly.

What are they waiting for? I have no idea what will happen.

"Is it safe for them to be here?" I ask.

Ava'Kara nods. "You will expend so much power to me, there will be none left to go anywhere else."

She glances at her sister, who gives her a look. Kara sighs. "There's something I need to tell you," she says.

"Okay... "

Lyx nudges Kara who sighs again. "Performing this ceremony might drain you."

I shrug. "I'll plan on getting extra rest until it all comes back."

Ava'Kara frowns. "Permanently. It might drain you permanently. You might lose all your powers. I don't know. I...we...thought you should know the risks before you agree."

I won't lie. This gives me pause. I could end up stripped of powers I just got? Powers I still don't know the full potential of. Am I willing to give all this up?

I know the answer the moment I think the question. Of course, I am. How could I not be? I may not be all light, but I have to live by a code of some kind. And I can't hoard power if it means so many others suffer.

I nod and the water dragon lets out a breath, then smiles. "You are braver and more generous than I expected, Eve Oliver."

The baby dragon turns back into a child, and Ava'Kara holds her daughter, kissing her head, then passes her to Lyx while she shifts back into her dragon form and positions herself in front of the wall of Dragon's Breath.

"It's very simple," she says. "Channel all the elements and pour them through your hands and into me while chanting *terry autumn usque ad terram.* Of earth, to earth."

I repeat the words in my head then nod and close my eyes. My power is there. It has returned in full form, and I have a feeling I will need every drop.

Hands held out, facing the water dragon, I begin to chant the words and funnel all of my power at the same time through my palms.

The wind whips around us.

A bush catches fire and burns.

The earth rips apart, leaving gashes around my feet.

Water falls from the sky, soaking me to the bone.

Still I chant.

Still the magic flows.

Golden light builds around me, mixed with dark tendrils of smoke. It all surrounds Ava'Kara, who glows a translucent blue, like waves in the ocean.

My knees buckle under me and I land hard on the ground, but I don't stop the ceremony.

Tears stream down my face.

Fire boils under skin.

I'm being drained, as surely as if a vampire was drinking the last drops of my blood.

My vision flicks in and out.

I can't hear anything over the storm wreaking havoc around me and within me.

And then, there's a great blast that knocks me flat on my face.

Everything goes quiet. Still. And I glance up and see that Ava'Kara is gone. Disappeared entirely.

A low murmur of voices begins behind me, and then the earth under us shifts, and the wall of Dragon's Breath begins to drift away like smoke until we are all staring at a lush new land that goes on as far as the eye can see. Grass green as emeralds, rolling hills, piney forests, the sound of the ocean in the distance. It's paradise.

Lyx wipes a tear from her eyes, holds the baby close to her chest, and nods at me, then steps forward, leading her people into the promised land.

I lie on the ground for I don't know how long—too exhausted and sore to even move—before I hear a familiar voice.

"I got a note to find you here. What happened?" Lily looks around, her face full of shock.

I clutch her arm for strength as I pull myself up. "Let's just go home. I'll explain on the way."

Kaya comes over to us and leans in to hug Lily and whisper something in her ear. They kiss and then Lily guides me to the carriage.

I pass out on the way home and Lily has to actually carry me inside. The dryad is stronger than she looks.

And my mind still hasn't processed all that just happened.

Liam, Sebastian, Derek, and Elijah are all drinking hard liquor in the study and turn to us when Lily arrives with me in her arms.

Sebastian reaches me first in three long steps, his arms propping me up as Lily releases me to him.

I smile up at him and laugh in a slightly maniacal and exhausted kind of way. "I watched a baby dragon hatch, and then I killed her mother and helped create a new extension to this world with my powers."

The room falls quiet, and the brothers exchange glances.

Elijah looks ready to burst with questions, and I can see him itching to write everything down. But I shake my head. "I need sleep. Food. Wine. I don't know. But definitely quiet. I love you all, and I'll explain everything tomorrow."

My eyelids are hard to keep open, and I step away from Sebastian, but have a hard time steadying myself. Then I feel someone help me, and I'm about to refuse it—because I really do want to be alone for a while—when I realize…it's a ghost. I can't see it, but I can feel it like it's solid.

I tentatively place a little more weight on it, and it shifts to offer more support, walking like this all the way to my room.

When it deposits me into my bed, it stokes the fire, opens a window for fresh air and is about to leave.

"Thank you," I say. "For all your do. Thank you. I will always help maintain your graves, and if you ever can show me where yours is and what your name is, I'll add it to your tombstone."

A gentle breeze blows through me, like a tender caress, and I smile as the door closes and I know I'm finally alone. I flop back onto my pillow, Moon purring at my side, and feel the crinkle of paper under my head.

I reach for it and stare at the script. I've never seen Cole's writing, but I know this is from him. My heart constricts as I open it. Inside the envelope is my onyx ring and a note.

MY DEAREST EVE,

YOU WILL LIKELY NOT BELIEVE me, and I wouldn't blame you at all, but not everything I said and did was a lie. You weren't a lie. I promise you that.

My brothers deserved what they got, and I think they know it, too.

But you didn't. You were a casualty of a war that wasn't your own, and for that I will always be deeply sorry.

I'm returning your ring, in hopes you will keep wearing it. It fell off that night.

I didn't get a chance to tell you this, but the ring is a protection ring. That wasn't a lie. I made it with my own powers, which means it even protects you from me. I never wanted you to be caught in something that could harm you. But I failed to consider the emotional cost of what I've done.

It has been too long since I have had any emotion but anger.

But you made me feel something more. Something true and deep and everlasting, even if I never see you again.

I returned the egg. I assume you know that by now.

And I know what you are. I always have.

I still believe you and I are stronger together.

If you ever change your mind, I'll know, and I'll be here.

Je t'aime,
    Cole Night

A TEAR FALLS from my cheek onto the paper, casting an inky smear over his signature. I set it aside, but clutch the ring in my palm, then I stand and walk to the balcony and gaze into the distance.

"Oh, Cole," I say into the wind. "How could I ever live with you?" I ask, not expecting an answer. "But how will I ever live without you?"

Already my heart is breaking. I feel like I lost both my brother and Cole in a single night.

I hold the ring to my heart, letting a sob break loose from my throat. I let the tears come, let the emotions wash over me. I give myself permission to feel pain. To feel grief. To not expect happiness for at least a few moments.

We place such a premium on happiness that we deny the reality of our own existence in seeking it. We devalue pain in all its forms, not realizing that the pain can teach us so much more than the joy. The joy is our reward for the lessons learned through pain. We wouldn't have the joy without it.

So, I embrace my own pain and I cry until there are no more tears.

I cry for Cole. For Adam. For myself. For this family that is broken and may never truly be mended.

I cry for Ava'Kara, who was the first of the dragons with the courage to sacrifice herself to save this world. Even the Beggar Queen chose a path that kept her alive. Sure, she drained her magic to help, but she didn't make the ultimate sacrifice and she could have. In the end, it was Ava'Kara. Maybe that was because the water dragon had an heir, but that doesn't make her sacrifice any less noble. I wear her ring on my right hand now, at her request before she died.

Someday I will give it to her daughter, when she is ready.

I open my palm and study the other ring recently given to me. Now that I know what I'm looking for, I can feel Cole's energy in the stone, pulsing at the same frequency that he does. It sends warmth through my body when I slip it on my finger, and I know the moment I do that I won't be taking it off again.

Someday, I have hope that Cole will come home for good. That this family will be complete.

Until then, I will be the best mother to Alina I can, and the best partner to other brothers. I will hold us together and help make us stronger.

There's a knock at the door, and a platter of food flies in seemingly of its own accord.

One of the ghosts has brought me food and wine and water, as requested. I smile.

And when I look down at my plate, I realize my vegetables spell something.

Mable.

A name.

"Are you Mable?"

The fire flares, and I know it's not my doing. I have nothing left in my magical reserves. "I take that as a yes. I'm Eve. It's such a pleasure to meet you."

Once Mable leaves, I head to the bathroom to ready myself for bed.

When I come out, I nearly shit myself in shock.

Standing in my bedroom by the fire is the woman I've been seeing flashes of since my interview for the Night Firm.

Tall, ebony skin with silver hair and large luminous silver eyes. And a silver horn sticking out of her forehead.

She looks like the human-ish version of a black unicorn.

"Eve Oliver, I would say it's about time, but I know this must be quite the shock. But do understand, I have been waiting for one of the Fates to release me from my binding for millennia. I just never expected until recently that it would be you." She walks over to me and holds up my arms, studying me. "And look at you. You really have returned."

"What are you talking about?" I ask.

She cocks her head. "I'm talking about you, Eve Oliver. The Maiden Fate has finally returned. In you."

KEEP READING for the final book...

I AM the NIGHT

BOOK THREE

CHAPTER 1: THE TREE

THE CAGED bird sings
  with a fearful trill
  of things unknown
  but longed for still
  and his tune is heard
  on the distant hill
  for the caged bird
  sings of freedom.
  -Maya Angelou, Caged Bird

A VAST CANVAS of emerald green stretches before us, dotted with colorful wildflowers, towering trees, moss covered boulders, bushes and plants and all manner of nature. The day is warm, and a cool breeze teases my skin. Sebastian rests his hands on my shoulders and uses his strong fingers to rub the knots of tension out of my muscles. I lean into him, closing my eyes, enjoying the feel of him at my back as he massages me. The scent of wildflowers carries on the wind, and I breathe it all in and smile.

"You've been at this for hours," he says, his lips brushing my earlobe as he speaks. "Ready for a break?"

I open my eyes and look around, then sigh. "There's still too much to do," I say. "The people need food. What good is this new expanse of Otherworld Ava'Kara gave her life to create if it's not livable?"

In the wake of what happened nearly a month ago, I thought things would be easier for the magical folk who claimed this new land as their home. It didn't take long to realize the world expansion created new problems. There were no homes, no farms, no food sources. It was an untamed wilderness that was raw and uninhabitable by anyone but woodland creatures and dryads.

And few of us had the kind of magic needed to make this part of the world more hospitable. Which meant for the past several weeks, the Night brothers, Lily, and myself have been working tirelessly to cultivate this new land for those displaced.

For many long days after that night, I feared my magic would never return. I was more exhausted than I'd ever been in my life. Even the revelation that I was one of the Fates returned couldn't penetrate the fog that surrounded me. I spent most of that time unconscious.

Callia, the unicorn I inadvertently pulled into this world, disappeared shortly after telling me I was one of the Fates reincarnated. For a time I was convinced I hallucinated her.

The brothers nursed me back to health with Liam and Matilda's disgusting potions, Sebastian's back rubs, Derek's wry jokes to make me laugh, and Elijah's gentle voice reading to me when I couldn't keep my eyes open long enough to read for myself. I snuggled Liam's baby, cuddled in front of the fire on long nights, listened to Liam playing his violin, and I soaked in the love and affection offered to me. I tried hard not to think about Cole, but his ghost haunted me. It's now impossible to feel like we are a complete family without him.

I glance down at my ring, his ring, and twist it on my finger, a melancholy settling over me. Sebastian notices and pulls me tighter into an embrace, his arms circling my waist as I lay my head against his chest and settle my hands over his heart.

He kisses the top of my head and sighs. "I think about him too."

"He belongs with us," I say sadly.

Sebastian doesn't respond. I know it's complicated for him. For all of the Night brothers. They feel guilt and anger in equal measure. I have no guilt, but somehow my anger is dimmed. Despite the fact that Cole betrayed me in such a heinous way, taking the form of my twin brother, convincing me Adam was not only still alive but had committed monstrous acts of violence against the innocent, *I can't help but think of all that he went through that led him up to that moment, and then I forgive him.* Cole is a man tortured by his past, both by acts done to him as well as those he himself committed out of anger and vengeance. Did his brothers deserve his wrath? Perhaps. But justice without mercy becomes tainted by its own misguided right-eousness. We need the tempering influence of compassion and forgive-ness, otherwise we risk perpetuating a self-destructive cycle that can only end badly for everyone.

I could stay angry at him forever. He would deserve it, if that's how we were meant to measure justice. But if I consider what he's been through, where he came from, what his life cost him...it's harder to stay angry. Perspective shapes our perception of life. And his story gives me a different perspective of his actions. They have to be seen together. His choices don't exist in a vacuum. We are, all of us, stories told and retold with layers that cannot be ignored if we want the truth of a thing. So who can possibly measure the weight of a person's soul? Who among us can ever truly know what another deserves?

I choose to believe we all deserve forgiveness. Mercy. Love. Compassion. Perspective.

I can offer that to Cole at least.

I can't yet offer it to Jerry, but someday maybe I'll be able to see the brokenness in him and forgive him for what he did to me as well as to Mary and her child.

Near us, something explodes, sending dirt and rock flying through the air. Sebastian attempts to shield me with his body, but I use my power to subdue the debris, letting it fall harmlessly back to the ground with ease.

He shakes his head, grinning, his forest green eyes sparkling. His wild, dark hair is dusted with specks of dirt, and his simple shirt clings to his broad chest and shoulders, muscles rippling under the stretched fabric. He's like a sculpture carved from the very earth. He's definitely in his element here. "I'm still not used to how powerful you've become since the spell you performed."

"Neither am I," I say. "But it feels good. I can tell there's still so much untapped in me that I want to explore."

"Slowly," he says. "Don't push yourself too hard. We still don't know what you being a Fate means or how it will impact your abilities, your health, or even your life span."

I roll my eyes. This has been a constant discussion since my powers returned. Once I was well enough to get about on my own, I accidentally blew up the kitchen trying to light the fire. We all realized then that not only had I not lost my powers, but I had unlocked them to the Nth degree. They flooded me in a dizzying avalanche of magic I am slowly learning to control.

That's when Callia returned. She showed up after the explosion and smiled widely. "I've been waiting for you to wake up and recover your strength," she said. "I'm here to train you, as I have trained all the Fates before you."

"You'll teach me how to use my powers?" I asked, stunned.

But then everyone looked at me strangely. "This is Callia," I told them, gesturing to her, but she shook her head.

"They cannot see me. Only you. While you have brought my spirit back, my body is no longer viable."

And so I had to explain to the Night brothers that I had an invisible unicorn to train me.

There was some concern I'd done damage to my brain after the spell, but Elijah was the first to point out that the Fates have always been able to see what others couldn't. He felt it made sense, so the others backed off. They're still wigged out by it though, I can tell.

It was actually Callia's idea to use my powers to cultivate this land, and it was a brilliant one. Not only am I doing good, but it's a practical way to stretch and test what I can do.

Everyday I'm gaining discipline under the scrutinizing eyes of the brothers and the fleeting attentions of Callia who comes and goes at her whim.

Liam strolls over, a huge grin on his face, his golden eyes flashing and his auburn red hair in sexy disarray. His simple trousers and sleeveless shirt are tinged with burn marks. "Sorry about that. I was trying something new and it got a bit out of control."

"Let me guess. You thought blowing shit up would be a faster way to get the job done?" A smile tugs at my lips and Liam grins sheepishly.

"Maybe," he says.

"Did it work?" Sebastian asks.

"Not really." Liam shrugs and we all laugh.

I reluctantly pull out of Sebastian's embrace and crack my knuckles. "All right, boys, back to work. These trees won't move themselves."

Sebastian groans and I clap my hands together and close my eyes, re-centering myself in my power. I tug on the chord of earth magic I need and carefully release it, moving it into the roots of the great conifer before me. This is a delicate process, uprooting an old growth and replanting it. Initially I destroyed several trees, but the dryads performed a transformation ceremony for them so we could use them to build houses and tools instead. Still, we've been trying to save as much of nature as we could. Like this beauty before me.

I can hear the tree speaking to my soul and I realize it doesn't want to move. It likes its spot just fine, thank you very much.

I frown. *"Would you be willing to reshape yourself? To become shelter for a family in need?"* I ask through a mental connection that has formed between us. *"We are cleaning this particular area for housing."*

This has been our work for a few weeks now. Using my combination of elemental magic along with each of the brothers' unique skills, we have been uprooting and moving trees, plowing fields, laying foundations for housing, paving roads, and creating infrastructures for a new town.

The tree considers my request, and I send it images of the people I'm trying to help. The children who will laugh and dance and play here, the mothers who will nurse their children, and the parents who will nourish their families, who will work the land to grow and thrive.

The tree agrees to a transformation, and I have to think fast, as I haven't tried anything like this before.

"Change of plans," I say as I grab my bag and pull out my sketch book. I quickly draw an idea forming in my mind. I study the structure of the tree to create the body of the home, and as I do, another consciousness tugs at me.

The tree, sensing my thoughts, helps me form an image of what it would like to be. It has a grand trunk, large enough to drive several carriages through, and it wants to expand, to be even grander.

In surprise, I realize it wants to connect to the tree near it, to bond with her, to create something with her, so I stretch my magic and seek her permission for this plan.

She agrees, and somehow this spell becomes something more. A partnership. A marriage of a kind. Their roots have been touching, connected, and now they will become one.

Callia appears beside me, as suddenly as she always does. "This is a wonderful test of your magic," she says, delighted. Her ebony skin shines like liquid and her silver eyes practically glow as she instructs me. "You'll need to use all of your elements for this. Air and Earth to help shape. Fire to burn away what's not needed and water to temper and strengthen what is. Light to give it life and Darkness to strip that which no longer serves. For in any transformation, there is death. We cannot give birth to new life, to new forms, without it."

I sigh but nod. I still have a hard time using the Darkness within me without worrying it will corrupt my soul, but I know I must embrace all the elements for there to be true balance.

I reach for Sebastian and Liam's hands and grip them hard, pulling their power into me as well.

We all work better when we are together, we have found.

Cole pushes into my memories, and I shake off the thought of what our family could be if he were here to complete it. I can't think of him right now. I must focus.

Exhaling, I release my magic into the trees and their roots expand as they twist and reshape, growing in new directions, intertwining as they form themselves into a new kind of creation that so far only exists in my sketchbook.

Sweat beads on my lip. Heat pulses in me. I feel Elijah and Derek approach. I sense when they take their brothers' hands, forming a circle, sending me more magic, more power.

The energy within me builds and builds and is expelled in a wave of magic that pulses out of us all and into the ground, the trees, and the air around us. The earth shakes and cracks as the wind rises, whipping my hair into my face.

I grip Sebastian and Liam's hands harder to preserve our connection.

And when the earth and wind settle, when the magic retreats back into me, I open my eyes and gasp.

Before us stands a beautiful new house, an organic and living structure made from the trees themselves, with gently curved walls and a sloped roof twined with vines.

"How did you do that?" a voice behind us asks.

I turn to see Lily looking on in awe.

"I don't know," I say, releasing my death grip on the brothers and stretching my sore fingers. "The trees helped."

Lily smiles, and it lights up her face. "They are so happy. None of us have ever seen anything like this."

She runs a hand through her hot pink hair—the new color of the week—and looks around, stunned. "The others want this too. The entire grove wants to be made into houses," she says. "Except that one," she says, pointing to one off to the side. "He would like to be moved closer to the water. He's thirsty."

I laugh. "I think that can be arranged."

The Night brothers are still silent, staring at the house we just created, then staring at me with stunned expressions.

Liam pulls me against his chest and brushes a lock of hair out of my face. His golden eyes are full of admiration and awe. "You amaze me," he says, and before I can respond he leans in and claims my lips with his. A spark ignites between us, as it always does when we touch, and I lose myself in the softness of his lips and the hardness of his body pressed against mine.

His tongue teases my bottom lip, and I moan in desire as need flares in me.

But before we set the forest on fire, I pull away, panting.

He releases me reluctantly with a wicked grin. "Later, we will finish what we started."

I flush red and sigh again, wishing later was now.

Instead I turn to the home we just helped build and step through the impressive French doors making up the entrance. Not only have the trees formed this structure, but they have furnished it as well. A table, counters, chairs, bed frames, all made from the living trees. It's incredible.

Derek steps next to me and slips an arm around my waist. The Water Druid always has a calming effect on me. And though he's been working just as hard as all of us, he's managed to stay much cleaner. His close-cropped dark hair is still neat and tidy. His button-up shirt and pants dust free. I don't know how he manages it. He glances down at me with his sapphire eyes and smiles. "You've truly surpassed yourself."

My magic is still radiating out of me as I look up to him. "Do you think Lyx'Ara and her people will like it?"

"They will love it," Derek promises.

The Light Dragon lives with her people, and has been foraging the forests helping them make ends meet since the world's expansion. Some have died without proper shelter and food, thus creating the urgent need for a town, for protection, and for sustenance. She asked us for help and we were happy to offer it, though it meant putting nearly all of our legal work on hold.

Derek has handled a few minor cases as needed, but mostly we have been here, all day, every day, working tirelessly to create a new world.

"Sebastian is right, this would be a good time for a break. We should give Lyx a report on our progress and let her know about this," I say, waving a free hand at the house we just helped create. "This will change how we approach the rest of the development."

I look around, frowning. "Come to think of it, I'm surprised she hasn't been here today, yet."

"She has a lot going on," Derek says pragmatically. "But I know she will be happy to hear what you've accomplished."

"We," I clarify. "What we've accomplished. I couldn't have done this—any of this—alone."

As we head to the carriage, it begins to rain, and a flash buzzes in my brain, giving me a low-grade headache.

We were already headed to see Lyx, but now I know, we must hurry. I just don't know why.

CHAPTER 2: THE DRAGON

Do NOT STAND *at my grave and weep*
I am not there; I do not sleep.
I am a thousand winds that blow,
I am the diamond glints on snow,
~Mary Elizabeth Frye, Do Not Stand at My Grave and Weep

MY HEART HAMMERS in my chest as we head to the carriage. Lily rides up front to drive and the five of us pile into the back.

It's a bumpy trip to the Light Dragon's home base, and not one particularly suited for a horse and buggy, but it's the easiest way for all of us to travel. I make a mental note that we should pave some roads along this path soon. For everyone's sake.

While I didn't know Lyx well before, working with her these past few weeks has brought us closer. Even her relationship with the Night brothers has mended as we all worked side by side to build her and her people a new home. I've witnessed her devotion to Ava'Kara's baby, watching as she has cared for the dragon child as her own. I've seen her dedication to her people, tireless and unconditional. She gets her hands dirty, working with us day in and day out. At night, after a long day, we often sit with her around a campfire, stew cooking over the flames in a cast iron pot, as we share stories, make music, form friendships.

This work has been immensely fulfilling, and it's largely thanks to the Light Dragon and her vision for what could be. I can't wait to tell her what's now possible thanks to the trees' willingness to transform themselves. It's truly a game changer.

The carriage wheel hits a stone and wobbles to one side, but Elijah uses his wind magic to help it stay righted as we hastily continue our journey.

We stop abruptly and I lurch forward into Derek, who catches me in his lap with a cheeky grin. "If you wanted to get closer, all you had to do was ask." He winks and helps me exit the carriage with some manner of dignity left.

His flirtatious smile lingers as we look around for Lyx.

We have come to a hidden cove carved into the side of a massive mountain. The shore is covered in a carpet of mossy green, dotted with brilliant yellow flowers that lead to a glassy clear stretch of water being fed by a tall waterfall crashing off the jagged rocks of the mountain.

But a scream catches in my throat when I look at the water more closely.

Floating face up is Lyx'Ara, her eyes open, a wound in her chest oozing a viscous purple.

"Lyx!" I scream and run to the edge of the water, using my magic to pull her to shore.

"Is that...her blood?" I whisper, unable to pull my eyes away. She practically glows in the water, her Light magic clinging to her and giving me some hope that despite all evidence to the contrary, she might still be okay.

"Yes," Elijah says. "Dragons bleed purple."

With tears stinging my eyes, I step into the lake and reach for her, pulling her to shore. Her blood stains my clothes and my hands, but I don't care. Once on land, I check her vital signs to no avail.

"Liam, help her!" I scream.

Liam is already by my side, examining her as thoroughly and carefully as he can, his face hard, his eyes serious.

Finally he looks up. "She's...dead."

"She...she can't be," I say, too astonished to form a clear thought. "That makes no sense. Try again!"

Liam shakes his head. "I'm sorry. But...it looks like someone murdered her."

"How?" I demand. "How can you even kill a dragon? I thought they were immortal? The most powerful beings in the world."

Elijah kneels beside us, examining her himself. "They are. And the only thing that can kill a dragon...is another dragon," he says.

"There's no murder weapon on her body," Derek says. "But it appears she was killed by a puncture to her chest from something cylindrical in shape with a very sharp tip."

"And her soul hasn't departed," Elijah says. "It should have."

"What do you mean?" I ask. I'm trying hard not to hyperventilate. My hands are still stained with her blood. I've still got her head in my lap.

"When a dragon dies, it's thought their souls depart and their bodies turn to magic and dissipate, putting themselves back into the universe to live again," Elijah says. "But her soul is still attached to her body, and she clearly hasn't turned to magic."

"Have you ever seen a dragon die?" I ask softly.

The brothers all shake their heads. "No one has," Sebastian says. "Except you."

He looks at me and I realize he's right. I was there when Ava'Kara died. And she did disappear into magic, though I assumed that was a byproduct of the spell, not the standard MO for magical spontaneous dragon cremation.

"We need to get Ifi and Elal here," I say to no one in particular.

Lily nods. "I can go. I don't need a carriage."

I'm about to ask how, but she's gone before I get the words out.

I return my focus to the Light Dragon and run my hands over her eyes, closing them. Even in death she is just as beautiful, with her silver hair and inner glow. It's then that I notice she's clutching something in her hand. I pry it open and find her signet ring within. I take it to study, wondering if this was some kind of clue about her killer. Why was she holding it instead of wearing it?

Knowing how the justice system works here—which is not well—I pocket it, hoping to uncover any secrets it might hold, and then look around. "Where's the baby?"

Liam glances at me, frowning. "That's an excellent question."

"We need to find her before whoever killed Lyx does. Maybe they were after the child?" The thought makes me sick, but I know I can't afford to overlook this possibility. Ava'Kara tasked me with looking after her heir until she came of age, and I will be damned if I don't do everything in my power to honor her last wishes.

Ava'Zara, the daughter and heir to the Water Dragon, has grown more than expected in the weeks we've been working with Lyx. The child mostly stays in dragon form, but every so often she'll change to her more human form, I suspect to marvel at it. But she seems to prefer being a dragon, and who wouldn't, if I'm being honest.

"Maybe they already have the child," Sebastian says darkly.

"I refuse to believe that," I say, as I gently move Lyx off my lap and onto the mossy ground so I can look for the child.

"Zara?" I call out to her softly, hoping she's nearby. The brothers join the searching, looking for clues, making notes about the crime scene.

As I look for the baby, Callia's training comes back to me. "Use your magic to amplify your senses," she would tell me. "You are so much more powerful than you realize."

So I do. I close my eyes and dig deep into myself, into the well of elemental power that lives within me, and I gently tug at a string. Another trick Callia taught me. To braid the elements into a string that I can use when I need a little bit of all six of my abilities.

My skin tingles as the magic dances over me, as if it's lighting me up. I send the string out, imbuing it with myself, with my senses. What it sees, I see. What it hears or feels, I hear and feel. And that is how I sense the presence of Zara, hiding behind the waterfall deep within the cave. She's scared. And she's not alone.

"I've found her," I announce to the guys, who all approach me. "She's close, but someone is with her."

Sebastian moves to leave. "Stay here, I'll be back."

I grab his arm. "We go together. I'm no damsel in distress, remember?"

As if to prove my point, I raise my arms, and as I do, the water before us parts, revealing the bottom of the pool and a path straight to the waterfall. Even Derek—the Water Druid himself—looks impressed, and we all walk forward, each of us on alert. We don't know what we'll find in the cave. Someone helping the child, or the person who killed Lyx.

My fingers ignite with flames as my protective instincts flare up, and Liam looks at my hands and shows me his. He's got a fireball ready.

I nod and we continue. The waterfall parts for us at my command and I guide the brothers past the damp entrance into the depth of the cave that divides into tunnels leading in several directions.

"Which way?" Sebastian asks, his muscles tense, his jaw clenched. All four of them look on edge, and I'm sure I look the same.

I close my eyes and pull on that thread of power again, letting it guide me. "To the left," I say, pointing.

The cave is musty and wet, and everything I step on produces a dead kind of squishy sound that makes my skin crawl.

I hear a tiny roar, like that of a baby dragon, and I move faster, using the fire in my hands as flashlights to see. The others don't need it, they can see fine in the dark.

The tunnel expands into an open space with crystals hanging from the ceiling and a small pond of muddy water in the center. A tiny blue dragon floats in the water, making growling sounds and spitting water from her mouth as she practices her dragon gifts.

"Zara!" She looks up at me and makes a cute chirping noise, then flaps her wings and awkwardly flies to my arms, landing heavily against my chest, soaking me with mud and water. But I don't care. I'm too relieved that she's unharmed. She nuzzles her head against my chest and I hold her more tightly as I look around.

"I know you're here," I say to the other person hiding in the cave. "You can come out now. We're not going to hurt you."

I wait a moment, the silence deafening, but I caution the brothers to stay still with a sharp glance. If we make a ruckus, the person won't come out.

Finally, a small shuffling sound alerts us to the presence of a young girl. She is soaking wet and looks about nine or ten years old. She wears rags that stick to her frail, bone thin body, her dirty blond hair caked with grime and clinging to a face that looks sunken in from hunger. Tears streak her skin, creating trails as they clear off the dirt from her cheeks.

I kneel down to her level. "What's your name?" I ask in my softest voice. The child looks like a wild animal ready to bolt at the slightest hint of danger.

"Ana," she says.

"What are you doing in here?" Sebastian asks, his voice gruff, and she shies back, sinking into the shadows around her.

"Sebastian, she's scared. Use your gentle voice." I reprimand.

I hand him the dragon, who curls up in his arms happily, and take small steps towards the girl. "I'm Eve," I say. "I'm a friend of Lyx. Were you her friend too?"

From the shadows I see her small head bob. "I tried to save her," she says softly.

My heart leaps at that. "Did you see what happened to Lyx?" I ask. "Who hurt her?"

The girl shakes her head, and my heart plummets. If only it had been that easy. "I was taking Zara for a walk. Lyx lets me help with the baby sometimes." She puffs out her chest, clearly proud of her trusted standing with the Light Dragon. "We got back and she was floating in the water, bleeding. I went to her, and she looked at me, like she was okay. But, but she was scared. She said to go, to... " She hesitates, her lower lip quivering. "To take the baby and hide. Then the light went out of her eyes and I ran in here with Zara. I... " She sniffles. "I didn't know what else to do."

The child begins sobbing, and I close the distance between us and pull her into my arms, holding her close. She cries on my shoulder until her tears are used up, then sniffles and wipes her face with the back of her hand. "Is it my fault?" she asks in a voice that cracks my heart open.

"No, love, it's not your fault. You did the right thing. You saved Zara."

Liam clears his throat. "We need to leave. Once word spreads, Enforcers will be here."

Shit.

"We have to get Zara out of here before they arrive. I don't trust anyone else to take her right now."

Derek looks like he's about to argue, but I stand firm. "She's coming with us until we know what happened. All I know for sure is that none of us killed Lyx, so we are the only ones I trust at the moment."

I take Ana's hand and lead her out of the cave. "Where are your parents?" I ask.

She shrugs. "Don't got none. Lyx took care of me."

Double shit.

"Would you like to come home with us? At least until we can find you a proper home."

Derek frowns again, but says nothing. Smart man.

The girl looks at the brothers, then back at me, and slowly nods.

"Good, let's get out of here and we'll show you the castle we live in. You're going to love it."

The girl's eyes widen as I once again part the waters so we can cross back to land. "How'd you do that?" she asks.

"It's part of my powers," I say. Then I point to our carriage. "I need you to go get in there okay? We'll be right behind you."

She reluctantly releases my hand and does as instructed, petting the horses on the way, and I approach the Night brothers. Sebastian still has the baby dragon in his arms.

"We shouldn't take the kids with us," Derek says, frowning. "It's a bad idea on so many levels."

"I know," I say, "but what choice do we have? Ana has nowhere to go. She's skin and bones as it is, plus she may have witnessed the murder, or at least seen more than she remembers. And Zara's life could be in danger. We don't know why Lyx was killed or how, so we have to assume the baby dragon's a target until we learn more. And that means hiding her from the Enforcers and especially the dragons."

Liam shifts, his posture still on alert. "I agree with Eve. We can't leave them behind."

Elijah nods. "It would be fascinating to learn more about the behaviors and habits of a newly hatched dragon. So little is known about them given how rare they are in general."

Derek sighs and looks to Sebastian for support, but Zara purrs against his chest, snuggled tight and looking quite content. The Earth Druid shrugs and I smile at the scene of him looking so nurturing.

"You all realize we could lose our license to practice law for this, right?" asks Derek.

"Maybe it's time we found a new calling anyways," Liam says, surprising us all.

"You don't want to be a lawyer anymore?" I ask.

"I didn't say that," he says, "but when you are immortal, it does well to change things up a bit from time to time. I've been thinking a lot about the past and what our future might hold. I'm just not sure I want to spend too many more years at this."

Derek looks beyond exasperated, but shakes his head. "We can't have this conversation right now. We have to go. Particularly if we are kidnapping two children."

"We are," I confirm, smiling at the baby dragon and trying not to look at Lyx's body lying by the water. "We should go." But we don't leave right away. Without exchanging words, we all pause before the water and stand in silence for a moment. In honor of Lyx's life, in mourning of her death. Then we turn to the carriage.

Derek, still annoyed with all of our plans, sits up front. Liam joins him, leaving me in the back with the two kids, Sebastian and Elijah.

The plan is to head straight to the castle and to avoid any confrontation on the way.

But, that plan is shit upon within fifteen minutes of driving.

The steady rainfall that began earlier turns into a full-scale storm, cracking the sky open and shifting the earth with its power and force. Everyone looks at me, but I shrug. "I'm not doing this."

The horses neigh in panic, pulling against each other and toppling our carriage to the side.

Sebastian clutches the dragon, and I reach for Ana, holding her close and cocooning us in a ball of air to cushion our fall.

Still, we land hard, and I know I'll have bruises tomorrow to tell this tale.

Liam rushes to help pull Ana out of the carriage just as a fire ball lands a few feet away, singeing the earth and nearly incinerating us.

The baby dragon hiccups and a stream of water flows out of her mouth, quenching the flames, but another fire ball hits to our right and Ana screams and hides behind me.

"What the hell is happening?" I shout, using my magic to quench the fires as quickly as they appear.

The wind is a frenzied thing, whipping around us as flames continue to rain from the sky and burn the earth. I look up and see them. Two giant dragons fighting amidst the thunderous clouds. I recognize the red one. Dath'Racul, the Fire Dragon. But the other is new to me. It's a pale blue dragon with shimmering white scales around its face. "That's the Air Dragon?" I ask.

Elijah nods. "Ventus'Arak. He and Dath'Racul don't always see eye to eye."

I snort. "That's pretty clear."

Through the wind we can hear them speaking...or rather shouting at each other. "You killed her!" Ventus says.

Racul roars, sending another fire ball flaming through the sky. "I did no such thing."

"If not you, then who? You always hated her for leaving the Council," Arak says.

"That does not mean I killed her," he bellows.

Two more dragons fly up. One a deep green and the other dark as pitch. Ra'Terr, the Darkness Dragon, I recognize as the one who guards the prison. But I've never seen the earth dragon before. She's magnificent. Her scales sparkle under the Dragon's Breath and look like emeralds shining in the sky.

"That's Brock'Mir," Elijah says. "And this is what remains of the Dragon Council," he says with sadness in his voice. "To lose two dragons so close together is a true tragedy for our world."

"Brothers, cease this bickering. We must work together to find out who killed our sister," Brock'Mir says, but they ignore her and continue fighting, shaking the earth and splitting the sky with their fury.

I fear their wrath will not end until another dragon has been killed, very likely taking us with them.

"We need to get out of here," I shout as I survey the damaged, overturned carriage.

Pulling on my power, I use the wind to right the wagon, setting it back on its wheels, but it tilts to one side since one of them is broken. The horses are still in a panic, and I approach them cautiously, infusing myself with light as I pour peace into them. They calm quickly, despite the tumultuous storm still raging around us.

I pat one on the nose, murmuring reassuringly to them.

Before I can figure out how to fix the wheel and get us back on the road, the Dragon's Breath above us begins to shimmer and stretch, a tear appearing in the fabric of the world itself, revealing a true wonder. A dragon, the largest I've ever seen—easily three times the size of the others, flies through the tear and hovers in the air. Her wings are stretched wide and she is covered in golden scales that glow like the sun. She lowers herself to earth, shifting into human form as she does, until a woman stands there, and everything about her is golden; long hair golden and wavy, an intricate golden crown on her head, and golden wings draped over her back like a cloak. Her skin is iridescent and shines brightly and her eyes are golden orbs. She wears a gown that shimmers with flecks of gold that catch in the light, and her presence causes all of the dragons to stop their arguing and land, turning back to their human form even as they bow before her.

"Who's that?" I whisper to Elijah, whose jaw has dropped in amazement.

"That...the gods help us, that is Amir'Amora'Akar. The Mother of Dragons."

CHAPTER 3: THE MOTHER

Out of the ash
  I rise with my red hair
  And I eat men like air.'
  ~Slyvia Plath, Lady Lazarus

I'M MOMENTARILY PARALYZED by the wonder of her, but then, as Elijah attempts to pull me into a curtsy, I take Ana's hand and usher her back into the carriage, which wobbles with her weight but doesn't tip over.

"Stay in here and stay hidden," I whisper, and I take the baby dragon from Sebastian and hand her to the girl. "And keep Zara hidden. Can you do that?"

Ana nods, her eyes wide and scared, but she doesn't hesitate to take the infant.

I close the door behind them and hope they go unnoticed, because shit's about to get real, and I'm just going out on a limb here, but I'm pretty sure it will not go well if all the dragons in the world discover we are trying to kidnap the only baby dragon in existence. I mean, I could be misreading the situation, but given the glares I'm getting from the Night brothers, I'm pretty sure I'm not.

"Why do my children fight amongst themselves?" the Mother of Dragons demands, her voice carrying over time and space and into the very souls of each of us, or so it feels.

Dath'Racul looks cowed—and I rather enjoy seeing the arrogant ass taken down a few notches by mommy. But then I look at the golden dragon again and feel my insides coil and wrap around themselves and my brief delight at his discomfort turns to reluctant empathy. This is not a woman to mess with.

"Mother," Racul says, his voice still powerful despite his humbled position. "Ventus attacked me, accusing me of taking the life of Lyx, but it is not true."

Amora seems to grow in size as her anger envelops her like a cloak. "Two of my children have died. Two immortal beings of ultimate power ripped from the worlds. It is unthinkable. Who has done this thing?" she demands. "It was not one of you; it cannot be one of you. That would be beyond blasphemous."

"I do not believe it was any of us," Racul says, tossing a cross look at his brother. "Ava'Kara gave her life voluntarily," he offers.

Amora scoffs. "I am well aware of what Kara did and why. To preserve this dilapidated, failed experiment of a world. As if the life and soul of a dragon was worth this scrap heap."

My blood boils at her words, and my spine stiffens. Derek shoots me a cautioning glance.

"What has become of Kara's child? Where is my grandchild?" Amora looks around as if one of the dragons might magically produce her from thin air.

I shift uncomfortably and pointedly do not look at the carriage, even though we might as well be invisible to the dragons. Which suits me just fine.

"We have not yet been to the scene of the crime," Racul admits. "We do not know where the child is."

"Because you were too busy fighting amongst yourselves," she shouts, her words like daggers piercing the hearts of her children. "Behaving much like the vagabonds you created this world for."

They all drop their heads. It's clear there's no good answer to that, so they don't try.

"And what of Lyx'Ara?" Amora asks. "Her death was not voluntary. Someone must pay."

"We will begin an investigation," Racul says. "Her killer will suffer."

"You are correct in that my child," she says, a saccharine smile spreading over her lips but never reaching her hard golden eyes. "That is why I have come. To punish those who would harm my children."

Ventus'Arak, the Air Dragon, glances up. "What is your plan?" he asks cautiously.

"My plan," she says, stepping forward, "is to end this little experiment. Once you have found my grandchild and left this miserable excuse for a world, I will destroy it and all who still remain, including my daughter's murderer."

My heart drops to my gut, and even the dragons look shocked.

"Mother, please reconsider," Racul says. "This is our home."

She holds up her hand, and a beam of golden light shoots from her palm, hitting Racul in the gut. He stumbles back, grunting in pain. "This is not your home, child. This is your creation, but it is not your home. Your home awaits you in our true world, unencumbered by the muddy mixed races of these substandard beings you've surrounded yourselves with. I've indulged you long enough, and this indulgence has cost me two of my children. I will allow it no longer."

"No!" I shout, stepping forward, the word rushing out of my mouth before I can change my mind. I can feel the frustrated and frightened looks of the brothers on me as I approach closer to the dragon.

She turns her attention to me, and it is a fright to behold her direct gaze. "Who dares speak to me!" It's not a question, it's a command.

"Eve Oliver," I say as my power fills me, just as it did the night I confronted Cole. "The Maiden Fate returned." The past, present and future collide, and I feel myself rising from the ground, glowing with light, tinged by darkness, all the elements swirling around me. Wind whipping my hair. The earth cracking under me, bubbling with spurts of water. Fire lighting my fingertips.

I hear the gasps of the other dragons as they witness my transformation, but I keep my eyes locked on the Mother of Dragons. Though the Dragon Council might once have seemed intimidating, they pale in comparison to her formidable presence.

"A return of the Fates," she says, gliding towards me until we are face to face. "What intriguing timing. Tell me, do you know who took my daughter's life?"

"Not yet," I admit. "But give me time. I will find the truth. I will find justice for your daughter, who was also my friend. But you cannot destroy this world."

Lightning cracks around her and her eyes glow a violent gold as power surges around us. "You dare tell me what I can or cannot do, Fate?"

My power pulses and grows, enveloping us both. It's a pissing contest, but a necessary one. She will only respond to power. I feel this instinctively and know I cannot back down. "I do. This world does not belong to you. It no longer belongs to just the dragons. It is all of ours. And it is mine. My soul flows in the lakes and streams, my blood feeds the roots of the trees, my magic powers the winds and sparks the fires...this world is now a part of me, and I cannot let you destroy it."

Her eyes widen and her golden light pools out into long tendrils that extend from her body and dive into the ground, as if testing my claims. "It seems you are correct. You have become part of this world." She doesn't sound happy at the proclamation, but I press my advantage while I can.

"There are good people here. Innocent people. They do not deserve to die for the crime of one."

She pauses, considering her next words. "You may very well be one of the Fates returned, but you are weak without an Order. In the past, the Fates were aided by the Druids, who shared their power and strengthened them. What do you have? You have no sisters. You have no Order. You are nothing."

My power seems to dim at her words, and I don't know how to respond. I hadn't considered the position the Fates had in the past and how that might impact me in the present. It's been a lot to wrap my mind around as it is.

My thoughts race as I flash through everything I've read and learned trying to think of an adequate response, but nothing useful comes to mind. Then Sebastian steps forward, joining me, and bends down on one knee. "I am one of the original Druids and I pledge myself to Eve. She is not alone."

I look down at the handsome Earth Druid, overcome by emotion at his declaration. But before I can respond, Liam steps forward as well.

"I too pledge myself to the Maiden Fate. My power is hers. My service is hers. I am hers."

"And I," says Elijah, joining his brothers.

"We all pledge ourselves," says Derek, taking his place. All four of the brothers are kneeling at my feet as Amora and I float above the ground in a cloud of power.

The golden dragon studies the Night brothers thoughtfully. "You were a powerful Order once," she says. "And I can see that your magic has returned. But I am surprised that after all that happened, you four would willingly commit yourself to the Fates once more, given all that entails."

I want to ask what "all that entails" means, but this doesn't seem like a great time to interrupt.

"We commit ourselves to Eve," Sebastian says stubbornly.

"Very well," she says. "Formalize your vows and I will reconsider." She holds up a hand and produces a golden ceremonial dagger and matching bowl, and hands it to Elijah.

Amora moves away from us and the Night brothers circle me as I lower myself to the ground. Then they each call upon their element, letting it dance between us. Fire, earth, air, water.

I can't help but thinking we're missing the light and darkness Cole would bring. But I push aside that thought and focus.

Elijah slices his palm, causing the blood to pool on his skin, then lets the blood drop into the bowl before he passes both to Sebastian. Around the circle they go, cutting into their own flesh, letting it drop into the bowl.

Once all four have done so, Liam, the last to use the blade, reaches for my hand, and I offer it to him, letting him slice into my palm. My blood mixes with the brothers' and Liam takes the bowl and sips it, then passes it around. When it finally returns to me, I realize I'm meant to drink the blood that is left. So I do.

As soon as the mixture of our blood slides down my throat I see the bonds between us form, like silver chords attaching each of us, and I'm suddenly much more aware of them, their feelings, their presence, their magic. It's heady, to feel this deeply intimate connection.

"Very well," Amora says. "I will give you a fortnight to discover who killed my daughter and bring them to me. If you do not, I will destroy this world and you with it. If you do, I will spare this world."

Two weeks. That's not enough time, but it will have to do. "I will need the cooperation of the other dragons to accomplish this in such a short time. And I will need full authority to do whatever must be done."

"As you wish," she says, gesturing for the Dragon Council to approach. "You, my beloveds, are under the temporary authority of the Maiden Fate, who is tasked with finding my daughter's killer. Give her your rings, and afford her every liberty and cooperation. I expect you will not disappoint me in this," she says, giving each of them, as well as me, a pointed glare.

They look none too happy at this proclamation and grumble under their breaths, but they do not argue.

The Earth Dragon steps forward first, tugging the ring off her finger and handing it to me.

Each of them follow suit, silently relinquishing their authority to someone they clearly consider a lesser being. Or at least they did before they found out who I really am.

Still, dragons are not easily humbled. They will obey their mother, but they don't have to like it.

Once I've slipped all their rings onto my fingers, I pause, studying them, wondering what use they are, other than implied authority.

As if sensing my question, Amora shows me her ring. "These symbols on the sides of the ring, if you channel your magic and trace them into the air, will summon the dragon whose ring you are using."

Wow. This is better than text messaging, at least in terms of access.

Though I don't particularly want to summon pissed off dragons to me at any given moment.

Racul's face is a study in frustrated anger. "Do not abuse this temporary privilege," he growls.

I smile charmingly at him. "My only goal is solving this murder and saving the world. I'm sure we both want the same thing in this, do we not?"

He glances away, unwilling to answer directly.

Amora begins to float upward, slowly shifting into her dragon form. "I will have eyes on you all. Do not disappoint."

And then she flies through the tear in the sky and disappears.

I look to the dragons, a bit flabbergasted by the shift in power dynamic. But we don't have a lot of time, so I need to start getting answers.

"First question for all of you," I say, skipping the small talk. "What, besides another dragon, can kill one of you?"

Racul glances at her siblings and then scowls at me. "There is nothing else that can kill a dragon."

"So it was one of you," I challenge.

"No." His answer is curt.

"I'm sure you can see how this creates a problem. You do want to save the world don't you?"

From the corner of my eye, I see Callia appear, her silver eyes glowing like the horn on her head, her skin and hair as black as ink. The unicorn woman shifts to my side and whispers in my ear. "They are lying to you. There is one other thing that can kill a dragon." She turns to face me, the horn on her head glowing a bright—nearly blinding—silver. "Me."

CHAPTER 4: THE VISION

THE NIGHT IS DARKENING round me,
  The wild winds coldly blow ;
  But a tyrant spell has bound me,
  And I cannot, cannot go.
  ~Emily Bronte, The Night is Darkening Around Me

THE DRAGONS each transform and fly away, leaving me stunned and deflated as my magic drains from me. Callia is still here, her eyes now locked on the tear in the sky the Mother of Dragons just disappeared into. I leave her to her thoughts and turn to the brothers, who stand beside me like sentinels.

"What the hell just happened?" I ask nobody in particular.

Elijah grins. "I think you just became the most powerful person in this world."

"Shit."

Sebastian runs a hand through his hair, a frown tugging at his lips. "This is...complicated. You bought us time, but if we don't solve this murder, she'll hold you personally responsible."

"I'm not sure how that's any worse than her destroying the world today with us in it," I point out as we walk back to the carriage.

"Good point," Sebastian says, though the worry has not left his face.

I look down at the rings lining my fingers. All six of the dragon rings plus Cole's ring. I can feel the power in them all zinging through my flesh, sending goosebumps up my arms. "We need to get Ana and Zara home," I say. "And then we've got to get to work."

We also need to talk about the oaths they all just took, but right now isn't the time. First, I need to find out more from Callia about how she can kill dragons.

"Explain," I tell her, and the brothers glance at me, then realize I'm talking to an invisible unicorn and studiously ignore us.

"The only way to kill a dragon—other than being a dragon yourself—is to puncture their heart with a unicorn horn," she says.

She glances away, as if caught in a long-forgotten memory. "There were many of us once upon a time. We galloped over the lands free and wild. Until one day, a unicorn and a dragon got into an argument, and the unicorn ran the dragon through with his horn. The dragon died, shocking everyone. This was so long ago, most on this world wouldn't remember it, but still the story spread, and then we were hunted, our horns fetching top price from illegal traders. The dragons, fearing the risk we posed, even those of us loyal to the Council, did the unspeakable. They quietly had all the unicorns killed and had all our horns destroyed by dragon fire."

"Did they kill you?" I ask, stunned by the cruelty of it all.

"Yes." But she doesn't expand as we reach the carriage.

I leave the questions for later as I examine the busted wheel. "Couldn't earth magic fix this?" I ask Sebastian.

"No, this is dead wood. I can't manipulate something that has no life left in it."

"You can," Callia whispers into my ear. "You have all the elements and can therefore sing to the parts that are dead, and the parts that yet live."

I'm used to these impromptu lessons from her, and I love stretching my powers, so I concentrate and focus on the wheel, on the molecules that form it, and I visualize it repairing itself like a broken bone. As I do, the wheel shifts, shakes, and begins to move together, the splintered pieces fusing back into one seamlessly, until it's entirely restored.

"Is there any limit to your power?" Sebastian asks in awe.

"I don't know. How would I fare in a straight up fight with the Mother of Dragons?" I ask. "Because if we don't do what she wants, it might come to that."

They all look like they're about to shit themselves at the suggestion. Even Callia shakes her head.

"You are not ready to face her," Callia says. "She's much more powerful than you can possibly imagine."

I detect equal measure awe and fear in her voice, and I wonder how well she knows the golden dragon. I'm still not entirely used to dealing with beings who have lived such ancient lives. It's a perspective that's hard to fit into a human-sized lifespan.

"You cannot fight her," Elijah says, speaking over Callia.

"Yeah, I just got the lecture from the unicorn. I get it. Let's do our jobs so I don't have to." I reach for the carriage to get in when Callia passes a hand over mine and a flash grips me so hard my stomach clenches and I double over in pain, vomiting what little food is in my stomach.

Liam rushes to my side, holding my hips as I continue to heave.

He's speaking, but I can't hear him as my head pounds with the grip of a vision I can't stop or control.

Callia stands before me, but she looks different. Her horn is missing, shaved off at the base. And then the vision shifts and I see a rider on horseback, making a mad dash through the woods towards the portal. He wears a black cloak and at his hip is a dagger that glows silver, made from unicorn horn.

And he's trying to leave the Otherworld. Ahead of him, the Dragon's Breath wall looms large, and he's heading straight towards it.

The vision begins to fade, and through the pounding in my head, I force it to last just a little longer. I need to get a closer look. To see who's on the horse.

Something burns my eyes and just before I slam back into my own body, I see his face.

No.

It can't be.

Pain grips me as Liam continues to hold me, his body hot against mine.

I realize I'm crying and swipe at my eyes, only to find crimson staining my hand. Was I crying blood?

"Eve!" Liam's voice finally penetrates my haze and I feel power from all four brothers pour into me, relieving the pain in my head and in my gut.

I struggle to sit up and find that the world is spinning just a little bit less. "I'm okay," I say.

I look around for the unicorn and find her standing to the side, her face unreadable. "What was that?" I ask her.

"I am still connected to my horn," she says. "And you just saw a vision of where it is right now."

I stand and Liam offers support, but I feel stronger and stronger by the moment. "I have to go," I say.

"We're going home," Liam insists.

"No, you all get the kids home. I have a lead on a possible murder weapon. I'll explain later but I don't have time now."

I look too Callia for guidance. "How do I get there?" I ask her.

She shrugs. "You could always try flying."

My eyes widen in stunned amazement. "Fly? I can fly?"

"Well, you have hovered before," Elijah says. "That's not how air magic is supposed to work but…"

"That's not how *his* air magic works," Callia says. "But you're different. Don't let them limit you. Try it. It's the only way you'll make it there before the suspect gets away."

I nod and focus, calling on my air and light magic. And just like that, I am airborne. I look down at the Night brothers. "I'll meet you back at the castle. Trust me."

I know they'll just argue with me, so I don't wait for their response. I take off flying high and fast, manipulating the winds around my body to give me speed without discomfort. I use my fire magic to warm me and earth magic to stabilize me. For a moment I forget what I saw in the vision. I forget about Lyx dying. About the orphaned children we are bringing home. And I am completely absorbed in the present moment, relishing the freedom and intoxicating wonder of doing something that previously I'd only done in dreams.

I truly can't believe I'm actually flying. Racing through the air like a bird, wind and freedom all around me.

But the flight ends too soon, as I reach the edge of the world, the grove where Kaya's tree lives, and the place where the rider was headed.

I see him now. He's moments from reaching the portal.

I drop down from the sky and land right in front of him. He swerves his horse to avoid knocking me over, and then topples off gracelessly.

He storms over to me, his face a confusing play of emotions when he sees me.

"Eve?"

"Hello, Cole."

There's a lump in my throat as I say his name. The last time we saw each other, I found out he'd been lying to me about everything, and he discovered I was the Fate who ordered his torture. Being this close to him now is almost painful. All the hurt and anger are there, but so is the love, the desire, the passion he ignited in me. He feels achingly familiar and like a stranger all at once. I want to reach out and touch him, to pull him into me, to feel his lips on mine, but he's standing here, trying to flee the Otherworld, with a weapon that could kill a dragon hanging from his hip.

"What are you doing here?" he asks.

"I was just going to ask the same of you."

He shakes his head, clearly confused. "I'm riding a horse."

"Obviously. I mean where are you going?"

He shrugs. "I'm enjoying the afternoon before a meeting I have scheduled."

"A meeting?" I scoff at that. "Does your meeting involve killing dragons?" I ask. Though I sound flippant, my heart is racing in my chest and I feel close to vomiting again. I can't bear for him to be guilty of this crime, but I can't ignore who he is, or what he is capable of.

"What are you talking about?" he asks.

"Lyx. She's dead. Stabbed through the heart with something that looks suspiciously like that unicorn horn dagger you've got there."

His face pales and he stumbles back a bit. "Lyx is dead? Are you sure?"

"I saw her body myself."

His eyes widen. "Her body remains? How? Why?"

"That's what I'm trying to figure out, Cole," I say with as much cool as I can muster. "The Mother of Dragons herself showed up and is pretty pissed. Things will not end well for me if I don't solve this murder, and right now, you look like the prime suspect."

"*Mon couer*, I didn't do this. You must believe me. Look at your ring if you think I am lying." He glances down at my hand and raises an eyebrow when he sees all the dragon rings lining my fingers.

I don't even bother considering his suggestion. "Do you really think I still believe this ring protects me from your lies?" I ask. "I've known for some time that it's a tracking device more than anything."

He cocks his head, his dark eyes unreadable. "You are a surprising woman. If you know, then why do you still wear it?" he asks, stepping closer to me until we are inches apart from each other. He raises a hand to caress my cheek, and though a part of me wants to turn away, I find I cannot. I'm mesmerized by him, as I always have been, and despite everything, I still crave him, body, mind and soul, and the bastard knows it.

I force myself to step back, just out of his reach, though the action pains me. "I wear it as a reminder not to fall for a pretty face."

He grins, stroking his chin. "I am rather dashing, it's true."

I roll my eyes but can't help but laugh. "You're impossible is what you are."

"By the looks of it, you're quite skilled at handling the impossible, *mon cher*."

"I'm not here to flirt with you," I say, though my voice lacks the confidence I try desperately to instill in it.

"Of course not. How can I be of service? If you do not believe me, how shall I prove my innocence to you?"

"Where did you get the dagger?" I ask. "And where are you going with it?"

"It was not easy to track down," he says. "When the Collector went missing, he left a certain gap in the underground industry. I, in my benevolence, have volunteered to fill that gap by acquiring that which is hard to find for people with the right resources."

My face hardens. "I hope you haven't picked up all his criminal behavior," I say, thinking of the girls he trafficked in.

Cole frowns. "No. Never. You know me better than that. I would never trade in lives. Not for any amount of money. Only hard to come by goods."

I nod, believing him this time. I know his past, know what he's been through, and I know he wouldn't put someone else through that.

He cocks his head, studying me. "You wouldn't happen to know what became of the Collector, would you?" he asks.

I shrug. "Why would I know anything about that?" I say. I mean, it's not exactly a lie. Just a question.

He chuckles. "Of course. How silly of me."

"So you were hired to find this dagger," I say, bringing us back to the point of the conversation.

"Yes," he says. "But I'm under strict orders of confidentiality."

I cock my hip and stare him down. "Cole."

He glances down at my hands again, at the rings lining them. "*Merdre*," he says, cursing under his breath. "I literally can't tell you. I'm bound. But there's nothing saying I can't show you. Come with me to my meeting."

"Yes. I will. But how is that better for you than telling me?"

He shrugs. "It's a loophole. And I get to spend more time with you this way. That constitutes a win-win in my mind."

"Fine. Take me to your meeting." I studiously ignore the flare of joy I feel at knowing we will have more time together. "But before you do, you should put a tracker on that dagger so we can see what happens to it."

"I could," he says. "But it would be better if you did it yourself. I can teach you how."

What is it with everyone wanting to teach me new tricks like I'm a dog to be trained? I sigh, but at the same time, this knowledge will come in handy. My powers are growing with each passing day, and though I keep waiting to hit the limits of what I can do, it hasn't happened yet.

"Fine," I say begrudgingly.

Cole smiles and approaches me. He pulls out the dagger and places it in my hand, then stands behind me, his arms circling my shoulders.

I suck in a breath at his closeness as I feel the dark tendrils of his magic interlace with mine so naturally, so organically, in such a way that I couldn't stop it even if I wanted to.

And I don't want to.

I want to stay here forever. I want to bring him home with me. I want him to be a part of my family.

But I can't always have what I want.

So instead I focus on the magic.

He recites ancient words in my ear, his breath sending shivers up my spine, and I repeat the spell and channel the darkness inside of me, as I feel him do.

The power is excited to be let out as Cole shifts closer to me. "Your darkness is tired of being stifled, *mon couer*. You must release it lest it eat you from the inside."

"That's a charming image," I say. "Thanks."

The dagger in my hand becomes shrouded in dark mist, then settles into its normal self once more. "Did it work?"

Cole nods. "When you want to know where it is, repeat the words I taught you."

I hand it to him and do as instructed, and when I close my eyes, I see the dagger in his hand, clear as day. Then the vision pans out so I see both of us, where we are, what we are doing. It's a bit disconcerting seeing myself as a third person in my mind's eye, but it's a useful trick.

I open my eyes again and nod. "It worked."

He grins. "You're a natural."

He holds out his hand then, and I reluctantly take it, relishing the cool comfort he offers. "Ready for our meeting?" he asks.

I nod.

"Do you trust me?"

I don't know how to answer that, so I say nothing.

He sighs. "Just hold onto me once we enter the portal. It's going to be a wild ride."

Merdre. It's my turn to swear under my breath. Because in this, Cole Night is not lying.

CHAPTER 5: THE DAGGER

Perhaps if Death is Kind, and there can be returning,
  We will come back to earth some fragrant night,
  ~ Sara Teasdale, If Death is Kind

It is indeed a wild ride, one that, had I anything left in my stomach, would have resulted in said content being spewed all over Cole's sexy black cloak. But, as it is, that gift had already been bestowed somewhere in the forests of the new world.

Entering the portal is easy enough—it's like sliding through warm butter. It's when he dematerializes us into black mist that things go from manageable to what the actual hell.

I feel as if I'm being turned inside out and shredded into tiny pieces, then blown apart like some kind of macabre wishing flower.

I exist in nothingness. It's not black, or dark, it's just nothing. Cole's voice reverberates around me, coming from all directions and no direction at all at the same time. "Embrace your darkness, Eve."

I swear to all the gods if I get one more bumper sticker motivational talk from him, Callia, or any of the other Night brothers I might scream.

Hell, I might be screaming at this very moment. Since I feel as if I've ceased to exist, it's hard to tell.

When we finally materialize, I hit the ground hard, knocking the wind out of my lungs, despite my budding mastery of my air magic.

"Was that absolutely necessary?" I ask Cole once I can speak again.

He is standing over me looking as if he just had a leisurely stroll through the Garden of Eden and not a hellscape ride through the Underworld.

"How else would you propose we get here?" he asks, gesturing around us.

For the first time, I take note of where we are. And how freaking cold it is. I tap into my fire magic to warm myself up, now that physical sensations are returning, and I turn slowly to look around. To the west of us is a vast expanse of pristine topiary gardens, featuring mythical creatures of all kinds carved from bushes the color of eggplants, dotted with pure white flowers that form their own designs. Everything is covered in a thin layer of fluffy white snow, though the sky is clear and sunny at present. To the east of us is nothing but sky. We landed dangerously close to the edge of the world, or so it would seem. We are surrounded by clouds, and it's impossible to tell how far up we are.

In the distance is a castle that looks made of crystal, glistening in the sun.

The sun! I look up and see it peeking through the clouds and close my eyes, enjoying the warmth against my face for a brief moment before I remember why we are here.

"We are back on earth?" I ask.

"We are, though you will not find this place on any maps. It exists in a hidden realm—a floating island that belongs to my client."

"The client you still can't tell me the name of," I say.

"Correct."

He holds his arm out to me in a gentlemanly fashion. "Shall we, *mon coeur?*"

Every time he calls me one of his terms of endearment, I melt a little inside, but I must be careful with him. So I ignore his offer of an escort and begin walking to the castle on my own. He dashes to catch up with me, the cheeky grin he wears never slipping from his face.

"I see we are still on the outs?" he asks, keeping pace with me as we weave through the garden.

"Cole," I say as steadily as I can. "You pretended to be my dead twin and confessed to a heinous crime, all in your efforts to hurt your brothers. Then you disappeared. So yeah, we're a bit on the outs."

For the first time, his grin slips and a look of serious contemplation replaces it on his devilishly handsome face. "I didn't think about what my pain would cost you," he says softly, and my heart cracks a little at his vulnerability. "When we are broken, we tend to break others until we mend our own brokenness."

"And are you mending yours?" I ask.

He stops walking to face me, taking my hand in his and running a finger over his ring. "I am trying my very best. When the cracks in your soul run this deep for this long, it is not an easy process to heal. But I will do anything to repair what I have broken between us."

"Swear to me you didn't have anything to do with Lyx's murder," I say.

"I swear it to you," he says. "I want to catch her killer as badly as you do. She was my mentor, and my friend. Her death is a great loss to all."

"Then let's solve this murder and see where things lead between us. And between your brothers."

He squeezes my hand, and he doesn't let go as we continue walking. This time I don't pull away as I tell him about my training, about Callia, and about my confrontation with the Mother of Dragons. "And you should know, the Order of Druids has reformed," I say. "Your brothers swore oaths to me, though I'm not entirely sure what it all means."

He stiffens and glances at me curiously. "That is significant. But if anyone is worthy of that power, it is you."

I wonder what is going through his mind at this news. The Order did not treat him well, to say the least, particularly the Maiden Fate, my past self, who destroyed his life. But that was such a long time ago and so much has changed. I may be the Maiden Fate reincarnated, but

I'm also still me. I will not become lost in who she was, which, by all accounts, wasn't always good. I will temper her influence with my own sense of right and wrong. Hopefully that will be enough.

We arrive at the castle a solid hour later, and I'm slightly out of breath from the altitude.

"Use your air magic," Cole says as the door opens of its own accord. "You have no idea yet how powerful you are."

"Yeah, so I'm told," I say as I manipulate the air currents around me to ease my breathing.

A man in a butler's uniform answers the door and without a word ushers us in, though he casts glances at me curiously. "He is expecting you," he tells Cole.

We follow him up a winding stone staircase to the very top of the castle, and as we step out, we are greeted by Cole's client.

"Ventus'Arak, the Air Dragon, is your client?" I whisper, as the dragon shifts from his true form to his human form.

"Why have you brought the Fate with you?" he demands of Cole.

"Is there a reason you don't want me to know you've gone to great lengths to acquire the only weapon that can kill a dragon?" I ask, holding up my fingers full of dragon rings to remind him his own damn mother sent me on this mission.

Cole raises an eyebrow and looks amused at the exchange, though he says nothing.

"I will know if it is the weapon that took my sister's life," Ventus says as he stalks over to us, his pale blue eyes narrowed to a slit.

The Air Dragon is tall, at least a head taller than Cole, which is saying something, with broad shoulders that taper to a perfectly toned six pack. I know this because his entire outfit consists of his iridescent blue wings that drape like a cloak, and what can only be described as a loin cloth. There isn't much left to the imagination, and even though the sight is impressive, I need to stay focused on something other than his abs.

"How can you be so sure?" I ask.

He holds his hand out. "The dagger, please?"

"Payment?" Cole asks, pulling the weapon from the leather sheath at his hip.

Ventus huffs as if he's been personally offended, but he grabs a leather coin purse from a wooden table nearby and tosses it to Cole, who catches it with one hand while handing off the unicorn dagger with the other.

Ventus studies it, waving a hand over it until it glows. And like Memory Catchers, the dagger projects holographic-like images of various beings dying at the end of the blade. There aren't many, but watching it feels awful, like some kind of medieval snuff film. When the images fade, I realize what he means.

"It holds the memory of all the lives it has taken," I say. "And Lyx isn't there."

Ventus nods, then turns to Cole. "Where did you find it?" he asks.

Cole glances at me before he answers. "In the private quarters of Dath'Racul."

Ventus looks confused for a moment. "This is the last of its kind that remains in our world. I suspected Racul of killing our sister, but he wouldn't need the dagger to do that."

"Do you really think he's guilty?" I ask. That would make this mystery easy to solve...if I could find proof.

He looks away from us, over the ledge of his castle into the distance. "I reacted impetuously upon her death," he says softly. "She and I were always close, even after she left the Council. I understood her in ways the others didn't, and she was a trusted confidant. I confess I lost a part of myself when I felt her die. But I no longer believe he killed her. Taking the life of another dragon would go against everything we are. Even Racul is not that ruthless."

He studies the dagger in his hand, running the pad of his finger along the razor edge. "Perhaps it is time for the Age of Dragons to come to an end. We began this world with noble intentions, but power and greed have corrupted even the best of us."

A strong wind blows through as he speaks, carrying the scent of snow about to fall as Ventus walks to the edge of the roof, his toes hanging off the ledge.

It's a long fall off the top of a castle this height, but I remind myself he's a dragon. Fear of heights is probably not one of his problems.

"We lost our way long ago," he says. "But we truly paved the path to our descent into darkness when we slaughtered the unicorns in an effort to preserve our own immortality. It's unnatural for any race to be so powerful that none can defeat it. The unicorns were our balance, and we killed them all out of fear."

Cole's eyes widen at that, and I'm surprised he's admitting this when none of them would speak about it earlier. Even with their mother's orders hanging over them, they hadn't wanted to admit that a unicorn horn could kill them. Something about the Air Dragon seems different this time. More melancholy and reflective.

"Do you know who might have killed Lyx?" I ask, hoping against all odds this whole trip hasn't been a dead end.

He turns to look at me, his eyes unreadable. "You should ask my mother," he says. "She carries within her secrets that could destroy worlds."

My ears perk at that, and I make a mental note to find out more.

He studies the dagger again. "It is time to step aside and let the world move on without me," he says, and before I can comprehend what's happening, Ventus thrusts the blade into his own heart.

I scream and Cole wraps his arm around my waist to keep me from rushing towards the dying dragon.

He smiles briefly, holding the dagger until his body disintegrates into a pale blue dust and is carried away on the wind, the blade dropping to the ground with a thud.

It shimmers briefly and projects a final image of Ventus dying, a new memory for its collection, before returning to normal.

Cole lets me go and I rush to the edge, looking over as if I might see the dragon reappear like this was a cruel and elaborate prank. But he doesn't. He's gone. Another dragon has died.

That's three since I arrived in this world.

A world that hasn't seen a dragon die for as long as the Night brothers have been alive.

What have I brought with me to cause this destruction, I wonder, as Cole pulls me into an embrace and the tears I've been holding back flow freely.

CHAPTER 6: THE SWIM

THE FOUNTAINS MINGLE with the river
  And the rivers with the ocean,
  The winds of heaven mix for ever
  With a sweet emotion;
  Nothing in the world is single;
  All things by a law divine
  In one spirit meet and mingle.
  Why not I with thine?—
  ~Percy Bysshe Shelley, Love's Philosophy

THE BUTLER INTERRUPTS US, his face grim as he studies the scene. "You both should leave. The dragons will know of his death and come to investigate. It would be better for all if you were not found here."

"How will you explain what happened?" I ask.

"I will not have to," he says and holds up a Memory Catcher. "My master left a message for his siblings, but it is private."

I look to Cole, who nods, and I realize we will have to dematerialize to get out of here quickly. The dagger is still lying on the floor where the dragon dropped it, and with a flick of my wrist I use air magic to fly it to my waiting hand, then tuck it into my waistband. Cole is the only one who sees, and he raises an eyebrow with a grin like he's proud of me. Then he pulls me against his chest.

"Ready, *mon coeur?*"

"No," I say.

"Just relax," he whispers as his hands rest on my hips. "Use your darkness."

I swallow and nod, then reluctantly tug on the powers deep within me, the dark depth I'm most scared of tapping into, and I let it flow into me, and then through me.

"Very good," Cole says. "Now stretch your darkness into me and feel what I do. You can do this without me, you just have to align yourself to the frequency of this spell, in a manner of speaking. And then picture where you want to go with as much detail as you can."

Per his instruction, I stretch the tendrils of darkness flowing out of me and attach to him, our magic merging, pulsing as one. The feeling is nearly erotic and brings to mind our love making, when our bodies were so connected they felt as one.

I can feel from the shift in his pants that he's thinking the same thing, and that only makes my own arousal more powerful.

He pulls me even tighter toward him until my breasts are pressed against his rock hard chest. My breath hitches as our bodies connect. And then we are traveling, our physical selves unraveling within the nothingness that consumes us.

But this time, I do not feel the panic and pain as before. Instead, I feel as if my spirit is set free, and I am everything, and nothing.

After an indefinite amount of time that could have been mere seconds or centuries, we arrive within the portal and are pushed through into the Otherworld, bodies intact, souls contained within our dense meat forms.

For a moment, I feel encumbered by the weight of my flesh, and I briefly mourn the feeling I had when we traveled through nothing.

Cole is still holding tight to me, his lips inches from mine. "You catch on fast," he whispers, his dark eyes luminous and intoxicating.

Still caught up in the swirl of emotions, I can't stop myself from pulling his head down and pressing my lips to his. I've dreamed of tasting his mouth again, of feeling his tongue flick over my lips, of reveling in the delight and desire that he brings.

He moans against my mouth, his chest rumbling with untapped longing, and I press my hips against him. He hardens against my stomach and I slide my hand down his chest until I'm caressing him.

He nibbles at my lip, then traces kisses down my neck to my collar bone, his teeth grazing me, nipping at my skin. My other hand is wrapped around his back, nails digging into him. I want more than I can have right now, and the thought sobers me. I gently pull away, my lips swollen with his kisses, my body empty without him.

"I should go," I say reluctantly. "This is too soon."

He caresses my head and nods. "*Je comprends*. But I am not giving up on us. I hope you do not either."

Tears sting my eyes as he steps back and disappears into smoke.

I look around at the forest, alive with the sounds of the wild, as I wipe my eyes and straighten my back.

Someday I might get him back, but today is not that day, and I need to go home. The others are probably losing their damn minds right now.

I contemplate the easiest way to go back to the castle. I could fly, but that will take a decent amount of time.

Or I could try my new shadow powers. That would get me home in an instant, but it also low key terrifies me.

I opt for being terrified. Because if I can master this, it's a useful trick to have in my tool box.

I close my eyes and pull out my darkness while reminding myself what Cole's magic felt like when he did this. Then I imagine the gardens just outside the castle, where I first found Moon.

It seems to be the safest place to aim for, and the one which will likely be the most discreet as well, since no one has seen me do this and it might freak them out a bit if I appear before them randomly.

Just as before, I disintegrate into nothing, into shadow and darkness, and then arrive just where I intended. Well, mostly where I intended. Since I was thinking of Moon and how I found him, I actually find myself stuck in the damn bush that he was stuck in when I rescued him. And it hurts like a bitch.

I slowly tear myself out of the dangerous barbed bushes and I'm covered in scratches that are starting to bleed.

That's how Liam finds me.

"What happened?" he asks, running over to me, his eyes filled with worry. "Who attacked you?"

He takes my arms and studies the injuries as I point to the offending bush. "We had a bit of a misunderstanding," I explain.

"I'm sure there's a story in that somewhere, but come in and let's get you cleaned up. Everyone is worried sick about you. Where did you go?"

"I'll explain once we're all together."

Liam slips an arm around me and we walk into the castle, then he leaves to round everyone up and find some ointment for my cuts. Moon greets me in the hall and rubs up against my legs, purring aggressively. I pick him up and nuzzle his soft black fur to my face. "I've missed you," I whisper, and I swear he purrs even louder. I set him down and he follows me as I head to the library.

The great hearth is stoked with a blazing fire and Alina and the baby dragon, Zara—who's presently in her human form—are both in the crib together. They are playing with colorful blocks of wood. Alina lights them on fire and Zara giggles and spits water onto them to put the fire out. Then they both laugh and do it all over again.

Liam arrives with the ointment and smiles when he sees the babies. "They've been like that since the moment they met," he says.

"It looks like the fire proofing has worked," I note. We've been trying a lot of spells over the last several weeks to keep Alina from burning down everything she touches, and nothing has worked until now.

He nods. "I think adding the phoenix feather to the spell really helped," he says. "Good call."

I grin at the compliment as he begins applying the ointment to my skin.

It burns a bit, then creates a cooling sensation that sucks the pain away. By the time he's done, I feel as good as new, and I know my skin will heal in no time. Magic medicine is the best.

Sebastian arrives next and pulls me into a bear hug that heals a much deeper part of my soul. Everything about this man makes me feel safe and cared for, and yet there is still a wall between us I don't know how to break down. But I'm determined to. Something always seems to get in the way of us being together more...intimately. That's going to end. Soon. I need this man. All of him.

As if sensing the direction of my thoughts, he tilts my head up and looks down at me, his forest green eyes full of so much unspoken longing.

"We should talk soon," I say softly. "Privately."

His pupils dilate and I feel how ready he instantly is for our 'talk.' "Just name the time and place, and I'm there."

But of course we are interrupted again when Elijah and Derek join us.

"Are Matilda and Lily coming?" I ask.

"Matilda is getting Ana to bed," Derek says. "And Lily is out with Kaya still."

"They haven't come back yet?" I ask, surprised. I know Lily went off to find the coroners, but I assumed she'd be home by now. Then again, Lily is home a lot less since she started dating Kaya, and I don't blame her. Being in a forest with her lover is likely far more exciting than being in a stuffy old castle.

"I'm sure she'll be back soon," Derek says. "Now please, share with us where you went. And how you suddenly learned to fly."

Oh right. Forgot about that.

That says something right there about how much has happened today, that learning to fly doesn't even register as worthy of mentioning.

We take seats around the fire while the babies continue to play with their magic. Elijah brings me a glass of wine and he and Sebastian claim the spots to either side of me.

"Before I begin, I need you to all promise to zip your lips until I'm done. No matter what. Got it?" I glare at them each sternly until they all reluctantly agree.

And so I begin with the vision I saw of Cole in possession of a unicorn dagger heading out of the Otherworld.

"That puss-filled rodent," Sebastian seethes, and I shush him with a pinch to his arm.

"I said zip your lips."

He glowers but stays silent as I continue.

I finish my wine just as I finish my story, and Derek rises to refill my glass before pacing in front of the fire.

"The situation is escalating," Derek says. "We need to consider all our options. Having Ana and Zara here could backfire spectacularly."

"And where do you propose we send them?" I ask.

He glances away, because there's no good answer to that. "Anywhere that does not put you at risk and compromise our investigation."

"Ana is a potential witness," I say, "if you want to be so bloody pragmatic about it. And Zara is a potential victim in need of protecting. Since we don't know who to trust outside this room, that leaves few options."

Derek, who is usually the even tempered one, snaps. "Damnit, Eve. You're thinking with your heart and not your head in this one!"

I stand, tired of this discussion. "Maybe this world needs more damn heart. It seems too many of you immortals get far too callous as the years tear out your emotions in favor of greed and self-serving nepotism."

And with that I storm out, too worn down to fight anymore.

Once in my room, the weight of the day adds a decade to how I feel, and I slough off my clothes and sink into the hot bath that's already waiting for me complete with scented oils. "Mable, did you do this?"

I look around for any sign of the ghost that looks after this castle and see my towel float to the edge of the bath.

I smile. "Thank you. It's much appreciated."

Moon takes his spot at the foot of my tub and proceeds to dip his paws into the water, splashing at things only he can see. I ignore him and close my eyes, content to let the heat soak out the exhaustion I feel.

I'm one giant prune and my limbs feel like noodles by the time I crawl out of the bathtub and dry myself, then slip into a silk robe and head to my room.

The sexy Fire Druid is sitting at the foot of my bed with a vial of liquid in one hand and a jar of ointment in the other.

"This," he says, holding up the ointment, "is for the rest of those cuts."

I glance down at where he's looking and see my legs are pretty scratched up.

"And this," he says, indicating the vial, "is for the headache you have."

I raise an eyebrow. My head started pounding while I was in the bath. But... "How did you know?"

"It's a natural byproduct of pushing yourself too hard. You used some really advanced magic today and didn't give yourself time to recharge. There are going to be consequences."

I take the vial and down it in one gulp, cringing at the foul taste. "Why do these always taste like ass? Can't you make something that tastes like strawberries?"

"Sure, I can, but it won't be medicinal. It's the rule. The worse it tastes, the better it works," he says with a wink.

"That's a terrible rule. By the power vested in me by the Mother of Dragons, I petition a change to this rule."

Liam laughs and pats the bed. "Settle in and I'll rub the ointment on you if you'd like."

By the gods, I would like nothing more than to feel his hands all over my body, though I'm still too bloody pissed at Derek.

Still, I nod and let my robe fall to my feet. He studies my body with clear desire, but doesn't move until I'm lying on my stomach, eyes closed. Then he proceeds to massage out all the cuts and bruises, as well as the sore muscles that a day of intense—everything—has left. By the time he's done, I feel more relaxed.

"Thank you," I say, turning over to look at him. "I needed that."

He nods and heads to the door, then pauses. "I know we are all a pain in the ass at times. But know that Derek is just trying to protect you. We all are."

I sigh. "I know. But I'm not a broken little girl in need of protecting. Ana is though."

"I think Derek knows that. It's a complicated situation and he feels lost. He's used to being in charge of things, and he doesn't feel in charge of this. It scares him."

Damnit, I wanted to stay angry longer, but his words are softening my resolve.

"He's at the lake," Liam says. "In case that matters. He feels badly about the fight."

Well, shit.

Liam closes the door softly behind him and I sit in my bed stewing and trying to decide if I should go to the Water Druid or try to fall asleep, but thanks to Liam's words, sleep seems impossible now.

"Damn them both," I say as I climb out of my comfortable bed and aggressively put my robe on.

I make my way to my balcony and sigh. I guess I'm doing this.

Using my magic, I fly towards the lake just over the rise of trees to the north. It's part of our property, so it doesn't take too long, and I land at the edge of a large body of water, the Dragon's Breath shimmering off the glassy surface, making it look like a different kind of portal.

It's surrounded by trees, and in the stillness of the evening it feels like the middle of nowhere.

Derek's clothes are folded neatly into a pile on a rock, and he is swimming laps in the water. When he turns to swim towards the shore, he sees me and stops. "Eve, what are you doing here?"

"Liam told me you were out here," I say. "I... I'm not sure why I came. I just don't like fighting with you."

"I don't like it either. Join me for a swim?"

I hesitate, but it's been so long since I've swam, and the night is perfect, and why the hell not? I let my robe fall to the ground and step into the lake, Derek's gaze unwavering from my body.

The water is cold and refreshing, and I don't cheat and use my fire magic to warm it. Instead, I let my body adjust to the temperature until I am submerged. Then I dunk under and swim towards Derek, popping up just in front of him.

"I'm sorry I lost my temper," he says softly, his dark, wet hair gleaming under the Dragon's Breath. "I'm still conflicted. Protecting you and our family is my top priority, so it's difficult making decisions that go against that."

"I know," I say. "But we have to expand who we think of as worthy of our protection," I say. "Especially when it comes to children. Those kids need us."

He raises his hand to caress my face, moving closer to me in the process.

My breasts graze his chest under the water, and my body responds instantly.

"You're the kindest soul I know," he says, and then his lips are on mine and all I can think about is him. Us. Our watery world where nothing else exists.

He was the first to offer me the job that changed my life.

He defended me when his brothers didn't want me in this world.

He brought me back to life.

And as his arm slips around my waist and I wrap my legs around his, I feel us both coming to life once again.

He tastes of the sea, or sunshine and rain and sunsets on the beach. His lean, muscular body easily supports us both and I feel how urgently he wants me as he presses against my spread legs.

His hands slip down to my ass, his fingers digging into my flesh as he tightens his hold on me, and our magic blends, water splashing against water, as playful as dolphins at sea.

Our kisses deepen, his teeth tugging at my lower lip, then diving down, exploring my throat as I lean back.

I use our joined magic to push us up to the surface of the water, making a kind of waterbed for us that we spread out on, my body pinned beneath his.

Enjoying the access this position gives him to the rest of me, he teases and tastes every part of me, using his magic in thrilling new ways to take me to the edge.

We are cushioned by the element we both love, supported in this lake like a dream come to life, and when pleasure crashes into me in waves of nirvana, he does as well, filling me and driving me to new heights.

As he reaches his own climax, I join him again, and the bed beneath us pulls us under, letting us sink to the bottom of the lake, locked in our embrace. I use air magic to create a buffer around us and light magic to illuminate the underwater world we find ourselves in, as exotic fish swim past us and coral-colored plant life sways in the currents.

He holds me tightly and I tuck myself into his arms, enjoying this unusual and magical moment for as long as I can.

Later, when our energy returns, we make our way to shore and dress.

Then we walk back to the castle together, hand in hand, enjoying the quiet moments of the evening, and when we reach my room, he hesitates, but I hold open the door. "Stay?"

He does.

That night I don't dream, but I do feel a deep warmth and safety as I drift on the clouds of my subconscious, and when I wake in the morning, Derek is still there, still holding me, his presence eternal and his love unshakable. He pulls me closer against him, his body wrapped around mine, my back pressed against his chest, and I feel his arousal as he drops kisses onto my neck.

I moan and press into him. "How long have you been awake?"

"Not too long."

I don't believe him, but it doesn't matter. I'm glad he stayed.

I press my ass against him, and he growls under his breath. "Don't you have to go to see Ifi and Elal soon?" he asks, his voice heavy with longing.

"Yes. So, we can't do a three hour marathon, but surely we have time for something?"

In a flash, Derek flips me over and pins me to the bed, pressing the weight of his body between my legs. "I can definitely give you something," he says as he trails kisses down my neck and to my breasts, stopping to give each their share of attention before moving further south. His fingers dig into my hips as he uses his tongue to push me to the edge of the cliff.

And then I'm falling. Pleasure crashes through me as he continues his attentions with his fingers while positioning himself to plunge into me.

I bite his shoulder to keep from screaming in ecstasy as he fills me, while he uses his hands to tease and torture other parts of me.

Once he climaxes, I'm ready again, and together we drown in each other's arms.

CHAPTER 7: THE WEAPON

I AM SO small I can barely be seen.
How can this great love be inside me?
Look at your eyes. They are small,
But they see enormous things.
~Rumi, The Turn

AFTER THAT WAKE-UP WITH DEREK, I'm ready to have a productive day. I try not to let the weight of the world—literally—derail me from finding joy in the moment-to-moment blessings. So while I will do everything in my power to stop the destruction of the Otherworld—obviously—I also can't ignore the love and beauty I have around me every day. If anything, knowing how easily something can be torn from us, seeing the immortal greatness of dragons die, it has reminded me to stay present and be grateful for every moment I have with the ones I love.

I find Sebastian in the library, sitting by the fire and reading an old leather-bound book to Ana—who looks like a whole new child now that she's been bathed and dressed in clean clothes which fit her properly. Her golden hair shimmers against the fire light. Her cream skin is nearly translucent. And her eyes, a silvery blue, seem to shine when she looks at Sebastian.

He doesn't notice me yet and continues to read from the book, which is red with a silver title that reads, *"All the Fairies Dared to Do."*

"Platious never felt that she was brave or strong or right or good, and her name spoken aloud made her want to cover her ears," Sebastian says, pointing to a picture on the page. "Her wings sagged, and her hair never stayed where it was meant to, and her skin did not sparkle like the other fairies of the garden. So she felt herself plain. She did not yet know that within her, she held the seed of truth, and once planted, it would give her wisdom beyond measure."

Ana sees me and smiles, leaving Sebastian and running over to me for a hug.

"Hey, honey. Did you sleep well?"

She nods. "It was the most comfortable bed I've ever felt. Even my friend liked it."

"Your friend?"

Sebastian nods. "Every child needs an imaginary friend," he assures me with a wink.

"Of course," I say, smiling. "I'm glad you and your friend were comfortable." I put an arm over her shoulder and walk back to Sebastian. "Sounds like you were getting a fun story."

"Oh, yes. I love Platious. She thinks she's not good, but she's *so* good. She just doesn't see it yet."

I share a glance with Sebastian, and I can tell we are both thinking about Cole. "Sometimes people need to be reminded of who they truly are before they can see the truth in themselves."

She nods sagely, then takes the book from Sebastian. "Can I keep reading while you're gone?"

I raise an eyebrow, surprised she knows how to read. But I assume Lyx helped with that. She was pretty committed to helping her people learn to read and write so they could engage more fully in their world.

Sebastian grins. "Yes, enjoy. But promise to tell me what happens when I get back."

"Deal!" she says and runs out of the room clutching the book against her chest.

I sink into the couch next to the sexy Earth Druid, sliding easily against his heavily muscled body. "That was adorable."

He blushes. Actually blushes. "She's a sweet kid. You were right to bring her home."

I lean a head against him. "Thanks. I couldn't just leave her. But I realize we are going to have to figure out what to do with her long term." I glance up at him, catching his gaze. "What happens to kids like her here?"

He frowns. "We don't have a great system for caring for orphans. If no one claims her, or takes her in, she'll end up on the streets where she isn't likely to survive long."

"Shit. That's ridiculous. Why? This is a small, wealthy community with many beings who are nearly immortal or at least long lived. Can't you figure out something better than 'kick 'em to the street and let 'em die'?"

"It is something that needs to be changed. There are many things that need to change in this world." He pulls me into him and kisses my forehead. "Maybe you'll be the change we need."

"On that note, we should get going. I want to see what Ifi and Elal learned about Lyx's death." I move to stand but Sebastian pulls me back to the couch.

"Not until you've eaten. Liam told me how drained you were last night." He grabs a plate from the side table and hands it to me. It's piled high with eggs, bacon, fresh baked bread with a thick pat of butter, and a bowl of berries and cream.

I'm about to tell him I'm not hungry but my stomach rumbles, betraying me.

Sebastian raises an eyebrow and I smile. "Thank you. This looks delicious."

While I eat, Derek and Elijah join us, with Liam following behind holding a baby dragon in one arm and Alina in the other. "She ate!" he says to Elijah. "You were right. Cooked shark was the way to go." He glances at me in exasperation. "We tried every kind of meat we could think of. Then it occurred to us maybe seafood since she's a water dragon. It took a bit to get to shark." The Fire Druid grins at the dragon in his arms. "You're such a good eater, aren't you?"

"This might be the cutest thing I've ever seen in my life," I say, watching them.

Elijah rises and takes the dragon from Liam. Zara hiccups and spits water all over him, but he just laughs and puts the baby in the crib so he can dry off.

"Here, let me," I say, and I place a hand on his chest and channel fire and air together, drying him in an instant.

"Thank you," he says, his smile almost boyish.

"What will the rest of you do today?" I ask as I take Alina from Liam and give her some love. She pulls at my hair and laughs as she singes the edges with her fire.

"I'm staying with the kids," Liam says. "I thought I'd take them all on a hike and let these two practice their magic somewhere safer."

"I'll join you," Elijah says. "I need to get out of the castle for a bit and enjoy some fresh air. Plus, you'll have your hands full with three kids."

I look to Derek who shrugs. "I'm going to go back to the crime scene to see if I can find any new leads."

"Where's Matilda?" I ask. I haven't seen her around much since Lyx's death.

"She left last night and said she'll be back soon, that she had something to look into," Sebastian says.

With plans in place, Sebastian and I head to the carriage. I could offer to fly us or teleport us, but I'm just learning these abilities and taking another person with me seems risky at best. Besides, there are worse ways in the world to spend a morning than in a carriage with a sexy vampire druid.

I'm about ready to climb into the front, assuming Sebastian will be driving, but he ushers me into the back. "We've got a driver," he says.

"Who? Lily isn't home and everyone else is busy."

I watch, and see the reigns to the horses shift and move through the air... and I smile. "Mable?"

She flicks the reigns to let me know she's there, and Sebastian raises an eyebrow. "You learned her name? How?"

"I have my ways," I tell him with a wink as we crawl into the back of the carriage.

He sits across from me, our knees touching as he leans forward so we're closer. "I'm glad we'll have some time together," he says reaching for my hand.

I take his, squeezing it, and enjoy the feel of our skin touching, even if it's just our palms. "Me too. I feel like we haven't had a minute to ourselves in ages, with all the work we're doing in the new world and now this."

"You've done an incredible job helping build a new community," he says. "I see how the people look at you. You're a hero to them, and they don't even know you're a Fate."

I laugh at that. "I'm 100% sure they do. Nothing stays a secret in this world for long. Y'all are quite the gossips."

He grins, unable to deny it. "Either way, you've healed a lot of hearts. Mine included."

I know he's still broken about Cole, but it's good to hear some healing has occurred. "This is my home now too. I wasn't exaggerating when I told the Mother of Dragons that this world is part of me now. Or maybe it's more correct to say I'm a part of it. I don't know how it happened exactly, but when I did that spell, it changed something inside me, and added something of me to the fabric of this world. I haven't wanted to admit this to myself, let alone anyone else. But Sebastian, if this world is destroyed, I think I might be destroyed along with it, regardless of where I am. I don't think I'll survive if Amora gets her way."

Sebastian sucks in a breath, his grip on my hands tightening. "How certain are you?"

I drop my head, not wanting to see the heartache in his eyes when I tell him. "I could be wrong, of course, but I don't think I am. I'm... " I look up, unable to pull my gaze from his any longer. "I'm pretty certain. I can feel my life force attached to this world. I know after we found out what I am, we all speculated about my life span. But the more I've used my powers, the more I've felt this connection. I don't think I'll die naturally unless this world does. Which felt like it would be a long time, but now it has the life expectancy of less than two weeks. And so do I."

He's quiet for a few moments, his face hardened against this news. "Maybe Elijah's books can uncover someway to fix this," he says.

"I think the only fix is solving the murder," I say.

"Assuming the Mother of Dragons honors her word," he whispers, pressing his lips into a tight line.

"Why wouldn't she?"

He shrugs. "The dragons follow their own rules. They always have."

"We'll just have to make sure she honors her word this time," I say. "Not just for my sake. We wouldn't be able to evacuate the entire population of this world in time, even if we started now." I pause, thinking. "Should we start now?" I ask. "Should we go public and encourage everyone to leave? To save as many as we can, at least."

He looks pained as he considers the possibility of failure. "If we did that, we would reduce our odds of finding the killer. They would leave, and we wouldn't have any chance of saving the world. And as you said, we still wouldn't be able to evacuate everybody. And where would they go? Not everyone here can pass as human, and even those of us who can would become targets in your world. It would lead to more deaths."

I sigh. "Yeah, I know. But I was hoping I was wrong. Because I'm worried about our odds. We have so little evidence to go on."

"We'll find more," he says. "We have to."

The carriage begins to slow and I look out the window, surprised to find we have already arrived at the cemetery where the morgue is located.

Unlike the first time I came here, today is a bright day with a light breeze that makes the grass covering the graves sway in synchronicity.

Mable stays with the carriage—presumably, I can't actually see her —and we walk across the cemetery towards the mausoleum when a thought occurs to me. "Are there ghosts here?" It seems the logical place for them.

Sebastian shrugs. "Most likely, why?"

"I just realized Mable might enjoy visiting with others of her kind. They must be a very underrepresented group in the Otherworld."

Sebastian tilts his head and looks around, as if seeing the area with new eyes. "I never actually thought of it like that before."

We approach the mausoleum— a towering gothic building that casts a long shadow over the cemetery with its clustered columns and sharply pointed spires. The stained-glass windows are filled with light today, as the brightness of the Dragon's Breath spills through them.

I pick up my pace when we are close, excited to see the gargoyles that guard the doors.

Okura comes to life first, her stone wings stretching and flexing as she flies down from her perch to land in front of us, a pouch at her stomach heavy with her baby, like a kangaroo.

"Okura!" I run up to her and hug her stony body.

She laughs, and the sound is much like rocks tumbling down a mountain. "It has been too long. And I have heard tales that your truth is finally known, Fate." She bows her head in reverence.

"Oh, please, not you too. I'm still just me. How's the baby?"

Akuro lands beside his mate and grins widely. "She is the sun and moon and the stars all in one," he says proudly as Okura pulls the sleeping child from the pouch and hands her to me.

My body sags under the weight of the baby, and Sebastian wraps his arms around me to help support us both. The child blinks, its eyes large and curious, and then she smiles and reaches out with a little fist to grab my hair.

I laugh. "It seems babies everywhere are all the same."

We spend a few more minutes visiting, with promises to get our families together soon, and they open the doors for us.

As we walk in, Okura says, "We are here if you need us in the upcoming struggles."

I turn towards her. "What do you mean?"

She closes her eyes. "A war is brewing. The Age of Dragon is coming to an end. Much will be decided in the coming days. Be well, Fate. Count us amongst your allies."

"Thank you," I say, then Sebastian and I continue our walk through the dim halls, and today the smell of death and old flowers is even stronger than normal.

We stop before the large arched double doors I recognize from our first visit here, and this time I'm prepared for the scene as we walk in.

Since my powers have manifested so strongly, I'm no longer impacted by the heat and the flames dancing along the edges of the marble walls. It's a large room with dead bodies lying across tables scattered throughout, and long stretches of glass tubing connecting beakers of bubbling liquid in varying shades of green, orange, grey, and purple. I ignore the specimen jars that line the shelves. They creep me out.

Instead, I focus on the two men standing over a body. Both are ablaze in flames that would have seared me in the past. Now, I can walk right up to them and hug them if I want, though I might still burn my clothes off. So I wait for them to de-flame, which they do the moment they see us.

"Eve, Sebastian!" Ifi grins and throws himself into a hug, first with me, then with Sebastian, who looks a little taken back but recovers quickly enough and embraces the Ifrit. I smile at the exchange, glad we have these guys as friends.

While Ifi regales Sebastian with his latest drama, Elal hugs me, his golden eyes more serious. "Sounds like you have had quite a time with the dragons," he says.

I snort. "That's the understatement of the century. What have you heard?"

Ifi joins us, dragging Sebastian by the hand. "Oh, darling, what haven't we heard? Dead dragons, a visit from the Mother of Dragons, your Fate powers going super nova. The Otherworld is getting lit!" he explains with a swivel of his hips.

I burst out laughing and Elal chuckles. "We took a visit to Earth recently. Ifi really liked the socializing on media part. He learned some new words."

"Yeah, I can see that," I say, still chuckling. "But honestly, how do you guys know so much about what happened already? There were only a few of us there."

They share a glance. "We have our ways," Ifi says with a conspiratorial wink.

447

Elal frowns. "We also know of other, more disturbing things," he says. "End of the world rumors."

I suck in a breath. "How?"

"It is hard to explain. But rest assured this is not common knowledge, and will not become so, not by us at least. While Ifi might be an irredeemable gossip, even he knows when to keep his mouth shut."

I look over at Ifi, who makes a motion to zip up his lips and toss away the key.

"We need to solve this case," I say. "Everything depends on it."

"Then let's get to it, shall we?" Elal says, and with a flick of his finger he gestures for one of the cooling units to open, and a table comes rolling out with Lyx's body laid out reverently on top, covered in a white sheet.

"We have never autopsied a dragon before," Ifi says, clearly trying to contain his excitement.

"Normally their bodies disintegrate upon death," I say. "Why didn't hers?"

"Our working theory," Elal says, "is that their body remains if their soul was torn from them without their willing consent."

"Does this mean Lyx can't move on? To...wherever dragon souls go when they die?" The afterlife is still a mystery to me, clearly.

"We can't answer that," Elal says.

"Can you tell us what killed her?" Sebastian asks, his voice soft, his demeanor more subdued than normal as he gazes at Lyx.

Elal reaches for a clay sculpture on one of the shelves and holds it up. "Something this shape and size," he says. "I made a mold of the puncture wound and created a sculpture from it."

I take it from his hand and examine it, turning it over in my hand. It's made of grey clay and has a cylindrical base that narrows into a sharpened tip with ridges spiraling it. "What does this look like to you?" I ask Sebastian.

He frowns, studying it. "A unicorn horn."

"Right. But there's presumably only one left, and it wasn't the murder weapon, so where does that leave us?"

"With another mystery to solve in just a few days."

"Can we keep this?" I ask, holding up the sculpture.

"Sure thing," Ifi says. "It's some of my best work." He winks and I grin at him.

"Now, are we ready for the last wish?" Elal asks.

"Yes," Sebastian says softly.

We all step back several feet in anticipation of Ifi's transformation.

He walks over to Lyx's body and stands by her side, then bursts into flames. The fire burns brightly and Sebastian shifts uncomfortably, sweating. I reach for his hand and use my water and air magic to dampen the heat for him. He pulls me closer to him and kisses my head as Ifi begins chanting in his own language. As before, his voice becomes layered with other voices, the vibration of them shaking the room. It feels like an earthquake moving through the mausoleum and then a loud screeching fills the air. Flames dance against the marble walls and ceilings, and the body of Lyx begins to shake as Ifi's magic fills her, animating her from within.

She sits up and turns to us, light filling her body, her soul returning to her eyes. She looks at Sebastian first. "Son," she says, "Keep your light close."

Then she looks at me and her face contorts in terror. "The mother must be stopped."

I expect her to drop back to the table, dead once again, but instead, she bursts into explosions of light that go off like fireworks in the contained space.

As vials of liquid begin exploding, I grab Sebastian and put up a shield, using a blend of light, air, water and darkness. It seems to do the trick as sizzling chemicals splash against the shield and slide off harmlessly, and projectile balls of fire and light crash into it and fizzle out. I feel the hits to my magic but withstand it easily as Elal and Ifi rush to contain the damage.

Eventually the light show dies down and then Lyx's body bursts into dust and disappears, leaving nothing but a massive mess behind.

"That was fire!" Ifi says in awe.

Sebastian looks confused, so I clarify. "It's a meme thing. It means cool."

"Fire means cool? That wasn't any more clarifying."

I snort. "Welcome to my world."

449

CHAPTER 8: THE NOTE

We are weaned from our timidity
 In the flush of love's light
 we dare be brave
 And suddenly we see
 that love costs all we are
 and will ever be.
 Yet it is only love
 which sets us free.
 ~Maya Angelou, Touched by an Angel

SEBASTIAN and I wait in Ifi and Elal's private quarters while they put out the last of the fires in their lab. I offered to help, but they insisted there were too many variables to allow other magic to interfere.

I look around in surprise at their very modern studio situated upstairs in the mausoleum. It's all leather and steel, tasteful and sparse, juxtaposed against stone walls and marble floors. Their kitchen is small but gourmet, with some definite black trade gadgets from my world. "How do they even make a cappuccino machine work without electricity?" I ask.

"Magic?" Sebastian postures as he takes a seat on the leather sofa.

He's been pretty quiet since we got up here, so I take a seat next to him and place a hand on his knee. "You okay?" I ask.

He grunts.

It was unusual that she had two 'last wishes'. Not to mention that she blew up after. The Ifrits look shook—as Ifi might now say with his new grasp of earth modern lingo.

"So that's a no," I say. "I know you all have a history with the Light Dragon. Do you want to talk about it? This must be hard for you."

"She was my mentor," he finally says. "Before I became a Druid."

I nod. "I knew you'd been close at one point, before your falling out."

"Falling out," he says with a bitter undertone to his words. "Yes. We certainly did. She turned her backs on us—on me—because she didn't like the direction the Order was going."

"Because of the Fates," I say, and guilt floods me even though I'm not really the same person as back then. At least I don't feel like I am.

"Yes, in part. There were a lot of complicated politics at play. And then Cole did what he did, and she sided with him against the Order and the Fates, severing ties with us all, just as Cole did."

"And you lost your brother and your mentor all at once," I say. "That must have been heartbreaking."

"I spent the first two decades of my life being trained by her to prepare for my initiation into the Order. Hours every day which became longer the older I grew. She taught me the history, the lore, the use of my powers, the control of my emotion. She was the only mother I really ever knew."

"Who were your parents?" I ask, shocked that I've never had this conversation with any of them.

"I don't really remember them," he says, his eyes losing focus as his mind is drawn into the past. "My brothers and I were born on a farm. Our parents were poor, and when they discovered we had powers, they feared us cursed by demons. The Druidic Order heard about us and sent Lyx to acquire us. My parents were more than happy to take the gold to get rid of us. Hell, had they had any money to begin with, I think they would have paid to have us taken away."

"Did you all develop your gifts at the same time?" I ask, my heart breaking for the little boys whose parents didn't want them.

"Strangely, yes," he says. "It was after Cole was born, once he developed his light powers at age two. Somehow that triggered it for all of us. Liam burned down part of the barn that day—which likely explains why our parents thought we were a curse. Our magic was so raw and untapped, we caused only grief for them."

I reach for his hand and hold it in mine. "Did you ever see them again?"

He looks away, unable to meet my eyes. "Their village was destroyed when we were cursed and lost control of our powers." He pauses, and the weight of his words hit me with a visceral force. "That's when we decided to end our lives."

Now tears are burning my eyes, and I let them fall. I know how awful that time was for them. I remember the pain when they first told me what happened. But this…this is so much worse than I even imagined. I want him to know that I see his pain and hold space for him.

He lifts his free hand and runs the pad of his thumb across my cheekbone, stealing my tear. "It has been many, many lifetimes, and I am not who I was then."

His hand, still caressing my cheek, moves to the back of my head, his fingers tangling in my hair as he pulls me forward.

With an urgent need he claims my lips, pulling me onto his lap as he does.

Like an earthquake, everything shifts between us, and I adjust my legs, straddling him on the couch to get closer. His hands fall to my ass, pulling me even nearer, fingers digging into my flesh as he deepens our kiss.

I nip at his lower lip and he growls and hardens beneath me, pressing himself between my legs. An agonizing need crashes through me, creating a temporary amnesia as to where we are.

It's not until the door opens that we both remember we are guests at the Ifrits home. Startled, I roll off his lap into the couch next to him and he casually covers his pants with a throw pillow.

I can feel the blood rushing to my face and know within moments I'll look like a disheveled beet.

Ifi raises an eyebrow at us as he walks in. "Looks like you two have been having fun without us," he teases.

They both left their white lab coats downstairs and Ifi is dressed in torn jeans and a band t-shirt. Elal is wearing more of a Renaissance style outfit of dark leggings with a long sleeved shirt and doublet. Elal heads to the pantry and pulls out a bottle of wine. "Ifi, leave them be." He glances at us. "Care for a glass?"

"Sure," I say. "Thank you."

Elal pours four glasses and brings them over, then they both take a seat across from us.

"Was the lab too badly destroyed?" I ask, sipping my drink.

"Thank the fires, no," Elal says.

"But it's an unholy mess nonetheless," Ifi interjects, already on his second glass of wine. "Still, worth it. Who else can say a dragon blew up in their morgue?"

Elal shoots Ifi a glance that is absolutely couple-speak for, "she was their friend, don't be such an ass." And Ifi's face changes to, "by the fires you're right, what a nob I'm being."

At least that's how I interpret it. But Ifi stammers an apology. "I can be an insensitive prat sometimes."

"It's fine," Sebastian says, finally able to move the pillow off his lap. "It was pretty remarkable. What do you think caused that?"

"My best guess is when Ifi pulled her dying wish from her, it cleared her soul of the karmic energy to move on," Elal says. "Or another magic interfered because they didn't want her sharing anything more."

My breath hitches at his words. "Is that possible? Could she have said more? I thought you only got one wish, but she had two."

"Oh, the dead can say whatever they damn well please," says Ifi. "They just usually don't have much umph left in them, if you catch my drift. But the Light Dragon, she was one of the most powerful beings alive. I'd bet she could have solved her own murder if she could've spoken longer."

"But who could have done that to her?" I ask. "What kind of power?"

"That's why that particular theory seems most unlikely," Elal says, casting a frown at Ifi. "Because it shouldn't be possible. Not with the spells and counter spells on this place, plus Okura and Akuro guarding it. Likely she'd fulfilled her death wish and moved on."

Once we are done with our drinks, Sebastian and I stand to take our leave. "It's been so good seeing you again. Come over for dinner sometime," I say at the door.

Elal gives me a hug and Ifi screeches and bursts into flames, startling us all.

"What the hell?" Sebastian says, rushing out of the way of the flames.

Ifi simmers down and apologizes. "I've been having hot flashes lately," he says. "Especially when I remember something important."

"I'm thinking hot flashes mean something different for you than they do for my world," I say. "But regardless, what did you remember?"

Ifi heads over to a desk and pulls out an envelope. "We were asked to give this to you, and only you."

Curious, I open it, and find a note written in heavy script font with dripping black ink.

MEET me at Landal's Tomb when you get this. I have information that could help you. Come alone or I won't be there. ~Dath'Racul

"WHAT'S LANDAL'S TOMB?" I ask.

"Doesn't matter," Sebastian says, reading over my shoulder. "You're not going."

"You know I have to," I say. "Too much is at stake and we know too little right now."

"Then I'm coming with you." Sebastian crosses his arms stubbornly over his chest.

"No, you're not. He won't show if you do. Besides, I think I've proven I can take care of myself."

"Uh oh," Ifi singsongs. "A lovers' quarrel. But they do make for the best make-up sex."

Elal shushes his lover and I blush for the second time today. Sebastian looks away, and I know we are both thinking about being in bed together for the first time. That moment needs to happen sooner rather than later.

"He could be the killer," Sebastian says.

"That seems unlikely. The dagger isn't the murder weapon."

"Dragons don't need a horn, remember?"

I sigh, wishing we had more clues. But that's exactly why I need to meet with him.

"Even if he didn't do it, he's dangerous," says Sebastian.

"I faced off with his mother, I think I can handle him," I say. "Besides I'm not going there to fight him, just to hear what he has to say." I turn to the Ifrits. "Where, and what, is Landal's Tomb?" I ask again.

Sebastian falls into a melancholy sulk while Elal answers my question.

"Landal's Tomb is where one of the three original Fates was buried."

My ears perk up at that. "Are there tombs for all three Fates?" I ask. In my mind I'm wondering if *I'm* buried somewhere, which is such a weird and creepy thing to contemplate.

"Nope," Ifi says, linking his arm through Elal's. The bigger Ifrit pulls Ifi closer, their bodies conforming to each other's as they speak. "She was the only one whose body was found after they disappeared. The other two were presumed dead, but no one knows for sure what happened to them."

"How did she die?" I ask.

"She was murdered," Ifi whispers, as if this is top secret information. "But no one knows by whom. However, there aren't many beings that can kill a Fate. The list is short."

"Ifi," Elal says sternly.

"What? It's not like she can hear us. Not here."

Elal frowns. "It's best not to speak ill of her regardless."

"Speak ill of who?" I ask, though I'm beginning to suspect who they're talking about.

They share a concerned glance and Elal sighs. "All I can say is this. Be careful with the dragons. And go to that meeting."

Sebastian grumbles but doesn't argue.

"I need to know where it is," I say.

"Well you're in luck, darling," Ifi says, throwing an arm over my shoulder and walking me to the window. He points across the field of gravestones to the far end where a larger structure stands. "That's the entrance. The rest is underground. Go in and follow the steps down. You'll find what you're looking for."

I glance at Sebastian. "Will you wait here for me?" I ask.

"I guess I have to," he says, reluctantly sinking back onto the couch.

Elal holds the door open for me, but I shake my head. "I've got a faster way to travel these days."

I close my eyes and think of the location Ifi just showed me, tapping into my darkness, and then I disintegrate.

I land just where I plan, outside the door to Landal's Tomb. It's getting easier to do this teleporting thing, which pleases me.

Vines and moss cover the stone structure before me with lifetimes of growth, and creepers hang down over the entrance, covering the door. Though it looks to have been recently disturbed.

I push through and open the entrance. It squeaks and cracks as it opens and the scent of mildew and dust clogs my throat. I cough, choking a bit before I remember I can use air magic to clear some of this up. A flick of my wrist and I can take a deep breath with more ease. That handled, I navigate down the stairs, casting a ball of light on my palm to guide the way.

Cobwebs catch in my hair and something squishes under my feet, but I don't look to see what. I don't really want to know.

When I finally get to the bottom, I enter a cavernous space full of candles. The room has a tall ceiling, and in the center is a sculpture of a beautiful woman draped in a see-through gown. The stonework is incredible, truly magnificent. It's as if her soul was brought to life, and a chill runs down my spine as I stare at her form.

In another life, she and I were friends.

Or sisters.

I'm unclear.

But we were close.

Who were the other Fates? What were they like? I have so many questions I can never hope to get answered.

"She's stunning, is she not? I tried to capture her essence."

I turn to see Dath'Racul leaning against the stone wall studying me, his long red wing-cape draped over his broad shoulders, his eyes hooded in shadows.

"You sculpted this?"

"I did," he says, stepping forward, into the flicking candlelight. "She was my lover. When she died, a piece of me died with her."

CHAPTER 9: THE FORBIDDEN

"Your task is not to seek for love, but merely to seek and find all the barriers within yourself that you have built against it."
~Rumi

His words leave me stunned. "Lover?"

"Does that surprise you, Miss Oliver? That I would be capable of love?" He steps closer, now standing inches from me, his massive form towering over me, his golden dragon eyes studying me with a penetrating intelligence that is unnerving. The candlelight plays off his deep burnt red skin, giving him a demonic quality that actually seems to amplify his attractiveness.

"We are, all of us, capable of love. The depth of that love is determined by the depth of our own souls," I say.

He tilts his head, studying me. "I was surprised to learn you were one of the Fates," he says in a non-sequitur. "But the more I study you, the more I see the wisdom of your past bleeding through the frailness of your small human life."

"That almost sounded like a compliment," I say. "If you keep working at it, I think you'll nail it one of these days."

His lips twitch as if he's tempted to smile, but he resists the impulse. "I wasn't sure you would attend this meeting."

"Why wouldn't I?" I ask. "I'm committed to solving this murder. I want to see the Light Dragon's killer brought to justice, and I obviously don't want to see your mother destroy the Otherworld."

"Yes. You are an altruist through and through. Tell me, do you share the ruthlessness of the Maiden Fate of the past? Will you cross lines drawn in blood to do what you think is right?"

His gaze bores into me as if he's trying to pillage my soul of all its secrets. Secrets even I'm not privy to.

"Whatever choices we make, whatever actions we take to protect, to guide, to lead, to bring justice, they should not and cannot undermine our basic goodness and decency, otherwise what is it all for?"

He steps back from me, half his face falling into shadows as he does. "So you would let the innocent die if the alternative required acting in a way against your conscience?"

I glance up at the sculpture, letting my hand study the delicate artistry of it. "This is the first representation I've seen of a Fate where her face is shown," I say, changing the subject. "Why is that?"

I've noticed he's studiously avoided looking at the image of his lover, but now that he does, his eyes soften briefly. "The Fates never showed their faces. Not to the dragons, not to my mother, not to anyone. They were more myth than anything." He turns his attention back to me. "Which is why no one knew who you were," he says.

"Do you mean I would have looked like this in my past life?" I ask. "I thought with reincarnation you come back in a new body, new look and all that?"

"Perhaps under normal circumstances. But you are not normal. You are not reincarnated. You are a fate reborn. You'd do well to remember that. You may not wish to face your past deeds, but they remain part of you regardless." He looks away, his face showing a moment of brokenness that surprises me. "We all must deal with the consequences of who we were, whether we recognize that person now or not."

"And who were you, once upon a time?" I ask in a whisper.

The air around us feels heavy with the weight of the past, with ghosts that still haunt us both, even if I can no longer remember them.

"A man in love," he says without looking at me. "Who didn't want to see what my choices would do to the one I loved."

I look back at Landal, who looks suspended in time, mid-dance, her body twirling, the sheer dress she wears flowing around her, her head turned to glance over her shoulder at someone, her face lit up with joy and love.

"What was she like?" I ask.

"Do you not remember anything?" he asks with a frown.

"Not really. It hasn't been that long that I've really known who I was. And I've only had flashes of memory. Nothing I can hold onto. But I feel her inside me, writhing like a living thing trying to escape. Sometimes I don't know where I begin and she ends," I admit, surprising even me. I haven't articulated these thoughts to myself, let alone anyone else. I never imagined Dath'Racul would be the one I could confess to.

By the look on his face, he didn't either.

I expect a sharp retort, a biting insult, a cutting jibe. But instead, he walks over to a bench I didn't notice before. One in the shadows, but that has a perfect view of the Landal.

He sits, and gestures that I should join him.

There is barely enough room for both of us, and our thighs press together as I take my seat, sending a jolt of electricity through my skin. My fire magic flares, being this close to the Fire Dragon, and his eyes widen, suggesting he feels it too.

"Your powers have grown substantially since we met at the Collector's party," he says. "I was a bit distracted that day with my mother that I didn't feel the full weight of it then, despite your rather impressive grandstanding."

I ignore the grandstanding comment, because I can be a bigger person. "The spell with Ava'Kara seems to have unlocked what was trapped in me."

I swear his eyes seem to mist over when I mention her name.

"I wish she would have talked to us before sacrificing herself. We could have found another way."

I turn to him, my face hardening. "I think she didn't go to you because you seemed determined to use your power and position to take advantage of the fear that people lived in. You stoked that fear and used it to make yourself stronger. She wanted to help. But you wanted control."

"I know it may seem that way in your minuscule and insignificant human life of what? Twenty or thirty years?" he says, his voice hardening. "But I created a world for the people you say I just want to control. It was Landal and I who talked my brothers and sisters as well as the other Fates into forming the foundation of the Otherworld. You cannot possibly know what that entails. What responsibility that involves."

There was a lot to unpack in his little speech, but my tolerance for his dismissive attitude had worn thin.

"Listen up, Racul, can I call you Racul?" I say, not waiting for him to answer. "Things will go a lot better between us if you drop this bullshit about my age, okay? You think because you've been around a few more years you're so much wiser? So much better? And yet here we are, dealing with dead dragons and a world apocalypse because you and your sibs can't find a way to get along." His eyes narrow at that, but I don't give him time to respond. I'm too pissed. "You keep this world stuck in the dark age. You prohibit advancement. You don't take care of the most vulnerable of your population. You disparage anyone who disagrees with you. You don't listen to anyone but yourself. You've become so myopic you don't even see that you are destroying the very thing you created."

When I finish, I'm nearly out of breath. My cheeks are flushed and I'm riled up.

I wait expectantly for him to say something.

But instead, he leans over and kisses me.

What the hell?

His lips are hot, searing, and burn straight through me, and I respond to him for a moment, drawn into his fire and power, but then I regain my senses, pull back and slap him across the face.

I think it hurts my hand more than his face. And he doesn't look at all phased or apologetic.

"What the hell was that!"

My body is tingling, and I don't even know what to do with all the emotions roiling through me like lava.

"It has been a long time since a woman spoke to me like that," he says, glancing at the statue again.

"That doesn't entitle you to my lips," I say, softening slightly but still low key pissed.

"Forgive me. I am too accustomed to getting what I want." He doesn't look sorry, though. Just arrogant.

"No shit. That's abundantly clear, and part of the problem. You created this world, but you don't own the people in it," I say. "You have to change with the times. Learn and grow. I'm always so stunned at how little self-development you long-lived beings accomplish. Humans have got you beat in that, for your information. For all that you criticize our puny mortal life spans, most of us bust our asses to grow and learn and accomplish as much as we can in that time. You, for all your lofty greatness, have done what in the last thousand years? How have you changed? Grown? What have you learned?"

He looks lost in thought, and then his lips twitch into a smile. "I was about to say that Landal would have liked you, and then I realized you two were close once. She shared your zeal for the downtrodden and abused. This world was actually her idea. She was tired of seeing so many of the magical community hunted and killed just for being different. She had a vision of a world where all could live in safety."

His words give me pause. "Did...did you know *me*...the me back then?"

"Only casually. I never saw your face, as I said. Or the Crone Fate. She spoke about the two of you from time to time, but Fate business and Dragon business were things we didn't share with each other freely. When we were together, we tried to let go of that and just be us."

"How did she die?" I ask, recalling what Ifi said before I came here.

Racul looks at Landal's statue, his expression almost heartbreaking. It is the look of a man trying hard to control emotions that he's suppressed for too many years. Emotions of love, pain, loss, betrayal, anger.

On impulse, I take his hand. It burns hot in my own but doesn't hurt me. He looks down at our hands, and I think he's about to pull away, but instead he squeezes mine and turns his gaze back to me.

"The truth of her death has never been uncovered," he says. "But I know what happened."

I bite my tongue to keep from asking more questions. I have a feeling if I wait, he'll speak more freely than if I interrogate him. He looks as if he's standing on the edge of his past, waiting to fall into it.

The silence lingers between us. Something scurries in the shadows across the room, disturbing the cobwebs. Dust mites dance in the fractals of light cast by the candles. The stagnant air settles around us. Still I wait.

When he finally speaks, his words are hushed, his deep voice laden with pain.

"My mother is a formidable being, as you have seen."

I can't help but snort at that. Understatement of the year.

"She did not support the formation of this world. She feels that dragons are the only pure bloods, and any other beings of magic are bastards, weakened by lesser blood. Not worth our time or energy. Certainly not worth creating an entire world for, abandoning our own in the process."

He pauses, swallowing, lost in thought. "She did not know about my relationship with Landal. Just that we had worked together to convince the others to join our quest. She was livid, but what could she do? We outnumbered her, and she knew if she pushed too hard, she would lose us entirely. So she relented."

He shifts in his seat, pulling my hand closer to him, still holding it tightly as if it's a lifeline for him. On instinct, I send a thread of my magic, the blend of all the elements, to him and I see his skin glow at the contact for just a moment before it fades.

He gapes at me, astonished. "Thank you."

I nod.

He clears his throat. "We celebrated when the world formed. We rejoiced when beings entered here, forming towns, homes, lives. We did our best to set up a fair and just system to manage the growing population. The Fates did not take an active role here, as they still had commitments on your world, but Landal came as frequently as she could to be with me."

I can feel the story shift, feel the tale turn dark as his eyes themselves darken in the telling. "My mother discovered our relationship a few thousand years ago. It all came to a head at a very unfortunate time in our world. There was already a...war with the unicorns. Strange things happening. And then... "

My breath hitches. "Did you mother kill Landal?" I ask.

His golden eyes fill with tears that turn to steam before they can find release. "I've never had proof. But yes, she did."

"Racul," I say, my voice more tender than it was. "Why did you ask me to come here?"

"When I built this memorial for Landal, I had it spelled. My mother does not know of it, and cannot hear or see anything that goes on within these walls. She will not even see that it exists. She will only see a vacant stretch of cemetery land," he says.

"Why?" I ask.

"Because I needed one place in the universe where I was free from her. I am the eldest of my siblings, and until I met Landal and we decided to create the Otherworld, I was in line to succeed my mother in our own world, where only dragons live. We are not the only dragons that exist, but we are the only dragons of the royal line. I was to be king. When I relinquished that to come here, my mother disowned me, and I have never lived up to her expectations since. Similarly, Lyx always defied her. Lyx had a big heart, too big. I feared for her. I was angry at her for leaving the Council, for becoming the Beggar Queen as they called her. Not because she was helping the poor, as many think. But because I knew she was putting herself at risk with our mother."

"Are you saying.... "

"I'm saying, I think my mother killed Lyx for defying her, just as she killed Landal for my defiance. And I think you were never meant to solve this murder. I'm saying, the world is going to end in less than a fortnight, and you should leave now."

Shit. Double triple shit.

"Racul, I can't. The spell…it made me a part of this world. I will die if it is destroyed."

His face shifts subtly, and I'm surprised to see that he actually cares about my fate.

"Then you need to find a way to stop my mother. I will help. But first, we need to go to the Ancient Library. It might hold information, or at least some sort of evidence that could help us take her down."

"What's the Ancient Library?" I ask, my pulse quickening.

"It is a secret place my mother built to hide all her secrets," he says simply.

"Why haven't you already gone?" I ask, my heart fluttering at the thought that we might have a new lead.

"Because only the Fates and my mother are able to open it. I need your help."

I can see how hard it is for him to admit this. "Okay, I'm in. When?"

"Tomorrow morning," he says. "I will pick you up."

"I'll be ready," I say, knowing the Night brothers are going to *looooove* this. Not.

"We will find a way to defeat my mother and save this world. Together."

CHAPTER 10: THE LIBRARY

"I SAID TO THE NIGHT,
"If you are in love with the moon,
it is because you never stay for long."
The night turned to me and said,
"It is not my fault. I never see the Sun,
how can I know that love is endless?"
~Rumi

DATH and I leave the tomb together and he takes my hand once more as we stand outside. "Apologies for stealing a kiss. You reminded me so much of her, it was...well, it doesn't matter. You're right. You're not mine to claim."

My heart feels a pang of regret that his relationship ended the way it did. It seems he's not found love again since. "It's not too late to find companionship once more," I say. "You have a long life ahead of you. Let yourself open up to something new again. I think she would want that for you."

He tilts his head. "Is that from memory?"

"No," I say. "But it's what I would want for someone that I loved. It's what I would want for you."

"Be safe, Miss Oliver. I will see you tomorrow."

He pulls away from me and transforms into a giant red dragon, fire sparking from his mouth. He gives me a brief nod and flies away, disappearing into the Dragon's Breath-covered sky.

I glance back at the mausoleum where I know Sebastian is sitting in Ifi and Elal's home, worried sick. Poor guy. I close my eyes and teleport to their apartment.

I rematerialize…awkwardly, landing in Sebastian's lap, as he's still sitting on the couch where I left him.

He grunts, catching me and preventing me from hitting my head on the edge of the metal and glass coffee table.

"I'm so sorry," I say, my arms wrapped around his neck to keep from falling.

He tightens his grip on me rather than letting me go. "I'm not," he says softly, his forest green eyes locked on mine.

"We have not stopped talking about you," Ifi says, with an excited clap of his hands. "Your powers are on fleek!"

I laugh and scoot off Sebastian to stand and stretch. "Thanks."

I give the Earth Druid a meaningful glance. "We should head home. There's a lot to discuss."

He raises an eyebrow and stands while I hug the guys and thank them for everything. "Any luck on the baby front?" I ask, knowing they are trying to adopt.

Ifi grins. "We might have a lead. But it's too soon to tell. Crossing fingers and toes. The need is real. My biological clock is ticking."

"Calm yourself, love. We are immortal. There is no clock," Elal says.

"Okay, Boomer," Ifi says, and I nearly die.

"Ifi, love, that's not quite what that means," I say, through fits of giggles. "But solid effort."

We leave and I'm still laughing as we head back to the carriage. "He's a crack up."

"They are quite entertaining," Sebastian agrees. "Now, tell me, what happened."

"First off, you're not going to like a lot of what I say, but I need you to chill, okay?"

He glares at me.

"Sebastian, I need your word."

With a huff he relents. "Fine. Tell me."

We climb into the carriage and Mable spurs the horses into movement.

Once we are on our way, I tell him everything. Including the kiss.

Sebastian clutches his hands into fists but doesn't say anything until I'm done.

"I know if I forbid you to go to the Ancient Library tomorrow, you'll just do it anyways," he says after a moment of silence.

I smile. "You're finally learning."

He narrows his eyes at me but continues. "You and Elijah should hit the books tonight to see what you can learn about it before you go. There might be traps. Spells. Best to get as much information as you can, for protection at least."

I'm about to say that Racul will be there too, but I don't think Sebastian will find that as reassuring as I intend it to be. Quite the contrary, so I keep my mouth shut.

When we get home, Lily arrives at the same time, and she grins when she sees us.

"I've missed your face," I say, reaching to hug her as she approaches.

"Yours too," she says. "Which is why I thought I should come home, at least for a few days."

I tilt my head at her. "Is everything okay with Kaya?"

"Oh, totally. She's going to swing by later to stay in my tree for a bit. Seems only fair."

"That's wonderful," I say.

We enter the house together and Liam and Elijah greet us with exhausted enthusiasm.

"Thank the gods you all are home. These kids are running us ragged."

Lily laughs. "Kaya and I can take care of them tonight. Give you a break."

The gratitude evident on their faces makes me laugh out loud. "Come on guys, it couldn't have been that bad."

"Alina burned down a tree. And Zara nearly flooded a village."

I gasp and Elijah raises a hand. "I stopped her. I used wind to move the water, but now we have a new lake."

"How's Ana?" I ask.

"Already in bed," Liam says. "She was lovely, though a little sad that her 'friend' hadn't come to see her recently."

I shake my head sadly. "She must have led such a hard, lonely life. At least when I lost my dad, I still had Adam. We might have been in and out of foster homes, but we always had each other. Poor girl. Even her imaginary friend isn't always there for her."

Liam nods. "I think being here is good for her. She's surrounded by a family and love. Healing will take time, but like the body, the soul can heal with the right ingredients."

I've always been intrigued by the juxtaposition of Liam's hot-headed anger and his heart and skill for healing. He really should have gotten the water element, but he's made it work.

"How are the babies?" I ask.

Liam rolls his eyes dramatically. "They will be the death of me. I thought one was a handful. Two is triple the damage, especially when one can turn into a dragon and fly."

Elijah chuckles. "I had to keep using my air power to prevent Zara from flying away entirely."

"Sounds like you two had an exciting day. How about we all get dinner and I'll tell you my news?"

Dinner for them will be blood. But I need real food. As if to prove my point, my stomach begins to rumble.

"Where are the kids?" Lily asks.

"I got them to bed, but those babies won't stay asleep. I tried separating them but then they scream and cry, so...I don't know what to do," Liam says, looking despondent.

Lily giggles. "I'll take care of it." She heads upstairs while we settle into the library.

Elijah brings me a tray with steak, potatoes, green beans and a fresh salad. "This is normal meat, yes? Nothing weird...or talking?"

You really can't be too careful about the meat in this world, I've learned.

"I would never feed you anything else," he assures me. I smile and thank him and dig in.

"Where's Derek?" I ask.

Liam shrugs. "He hasn't come home yet. Hopefully he's chasing down a lead."

This is when cell phones would be super handy. I don't often think of the things I gave up to live in the Otherworld, but every once in a while the thought crosses my mind when a modern convenience could solve a host of problems.

Also, I miss him. After last night, I find myself thinking about his lips…and other body parts at random. I'm looking forward to another round with the Water druid.

Pulling my mind out of the…water…I tell the remaining brothers about my meeting with Racul.

They are stunned silent.

"I told her this is a bad idea," Sebastian says.

No one disagrees with him, but I see the spark of intrigue in Elijah's eyes, so I pounce. "Have you heard of the Ancient Library?" I ask the Air Druid.

"Not specifically, but there have always been rumors of a secret library filled with cursed spells and dangerous magic. If you really do get in, please take notes on everything you find and bring back as much as you can. That's a gold mine." He pauses, his pale blue eyes full of thought. "I should go with you," he says finally.

"I wish you could, but that wasn't part of the deal. I'm not sure Racul will be okay with anyone else coming."

"Racul isn't to be trusted," Liam says, his eyes blazing.

Oh the irony that the Fire Druid and Fire Dragon, both sexy, arrogant hot heads, hate each other so much.

But Racul did try to execute Liam for a crime he didn't commit not so long ago, so I don't blame him.

"This isn't about trust. He doesn't want the world to end. Neither do I."

Sebastian opens his mouth to say something, but I shake my head.

Not right now. I don't want to explain to everyone else what's at stake. I probably shouldn't have even told him, but I needed someone to confide in. I won't deny I'm scared. But I'm not trying to save the world just to save my own life. There are many lives on the line, and I need the Nights focused on that, not on me.

Sebastian clamps his mouth shut and frowns at me.

"It sounds to me like Racul has mommy issues," Liam says, still pissed. About the kiss or the whole thing, I have no idea. Probably everything. It doesn't take much to rile him up, in or out of the bedroom.

"That may be, but if the Mother of Dragons is behind it all, how do we handle this? You guys nearly had a fit at the thought of me going up against her, but we will have to if she tries to destroy the Otherworld. So, any ideas how to defeat her?"

Elijah stands. "I need to do some more research. On the library and on dragons. When reading up on how to take care of Zara, I came across some references to other books which I have since acquired yet haven't had a chance to read. I'll get on that now."

I'm done with my dinner and set the tray aside, standing. "I'll join you. Two eyes are better than one."

He smiles. "Your mind—and company—will be much appreciated."

As we leave, Sebastian pulls me aside, holding my hand. "Why don't you want me telling them?"

"Because they need to focus, and so do we. We'll tell them if we have no choice."

"Fine. But we have to tell them eventually."

"Not if we save the world," I say with a wink and a nonchalance I'm totally faking.

I find Elijah already bent over a stack of books at a table in his office library. I sit across from him and without looking, he pushes a pile to me. I take a quill and parchment and open up the first book in the pile. I basically have a photographic memory, so the notes are more for Elijah than for me.

I speed read the first book, but nothing stands out as helpful other than one story of a dragon killed by its own reflection in a children's myth. It seems sketchy at best as reliable information, but I take notes anyways and move on.

Several hours pass and my neck cramps before I set another book down to stretch. Elijah is gone, and reappears moments later with a plate of fresh chocolate chip cookies. "I know they're your favorite. I thought you could use the sugar."

"You are my favorite person in the world right now," I say as I munch on one. "Seriously, I wish you could still enjoy food. These are the bomb."

When only crumbs are left on the plate, Elijah stands behind me and massages my shoulders.

"Oh my god, that feels amazing."

"You're tense. I shouldn't have kept you up this late. You have an early morning."

"I know, but this is important. One of these books might hold some useful information," I say. Though so far none have yielded much. My parchment only has a few notes on it and none particularly relevant.

His massage finishes, leaving me much more relaxed, and I stand and lean against the table to face him, half sitting on it as I do. "We have the unicorn dagger," I say. "That could kill her, couldn't it? If it came to it?"

He takes a step closer to me, and I'm reminded again of how delicious Elijah really is, with his silver blue eyes and perfect porcelain skin. He's tall and lean, with a chiseled body that would be the envy of any underwear model. When he takes a step closer to me, it becomes a little harder to breathe.

"Theoretically it could," he says. "But the challenge would be getting it into her heart without her killing you first. From all accounts, she is the most powerful being in the world. In any world actually."

He comes closer still, and lifts a finger to wipe at my lower lip. "You had a bit of chocolate there," he says softly, his eyes dropping to study me—all of me.

"I know I've told you this before," he says. "But I've never known a woman—or anyone—like you. And I'm not talking about your powers. I'm talking about your mind. And your heart." He pauses, as if considering his words. "I have lived in my head so long, it has distanced me from my emotions. I considered them a weakness to overcome, rather than a necessary part of my being."

He brushes a stray hair out of my face as he studies me. "But you. You have the mind of a genius. Unparalleled. Even by me, if I'm being honest. And yet it hasn't numbed you to your heart. You still care. You are still full of compassion. And…Eve, you made me feel. You made my heart beat again—metaphorically of course."

I chuckle at that. "Of course."

"What I'm trying to say is, I know I'm not the most expressive or romantic person, but I am drawn to you like I have never been to anyone before in my very long life. I hope you know I would do anything for you. Sacrifice anything for you."

And in that moment, I know that if the Air Druid doesn't kiss me soon, I will throw him to the table and make shit happen myself.

But he surprises me and makes the first move, leaning in to claim my lips.

The touch is just a breath between us, stirring my air magic as he deepens the kiss into something that blows through me and leaves me weak-kneed. He lifts me up to the table and spreads my legs to press himself between them as he runs his hands down my back, clutching my ass to pull me closer.

His breath hitches as my hand slides down between us.

Then it's my turn to lose my breath as I feel the length and girth of what's being offered.

He grins into my mouth. "I take it that's satisfactory?"

"It'll do," I joke, and he lifts me from the table, my legs straddling him, his muscles bulging as he carries me to the middle of his office where a bear skin rug is spread out before the fire. He lowers me to the rug carefully and once he does, he pulls off his shirt.

I admire the ripples of muscles and run my hands over his abs, then raise my own arms so he can help me undress.

"Gods you are beautiful," he says as my breasts are freed.

I lie back as he tugs off my pants and underwear, and I return the favor until we are both naked, the light of the fire dancing over our skin.

He lies beside me and uses his mouth and hands to memorize every inch of my body. With air magic he teases and tickles my most sensitive spots, creating a delicious tension within me that builds and builds like a tornado at my center.

Then I take control, pressing his back to the rug as I straddle him, teasing his hardness before I move up his body to feel his tongue.

And feel it I do.

He takes me in his mouth with such passion and attention to detail that I have to pace myself to keep from losing it too soon.

Finally, I can no longer handle more, and my body is pushed over the edge, into sheer bliss.

Without hesitation, he readjusts my hips to his own, and as I slide onto him, I moan and melt into the pleasure he brings with his every thrust. His hands hold my hips, while his magic explores my breasts.

On impulse, I channel my own air magic and use it to push us off the ground, so that we are both hovering in flight as we make love. He joins his magic to mine and the intimacy and connection from this shared elemental power is intoxicating. I feel drunk on it, on him.

When I fall over the edge again, he joins me and together we soar.

We slowly fall back to the carpet and with deep satiation, fall asleep in each other's arms.

CHAPTER 11: THE PAST

THE CHANGING heart turns evermore
  And changes that of more and more
  Now I see forever lost
  These broken things of little cost
  ~Neil Stevens, The Changing Heart

I WAKE in Elijah's arms, his breath on my neck as he spoons me in front of a dying fire. I send a spark of fire magic to fan the flames, giving the room a much-needed burst of warmth, then turn over to face him, our legs entangling underneath a feathered blanket. He must have brought it at some point in the night. I kiss him tenderly on his lips, and he stirs, waking, kissing me back.

A banging on the office door interrupts our moment. "Derek's home and has news," Liam shouts through the door, then takes off down the hall, probably to get everyone else.

I groan my disappointment and pull out of his arms reluctantly. "Guess we'd better get dressed," I say.

He sighs. "I prefer you this way," he admits with a boyish grin.

"But I suppose you are right. I wish we'd found more that could help you today. I'll keep looking while you're gone."

I kiss him and let my lips linger as he cups my ass and grows hard against my stomach. "You're not making this easy," I say against his mouth.

"I blame you entirely," he says, smiling and releasing me. "But alas I am a patient man. Let's go see what Derek found."

I collect my clothes from last night, and rather than putting them on and trudging through the castle, I have a better idea. "I'm going to dematerialize, so don't be alarmed."

"I've wanted to see this," he admits.

Still naked with an arm full of clothes, I close my eyes and imagine my bathroom.

And just like that, I'm there.

Damn, I love this.

I shower the sex and the previous days romp through the cemetery off me and dress in a clean outfit, then meet the brothers in the dining room, where the children are finishing up breakfast.

Alina is in Liam's arms with a milky bottle of blood, Zara is on the floor with her grilled shark, and Ana is in a chair eating pancakes with syrup and blueberries.

"Yum, that looks good," I tell her.

She grins through syrupy lips. "It is!"

"I'll have what she's having," I announce to whatever ghosts are listening, but it's Matilda herself who comes out carrying more freshly made pancakes.

"Thank you," I say, accepting my plate. " I feel like we haven't spent much time together recently," I tell her as she sits next to Ana across from me.

"It is a strange time," she says ominously. "Join me for tea when you have a moment. Let us catch up."

"I will," I promise. With this ticking time bomb over my head, I'm becoming more aware of how precious these relationships are and how important it is to make time for the people I love, no matter what else is going on.

"What are you kids up to today?" Matilda asks.

"Research," Elijah says, sharing a meaningful glance with me.

"I'm going to try to get into the Ancient Library," I say. "Have you heard of it?"

Matilda's eyes widen, and then Alina begins crying and Zara joins her.

"Oh my," Matilda says, standing. "Let me take the babies upstairs so you kids can have your meeting."

Ana finishes up her last pancake and helps by picking up Zara, who clings to her. The five of them head upstairs, leaving me with the Night brothers.

Derek has been pacing, waiting until the kids were gone to speak.

"What did you find?" I finally ask, once we are completely alone.

"This," he says, holding out a Memory Catcher.

My heart nearly stops in my chest. "What does it show?" I ask.

"The murder," he says.

"Holy shit. How?"

He runs a hand through his hair, and I realize how disheveled he appears. He normally looks like he just stepped off the cover of GQ but this morning his hair is a mess, he's got a day old stubble covering his chin and his clothes are dusty and torn in places.

"I've been up all night hunting," he says. "Looking for animals that might have seen what happened. I must have caught the memories of every wildlife in the area until it occurred to me to try the fish in the pond where she was found."

He looks exasperated with himself for not thinking of that one sooner, and I let our water magic connect, giving him a little boost of love and confidence. His gaze lands on mine and he grins just a little as acknowledgement.

"Don't keep us in suspense, brother. Who killed her? If it was Dath'Racul I'll ring his neck myself," Liam says.

Derek frowns. "It wasn't the Fire Dragon."

He lays the crystal down and activates it.

I hold my breath as the holographic image starts to play and we see Lyx standing near the pool of water talking to someone, though we can't see who it is.

She looks happy. Excited. Probably about the work that's being done for her people. We were just about to move some families into their new homes that day.

Then there's a blur.

Lyx screams.

And a monstrous creature appears, reflected oddly through the water. It's golden and black, with malformed wings, a body covered in boils, a head that is misshapen with eyes too small and too wide apart, and a mouth too big. But what stands out the most is the protrusion coming from the side of its head. It's the exact size and shape of a unicorn horn, though it doesn't much resemble one in color and form.

The creature's wings expand, and it crashes into Lyx, impaling her with its horn and shoving her into the water, where she falls.

Then the memory ends.

"The fish swam away when Lyx fell into the lake."

We all sit in stunned silence. "So, Racul is wrong, it wasn't his mother. It wasn't any of the dragons. But...what *is* that creature?" I look around the table hoping one of the brothers can shed some light on this.

Derek shrugs. "I've never seen or heard about anything like this in my life."

Well, shit. That's not good. "Elijah?"

"I've never come across anything like it in life or in my books. It's...a bit curious. We have lived in both worlds for many lifetimes and have represented and come across beings of all kinds. It seems unlikely there would be one we have never at least heard of." He hesitates a moment before saying, "Perhaps you can find something about it in the Ancient Library, if you're able to get in."

"Can I take that with me to show Racul?" I ask Derek.

None of them look thrilled at the idea but I persist. "He's a dragon. He might know something you don't. At the very least, it will show him it wasn't his mother. And if that's true, then maybe I don't have to find a way of fighting and defeating the Mother of Dragons in order to save this world."

"That is the good news," Sebastian agrees. "But Elijah, you should continue to research just in case. I still don't trust her. And if we have to go up against her, we need to be prepared."

"Agreed," Elijah says.

There's a knock at the door, and I stand. "I think my ride is here. Wish me luck."

I can tell none of them want to let me go, but we all know I have no choice.

Racul greets me when I open the door. "Have I arrived too early?" he asks.

"Nope. I'm ready to roll," I say, closing the door behind me. "How far is this place?" I ask as I look around for his carriage, but none is in sight.

"Too far for horses. You will ride me," he says, shifting into dragon form.

"Yeah, um, as tempting as that offer is," I say trying not to laugh. "I can actually fly, so let's try that first?"

"You think you can keep up with a dragon?" he scoffs, his voice even deeper now.

"Why don't we do this thing and find out?"

"Very well, Fate. But I'll be here when you tire."

Oof, the arrogance.

Racul takes off into the sky and I summon my magic to follow him.

He continues to accelerate, pushing his speed faster and faster. I'm pretty sure he's just trying to show off, but he doesn't know who he's messing with. I wrap air around me, using fire to stay warm, using light and darkness to give me an extra edge, and I keep pace side by side with him. I even give him a thumbs up when he glances my way, an incredulous look on his dragon face.

We fly like this for some time, and I do start to tire out, but I can't give him the satisfaction of knowing, so I push harder, determined that he and I will arrive together, as equals, and he can shut his mouth about it all. We are heading west and soon begin to pass over areas I've never been, though I recall these parts from the maps I studied in Elijah's office. Somewhere around here is giant territory, though I see no evidence of them at present.

And then we reach a place that doesn't exist on any maps I've seen.

A body of water that spans miles, with an isolated island stuck in the center. That appears to be our destination.

When he finally begins his descent, I'm so relieved I nearly cry, but I land like a boss and grin like it was nothing.

He shifts back into human form, and I pretend like I'm not completely exhausted.

"I was not expecting that," he says, a curious look on his face.

I'm pretty sure he keeps seeing his dead girlfriend in me, which is a bit creepy but also super sad, so I give him a pass and instead ask, "Where now?"

We are in a dense jungle in the middle of an island that looks like it shouldn't exist. The temperature is sweltering so I use my air magic to cool myself. Vines coil around tall trees and fall from thick branches like snakes waiting to snap. The dense undergrowth is teeming with a hidden world of insects. A canopy of lush foliage blocks out the view of the sky, and in the distance a strange kind of shriek that might be a monkey calls out.

Racul points west and I can see through the trees the ruins of an old castle that looks like nothing more than crumbled stone at this point. I follow the Fire Dragon to a spot in the center, stepping over heavy roots that have taken over the area, my boots sinking into the decomposing plant life of the jungle.

He points to an area thick with vines and undergrowth. "There should be a door here that only you and my mother can open."

I nod and use my earth magic to clear everything away, revealing a circular metal door with a handprint in the center. I place my hand on it, but nothing happens.

"Um, do you know what I'm supposed to do?" I ask.

"I've never actually seen it opened," he says. "Though I have tried myself."

Shit.

First, I go with Liam's approach to life. I try to blow shit up.

The fire ball lands on the metal door and fizzes out, having zero effect.

"I'm not impressed," Racul says, dryly.

"Good thing I'm not actually trying to impress you," I say.

Next I use my air and water magic it to create lightning that I zap from my hands, but again, nothing.

"This is getting us nowhere," the impatient dragon says.

I step aside and gesture to the door. "Would you like to try?"

He glares at me but says nothing.

"I didn't think so."

I kneel down again, studying the handprint. "Maybe if I channel my power into this?" I say, thinking out loud.

Pressing my hand against the cold metal, I rotate through my elemental powers, but none of them work, and I'm getting a headache.

"This was a long trip for nothing," Racul says under his breath.

"You can shut it now," I say, pinching the bridge of my nose. There's one thing I still haven't tried.

Closing my eyes, I channel all six elements at once into the door, and finally I'm rewarded with a series of clicks and the sound of grinding as the cool metal beneath my palm falls away, revealing a long ladder into a dark hole.

"About time," Racul says.

I scowl at him. "How long did it take you to get in?"

He doesn't respond to that, but instead peers down into the darkness. "Ladies first," he says.

"Age before beauty," I say, and he frowns, but begins the decent.

I'm not ashamed to say that if there's a trap in there, I'd rather let him deal with it first.

"All clear, you can come down now," he shouts from below.

I descend quickly, cheating with some magic. It's dark and dank and I wonder how any books survived in these conditions. I hold out my palm and produce an orb of light to guide us through the tunnel. I have no idea if dragons can see in the dark, but it doesn't seem to be one of my superpowers.

We arrive at another door at the end of the long hallway, and it has another handprint on it. I sigh at the excessiveness of it all and use my palm and magic to open it.

It's pitch black within, so I shoot hundreds of orbs of light into the room to illuminate our way, and we both gasp at the same time at what we see.

The library is huge, and was clearly lined with thousands of books and scrolls. But it's been ransacked. If I didn't know better, I'd say tomb raiders have been here.

Everything is torn apart and all the books and whatever artifacts may have been preserved in the glass cabinets are gone.

Racul walks in, his eyes wide. "Who could have done this?"

"Logically, if only the Fates and your mother could gain access, and the Fates have been gone for thousands of years...then... "

His face is grim at the thought. "She did this to cover her crimes."

Oh right. "Speaking of, I meant to tell you. I have a Memory Catcher of Lyx's death. It wasn't your mother."

"Show me," he says.

I pull it out and play it for him. He watches silently and when it's over he just shakes his head. "I still believe she is behind it. Somehow. Maybe she is controlling the creature?" he asks.

"Or maybe she didn't do it, and we need to be looking at this differently. Do you know what manner of being this is?" I ask.

He shakes his head. "I have never seen something like that in my life. It appears to have traits of a dragon and maybe a unicorn, but that does not make sense. Our species cannot interbreed. It is impossible. Besides that, it is clearly the product of some great evil, which neither dragons or unicorns are."

His logic seems a little self-serving and flawed, but I can't deny this creature seems to defy the natural order according to everyone who knows about such things.

"Let's look around," I say, disappointment flooding me as I realize I'd hung all my hopes on finding answers here, and now they were as useful as dead butterflies pinned to a cork board for display. Still, I hold onto what optimism I can summon. "Maybe we will find something."

He looks as doubtful as I feel. The place, after all, has been well and truly ransacked, but still we begin sorting through the scarps that remain.

There are a few books left, but they offer nothing useful. I'm not sure why they were kept here at all, to be honest. *A History of Cheese in Northern Europe*, for example, which looks brought over from my world. Like, okay, thanks. That's super-secret shit to save in an underground Ancient Library. Still, I add it to my bag in case Elijah finds it interesting.

I spend another hour scouring every inch of the place, and in a dusty corner under a thick coating of cobwebs I discover a trunk that looks promising. "Racul, check it out."

He saunters over, his face reflecting my own lack of success. But something in this chest feels important. My magic is tingling in my fingertips, and I use that power to unlock the trunk and open it.

The only thing inside is a deep velvet purple cloak with silver trim and embroidery, and a mother of pearl clasp that holds it at the neck.

I pull it out, shaking off the dust, and hold it up.

Racul 's eyes narrow. "I recognize that," he says. "It belonged to the Maiden Fate."

Me.

This was mine?

Or my past self at any rate.

I drape it over my shoulders and I am thrown into a memory that feels so vivid, it's as if I could be living it right now.

I stand next to my sisters. They are not sisters by blood, I know this, but by power, by destiny, by Fate. We are the Fates and we are draped in our royal robes. I wear purple, the Crone wears emerald green, and the Mother wears sapphire blue. We have silver masks that cover our faces, allowing us to keep our mystery, and we stand before the Mother of Dragons, who is angry, but I do not remember why.

We turn to leave, and once we are alone, the Mother takes off her mask, and I see the beautiful face of Landal, her blue eyes that match her robes glistening with tears. "We have made a grave mistake in what we have done," she says.

The Crone nods. "It is as you say. We should never have agreed to this."

I take off my mask and see in a mirror my own face, similar to what it is now.

And then the Crone removes her mask, and my present self gasps as I collapse to my knees.

The face unveiled before me is one I know.

One I trust.

I am looking at the face of Matilda Night.

CHAPTER 12: THE MONSTER

"We delight in the beauty of the butterfly, but rarely admit the changes it has gone through to achieve that beauty."
  ~Maya Angelou

Racul insists on returning with me to the castle, though I'm not sure his presence will make this conversation go easier. Since time is of the essence, and I need to know what the hell is going on, I suggest teleporting us both.

"I prefer to fly," he says.

"That's fine. But I'm not going to wait for you, though."

He pauses, clearly torn between wanting to be a part of the conversation, and not wanting to trust me with dematerializing him.

"Clock's ticking, buddy. I'm leaving now." I have the cloak—my cloak—stuck in my bag. Touching it, holding it, feels like connecting with a part of myself I'm still trying to find.

And Matilda must have known this whole time who, and what, I was. Why didn't she tell me? Why didn't she help me? Why has she kept her identity a secret?

Racul cocks his head, studying me. "You feel betrayed. But you must know, the Fates' identities were never revealed to anyone. Not even my mother knew who they were. Nor did the Druids. Their secrets are what kept them safe."

"Except I am a Fate. She knew that. She could have told me." I pause. "And besides, Landal told you, didn't she?"

He glances away. "And that trust ended her life."

My own feelings give way to compassion as I see the hurt he carries with him. He's a giant ass. He has been ever since I've known him. But he's also someone in pain, like all of us. Someone who lost a person he loved. I can relate to that. My brother's death still tears at the fabric of my soul on a daily basis, though it's getting easier to bear, if easier is the right word.

I take a step closer to him. "You don't know that for sure," I say. "And even if it's true, I believe she would still make the same choice, to share the life she had with you while she could. I don't remember much of my time as a Fate, but I do know that life is never guaranteed, even for immortals. And spending your days hiding behind a mask is no way to live. She had love. She gave love. That's a lot for any life," I say. "Really, that's everything."

He sucks in a breath. "Take me with you," he says. "Just try not to kill us both."

I grin. "I'll do my best, but no promises."

I take his hand and close my eyes, this time avoiding the gardens and instead imagining the open area in front of the house. In a flash, we arrive, and Racul staggers as we land. I steady him and smile at the fact that I didn't send us anywhere too terrible.

"That was...awful," he says.

"It was rough my first time too," I say. "You get used to it."

"I will not be doing this again to get used to it," he says in a clipped bass voice.

We walk into the castle and find Liam first. The dragon and the Druid stare each other down, heat building in the room and their bodies sizzling with fire.

"Settle down boys. Bigger fish to fry right now." I turn to Liam. "Where's Matilda? And where's everyone else?"

Liam doesn't stop staring Racul down as he answers me. "My

brothers are around here somewhere. Lily and Kaya are at the grove. The babies are napping, and Matilda is upstairs with Ana. Why? What's wrong?"

I don't answer, I just head straight to Matilda's room, my heart and head at war for how to approach the woman I have come to love like a grandmother.

Along the way, we seem to collect the remaining brothers, who are all wondering what's going on and why we have one of the dragons in our house.

Matilda sits in her rocking chair in front of the fire, a cup of tea at her side. Green beads woven into her gray hair. Her eyes heavy and dark. Ana is napping with a new doll Lily made her in the corner on a mat. As soon as Matilda sees my face, she knows.

She stands and gestures for us to leave so we don't disturb Ana's nap.

"The girl hasn't been sleeping well," Matilda says. "She has night terrors every evening. She can only seem to get any rest during the day."

We walk down the hall into a sitting room that's seldom used. It has a large glass door that leads to a spacious balcony overlooking one of the gardens with overstuffed chairs and couches that are arranged for conversation in the center of the room, and a fireplace in the corner to ward off the chill that all castles inherently have. Thick rugs cover the stone floor and tapestries of gardens hang on the walls. Matilda and I sit across from each other. Liam and Sebastian sit on either side of me, Elijah takes a chair by the fire, and Derek and Racul flank Matilda on the other couch. It's an incongruous group, and we are awkward with each other.

"Why?" I ask. "Why didn't you tell me?"

The Night brothers look to each other in silent question, then to me to find out what I'm talking about. My relationship with their grandmother has always been affectionate, loving, close. They've never seen me upset with her.

Matilda sighs sadly. "I wanted to. Many times. I tried. But I have spent thousands of years keeping my identity a secret. And when I saw you, when you responded to the ad, I just couldn't believe it. At first, I thought it must be an unlikely coincidence. What were the odds that the Maiden Fate would return in the human world, so unprepared for her own life and powers? Then your magic began to manifest, and I couldn't deny the truth, but I convinced myself it would be better for you not to know."

"I'm confused," Liam says, looking between the two of us.

"That seems a common state for you," Racul says snidely.

I glare at the dragon and then look to Liam, waiting to see if Matilda will fill him in.

"My boys, there is something I have been keeping from you for many years." She pauses, the truth clearly so hard to say, even now. "I am the Crone Fate."

Her words land like a live bomb in the room, and no one speaks, so she continues.

"When my sisters died, I went into hiding and gave up my role as Fate, instead, committing to my life as Matilda alone."

Liam sits stone faced, his emotions burning deep within him. I can feel the flare of his fire, his anger, pain, confusion. The tether between us lights up with it, and I send along a soothing stream of water and air magic to calm him.

Sebastian is stoic, as always, pushing his feelings down deep. Elijah is curious but I feel the strain of hurt underneath, and Derek is awash in deep and roiling emotion that he's barely holding onto.

But I understand their feelings. I haven't known Matilda nearly as long as they have; their betrayal must feel much greater. Especially given all the shit that went down with the Fates. I know my past self-role in their lives wasn't stellar. I made Cole's brothers torture and punish him. Or she did. It's so hard to see that person as myself, when she did things I couldn't imagine ever doing.

And why didn't Matilda stop that from happening? What role did she have in all that?

I feel even worse as I recall their story of being banished from the Order and destroyed with the Unforgivable Curse. They never said who cast the curse, but it must have been the Fates. That would make the most sense. Does that mean Matilda and I were responsible for their descent into madness? For their destruction of villages, animals, and lives?

A wave of nausea overtakes me and I sit forward, my head pulsing with heat and pain. A flash hits me but I can't quite grasp it. I'm too overwhelmed by grief for the karmic pain I've wrought.

Liam puts a hand on my back. "Are you sick?"

I look up at him, my eyes filled with tears. "I am so sorry for what we did to you back then."

He frowns. "That wasn't you. Not really." He looks over to Matilda. "But it *was* you. *You* are still the same person you were. You didn't stop the Mother Fate when she cursed us. You didn't stop the Maiden when she made us punish our own brother. You knew us. And you didn't protect us."

The other three brothers are silent, letting Liam speak their rage for them.

Tears fill the old woman's eyes. "I should have done more. I did what I could behind the scenes. It wasn't enough, but I tried. I was one voice amongst three and towards the end we didn't agree on a lot. Landal—the Mother—she wanted to kill Cole for what he did. And she wanted to kill all of you when you rebelled. When you stopped doing what you were told."

"Death would have been a kindness compared to what was done to us," he says, the fire leaving him as sadness takes its place. "We destroyed so many lives because of that curse."

"I know, my boy," Matilda says. "I know. And I cannot be more sorry for my role in all of it. But I couldn't let any of you die. I loved you all too much."

I glance at Racul and his face is impassive. Hard. I wonder what he knew about Landal's role in all of this. Or if he even cares about any of this.

I take Liam's hand in mine, holding it tight, letting him know he's not alone. Not anymore. Not ever again.

As reluctant as I am to change the focus of this conversation, I know I must. We haven't a lot of time. "Matilda, I had a vision when I was at the library. The three Fates were together after a confrontation with the Mother of Dragons. It seemed we all regretted something we'd done. What did we do?"

Matilda gasps and puts her hand to her mouth. "We can never speak of that. It doesn't matter. It was destroyed."

"What was?" I ask.

"The abomination we helped create."

A sinking feeling fills my gut and I pull the Memory Catcher out of my pocket and play the memory for Matilda. When it comes to the creature that killed Lyx, I pause it. "Was that what we made?"

Matilda's eyes widen. "It's not possible. It was destroyed. The Mother of Dragons knew what she'd done was wrong. She…"

"This is what killed Lyx," I say. "You must tell me the truth. What is this creature?"

Gods, if only I could remember myself.

"It's time you knew everything," she says. "The Mother of Dragons was in love with the Queen of the Unicorns. They wanted a child together, but their races could not mate, nor could two females. So, they petitioned the Fates to help them merge their magic into a child."

I can see my own emotions reflected on the faces of the others. None of them knew about this, though Racul certainly suspected his mother had been up to shady shit. But this? Gods be damned, how stupid could they all be? That was clearly a recipe for poison cookies right there. And I was a part of this? I was a moron.

"So that clearly didn't go well," I say.

"No, it didn't." She rubs her eyes. "What we made…well, you've seen. It was…monstrous."

"And my mother killed it?" Racul asks.

"Yes," Matilda says. "Or so we thought."

Pain lances through my brain and I grip Liam's hand tighter as a flash rushes through me. "Something is coming," I whisper through gritted teeth, but before anyone can do anything about it, the door to our room explodes in shards of splintered wood and the most hideous creature I've ever seen bursts in, sharp teeth dripping with saliva, yellow eyes crazed.

It's so much worse in person than in the memory, I realize.

Matilda stands and pulls out a wand from her robes, channeling her magic through it to blast the monster with an electric bolt.

It absorbs the impact of the attack and seems to grow stronger from it. The horn on the side of its head spins like a drill, and its wings extend, propelling it through the room. I'm still too sick to be of much help, my brain feeling as if it will explode.

Liam hits it with a blaze of fire, but once again, the attack has no impact other than seeming to make it stronger and faster. It now crackles with lightning and burns with the fire of the Druid.

Derek tries to drive it away with wind, but it uses its wings to push through.

Lovely.

Matilda shouts at the monster. "Be gone you beast, you abomination. Be gone!" Once again, she uses her wand to attack, but this time the bolt of lightning is directed back at her and she's hit in the chest and collapses to the floor.

Ignoring my pounding head, I run to her, nearly vomiting at the movement.

I can't tell if she's alive or not. "Liam! Help her!"

Despite his own anger, he comes to her and checks her pulse, but the monster descends on us, and I am in the direct line of its fire. I attempt to create a shield to protect us, but I'm not fast enough.

Just as the monster is about to impale me with its drill horn, Racul jumps in between us and the horn plunges into him instead. He's hit with such force that both he and the creature crash through the glass window, over the balcony and into the garden.

The light rain that had begun earlier is now a raging storm, darkening the Dragon's Breath in the sky and turning everything murky and wet.

With fear pulsing through my veins, I plunge into my power and pull on every strand I can find, then fly through the broken glass and down to where Racul and the monster are.

Racul lays unconscious in a bush as rain pelts him.

The monster turns to me, and using all the elements, I weave a cocoon trap that I throw on it. This seems to work for a moment, as a magical net wraps around the beast and slows its progression.

But it breaks free too soon and lunges at me.

In a blink, the four Night brothers jump off the balcony with ease and join me.

I grab the hands of the two nearest brothers while they form a circle around the monster, hands held. I channel the power they offer in addition to my own and cast another shield around the creature, this time creating a dome prison in which to trap it.

The monster screams and thrashes against the barrier but the power I've thrown into the barrier zaps it back each time it hits.

"I think it's holding," I say, my body buzzing and my head pounding.

I feel as if I'm about to vomit.

I sag into Sebastian's arms and he catches me, holding me close.

"Matilda?" I ask.

"She's alive," Liam says.

"Racul!" I scream and pull out of Sebastian's arms and run over to the Fire Dragon. His body is crumbled in a bush and I tug at him to turn him over. There's a horn sized hole in his chest and he's not breathing.

"Liam?" I ask, knowing he won't love helping but he's a healer before anything.

True to form he rushes over and examines the dragon. There's no gloat in his face when he turns to me and frowns. "He's dead."

CHAPTER 13: THE TRUTH

"Look for the answer inside your question."
~Rumi

The storm continues to rage around us and a deep dread builds within me. I stare at Racul's body and can't stop shaking. He died to save me, which goes against everything I thought I knew about the Fire Dragon.

His burnt red skin looks paler in death, as if the flames of his soul are being extinguished. I take his hand, but it is heavy and limp. A tear slides down my cheek. I didn't exactly like the man, but over the last few days I had developed a kind of bond with him, and this death hurts. They all hurt.

I turn to look at the creature in the makeshift cage we created. Its thrashing has calmed, and it seems to be tiring out.

In fact, it looks to be curling up to rest. The fight must have drained it.

As it falls asleep, we all watch in stunned silence as its body begins to glow and its shape changes. Its legs lengthen, its body shortens, its head becomes smaller, until it's no longer a hideous monster at all.

It's a girl.

A girl we all know.

It's Ana.

I place Racul's hand on his chest and walk over to look more closely.

Ana sleeps fitfully, crying out until she wakes herself with her own terrors. When she sees where she is, she screams and cries. "Please let me out, I'm scared."

I kneel to speak to her. "Ana, do you know why you're here?" I ask.

She shakes her head. "I'm scared."

"You turned into something else," I say, unsure of how to phrase this. "Do you remember that?"

"No. I don't know what you mean?"

"You attacked us," I say softly. Nothing about this feels right, and I don't know how to process what's happening. My flash is buzzing madly.

Her eyes widen and she begins to cry. "I didn't. I promise. It wasn't me."

She's either the world's best actress or she really doesn't remember doing it.

"What's the last thing you remember?" I ask.

"I was sleeping in Grandmother Matilda's room and I heard someone calling me. I opened my eyes, felt a pain, and then I was here."

"You remember nothing else? Nothing at all?" Sebastian asks, kneeling next to me.

"No. What happened? What do you think I did?"

Shit. How do you tell a small child she's a killer?

I look over at Sebastian, whose jaw is locked. He shrugs, but doesn't take his eyes off Ana.

Ana looks past us, her eyes widening when she sees Racul in the bushes. "Why is he like that?" she asks, breaking into sobs again.

I want to reach through the barrier and hold her. She's so small and scared and I just don't believe she's done this on purpose. But the fact is, she did do it, and I can't risk letting her free to do it again.

"Is he dead?" she asks. "Why is he like that?" She's screaming and shaking, and I can't leave her alone like this.

Against my better judgement, I move through the barrier and into the space with her. Sebastian shouts for me to stop, but I can't let this poor little girl suffer alone.

She clings to me, sobbing into my shoulder, her frail arms wrapped around me. "Tell me what's happening? Why do people keep dying?"

"I don't know what's going on, honey. But we're going to figure it out. Until then, you're going to have to stay in here. For your own safety."

She looks up, eyes wide. "No. You can't leave me in here alone. No! I'm scared."

It's a terrible place to leave a child, but she's not just a child. She's a creation gone wrong. And where has she been all this time? What brought her back if the Fates were so certain she was killed?

"I'll make it nicer for you," I say. "Watch."

I don't need to be touching the Nights to do this anymore. Instead, I place my hand in the earth and request help from the flowers surrounding us. I telegraph the image of what I want to do, and they agree.

My magic is connected to the brothers through our new bond, and I tap into that to help. As my power flows, a small room forms around me and Ana, made of beautiful flowers and vines and leaves. It's tall enough for her to stand and walk around, and mounds of mossy grass make up a bed and small couch.

She looks around, her fear momentarily forgotten as she watches in awe at the earth reforming itself for her.

When I'm done, I feel exhausted, but she smiles. Then her mouth drops when she realizes she has to stay here. "Please don't leave me," she begs.

"I'm so sorry honey, I have to. But I'll send out your doll, and I'll come visit you often while we figure out what to do, okay?"

She sobs softly as I leave.

The other brothers have gone upstairs to check on Matilda, but Sebastian stayed behind to wait for me. He takes my hand as I leave the barrier. "That was risky," he says, as we walk back to the house.

"I know. But I couldn't just leave her."

"I know," he says softly, squeezing my hand.

I glance back at Racul 's body and my heart lurches. "What do we do about him?" I ask.

"We'll send for Ifi and Elal. But we will have to explain this somehow. We have to turn the girl over to the Mother of Dragons."

I pull back from him. "We can't. She didn't mean to do this. We have to figure out what's going on."

We enter the house and Elijah is coming downstairs, his face distraught. "What's wrong?" I ask, releasing Sebastian's hand to rush over to him.

"Matilda is unconscious and can't be woken. Liam doesn't know why. She's alive, but appears to be in a coma. We've put her in her room for now and Liam is working on potions. I'm heading to my office to look for a book that might help."

Oh gods, this is awful.

I want to check on Matilda, but I know my presence won't help anything, so instead I retrieve Ana's doll, along with some food and water and take it to her, then join Sebastian in the family library. He's staring into the fire as I take a seat next to him.

"How was she?" he asks.

"She'd already fallen back to sleep. Poor kid."

"You don't know for sure that she's innocent of intent," he says. "If she's doing this deliberately, then she could be very skilled at lying. She was created a long time ago. She's not an ordinary child. She might not be a child at all."

My stomach turns at that. I hadn't considered the possibility that her entire presentation was a lie. Still. "I felt something from her. A connection to her magic. It doesn't feel evil to me. With my darkness and light, I can suss out intention better than most, and hers feels pure. She's genuinely scared. Maybe she just needs to learn control."

"And yet she's only killed dragons," he says. "And not all dragons. She didn't harm Zara. That doesn't feel random or lacking control to me."

Liam, Elijah and Derek join us downstairs, Liam carrying Alina and Derek carrying the baby dragon.

They put the babies in the crib and take seats in front of the fire with us.

"Any news?" I ask Liam.

"It's a waiting game now," he says.

Derek stands and begins pacing, his trademark go to for stressful times and thinking. "At least now we can resolve these murders and save the Otherworld," he says. "When we turn over the monster, Amora should honor her word and leave us alone."

Oh boy. "We're not turning over the child," I say.

They all look at me with unreadable expressions.

So I make the same argument I just made to Sebastian. "I felt it in her. She doesn't know what she's doing, but from what I've seen of the Mother of Dragons, she won't care. In fact, she's the reason we're in this mess to begin with. She created this child and tried to destroy her. Now the child is back."

And the timing is awfully...coincidental.

"Callia!" I shout. "Show yourself!"

The unicorn always turns up when she feels like it. I've never been able to summon her, but she has to know what's going on.

"Callia!"

Finally, the unicorn appears before me, her face grim. I glare at her. "Did you know all along?"

She shakes her head. "I didn't. Not at first."

"So it's true? This is the child that the Queen of the Unicorns and the Mother of Dragons created together?"

Her head drops. "It is. She is. And I loved her with all my heart. I did not want to destroy her, even though she wasn't what we expected."

"We?" I ask, the puzzle pieces in my mind suddenly rearranging themselves once again.

Her large silver eyes gloss over. "I am...was...the queen of my people. My relationship with Amora was...unexpected. We were enemies but we fell in love. We thought a child together could bridge the gap between our kind."

"Then why did you let Amora kill her?"

She looks up at me, her expression filled with complex emotion. "I didn't let her. I told her she would have to kill me first. So, she did."

I gasp and tell the brothers what Callia just told me. It would be a lot easier if everyone could see the damn unicorn.

"Do you know what happened after?" I ask. "To your child?"

I can tell she does. She sighs and gazes into the distance, into a past so far gone it's hard for me to imagine. "As I died, I used the last of my power to create a small slice of a new world, and I pulled my dying child into it and left her there. I thought it would be better, for her to live, but I was wrong."

And then it all clicks. "When Ava'Kara and I expanded the world, we pulled her into it, didn't we? That's why she's back?"

Callia nods. "I do believe that's what happened, yes."

My stomach sinks with the unintended consequences of my actions. "Why is she targeting and killing the dragons?" I ask.

"That I do not know. But she is innocent, you have seen that yourself. Please do not sacrifice her to Amora's ambitions."

A tear slides down Callia's cheek. "I'm going to see my daughter now," she says, and blinks out.

I face the Night brothers, prepared to fight for this girl's life. She's already been tormented too much.

"We cannot harbor a serial killer," Derek says. "She puts all of us—this entire world—at risk. She was never meant to exist at all," he argues. "We must let her go. It's the only way."

I expect Liam to side with Derek, but he surprises me. "No. I'm with Eve on this. If there's a chance she's innocent of intent, we must find another way. We have spent lifetimes defending the guilty, making sure they get a fair trial. We cannot turn this child over to someone we know will torture and destroy her. That's not who we are."

Elijah cocks his head, taking in all the information. "I think we should hold off making any decisions until we know more. I can't deny turning her over would be the most expedient solution to our problems, but I also do not feel it wise to turn our back on our own values for sake of the convenient solution. That is not who we are, nor is it who we have ever been."

Sebastian shakes his head. "I'm sympathetic, I am. But... " he glances at me and I know what he's about to do.

"Don't," I say.

"I'm sorry," he says. "But they have to know. It's too important."

I close my eyes. In a moment, everything will shift, and it will be my fault.

"What do we need to know?" Liam says, glancing at me.

I can't speak it, so Sebastian does.

"Eve is connected to this world," he says. "As a Fate, through the spell work she did to expand it. If the world is destroyed, she will die."

The room falls silent as they each process what this means.

Elijah speaks first. "This changes things," he says, turning sad eyes to me. "We cannot risk your life for this."

"My life is a small matter in the bigger scheme of things. Let's say we hand over Ana to her. Then what? She tortures and kills the child she created? Or who knows what? Are we sure she'll honor her agreement to spare the world? Racul didn't think so. And what happens next time she gets a wild hair up her ass? She comes at us again with different demands?" I ask, making eye contact with each of them. "No, we cannot allow her to hold this world hostage."

"What do you propose?" Elijah asks.

"I don't know," I admit. "But at least give me time to think about it before we ruin this child's life. There's a piece we're missing. I'm sure of it."

An urgent knock at the door interrupts us and when no one makes a move, I go to answer it.

I'm stunned to see the tall, stunning Earth Dragon in human form standing there. Her skin is a deep ochre and her eyes are emerald green with touches of brown. Her wings are also flecked with the same green, and drape around her like a cloak. Her hair falls to her knees in thick waves of different shades of earthy brown mixed with the greens of a lush wilderness, with thin vines woven through tiny braids.

"Brock'Mir," I say, instinctively touching her ring on my hand. We met briefly of course, the day I got her ring, but we've never really spoken, and I certainly didn't expect her to show up at my front door.

"Maiden Fate," she says formally, her voice husky and full of earthy resonance. "You must come with me. To the Broken Cathedral. We have all felt the death of two more of my brothers." Her face is pained when she says this, and the reality of what is happening hits me harder than it did before.

In the chaos of the world ending and trying to solve the mystery, somehow, I lost sight of the fact that these immortal creatures are losing their family, their siblings, one by one. My brother's death is still raw in my heart, and on instinct I pull the dragon into my arms, though she towers over me. "I am so sorry," I say through thick emotions. "I have been through some fraction of the pain you are going through and I know it is hell."

She stiffens a moment, then relents and returns the affection of the hug briefly, before pulling away. Her eyes glisten with emotion but it is quickly wiped way by her pragmatism.

"Thank you, Eve," she says. "But I'm afraid there is no time for mourning right now. My mother has arrived, and she is threatening to destroy the world now, not in the timeframe she originally promised. You must come and help me stop her, or everyone in the Otherworld will die tonight."

CHAPTER 14: THE CAVE

So close that your hand on my chest is my hand,
So close that your eyes close as I fall asleep
~Pablo Neruda, Sonnet XVII

SHIT. Double and triple shit.

I rush back into the house to explain to the guys where I'm going.

"We're going with you," Sebastian says, standing.

"I'll be fine," I say. "Besides, Racul's body needs to be handled, the babies need to be watched, someone needs to keep an eye on Ana, and we can't leave Matilda alone. Also, someone needs to get word to Lily about what happened. She's probably at the grove with Kaya."

"I'll send a note out to let Lily know what happened, and I'll send a runner to fetch Ifi and Elal to handle the body," Elijah says.

"I'll keep an eye on Matilda," Liam says. "And take care of the babies."

Derek looks over. "I can make sure the dome holds for Ana until we figure out what to do."

"So everything is handled," Sebastian says. "Which means I'm coming with you."

I'm about to argue when Liam interrupts. "You're going to face off with the most powerful being in the world, who wants to destroy everything today," Liam says, his face stoic. "You should take at least one of us for the extra power."

"I know, but like I said, I'll be fine." I grin but he's not buying it, and my smile drops. "Look, I won't lie. I'm nervous as hell, but we don't have time to argue. I've got to go now."

As if on cue, my head splits and I double over in pain. Sebastian catches me in his arms before I fall to the ground. "What happened?" he asks, concern written all over his face.

"She's starting to tear the world apart. I have to go now!"

"You can't go alone like this," Sebastian says, sending earth magic to steady me through our bond.

When I can stand, I nod reluctantly. "Fine, let's go," I say. We rush back to Brock and I grab her hand. "He's coming with us," I say to the dragon, who looks skeptical but there's no time to argue. "Ready?"

She nods, and I focus. I've never done this with two people before, but how much harder can it be?

Ha! Famous last words.

I feel like I've contracted food poisoning as I dematerialize us and travel to the Broken Cathedral. Waves of nausea crash through me but I somehow manage to avoid vomiting into the void. Amora and the Darkness Dragon are arguing when we land on top of the Cathedral, in the same spot where I killed Jerry—or he killed himself through me —and I break out into a sweat at the memory, which doesn't help the nausea one bit.

Amora is in her dragon form, hovering over us and casting a giant shadow over everything. Golden light blazes forth from her mouth as she screams out her pain into the world, shaking its very foundation. The storm we've been dealing with all day rages uncontrollably around us.

My hair whips in the wind, cutting into my face as it does. I'm soaked to the bone despite my fire magic blazing within me to keep me warm. Lightning flashes in the sky, splitting a tree on the ground near us. It catches flames but is put out by the rain.

"Stop!" I scream, channeling my Fate powers until I'm glowing with them. I ride a wind current and rise above the building to face her. "You cannot do this. Not now! Not yet."

"More of my children are dead," she screams, her eyes glowing with fury, her voice layered with power that nearly undoes me.

"And so you would murder even more innocent people?" I shout. "You gave your word. Does that mean nothing?"

"This world does not deserve to live!" As she screams, thunder crashes through the Dragon's Breath, shaking the ground.

"This is our world," Brock says, transforming into her dragon form and rising up with us. "You cannot take it from us."

Ra'Terr takes longer to join, and when he does arrive, his deep ebony black looks greyed out and he appears less vibrant than he was.

Sebastian remains on the roof watching from below. But I can feel him sending me as much power as he can, and I'm glad he came with me.

This is all terrifying, but I put on a brave face against the Mother —and Queen— of the Dragons.

"You are my children," the queen says. "I must do this to protect you."

"You are taking from them a piece of them," I say. "What do you think it will do to your remaining children if you destroy the world they helped build? A part of them will die too."

She pauses at that, looking at the two dragons flanking her. "I should never have let you do this thing," she says. "If we had stayed in our world, all would be well. Dath'Racul would rule by my side. You would all have your own kingdoms. Our world would be at peace. This world would never exist."

"If we had stayed in our world," Brock says, "we would have let all these people die. They cannot survive in the mortal world any longer. The humans have taken over and made it inhospitable for anyone else. And we are the reason these people exist."

My ears perk at that. This is the first time I've heard that particular news.

"What does that mean?" I ask.

Brock looks at me. "Magic exists because of dragons. When our kind began breeding with human, mixing our blood with them, it created all the races that now exist. These people are our people. These races exist because our kind fell in love with humans."

The queen rages again, spewing boiling golden lava from her mouth that destroys a side of the Cathedral. Sebastian has to dodge to avoid being hit himself.

Brock continues, now focused on her mother. "We owed it to them to create a world of safety for their kind."

"We owe these mixed bloods nothing," she sneers. "Dragons should have never shared their bloodline with such inferior beings."

Ha! That's rich coming from the woman who created a magical baby hybrid monster with her lover. But then, maybe that's part of the problem. She's punishing the world for her own mistakes.

"And yet they did," Brock says. "We cannot turn our back on our people." She pauses. "If you destroy the world now, I will not leave. I will die with it."

Ra'Terr nods his giant black dragon head. "As will I," he says.

"And your grandchild will also die," I say, pulling my last card. "We are still searching for her, but she's in this world somewhere. If you destroy it now, not only will you never find out who killed your children, but you will lose your last two children and your only grandchild."

I swallow a lump in my throat and pray to whatever gods are listening that she will be swayed by our words.

Finally, she lowers herself back to the roof, turning into her human form. The other dragons do as well, until we are all facing each other. Sebastian rushes to my side as support.

"I do not understand your loyalty to this wretched place," she says. "But I will honor my word. On one condition," she says, looking to her children. "When this is over, however it ends, you agree to come home with me and take your rightful places in our kingdom. Swear to it on the blood of the dragons."

I hold my breath, waiting.

Ra'Terr nods. "If we all make it through this, I will come home."

Brock hesitates, but eventually nods too. "Very well. I swear it on the blood of the dragons."

The queen doesn't look happy, despite getting her way. "I will hold you all to your promises." Then she turns her golden eyes to me. "You are running out of time, Fate. Bring me my children's killer and my grandchild, or be prepared to face the consequences."

Then she returns to her dragon form and flies high into the sky, her wings expanding to cover so much of the Dragon's Breath I can barely see anything beside her as she uses her magic to tear a hole in the fabric of this world and disappears.

I half expect the storm to stop the moment she's gone, but it continues to rage around us, and the Darkness Dragon slumps against his sister.

"Fate, before you leave, I must speak with you. Privately," he says, glancing at his sister who seems to know what this is about and nods.

Sebastian looks reluctant to let me go, but he waits with Brock as Ra'Terr and I walk to a corner of the Cathedral where there is a bit of shelter from the rain.

We both sit, our backs against a wall.

"There is something you should know," he says, his voice sounding weak.

"What is it?"

"I am dying," he says bluntly.

"What? How?" My mind tries to wrap itself around this news, but I am too stunned to make sense of it.

"In the darkness of my own cave, I was attacked." He pulls up his shirt to reveal a deep wound that is turning black at the edges. "Whatever did this to me, it left its poison in me and I will not last much longer."

"Did you see what attacked you?" I ask, my heart sinking with the answer I know is coming.

"A monstrous creature, though I only saw it for a moment."

Ana.

Gods. That means... The Mother of Dragons is going to lose her shit when she realizes Ra'Terr is dying too. There will only be one of her children left then.

And Brock'Mir will have to live the rest of her long life without her siblings. The truth of that crushes me.

I don't know the Darkness Dragon well at all. He is like a shadow, dark and mysterious. He keeps to himself. But I take his hand none-theless, and let my dark magic flow into him, but I wrap it in light, because the two cannot exist without each other.

Cole taught me that.

His ebony eyes fill with tears, and I have a feeling this isn't a man who cries often. "I have not told anyone this, not even my sister, but since the attack...I have felt fear. It is the first time in my long life I have felt such a thing. The darkness used to be my haven, my element, and now I find myself scared of the dark." He chuckles, but it is a humorless sound of self-deprecation. "How silly is that? For a being of darkness to fear the dark?"

"None of us are made of just one thing," I say. "There is light in your darkness, just as there is darkness in light. Maybe it is time to step into the light, just a little. My father used to tell me *in lumen et lumen.* To be in the light and of the light."

His hand squeezes mine. "I have spent millennia in the dark. I do not know what to do with the light."

"I spent so much of my life fighting to live in the light, that when I found out I had darkness in me, I feared it," I confess. "Perhaps we all have to face the parts of us we fear and embrace them. This could be your time to do just that."

We sit there in silence a moment, then Ra'Terr stands, and I join him. "Thank you, Eve, Maiden Fate. You have brought me hope."

We walk back to Brock and Sebastian and Brock rushes to her brother. "I must get him home," she says, reaching for Ra'Terr. "Let us meet soon to discuss next steps." She pauses, looking at me carefully. "But before we go, I must say this. I know you have Ava'Zara, my sister's daughter."

I open my mouth to say...well, I'm not really sure what I'm going to say, but she holds up her free hand. "Wait. I understand why you took her. I believe you have a good heart, Eve Oliver. And you didn't know which amongst us you could trust. You were keeping her safe."

Relief floods me at her words.

"Are you going to take her away now that you know?"

She hesitates. "I want to. You are not equipped to raise a dragon. I do not know how you are even feeding her."

"Cooked shark is her favorite," I volunteer.

She raises an eyebrow. "Be that as it may, you are not wrong that she might be safer with you for now. As dragons are being killed off, we cannot be trusted to keep her safe. So take care of my niece, but when the time is right, I will bring her home."

My heart tugs at that. Ava'Zara has already become so close to Alina. The two of them are nearly inseparable. But Brock is right, we aren't in a position to raise a dragon. She will quickly outgrow our space and she needs her own kind to teach her their ways.

But that's a problem for another day.

"Take care of your brother. We will talk soon." She transforms and her brother climbs onto her back, looking weaker by the minute. But before she leaves, I add, "And come visit Zara when you'd like. She would enjoy that."

Brock nods and then takes off, soaring into the sky with Ra'Terr clutching her back.

Once they leave, Sebastian turns to me. "What was that about?"

I tell him what Ra'Terr shared.

"She's even more dangerous than we thought," Sebastian says, frowning. "We should get back to tell the others."

I nod and take a step toward Sebastian, but I stumble. I feel sick and weak and dizzy.

"You need to rest," he says.

I shake my head. "We need to get home, like you said."

I grip his hand and try to teleport us back to the castle. But even as we begin to disintegrate, I can feel it all going wrong. I'm too tired, too drained from all the magic I've been expending.

I screw up, and when we land, it is with a crash that results in bone deep pain that makes me almost pass out.

We look around to find a wilderness with mountains surrounding us. The storm is still raging on, so violently it's already pulled some trees from their roots.

Sebastian looks pale, but his stoicism holds him in good form, and he kneels at my side, examining me. "Is anything broken?" he asks, concern edging his voice.

I can barely hear him through the screams of the wind and the damage it's doing to the nature around us. "No. I don't think so. Just the wind knocked out of me," I say as loudly as I can, trying to catch my breath.

"We need to find shelter," he says.

I want to argue, to say that we should try again, but I know I can't. Not just yet. I need time to recover. And he's right, we can't stay out here in this. It's too dangerous and honestly, too damn miserable.

I can't get dry no matter how much fire I build in myself, and that isn't much at the moment. I need to save my magic for later.

I try to stand, but dizziness overtakes me, so Sebastian lifts me into his strong arms and carries me instead. I wrap my hands around his neck and let my head fall to his shoulder. He's wet, we both are, but he feels so solid and safe, I smile as I close my eyes and he begins to walk towards the closest mountain.

It feels like we are trekking through a tornado, not that I specifically know what that's like, but I imagine it to be like this. Without Sebastian's earth magic and strength, I'm positive we'd be swept up in the air currents like Dorothy and Toto.

We walk for what feels like forever before we reach our destination. Sebastian scans the area and grunts. "I'm going to have to make us a cave to take shelter in," he says.

I just nod. It's all I can do at this point.

But I feel as he pulls at his power, channeling it at the base of the towering snow-peaked mountain.

Rocks grind and dirt shifts beneath us, and it sounds as if there's an earthquake. Feels that way too, but Sebastian holds on tight to me and I pry my eyes open to watch as a hole forms where once rock and dirt filled. He walks us into the new cavern and uses more magic to cover the opening with thick vines that block out the wind and rain. It's a small space with crystal stalactites hanging from the ceiling.

Sebastian props me against the wall. "Stay here, I'm going to get us some supplies."

I don't have time to ask what kind of supplies when he's gone, dashing away using his vampire speed.

He's back in record time with wood and animal fur. "Um, did you just go hunting?" I ask.

"No, the bear was already dead. I just borrowed his pelt."

Somehow the Earth Druid has also cleaned it so that it was not covered in the blood and guts of said bear. A gesture I am grateful for. He quickly gets to work building a small fire in the center, laying the fur to the side for me to use.

I summon the last of my strength to dry us both, against his objections, and then I lean against him as the fire before us blazes to life, warming the cave and casting lights off the crystals surrounding us.

"You saved this world," he says against my ear, his arms wrapped around me as I snuggle against him. "Again," he adds.

"It was a group effort," I say sleepily, the warmth of the fire, the steady drone of the rain and the feel of Sebastian's body all working together to lull me into unconsciousness.

"Led by you," he clarifies. "You're the bravest, most selfless person I've ever met."

I look up at him and caress his handsome face, losing myself in his forest green eyes. "Meeting you changed my life," I say. "That day on the subway, I had lost hope. I didn't know where I was headed or what my life would look like after Adam died. I had nothing left. Then I saw you, full of color and life, juxtaposed against a world of grey, and I couldn't stop thinking about you. Your eyes pulled me in to a new world, before I ever knew how literal that new world would be. You gave me a reason to live again. You saved me," I say. "So whatever you think of me, know that part of that is because of you."

He bends forward to press his forehead to mine. "You saved all of us," he says softly. "We would be dead right now if not for you."

Tears burn my eyes as I remember how close I had come to losing all of them. "Then we have saved each other. And now, we will save all of the Otherworld, and free it from the tyranny of the Mother of Dragons."

His lips find mine and despite my exhaustion, I can't help but respond in kind, pressing myself against him, intertwining my fingers into his hair as he claims my mouth with his. His arms pull me closer to him, and our bodies press together, feeding on each other's warmth and energy. I feel the stabilizing strength of his earth magic flow into me, giving my own powers a boost, giving me energy, healing me. And I melt into him as he moans against my mouth.

"Eve," he says breathlessly, pushing me away gently. "I want you, but I don't want to hurt you."

I push myself against him, again. "You could never hurt me."

And it's true, I realize. It has always been true. From the beginning, Sebastian has been my rock. The foundation that this entire new life was built upon. Without him, none of it would exist for me. Without him, I would still be sorting through the tattered shreds of my old life wondering how I ended up there, wondering where to go next. It was Sebastian's strength that has helped me heal from the death of my brother. His steadfastness that has gotten me through these recent trials and struggles. Even now, as the winds blow outside, as the world feels as if its ending, it's his arms around me that are holding me together, filling the holes in my magic, mending the tears in my heart.

"It has always been you," I say, and then there is no more space for speech.

There are some emotions that are too powerful to be contained in words. They require the entire body to act as their language. To communicate the depths of my love for this man, I use everything I am. Body, mind, and soul.

Any walls between us crumble and new roots form, binding us, connecting us forever.

The power we share fills me with a new kind of strength that I grab onto with everything in me.

The fire crackles beside us, the crystals shining above us, and I straddle the sexy Earth Druid, enjoying the feeling of him between my legs as my weariness evaporates as quickly as dew when the sun comes out.

His lips trail down my neck. "I have missed the feeling of the sun since being turned, but being with you is better than the warmest day, then the freshest morning breeze. You bring light into my life, joy into my heart. "You are my sun, Eve Oliver. You are my everything."

He whispers these words against my collar bone, against my lips, against the hollow of my neck, and my skin absorbs his promises like a thirsty child on a hot summer day drinks his water. His declarations quench the thirst of my soul and fill me with love so deep and joy so pure I can't contain it. I feel it spilling out of me, shining through my skin like magic.

I look down at us and realize we are both glowing a golden light that radiates throughout the cave.

As he hardens beneath me, I realize we have too many clothes on, so I pull my arms away from him to quickly shimmy out of my shirt, until my breasts are free and tantalizingly close to his lips.

He claims one of my nipples in his mouth and sucks, and my undressing is paused as pleasure strikes me like lightning, zapping through my body, spreading warmth everywhere.

I need to feel more of his flesh, so I tug at his shirt until he helps me get it off. I place my hands on his chiseled chest, enjoying the roped contours of his muscles. God he feels so good.

My breasts brush up against his bare skin and tighten in need. I grind against him but our pants are in the way of our pleasure, and there's no easy way of undoing this.

Unless…

I close my eyes and imagine just teleporting our pants and nothing else.

This is new for me.

But my power has returned. Being with him has strengthened me beyond what I could have imagined.

And in a blink, we are both naked, our clothes lying next to us now.

His eyes widen. "Neat trick." His voice is thick with desire, as he presses himself between my legs.

He resumes his attention to my breasts and drops his hand between my legs to heighten my need with his fingers.

At first, his touches are feather light, teasing my flesh. I arch closer to him as his tongue flicks at my nipple. When he presses his fingers deeper into me, I moan, desperate for more, unable to stop from moving my hips to feel him more deeply.

"I need you," I beg, ready for more than just fingers and tongue.

He groans, his mouth tracing a line of fire back up my chest to my neck.

He removes his fingers and uses both hands to grab my ass as I reposition myself to take him into me.

The moment I do, his teeth sink into my neck, and I cry out his name and thrust my hips, taking him as deeply as I can, my knees digging into the fur, our bodies pressed together, everything else disappearing but us.

It feels as if the entire mountain erupts as pleasure explodes within me and we both crash into each other, riding the high together as the storm thunders outside.

Spent and panting, we lie in each other's arms beside the fire, and I run a finger over his chest as my head rests on his shoulder and his arms grip me firmly. My legs are wrapped around his and I relish the feeling of our skin-to-skin contact.

He kisses me and smiles. "That was definitely worth the wait."

I laugh and kiss him again. "It's the first of many," I say. "We will get through this, and we will have lifetimes to enjoy each other."

CHAPTER 15: THE PLAN

LYING, thinking
Last night
How to find my soul a home
Where water is not thirsty
And bread loaf is not stone
I came up with one thing
And I don't believe I'm wrong
That nobody,
But nobody
Can make it out here alone.
–Maya Angelou

WE BOTH FALL ASLEEP, and when we wake, the fire has died down, as has the storm. I sit up and stretch, grinning through a yawn. "That was... "

"Incredible," he says, kissing me and pulling me against him.

When he hardens against my stomach, I moan. "We should get back," I say, but it's not a convincing argument.

I'm ready for round two, and clearly, so is he.

With the first wave of passion spent, we now take our time. He explores my body slowly, studying the dips and valleys with his mouth, using his tongue rather than his fingers to tease me.

And when he enters me, it is deliberate, our gazes locked on each other, and a well of emotion consumes me, like the view from the top of a mountain after a long and arduous hike. I have waited so long for him, so long to feel him inside me, to complete this dance we started on the subway in what feels like another life.

I wrap my legs around him and take him all the way in, enjoying the slow, delicious way he moves within me.

This time when we climax, it is like hang gliding off a mountain. His hands are gripped in mine, pinning them to the fur. My breasts are pressed to his chest, his lips are on mine. We are one.

We cuddle after for as long as we can justify it, then we reluctantly collect our clothing and dress.

"I'm guessing everyone will be worried sick about us," I say.

He shrugs, then winks at me. "Still worth it."

I chuckle. "You know I always wondered how people in thriller movies could take time from being stalked and nearly killed to have sex, but now I get it. In life or death situations, you realize the importance of that intimacy more than ever." I walk over to him and lay my hands on his chest. "If the world is going to end, I needed to be with you today, and as many times as I can before that happens."

"We are not going to let the world end," he says, frowning. "Because I don't think any of us will survive this life without you."

I blink away the tears when I realize what he's saying. "You have to," I whisper. "Alina needs you. You have to make it. For her. For me. Swear it."

He closes his eyes, his face a portrait of grief to come. "I swear it." He opens his eyes and caresses my face. "But know this. I will do whatever must be done to save you."

I know what he's saying, and I frown. "Let's first try it my way. Before we talk about turning over the child, let's try to find out what's going on with her powers and why. Let's find another way."

He nods and leads me out of the cave by the hand. But before we leave, I grab the fur. "For later," I say, winking.

He chuckles. "For later."

Outside, evidence of the storm is everywhere we look. Trees are toppled, pulled from their roots or split in half like twigs. Foliage is ripped out of the ground. Boulders have been tossed about like pebbles. In short, it's a mess.

"We'd better get home, make sure everyone's okay," I say, reaching for Sebastian's hand.

"Are you sure you're strong enough to teleport?" he asks.

"It's easier than walking from... " I look around. "From wherever we are. Do you even know where we are?" I ask.

"No, not really. This must be part of the new world we haven't been to yet."

"Okay, well then we teleport. Besides, I feel as good as new." And it's true. I've made a remarkable recovery and feel stronger than ever.

It only takes me a moment to take us back to the castle, and we land by the front door, just as intended. Sebastian sways a bit and then steadies himself. "That's still very strange," he admits.

"I think it must be easier if you have Darkness," I say. "Otherwise you're fighting the magic."

He nods and the moment we step in the door we are greeted by three very worried men, two babies, and a pacing Dryad.

Derek pulls me into his arms. "We've been worried out of our minds. Where have you two been?"

I explain our confrontation with the Mother of Dragons, then the storm, then my powers conking out followed by our makeshift habitat for the night.

"Good thinking," Elijah says to Sebastian. "The cave was smart. That storm was the worst this world has ever seen. Buildings are damaged. People are panicking."

Lily steps forward. "Kaya says more people than are requesting transport to Earth. Especially those who can pass as human. Everyone knows something's up here, most just don't know how serious it is."

"What does Kaya say about the chances of getting everyone out if we need to," I ask.

Lily frowns. "It would take at least a month to evacuate this world, but that would create a massive influx in Earth that could trigger a whole new witch hunt."

"In other words, it would be a massacre the moment they arrived," I say.

Lily nods.

"So we have no choice," Derek says. "We need to turn the girl over."

"I don't think you understand," I say to Derek. "She's not going to leave this world intact. I'm sure of it. Once she has the murderer and her grandchild, she'll take her kids and head to her world, and snap her fingers to get rid of this one. I know it. I can see it in her."

They look at each other, and Liam shakes his head. "Eve is a Fate. If she sees this, we have to trust her."

Sebastian comes to my side. "I believe Eve as well," he says, surprising me. "I saw how unhinged the queen was. She will not leave us alone until we defeat her."

Elijah frowns. "You realize that's impossible, right? I have searched every book I can get my hands on. There's nothing powerful enough to defeat her in this world."

"There has to be a way," I say, standing. "I'm going to visit a friend. I have an idea. I'll be back soon."

I close my eyes and imagine the place I want to go, then I open them and find myself standing before an ornate door carved of cherry wood. I use the door knocker and a moment later, a young woman with cat ears and a tale opens it. She's wearing a white fur jumpsuit and smiles when she sees me. "Eve!" she hugs me, and I laugh as I return the hug.

"You look happy," I say, so pleased she seems to be settling in well to her new life, after being a sex slave to The Collector.

"I am, thanks to you." She turns to escort me in. "Mistress Lilith will be delighted to see you."

"Hopefully that's still true after she finds out why I'm here," I say.

Lilith's mansion is a vision of class and sophistication, much like the ancient vampire herself.

She's sitting at a white grand piano in her all white living room, playing a complicated piece I don't recognize. She stops when she notices us, and stands, adjusting her crimson red dress as she walks over to greet us.

She looks like a drop of blood in her pristine parlor, and the contrast is striking. Lilith is one of those beings who always stands out from their environment, but in a way that is complimentary, as if the world is orientating itself around her.

"Eve, how lovely to see you," she says, kissing both my cheeks, then offering me a glass of wine.

"Actual wine, I hope?" I say, sniffing at it.

She laughs. "Of course, darling. I know you haven't yet developed a taste for the finer things. But give it time."

It's my turn to laugh. "I think I'm good, thanks though."

We sit across from each other and she leans back and studies me, her long sharp nails clicking against her wine glass which is definitely not filled with actual wine.

"It's been ages since you've come by for a visit. I hear you've been digging in the dirt with the peasants."

"Your elitism is almost offensive," I say smoothly, "were it not for the fact that I know you donated the money to feed and clothe everyone for nearly two months while we worked."

She wrinkles her nose. "How did you find out? It was meant to be anonymous."

"You just told me," I say, winking.

She rolls her eyes. "I cannot believe that trick worked on me. I must be losing my edge in my old age."

Lilith might be the oldest person alive, or undead, rather, but she looks in her prime, with flawless skin and luminous dark eyes that are keenly intelligent and full of secrets.

I fill her in on the details of my life the past few months, then I get to the crux of it. "I need your help."

"Of course you do," she says. "You have that look about it. Always getting into some kind of mischief. It's part of why I adore you. It's never boring when you're around."

"The dead dragon body count would disagree," I say.

"Tragic, truly, but still not boring."

To Lilith, boring is the worst offense. I guess when you've lived that long, everything else is just shades of perspective.

I decide to say this as bluntly as possible. "The world will end in less than two weeks, and I will die with it, unless we can defeat the Mother of the Dragons. Will you help me find a way to stop her?"

Lilith leans forward, putting her glass of blood down. "Oh my, this truly is the most excitement I've had in quite some time. Amora is back is she? I had a fling with her once ages ago, but she is too racist for my taste."

"Is there anyone you haven't slept with?" I ask with a laugh.

She winks. "You, for one."

"Well, if we don't stop her soon, I won't be around as an option for much longer."

"Then I guess we're going to have to play chess with the most powerful being in all the worlds I know of," she says with a conniving smile. "And in this game, there is no king."

I take a sip of my wine before asking, "Where do we start? How do we get to her?" I tell her about the unicorn horn dagger I have, and her eyes widen.

"How did you come across one of those? I thought they'd all been destroyed during the war."

"War?" I ask. "I thought it was more like a slaughter?"

Lilith shrugs sipping her blood. "The unicorns killed off many dragons in other worlds before coming here. They had their horns set on the Council, but before that could happen, the Council got wise and had them killed off first. So, who's the villain in that story? It's impossible to say. War begets war begets war. It's the same with all races and species on all worlds."

That's news to me, and something Callia didn't share. I wonder why.

"Elijah says there's nothing in the world he can find that will kill a dragon like her," I say.

A mischievous sparkle lights up Lilith's eyes. "Then we'll need to look outside of this world."

"Earth," I ask, doubtfully.

She shakes her head. "Only the Dragon's own world will have the answers, I fear. But fortunately, I still have a secret way in, thanks to our long ago tryst. I'll go, do some digging, see what I can find, and come back. In the meantime, go prepare yourself for the battle ahead. This is going to be one hell of a ride, and we can't have you damaging that gorgeous face of yours."

I'm still chuckling at her childlike enthusiasm for war as I blink and send myself back to the castle.

No one is downstairs, so I venture out back to check on Ana. She's curled in a corner playing with her doll.

"Hey there, honey. How are you?" I ask.

She shrugs, not speaking.

Gods I feel like such an ass.

"Are you hungry? I can get you some food."

She shakes her head.

"Do you want me to read you a story?" I ask, though I don't have time for that, but I'll make it work for this poor kid.

She shakes her head again.

I sigh. "Okay, I'll come check on you soon."

I glance at the bushes on my way back in and see that Racul's body has been removed. The memory of him throwing himself in front of me to take the blow sends shivers up my spine, and I still don't know how to factor that Dath'Racul against the giant ass from court. People —and dragons—aren't always what you think.

I head upstairs, hoping there's not more bad news awaiting me. I fear the worst as I approach Matilda's room, but when I push open the door, my heart warms to see all four brothers sitting around her bed as they talk. She has tears running down her weathered cheeks, and Liam holds her hand. The babies are in a crib in the corner napping.

I don't want to interrupt, so I pull the door closed behind me and head to my room to take a bath and have a minute alone before reality sets in too hard and we must make our next plan.

Moon is excited to see me, and curls around my ankles purring as I prepare my bath. I pick him up and hold him against my chest, enjoying the velvety softness of his fur.

He takes his customary spot at the edge of my tub as I heat the water with my magic and step in.

519

I try to pause my mind for just a few minutes. To forget about the end of the world and the dead dragons, and the monster killer who's just a child. I push it all away and meditate on just the present moment. The bubbles tickling my skin. The heat of the water soaking away my weariness. The scent of lavender oil. The sound of Moon purring.

"You look like a goddess," a familiar voice says, startling me out of my meditative state.

I sit up with a jerk, splashing water over the sides of the tub as Cole Night saunters over and takes a seat next to me, my bathrobe in his hands.

"What are you doing here?" I ask, my heart palpitating at his presence. And even though I really don't want to want him. I totally want him. Damn this man and the effects he has on me.

"I heard you have a problem with a queen. I'm here to help."

I sigh. "It truly is impossible to keep secrets around here."

I stand and grab my robe from his hands, slipping into it as I climb out of the tub.

Then I realize there's other news he may or may not know. "Matilda... " I say, unsure how to proceed.

"I know she was attacked," he says softly.

"Yes, but she's okay now I think. But that's not all," I say, struggling to find the right words.

Understanding dawns on his face and he nods. "So, she finally told you?" he asks.

I narrow my eyes. "Told me what?"

"That she's a Fate."

"No! She didn't tell me, but yes, I did find out. I had a memory of it. But how the hell did you know?" I ask, confused.

We walk back into my bedroom, and I take a seat in front of the fire as Moon makes a spot on my lap. Cole takes the chair next to me. "I didn't know for sure, but I've suspected for some time. She's always had visions and known things she shouldn't. She's been around forever but no one has ever really known what she is, or where her power comes from. It just made sense."

"Why didn't you tell your brothers? Or me?"

"For one, it wasn't my secret to tell. Matilda had her reasons for keeping her identity to herself and I wasn't going to betray that. And two, I didn't know for sure. Also, it's not like my brothers and I have been close," he says.

"Why aren't you angry with her if you've stayed angry with your brothers for so long?"

"Because I don't know what her direct role was in what happened to me. I know what theirs was."

"Oh Cole," I say, my heart breaking for him all over again. "They aren't the same men they were back then. They weren't strong enough to fight the powers that controlled your lives."

"And they are now?" he asks bitterly.

"We're all stronger," I say. "Together." I look pointedly at him. "I'm working on a plan to stop the Mother of Dragons, but I'll need everyone's help. Including yours. We can't do this without you. Can I count on you to help?"

Cole looks at me, his dark eyes hypnotizing and full of so much pain. "I'll do what I can. But this isn't a battle that will be easily won. What's your plan?" he asks.

"Like I said, I'm still working on it." Sheesh, doesn't anyone listen? "But I'm open to suggestions."

CHAPTER 16: THE GOODBYES

"GOODBYES ARE ONLY for those who love with their eyes. Because for those who love with heart and soul there is no such thing as separation."
Rumi

COLE JOINS HIS BROTHERS, spending time with Matilda, and when they are done, we all meet in the library and spend hours brainstorming ways to defeat the queen, but the fact is we just don't know enough. We only know one way to kill her—the unicorn dagger—but no one has a solid plan for how to get it into her heart, which seems to be the sure fire way to get the job done. Ra'Terr was simply injured with a horn, and his death is coming slowly, too slowly to stop the queen.

It's a tedious back and forth that ends with Cole jumping up in frustration. "We should all just leave. Get out of here. Get as many people off this world as possible, sure, but then we leave. We can't win this."

"He doesn't know?" Liam asks.

I shake my head. I really don't want to have this conversation. Again. But it seems I must.

And so I tell Cole what everyone else now knows. That I won't survive the destruction of this world.

That silences him, and without saying another word, he storms out of the library.

I lean back in the couch and close my eyes, pinching the bridge of my nose to alleviate a headache. The fire crackles and candles are lit around the room creating an ambiance I don't feel. I'm tired of arguing. Of planning. Of worrying.

Standing, I pick up Alina from the crib and hold her against my chest. Her baby fists reach for anything they can grab, settling for a bit of my shirt that she tries to shove into her mouth.

"I'm going for a walk," I say.

Sebastian stands. "I'll join you, if that's all right?"

I nod. "Only if you promise not to mention anything related to end of the world shit. I need a mental break."

"Agreed."

Elijah stands and stretches. "I think you're right. We're talking in circles. I'll keep researching and see if I can find anything in my books. But there might not be an easy solution to this."

"There might not be any solution to this," Liam says, his brow creased in worry.

"Then we do what we can," I say. "And we keep on living until then. What else is there?"

Derek frowns but doesn't say what I know he's thinking. That we could at least try and turn over Ana. It might work.

But I know it won't. I feel it so deeply within me that it's more than just a hunch, or even a flash. It's a Fate premonition, or whatever that is.

The evening is chilly, and I wear a cloak and wrap Alina in a blanket before putting her in the stroller.

Moon joins us as we head to the gardens and stroll over the cobbled paths that wind around the property.

Sebastian pushes the baby and I loop my arm through his as we walk slowly, enjoying the stillness of the night. While there are no sun and moon in this world, and the shift from day to night is much more subtle, I've lived here long enough to understand the different shades of color and light in the Dragon's Breath.

We stop beneath a weeping willow near a pond and I take Ana out and spread a blanket for her so she can stretch, then Sebastian and I lean against the tree and I tuck myself into his arms and try to clear my mind of everything but this moment.

It occurs to me we are never guaranteed a future, whether it's measured in minutes, years or lifetimes. Anything could happen, and so all we can do is stay as present as we can in the moments we are assured.

So I take it all in. The baby playing at our feet. The black cat curled up next to me. The beautiful man at my side. The fish swimming in the pond. The birds flying overhead.

All of it is a miracle.

"What are you thinking about?" Sebastian asks after a time.

I tilt my head up to him to look into his gorgeous green eyes. "You. Us. The wonder of it all. I've been given more than I ever thought possible. No matter how long it lasts, I can't complain."

A flood of emotions fills us both and he kisses me, drawing out my love for him, his love for me, in that one intimate exchange.

Then Alina begins to cry and we pull away from each other and laugh.

Sebastian checks her diaper and crinkles his nose. "I'll take her back to the house and give her a bath before putting her to bed."

I nod. "I'll be back in a bit."

I watch them walk away, then I head towards the ocean, Moon still at my heels. He seems to know something's up and hasn't wanted to leave my side lately.

Despite not wanting to dwell on what could be, I know I need to make plans if the worst-case scenario happens. So, I make a list in my mind of what that will look like. People I need to talk to. Letters I need to write. People I want to draw before my time might be up.

Was this how Adam felt as he was contemplating the end? Did he look at his life lived and weigh what he would need to do to close out the final chapter?

The ocean air invigorates me, and I slip my shoes off and stand at the shore, letting the water lap over my toes as Moon dashes back and forth, dodging the tide, then chasing it when it flees.

"Are you really so connected to this world that your life will end if it does?" Cole asks from behind me.

I should be used to him just turning up randomly, but the man still startles me.

I turn around, frowning. "I wouldn't lie about this."

He shrugs. "It would be a good way to motivate my brothers to stay and help."

I huff at that. "They don't need my potential demise to want to save thousands of others," I say. "They are good men with good hearts."

"Unlike me," he says softly.

I consider him a moment before replying. "Our goodness lies in our choices, which means we are, each moment, given opportunities to reinvent ourselves. You can be whoever you choose to be."

"I wish I believed that," he says, staring into the ocean.

"Have you come to say goodbye again?" I ask, my heart hurting.

"I don't know why I'm here, except that whenever I'm away from you too long, a heaviness grows in me that I cannot carry."

"Then stay," I say simply, but I know he will not. It is not yet who he is choosing to be.

"Can I kiss you?" he asks, and I'm surprised, not by the fact that he wants this, but that he asked permission.

I answer by turning to him and tilting my head up.

His arms encircle my waist, landing low on my hips as he steps closer to me, so that our bodies are pressed together.

My darkness reaches for his, my light as well, the two mingling with his dual magic, and the completion I feel at his closeness is a bittersweet balm that soothes even as it burns. I feel my heart breaking again, just a little, as he teases at my lips, tasting me. I slide my arms over his shoulders, through his thick black hair, deeming the kiss he began, tasting him in all his darkness and light.

And I feel the moment he begins to dematerialize, disintegrating like mist in my arms. When I open my eyes, he is gone, and I wonder if I will ever see Cole Night again.

~

OVER THE NEXT FEW DAYS, I bury myself in my art. I feel a compulsion to draw, to create portraits of the people I love most in the world. I try not to view it as saying goodbye, but there's no denying there is an element of that in all that I do.

Still, I'd like to think that I would have come to this place eventually, that space within myself where I see how important it is to show people how you feel about them before it's too late.

I still haven't heard from Lilith, and none of the brothers have found anything new, so our plan basically relies on luck.

With that in mind, I teleport myself to Kaya's grove where I know Lily will be.

I find the two of them leaning against Kaya's massive tree, arms intertwined, love glowing in them both.

When Lily sees me, she frowns and stands. "Eve! Is everything okay? Did something happen?"

"No, everyone is fine. I just… " I pause. This is harder to do than I'd imagined. "Can we talk? All three of us," I ask, glancing at Kaya.

They invite me to join them and I take a seat on the soft mossy earth and pull out the drawing I have for them. "I made this for the two of you," I say, handing it to them.

It's one of my most unique drawings, done on a large dried leaf using only pigments made from natural sources. I've secured it to a piece of wood that was donated by one of the trees I worked with in the new world. It's a portrait of both of them, their more human forms in front, with their trees behind them.

Lily's eyes fill with tears. "This is amazing. Thank you!" She leans over to hug me and I squeeze her tight, then pull away.

"There's something else," I say. "I need you to promise me something."

She nods, and Kaya holds her hand.

"If this showdown with the queen goes south, as it very well could,

I need you to get our family and our friends out of this world as quickly as possible. The Nights, the kids, the Ifrits, the Gargoyles, Lilith and her household, everyone. Can you do that?"

"You mean if the world ends and you die?" she asks softly.

"Yes. That's what I mean."

Tears fill her eyes and she looks to Kaya, who nods. "We will," Kaya says as Lily swipes at a tear. "You have our word."

Relief floods me. Knowing my loved ones will be safe makes this a little easier, though I wish there was a way I could save everyone in this world, not just the ones I know personally. It's not fair or right, but I'm doing my best. This is all just a shit situation however you look at it.

I take Lily's hand. "I'm so glad to know you," I say. "You are full of life and love and laughter, and you have become one of the best friends I have ever had. Thank you."

We spend the afternoon visiting, walking through the groves and talking about our lives, then I head to the Mausoleum and repeat this all with my friends there.

Okura and Akuro greet me first, landing before me when I materialize at the entrance. The baby is with them and I show them the portrait I created for the three of them. This one is etched into stone, which seemed fitting.

I don't know if Gargoyles decorate or enjoy this kind of thing, but I wanted to do something for them.

They are speechless. "I've never seen a likeness made of our family like this," Okura admits, her deep voice thick with emotion. "Our kind doesn't really get gifts. Ever."

"I hope I haven't offended you with this," I say, wondering if I should have checked the protocol first.

"Not at all," Akuro says. "We are pleased."

I take the baby when Okura offers her to me and cuddle her. Well, as much as you can cuddle animated stone.

I also hand them a Memory Catcher. "Please do not watch this unless something happens to me."

Okura frowns. "Is something meant to happen to you?"

I give a sad smile. "None of us are guaranteed a tomorrow. But if the worst happens, watch it and you'll know what to do."

I swear I see a tear slide down Okura's stony cheek as I enter the Mausoleum.

Ifi and Elal aren't in the morgue, so I head to their apartment, and there I find them cooking dinner.

Their door is left open, likely to air out the smoke building in their home.

"What are you two doing?" I ask, choking as I use a bit of air magic to help clear out the kitchen.

"Oh thank the gods you are here," Elal says, sounding more like Ifi than himself. "My husband has decided to take up cooking. That's normally my job but he insisted he wants to be more helpful in the kitchen." Elal waves a hand as if to say, 'look how helpful he's being.'

I chuckle. "At least he's trying."

Ifi huffs as he stirs a large pot. "I am creating a masterpiece. Both of you take a seat at the table and stop your whining. A little smoke never hurt anyone."

I could cite studies that would disagree with that, but instead I follow Elal to the table and we both sit, eyeing the Ifrit nervously as he serves up whatever is in the pot into large bowls that he places before us with a flourish.

"Now, dine on the most magnificent food you will ever experience in your lives," he says.

Whatever is in the bowl…and I really do mean *whatever*…is green and slimy, and my stomach flops over at the thought of introducing it to this substance of questionable edibility.

"Um, Ifi," I say, not quite sure how to phrase this. "You know that though I'm a Fate, I'm still in a mostly human body, right? So, I have to be careful what I put inside it, lest I end up on your table prematurely."

He cocks his hip and rolls his eyes. "I know, I know. Rude. I assure you, this is safe for human consumption."

Elal moves the gelatinous sludge around with a spoon, not looking the least bit convinced by his husband's encouragement.

He looks up at me. "Ladies first?"

I fall back on my standard line in this world. "Age before beauty."

"How about we do this together?" Elal proposes as a compromise. "On three?"

"Fine."

"One. Two. Three."

I take the smallest taste I can, while still managing to get some on the spoon. I'm definitely expecting to gag. Possibly die.

The flavor takes a moment to hit, and when it does, I see Elal's eyes widen just as mine do.

I take another bite just to make sure I'm not hallucinating, and yep, I was right. "Ifi, this truly is amazing."

Elal nods his head. "The key is not looking at it while eating it, I think," he says, patting his husband on the hand.

Ifi walks back to the kitchen, beaming. "I told you. Best chef ever."

"Can we work on the presentation?" I ask, avoiding direct eye contact with the green goo while I eat.

"I'll see what I can do."

We visit for a bit before I pull out the sketch I made for them. This one was a bit tricky to create, and I actually used my magic for the first time while drawing. I hand them a piece of wood with their portrait burned into it. In it, they are looking at each other with such love and devotion, you can feel it in your heart.

Ifi starts crying the moment he sees it, and Elal pulls his husband into his arms.

"This is just the most touching gift we've ever gotten," Ifi says. "And I look hot!" Then he looks to Elal. "So do you, of course."

Elal smiles. "Of course."

Our goodbyes are bittersweet, and when I hand them their Memory Catcher, they know what it contains, but Elal pockets it anyways. "This isn't the end," he whispers as he hugs me. "You may be a Fate, but you're also a Phoenix at heart. You will always rise from the ashes to be reborn."

His words stay with me long after I leave.

OVER THE NEXT FEW DAYS, I wait to hear from Lilith. I have a portrait for her as well, drawn with blood, which was…an interesting medium. In the picture, she's at the tree of knowledge licking blood off an apple while a snake slithers around her ankles. I am eager to show her the gift, but Lilith is still not back from her trip.

And then finally, the day has come. We have run out of time, and our plan is iffy at best.

"One hour," Liam says, staring into the dancing flames of the fire.

"Lily and Kaya will be here soon to take the kids away," I say. We decided it would be best for them to be out of the world ahead of time, just in case. I wish I could convince the Night brothers to go as well, but without them to help me, we don't stand a chance, and we need to try at least. Too many lives are at stake.

I walk over to Alina and pull her from the crib, cuddling her against me. I try not to cry as I imagine what will happen if we don't succeed.

The Night brothers surround us, forming a group hug with me and the baby in the center. Their power flows through me and I soak it up, hoping it will be enough.

Lily enters the room, Kaya at her side. "We're ready," she says.

I hand Alina to Kaya and Lily goes to pick up Zara who instantly starts screaming. She shifts from baby to dragon form, and her screams become the shouts of a dragon in distress. They echo throughout the castle and reverberate in our bones. Water begins spewing from her mouth, and Alina joins in, screaming, crying, thrashing and throwing fire balls indiscriminately.

"What the hell is going on?" Liam shouts over the noise.

"I have no idea," I say, scrambling to catch Alina's fire and neutralize it before she burns the damn castle down. "They were fine a second ago."

"Maybe they know we're trying to take them away," Lily says, nearly dropping Zara when the baby dragon spreads her wings and tries to fly.

The pitch of the dragon scream changes and nearly splits my eardrums, and then my flash buzzes and I clutch my head. "Oh, shit."

Outside, thunder rattles the rooftop as a new storm brews from a previously clear sky, and the sound of dragon wings fills the air.

A loud roar shakes the foundation of the castle and a dreadful cracking sound is the only warning we have before the entire top half of the castle is torn off to show a giant golden dragon looking down at us, lightning pouring from her. "Give me my grandchild!"

CHAPTER 17: THE STORM

"Love makes the ocean boil like a pot. Love grinds mountains down to sand. Love splits the heaven into a hundred pieces. Love shakes the earth with a mighty shaking...If not for pure love, why would I give existence to the spheres? I raised the Celestial wheel on the high so that you might understand love's elevation."
~ Rumi

With the lower level of the castle now exposed to the elements, rain pelts us, soaking everything. Lily backs away, still holding a screaming baby dragon.

Everything is chaos.

Before the Night brothers and I can scramble to protect the kids, the queen of dragons shoots a bolt of golden light at Lily, hitting her in the arm and knocking her down. Zara attempts to fly unsteadily, then drops to the ground crying. Kaya looks frantically between Alina in her arms, and her unconscious lover on the floor. I try to distract the queen to give the dryad a chance to help them both.

"Amora!" I say, filling myself with power, my voice projecting into the heavens. "Stop! We have not harmed your grandchild." I think quickly, trying to mitigate the damage. "We were about to bring her to you at the meeting time. Why are you attacking us?"

"You lie," roars the queen, flames flicking from her lips. Her golden eyes look past me, to what remains of the balcony, to Matilda, who is dressed in her Fate robes for the first time since I've known her. The Queen sneers, "Another Fate. I remember you, though you now deign to show your face. Your kind has brought me nothing but pain. This world ends now!" She begins chanting, her voice echoing on the wind, and her body begins to glow like the sun.

Callia appears by my side. "You must kill her. Now. It's the only way," she says.

"No." I'm not a murderer. We can still execute my plan.

"Elijah." I call out. "Sebastian. Liam. Derek. It's time."

The Night brothers snap into action, rushing to my side as we discussed. We all clasp hands and form a circle. The earth druid to my right. The water druid to my left. Fire and air across from me.

I channel my powers, seeking to create a barrier like the one I did to hold Ana. I only had a few of the brothers lending me their strength that time. With all four it should be enough to hold even the Mother of Dragons. It must be enough. The elements swirl together, creating an intricate web of white light that covers the giant dragon. Magic seals, runes that I once knew in a past life, begin to appear around her. The barrier is forming. Her glow diminishing. She is trapped.

Matilda makes her way downstairs and joins our circle as Kaya manages to take Lily, Alina and Zara outside the castle. The barrier strengthens, becoming almost blinding with its light, fueled by the power of two Fates and four druids.

But as the queen fights against her captivity, I can feel my magic stretching, pulling, and tearing apart. For a moment, I connect with the Queen, with her power, and I feel an energy so hot, so overwhelming, it burns like an inferno. A heat so blistering even a fire druid could not resist its flames. There is so much power here. More than I have ever felt. The blaze grows. The queen screams.

And the barrier shatters.

A shockwave erupts from the golden dragon, knocking all five of us to the ground, breaking our circle as wooden furniture splinters apart and stone cracks to pieces.

"I killed a Fate once," roars the queen. "You think I can't kill more?" She resumes her chanting, and the ground beneath us begins to crack as the world is undone piece by piece.

The northern wall splits in half, crumbling under the weight of its own stone, and then it falls, leaving us in only a partial shell of a castle, our library now extending into the side garden.

I think of all the lives that will be lost and wonder if I could have done more. If I should have tried to save as many as possible before it came to this. But I don't have time to second guess myself.

I channel all my power, my body glowing white, and I float into the sky and summon lightning at my fingertips, flinging it at her, but the bolts bounce off her golden scales like pebbles.

I try fire next, and it slips off her like oil. Nothing is working.

Below me, Sebastian tries to hold the earth together. Elijah and Derek work as one to keep the storm from tearing us all apart. And Liam launches his own useless attack.

It's over.

Unless…

I tap into my Darkness, using the tracking spell Cole helped me to perform, and search for the unicorn dagger. It should be somewhere below. Amongst the rubble.

But it's not.

It's above me.

Close to the queen.

I don't understand.

Until I see the dark mist.

See his body appearing midair, black cloak flapping in the wind, unicorn dagger in hand.

Cole.

He materializes at her chest and plunges the dagger toward her heart. It breaks through a scale, and the queen roars in agony, golden blood spilling from her wound, her wings flapping erratically. Cole places both hands on the hilt, driving the dagger deeper. Deep enough to pierce her heart.

But then she swipes at him with one of her massive talons, hitting him in the side. And like an insignificant mosquito, he is flung through the air, dagger slipping from his palm as it falls into the shadows. I create a pocket of wind to catch him, slowing his descent to the ground. His face is bloody and purple, but he manages a grin through scarlet lips.

The queen of dragon roars, holding a claw in front of her chest to protect her gaping wound. "I should have destroyed this cesspool without warning. It is over. You cannot defeat me. Give up!" Her voice carries through the sky and the destruction continues.

But then she glances behind us and her eyes widen. Her words stop. Her glow fades. For the first time, I see the dragon queen afraid. "No. It can't be. I killed you a millennium ago. You cannot be here. You're supposed to be dead."

I follow her gaze behind me, to the garden.

To the creature that is now free. A black and golden monstrosity, with wings that look crooked and torn, and a venomous drill-like horn. Ana. In her true form. She grows in size, flying towards the Queen—her mother.

How did she get out? But then I realize...the Queen freed her child herself when she tore apart the earth. It must have broken the magical seal we created.

The two clash in the sky, the dragon queen moving desperately to avoid her daughter's horn, striking out with her claws, cutting into the hybrid-creature's shoulder. Ana cries out into the storm, a hideous sound of pain and anguish and fury.

And in that moment, with the Queen of Dragons and her abandoned child fixed completely on each other, I see my opportunity. I use my Darkness to track the dagger once more, and with my Air, I retrieve the blade, hovering in midair before me, and aim it at the Queen's heart.

That's it.

I have the shot.

All I need is a push.

But something shifts within me.

A struggle at my very core.

535

I've taken a life before. But my past self was in control then. The ancient Maiden Fate. But now... Now I am in control. The dragon's blood will be on my hands.

I can't take another life.

But I can't let her take my world.

"*In lumen et lumen*," I whisper.

And with flick of my wrist, the dagger flies true.

And penetrates the Queen's heart.

SHE SCREAMS and drops from the sky, but as she does, she shoots one last golden arch of lightning at Ana, hitting her in the heart.

They both land hard on the wet crumbling earth, creating a wave of earthquakes that is felt across the world.

I lower myself from the sky and race to them, praying it's over, that we are safe.

As I approach the Queen, she shifts into her human form, clutching the dagger in her heart. Golden blood seeps out of her wound and mouth, but still she smiles. "At least I will die knowing I am taking this wretched world with me. It is over. It is done. I have completed the spell to end the Otherworld."

I reel back, terrified, sickened, my soul feeling as if it's being sucked from my body. "What did you do?" I scream at the dying dragon. "What have you done?" I can't control my tears, or my rage, as her life fades away and my world continues to crumble.

Near her, Ana lies still. Too still. Her body now that of a little girl, but not as before. A small unicorn horn protrudes from her forehead and delicate dragon wings span out behind her.

I crawl over to the motionless form, my body hurting as if it too is being torn apart.

I am dying.

As the world dies, I too am becoming undone.

I take Ana's hand, and her eyes flicker open. "I remember now," she says, words barely a whisper. "But I didn't mean to. You have to believe me. I didn't mean to. My friend... she made me... " Her eyes flicker closed again, and she goes still. Her hand goes limp in mine.

I can't see through my tears. Through my pain. Through my rage.

And then the Night brothers, all five of them, surround me. They hold me, support me, and give me strength.

And a thought begins to form.

"What if... "

I look at them all. Each representing the elements that live within me.

I glance at Amora, whose body remains.

And I wonder.

"We can save the world," I shout over the storm. "But we have to work together."

I look to Cole, the prodigal brother, the lost soul. "We need you," I say.

Tears fill his dark eyes and he nods.

I glance at the rings on my fingers and trace the symbols of darkness and earth in the air. The Night Brothers and I form a circle once more, all of us holding hands, but this time Cole is with us. Six elements. Like the six dragons who first formed this world. I recall the spell Ava'Kara taught me. The one I used to expand the Otherworld. But this time, I'll use Amora, the Mother of the Dragons, as the focal point.

"It won't work," Ra'Terr says, his body wrapped in his dark wings as he lands from the sky with Brock by his side. They glance quickly at their mother's corpse, and for a moment I see a hint of sadness in their eyes, but it is quickly gone, replaced by a hard resolve. "The sacrifice has to be from a living dragon." He clutches the poisonous wound at his side, leaning on his sister for support. "Use me," he says simply. "I can be the sacrifice."

Brock turns her head, auburn hair wild in the storm, emotion clouding her eyes. "No. You…"

"It's the only way," he says. "I'd rather die like this, then live a moment longer knowing I have failed my people. Use me. I will be the sacrifice. Let me amend for any harm I may have caused those I swore to protect."

I nod, tears streaming down my face and flying away in the wind, and I resume the spell, this time focused on Ra'Terr. Brock stands away, and they maintain eye contact with each other as I channel all the power the six of us have into the body of Ra'Terr and into the body of this world.

The storm rages even stronger.

Wind nearly blinds me.

Debris flies through the air.

Still I scream out the words Ava'Kara taught me, infused with every ounce of magic I have left in my body.

"Terry autumn usque ad terram!"

Everything around the Darkness Dragon turns dark, like a black hole spreading from his body, consuming him. Within, a small spark of light begins to glow, growing brighter until it explodes like a dying sun, creating a shining dust that falls to the ground and dissipates into nothing.

Instantly, the storm dies down, the earth stops shaking, and the world becomes eerily silent.

CHAPTER 18: THE FRIEND

Tell all the Truth but tell it slant —
Success in Circuit lies
Too bright for our infirm Delight
The Truth's superb surprise
-Emily Dickinson

Two Weeks Later

THE DAYS PASS LIKE A DREAM. I am weak for many of them, drained from my spell, and nearly helpless when the people begin to rebuild what was broken. Two weeks pass before my strength returns, and it is time to go.

The Night brothers and I arrive in the grove early, but already it's crowded with Otherworlders of all kinds. Lily and Kaya are there waiting for us, and hugs are exchanged as we take our places near the front. Matilda insisted on staying behind to care for the children, but I honestly think this was too much for her. She has kept her identity a secret for so long, I think it's hard for her to be known and to face her past. Healing will take time for everyone, but there is enough love to guide us through.

There's a sense of solemn festivity that often accompanies funerals, which are inherently strange, I've always thought. They are a blend of celebration, mourning, and socializing that lends itself to a singularly unique experience equivalent to an emotional milkshake. Throw every feeling you've ever had together and blend.

Brock'Mir stands on a platform built for this event. There are no bodies left of her siblings, so she asked me to paint portraits of each of them for the service. Those are placed around her as she addresses the crowd.

"Today we come to honor the sacrifices of my brothers and sisters, and to say goodbye to the Age of the Dragons."

A murmur spreads through the crowd as everyone wonders what that means.

"Ava'Kara was the first amongst us to die. She gave her life willingly to expand this world so that there would be room for everyone who needs sanctuary and safety. For all those who share our bloodline and our magic. We honor her."

There is a moment of silence as I use my magic to bring water up from the land, creating a natural fresh water source. It will flow always, giving refreshment to weary travelers in Kara's name.

"Lyx'Ara spent much of her later life living amongst you, helping you, leading many of you into what is called the New World. She believed in a system that recognized everyone as valid, as belonging, as deserving, and we honor her."

There is a moment of silence and I create a ball of pure white light that brightens the forest around us and will remain there always as a symbol of the light Lyx brought to the world.

"My brother, Ventus'Arak took his own life. In his final message to us, he expressed his deep grief over the unraveling of our world and our family. My heart breaks for his life, and I honor him."

This silence is the most painful for my heart. Suicide cuts twice as deep. But I pull my air magic out and allow a gentle breeze to caress the crowd. Anyone who ventures into this forest will feel the touch of the wind in the Air Dragon's memory.

"As many of you know, my brother Dath'Racul was also murdered, defending the life of one of the Fates. And we honor him."

I create a great bonfire with my magic, the fire burning brightly and providing heat to all around it. It is a fire that will never spread, but will always bring warmth and comfort to those who come here. Racul will be remembered.

"And finally, Ra'Terr gave his last moments of life to aid in saving this world from destruction. To save your lives. And we honor him."

In discussing with Brock how to honor her siblings, this was the hardest and required the most thought. I pull a strand of Darkness from my soul and cast a shadow in the shape of a dragon over the land near us. Anyone who walks through the darkness will feel the power of their own shadow self rise up in them, and will be encouraged to embrace that part of them to become whole.

"We come to the end of our ceremony," Brock says, "but there is one last thing that must be done. I am leaving the Otherworld."

There are gasps and protestations. People crying out asking who will lead them?

She waits until they die down before calling me over to her.

A lump forms in my throat as I walk onto the stage and take my place by her side, tugging at my purple cloak from my past life which Matilda altered to fit my current life.

"Eve Oliver is the Maiden Fate reborn."

This brings a few gasps, but I'm pretty sure that rumor has already spread everywhere.

"She contains within herself all the elements of each of the dragons."

That gets people talking.

"And she has saved our world, twice. First when she expanded it. Second when she stopped my mother from destroying it. Her life is bound to this world and to you. As my last act as High Dragon of the Council of Dragons, I name Eve Oliver my successor on this world and Guardian of the Otherworld."

She pulls from her robe a staff made of a deep black wood with a crystal tip. "Do you accept this responsibility and all it entails?" she asks me.

"I do," I say.

"Then it is done. Eve, Guardian of the Otherworld, High Priestess of the Council of Dragons, Maiden Fate Reborn. My people, you have a new leader, and I know you will be in the best of hands. The Age of Dragons is over, but a new age has arisen, and it is one for all the people of the Otherworld."

A great cheer fills the forest and I can't help the tears that flow down my cheeks. I look to the brothers, all five together, a family as we were always meant to be, and I feel their love and magic pouring into me.

LATER THAT NIGHT, after much celebrating, drinking and eating, we return to the castle with Brock, who looks as tired as I feel. "Are you sure you want to do this tonight?" I ask, for her sake but also mine. This goodbye will be hard.

She nods. "My people are waiting for me. My kingdom, in my true world, does not have a leader. Given my mother's frame of mind, perhaps they have not had one for a very long time. Now that I know my people here are safe, I need to take my place as Queen there."

We walk into the library where Zara and Alina are playing in the crib together. Matilda is asleep in a corner chair so we do not wake her. Liam picks up Zara and holds her close, kissing her forehead, then passes her to the other brothers.

And then she's given to me, and I hold her tightly and whisper words only meant for her before I hand her to her aunt.

"I wish she could stay with us forever," I say, "but I know she needs her own kind."

More tears flow, and the Earth Dragon looks on sympathetically. "I will bring her back for visits," she says, as Alina begins to cry when she realizes her best friend will not be returning.

Liam picks up his daughter and rocks her to soothe her feelings.

"And what of the girl," Brock says. "Ana?"

"She has shown no signs of the monster since that night," I say.

Liam nods. "All of my examinations have indicated that in her death, the monster part of her died and the child yet lived."

"A child who is part unicorn, part dragon," Brock says.

"Yes. And maybe one day she will exhibit shifting abilities," Elijah says, "but we have seen no evidence of this."

"So you will keep her and raise her?" Brock asks.

I look to the brothers and nod. "Yes. She is family now."

Brock smiles. "Very well. If she ever does show signs of shifting into a dragon, don't hesitate to reach out. She may need guidance from us to know herself."

"We won't," I assure her.

Tension coils in me as our time nears to an end.

And out of the corner of my eye, I see a small form sneaking through the shadows behind the Earth Dragon, wielding the unicorn horn dagger.

I hold out a hand and cast a shield, just as Ana strikes against the dragon, and trap her in a barrier before she can do any harm.

There's chaos for a moment as Sebastian pushes Brock out of the way and everyone stares wide eyed, shocked at the little girl holding the weapon mid-air, ready to kill the last remaining adult dragon on this world.

I remain calm.

And approach the child. "Ana? Can you hear me?"

But she doesn't respond. Her eyes are black pools floating in silver and I know she's not acting on her own accord.

She never was.

"Callia, show yourself!" I shout, and then I repeat the words Lilith taught me. The mother of all vampires did not discover how to defeat Amora in her time away, but she did bring back some very useful information. And it helped me put all the pieces together.

Callia appears, locked in a barrier much like the one holding Ana, looking angry and confused. "How did you summon me against my will?" she demands. She thrashes, but no amount of force allows her to escape.

"You can't leave or hide any longer. You have been behind the murders the whole time, haven't you?"

Her eyes shift, and she realizes that everyone can now see her. Her mouth is agape as her new reality settles in on her. "I...how did you know?"

"I never believed Ana was acting out these attacks on her own. She was having night terrors and talked of an imaginary friend. I suspected she was being controlled, but didn't put the pieces together until Lilith returned from the dragon world with some very interesting information about the war between the unicorns and the dragons, and a specific ability the unicorns had to control other sentient beings, making them particularly dangerous. She found a spell that I could use to bind you here."

Callia turns to Brock, rage simmering in her dark gaze. "You killed my brothers and sisters. You all did. You massacred us out of fear, and then your mother killed me to hide her secret. You all deserved your fates."

Brock frowns. "Hate begets hate. Violence begets violence. I could justify what we did by pointing out what your people did to an entire generation of our eggs. And maybe you could go back further and argue we deserved that. Does it matter? If we continue this path there will be no more of either of our kind left."

Callia spits. "There are no more unicorns left. I was the last one."

I point to Ana. "There is her. She is part of you and part of the dragons, yet you would use her as a weapon to murder? A child? Your child?"

Callia's face drops as she sees her daughter, truly sees her. Ana's eyes have returned to normal and she looks as she truly is, a little girl who is lost, alone, and scared. And tortured by the memories of what she has done under the control of someone else.

"Gods, what have I done to you, my child? What have I done?"

Callia drops to her knees. "Most of them are dead and yet I feel no relief. No hope. No peace. I am stuck forever in this hell Amora sent me to when I would not let her kill our daughter."

Brock turns to Callia. "I am tired of the wars. Of the fighting. Of the killing. We will not be friends. And it will take me lifetimes to forgive what you have done to my family. Just as it will take you lifetimes to forgive me for what I've done to yours. But perhaps we can try? For our children's sake?"

Callia's eyes flick to the side, shame filling her face. "I do not know how to stop, but I agree, the bloodshed cannot continue. Vengeance has not given me what I'd hoped, but neither will forgiveness, I fear. I am too lost for both."

She turns to me. "What will you do to me now? Where will I go?"

"WHERE YOU DESERVE," I say softly.

CHAPTER 18: THE PUNISHMENT

"If you are seeking, seek us with joy
For we live in the kingdom of joy.
Do not give your heart to anything else
But to the love of those who are clear joy,
Do not stray into the neighborhood of despair.
For there are hopes: they are real, they exist –
Do not go in the direction of darkness –
I tell you: suns exist."
~Rumi

THE TENSION between Callia and Brock is thick, and with the dragons leaving this world and the unicorns extinct, Ana is now all that's left of the two races, and none of us know what that will mean for her as she grows into her own powers—if she has any left at all.

Only time will tell what the future holds for the child.

We stand by the ocean near the castle, the five Night brothers, myself, Ana, Brock and Zara, and Lilith, who has just arrived.

Callia awaits her fate nervously.

"Are you sure this will work?" I ask Lilith for the umpteenth time.

"Yes," she says with slight exasperation. "I obtained this spell from a solid source."

It is meant to open the door to the world of spirits, but I'm nervous as I begin the incantation. So much could go wrong. The last thing I want to do is create a tear in the fabric of reality and unleash the undead into the Otherworld.

We just narrowly avoided an end of the world scenario. We don't need a ghost apocalypse now.

But we have to do something with Callia. She can't stay in this world as she is. She's a risk to others and she cannot heal while living in limbo.

The Night brothers stand near me and I channel their power with mine as I speak the ancient words. They are unfamiliar on my tongue, but Lilith and Brock both helped me learn the proper pronunciation.

As I speak, my hands begin to glow and a streak of light and darkness woven together spreads, creating a portal that peels open, and producing a window into the realm of the dead.

"It is time," I say to Callia.

I could force her into the portal, but I remain hopeful that won't be necessary. It will be better for her own soul's journey if she steps in on her own.

She looks around, fear etched in her face.

She has clung to hatred and revenge for so long, she knows nothing else.

Brock can barely look at her, but as Callia takes a step forward, something within the portal shifts as a green landscape of rolling hills comes into focus. And then I see them.

Hundreds of unicorns prancing and playing. One gallops over to the portal and shifts into a beautiful woman with deep mahogany hair and matching skin. She peers through, as if looking into a dream, and then she drops to her knees. "My Queen."

Callia startles, then steps forward, reaching out a hand. "Lumara? Is that really you?"

Tears stream down both their faces as the Queen of the Unicorns steps through the portal and joins her people after millennia apart. They take hands and walk towards the others. When they reach the glade, they shift into their unicorn forms and Callia is surrounded by her people.

Brock's face is hard, impassive as she watches this, and I can only imagine what she's thinking or feeling. Callia, who killed her siblings, now gets to be with her kind. And Brock is alone.

I glance at Lilith, who seems to read my mind and nods.

I concentrate and the scene shifts to one of mountain tops and endless skies. And five dragons flying against the backdrop of a beautiful, warm sun. Brock gasps and moves closer. "My family," she says, softly.

"Would you like to speak with them?" I ask.

She reaches her hand out, nearly touching the portal, her eyes misting over. "Can I?"

I nod and move away from the gateway so she has some time alone with her siblings.

I take this moment to enjoy the crashing of the waves against the shore, and Cole joins me, his arm sliding around my waist.

"Are you coming to say goodbye again?" I ask without looking at him.

I've been in fear of this moment since the battle with Amora. He saved us, saved the world, by showing up. I couldn't have done that spell without him. Without all five of them. When I expanded the lands here, I was building on what already existed. I had enough power to do that. But this time, it was different. I had to stop the destruction of the Otherworld, which basically meant rebuilding it from within. I needed every element amplified to accomplish that. Cole was integral in that.

Since then he's stayed, though he is often missing for long periods. Each time, I expect he won't come back, but he does.

But I've been waiting for the final goodbye.

And here it is.

He moves to stand in front of me, his dark gaze capturing mine. "I've spoken to my brothers," he says softly, his lilting French accent like music. "And if it's all right with you, I'd like to stay."

My eyes widen. "For good?"

He nods. "Forever."

Tears blur my vision and I hug him fiercely. "Of course it's okay with me," I say. "We are all meant to be together."

We walk hand in hand back to the portal and Brock is saying her final goodbyes. Ava'Kara is there in human form, gazing longingly at her daughter. When she sees me, she smiles. "You have done well, my friend. This world is in the best of hands with you."

After saying her last goodbyes, Brock turns to face us with tears in her eyes. "We must go now. My world awaits."

We've already said our goodbyes, but we exchange one last hug and watch as they fly into the sky through the tear Brock opens. When it closes behind them, I sigh and turn to finish sealing the portal I created into the world of the dead.

But just as I'm about to, Lilith puts a hand on mine. "There's one more who wants to come through," she says, her gaze distant.

I wait, watching as the portal shifts once again and standing by a cottage is…Adam.

I cry out, and step closer, wanting desperately to go through and hug him once more. Cole takes my hand to keep me in this world as Adam moves closer to the doorway. "Evie," he says softly, his big blue eyes so achingly familiar. "I am so sorry I left you the way I did."

Tears stream down my face. "Oh, Adam. I wish you were here," I say. "I would give anything for you to be back with me."

"It's all okay, sis," he says. "I'm healing. My heart and soul are healing. And someday I will come back to you. Someday we will be together again. Just know, I'm safe. And I'll love you forever. It's always going to be you and me against the world."

"See you soon, then," I say. "I'll be looking for you."

He smiles. "We will always find each other. We always have."

And then he is gone.

CHAPTER 19: EPILOGUE

"This is love: to fly toward a secret sky, to cause a hundred veils to fall each moment. First, to let go of life. Finally, to take a step without fear."

~ Rumi

1 year later

Lily and Kaya gaze deeply into each other's eyes as they take their vows to one another. We are in the center of the majestic grove surrounded by trees. They are both dressed in full dryad style, with wildflowers and vines flowing from their beautiful gowns.

Alina, barely walking, totters nearby, with Moon to keep her steady, and she randomly tosses rose petals at people.

All our friends are here to celebrate the mating of these remarkable dryads.

"I now give to you the beautiful mating of Lily and Kaya, forever bound by love, by respect, by compassion, and by the elements that shape our world."

They kiss and our friends cheer, tossing flowers at the happy couple.

The ceremony was short and sweet, but the afterparty will last all night, as is tradition.

There are tables set up with drink and food, mats for resting when people need to, and music for dancing. It is festive and lighthearted, and everyone we care about is here.

This last year has brought so much change to the Otherworld. A new form of government, rebuilding areas that were destroyed by Amora, and a shift in the way everything is managed.

It hasn't been easy. Many have been resistant to change. But slowly we are showing people that the best way to move forward is actually going forwards, not backwards. We can no longer live in the past if we want a world where everyone is safe and happy.

Ana comes over to me carrying two drinks and hands me one. "It was beautiful," she says shyly.

She is still coming out of her shell, and her healing will take time. But she is finally excited to start school with other kids her age.

I watch as the Gargoyle's daughter plays with Alina. The Ifrits join them, their new baby in hand. He's six months old now and already bursting into flames at random times. Alina loves him and is one of the few kids who can actually hold him without injury. Fortunately, the Gargoyles' child is immune to fire as well, being stone and all.

Lily and Kaya dance in blissful synchronicity, swaying to the music, lost in their love.

Lilith comes to me, a smile on her lips. "Will there be a wedding in your future?" she asks.

I laugh. "I'm not entirely sure what the logistics would be to marry five men at once," I say. "But I think our bonds are pretty well established without all this."

This year has brought a lot of personal healing to our family. The Nights and Matilda have sorted through their complicated history. The brothers have had ups and downs with Cole, but all in all we've made it work.

Lilith moves on to chat with others, and Cole joins me. "Did I hear something about a wedding?" he asks.

I slide an arm through his. "I don't think we need one to make what we have count, do you?"

He looks down at a me. "No, but there is something I wanted to talk to you about. I want to bind myself to you, as part of the Order of Druids," he says softly.

I pause. This is huge for him. We've never talked about it. I've never demanded it. With what Cole went through, I never expected it, to be honest. "Are you sure?"

He nods. "It's the one piece missing, and I want that with you. Only you."

"Do your brothers know?" I ask.

"I wanted you to be the first, but I'll tell them."

I hold him back. "Not today. Let today be about Lily. We have plenty of time."

That night there is much celebration, laughter and joy, and as I take turns dancing with each of the brothers, I'm reminded of just how lucky I am to have them in my life. They each bring a special kind of magic to my heart. Not just their elemental magic, but their soul magic, that connection that fills me and makes me feel like I've finally found home.

Elijah matches my intellect. Pushes me to new knowledge and understanding. I can stay up all night talking and reading with him. He shares my passion for books like none other.

Derek makes me laugh, soothes over hurt feelings with his calming water magic and verbally spars with me.

Liam is my fire. He burns as hot as I do and fans the flames of my passion, in and out of the bedroom. He is my music and my warmth.

Cole... Cole helps me to embrace my shadow self, the light and the dark within me. He shows me how to hold the duality of my nature together in a way that makes me stronger.

And Sebastian...he is my rock, my foundation, the man I know will hold me up when I need extra strength. He supports me and loves me through it all.

These men together create the family I have craved my whole life. They form the unbreakable circle in which I stand.

~

THE NEXT DAY I have a job interview. Not for myself, of course, but for a new assistant for The Night Firm.

It has to be held at the courthouse, since our castle is still full of people celebrating Lily's wedding.

I'm sitting at my desk when she arrives, and I have her escorted in.

"I'm Kass," she says smiling.

She's a beautiful woman with a scanty resume and I've been curious about her since reviewing her application.

"Tell me why you want to work for the Night Firm," I say.

She hesitates. "I... I've only been in this world a short time, and I'm still trying to figure out where I belong. I was recently turned into a vampire and most of my human life was wasted on...well, let's just say I didn't have that great of an upbringing or even direction, really. I know the Night Firm is no longer a legal defense, but is now about making sure the disenfranchised of the world get equal access to resources and opportunities. I want to be a part of that. I want this new life to matter. To make a difference. I know I don't have experience, but I'm a fast learner and I will work hard, I promise you that."

I study the woman before me. She and I are very different in many ways. She's less polished, less educated than I was when I came to the Firm. But she has the same haunted look in her eyes I did. A look that speaks of pain and loss. Like me, she needs a new path that will give her life meaning.

Before I can comment, she shifts uncomfortably. "I understand if I'm not a fit...or if, if the Night brothers won't want me."

She may not be the perfect fit on paper, and it might be complicated, all things considered, but my flash buzzes and I know what I must do. I stand and offer her my hand. "Welcome to the Night Firm."

≈

THE END

≈

You made it to the end of The Night Firm! What a journey you have been on. We hope you enjoyed the magic, mystery and madness of it all. But don't close the book just yet. We have some fun bonus content for you. Keep reading for sneak peeks of 4 other books (including Wanted, which is a standalone spin off of The Night Firm), as well as an original KK short story, Night Terrors.

We'd also love to send you a newsletter the moment we have a new release. Sign up here: http://bit.ly/kkbooknews

And if you're on Facebook, come join us in the KK Coven and Bad Witches Coven for monthly live events, giveaways and more.

Finally, if you want all our content early, consider becoming a patron at Patreon.com/KarpovKinrade. You get all our books, music and anything else we do before anyone else, plus bonus content no one else gets!

Ready for your next read? Check out the following:

The Winter Witch, co-written with Heather Hildenbrand. A standalone fairytale-esque fantasy romance full of magic. Grab it on Amazon.

Wanted, co-written with Liv Chatham. A standalone dark paranormal romance that's a spin off of The Night Firm. Grab it on Amazon.

Dungeon Queen, co-written with Liv Chatham. A fantasy romance RH series with Greek Gods, mystery and magic. Grab it on Amazon.

Mad Girl: Locked Up, co-written with Heather Hildenbrand. A paranormal romance RH where nothing is what it seems and everyone is mad... some are just more dangerous than others. Grab it on Amazon.

Vampire Girl: A USA Today bestselling complete 7 book vampire fantasy romance. TheVampireGirl.com

We hope to see you around!

Love, Lux & Dmytry

BONUS: THE WINTER WITCH
—CHAPTER 1

BY Karpov Kinrade & Heather Hildenbrand

CHAPTER 1

A WISP of light pierces the darkness, the candle flickering bravely against the penetrating night, and then, in a blink, thousands of flames join the first, illuminating the ancient forest in which we are gathered.

Our matriarch stands before the largest Sophos Tree in our village, her arms outstretched, the long white robe she wears blending into the white bark of the tree and the winter snow that blankets our world. Her voice is melodic and firm. "Each light, alone, is nothing. But together, we can outshine the sun."

The villagers chant back, repeating her words.

I'm kneeled before her in my own white cloak, my long dark hair undone and trailing down my back in soft curls. The cold bite of our never-ending winter nips at my ears and nose, and I sniff as quietly as I can and pray to the goddess I do not sneeze and ruin the ceremony.

"Tonight, we baptize Adara Alexander with the sacred waters of the

Ice Rivers. Adara is the flame born in the cold, the defender of humankind, sent to free us from the curse that plagues our land and our people. A Winter Witch, the first to be born in our village in over a thousand years, and the strongest we have ever seen. Our prayers to the goddess have been answered. We have been sent a savior. May the goddess bless Adara," she says.

"May the goddess bless Adara," the villagers respond.

I look towards the ground, focusing my attention on the crust of snow forming over the forest mulch, and she pours the pitcher of ice water over my head. I force myself not to shiver as my hair instantly freezes.

"May the goddess guide her path," she says.

The villagers once again repeat her litany, a chorus of voices adding their magic to the words spoken each year over a new sacrifice.

But this year the words are different.

This year, *I'm* the difference.

Normally, the chosen one would be selected by lottery. There isn't a family in Willowdale who hasn't lost someone to this annual slaughter. But this year, we all knew I would be the one to go. I came of age last month, just in time to be offered.

But I am not being sent to die like the others.

I'm being sent to kill.

I've known it my whole life. Trained. Studied. Prepared. And now it is time.

As she completes the ceremony, I stand to face her, and she pulls me into a hug, kissing both my wet cheeks. "Carry the flames of the sun in your heart, my sweet granddaughter. And come home to me."

Tears sting my eyes as my grandmother releases me and turns me to face our clan. "Tonight, we celebrate the Festival of Lights. Drink, Eat and Be Merry, good people. Our fates will soon turn toward the better. I have spoken."

The crowd cheers, and as I help my grandmother slip her thick cloak over her frail shoulders, someone begins playing a fiddle. I toss my own cloak on, wrapping my wet hair and tucking it away. Then I smile as everyone begins singing the familiar folk song as they make their way back to town.

. . .

THE CANDLES LIT
   Darkness outwit
   We sing to usher in the dawn

THE SUN WILL RISE
   As winter dies
   We sing until the snow is gone

HO HO HALLIHO the light
   No No Nevermore the night
   Ho Ho Halliho the dawn
   No No Winter now be gone

AFTER THE FIRST ROUND, harmonies are added and the melodic refrains echoes throughout town, which tonight is decked out with tables laden with food and wine. There will be dancing, entertainment, and all manner of revelry that lasts until morning.

It's normally my favorite night of the year. Even as a child I was allowed to stay up all night, eat whatever I wanted and run wild with the magic of the evening.

But tonight, I will partake of very little, as I need my sleep before my treacherous journey tomorrow. Always, I've wondered what it would be like to be on the other side of the merriment. To be the sacrifice, celebrated in glory for one night, only to die the next. Now I know. It is a somber thing even if I'm not going to my death.

My grandmother takes my arm, and we walk slowly together, trailing the others and enjoying the stillness of the cool winter night.

"What if I fail?" I ask, the fear weighing heavy on my soul.

I clutch at the vial that hangs around my neck and feel the warmth of it to the depths of my soul. I have collected a drop of blood from every villager and mixed it with the sap of the Sophos Tree and a crushed petal of a Fire Flower. Legend has it these bold red beauties were a summer flower before the curse, yet they continue to dot the snowy landscape of the mountains to the west even still, and are a symbol of the enduring persistence of hope. The last ingredient was my magic, infused into it over the course of a full moon cycle using a spell I created over many years; the most complicated one I've ever performed. It is now ready, and so am I.

At least, I hope I am.

"You will not fail," my grandmother says softly, her lilting voice a comfort as it has been all my life. "You have the sun's fire in your heart. It will guide you."

We walk the rest of the way in companionable silence, the sound of music and laughter spilling out from the village square, audible even from this distance.

A symphony of night birds sings from the highest branches of the trees, sharing their secrets with one another. *What do you see, little birds?* I wonder, glancing up into the canopy that shines with moonbeams and twinkles with starlight. *What do you hear?* And not for the first time I wonder, what will it be like to see the snow melt and the ice crack and then disappear, to see fresh flowers and leaves exposed to the sunlight, glowing in color, iridescent in their brilliance? What will it be like to feel warm from head to toe, without the aid of fire? How will our lives change when we can plow and farm and forage again? When we can support ourselves and use trade for mutual gain rather than survival?

Our entire culture and way of life is oriented around winter, cold, snow. If I do succeed, our village—our whole kingdom—will need to adapt to entirely new lives. We've, of course, heard the stories of summers and autumns and springs in other lands, but those who venture from our village never return. And many of the elders fear an unspoken rule that we are not meant to leave. Few have dared to try since, and so we live on stories and hope.

The year I was born, when it was clear I had magic of my own, the village began preparing for spring. They purchased seeds and wove lighter fabrics for new clothing. They made maps of the best lands for farming, raising cattle, and building on. They gave everything to the hope—the belief—that I would be their savior. Thus, my name. Adara means fire. Alexander is defender of human kind.

It's a big name to live up to, but the moment I was old enough, I began to study the books kept in a locked library and guarded by my family for generations. Books left by the old ones who had magic running in their veins. Books that taught me everything I know about magic.

My bag for tomorrow is already packed. I have a change of clothes, dried meats and fruits, wine, hard bread, and cheese. And I have my herbs, my potions, and my Grimoire. I would never leave home without them, despite taking up valuable space in my pack.

There is nothing for me to do but wait out the night. Still, I must eat, and as we enter the town, the thatched roofs shimmering under the moonlight, the villagers dressed in their most colorful cloaks and scarves, fire pits burning at every corner for light and warmth, it all invites me in, to dine, to smile, to laugh, to enjoy one more night with the people who have bound my heartstrings to them.

As people mill about, my grandmother pulls away to make her rounds and many stop to chat with me, to ask me how I am, to offer me words of support or gratitude.

Conversations about the curse float around me as people share stories they heard from long-dead relatives.

"I hear he sucks the blood from his victims to stay alive," the baker says, shaking his head.

"He is a vampire of old, though they were thought to be long dead," the librarian says. "But thousands of years ago, the wicked prince was cursed with this ancient demon, and now he walks the nights devouring the souls of his victims along with their blood."

I shiver and move away from that group. I don't need more horror stories filling my head. I've got enough of my own to keep my imagination active.

While many continue to greet me, none stay and chat. I'm a bit of an oddity in the village.

I had a different upbringing than others. While most kids went to the small schoolhouse and studied together, I was tutored in private, by my grandmother and others, for the one job I would have in this life.

Now I smile as my combat instructor approaches. She is tall and lean with dark eyes, even darker skin, and is never without her bow and arrow, though she is just as deadly with a sword.

"Adara, well wishes to you," she says in her thick eastern accent, holding out her forearm.

I grasp it in the traditional greeting and nod. "Thank you, Kadere. I wouldn't be this prepared without your years of training."

"You made a fine pupil," she says, then turns to leave.

Kadere is from a kingdom to the east. She came here to train me for a season, then met a woman with whom she fell in love and never left. She's not one for words, but she's been a dear friend these many years.

I watch as she joins her wife, their daughter spinning in circles laughing. The girl was an orphan whose father was killed by the beast on the mountain and whose mother died of heartbreak not a year later. Now she has a happy home, but that does not erase the blood debt the monster owes to my village.

A tall, handsome young man rushes over to me carrying a plate of food and a goblet of wine, distracting me from my dark thoughts. "Adara, I was hoping you would come," he says, a blush rising on his cheeks.

I've known Arthur since we were both crawling in mud with pigs. He hands me the plate and cup. "I thought you might be hungry," he says with a shy grin. "And thirsty," he adds quickly.

"Thank you, I am." I sip the wine and try to sort out how to eat while holding both the cup and the plate. "Walk with me?" I ask as I tuck the plate into the same hand as the goblet so I can more easily pluck a chunk of honeyed ham from it.

He falls into step beside me. "Are you scared?" he asks.

"Yes," I say honestly.

He raises an eyebrow in surprise. "I've never seen you scared before," he says.

"Sure you have," I say, layering a bit of cheese and salami onto a cracker. "I get scared loads of times."

"But you never seem it. You're always so sure of yourself."

I shrug, licking my fingers and then dipping a strawberry into whipped buttercream. "I feel the fear, and I do it anyway. That's all you can ever do."

He pauses, and we watch a group ice-skating on the lake under the bridge we stand on.

"So that's what you're doing now? Feeling your fear but doing it anyways?"

"Yes," I say, closing my eyes as I conjure up the thing that terrifies me the most and mentally stare it down.

"I don't think I could do it," he says.

I turn to him. "Do what?"

He shivers. "Face the monster that killed my parents."

A cold wind whips around me, and I stiffen my spine and look into the distance, toward the snowcapped Ice Mountains. "That's why I have to do it. He killed my parents. Now, I will kill him."

To be continued….

ONE CLICK on Amazon.

BONUS: DUNGEON QUEEN —CHAPTER 1

BY KARPOV KINRADE & Liv Chatham

CHAPTER 1

RED EYES GLOWING in the crisp fall night.
 Terror pulsing through my veins.
 My breath comes in short gasps as panic clutches my gut.
 And then…the screams.

I WAKE WITH A START, my heart beating with such force I fear my ribs will crack. A sheen of sweat soaks my clothes, making my skin itch, and my head feels crushed in a vice. My eyelids peel open but the light is too bright, and I squeeze them shut against the glare. Every part of my body aches, and a dread I can't define has me in its grip.

A nightmare. I must have been having a nightmare…but why do I feel as if I've been hit by a truck?

Through my anxious haze, music floats to me as if in a dream.

Something stringed— a harp, perhaps—plays a calming melody that dances in my mind. I try to move, to sit up, to see where the music is coming from, but my body feels tethered to some dark place, and I moan, finally giving up, still keeping my eyes tightly shut.

The music pauses.

"Easy now," a deep voice soothes. "You will feel a bit discombobulated for a time. That's perfectly normal."

Someone's in my room? Someone definitely not my roommate, who 1: isn't a dude, and 2: would never use the word 'discombobulated,' and 3: doesn't have an unusual accent. Greek, maybe?

I force my eyes open once again, blinking rapidly to ease the strain of the bright golden light saturating the room. Our dorm has only one tiny window that doesn't face the sun and a light bulb so old the space feels like a cave most of the time.

So where is this blinding brightness coming from?

I peek through my eyelashes as gradually, my vision focuses.

Standing over me, I see a beautiful man. His short golden hair curls around a face so chiseled he could be carved of marble. Thick lashes frame his large, hazel eyes and his lips are full, sensuous. But his attire is distinctly odd. A white tunic made from obviously expensive fabric stretches across his defined chest, and over his broad, muscled shoulders he wears a luxurious gold cape with matching gold trim around the hem. A gold sash, gauntlets, and a golden leaf headpiece— that I'd swear is made of real gold—accent his attire.

This is no cheap Halloween costume, and we're not even near the holiday, anyway.

I blink once, then twice. "Who... who are you?" My voice sounds strange, unfamiliar.

The man leans down and slides a bare arm behind my back, his muscles flexing as he helps me sit.

The room spins, and I clutch my head to ease my dizziness. "Am I sick?"

He sits in a chair next to my bed and presents me with a golden, emerald encrusted goblet. "Drink," he says. "You have been through an ordeal."

I have so many questions, but the temptation of liquid stills them all. I accept the ornate cup and take a test sip. The amber liquid is sweet with hints of honey and cinnamon, so I drink more deeply, delighting in the flavors playing over my tongue. When I drain the cup, he lifts a matching pitcher from the side table and refills it. By the time I've emptied the goblet a second time, my head is clearer and my vision sharpens.

I look around. I'm definitely not in my dorm room. I'm propped on a canopied bed made of olive wood, and on each post, deep green vines crawl with glowing crystals that hang where flowers might normally bloom. The walls are painted with intricate murals of Fae dancing under moonlight, the forests glittering with magic. At one wall, a fireplace blazes with warmth, and on a stand nearby rests an ancient lyre with tortoise shell adorning its silver inlaid cross bar. Was that the source of the music?

"Where am I?" I ask the beautiful man, even though he hasn't answered any of my previous questions.

"What do you remember, Lily?"

My eyebrows shoot up. "How do you know my name?"

"I know much about you," he says, his carved lips curving into a secret smile. "But first, it is important you remember what brought you here. I've found, over time, it makes the transition much more seamless if you arrive at the answers on your own."

What do I remember? I search my mind, but it is blank. My pulse races and my breath hitches, but the man puts a hand on mine that ignites a spark of electricity between us.

"Breathe slowly." His voice is calm and comforting. "Temporary memory loss is perfectly normal. It will come back."

"Perfectly normal for what?" I search his face for answers, but none present themselves.

"What can you recall of yourself?" he asks instead.

I close my eyes and inhale, breathing in through my nose and out through my mouth. And as I relax, I scan my thoughts for clues of my arrival in this strange place.

***

565

. . .

My name is Lily Lemon, and my life has always come in threes, this I know for certain. I remember my sisters first. I was born the third of three girls to a middle-class family whose only remarkable quality lay in how exceptionally unremarkable we actually were. We even looked alike, dark hair, green eyes with the same dusting of freckles over the same pert nose, and lips a shade too wide. As the most academically driven of the three of us, I graduated high school in three years, and then spent the following three years working three jobs to save up for college.

Nourished by hundreds of books and movies about this formative coming of age experience, I had high hopes for the college stage of my life. I'd develop everlasting friendships, acquire a reluctant—but devoted—mentor who would see my hidden genius and mold me into a work of intellectual art, and I'd come into my own as I mastered the subjects that spoke so deeply to my soul.

This was my frame of mind when my parents and sisters loaded into our mini-van and drove me across two states to Bard University.

Along the way, we played silly, road-trip car games, just as we had when we were children, and when we stopped for the night at the cheapest motel we could find, my sisters and I squeezed together into a too-small bed with me sandwiched in the middle.

Sarah—the mischievous middle child—held one hand and Melanie—the most beautiful of us—held the other. We were each born a year apart, and though I was the youngest, I was the first to leave home for college.

"It's not going to be the same without you, Lil." Sarah's voice wavered in the darkness.

"I'll be back for Thanksgiving," I promised, my own throat tightening.

Melanie squeezed my hand. "You're going to do great things," she said. "Museums the world over will vie to hire you after you get all your degrees."

"Or you'll travel and collect stories and become a famous anthropologist," said Sarah, who fancied traveling above all else.

"Or I'll end up teaching community college while struggling to pay basic expenses," I inserted, voicing my greatest fear. "No one touts Classical Studies as a must-have career path."

"Nonsense," Melanie snorted. "There will be plenty of great jobs open to you. You could be a professor, a lawyer, a museum researcher… "

"I definitely do *not* want to be a lawyer." I rolled my eyes.

"But you're so good at arguing," Sarah said with a giggle. "Mom and Dad think you'd be *great* at that."

I nudged her with my shoulder but smiled, nonetheless. The fact that I tended to win the debates in our house no doubt had a part in why my parents were willing to sacrifice so much for my higher education. Out-of-state college wasn't cheap. But still, I didn't see law in my future. I'd always felt more drawn to the past. To myth and stories of old. To dead gods and even deader languages. Could I just get paid to study Greek Mythology? That would be the dream job.

"I'll miss you both so much," I said over the sounds of our dad's snoring filling the room.

When he snorted loudly and rolled over in bed, Sarah giggled. "At least you won't have to deal with that anymore. I'd give anything for a night of silence."

I didn't blame her. Every night, the terrifying snores of our father resonated throughout our small two-bedroom cottage. But I knew she was wrong. I'd miss even that.

The next day, my family joined me as I waited in the long registration lines, Sarah and Melanie taking turns pointing out every cute guy they saw. Then, they all helped carry boxes and suitcases up the three flights of stairs to my dorm room.

As I schlepped the last box through the long hall, I tripped, falling unceremoniously on my ass and spilling all my precious books onto the floor.

"Are you okay? Let me help."

I looked up and into the eyes of a guy who could definitely pass for a Greek god. He practically glowed with gorgeousness. His dark hair heightened his pale blue eyes, and the sexy smirk playing over his lips would have made my knees weak if I'd been standing.

He knelt down to quickly repack my books, then tucked the box under one arm while offering me his other hand to help me up.

At his touch, my skin tingled and my cheeks flushed hot. "Uh, thanks."

"You on this floor?" he asked as I righted myself and reluctantly let go of his hand.

"Yes, room 306."

His smile widened. "We're neighbors then. I'm 308. Let me walk you back." He winked as he added, "Wouldn't want you to fall again."

My faced burned with embarrassment, but I fell into step beside him until we reached my door. "I'm just there, if you need anything," he said, nodding his chin to the room next to mine.

As he handed my box back, my door suddenly flew open to reveal Sarah, standing there and grinning. "Lil, I—" when she saw the boy next to me her eyes widened. "Hello, I didn't realize Lily brought a friend over."

"Oh, this isn't—"

But 308 beat me to it, holding out his hand to Sarah. "I'm Clay. Lily's neighbor."

Sarah blushed, her fair skin turning a pretty pink. "Sarah, Lily's sister."

"Well, Lily's sister, I'll let you get back to it." He turned and bowed dramatically as he took my hand. "Lady Lily, we shall undoubtedly meet again soon."

Then he brought my hand to his lips and brushed a kiss against my skin. This time, my knees definitely did wobble.

He left, and my sisters pulled me inside, grilling me for the details on how I'd met the gorgeous Clay from Room 308.

After I told the story, Sarah snorted. "Only *you* would meet the sexiest guy on campus by tripping over your own feet."

I wanted to argue, but she wasn't wrong. "Where are mom and dad?" I asked.

"They went to get you snacks from the vending machine." She laughed. "Mom was worried you'd starve to death before the cafeteria opened tonight."

They arrived a few moments later, and my mother looked around the room, sniffing in distaste.

I couldn't blame her.

The room itself was the size of a glorified shoebox, and to make matters worse, my roommate took up more than her share of space. Even though she couldn't have been here more than a few hours longer than myself, she'd left her dirty clothes littering every square inch of the floor.

"This place is a mess," Sarah said, wrinkling her nose.

Melanie guffawed. "Says the Lemon who has yet to learn how to put away any of her own laundry."

Sarah shrugged. "I'm not *this* bad."

She actually was worse, but none of us had the heart to tell her that. She was a whirlwind disaster who has always left a mess in her wake.

Of the three Lemon girls, Melanie was the tidiest, and as the oldest, always picking up after us both.

I fell somewhere in between, the dreamer who left piles of books in odd places, but otherwise, generally kept my belongings neatly put away.

My mother, a tall woman with an aristocratic face that often looked harder than she meant it to, dabbed her eyes as I finished unpacking the last box. "So this is it," she said.

"Just for now," I said, letting her wrap me into a hug. She towered over my 4'9" frame, but then, so did everyone in my family. I was definitely the shrimp.

"Oh, my little Lemon." My dad sighed, pulling me into a bear hug. With a paunch for a belly and beefy arms from his years hauling garbage as a sanitation worker, the combination made his hugs a little dangerous—but always wonderful. "Be good and work hard," he said, releasing me.

"I will, I swear it. I won't let you down." They'd put everything on the line to help pay for my education. I'd worked and gotten scholarships but still hadn't managed to cover everything. They didn't know I'd overhead them talking about getting the second mortgage on our house to cover the difference. It made my heart ache to think about the sacrifices they'd made for me.

Finally, it was time to say goodbye to my sisters. "Lemonade squeeze," Sarah said, recalling our childhood nickname for our group hugs. I embraced them tightly, the tears now flowing freely on all of our cheeks.

Melanie twirled her dark braid as she studied me. "Remember, Lily, when life gives you lemons…"

"Make lemonade of their heads," I finished. Another childhood saying we crafted in a fort one day. It didn't make a lot of sense on the surface, but for us three, it made all the sense in the world.

The moment they left, my world felt empty, and yet a new stirring rose in me, one of hope and excitement for what was to come.

To be continued..

ONE CLICK on Amazon.

BONUS: MAD GIRL: LOCKED UP—
PROLOGUE

BY KARPOV KINRADE & Heather Hildenbrand

PROLOGUE

I NEVER KNEW what I was, until the day I discovered what I was not.

The ripples of the river *Le Seine* send shimmers of light reflecting over the dark depths, and I can't avert my eyes from the temptation to see, to know.

I try. With everything in me I try. For several footsteps I keep my face forward, my eyes following the lines in the cobblestone, my mind focused on the sound of my heels clicking against stone. The chill of fall forces me to pull my wool coat around my shoulders, to tighten my red scarf against the breeze caressing my skin as it brushes through my dark hair like cold, invisible fingers that send shivers up my spine.

This is my favorite time of day in Paris; twilight. Studying here for the past year was a dream come true—a dream turned nightmare. As the evening shadows dance with the remnants of afternoon sun, the sky turns shades of purple and red. I never tire of it, of the vision of colors swirling together like one of Monet's paintings. As much as I love spending my days at the Sorbonne studying art, and my afternoons at the Louvre, gazing at the greatest paintings in the world, nothing can compare to the masterpiece mother nature creates nightly.

At least, that's how I used to feel. Until that night.

Nothing has been the same since *that* night.

An older couple passes me on the bridge, the woman smiling in my direction as she wishes me a good evening. I try to smile back, but my face freezes in the effort, the weight in my heart too heavy to give the fake gesture much sincerity.

A teenage couple stands at the foot of the bridge kissing, laughing, whispering to each other. A business man paces near them talking on his cell phone. All of the voices—French, English, Italian— blend together—into a music that turns sinister the longer I listen.

I stop walking and turn toward the water with pain and reluctance, but also with a compulsion that leaves little choice.

When I peer over the side of the bridge and into the dark murkiness, at first I see nothing unusual. I smile for the first time that day, a real smile, and almost laugh out loud at the relief that courses through me as the ball of anxiety that has been tightening in my chest slowly uncurls.

But my relief is short-lived.

At first it appears just a trick of light, something explainable by science. Anyone might see it if they tilted their head just so.

But I know it isn't the light, and that no one would be able to see what is about to show itself to me.

The form clarifies into an image so achingly familiar a bolt of pain shoots through my heart. It's me, but not. A reflection of the woman whose face I have shared since birth.

She smiles in that sad way that resonates so deeply, and I can't turn my head, can't look away, even knowing what's about to happen.

The smile fades on the beautiful elfin face, wide green eyes almost too large, skin too pale, the color of porcelain.

No longer my own reflection, my twin stares back at her, mouth twisting into something grotesque as the voices return in whispers that grow into screams. *Celeste, save me. Help me. He's hurting me. Why won't you help me? It hurts. Celeste!*

I cover my ears, but the voice doesn't just live outside my head, and nothing can shut out the sound once it begins. Whimpering, scared, unable to face this ghost yet again—this mental madness brought on by loss and grief and an unfortunate spin of the genetic lottery— I run.

I run off the bridge, away from the cursed water, away from my own insanity. I've taken the pills, done the counseling, followed all the rules, but it hasn't gone away.

I know only one thing can stop it now.

As I stumble toward my flat, latching onto my keys, I feel someone watching me from the shadows, but when I turn to look, no one's there. Still, my skin prickles and the hair on my arms stand on end. I'm not alone.

But it doesn't matter.

Only one thing matters right now—quieting the voices once and for all.

For years, I hated my mother for what she did to find relief from her madness.

It wasn't until recently that I finally understood. That I finally felt compassion. That I finally realized this was the true curse of our family.

I've had the plan for weeks, ever since that night, but I never really thought I'd follow through with it. Tonight, I know I will. There is no more doubt. No more fear. Only a deep relief that soon it will all be over.

Once inside my flat, I don't bother kicking off my shoes or placing my keys on the hand-painted table under the mirror in the entryway. I drop everything on the floor and make my way to the small bathroom adjacent to my bedroom. I've already written the note. They will find it on my desk next to my laptop.

I don't bother taking off my white dress, though I do pull off my coat. I almost laugh at the absurdity that the moment before my death I would be worried about ruining my favorite—and most expensive—indulgence, my beautiful red wool coat.

I take the razor blade I purchased just for this occasion, turn on my bath, and sink into the warm water. My red scarf floats around me like blood. How fitting, I think, as I place the silver blade against my left wrist.

I know how to cut, vertically not horizontally. I know which veins to hit to get the job done correctly. Living alone helps. No one will look for me until tomorrow when I don't show up for school.

I idly wonder who will come checking in. Probably Mike, from Art History. He's been asking me out for months and would want to be the first to 'help'. But maybe Lacy will insist, knowing I don't fancy Mike at all. I actually hope it's Mike and not Lacy. I don't want my friend seeing me like this.

The slice doesn't hurt like I imagined it would. It almost feels good, like it's cutting into an illness and letting out the infection. As the blood flows into the water, covering my pale skin, staining my white dress, I imagine all the crazy bleeding away. Soon I'll be with my sister and my parents again.

Soon, I will be free of the madness that has taken the sanity, and lives, of every woman in my family for generations.

My eyes are closed, lost in dreams of death, when a stranger's arms pull me out of the water.

"You poor girl. There's hope for you yet." His voice is the last thing I hear before I fade into nothing.

To be continued…

ONE CLICK on Amazon.

BONUS: WANTED—CHAPTER 1

BY Karpov Kinrade & Liv Chatham
A spin off standalone of The Night Firm

CHAPTER 1

I'M RECORDING everything that happens in the very likely scenario that my whole plan goes to shit and all that's left to tell the story is this journal. If you're reading this, I'm probably dead, and it's too late to do anything about any of it now. But, at least, you'll know the truth. And I won't hold back. I won't try to make myself look better than I am. I have no delusions about myself.

I began the day stealing from a department store and ended with lying to my new boss.

I'm no saint, but I'm far from the worst that exists. No, there are much worse specimens of humanity than me. They're the ones to be afraid of and the kind I'm trying to get away *from*. But I don't think it's going to work.

After all, nothing in my life has ever worked.

I'm not trying to wallow in self-pity. I'm just being honest. Some lives shine with a kind of preternatural luck that follows them around. Others live under a perpetual storm cloud.

My life is the latter.

But who knows, maybe the weather is turning in my favor for once.

You never know, right?

***

STEAL a little and they'll jail your ass, steal a lot and they'll make you queen. It's a Bob Dylan quote with my personal spin on a few of the words. And it's all I could think about as I walked casually through the exit of the department store with new as-yet-paid-for dress and shoes shoved into my oversized purse.

It was only a borrow. I'll return them tomorrow.

However, stores generally frown on you taking their shit without paying, so I schooled my face into a bored housewife expression and causally browsed a few items lining the back of the store on my way out.

Why do they put shit past the checkout stands? You don't pass them when you come in, only when you go out, and by then you've already paid. What's the point?

Fortunately for me, the store alarm didn't go off. No one tried to stop me. In fact, one of the employees nodded his head in my direction with a smile as I left. "Have a nice day," he said with a wink. "And come back again soon."

He looked college-aged, with a sweet grin and kind brown eyes.

"Thanks," I said blandly, not giving into the temptation to flirt back.

He was cute and it could have been fun, but he looked too innocent to handle the skeletons piling up in my closet. And by the time this blistering summer is over, there will be more.

I sighed deeply once I was safely in my beaten-up old car, doors closed and locked, air conditioning drying the sweat dotting my skin.

I studied my hands gripping the steering wheel as they shook, my fingernails bitten down to stumps, my cuticles in need of some serious TLC. You'd think this was my first time stealing, the way my heart fluttered in my chest like a hummingbird on crack.

Closing my eyes, I steadied myself with a few deep breaths.

A sharp knock on the window startled me back to the present and scared the living hell out of me.

It was the cute store guy.

Jesus.

I rolled down my window and put on my best 'polite but I'm in a hurry' smile. "Is something wrong?"

If I got caught, I'd be ruined, and I wouldn't be the only one to suffer.

He held up a cell phone. "I think you left this in the store?"

With a relieved sigh, I took it from him, feeling twice the idiot. How could I be so stupid? "Thank you. It must've fallen from my purse."

This time, my smile was one hundred percent genuine. Losing my phone would have been Bad-with-a-capital-B.

He glanced inside my car, towards said purse, but fortunately, I'd zipped it shut, the stolen items safely tucked out of sight.

"Hey, so, I was wondering..." he began.

I inwardly cringed, just knowing what was next. Could I start the car and hightail it out there fast enough? *Would* I?

Then, he stunned me with a nervous slur of, "Would you like to grab a coffee after my shift?"

I blinked. "Thanks, but I have a job interview today." This was it? Really?

His smile faltered. "Oh, right. Well, good luck."

Before he could ask for my number, I rolled up my window, waved, and then drove off.

A quick glance in the rearview mirror revealed him standing there, a bit forlorn. He watched my car leave the lot before he turned back toward the store.

"Your lucky day, bud," I muttered under my breath.

Boys like troubled girls before they know what kind of trouble they're really in for. I'd just saved him a shit ton of heartache.

My phone binged just as I pulled up to the curb and parked in front of my house. I already knew who it was, and a blanket of depression dropped over me as I checked the messages, proving myself right.

ARE YOU READY?

WITH SHAKING HANDS, I replied.

YES.

GOOD.

I SAT THERE, waiting for the three dots to blink, signaling a reply, but when nothing appeared on the tiny screen, I felt the anger beginning to bubble. That was it? That was all I was going to get? I mentally screamed a few choice words at the sender of the texts, then grabbed my purse and headed into the house.

I heard the sound of an argument even before I set foot on the cracked concrete steps. One kick of the screen door later, I was in the living room, tense and ready.

My father, a tall brute of a man with beady eyes, a rounded stomach fed by liquor, and meaty fists, towered over my little brother, wielding a broken beer bottle like a knife.

"You do as you're told," he was shouting. "Or I'll shove this so far up your ass you'll be eating glass and shit for a *week*."

My little brother stood there, trembling, with his thin forearm protecting his face. At fourteen, he was small for his age and much preferred reading books to fighting.

As my father lurched forward to backhand my brother, I shoved Jeremy aside and stepped between them.

The blow jarred my teeth and pain exploded across my cheekbone. If there weren't any broken bones, I'd be shocked. I choked, clutching my face as tears stung my eyes.

My dad's eyes widened. "What are you doing, you little slut?" He snarled, sending spittle straight at me. "You're nothing but a worthless whore." He stumbled to the couch to grab another beer.

Now was my chance, before he could wind himself up for another strike, a strike I sure as hell wasn't going to be around to take. I grabbed Jeremy by the arm and dragged him out of the room to our shared bedroom at the end of the hall before that blow could land.

Once locked in the safety of our shared bedroom, I checked him over quickly. "Are you okay? Did he hurt you?"

Jeremy shook his head, but tears glistened in his large eyes.

My heart broke and I pulled him close, hugging him tight. "I'll get us out of this. I promise." And I would get us out, by any means necessary, even if it involved me dying.

My little brother's shoulders shook in mute sobs, silent as they must be in this house. We are the children of the silent pain. I grimaced. If nothing else, Children of the Silent Pain would be a cool band name.

When he calmed down, I released him and wiped his face with my sleeve. "I have to go, but you should climb out the window and stay at Rick's tonight. Go to school with him in the morning."

Jeremy's caramel eyes widened. "But won't you get in trouble if I leave?"

"I'll be fine. Don't worry about me. I can take care of myself," I said. We are twelve years apart, and I only came back to this hell hole to rescue him. Well… mostly for him. I had a plan. Kind of. I shoved him toward the window. "Now, go!"

He nodded and detoured to grab his backpack, then returned to the window and climbed out.

I exhaled and turned my attention back to my father. He had the TV in the living room on as loud as it could go and now, he was bellowing at the game.

Hoping he'd remain distracted, I crept down the hall and snuck into the kitchen with as much stealth as I could muster. After snagging a bag of frozen peas from the freezer and grabbing the ibuprofen, I scuttled back to my bedroom and locked the door.

Suddenly drained, I collapsed on my bed and then slid to the floor, pressing the frozen peas to my cheek.

I tried to cry.

I wanted to cry.

Hell, I *needed* to cry.

But… nothing. I felt dead inside—and that scared me more than anything.

I needed to feel. *Do* something to numb the pain that shriveled my soul, made me feel like I was a shell of a person, already dead, a ghost of myself haunting my own life.

I felt under my bed until my fingers tripped over the small silver box that held a razor blade and alcohol wipes. Still numb, I pulled it out and flipped open the lid. It took only a second to clean the blade, and then, I was pulling my shorts up as far as I could, eyeing the small white scars crisscrossing my inner thighs.

With a deep breath, I pressed the metal blade into my flesh, gently at first, then with more pressure until I felt the skin brake under that sharp edge of pain.

Crimson blood spilled and dripped down my pale leg.

Relief surged through me, almost as if the seeping blood released the poison lurking in my soul. I sighed as the tears finally began to fall.

I'm not proud of it, and I'm not writing for sympathy. But I promised I wouldn't paint myself in a false, flattering light, and I'm keeping my word—at least, in this instance.

Carefully, I cleaned myself with an alcohol wipe, applied a bandage, and then shoved the container back under my bed.

It was time to move on. I had an interview. I opened my purse and grabbed my 'borrowed' outfit, a conservative navy-blue, button-up dress with matching slip-on ballet shoes. Everything fit to a T and minutes later, I stood in front of the mirror, staring at the image reflected there.

"Not bad," I murmured. No, I looked damn good. Striking, even.

The color brought out the blue in my eyes and complemented my dark hair and fair skin. Of course, I could still see the tattoos on my arms, but as practically everyone had them these days, I didn't see how that would be a problem.

Then, I glanced at my cheek and winced outright at the dramatic array of reds and blues standing out against my white skin in a nice bruise despite the ice and meds.

It took a good twenty minutes to do my makeup, thanks to the purple spreading over my cheekbone. I flinched each time I dabbed on the concealer, but finally, I'd finished and even I couldn't tell I'd been hit. I just had to keep my fingers crossed that my eye wouldn't swell. Then, there'd be no hiding my injury.

After one last dab of lip gloss, I followed my brother's path and shimmied through the window. I made it back to my car and then I was off again, before my father knew I'd even left.

It was dusk by the time I reached the address for my interview. I switched off the engine and settled in my car, preparing to wait, as instructed, until full darkness descended.

I didn't mind. It gave me the chance to study the mansion I'd be cleaning, provided I got the job, of course.

The place was massive, by far the largest and remotest estate in and around our small town. A forest of trees blanketed the mansion from the road and you had to drive down a long, winding driveway before you'd even catch a glimpse of the slate tile roof. It wasn't until the last bend, when you were upon the place that you got a good view.

Other than the ornately carved tall, black double arched front door, the mansion was entirely white with stately columns that gave it a Roman villa vibe. Fountains graced the lawn and a meticulous garden of red roses lined the walkway from the drive to the front door.

For a place that had been vacant forever, it looked remarkably well kept. The man who'd bought it last month was a mystery in our small Northern California town. No one had seen him, but everyone had heard the rumors of his wealth and that he'd paid for the place in cash. With that kind of money, he had to be dripping with diamonds. He'd have to be to buy the place. Few could afford it, and those who could didn't want it after... well, after everything went down. A real estate agent is required by law to disclose when a murder's been committed on a property. That typically doesn't help sell a place.

I sat in my car, tapping a beat on the steering wheel as I watched and waited. Finally, the sun sank out of view and when the full moon hung over the treetops, fully visible, I checked my phone and scanned the job details one last time.

Job details. Check. Like I hadn't had them memorized already. Well, there was nothing left to do but get the show on the road.

Inhaling a deep breath, I exited my car and walked to the entrance. After lifting the brass knocker and giving the door a sharp rap, I rubbed my sweating palms against my thigh without thinking. Damnit. I'd just left a dark wet smudge on the borrowed dress.

I drew a deep breath and glanced around. I'd been here, at the house, once before, but it wasn't a night I liked to recall.

Fortunately, the door opened, sparing me the memories, and I straightened my spine and tried to act like someone else. Someone poised, polished, and well-spoken. Someone who deserved to scrub the toilets of the filthy rich.

A tall, rail thin man wearing a traditional butler uniform greeted me. "You must be Miss Kassandra Blackwood," he said as he ushered me inside. "Welcome."

"Thanks... er...thank you," I replied, belatedly polishing my speech so I could later polish the silver here.

My phone buzzed in my purse, and I scowled at the annoyance.

The butler's eyes flicked down, but he said nothing. Instead, he escorted me to a small room a few doors to the left of the foyer and offered me a seat on a plush leather chair. "Please, wait a moment. The Count will be right with you."

Count? I raised an eyebrow. Had he said...Count? Just who the hell *was* this guy? I scanned the room assessing the value of the rugs, furniture, and knickknacks in a cursory calculation. It didn't take long to determine that, most likely, just one of the knickknacks on his shelf was worth more than my whole life. I couldn't imagine being so wealthy that you'd spend insane amounts of money on painted eggs or some shit just to display them behind locked glass doors. It was vulgar.

But who was I to judge? After all, I didn't have two pennies to rub together.

Then, the butler returned, and I stood as he smiled and gestured for me to follow. "Right this way."

He led me through gilded hallways with more molding than wall, and past rooms filled to the brim with priceless antiques. Obviously, the Count had changed a lot about the house since I'd been there last.

Finally, the butler escorted me into an office lined wall-to-wall with leather-bound books. The room was dark and very Gothic, without windows. The only sources of light were the ornate iron candelabras, each boasting five beeswax pillar candles. Strange. The room was an odd choice considering the rest of the mansion had electricity.

Under any other circumstances, I'd have hightailed it out of there. The whole place screamed sexual-assault-that-gets-thrown-out-of-court —that is, if it ever made to court in the first place with me. After all, they'd take one look at how I'm dressed and then another at my past and conclude I'd clearly asked for it.

Yet the more I inspected the place, the more the highly tuned street-smart side of me kept telling the rest of me to calm down, that it wasn't getting any real rapey vibes.

I hesitated, on the fence, but deep inside, I knew I couldn't just walk away. I didn't have a choice.

Trusting the street-smarts knew what they were talking about, I stepped inside.

Immediately, the butler left, closing the door behind him with a click.

It was then I saw the man, standing in the shadows. As I watched, he emerged into the circle of candlelight, book in hand.

It took a moment for my eyes to adjust to the lighting, but when they did, my jaw dropped.

He was tall, at least 6'3", and elegantly lean in a black suit tailored to his trim, muscular frame. Yet it was his face that drew my gaze, so fine, ageless, and all chiseled angles. His dark, nearly black eyes glinted in the candlelight or perhaps with a hint of madness.

He looked so elegant, suave, and fierce at once.

He snapped his book shut and set it on a nearby shelf, his gaze never once leaving mine. "Good evening, Miss Blackwood," he said as he reached out his hand in greeting.

A shiver ran up my spine the instant our hands met, and almost at once, a wave of unexpected desire rolled over me, making my legs tremble and taking me by surprise. Shocked, I drew a silent, fortifying breath and stood firm, willing myself not to flinch under his gaze or touch. "Thank you for the interview, Mr. ...?" I never got a name. Just an address.

He tilted his head, causing a lock of dark hair to fall across his forehead as his long, elegant fingers tightened ever so slightly around my hand. "It's Count... actually."

I narrowed my eyes. "That's rather grandiose," I teased and then promptly bit my lip. *Don't freaking forget your place, Kass.*

Fortunately, he didn't appear offended, judging by the wry smile that curved his lips, anyway. "It is a title well-earned," he said mildly. Then, his eyes dropped to my hand, still clutched in his, and I stared at the line of his thick, black lashes as he studied the ink on my arm.

Suddenly self-conscious, I pulled free of his grasp. Instantly, part of me felt a loss at the lack of contact, which was, of course, a shit-ton of pure stupidness, so I mentally clocked myself in the head, hoping to knock some sense into my brain.

"Please, sit," the Count waved a hand at a tufted leather chair as he took the seat behind the mahogany desk nearby. "Tell me, Kassandra. May I call you Kassandra?"

To be perfectly honest, the way he said my name made me a bit lightheaded. I sat down, mentally kicking myself again and forced my mind back to the interview. For the first time, I realized he'd never actually told me his name, but now it felt weird to ask again. "My friends call me Kass," I said, clearing my throat. "But Kassandra is fine too."

"Tell me, Kassandra, why are you applying for this job?"

This was it, my moment to shine. I looked him straight in the eye and recited from memory the script I'd been given to say, "I'm passionate about housekeeping and finding new and innovative ways to keep a home clean and inviting. I'm organized, strong, and can work long hours without tiring." Ha! What a crock. "I would be an asset to any house." There, I'd nailed every word *and* emotion.

The Count leaned back, steepled his fingers, and studied me in the candlelight. The flickering of flames lent him a menacing look but strangely, that only somehow amplified the attraction I felt. This wasn't an innocent boy who didn't know which way was up. This was a man… a man who had clearly walked with darkness and lived to tell the tale—and a man who obviously knew his way around a woman, maybe even women with my kind of demons. My libido warmed at that, a libido that had been very much neglected of late due to my inability to make good decisions on the men front. Yet, while I was a year into taking a sabbatical from men entirely, my libido whispered I just might want to make an exception for *this* tall drink of water.

Then, I became suddenly aware of the silence hanging heavy in the room and the fact that the Count was just sitting there, watching me.

I gritted my teeth. *Quit thinking with your pants and think with your head, Kass.*

As if aware I was suddenly paying attention again, the Count arched a cool brow and said in a low, menacing voice, "I have three rules for anyone who works with me or lives with me, Kassandra."

I froze as a prickle of foreboding crept down my neck.

"The first rule, Kassandra, is no lying. Ever. Without exception. So, before I terminate this interview and have you escorted out, I will give you one more chance to answer my question. Why are you applying for this job? This time, I want the truth."

He never raised his voice, but there was such power behind his words I felt compelled to obey, and that terrified the ever-loving shit out of me.

This was the moment I should have gotten the hell out of there. But I didn't. I couldn't.

Still, I needed to know what I was playing with, so I asked, "And what are the other two rules?"

His dark brows creased with displeasure. "We will go over those should you get the job."

It was my turn to frown. What a freaking strange interview. I sucked in a breath as I prepared a suitable combination of the truth.

Then, I smiled, knowing exactly what I'd say. After all, a lie is always most believable when it contains a kernel of truth, and my lie had the advantage of being entirely true and entirely a lie at the exact same time.

"The truth is, I came back home after being gone for some time to help take care of my little brother after my mother died. I need a job, and this town isn't exactly overflowing with them. I'm a shit house-keeper and I couldn't care less about 'innovative cleaning techniques', but I *am* a hard worker and I will learn to do what you want and do it well, should you hire me." Let's see what he did with that. I raised an eyebrow at him as if to say, "*ball's in your court, buddy.*"

He studied me for a long time. I didn't know if he was waiting for me to crack or what, but I didn't play his game. I just sat patiently, waiting. I could do that all night.

Finally, he smiled. It was brief, and it didn't reach his eyes entirely. Eyes that looked weighed down with so much pain it couldn't be hidden.

"Very well, Miss Blackwood, you're hired. You may move in tonight and start tomorrow."

"Thank you, I—" I paused as his words sank in. "Wait, what? Move in?"

He nodded. "Were you not aware? This is a live-in position. That's non-negotiable. Will that be a problem?"

I gulped. *Yes.* "No, not at all."

I plastered a smile on my face but inwardly I was already swearing at myself. *What the hell are you going to do now? You're really up shit creek, Kass.*

To be continued…

ONE CLICK on Amazon.

BONUS SHORT STORY—NIGHT TERRORS

NOTE FROM AUTHOR: This was originally published to our patrons (Patreon.com/KarpovKinrade) after they voted on an image to inspire the story. We hope you enjoy this bonus short story.

NIGHT TERRORS

I WAKE ONCE AGAIN from a fear I can't remember, my body shaking, covered in cold sweat. My face is streaked with tears I do not remember shedding. My heart breaking from experiences I do not remember having. And like all the other nights, I am not in my bed.

My black cat, Loki, is at my feet, and a fresh claw mark oozes a bit of blood on my ankle. I pat the feline on the head. "Thanks for waking me again, buddy."

The evening air is chilling against my damp skin and I shiver and turn back to my house, Loki following. My feet are bare and covered in mud. My nails are chipped and dirty. My pajamas haven't fared much better.

I used to sleep naked, until I started wandering unaware. I should probably start sleeping with shoes on at this rate.

When I reach my bedroom, I check the time on my cell phone. 3:30 a.m. Same as every night. I grab the notebook I keep by my bed and try to jog my memory with notes, sketches, anything I can recall. My therapist thinks this will help, that if I can consciously process whatever my subconscious is torturing me about, I will be free of these night terrors.

So far it hasn't worked.

So far it has only led to a notebook full of darkly sketched images with no faces.

So far, it has only gotten worse.

I can't go back to bed, not this filthy and jittery. So I start the shower and throw my soiled clothes in the laundry.

Loki rubs against my legs and meows. I pick him up and bury my face in his fur as he purrs against my chest. Just holding him calms my nerves and soothes me in ways nothing else does.

He joins me in the bathroom as I shower, laying right outside the tub.

As the water pours over me, I close my eyes and hum a tune that feels familiar though I don't know why. But I'm used to this now.

I always come back from these terrors with something new in a my brain. A vision to sketch. A song to compose. A story to write.

I say 'come back' because that's what it feels like. Like I'm traveling somewhere and going through hell, then coming back into my own life inspired in some way by the journey.

But it's taking a toll. My creative life is rich. But I am exhausted all the fucking time. I feel as if I haven't slept in months. Ever since this started.

My relationships have suffered. I rarely see my friends and my boyfriend dumped me because he was convinced I was sneaking off in the middle of the night to fuck someone else—despite all evidence to the contrary. Really, I think he grew tired of having such crazy shit happen and he needed an excuse to hook up with the new barista at our local coffee house.

I don't blame him. I'm a hot mess right now, and she's just hot.

I step out of the shower and put on fresh clothes, then pull Loki into my lap and turn on the tv, looking for something—anything—to keep my mind distracted and my sanity in place.

I find something that looks like it'll be a buddy comedy, and I play it, letting it drone on in the background as I pet Loki and sip a cup of tea.

Maybe I'll be able to go back to sleep?

Unlikely.

When the movie fails to keep my attention, I grab my iPad and search the internet for any answers to my strange dilemma.

I do this every night. Look for answers.

I've never found any, but it helps to feel like I'm being proactive.

But tonight something new pops up.

Something I've never seen before.

A drawing someone did in a chat group I'm in. A drawing that's a near replica of the one I did tonight.

I run to grab my notebook and open it up, staring at the sketch of a woman with blue hair laying on her stomach, looking into a glowing pool. The person who posted his picture has a different artistic style, but it's the same setting, same woman, same everything.

I private message him.

DreamerCat39: That drawing you did. Where did you see it?

ForestDwellerZombie: I don't know. I woke up from a nightmare and drew it.

DreamerCat39: Tonight? Just now?

MY HEART IS RACING in my chest. Could he be having the same experiences as me? How would that be possible?

ForestDwellerZombie: Yes. Just now. Why? Who are you?

DreamerCat39: Someone who also woke up from a nightmare and drew that same image.

589

. . .

I TAKE a picture of it and upload it to the private chat.

There's a long pause while dots appear to show he's writing a response. I wait, my tea growing cold, Loki growing impatient with my lack of attention on him.

Finally his response comes through.

FORESTDWELLERZOMBIE: I'm not trying to be a creep, but can we talk? Skype or something? This is freaky.

NOW IT'S my turn to pause. There are too many crazy stories about assholes online, but he's not asking to meet in person, just through the computer. Where's the harm in that? And if he has answers, or even just the same questions, maybe it's worth it?

DREAMERCAT39: Okay. Yes. My Skype name is the same. DreamerCat39.

A FEW MOMENTS LATER, my iPad buzzes with an incoming call. I nervously answer, realizing that it's the wee hours of the morning and I look like shit.

Oh well, this isn't a date. It's an emergency.

When the call connects, the man on the other side of the screen leaves me breathless for a moment. He is quite possibly one of the most beautiful people I've ever seen. His eyes are a rich emerald green, his hair dark blond and slightly disheveled. He's got a sexy stubble along his chin and a chiseled face that could grace the covers of magazines. And he's not wearing a shirt, just pajama bottoms, as he sits in bed, and damn the dude must work out.

I self-consciously tug on my ponytail and hope my eyes aren't too swollen and red from the crying.

He smiles sheepishly. "Thanks for agreeing to the call."

I nod. "I'm Amber," I say.

"Derek," he says.

We both hold up our drawings for each other to study.

"It's weird," he says. "Why would we both draw this?"

"Maybe we saw the same movie or show or something and we both happened to pick up on it?"

That idea is week, but we spend a moment exploring it. We have similar taste in entertainment, it turns out, but nothing that would have had this woman in it.

"Has this happened before?" I ask.

I link him to my website that lists the stories and music and art I've created after my nightmares.

His eyes widen as he scrolls through.

"Yes," he says finally. "And there's something you need to see. But it has to be in person. It's a place. And I think it might have the answers we are seeking."

All the red flags rise before me, but I ignore them. If he's a serial killer or a stalker... I'm just going to have to take my chances. I need answers more than I need safety at this point. Because if this keeps up, I will lose my fucking mind and then what's it's all for anyways?

"Where do I need to go?"

He gives me coordinates that are about three hours from where I live.

"We have to meet there tonight, at 3:30 a.m., under the full moon," he says. "It won't work otherwise."

"What won't work?" I ask, suddenly nervous.

He closes his eyes and shakes his head. "I don't know. I know this sounds nuts. But I don't know. I just woke up tonight with these coordinates and this time written down next to my bed. I don't remember writing it. But maybe it's the answers we're looking for?"

I can see the desperation in his eyes and it mirrors my own. "I'll be there," I say.

We talk for a few more minutes, sharing stories of the places we've woken up in, the things we've created after, and the similarities are too many and too specific to ignore. Whatever is happening to me is also happening to Derek.

The next night I do not sleep. Instead, I put a leash on Loki and he hops into the car, waiting patiently in the passenger seat as I program in the coordinates and begin our drive a little after midnight. I chug coffee to stay awake—a staple in my diet lately— and fight the impulse to close my eyes for more than a blink.

It's a fight I fear losing, so I roll down the windows and blast some music, singing at the top of my lungs as Loki looks at me like I've lost my bloody mind.

Maybe I have. Might as well enjoy it then, right?

As I drive and sing and think about what awaits me at the end of this trip, I reflect back over the last few months and marvel at how my life has changed. I feel like a shell of myself. The world around me has become so gray and lifeless. Nothing seems real anymore. Nothing seems meaningful. Loki is the only thing left in my life that still brings me joy and comfort. And he has been more than happy to take an active role in my day to day activities. Coming with me on trips, going on walks, even following me during my night terror sleep walking. I often wake up to him nudging my ankles or scratching my calf. He's been my protector and friend during it all, which is why he's with me tonight.

For better or worse, he and I are in it together.

When we're close to our destination, the GPS directs me onto a sketchy-looking dirt road, and we turn right, bumping along painfully down the rock-strewn path until we finally reach a clearing with another car parked there.

I clutch Loki in my arms and get out of my car, then put him down and walk him on the leash towards the other car.

The driver door opens, and a tall, beautiful man steps out. He glances at the cat and then laughs.

I see why when he approaches.

He brought his dog. A gorgeous husky with blue eyes and thick white fur.

"His name is Thor," Derek says, and now it's my turn to laugh.

"My cat is Loki."

We watch as the two animals greet each other cautiously.

"So, what do we do now?" I ask, noticing that Derek is even more handsome in person, and the flicker of desire I feel is not lost on me. I've missed having someone to share life moments with, to share a bed with. Loki's great, but there are some needs even the best of cats can't meet, ya know?

Derek smiles as his eyes quickly take in my black leggings and tank top. It's a warm night and a long drive, so I dressed for comfort. But I did put on some lip gloss and mascara. Just in case.

It seems the attraction I feel might be mutual, and butterflies swarm my stomach at the possibility that this nightmare might ultimately lead to something good.

Unless he actually does turn out to be a crazy serial killer. In which case, bummer, and kids don't try this at home.

"I'm not entirely sure," he says, running a hand through his hair. "But come, I want to show you something."

He takes my hand, sending shivers up my spine, and leads me to a place just beyond where we're parked. There we find a pool of water—black and sluggish— reflecting the full moon in it.

I feel drawn to this pool and I bend down and dip a finger in it, the water shooting some kind of electricity through my body. I pull away, frightened and intrigued.

"Did you feel it too?" he asks.

I nod. "What does it mean?"

He looks at me, then looks away. "You're going to think I'm crazy."

I bark out a very unladylike laugh. "Try me."

"I think we are supposed to jump into it," he says, finally making eye contact again. "Together."

I swallow, my throat suddenly dry.

Thor barks at the pond, and Loki sniffs around it, dipping a paw in to test it out. Neither shy away, and I wonder at it all.

"Okay," I say finally, surprising myself. "What's the worst that can happen?"

He chuckles. "Probably a lot, but I'm willing to risk it if you are."

He holds out his hand and I take it. Our pets stay by our side on their leashes. And without anther thought, we both jump into the water together, our animals following.

I expect to feel wet.

To maybe land in shallow water.

Or possibly it's deeper than it looks and we sink a bit and have to swim and pull our way out.

I definitely don't expect what actually happens.

Darkness surrounds me. Electricity zaps through me. I can't see anything. I can't breathe, but I'm also not short on breath. My body is suspended in limbo.

And then.

The four of us fall to the ground.

Loki meows loudly and Thor barks, but when we look at our pets, they are changed. Loki is a black panther, sleek and large. Thor is a wolf, twice the size he was before.

And Derek and I....

We have changed too.

He's dressed in medieval style clothing made for royalty, complete with a crown on his head and a sword at his hip.

I too have a crown and sword, and am wearing a beautiful red velvet dress.

And before us is the woman with blue hair and glowing eyes, the woman we both drew. She smiles and stands, bowing before us.

"Welcome home, King Derek and Queen Amber. We worried you would forget your true selves and never return from your journey to the mundane, despite your familiars joining you," she says, looking at the animals. "But the magic in that world died long ago, and my powers do not reach there. I had to use dreams to remind you. Did you find what you were seeking?"

Derek and I exchange alarmed glances, and then, it all comes back to me in a rush of memory that makes me dizzy.

"This is our home," I say. "We were never from that other world at all."

But why did we leave? I search my mind for answers, but none come. And then Derek pulls out something from his pocket and I see what he's holding.

It was with us all along, we both realize.

We have what we need to save our world.

The answer was in the question the whole time.

***

THE EMOTIONS FLOOD ME FIRST. An overwhelming love for Derek, for this world, for my life. The specifics trickle in slowly, like trying to remember a dream. I can tell by his face, that Derek is going through the same process, experiencing emotions that are no yet based in memory.

I study the small object in his hand again, marveling that what we needed this whole time was something so simple. So obvious.

And yet.

My mind still feels full of strange ideas and missing pieces. "Is this real?" I ask.

Derek shrugs, but the woman with the blue hair smiles. "What is reality, after all? Are dreams less real than your waking memories? Are thoughts less real than objects? All things begin with thought and are formed from will and intention. This is one reality of many. What you choose to do with it is up to you."

As if on cue, two white horses walk out of the forest and up to us. They both have mounts and seem to know us. I feel great affection for them both, but particularly the one on the right, though they are nearly identical.

I walk over to her and stroke her behind her eyes, just as I know she likes it. "I have missed you, haven't I?" I say pressing my forehead into hers.

The horses don't seem spooked by a black panther and a wolf, and Derek and I mount as our familiars gallop by our side. "Where are we going?" I ask.

"I think the horses know!"

Over the course of the next few weeks we travel across our kingdom. When we reach towns, our people recognize us and welcome us with open arms, giving us their best rooms for us to rest. They share their meals and make sure we are always equipped with wine, water and food for our journey. The memories of this world come to us slowly, in pieces, a fragment here and there. But our connection to each other is steadfast. I know with the greatest assurance of my soul that Derek and I belong together, whatever world or reality we are living.

He is my steadfast north star, my hope when all hope is lost, my guiding light in a world of darkness.

And this world does have darkness.

We discover this several days into our journey when we are forced to sleep in a dark and strange forest plagued by unnatural sounds. It is the only night we have slept outside, and when darkness descended, the creatures of nightmares came out. We lost Derek's horse that night, to a hungry beast with glowing eyes and a body I still can't fully fathom in my mind.

It was a night of terror, and I have a wound across my shoulder from our battle with the darkness that still hasn't healed. Each night it seems to open back up, pushing and oozing.

"We need to get you to a healer," Derek says one night, as he cleans it out yet again.

"We have seen a healer in every town we've stopped. None know what to make of it," I remind him.

We have this conversation every night, and every night we end it in the same way. With uncertainty.

It isn't until we finally reach our castle that we are granted renewed hope. By this time, I am weaker than I ever have been. The fevers caused by this injury have gotten worse, and I can barely stand on my own.

Memory of our life before this are fading, but I still can't wrap my mind around all the details of this life, of this world. I feel incomplete, like a ghost of myself, and I don't know if it's the illness caused by this injury, or a byproduct of this strange magic that lets us travel through worlds. Derek seems to be recalling things more easily than I. He is the first to remember someone's name and the names of their children. To notice when we reach a place we've been to before. To remember a food that that's unique to this world.

But I hold the emotions of this place. When I see a familiar place,

I don't remember it so much as I feel my connection to it. Longing, or joy or even fear. When I meet someone, if I've known them before my impression of them is strong. I instantly like or dislike them, trust or mistrust them.

Unfortunately, as I fall more and more into my fever, as my arm swells and feels like it's going to fall off, everything is displaced by pain.

So when I see our castle for the first time, I'm hardly aware of the pristine white stone that shimmers under the soft glow of the full moon. I expect that normally the view would steal my breath, so magnificent is it.

Derek carries me in, my body limp in his strong arms, Loki and Thor flanking our heels and growing at anyone who gets too close.

We are greeted by a woman who looks wise and kind, and the moment she sees me, she leads us deep within the castle to a room that smells like all manner of herbs.

"Lay Her Majesty there," the old woman says, pointing to a mat on a small platform frame. Derek does as instructed, and the woman gets to work immediately, draining out the wound and drinking herbs to bandage my arm with.

She gives me something to sip, a bitter brew that burns going down, and she looks gravely at Derek. "Did you get what we need?"

He nods, handing her a small velvet pouch. She peers in, then sighs in obvious relief.

"We might survive this yet," she says ominously. And I know what she's talking about, but I can't quite call it to mind. I can't quite call anything to mind.

"Will Amber be okay?" Derek asks. His accent has changed since we've been here. As has mine. We are more and more fitting into this world we are from.

"Only time will tell," the woman says gravely. "She needs to rest. And we must pray for the gods to show mercy."

Derek bends at my bed and clutches my hand, kissing it. "Be well, my love. We have found what we need to save our people from the darkness. Now, you must heal so we can rule in peace and prosperity all of our days."

I smile at the image of that, my eyes fluttering closed as the potion I drank takes effect until darkness overcomes me entirely. The last thing I see is Derek's kind eyes, his beautiful face, and I feel his love to the depths of my soul.

***

I WAKE IN A START, from a fear I can't remember, my body shaking, covered in cold sweat. My face is streaked with tears I do not remember shedding. My heart breaking from experiences I do not remember having. And I am not in my bed.

My black cat, Loki, is at my feet, and a fresh claw mark oozes a bit of blood on my ankle. I pat the feline on the head. I lift the feline into my arms and look around, confused.

I know there's something incredibly important I need to remember. But no matter how hard I tug at the edges of my mind, I can't shake loose the memory.

The evening air is chilling against my damp skin and I shiver and turn back to my house. My feet are bare and covered in mud. My nails are chipped and dirty. My pajamas haven't fared much better.

And a deep ache is spreading over my shoulder.

When I get back into the house, I set Loki in front of his food bowl and head to the bathroom to examine myself in the mirror.

I look tired. Like I've been ill, though I don't recall having even so much as a flu in some time.

But when I pull off my shirt, I gasp.

I have a deep gouge on my shoulder, that pusses and oozes.

No wonder I feel like shit. Did I get this while sleeping?

I pull out my first aid kit and clean it as best I can, but I worry I will need the ER.

First, though, I need to sketch what little I can recall from my dreams.

I draw furiously into the morning, creating monsters with glowing eyes and castles and a beautiful man with kind eyes.

I post a few online, and as I'm about to head to the hospital to have my cut checked, my computer bings with a message.

DREAMERCAT39: That drawing you did. Where did you see it?

I SIT DOWN, thoughts of the hospital long forgotten, and reply.
ForestDwellerZombie: I don't know. I woke up from a nightmare and drew it.

HIS RESPONSE IS INSTANT.
DreamerCat39: Tonight? Just now?

MY HEART IS RACING in my chest. Could he be having the same experiences as me? How would that be possible?

FORESTDWELLERZOMBIE: Yes. Just now. Why? Who are you?
DreamerCat39: Someone who also woke up from a nightmare and drew that same image.

HE ATTACHES his drawing and my eyes widen.

FORESTDWELLERZOMBIE: My name is Derek. What's yours?
DreamerCat39: Amber.
ForestDwellerZombie: Amber. It's nice to meet you. Do you think... do you think we could meet for coffee and talk? I have a feeling we might have be the answer for each other.

*** THE END ***

ABOUT THE AUTHOR

Karpov Kinrade is the pen name for the wife and husband writing duo of USA TODAY bestselling, award-winning authors Lux Karpov-Kinrade and Dmytry Karpov-Kinrade.

Together, they live in Ukiah, California where they write fantasy romance novels and screenplays, make music and direct movies.

Look for more from Karpov Kinrade in *Dungeon Queen, Avalon Academy, Mad Girl, Bad Witch, The Night Firm, Vampire Girl, Of Dreams and Dragons, Nightfall Academy* and *Paranormal Spy Academy*. If you're looking for their suspense and romance titles, you'll now find those under Alex Lux.

They live with their three teens who share a genius for all things creative, and seven cats who think they rule the world (spoiler, they do.)

Want their books and music before anyone else and also enjoy weekly interactive flash fiction? Join them on Patreon at Patreon.com/karpovkinrade

Find them online at KarpovKinrade.com

On Facebook /KarpovKinrade

On Twitter @KarpovKinrade

And subscribe to their newsletter at ReadKK.com for special deals and up-to-date notice of new launches.

~ ~ ~ ~ ~

If you enjoyed this book, consider supporting the author by leaving a review wherever you purchased this book. Thank you.

ALSO BY KARPOV KINRADE

Dungeon Queen

Warrior Queen

A fantasy romance reverse harem with greek mythology and badassery.

The Winter Witch

A standalone fairytale fantasy romance retelling with magic and wonder.

Mad Girl: Locked Up

Mad Girl: Fights Back

A paranormal reverse harem romance with magic, mystery and madness.

The Night Firm

I Am the Wild

I Am the Storm

I Am the Night

A fantasy reverse harem romance with mystery and depth.

Wanted

A standalone dark paranormal romance that's a spin off of The Night Firm.

In the Vampire Girl Universe

A fantasy romance series with mystery and magic.

Vampire Girl

Vampire Girl 2: Midnight Star

Vampire Girl 3: Silver Flame

Vampire Girl 4: Moonlight Prince

Vampire Girl 5: First Hunter

Vampire Girl 6: Unseen Lord

Vampire Girl 7: Fallen Star

Vampire Girl: Copper Snare

Vampire Girl: Crimson Cocktail

Vampire Girl: Christmas Cognac

Of Dreams and Dragons

Get the soundtrack for I AM THE WILD, OF DREAMS AND DRAGONS and MOONSTONE ACADEMY wherever music can be found.

Nightfall Academy

A fantasy dystopian academy series with double lives, intrigue and romance.

Court of Nightfall

Weeper of Blood

House of Ravens

Night of Nyx

Song of Kai

Daughter of Strife

Paranormal Spy Academy (complete academy sci fi thriller romance)

A paranormal romance with mystery and superpowers.

Forbidden Mind

Forbidden Fire

Forbidden Life

Our ALEX LUX BOOKS!

The Seduced Saga (paranormal romance with suspense)

Seduced by Innocence

Seduced by Pain

Seduced by Power

Seduced by Lies

Seduced by Darkness

The Call Me Cat Trilogy (romantic suspense)

Call Me Cat

Leave Me Love

Tell Me True

(Standalone romcon with crossover characters)

<u>Hitched</u>

<u>Whipped</u>

<u>Kiss Me in Paris</u> (A standalone romance)

Our Children's Fantasy collection under Kimberly Kinrade

The Three Lost Kids series

Lexie World

Bella World

Maddie World

The Three Lost Kids and Cupid's Capture

The Three Lost Kids and the Death of the Sugar Fairy

The Three Lost Kids and the Christmas Curse

Printed in Great Britain
by Amazon